Nothing Lost

a novel

S.E. Beathan

BR

Dedication

For the man in the season that passed—

and the love that never did.

Chapter 1

Chicago — Fulton Street Loft — *Mar. 25, 2002 — 10:15 a.m. — James*

Today did not feel like any other day—it absolutely did not. It's not that James had sunken into a mild mind dip, like a slight depression leaving an impression on Ma's couch—gone, but not, because here's visible proof of the weight you carry. No, this morning's golden sunrise wasn't a clarion call begging him to lighten up—lighten up!

It wasn't like that at all.

He had been fine for years and years—well, high functioning—and he wasn't prone to exaggeration, but this day felt... different. From the moment he'd awoken, James felt a soft, sweet sensation around him, like a bubble. It was as though he were walking on pillows. And so, with a gentle pitty-pat, he tread from the master bedroom across the refurbished wood floor. He passed through the open expanse of his working studio and into the living area, each step a buoyant tribute to inexplicable lightness.

Wow.

James's assistant, Val, had the long table adjacent to the kitchen area already prepped for the mid-morning meeting; chairs were in place, project folders stacked, and the projector set and aimed at a white wall. All was good—nothing needed to be done by him. Val had some incidental tasks to complete, such as setting out the food and beverage carafes. In fact, she was already bustling about in the kitchen, so instead of harassing her and fretting over moot points, he made a beeline for the tall windows overlooking a northwest view of the Chicago skyline to see the sun. To espy the source of this golden light flooding the space and, yes, maybe his heart too. He felt lighter—so why not enjoy the source of light?

What a day, and it was just beginning.

And so was the sun—it was just peeking up over the tops of the buildings on the horizon, but it was moving on up like it meant business. And... it might have been smiling at him. James chuckled. Crikey, he was in a mood.

His studio loft on Fulton Street was in a rehabbed warehouse just west of the Loop, so he was near the center of the city, but not quite. It was located on the third floor and elevated enough to overlook the neighboring buildings and enjoy a northwest view of the skyline, as well as see the sun come up over Lake Michigan. It was what drew him to this space and what he enjoyed now.

James stood by the front window of his loft studio, his tall, lean frame silhouetted against the vast expanse that was called Chicago. His brown hair was slightly tousled from running his hands through it—a habit he'd never quite shaken. The early morning light caught the faint silver strands at his temples, a testament to time spent on Earth, but still counting.

James stood by the front window of his loft studio, looking at the vast expanse that was called Chicago. *Onion field*, right? Wasn't that what the Algonquin had called the wetland area? You better believe it was the first thing he'd looked up since moving here only a year before. He was done with New York, and Chicago had welcomed him with open arms and, well... big shoulders. Thank you, Carl Sandburg.

It had put him in mind of his birthplace in Newcastle upon Tyne—the working middle class growing up from industrial roots; the pubs, the bars, the keen devotion to sports teams—so many touchstones. And tombstones too—James looked at the old warehouses that were his neighbors now, backdrop to the sparkling city skyline. Some of these old buildings were being refurbished; some stood their ground as weary brick and boarded windows, hanging onto the memory of their heyday.

Then the soft golden morning light of this sweet bubble morning spilled in and soaked every sore spot in view, glowing into an unparalleled vista. Some Grand Canyon moment, right here in his front yard. James shook his head at the sight and thought, *God, I'm lucky, I am.* And then, as if to confirm this gentle observation, the yellow light softly—oh, so sweetly, with a *don't mind me, beg your pardon* pose—glowed through the glass and into the palm of his hand. Took him by the hand. He almost felt it.

James Watson laughed, his eyes shining in a way that softened his otherwise sharp features.

"What? What is it?" It was Val calling out to him across the room from the open kitchen. "And good morning to you, by the way."

"Oh, nothing… nowt. Just enjoying the view, thinkin' a bit," James returned, the slight Geordie accent he'd retained becoming more pronounced in his relaxed state.

Instead of answering directly, Val was already crossing the room with a large steaming mug in her hand. "I fixed your *cuppa*, as you say, but only because I know you're gonna be busy this morning—so don't yous' guys get used to it."

She deliberately played up her Chicago accent as she extended what looked to be a hand-pinched, handmade, thick-walled ceramic mug with a particular glaze shade of chartreuse green that could only be described as *vivid*. In addition, it sported three yellow mod-style flowers affixed around the side. You know how it is—you're never really sure you got the job done, so you have to stick on something super special to seal the deal.

Val O'Reilly stood straight and slim as an arrow, her simple, impish oval face turned upward to look him square in the eye, and there was that sparkle of good cheer and diamond glint of intelligence shining out to him—definitely her best feature. Her grin was already giving away the game, though; she was only twenty-four years old and hadn't quite mastered her poker face in every humorous gambit.

James stared at the mug for a full five-count, then finally: "Seriously? Please tell me you got that for five cents at a garage sale and you haven't been playing with my kiln on your off-hours?"

"Not me," was all Val said, and she waited to see if he would accept the mug. When he said nothing more but pursed his lips, she added, "The kids from Gerardo's youth class made it for you..."

"Oh, well... context is everything. In that case, job well done," James observed sagely, finally taking the steaming mug. "I was afraid for you for a few moments."

"Afraid I was going to foist a secret portfolio on you?" Val asked, arching a brow.

"Something like that, yeah," James observed, his tone still cautious.

Val laughed and flipped her long, thick brown braid over her shoulder. "Nope. Some of us have photos to take, tasks to run."

"Ta, Val... I appreciate all you do—hope I say it enough."

"Almost enough, close enough... oooh, watch it, it's h.o.t.," Val advised as James took a sip from the greatest, bestest, greenest mug he'd ever seen.

James chuckled. "You're enjoying this, aren't you?"

"Little bit, yeah... you know kids—when they appreciate their teacher, they've gotta give him an apple. Kids must like your... um... your dishwater-brown hair, I suppose... flour-colored skin... your lazy eye..." Val began as she went back to the kitchen. She brought out a tray of pastries and placed them on the side table set up for refreshments, continuing her list of his dubious assets and suspect qualities as she brought out the rest of the food.

"And... you're... ah... funny. Kids like that. And tall—well, medium tall, or tallish... and cheekbones that could carve cold granite. But wait—that's a different craft class. And that intense brooding look you do when you've lost track of the conversation and are buying time until you *catch up*... oh, and let's not forget that adorable gap between your front teeth... and your uncanny ability to quote obscure phrases from Sanskrit, of all things, and for no apparent reason..."

"Everyone's tall to kids, and you're making me sound like an undernourished waif wearing a hairpiece that's squeezed me brain so tight leftover pretension pops out," James said with a straight face, then took another sip from the mug. "Absolutely nothing wrong with my teeth, no gaps—all English, au naturel."

Val laughed. "See? That was funny. So—you like the mug? Really? I can get you another one for the meeting if you want. You are the lead designer on this project, after all, and you may need to set an example. Or high-water mark... or whatever."

"Actually, I'm liking this mug more and more. No matter the age of who made it, there's something about homespun with heart that does the job—makes every beverage taste better. Don't you dare take it."

Val nodded her approval. "Good on you—hotshot artiste seen drinking from the results of a second-grade arts and crafts session. You'll start a trend."

"Move over, Op Art."

Val laughed. "Pave the way... you are a way-paver. Road construction; that's bona fide working class."

"I'll wear the yellow safety vest like my alma mater keepsake tee."

They shared a laugh, and Val leaned back to peer at him. "You look especially... sparkly today..."

"Ta—though I suspect *sparkly* should be reserved for describing wee pink unicorns, but I'll take it." James sighed and smiled. "I'm very pleased to get this project up and rocking—gonna be a good day."

"Indeed," Val said as she crossed back to the kitchen to survey the conference table. "How many board members of the Epoch Alliance are coming? Just two, right? Alfred and Mabel?"

"That's right, far as I know," James called over his shoulder. He was back at the window again—wanted one last look before completely shifting gears. Some of the warm morning glow had faded, but it was still there, still soft. He wanted to be quiet for a few moments more, to dwell here and clear his mind for the coming presentation.

Interesting. He hadn't felt this way for years and years... maybe as far back as when he was a student coming across the big water to New York, twelve years ago now. Yeah, maybe that's it—that wonderful feeling of beginning again, with nowt but tuppence in his pocket.

Fresh start—big horizon—unknown adventure.

He sipped his tea, the familiar bitter taste grounding him momentarily as he looked at the sun climbing higher in the sky, dissolving the secret shadows and exposing all to the discerning eye. Maybe he was simply feeling positive about the upcoming Epoch Alliance project. The massive mosaic wall they were planning to install at the new Eco United Building was certainly a bold undertaking on the face of it. Maybe. But James Watson had learned long ago to listen to his instincts, and if he was getting a sign that *something* ethereal was trying to make itself real, he would pay attention to it.

As he stood there and finished his tea, he watched the city move on. It was as if the whole town had paused for him to take a mental snapshot, and once that spot of tourism was complete, the whole works could move along and talk amongst themselves. He smiled at the thought. He was in a mood, wasn't he? Might burst out in song at any moment.

He walked across the studio, his footsteps echoing softly on the wood floor. Every detail seemed heightened—the texture of his worn blue t-shirt against his skin, the slight breeze from the open window, the faint smell of paint and clay that permeated the space. He ran his hand along a worktable, feeling the smooth wood beneath his fingers.

"James?" Val's voice called out. "Do you wanna do seating arrangements for the meeting?"

He chuckled softly. "Nah, let gravity do its thing. Everybody lands in the right spot at the right time."

James's thoughts wandered to the team he was expecting today. Each member brought their own unique skills and vision to the project, and he absolutely loved the brainstorming of a group mind—different ideas ringing out to chime in like bells, searching for a place in the pattern and overall harmony.

James stood poised with arms crossed, surveying the table, the refreshments, just checking for any loose end to tuck. He knew better than to interfere—he really did—but just had to ask:

"Oi, Val!" he called to his assistant, who was bustling about the long table, straightening chairs and placing a project folder in front of every seat. "You haven't put the jelly doughnuts next to those cardboard granola bars, have you? We want to provide options, not break their hearts with a life-altering decision."

Valerie rolled her eyes good-naturedly. "Relax, boss. Everything's perfect. I've even color-coded the fruit platter. Although I still think the kiwis clash with your *lucky* shirt."

James glanced down at his worn blue t-shirt and grinned. "Watch it. This shirt's got more style than your entire wardrobe, I'll have you know."

"If, by *style*, you mean ancient stains that look like a whimsical Dadaistic rendering of the Hawaiian islands, then sure—that's a lay-up," Valerie quipped, adjusting a stack of blueprints. "Slides are ready, by the way. Though why we're using actual slides in 2002 unleashes a baffled bird in my brain. You do know computers exist, right?"

"Computers, eh? I suspect I've heard of those, but deliberately chose to forget. Next thing you know, we'll be communicating through magic boxes in our pockets," James retorted, eyes twinkling. The banter with Val was familiar, comforting. He was admitting to a wee bit of stage nerves, just a sense of anticipation for the coming presentation.

The door buzzer sounded, and James straightened, tugging at his shirt. "Right then, bottoms up."

* * *

Alfred strode in first, flanked by two assistants James didn't recognize. The older man's imposing figure filled the doorway, silver hair gleaming in the sunlight streaming through the windows. Despite his advanced years, Alfred Worthington carried himself with the vigor of a much younger man, his broad shoulders squared and his steps purposeful. The fine lines around his eyes spoke of a lifetime of laughter and hard-won wisdom.

"James, my boy!" Alfred boomed, his rich baritone filling the room. He clapped James on the shoulder, his grip still strong and sure, then grasped his forearm with the fervor of a fellow gladiator surviving another round in the ring. His bright blue eyes, as sharp and keen as in the salad days of his twenties, twinkled with genuine warmth. "I see you've done a lot with your space, made yourself quite at home here, glad to see it, so glad. I want to take a look at your new work over there on the bench, but later, yes?"

James was always so pleased to be with Alfred; they had hit it off from square one a decade ago, and their friendship had only deepened over the years. He couldn't help but notice how, instead of Alfred's usual upscale, well-tailored attire, he was dressed in a more casual way this morning. James smiled—it suited him.

James chuckled. "Of course, and yes, I'm feeling quite at home, thanks." He gestured toward the kitchen area. "Coffee? Tea? We have decaffeinated... I'd offer you something stronger, but we'll be talking nuts and bolts, won't we? And it won't be the best idea to have you breaking into the stage version of 'Trouble in River City.' Gotta stay on track, mind the horses."

Alfred laughed, the sound deep and hearty, causing the crow's feet at the corners of his eyes to deepen. "Too true, it's funny because it's true. At least you didn't make a sideways comment about my dusty voice."

"Never. You and Mabel are timeless and priceless," James replied, admiring how Alfred's vitality seemed to belie his years. "How is Mabel? She joining us today?"

"She'll be here shortly," Alfred replied with a wink, his eyes twinkling with mischief. "Said something about picking up several cheesecakes from a European bakery on Lincoln Ave. She'll be here soon—wouldn't miss it for the world."

As they chatted, more team members trickled in. Max Henderson, the liaison from Eco United, was here. James greeted each with a smile and a quip, falling easily into the role of charming host. But he found his attention shifting toward the front door of the loft space, as if waiting for a curtain to part and a big reveal. Energy was humming under his feet like the thrum of a steady drum rolling up to a cymbal crash. That's an odd thought. He smiled—he certainly was in a mood.

Alfred pulled James aside as he was noting Val instructing folks where to leave their coats and the lay of the loft. "Listen, James, are you listening? Good. About our color glaze specialist... bit of a coup, really. New to Chicago, had a well-received showing at the Art Institute, and is quite the name in London, L.A., and parts of Europe—Dresden... I think you'll be impressed."

Before James could respond, the door opened once more. Rhonda Morrison strode in, her presence commanding attention. She was tall, a full five-six inches of stately African American woman, her light brown skin glowing with vitality. Her short, natural hair was impeccably styled, framing her strong features and intelligent eyes; cool, coiffured, and she momentarily filled the door from stem to stern. Rhonda was talking to someone over her shoulder—James caught something about "earliest start date." And behind her...

Emma.

Emma stood in the doorway, her eyes meeting his across the room. There was no surprise in her gaze, just a quiet resignation tinged with... what? A soft "hello you," perhaps.

James felt as if sixty-five percent of the air in his lungs had just been mercilessly sucked out, leaving just enough—just enough—to remain upright and conscious. No kidding; he had just enough air to tip the scale to a command stand and avoid a Victorian-era attack of the vapors. He didn't have a tightly wound corset to blame or smelling salts to come to his rescue, but he did have... the years in between, and time-tested emotional shock absorbers. His hand absently touched his lucky shirt, which suddenly felt too tight, too warm, but real.

Emma moved into the room, her steps measured and careful, as if she were approaching a wild animal. Which, James thought hysterically, wasn't that far off the mark.

In a tidy, lazy-Susan cupboard in his mind where observations were constantly clocked and his sense of humor remained perpetually intact, he observed this worn cliché: the world seemed to tilt on its axis. How fatiguing to find it true. James, indeed, felt as if he were standing on the edge of a vortex, with every table, chair, kiwi, and odd breakfast bar, et al. fading away except for her. It was an indiscriminate dissolution of time and space, save for her. He couldn't speak, couldn't move, could barely breathe. Except for this:

Emma... Em...

She was in a patch of sunlight now, her dark brown hair, touched with hints of auburn where the light caught it, fell in soft waves around her face. Her high cheekbones and full lips—the same, just the same. Perhaps more finely tuned, more a woman now, but it was herself. The same soul.

Val's voice broke through the fog. "Everyone, please help yourself to refreshments."

The sound of Val's voice pierced the bubble—well, at least enough to release the handbrake on his mind.

James turned abruptly, walked deeper into his studio, his back to the group. He needed space to breathe, a few moments to get his bearings. He took a deep, shuddering breath, then slowly turned around.

Emma stood just three feet away, her eyes meeting his. He was looking into the unflinching, steady beams of "Emma eyes." A warm brown that seemed to shift to hazel in certain lights—absolutely Emma eyes.

It was a shock, of course. One could have someone on their mind, so much a part of their mind, they thought of them untold times in a month, but that wasn't the same as seeing said person suddenly in the flesh. James was tempted to reach out to touch her arm just to satisfy his doubting mind that she was really here, but thank God, he heard himself ask this instead:

"What are you doing here?"

She swallowed hard before answering, her low voice—her speech pattern sending a thrill to his inner ear. "Hello, James… I'm here to help. This is a big project, bigger than you imagine. I'm here to help you," she said softly, her voice carrying easily to him, private to him.

James opened his mouth, closed it, opened it again. What came out was: "Didn't expect to see you on this side of the pond."

Emma's face remained expressionless, but her voice was soft as she offered, "I go where the work takes me."

"Right," James said, his voice just a wee bit too tight. "'Cuz that's your M.O., isn't it? Following the work. No matter what." His Geordie accent was a bit thicker now.

"I always do my best, you know that," Emma said clearly, calmly.

They studied each other for a long moment, maybe two... for maybe two moments straight James looked into her eyes, to assess, to study, to espy who in the world she was now compared to the girl he'd thought he'd known. She let him look, she wasn't hiding—her soft brown eyes, warm and yielding, and still she was a mystery. He simply did not know what she was about. He couldn't find... the reason.

Maybe it was about the work. Maybe he'd been right and it was always about the work for her, but that meant she'd always put herself first—and that placed this very important project second. That was an inconceivable situation.

Emma was speaking again.

"I'll do my best, James... I... I have a knack for color, I'll be a good co-lead designer, I'm your girl—"

It was an unfortunate choice of words, and Emma had stopped herself but not soon enough. The slip hardened his heart and made his mind up.

James glanced over his shoulder. The others were settling around the table. He looked back at Emma, his face carefully neutral. "Not for long, if I have anything to say about it."

Some people were lingering by the refreshment table, some were staking out their place at the conference table, others were looking at the sample photos James had posted on the wall of the installation site at the Eco Building. James noticed Emma had moved to look at the photo of the wide lobby wall of the new Eco Building. It was the selected site for the mosaic wall.

She was studying the location and tapping her chin with small, simple pats... that meant something was brewing in her noggin.

"Oh my God," James muttered under his breath, "am I really seeing this? Am I really casually observing the woman that split me in two and almost broke my mind munching on a bagel and strolling the gallery in me house?"

A soft inner voice immediately broadcast: *Well, she didn't break you in two... you broke yourself in two.* James was an honest man, and so he acknowledged the truth—but still... Emma had been a catalyst. Whatever—didn't really matter. That was then and this was now, and he needed to talk with Alfred.

James spotted him looking out the window and, as he approached, Alfred said, "So sorry, Mabel is running late, she'll be here any minute. Can we wait until she's here? She'd hate to miss one word."

"Of course, of course," James assured him, and then lowered his voice in a way that suggested the next part of this conversation ought to be considered private. "Listen, Alfred," he murmured, "about Emma... I'm not sure she's right for this project. I know some other glaze color specialists who might be a better fit for the long haul."

Alfred frowned. "But her portfolio is impressive, James. Her work with glazes is beyond amazing. What's the problem?"

James ran a hand through his hair. "It's... she works abroad, doesn't she then? Always has something cooking in the small parts, which suggests distraction—maybe her own priorities... just consider it, yeah?"

Alfred's expression sobered, and he looked at James and finally said, "Well, you're not prone to exaggeration; I've never known you to overreact. But this is meeting number one, and let's see how this goes. Let's not put words in her mouth or jump to conclusions."

Alfred looked around the room to make sure they weren't being overheard, and once content, he continued, "James, my dear boy, the interview with her went very well indeed. In fact, some of her understanding of how art can function as a living, healing expression in society is very similar to yours—and mine, not to mention Mabel's. We both agreed that Emma Hawkins would fit well with you, not to mention her portfolio. Let's not..."

"Put the cart before the horse? Throw a bag of ice into the sauna?" James offered.

"If I understand the juxtaposition of those expressions correctly, then yes—some marriage between the two. Ah! Mabel is here. I need to see if she needs help with the dessert boxes. She knew you wouldn't have many sugar treat options, and some people enjoy rich treats with coffee. Don't worry overmuch; things have a way of working out."

And with that, Alfred was at his wife's side to greet her and help carry the boxes to the refreshment table.

All right. It was time. James was ready—like it or not, ready or not—this was going to be the biggest pitch of his life thus far. And looking at Emma, sitting frozen in her chair with her face averted from his, he suddenly wanted to spark her mind, melt her stoic expression. Em wanted to be here?

Fine.

All at once, in one massive download, James knew what to say and how to say it.

James stood at the head of the table, his posture straight but relaxed. He took a moment to survey the faces before him, noting Emma's careful mask and the expectant looks from

Alfred, Mabel, Rhonda, Val, Harry, Stan, and even Max from Eco United.

James looked inside himself for a moment and then began, his voice low, confidential, casual, and unforced. "The past makes us what we are." He paused, and then: "The future is our hope, our dream, and the result of thought-form building, but the present—the present is our resting place. It is the kettle where we blend the best of the past, clean the dross, and pave the way for the best possible future. Being present in the present, and aware of this responsibility, is the highest honor and noblest task a person or people can hope to have."

"My friends," James continued, his voice steady, "we've been tasked with creating a mosaic for the Eco Building. I believe we have an opportunity to do something profound with that trust. Let us consider what Eco United is going to accomplish. They have expanded research into alternative energy systems—electric cars, solar energy, even wind energy are dreams to most of us—but Eco is looking forward. And to get forward, to succeed in the long view, there will need to be a parallel current of thought-form building in the public. People will need to buy these products for the vision to work. And so, the stake needs to be personal. The people are the source for continued economic support for this type of enterprise—for any enterprise, really—and so what I am suggesting is that every hope that we have for a well-constructed, well-earned good future comes from the minute desires inside ordinary people."

He paused, gauging the room's reaction. Rhonda leaned forward slightly. Alfred drew in a deep breath. Mabel was smiling, silver curls framing her heart-shaped face, crow's feet wrinkling at the corners of her bright blue eyes. Emma's face was as still and quiet as a Japanese Noh Theatre mask.

James nodded to himself, looked inside to find the thread, and then continued. "Our mosaic can be a bridge—connecting past, present, to the future. It's a chance to show how ordinary people, in our ordinary ways, are the actual building blocks for every great enterprise. Every. Single. Person. Is seen, is important, and is part of the large picture perpetually expanding to the cosmos itself."

Here, James took a breath and signaled Val to show the next slide. It was a photograph of a happy family—mom, dad, and two children smiling at the camera. James took a sip of tea from his bright green mug, looked at the photo, and thought for a moment. The room was silent, waiting to see where he was going next.

"So what do we do to make that happen? We don't suddenly wake up one day yodeling, 'I got the power!' and instant-Bodhisattva everybody... at least not yet. So we begin with what we know—we begin with what we want—in a way that feels real and personal."

James nodded to Val, and the next slide came up. It was a bright color rendering of a child's drawing of a happy family—much like the previous photo: mom, dad, two siblings, and a happy house.

"This," James pointed at the image on the wall, "is what children want. And it's still there inside us all—it's what we all want—for everything to be okay, always. And so what do you do with that hope? You draw it. Children draw this out as a daily meditation practice, for God's sake."

James nodded to Val again, and the next slide was the wide expanse of the lobby wall of the Eco United Building.

"This is the thought-form building boiled down to its most basic alchemy," James said, then added, "This works—from ancient cave drawings sporting a bison to spear for dinner, to now. All our lives, all our countries and cultures, boiled down to one single hope: 'Please God, let it be better. Let the world be how good we know it can be—and we know it can be good, because I felt it once upon a time, and here is the story to prove it.' And so somehow we gather stories from people in the community—from their personal past—something wonderful that has happened or is hoped to happen—and fill that wall you see there... with that."

They all stared at the image of the wall and imagined. Just imagined.

James continued, his voice low, "I know I'm speaking conceptually, and that we are at the very beginning of this proposal, but I wanted to bring it to you all in this raw form for the group mind to consider, to see what happens."

James noticed Alfred nodding thoughtfully, while Mabel's eyes sparkled with interest.

"Of course, there are technical challenges," James acknowledged. "The Eco Building's curved wall at the end there will require careful planning for tile placement. We'll need to consider lighting, both natural and artificial, to ensure the mosaic is visible at all times of day."

Rhonda scribbled notes furiously, appreciating the practical considerations.

"But the benefits are substantial," James pressed on. "The building's high foot traffic means our work will be seen by thousands daily. The eco-friendly ethos aligns perfectly with our community-focused approach."

James's gaze briefly met Emma's. He saw a flicker of something—admiration? Challenge? But there was a small signal of a pilot light there in her eyes before she looked away.

"This isn't a temporary pause, just another mural or mosaic wall. Eco is building for the future, and I'm proposing a way in which the community can help play an active part." James concluded, his voice gaining passion. "It's about capturing the spirit of our community—showing how our individual stories weave together into something greater. Stories from the past, right alongside what I had for breakfast today, my favorite food perhaps, and hopes for the future—and all told as images, simple such as the child's drawing to complex, micro to the macro. But the energy inside every single story is a prayer to God. It's ambitious, yes, but I believe we can do it—with bells on."

James paused, providing a small resting place, to allow everyone to catch their breath, like standing on a plateau to consider the view before moving forward to the wrap-up. He could almost see the wheels beginning to turn in each person's mind, considering the scope of what he'd proposed. He risked a glance at Emma, who was watching him carefully, listening intently. In the old days, she would have chimed in long before this point, unable to restrain herself from jumping into the pool to compete with him. Now, she had self-control. So, she had matured. Well, so had he. He supposed that was a good point on both their parts.

With that thought, James drew in a deep breath and turned his gaze upward this time, looking up toward the ceiling. When he spoke again, his voice carried a depth of feeling that commanded the room's attention.

"We don't know where we're going, we have no idea what's going to happen—not really, not in a way that feels real—so what do we do? Where do we begin?"

Alfred leaned forward, his eyes fixed on James with intense curiosity. Mabel's hand found her husband's, squeezing gently.

"Well, in order to build something wonderful, we need a solid foundation. And so, as individuals, we remember what has worked in the past, don't we? Holiday gatherings, simple moments become profound by their purity—and so we use that, don't we?"

A ripple of reaction passed through the small group. It seemed as if everyone shifted subtly in their chair—either to lean forward to listen harder or to push back to see him better. Rhonda's brow furrowed in concentration. Emma remained still, outwardly calm, but her eyes never left James's face; she appeared to be listening to every word.

Even Max from Eco shifted in his seat, leaning forward with a mix of curiosity and cautious optimism. This was beginning to sound more real.

And so James took a breath to clear the way to begin the ascent to the top of the point. "We use those memories—best-loved activities, appreciation of nature, and love for each other—as fuel. Even if it's just five minutes of love, we use that as fuel and inspiration to look forward. We focus only on the positive memory and moments and extend that forward as a kind of momentum and perpetual prayer. And sure enough, with that kind of kindling, the imagination begins to sparkle and shine a light on ways to improve and take the highest road into the future."

James took a beat to look around the room, and then on a more personal note: "When you shine a light, you can see in the dark. It seems so simple—but simple works. And so alternative technologies begin to become possible; science and healing, unhindered by negative thinking, begin to rise to the surface with no one to 'say thee nay.' And so positive approaches toward ecology become clear as well. This is the result of the subsequent healing power of the group mind focused on one central theme. Love."

Emma's careful neutrality began to crack. James watched her as she lowered her head to hide her emotions, her hands clasped together in her lap. To give her some privacy, he shifted his attention to look around the table at his friends, new and old, and continued.

"I propose all this as a concept and focal point for this mosaic project... and then..."

James smiled his most charming smile, and the effect was palpable. A collective intake of breath swept through the room. "And then witness what happens next. It's going to be something wonderful."

As James finished, a charged silence fell over the room. Mabel took Alfred's hand as they shared a look. Max Henderson was grinning broadly, already envisioning the artistic potential and connection to the community for Eco United. Rhonda, despite her initial reservations, looked intrigued, her notepad now filled with hastily scribbled ideas.

But it was Emma's reaction that James found himself most attuned to. The careful distance she'd maintained throughout the meeting had softened. There was a complexity in her gaze now; her eyes were moist—a mixture of professional admiration, creative excitement, and something deeper, more personal, that she seemed to be fighting against. For a brief moment, their eyes met, and James saw a flash of the connection they'd once shared—a spark of the creative synergy that had drawn them together in the first place.

Maybe, just maybe, it wouldn't be too bad to have her around.

As the room began to buzz with excited chatter, James knew he had struck a chord. The seed of something extraordinary had been planted, and he could feel the collective energy of the group already beginning to nurture it into life.

Alfred drew in a deep breath and said, "Thank you, James. Thank you from my heart for a concept and a beginning place. Let's all take a break and come back to discuss what comes next."

* * *

Back at the table, the discussion turned technical. James found himself caught up in the excitement of planning—almost forgetting Emma's presence. Almost.

James had more slides queued up in the projector, which Val revealed one by one. There were images of other murals, mosaic walls, and public art installations from around the world. There were examples of how big-concept ideas could be harmonized into a whole.

James had also thought to include a wide variety of images from nature, showing how the most complex landscape *worked*. There were also photos of large groups of people at public gatherings, smaller sets of children in school, plenty of images of family gatherings—both large and small. Plenty of food for thought and discussion.

Mabel had a list of questions and suggestions. "You mentioned getting stories from people—do you mean specific, or more general, as in events from history?"

"I was thinking both," James responded. "Representing smaller stories building up into larger themes—not using words, but drawings, images, both abstract and specific. Much like a montage—an all, broken apart to be put back together."

"Ah! Yes, that could work..." Mabel's eyes brightened.

Other ideas were offered, and all were jotted down and considered. James risked a glance toward Emma; she had been remarkably silent so far. It wasn't how he had remembered her—or was it?

He looked at her again, closer this time... ah! She was going deep. She'd either found something and was working it out... or absolutely couldn't take her eyes off his new green mug. James cocked his head and looked at the handcrafted gift from children. He had let Gerardo use his studio and kiln for his class when his was on the fritz, and the kids had made him a gift. It was sweet. His mind stopped—wait a minute. He began to think. He looked again at Emma.

As the conversation lulled, her soft voice broke the silence.

"We invite the public."

James drew in a sharp breath, his eyes meeting Emma's. She broke the contact and looked around the table, continuing—her voice gaining strength. "What if we invite the public? Ordinary people, creating their own pieces of the mosaic. Unprompted, unstructured. It would tie together everything James has proposed—everything: past, present, and future—all through the eyes of the community. Through their very personal history, family stories in clay, very real hopes... it would be true, and it would be... love."

The room fell silent as her words sank in. James felt a reluctant admiration stirring within him. It was brilliant, damn her. It took his ideas and elevated them to something he had been heading toward but hadn't quite conceptualized yet.

Alfred's face lit up. "That's inspiring!"

Rhonda nodded enthusiastically. "The logistics would be challenging, but the impact..."

James found himself nodding along, despite himself. He looked at Emma—really looked at her for the first time that day. She met his gaze steadily, a glimmer of hope in her eyes.

He cleared his throat. "It's... not without merit," he admitted grudgingly. Then, because he couldn't quite help himself, he added, "Assuming, of course, everyone stays on board and sees it through to the end."

Emma flinched slightly but held his gaze. "I'm not going anywhere, James." She didn't say it, but what she was telegraphing to him was: *Not this time.*

James took a deep breath, suddenly aware that he was standing at a crossroads. The peace he'd felt earlier that morning whispered at the edges of his consciousness. Could he trust it? Could he trust her?

Never mind the bollocks. He shook his head slightly. He often told people he loved the group mind—well, this was the fruit of that. So don't be daft; do it.

"Right then," James said, his voice softer than before. "Let's hear more about this idea of yours, shall we?"

As Emma began to elaborate, James found himself leaning in, drawn by her words. He made a conscious effort to give everyone a turn, listening intently to each contribution. The project was taking shape in a way he'd often dreamed about—a true meeting of minds. Even Max from Eco United, usually so buttoned-up, was pitching in with unexpected enthusiasm. There was a palpable sense of excitement as ideas bounced back and forth, each suggestion building on the last. James couldn't help but smile. This wasn't just work anymore—it was the purest form of play.

* * *

The meeting wound down, the excitement of new beginnings palpable in the air. As others said goodbye and filed out, Rhonda lingered, her enthusiasm barely contained. She approached James and Emma, who were gathering their notes.

"James, Emma, do you have a moment?" Rhonda interjected, her voice measured and polite. "I'd love to go over some scheduling details."

James nodded, stealing a glance at Emma. "Of course, Rhonda—fire away."

Rhonda launched into a series of questions, her words tumbling out in rapid succession. "How long do you think we'll need for the public sessions? How many weeks of tile-making to fill the entire mosaic? Should we stagger the times, maybe offer evening sessions for working folks?"

James chuckled at Rhonda's rapid-fire questions, still shot with zeal after a long day. He answered each in sequence, and Emma chimed in occasionally, offering suggestions. "We might want to consider weekend workshops too," she said, her voice soft but confident. "It could draw in families, make it a community event."

James found himself nodding along. "Yes, weekends are going to be key—for paving the way for the people that want to come, and for getting our crews in a steady working pace too."

The conversation continued, James and Emma falling into an easy rhythm of collaboration. All the while, they studied each other surreptitiously. James noticed the way Emma tucked her hair behind her ear when she was thinking—a habit he'd forgotten. Emma observed the crinkles at the corners of James's eyes when he smiled, a detail that sent a pang of nostalgia through her.

As the sky outside darkened to a deep indigo, Rhonda finally glanced at her watch. "Oh my, I didn't realize how late it's gotten. Emma, would you like a ride home?"

Emma hesitated for a moment, her eyes flicking briefly to James and then back to Rhonda. "That would be good, thanks. I know it's probably out of your way, but I'd appreciate that. It's been a long day."

As they gathered their things, James felt a strange reluctance to see them go. He walked them to the door, exchanging final pleasantries. And then he had the oddest thought pop into his mind, unbidden but binding, and it was this: in gratitude for that idea Emma had gifted to the project... *If she turns to look at me on her way out the door, I will accept that as "I'm sorry," and I'll let the past go... if she looks back...*

"Good night, James," Emma said softly as she passed him.

"Night, Em," he replied, their eyes meeting one last time before she turned away. He thought she paused a beat when he spoke his pet name for her, but she didn't look back at him.

She didn't look back.

The door closed behind them, and suddenly James was alone in his loft. The wonderful energy that had built up in the space all day had been vacuumed out. She had taken it with her.

The space seemed larger now—and quite empty.

James wandered back to the table, absently straightening papers. His eyes fell on a small sketch Emma had made during the meeting—a rough design for a tile. Without thinking, he picked it up, studying the confident lines. Wait a minute... he looked more closely. It was a sketch of his new flower-power mug.

The second sketch next to it was a simple line drawing of the flowers from the mug, as they might look on a clay tile.

"Well, I'll be a daft lunk of stupid... she *is* brilliant."

But there was no one to hear him. The quietness of the loft pressed in, and it wasn't an unfamiliar sensation—it was often a comforting way to cushion himself from the noise of Chicago. But not tonight.

Emma hadn't looked back, she hadn't said she was sorry. There had been plenty of opportunities all day to single him out and talk to him, to explain—but no, she hadn't said "boo," which could only mean she wasn't sorry.

It wasn't a dramatic realization—more of a quiet observation that settled in the center of his chest, the familiar pinprick of a hurting place that ran deep. And still... he missed her. God, love was strange.

Did he actually just think that? Yes, he did.

James sighed, setting the sketch down. He moved to the window and looked out at the city lights. The day had brought changes he couldn't possibly have imagined this golden morning. Emma was back in his life—at least professionally—and by her own words, wasn't leaving any time soon.

Strange, strange, strange.

* * *

Chapter 2

Chicago — Lake Shore Drive *— Mar. 25, 2002 — 7:35 p.m. — Emma*

Emma didn't realize that her hands were shaking until she had settled into the passenger side of Rhonda's Volvo. She intertwined her fingers, clasped her hands together, and willed herself to be still. Emma had held herself together for a good five hours; she had been poised, polite, and professional—the royal trifecta for the modern woman. So what was thirty minutes more in a meager car ride, more or less?

More, so it seemed, because her body wasn't listening to her anymore. All her body knew was that her mind had just left the man she loved... again. And so, her hands wouldn't take requests from her anymore.

The sun had long since dipped below the horizon, painting the Chicago skyline in hues of deep purple and indigo. It was cooling down too—typical for early March, because winter wasn't done. Emma settled deeper into the passenger seat of Rhonda's Volvo; the leather felt cool through her thin coat, and she waited for the car to warm.

Rhonda seemed to notice her trembling and offered, "This car heats up fast—an older model, but tried and true."

Emma nodded as an answer. Her teeth had begun to chatter, and she didn't quite trust herself to speak without stuttering, which wouldn't have been the greatest impression for the managing director of Epoch Alliance to witness. She'd been advised by her colleagues that Alfred gave Rhonda a lot of room to run around in, and it was best to tread softly until she knew the lay of the land.

When she didn't answer, Rhonda smiled and said, "Ah, you've been in L.A. It's going to take a while for your body to acclimate to the cold here. As you can see, this day ran warm, and now—cold."

"Yes…" Emma finally managed. "I remember, I have… family roots in Minnesota… it'll come back," was all she seemed able to manage.

For a moment, neither woman spoke. The only sounds were the soft purr of the engine, the blow of the heater on full, and the muted bustle of the city outside. They were getting ready to turn north onto Lake Shore Drive, which would mean a clear shot to Lawrence, so Emma assumed Rhonda was waiting for the straightaway before grilling her.

"Well," Rhonda finally broke the silence after she made the turn and merged with care onto the Drive, mindful of invisible ice, "that was quite a meeting, wasn't it? Your idea about involving the public in the mosaic project was inspired."

Emma nodded, her gaze fixed on the passing buildings. "Thank you," she replied softly, her tone polite but reserved. Then, "I got the idea from James—he provided the tipping point."

Rhonda thought back. "Really? I didn't notice."

"It was there," was all Emma would provide.

Rhonda, seemingly determined to draw Emma out, pressed on. "You and James seemed to have a great dynamic there—reading each other like that. Have you two worked together before?"

Emma tensed slightly, her fingers curling around the strap of her bag, hanging on for dear life, it seemed. Damn—was her body in shock or something? She took a deep breath and worked at keeping her sentences short. "We attended Cooper Union around the same time," she said vaguely, careful to keep her voice neutral. "That was years ago."

"Oh, really?" Rhonda's eyebrows shot up with interest. "Small world. So…"

There was a pause as Rhonda smoothly passed another car on Lake Shore Drive, the city lights reflecting off the lake to their right. Emma found herself holding her breath, unsure of what was coming next.

Rhonda turned to Emma with a smile that was both friendly and curious. "James—was he this hot back then?"

The question caught Emma off guard. For a moment, she was transported back to New York, to late nights in the studio—James with paint-stained hands and a fierce concentration in his eyes. The way he'd run his fingers through his hair when he was thinking, leaving streaks of color. The infectious laugh that could get everyone in their group going, riffing off each other.

Emma considered her answer carefully. "No," she said finally, a small smile playing at the corners of her mouth. "But yes—just in a different way. More wild, maybe."

"Wild. Wow. Interesting," Rhonda observed, her eyes back on the road but her mind clearly processing this new information.

Emma turned to look out the window, using the moment to compose herself. The lights of the city blurred past. She hadn't meant to reveal even that much, but something about Rhonda's direct question had caught her off guard.

Sensing the shift in Emma's mood, Rhonda fell silent for a moment. As they merged onto the exit for Lawrence Avenue, Emma decided to shift the conversation.

"So, Rhonda," she began, her tone carefully casual, "how long have you known James?"

Rhonda shook her head. "Oh, not long at all, actually. Alfred and Mabel brought him on board for this project. They're the ones who know him best." She paused, then continued, "They were set on him from the very beginning. I'm not even sure they actually considered all the other candidates I had lined up for the interviews." Rhonda shot Emma a quick glance and countered quickly with, "Oh, they interviewed everyone, don't get me wrong, but somehow I got the feeling they were just going through the motions until everyone on the board saw what they already knew."

She glanced at Emma again, saw she was listening closely, and so expanded slightly. "I was there at the interviews, same as at yours. Alfred always keeps me in the loop, so I saw for myself what was driving him... and damn, he created the impression he could pick up the whole project and carry it if need be. You just got this feeling it was personal. And of course, his work spoke volumes. He was the guy. Funny—both you and him spoke along similar lines... maybe it's the Cooper Union way or something."

Emma nodded, filing away this piece of information. "Maybe... it is a specific mindset. The students are vetted—it's an intense admissions process." She paused, then asked, "And how did he end up in Chicago? And working with clay? Last I heard, he was still in New York."

"From what I understand, he moved here about a year ago," Rhonda replied. "Needed a change of scenery, I guess. Maybe something about the events on September 11... Mabel might have mentioned something about that. I'm not talking out of turn—he hasn't made a secret of it. And... Chicago's art scene has been really good for him. He's made quite a name for himself already... in several mediums, I suppose."

Emma felt a pang in her chest. A year ago. Had it really been that long since she'd allowed herself to wonder about James? Since she'd forced herself to stop checking for news of his latest exhibitions or projects?

"That's... good to hear," Emma managed, her voice barely above a whisper.

They lapsed into silence again, and so Emma studied Rhonda's profile. Her face was serene, composed, and good-humored—especially here in the car and away from the official atmosphere of the meeting—but Emma got the distinct impression that James had not been Rhonda's first choice. Interesting.

As Rhonda navigated the streets of Lincoln Square, Emma risked a glance at her hands. They were still now, quiet and waiting for instructions. These same hands had reached for the door to James's studio. Waiting outside that steel door to follow Rhonda might have been one of the most telling moments of her life so far. Even then, committed as she'd been, forty-nine percent of her mind had been screaming at her to run far and fast. Dang mind. But trust your hands, feet, and instincts when it comes time to climb a mountain.

Good on you, hands. Thank you, feet—forget that dang mind. It had been hard, so hard on her pride after he had rejected her, to come here. But once begun—even now, hurting as she was—she knew it was the highest road.

Emma's thoughts returned to the moment she'd stepped into James's loft earlier today. The familiar scent of clay and paint, the eclectic mix of art and function that was so quintessentially James. And then, seeing him...

It had been like a punch to the gut. James, standing there in his worn blue t-shirt—so similar to ones she'd seen him wear at Cooper Union—and him, himself looking both exactly the same and utterly different. His hair was a little grayer at the temples, and he carried himself with a confidence that hadn't been there before. The boy she knew was gone. He was every inch a man now, his sparkling charisma now a steady, unconscious stream of power. He had become a strong man.

But his eyes... those hadn't changed. A little more reserved, perhaps—cards much closer to his chest—but still him. The same deep brown that had melted her mind still did the trick.

But seeing the shock on his face, then those deep eyes alight with an unguarded joy, which slowly turned to stone right before her eyes, had been hard to bear. James Watson had not been happy to see her. At all. Or at least, not happy enough to suit her—and sure, it hurt. It wasn't logical to expect more, but still—since when were human beings logical?

Emma recalled the details of James's studio. It was so perfectly him—organized chaos, with splashes of color and texture everywhere... and that mug... that outrageously beautiful splash of a mug had provided the key.

James had been holding a mug—a particularly piercing tone of lime green that shook the bones a bit, but was sweetened with three sunny flowers to complement the whole. The mug was clearly handmade and completely without guile or artifice. And of course, it was made by a child—and one who loved him well enough to work that hard. She had wondered—who was the child? His child? Emma felt a pang of remorse; it would have been unnatural if she didn't.

She had watched as James sipped from the mug, his fingers curled around the thick walls. There was something profoundly touching about seeing this accomplished artist—this man she had once known so well—drinking from a child's creation with unselfconscious ease. This was James with his heart on display—never mind the bollocks, he did what he wanted, and in turn, it elevated the value of the object. Love made the homespun, handmade craft not only beautiful, but resonated with that same tender vibration.

To make the ordinary extraordinary.

That was when she held her breath, becoming quiet in body and mind so as not to disturb the birthing of an idea. Oh dear God... it would mean an enormous amount of work and commitment from everyone involved—on a monster level—so she had sat on the idea for a few minutes as it brewed in her brain, drew a sketch or two to test the notion, and then she noticed James watching her, with his brow pulled slightly together, as if he were waiting for her to say what was on her mind. And so, without preamble, she had.

Also—she needed to earn her place on the project at an early phase so he couldn't kick her off the team. Oh yes, she could admit it. James would have found the idea too, sooner or later—she had merely beaten him to the punch.

Still competitive after all these years.

"Emma?" Rhonda's voice cut through her reverie. They had arrived at her apartment building. "We're here."

Emma blinked, coming back to the present. "Thank you for the ride—I think I might have dozed off for a few moments," she said, reaching for the door handle.

"Of course, that's fine—it's been an intense day." Rhonda smiled. "And Emma? I know we're all new to this project, but

I think there's something special happening, and you're a big part of it. Not all first meetings go as well. I admit James was on fire, but don't forget we need your voice too—your opinion, your work. You are clearly an asset."

Emma paused, her hand on the door. "Thanks—yes," she said softly, not quite meeting Rhonda's eyes. "Good night, Rhonda."

As she watched Rhonda's car disappear down the street, Emma felt the weight of the day settling on her shoulders. She climbed the stairs to her second-floor apartment. All she really wanted was to lie down somewhere—hopefully her bed if she could make it that far—and sleep.

And so, once inside her small one-bedroom space on the third floor, with the door shut firmly behind her, she felt her way to her bed and fell onto the duvet, with her coat still on and bag wrapped over her shoulder, and issued the command call:

No more thinking, please.

But as she fell asleep, there was one last thought to color her dreams:

He called me Em.

* * *

Chapter 3

N.Y.C. — Cooper Union Admin. — *Sep. 7 1987 — 10:20 a.m. —* *Beginning*

The crisp September air carried a hint of excitement as nineteen-year-old James Watson, recently of Newcastle upon Tyne, stood on the corner of 3rd Avenue and St. Marks Place, his senses overwhelmed by the cacophony that was New York City. The start of a new semester at Cooper Union brought fresh faces and endless possibilities, and James found himself at the heart of it all.

He loved it—absolutely, unequivocally loved it.

He closed his eyes for a moment, feeling the vibration of the city through the soles of his feet. It was as if the very concrete beneath him pulsed with life, a steady rhythm that matched the quickening of his own heartbeat. When he opened his eyes again, he tilted his head back, gaze traveling up and up and up to the imposing facades of buildings that dreamed of touching the sky.

"Bloody hell," he murmured, a grin spreading across his face.

His eyes settled on the iconic Cooper Union Foundation Building just down the street. The brownstone structure stood out among its neighbors, its Italianate style a testament to its 19th-century origins. The rounded arches of its windows and the intricate cornices spoke of a different era, yet the building seemed to pulse with the same energy as the city around it.

James had arrived in New York just days before, his talent having earned him a coveted spot in Cooper Union's prestigious art program. Everything about the city thrilled him—the towering buildings, the eclectic mix of people, the palpable energy that seemed to hum through the streets. It was so different from Newcastle, yet somehow he felt an instant connection to this urban labyrinth.

As he stood there, James couldn't help but reflect on the journey that had brought him here—the countless hours spent hunched over his sketchbook, the sleepless nights preparing his portfolio, the nerve-wracking interview. And now here he was, about to embark on a new chapter of his life in a city that never slept.

The energy of New York was unlike anything he'd ever experienced. It was as if millions of dreams and ambitions collided in the air, creating an almost tangible force that propelled everyone forward. James felt it coursing through him, igniting his creativity and filling him with a sense of limitless possibility.

A street vendor's voice cut through his reverie, offering hot dogs and pretzels. James's stomach growled, reminding him that he hadn't eaten since early morning. He approached the cart, his Geordie accent standing out as he asked for directions to the nearest café.

"Cheers, mate," he said, accepting a pretzel and the vendor's instructions. As he turned to leave, his eyes caught sight of the Cooper Union building again. The morning sun glinted off its windows, and James could almost imagine the generations of artists and thinkers who had passed through its doors. His heart leapt with excitement and a touch of nervousness.

His battered portfolio case tucked under his arm, James made his way toward the building, his long strides eating up the distance. The closer he got, the more details he noticed—the weathered stone, the play of light and shadow across its façade, the way it seemed to anchor the bustling street around it.

As he approached the base of the building, his eyes were drawn to a young woman sitting on the concrete steps. She was intensely focused on a large pad of paper balanced on her knees, her hand moving in swift, confident strokes as she sketched the bustling scene before her. The juxtaposition of her stillness against the backdrop of the historic building and the frenetic city street struck James as oddly poetic.

James paused, captivated by the fluid movement of her pencil and the look of total absorption on her face. There was something in her concentration that resonated with him—a familiar passion he recognized in himself. Without thinking, he moved closer, trying to catch a glimpse of her work.

And then he saw what she was drawing.

Him.

Standing on the corner, head tipped to the sky, grinning like a lad seeing the world for the first time. Had he really been that transparent in his awe of the city?

"You what?" he exclaimed, his accent thicker in surprise. "How'd you get that so fast? I was only standing for a moment."

The young woman looked up, her eyes meeting his for the first time. There was a spark of something in that gaze—recognition, perhaps, or surprise at seeing the object of her study now up close and personal. A small smile played on her lips as she replied, "Maybe a longer moment than you think."

He cocked his head to look at her more closely, studying her intently now, as if sending the energetic impression of her image back to his brain for further analysis and direction on how to proceed.

"Have I seen you somewhere?" he asked.

"You mean like in a movie or something?" The girl laughed; she seemed to think it was the best joke cracked on these concrete steps. "Not quite immortalized yet."

James plopped down beside her on the steps, the rough concrete cool beneath him. A gust of wind swept up the street, carrying with it the scent of coffee from a nearby café and the faint aroma of Emma's vanilla perfume. "Well, let's do something about that... here, give over," he said, grinning, gesturing for the sketchbook. "Fair's fair—lemme have a crack."

Emma laughed, a melodious sound that seemed to rise above the city's cacophony of honking horns and chattering pedestrians. She handed him the pad, her fingers brushing against his for a moment. James noted the callus on her middle finger, a testament to countless hours of drawing.

He immediately began sketching, his hand moving with swift, sure strokes. He found himself captivated by the way the sunlight caught the auburn highlights in Emma's very dark brown hair, the way her nose crinkled slightly when she smiled. In the background, a street musician's saxophone wailed a jazzy tune, providing an impromptu soundtrack to their encounter.

"Stop now, you're not playing fair," he protested as Emma continued to laugh—her soft brown eyes, with glints of... was that green? Her eyes fairly danced with mirth. Her heart-shaped face, strong cheekbones, full lips... and was that a dimple? James quickly added it to his sketch. "Think of... dead kittens—"

"What? No, not the tabby, don't touch the tabby!" Emma gasped, her hand flying to her chest in mock horror. Her silver bracelet caught the light, momentarily blinding James.

He squinted, his pencil pausing for a moment. "Well then, something else—sad, but not too sad," James amended, his eyes twinkling. He noticed a small paint stain on the cuff of Emma's denim jacket, wondering what masterpiece it might have come from.

"Anything else you require? Sir... what's your name?" Emma asked, tilting her head slightly. A strand of hair fell across her face, and James resisted the urge to reach out and tuck it behind her ear.

"James will do, to you and yours at this time of day," he replied cheekily, his Geordie accent rolling off his tongue. He saw Emma's lips quirk up at the sound, and he felt an immediate but unnameable pleasure.

"All right, Sir James," Emma said, her laughter under control now. She shifted on the step, crossing her legs at the ankle. James noticed her worn Chuck Taylors, covered in doodles and paint splatters—a canvas in their own right. "I'll think of..." Her voice trailed off, her expression softening, a hint of sadness creeping in.

As he continued to sketch, capturing the subtle change in her demeanor, he became oblivious to the bustling world around them—students rushing past with backpacks full of dreams and ambitions, a group of pigeons squabbling over a discarded bagel nearby. Yet somehow, in the midst of New York's endless motion, he and Emma seemed to exist in a bubble of calm.

James's pencil danced across the paper, trying to capture not just Emma's features, but the essence of this moment—the play of light and shadow on her face, the way she held herself, the complex emotions flitting across her eyes. He found himself wishing he had his paints with him, longing to capture the exact shade of hazel-brown in her eyes.

"Okay, done," he announced triumphantly, though his voice softened as he looked up and saw that Emma's expression had truly turned melancholic. The saxophonist down the street had switched to a more somber melody, as if sensing the shift in mood.

Without thinking, he wrapped an arm around her shoulders. The warmth of his touch seeped through Emma's denim jacket, a stark contrast to the cool September breeze. "Here now, here now, steady on... it'll be alright," he said, as soft as silk, his words wrapping around like a 'besty blanket.'

A siren wailed in the distance, momentarily drowning out the constant hum of the city. James felt Emma tense slightly under his arm, then relax. "They'll have potatoes and meat—well, some kind of meat—nearby, I'm certain, for lunch in the café. Get some food into you; thas' always a comfort—works for me," James continued, his eyes fairly singing a bright blessing as he tried to coax a smile from her. "What else can I say to cheer you?"

Emma's gaze remained fixed on the ground, where a fallen leaf skittered across the concrete.

"Lemme see the picture," she said quietly, her voice barely audible above the cacophony of the city.

James handed her the pad, his calloused fingers brushing against hers. A group of students rushed past, their excited chatter creating a momentary bubble of noise around them. Emma caught her breath as she looked at the sketch. The paper still held the warmth of James's hand, and she could smell the faint scent of graphite and something uniquely him—a mix of soap and perhaps sandalwood.

The sketch was a marvel of economy—just a few lines capturing her essence, her changing expression, the softness and sadness in her eyes. But more than the skill, it was how he saw her that astounded Emma. In just a few strokes, he had captured something only she had known was there—a vulnerability, a depth she usually kept hidden.

She looked up at James, really seeing him for the first time. The sunlight caught in his tousled brown hair, nature's own highlighter outlining his form. His eyes, she noticed, were a light, warm brown, flecked with gold. A small scar on his right jaw hinted at some long-ago mishap. "Who are you?" she asked, wonder and curiosity coloring her voice.

He met her gaze; the world seemed to slow around them, the constant motion of New York fading into the background. "Just a lad from Newcastle with a pencil and a dream," he said softly, a hint of self-deprecation in his tone. His fingers absently played with the frayed edge of his sketchbook. "And you? Who are you that can draw a proper classic rendering lickety-split, and feel so deeply the next I'm forced to drop me wares and sketch you?"

They looked at each other, and for a moment, the rest of the entire world became moot and melted into a background blur. The air between them seemed so soft now, so easy to be alive.

"I'm Emma," she said finally, her voice barely above a whisper. A small smile tugged at the corner of her mouth, transforming her face. "And I think... I think I'm very glad to meet you, James."

James smiled, a warm greeting that lit up his entire face and sent a flutter through Emma's chest. "The pleasure's all mine, Emma," he replied, his accent caressing her name in a way that made it sound new. He stood, offering her his hand. "Now, what say we go find a café that serves something resembling meat?"

"After we register for classes first, of course," Emma corrected. "It is, after all, free—"

"—God, isn't that brilliant? Don't you love it? No tuition at Cooper Union," James declared. "Means we can use our spare change to eat like kings and queens—of a lesser-known, rather diminutive kingdom perhaps, but still... more opportunity for eating versus starving artist. Don't you hate the cliché?"

Emma laughed, took his hand, and stood. The city continued its relentless pace around them—taxis honking, pedestrians rushing, the distant rumble of the subway beneath their feet. But for James and Emma, they had found a portable resting place called friendship.

They gathered their things, the sound of paper rustling and zippers closing momentarily drowning out the city's symphony, and then turned in tandem and headed toward the front doors of the admissions building.

* * *

The lobby of the Cooper Union Foundation Building buzzed with the energy of countless conversations, the high ceilings amplifying the excitement of new beginnings. James and Emma had just stepped through the ornate double doors, the cool air inside a stark contrast to the September heat outside.

"James! Oi, James!"

Before Emma could blink, two whirlwinds of enthusiasm descended upon them—a tall, lanky young man with a shock of red hair and a petite girl with a pixie cut and more piercings along the rim of her ears than Emma would care to see on a human being—(Ouch... how did she brush her hair?)—engulfed James in a tangle of arms and back-slaps.

"Bloody hell, mate! You made it!" the redhead exclaimed, his voice carrying a hint of an Irish lilt that echoed off the marble floors.

"We knew you would," the girl added, her grin threatening to split her face in two. "Told you the interview was just a formality, didn't I?"

James laughed, the rich sound of it momentarily drowning out the cacophony around them. "Maribel, Zane—or whatever name you're trying on this week," he said, shooting a pointed look at the redhead. "Good to see you haven't been deported yet."

Emma stood to the side, observing the exchange, not quite sure if she should lean in or drift back. The warm bubble that had enveloped her and James on the steps outside seemed to have dissipated, leaving her adrift in a sea of unfamiliar faces. She shifted her weight from one foot to the other, her eyes drawn to the intricate mosaic on the lobby floor.

"Come on," Maribel said, grabbing James's arm. "We've found a quiet corner over here. You won't believe what happened to Zane's sculpture during the summer program. It involved a fried egg on the sidewalk, a burlap tote of recycled Pepsi bottles, and Professor Herzog's bow tie—you were right, it was the ironic iconic cherry on top. He'll never speak directly to any of us again."

Zane groaned dramatically, his hand clutching his heart. "Must we relive my shaming in these hallowed halls?"

As the trio started moving towards a cluster of antique leather chairs, Emma felt a pang in her chest. James was swept along in their wake, his new friends monopolizing his attention with rapid-fire questions and inside jokes.

For a moment, it seemed James had forgotten her. Emma stood rooted to the spot, her portfolio growing heavy in her hands. The lobby suddenly felt too grand, too crowded. She glanced towards the exit, considering a hasty retreat—or slipping into the stream of students heading upstream to register for classes.

But then, just as she was about to turn away, James looked back over his shoulder. His eyes widened, as if suddenly desperate to save her from slipping away into a flash flood. He stopped so abruptly that Zane nearly ran into him.

"Emma," he called, his voice cutting through the noise. He extended a hand towards her—a silent invitation. "Come on, then. You've got to hear this story. Maybe you can help me decide if Zane's having us on."

It was a kind of word magic on Emma's state of mind. She had never lacked for personal confidence, but she'd never really found her peer group either, and so the prospect of being held in the circle—drawn in by one such as James—well, color her giddy. She found herself moving forward, drawn by James's smile and the rapid-fire sparkle in his eye.

As she approached the group, Maribel and Zane's curious gazes swept over her.

"Who's this, then?" Zane asked, a mischievous grin playing on his lips.

James's hand found the top of Emma's shoulder, gently guiding her into the circle. "This is Emma," he said, his voice carrying a note of pride that made Emma feel... well, almost fourteen-year-old girlish. "Best artist on the steps of Cooper Union. You should see her sketches—capturing my entire essence in the time it takes most people to blow their nose."

Maribel's eyebrows shot up. "Oh really?" she said, an assessing look passing between her and Zane. "Well, Emma, pull up a chair. Sounds like you're one of us already."

As Emma settled into a seat beside James, their shoulders brushing, she felt the last of her unease melt away as he made introductions. "This here is Maribel Smyth—with a 'y'?—from London, right? An' this 'un is Zane Thomason from some nether-land of Ireland, I forget where." They laughed, and James turned to Emma and explained, "We met in London along with about twenty others at the early admission stage... still can't believe we three beat the odds."

The lobby was still bustling, still overwhelming, still a raging river of students alternating between going with or fighting the flow, but now it felt alive with possibility. Emma caught James's eye and he winked—a silent reassurance that their moment on the steps hadn't been lost, merely widened to include an expanding circle.

Zane leaned forward, fairly overflowing with the tale he could barely wait to share. "Right then, gather 'round for the tale of the solar fried egg, the Pepsi bottles popped, and the Professor's unfortunate dark blue bow tie. I swear on my grandmother's secret pickle recipe, every word of this is true—or true enough for you lot."

As laughter erupted around them, Emma found herself swept up in the camaraderie. She'd come to Cooper Union hoping to expand her skill set and find her artistic voice, and now—alongside for the ride—she might be discovering something even more intrinsically valuable in order to grow: a place to belong.

As their laughter subsided, Maribel glanced at her watch. "Uh oh, we'd better get registered for classes soon. But after that, I'm starving. Where should we go to celebrate our first day?"

"Ooh, what about that Ukrainian place?" Zane suggested, his stomach growling audibly. "Veselka, innit?"

James shook his head, glancing at Emma. "Nah, we need proper meat. I promised Emma here some real food to cheer her up."

"There's that Jewish deli, B&H," Maribel offered. "Great soup, but no proper meat dishes."

"What about that place on Second Avenue?" Emma chimed in, surprising herself. "I saw it on the way here. Kiev, I think?"

James's face lit up. "Brilliant! They've got those massive sandwiches. Proper steak and potatoes too, if I remember right."

"Perfect," Zane nodded enthusiastically. "Nothing says 'welcome to art school' like stuffing our faces with Eastern European comfort food."

As they stood to join the registration queue, James caught Emma's eye again. "See?" he said softly, just for her. "Told you it'd be alright. Cooper Union's got history, new mates, and real food. What more could a starving artist ask for?"

Emma laughed. "Well, when you put it like that—so desperate you would lean on a cliché—who can say thee nay?"

James threw back his head and laughed.

* * *

The art studio hummed with the whir of pottery wheels and the soft squelch of clay being kneaded. Emma sat at her wheel, hands slick with slip, trying to coax a stubborn lump of clay into something resembling a bowl. Beside her, James was effortlessly throwing a tall vase, his long fingers shaping the clay with practiced ease.

"I swear," Emma grumbled, "this clay has a vendetta against me."

James chuckled, his eyes bright with a perpetual spark. "Nah, luv, you're just thinking too much. Let your hands do the work, yeah?"

Emma was about to retort—something very clever, to be sure—when Professor Hodges's voice cut through the studio chatter. "James! Could you come over here for a moment? I want to show you a new technique for attaching handles."

James shot Emma an apologetic look. "Duty calls. Don't let that clay bully you while I'm gone."

As James made his way across the studio, a small crowd of students gravitated towards him, eager to watch and learn. Emma sighed, her hands stilling on the wheel. It was always like this—moments of connection interrupted by James's magnetic pull on others.

"Quite the popular bloke, isn't he?"

Emma was startled, jumped a wee bit, looking up to find Maribel sliding onto the stool James had vacated. The petite girl's knowing smirk made Emma's cheeks warm.

"Oh, um... yeah. I guess he is," Emma mumbled, suddenly very interested in cleaning the slip from her fingers.

Maribel leaned in, her voice dropping conspiratorially. "So, what's the deal with you two anyway? Half the studio's trying to figure it out. Are you together? Just friends? Locked in some kind of artistic rivalry? Fighting over a bag of peanuts? What?"

Her hands stilled, her eyes fixed on the misshapen lump of clay before her. "We're... friends," she said, the word feeling inadequate on her tongue. "I mean, we hang out, we talk about art, but..."

"But?" Maribel prompted, one pierced eyebrow arching.

Emma shrugged, unable to find the words to describe the nebulous thing that existed between her and James. "It's different, I guess. Hard to describe."

Maribel nodded sagely. "I see. So, hypothetically, if someone else were interested in James..."

The implication hung in the air, making Emma's stomach twist. She looked across the studio to where James was demonstrating a newly acquired skill to a rapt audience, his hands moving with clear precision as he spoke. His easy charm was on full display, and Emma felt a pang of... what? Not quite jealousy, but some emotion that was super darn close—maybe some feeling of being left behind to clean up after the party.

"I don't know," Emma finally said, her voice small. "It's not like I have any claim on him."

Maribel hummed thoughtfully. "Now, I'm not talking about me—I've got my sights set somewhere else—but Em, old girl, what are you thinking? Someone like him won't wait. He is hot to T.R.O.T.—clear to see."

"I'm not letting anyone pressure me," Emma insisted. "I do what I want—"

"—Okay, okay... well, if you ask me, he's wasted on just one person anyway." Maribel leaned over and tapped Emma on the shoulder to make sure she was paying attention. "Did you know he helped organize an impromptu art show in the dorms last week? And he's already been asked to TA for Professor Simmons next semester. The guy's going places, and fast."

Each word was like a tiny needle pricking Emma in the patoot. She'd known James was special from the moment she'd met him, but hearing it laid out like this made her realize just how quickly he was outpacing her.

"That's... great," Emma managed, forcing a smile. "James deserves all the success."

Maribel patted Emma's arm, leaving a small clay handprint on her sleeve. "You're a good friend, Emma. Just don't let yourself get left behind, yeah? You are good—brilliant even—at everything you put your hand to... except, well, maybe that pot in your hands."

Emma chuckled, and Maribel continued, "So I'm speaking woman to woman—don't play second fiddle when you should be first violin. You don't have to be better than him or anyone; he's not the high-water mark. Just be yourself, be honest about what you want, and see what happens, thas' all."

As Maribel sashayed away, her flower-print skirt spinning a colorful blur, Emma turned back to her wheel, her mind whirling faster than the clay beneath her hands. She glanced up, catching James's eye across the room. He grinned and gave her a thumbs-up, mouthing, "Bloody brilliant!"

She smiled back, but it didn't quite reach her eyes. She pressed her hands into the clay, trying to shape it into something beautiful, but it just wasn't working, and she couldn't shake the feeling she was trying too hard. Maribel was right, James was right, the Prof was right—everybody was right—and she was totally wrong.

She was trying to prove herself rather than be herself. When did that bad habit begin?

The studio continued its bustling rhythm around her, but Emma felt oddly disconnected from it all. She had come to Cooper Union to find her artistic voice, to see what she could offer the world in exchange. But now, watching James shine so bright, she wondered how in the world she could ever catch up.

She looked at the squashed clay and had to admit it was time to scrap it and start again with a new shape—clear the decks, clear the mind. She knew what to do; she'd been making clay pots since she could use her hands. She just needed to wear a set of blinders to block a little of the James factor so she could focus.

Alright, back to squares.

* * *

Chapter 4

Chicago — Fulton Street Loft — *Apr. 1, 2002 — 9:50 a.m. — The Team Assembles*

The dark, freshly brewed coffee in James's mug looked inviting—hot and sharp—and even though it was decaf, there would be enough trace caffeine to jump-start his day. It looked good, it would do the job; he just wasn't quite in the mood to reach for it.

And so he sat staring into space, thinking nothing really—the blissful blank of *nada*—and then smiled. It seemed Val's odd observation about him was correct: he could "play possum" when he wanted, manufacturing a quiet corner in a crowded room for a portable respite. It wasn't exactly a crowd here this morning, but perhaps he felt crowded—that was the point.

He risked a glance to where Emma was standing at the far end of the conference table, as if she too found his presence bordering on barely tolerable. James sighed. Well, she'd come up with a brilliant idea at the first meeting, so she wasn't going "anywhere but here" soon—and truth told, he didn't want her to. Clearly, she had the brains and brawn to contribute, so he'd just have to suck it up and find the best way to work with her. They were both professionals, after all.

At 9:55 a.m., key members of the Epoch Alliance began to filter in, their faces a mix of anticipation and avid energy, as if they had stumbled en masse onto the best buffet in town and couldn't wait to grab their plates. Well, that was good—they had a lot to go over.

Val, his assistant, had been placed on door duty, greeting one and all to make sure everyone felt welcome. James wandered over to stand near his workbench, absently twirling a pencil between his fingers as he watched the others arrive. Val moved comfortably about the space, ensuring everyone had coffee or water, her efficiency a comforting constant.

Alfred and Mabel, the founding members of Epoch Alliance, were deep in conversation with Rhonda, who now and again used her right hand for emphasis—no doubt outlining her proposed schedule and logistical concerns.

The studio door burst open, and a booming voice filled the space. "Jimmy the James! My man, so glad to be on board—thanks for asking!"

James turned, a grin spreading across his face. "Gerardo Jimenez, as I live and breathe. You mean cajoling, or otherwise calling in twenty-six favors, don't you?"

Gerardo laughed, clapping James on the back. "Horse of a different color still gets the job done. Seriously, glad to be here—and so will my interns..." His voice trailed off as his eyes landed on Emma, who was examining some of James's preliminary sketches. "Is that *the* Em Hawkeye?"

Before James could respond, Gerardo made a beeline for Emma, scooping her up in a bear hug that lifted her clean off the floor.

Emma's laughter, tinged with surprise, rang out. "Have we met?"

"Well, I've seen your work in person, so that's as good as a formal introduction," Gerardo replied, still not setting her down.

"Okay, hard to breathe here," Emma gasped, though her eyes twinkled with amusement. "You can put me down anytime now." She glanced over at James. "Does he come with instructions?"

James chuckled, shaking his head. "I'm afraid not. Gerardo's a force of nature—you just have to weather the storm."

Amid the general laughter, Gerardo carefully set her back on her feet. "Seriously, I love your work—just love it. So glad to be working with you."

Emma adjusted her sweater, then slid into the nearest chair. She adjusted her coffee cup on the tabletop, turning the handle to the right—presentation grasp friendly—then reached into her bag for her notebook. In the process, something heavier shifted and slipped free, landing on the table with a soft *thunk* and a slow roll, coming to a full stop before clinking her cup with a kiss.

It was a sculpture—her lava rock mini mountain—larger than a fist, dark and ridged with the uneven surface of cooled earth, wind, and fire. The edges caught the light, revealing the subtle shaping of a careful hand with an iridescent color spectrum breathing: *ah me.*

James's gaze locked on it instantly. Recognition flared—swift, sure, undeniable. He didn't reach for it. Didn't speak.

His pencil paused mid-turn between his fingers. It was her work, his favorite—now seemingly, her good-luck-talisman. And the piece from her he'd wanted for himself.

Emma, without glancing his way, slid it back into her bag with one smooth motion, her face neutral, her attention already on her notebook. Of course she knew he'd seen it, everyone at the table had seen it. Moving on.

He gave the smallest of nods. "Ah... so that is how it is," he murmured under his breath. *The past is gone.*

Mabel's voice cut cleanly through the moment. "Speaking of forces of nature, perhaps we could harness some of that energy toward our project?"

"Right you are, Mabel," Alfred chimed in. "James, my boy, why don't you give us an overview of where we stand?"

Rhonda opened her mouth as if to interject, but Alfred's gentle hand on her arm stopped her. She nodded, understanding the hierarchy at play.

James cleared his throat with a small cough, nodded, moving towards the large drafting table in the center of the room. "Of course. If everyone could take a seat and gather 'round?"

As the group assembled around the table, Val quietly distributed folders. "I've prepared information packets for everyone," she murmured.

"Brilliant, Val. What would I do without you?" James said warmly.

Rhonda cleared her throat. "Probably forget half your meetings and lose the other half of your sketches."

A ripple of laughter went through the group. James mock-glared at Rhonda, but couldn't keep the smile from his face. "Right then—let's get down to business, shall we? We've got a mosaic to build and a community to inspire. Work, work, work."

James began to outline a plan, his voice confident and his gestures minimal except when driving a point home. The room seemed to come alive with his energy, everyone leaning in to catch every word. He effortlessly fielded questions, incorporated suggestions, and navigated potential conflicts with grace.

Emma found herself studying James's face, noting the passion that lit up his features as he spoke. Despite the years and the pain between them, some things hadn't changed—James still had the ability to command a room, to ignite excitement in others.

She felt a gentle nudge and turned to find Gerardo grinning at her. "Quite something, isn't he?" he whispered.

Emma nodded, a complicated mix of emotions swirling inside her. "He always was," she murmured.

As the meeting continued, the camaraderie in the room grew—old friendships strengthening, new ones beginning to form. They were an eclectic group, brought together by a shared vision, and as ideas flew and plans took shape, there was a sense that something truly special was beginning to unfold.

Rhonda was clearly itching to steer the conversation to logistics, and after the second nudge and suggestion, James nodded and stood at the head of the table, his energy infectious as he laid out the initial overview. "Alright, folks, let's talk logistics. We need a place where the public can come and make tiles. I'm thinking we've got a few options.

"Outside the Shedd Aquarium, around the side of the Field Museum, the Art Institute, the Lincoln Park Zoo has potential but it's a little far from downtown tourists. So, ideally, some kind of educational facility where we've got a built-in audience eager to participate."

Mabel nodded thoughtfully. "An educational facility would certainly align with our goals," she said, her voice soft but carrying weight.

"As for when," James continued, "I'm thinking weekends, geared towards families and individuals looking for creative expression. Time-wise, we're looking at this summer—I know it's coming up fast, but I'm thinking three or four weekends in July, the height of vacation season."

Emma leaned forward, her brow furrowed in concentration. She absently tucked a strand of hair behind her ear. "We're going to need a location on ground level where we can process and prep the clay, and also clean the tiles and prep for non- or partial-glaze firing." She paused, a thought occurring to her. "It doesn't need to be a lot of square footage at this stage—we'll be rotating clay and tiles in and out—"

"A processing station," James confirmed. It seemed he was talking with her directly now, albeit with a professional tone.

She nodded. "With tall windows, natural lighting—you know the drill."

"I do indeed...our good Val has been helping me these past weeks narrow down some possible locations that will accept a short-term lease—"

"Location is important," Emma reminded him. "Something on ground level, close to a very large kiln, or else this will take forever."

James's eyes lit up, a mischievous grin spreading across his face. "Gerardo, my friend," he said, turning to the man, "can we have access to the monster?"

Gerardo's face lit up. "We can have the big one at the studio on Lill Street."

"He shoots, he scores..." James drawled, making a mock basketball shot.

"The crowd goes sliced banana bread," Emma said dryly.

Everyone turned to look at her, puzzled expressions on their faces. James, however, chuckled. "God, you have an odd mind,

Em," he said, shaking his head, his eyes lingering on her face a moment longer than necessary for, let's say, ordinary social interaction.

Clearing his throat, James turned back to Gerardo. "Tell me about your interns. How many, and how much time are you asking them to put in?"

Gerardo scratched his chin thoughtfully. "We should probably pay at least three of them so we have steady hands showing up when needed, but I think I can get twelve in total."

The room fell quiet as everyone absorbed the information. Then, suddenly, several people started speaking at once, their voices overlapping in a cacophony of ideas and concerns. The energy in the room shifted, becoming more charged, more intense.

James held up his hands, laughing. "Whoa, whoa! One at a time, folks. Rhonda gets top billing. What've you got, Rhonda?"

Rhonda took a deep breath, her expression a mix of concern and determination. She smoothed down her impeccably pressed blouse—a gesture James recognized as her preparing for battle.

"I have a problem with only the weekends," she began, her voice clear and firm. "True, that would be geared toward families, but it leaves a lot of other people out in the cold. What about working adults who can't make it on weekends? Or students who might have weekend jobs?"

Alfred nodded, stroking his chin. "Rhonda's got a point, James. We want to include as many different people as possible."

"Not to mention," Mabel added, her soft voice somehow cutting through the tension, "limiting it to weekends might create overcrowding issues. We don't want to turn people away because we can't handle the volume."

James nodded, acknowledging their points. He moved to the whiteboard, uncapping a marker with a decisive click. "That's just it," he said, his voice steady. "We can't handle the volume from weekends *and* some weeknights. With two days straight on three weekends outside a large institution with a built-in flow of visitors, we'll end up with about thirty-five hundred tiles in total. More than that and we won't be able to use them all, and we'll be over our heads with work."

He turned to Emma, one eyebrow raised in a silent question. "That's enough for our final project, right, Em?"

Emma nodded, her eyes meeting his. "More than enough, actually," she confirmed, her voice soft but sure. "And I think it's important to use every single one."

"Agreed," James said, then turned back to the group, his marker squeaking against the whiteboard as he began to break down the logistics. "Here's why we need to stick to this timeline," he began, drawing seven rough boxes on the board in three rows. "Let's pretend this is a calendar and I can count."

A small chuckle came from Alfred and Mabel, and then James turned back to the whiteboard, his marker poised. The room fell silent, all eyes on him. Even Rhonda, despite her skepticism, leaned forward, unable to resist the pull of James's thought process.

"Let's break this down," James began, his voice taking on that particular cadence Emma recognized from their college days—the one that meant he was about to blow everyone's minds.

He started sketching a timeline on the board, his strokes quick and sure. "Three weekends, two days each. That's six full days of public participation."

As he spoke, he filled in the details, his handwriting a mix of precise architect's lettering and artistic flourishes. "Each day, we need to set up and break down. That's at least an hour on each end, which leaves us with about eight hours of actual tile-making time."

Gerardo nodded, his fingers drumming an unconscious rhythm on his leg. Mabel had pulled out her tiger-striped reading glasses and was squinting at the board with intense concentration.

James continued, warming to his subject. "Now, let's talk about manpower. We need at least five people on site at all times. Two to manage clay distribution, two to guide participants, and one floating to handle any issue that comes up."

He drew a quick diagram of the proposed setup. "Each participant needs about thirty minutes to create a tile. If we have eight stations set up under two tents, with five people at a table, that boils down to about eighty people per hour. With eight-hour shifts for six days, we're talking almost eight hundred tiles per day. If folks choose to do more than one tile—and we think they will—that figure increases. After three weekends, otherwise known as six days, we can be looking at thirty-eight hundred tiles. Let me write that figure here and circle it—really meaning we might top out at four thousand. Which is the absolute highest amount we can handle and stay sane."

Emma found herself nodding along, impressed despite herself. She'd forgotten how thoroughly James could think things through when he set his mind to it.

"Factor in cutting clay to make slabs, drying time, cleaning tiles, firing schedules, and the actual installation time," James said, circling his final number with a flourish. "Four thousand is the top end of what we can handle in all categories of the work process. Any more than that, and we risk losing quality and burning out. I've seen some of Emma's work—don't look so surprised, Em, I've kept tabs—and the layers of color we all want will need multiple firings and/or multiple layers of glaze, depending on her call, and that's more time on the backend."

He turned back to the room, his eyes bright with the thrill of problem-solving. "Questions?"

Rhonda cleared her throat, her lips pressed into a thin line. "I'd still like to hear from the other co-designer on this," she said, turning to Emma. "Do you agree with this… assessment?"

Emma felt all eyes turn to her. She looked down at her hands for a moment, gathering her thoughts. When she looked up, her gaze was steady.

"You can't speed the plow," she said, her voice quiet but firm. "It's going to take a certain amount of time to prep, teach the folks, and pull the finished tiles back into the studio to dry. Then, after drying, they'll need to be cleaned for a first edge glaze maybe. The clay can go into the large kiln in rotation, but it's all time on the clock, and you have to add in when things go… well, wrong. That's life—part of the process."

She paused, then continued with more confidence. "The weekend schedule is tight, but we can do it. James knows what he's talking about. The clock is the clock, and it's true—interns will get burnt out if they work too hard for too long, which means replacing staff, more training, and slowing down. But this current plan James put forward can work. Four thousand four-inch square tiles is a lot, but we can do it. If you add more days on top of this schedule, that's even more tiles—meaning a panic button in the future or a temptation to cut corners. I'd rather not do that."

James smiled, a mix of gratitude and something deeper in his eyes as he looked at Emma. "Ta, Em," he said softly, before turning back to the group.

"Any other questions or concerns?" he asked, his tone inviting but confident.

Everyone in the room was quiet for a moment, then Alfred spoke up. "I think you've covered all bases, my boy. It's a solid plan."

James watched Rhonda's face, noting the lingering dissatisfaction in her eyes. A slow smile spread across his face—the kind that usually preceded his most brilliant ideas.

"Rhonda," he said, his voice warm with sudden inspiration, "I've got a challenge for you. One that could solve our 'access for everyone' problem."

Rhonda's eyebrows rose, a mix of curiosity and wariness on her face. "Oh?"

James nodded, his enthusiasm building. "Publicity. We need to get the word out—make sure everyone knows about this opportunity. NPR, *The Chicago Reader*, free newspapers, TV spots—the works."

He started pacing, his energy infectious. "If we do this right, people will have three weekends to plan their visit. We'll be open from 8:00 a.m. until 6:30 p.m.—it'll be summer, we'll still have light. And I'll take the first and last shifts myself, keep the door open as long as we can."

The room buzzed with renewed energy. Alfred was nodding approvingly, while Mabel scribbled notes furiously. Gerardo let out a low whistle of appreciation.

James turned back to Rhonda, his eyes alight with the challenge. "What do you say? Think you can make this the most talked-about event of the summer of 2002?"

Rhonda sat up straighter, a slow smile spreading across her face as the possibilities began to unfold in her mind. "You know what, James? I think I can."

As the room erupted into excited chatter, Emma caught James's eye across the table. He nodded to her, with that familiar, mischievous glint in his eye that always meant trouble—and that he was having the time of his life. Despite herself, Emma felt a smile tugging at her lips. Some things, it seemed, never changed.

* * *

As the excitement in the room reached a fever pitch, with everyone talking over each other about publicity ideas and logistics, Gerardo leaned in close to Emma. His eyes were fixed on James, who was in the midst of sketching out a rough publicity timeline on the whiteboard—his movements quick and sure.

"Man," Gerardo said in a low voice, shaking his head in admiration, "if I wasn't straight as a board, I'd be in love with that man." Then, almost to himself, with a tone of wonder and affection, he murmured, "Jimmy the James."

Emma found herself nodding, her gaze also drawn to James. She watched as he drew circles in the air—she wasn't sure what point he was making, but he was clearly enjoying himself. A familiar warmth spread through her chest, a feeling she'd tried for years to forget. She drew in a breath and looked away—out the tall windows that framed the length of his loft to the city skyline beyond.

There were people—so many people—inside those rooms, inside those buildings, and all of them, whether they knew it or not, were searching for a way to ease the ache of unrequited love.

Unrequited love from parents, siblings, friends—it didn't matter who. That was the primary issue for all of humanity. And so, making something—some small something—became a way to forget the ache for a little while, and focus on the dream of feeling love on earth. The pleasure of being able to add their prayer to the pattern, as one small drawing or clay pot.

James Watson understood that. And what's more, he had become successful because of it. He wasn't the kind of creator who leaned on angst. He leaned on love. With or without her, James had leaned on love.

Emma looked around his loft—to the fine, bright work studio, the living area, the life he'd built for himself... without her. She nodded in silent agreement. Good on you, Jimmy the James.

It hurt too, in an odd way—that he could do this well without her, but in a better way... in a full grown woman *mature way*—Emma Hawkins was happy for James Watson.

She smiled to herself, thinking: *Hmm... that might look great on a plaque or something.*

Out loud, she simply said, her voice barely above a whisper: "Tell me about it."

* * *

The afternoon light slanted through the studio windows, painting the room in warm hues of amber and gold. James stood at the head of the table, his eyes scanning the faces around him. Rhonda's carefully crafted schedule lay before her, a testament to the day's productivity.

"Alright, folks," James said, his voice tinged with satisfaction. "I think we've covered everything. Any final concerns or thoughts going forward?"

Everyone present at the table was quiet now, taking a well-earned breather. They looked to each other with the soft expectation of the next issue—though not really expecting one—when, unexpectedly, Val raised her hand, her face a mix of apology and worry.

"Go ahead, Val," James encouraged, his brow furrowing slightly at her hesitation.

Val cleared her throat. "I have something kinda important—sorry, it can't wait. I just checked my email."

"Cough it out, Val," James said, his tone light but his eyes sharp. "Can't be worse than a fur ball—it'll only hurt once."

Val's words tumbled out in a rush. "According to what the clay company can ship us, we'll have enough red clay for the first weekend. We might have enough white clay for several weekends, but not red. They're sorry—they know they promised. Some other client took—I don't know—ranked over us. I'm not exactly sure how this happened. Personally, I think it had to do with the law of supply and demand and someone paid them more. They're sending a reimbursement."

James took a deep breath, his mind already racing through possibilities. "No need to ask if you checked around—I know you would."

Val nodded, her face a picture of the double "d": dejection and despair.

James felt the energy in the room slowly evaporate—from feeling on top of the world to being under the weight of it. Mabel's hand found Alfred's, their fingers intertwining in a silent gesture of support. Gerardo's usual jovial expression faded, replaced by a furrowed brow.

Long pause and then Rhonda suggested, "We could always do it with more white clay. Couldn't we?"

James thought about it. "Porcelain isn't as accessible as red clay. We ordered enough to use as accents—places to bounce light and color. Red terracotta grounds the work." He shook his head, his artist's soul rebelling against the idea. "The texture would be out of balance. Besides, we don't have enough white clay to do double duty anyway."

Everyone was quiet, too stunned to dare offer a suggestion with so little information available to them at the moment.

"Well, well—this is a pickle..." James mused. He walked to the window, gazing out at the Chicago skyline as if the answer might be written in the clouds.

James was at the center window, his eyes drawn to the clouds drifting across the skyline. There was something about their fluid forms that reminded him why he'd turned from painting to clay—the desire to be closer to nature, to shape something tangible with his hands.

As he watched the clouds morph and change, a thought began to form in his mind. Nature. Earth. Clay in its rawest form. His eyes found Emma's reflection in the glass, and he saw the same realization dawning on her face. Their eyes met in the reflection, a moment of silent understanding passing between them.

Emma approached James, her voice low. "I know what you're thinking," she said. "But James, this isn't something they sell to just anyone. It's sacred."

James nodded, understanding the weight of what he was asking. "Would he do it?" he asked, his voice soft, his timbre low enough to reverberate in her brain.

Emma hesitated. "I don't know. He's not in actual charge—Dad defers to the elders."

James nodded, the weight of the moment palpable between them.

Emma drew in a breath. "Where's your landline phone?"

Val was hovering on the perimeter, waiting for a command, and so she escorted Emma to the office to make the call. James called the group back to the table. "We're waiting on a call," he explained, his voice tight with anticipation.

As Emma made the call, all at the table maintained their silence. No one got up for coffee or a snack, or even shifted their weight in their chair, as if any sudden movement might put the project closer to the crosshairs.

James watched as Mabel leaned her head on Alfred's shoulder, their years of partnership evident in the comfort they drew from each other. Gerardo had his head in his hands, clearly thinking hard too.

Emma returned. Her face was tight, her expression unreadable, her brows pulled together as if she were still running the conversation she'd just had with her father through her mind. She moved to stand beside James, and he could feel the tension radiating from her.

"My dad—well, my people—are the Ojibwa of the Red Lake. Some know them as the Chippewa," she began. "They harvest raw red clay. It is… very pure, powerful, sacred. He doesn't think—"

The phone's shrill ring cut through her words. Val rushed to bring the cordless to Emma.

"Hi, Dad," Emma said, then quickly corrected herself. "Oh… I'm sorry—excuse me, sir, yes, I'm listening." There was a long pause as Emma paid close attention, her face impassive, and then finally: "Yes, I understand... when?" A semi-medium pause, and then: "That soon? I understand... James is standing right here, I'll ask him, hold on... and thank you, grandfather."

Emma turned to the group, her voice steady but her eyes wide with surprise. "The Ojibwa people will sell you the red clay. They'll do it, but the elder has a condition that must be met."

James nodded, his eyes bright with determination. "Oh God, thank you—thank them—and yes... whatever it is."

Emma continued, her words careful and measured. "This clay is sacred, and the path must be made clear, so there is a beauty-way, so the earth and the creation will be respected..."

She paused, her hand raised to stop James's eager nodding. "He is inviting the male members of the group to participate in a sweat lodge ceremony, if they want to. But you, James—you must attend a sweat lodge ceremony... all four rounds, without leaving. You cannot leave the lodge. If it gets too hot, you fry, but you can't leave. That's the way this can happen."

James felt a mix of elation and trepidation. He joked, "Of course I'll do it. I don't need my outer epidermis—summer's coming."

"James," she said, her voice low and serious. "This isn't an ordinary task, or even just a hard one. I've done a sweat lodge—all four rounds. This is the real deal. This won't be watered down for you—no New Age nonsense. It was excruciating for me, and I suspect if they're doing a private ceremony for men, it will be even harder for you guys; that's the way it is. Some things a person can only do once in their life."

He met her gaze, seeing the concern in her eyes and understood then that this wasn't just a physical challenge—it was a spiritual one, a cleansing, a purification perhaps. It made sense.

Despite the gravity of the situation, James felt a smile tugging at his lips. "Your dad set this up, didn't he then?" he asked, recognizing the cleverness of the solution. "Getting a wee kick in for his bonny lass?"

Emma's answering smile was small but genuine. "He might have had a hand in it," she admitted.

James took a deep breath, feeling the weight of the decision. This wasn't just about getting the clay they needed—it was about respect, about honoring traditions and connecting with the time-tested process.

"I would be honored," James said, his voice steady despite the flutter in his stomach.

Emma relayed James's answer and then listened attentively. "Yes, I'll let him know, thank you, grandfather. The elder says he heard your joke and, 'That's okay—you hang onto that. You'll need levity to rise above.' That's what he said to tell you."

James nodded—levity to rise above the pain, the elder meant.

As the room buzzed with a mix of excitement and concern, James felt a strange sense of calm settle over him. Whatever challenges the sweat lodge might bring, he might not feel ready at this very moment, but he would be.

Cleansing, huh? That actually sounded just about on time—and maybe even what he'd been looking for.

* * *

Chapter 5

The acrid scent of fired clay and chemical glazes permeated the air of the ceramics studio, a sharp contrast to the earthy smell of raw clay that usually dominated the space. Late-afternoon sunlight filtered through the dust-streaked windows, casting long shadows across workbenches cluttered with half-finished projects and glaze-splattered tools.

Emma stood before her workstation, her brow furrowed in concentration as she applied another layer of glaze to her piece. Her hands—stained with various hues—moved with a certainty that belied the frustration evident in her eyes. She'd been at this for weeks now, experimenting with different techniques, each attempt ending in disappointment.

First, she'd tried painting one glaze, letting it dry, then adding another coat of a different color. The result had been a muddy mess—the colors fighting each other instead of harmonizing. Next, she'd attempted wet painting, one color over another, mixing on the surface. But the glazes had run and blended unpredictably in the kiln, creating a chaotic swirl that bore little resemblance to her vision.

Professor Herzog's voice, tinged with disappointment, echoed in her mind from their last critique: *"Miss Hawkins, after your success in my advanced color theory painting class, I expected more from you. This lacks finesse. Patience. Understanding of the medium. Where is your singular approach to color? What are you trying to say?"*

Emma's hand stilled, the brush hovering over the clay surface. *Patience. Understanding.* The words tumbled in her mind, colliding with memories of childhood hikes with her father—examining rock formations, layers of earth telling stories of millennia.

Suddenly, it clicked. *Time. Layers.* The earth didn't rush its masterpieces; why should she?

With renewed determination, Emma began again. This time, she painted only the edges of her piece with a single glaze, firing it carefully. Days passed as she waited for it to cool, resisting the urge to rush. When it was ready, she applied a second glaze, then waited again for the second firing.

The project deadline came and went. Emma worked late into the night, the empty studio her sole companion as she patiently built up layer after layer, firing after firing. She lost track of time—lost in the rhythm of creation.

Finally, as dawn broke over the New York skyline, Emma stood back and looked at her finished piece. It was an abstract sculpture in the form of a rock, its surface a complex interplay of colors that seemed to shift and change in the early morning light. The glazes blended yet remained distinct, like geological strata compressed by time and pressure.

When Professor Herzog entered the studio later that morning, his eyes immediately locked onto Emma's piece. The usual hub of activity faded into the background as he approached, his lined face a study in concentration.

"Class," he said, his voice cutting through the chatter, "gather round. Miss Hawkins has something to show us."

As the students crowded around, Herzog lifted the sculpture, turning it this way and that to catch the light. "This piece here," he announced, "is the Cooper Union way. Not perfect, not even beautiful, barely working… but on its way, with a unique vision."

He set the piece down gently, fixing Emma with a penetrating stare. "Well done. You still get a low mark for being late, Miss Hawkins, so your challenge is to work in your way—this way—but within the time allotted. Right?"

Emma nodded, a mix of emotions swirling within her. She should have felt chastened by the criticism, but instead, she felt lifted. Someone had seen her—truly seen what she was trying to achieve.

Her eyes sought out James in the crowd. When she found him, his expression was soft, his eyes suspiciously bright. He gave her a small nod, as if to say, *I knew you had it all along.*

* * *

As the class dispersed, Emma remained rooted to the spot, her gaze fixed on her creation. The colors seemed to pulse with life, whispering promises of future masterpieces. For the first time since starting at Cooper Union, she felt the stirrings of true confidence. This wasn't just a technique—it was her voice, her vision. And she was only just beginning to discover its potential.

The art studio for the gesture drawing class had been transformed into an impromptu auditorium, easels and pottery wheels pushed to the sides to make room for a circle of folding chairs. Sunlight streamed through the high windows, catching dust motes in its beams and lending an almost ethereal quality to the space. Professor Linden, a wiry woman with salt-and-pepper hair and paint-splattered overalls, stood in the center of the circle, her eyes twinkling with excitement.

"Alright, everybody," she said, clapping her hands together. "Today, we're stepping out of our comfort zones. As artists, we often let our work speak for us, but there will be times when you'll need to articulate your vision, your process, your very essence as creators. So, we're going to practice the art of the interview."

A murmur rippled through the assembled students, there may have been groans. Emma caught James's eye across the circle, and they shared a quick, conspiratorial grin. This was their kind of challenge.

"Partner up," Professor Linden continued, "one of you will be the interviewer, the other the subject. Dig deep, ask probing questions, and most importantly, listen."

The art studio buzzed with anticipation as Professor Linden pushed the last easel against the wall, creating an open space in the center of the room. Sunlight streamed through the high windows, casting long shadows across the floor and illuminating the dust motes swirling in the air.

"Alright, everyone," Professor Linden called out, her voice cutting through the chatter, "let's gather 'round. We're going to make this a bit more...intense."

The students exchanged nervous glances as they dragged their chairs into a tight circle around the cleared space. Emma felt a flutter of anxiety in her stomach. This wasn't what she had expected.

"We'll do this one pair at a time...so we all can watch, witness...and critique," the professor continued, her eyes scanning the group, "who wants to go first?"

Before Emma could process what was happening, James's hand shot up. "We'll do it," he said, flashing that irresistible grin of his. He turned to Emma, eyebrows raised in a silent question.

Emma nodded, trying to ignore the sudden dryness in her mouth. As they made their way to the center of the circle, she could feel the weight of every gaze upon them.

"Right then," Professor Linden said, settling into a chair at the edge of the circle. "Emma, you'll be our interviewer. James, you're the subject. Remember, this isn't just about asking questions—it's about revealing the artist behind the art. Begin whenever you're ready."

Without hesitation, Emma and James gravitated towards each other, claiming the pair of chairs in the center of the circle. Emma perched on the edge of her seat, while James lounged back, his long legs stretched out before him.

"So, Mr. James," Emma began, affecting an exaggerated posh accent that made James snort with laughter. "Tell me, what drives your artistic process?"

James leaned forward, his eyes lighting up with that familiar spark of passion. "Well, you see," he said, his Geordie accent more pronounced under the pressure of performance, "art is more than just pigment on canvas or clay shaped by hands, isn't it then? It's an extension of the artist's state of mind, and oscillation of the soul."

Emma nodded encouragingly, and observed, "Oscillation is an interesting word choice, it would suggest an energetic variation, not a constant stream of energy, are you suggesting the soul varies?"

James grinned, "That might be exactly what I'm suggesting, of course there is no way to measure such variation, unless, unless we consider art, as the vehicle to observe changes day to day. Art therapy is often used to understand how children are relating to their environment, one day a painter is using bright green for valley vistas and two days later, dark purple and brown to paint a massive bruise. What happened?"

"But that could indicate simply a change of mood, or emotions, how does that signify..." and here Emma searched for what she was trying to understand "how are changing emotions indicative of an oscillating soul?"

James considered Emma, looked into her eyes and then said, "You may have something there, let me think for a moment..."

The room was quiet as everyone leaned in, it seemed Emma had James pinned, what would he say, concede the point or spin it?

James began slowly, thinking his way through to what he intended to communicate, "We think of emotion as being triggered by an external event but what if emotion is merely the ripple coming *from the soul* being triggered by the external event. It is the soul shifting and adjusting to the event to broadcast outward as an emotional response. Don't quote me or anything, just something I've been thinking about when I look at some art."

Emma nodded, "There is a tradition in many cultures where a Master Spiritual teacher can imbue blessing; actually imprint the vibration of their soul into matter, what you are suggesting is a very powerful cause and effect situation."

"Exactly! Exactly!" James effused and leaned forward in his chair, barely able to refrain himself from hugging her. "Exactly, what if we, as artists, through the sheer force of desire are imbuing the state of our soul into every whatnot nasty or nice thing we do?"

"Please go on, I will give you the floor." Emma was smiling at him, radiant and thrilled when he got like this. A small chuckle ran around the room.

"Every brushstroke, every sculpted curve, carries with it the energy of its creator," James continued, his voice growing more animated. "It's like... like a conduit, yeah? The artist guides their spiritual intention via the medium and into the piece itself with or without their willingness to do it."

As James spoke, Emma found herself drawn in, not just by his words, but by the sheer force of his presence. The sunlight caught his hair, turning the dark strands to burnished gold. His eyes, always expressive, seemed to glow with an inner fire.

Emma nodded, feeling herself relax into the familiar rhythm of their conversations. From the corner of her eye, she could see their classmates leaning in as well.

And then, it happened.

It started slowly, almost imperceptibly. A soft, white light seemed to emanate from James, outlining his form like a halo. Emma blinked, thinking it must be a trick of the light. But the glow intensified, expanding outward, enveloping James entirely.

Emma's breath caught in her throat as the light continued to spread, washing over them both and then filling the room. The circle of students, the studio, everything faded away, replaced by a vast, endless expanse of pure, radiant silent white.

It was as if the boundaries of her being had dissolved, merging with the light, with James, with everything. She was dimly aware of still sitting in the center of the room, and she believed she was still sitting on her chair, but wasn't sure—she heard nothing but silence and saw nothing but white. Her mind was alert and thinking clearly, she assumed James was still speaking, but couldn't hear a word. The white-out seemed to come from everywhere and nowhere at once.

Time lost all meaning. Emma floated in this sea of white, feeling both infinitely small and impossibly vast. There was no fear, no confusion, only a profound sense of peace and...love.

Just when she began to be concerned they would think something had gone wrong with her...slowly, gradually, the world began to reassert itself. Forms emerged from the white, colors seeped back into her vision. She was aware that she could feel the top of her chair now, so she knew she was still sitting, hadn't fallen on the floor...and then her feet. Emma blinked, finding herself once again sitting across from James in the sun-drenched studio, surrounded by their classmates.

"...and that's why I believe every piece of art carries a bit of its creator's soul," James was saying, wrapping up his impassioned speech. The room was silent.

Emma realized she had no idea what he had said for the past few minutes. She nodded sagely, hoping her face didn't betray her confusion.

James burst out laughing, the sound rich and warm, breaking the spell that had fallen over the room. "Ever the minimalist, eh our Em?" he teased. "I pour out my artistic soul, and you respond with a nod. Brilliant."

The class erupted in laughter and applause. Emma shrugged, grateful for the out he had inadvertently provided. Her mind was calm, almost distilled and distant. She wasn't worried exactly, more like being curious, had anyone else noticed? A quick glance around the room showed their classmates looking impressed and slightly awed, but no one seemed to have experienced the profound shift in reality that Emma had.

As Professor Linden stepped forward to offer her critique, Emma sat in stunned silence. She had touched something profound, something that defied explanation. It would be years before she would hear terms like "oneness" or "non-duality," years before she would understand that she had experienced a glimpse of Love with a capital "L."

For now, all she knew was that something had changed. As she looked at James, still flushed with the excitement of his performance, she saw him with new eyes. He was still James, her friend and artistic rival, but he was also something more—a catalyst, a key that had unlocked a door she hadn't even known existed.

The world looked the same, but she had been irrevocably changed. And as James threw an arm around her shoulders, and led her out of the studio with promises of coffee and continued debate, while their classmates trailing behind and peppered him with questions, Emma found that she absolutely had nothing to say.

* * *

Cooper Union – Student Commons– *Feb. 11, 1988 – 5:30 p.m.*

The group had migrated to their usual corner of the student commons, a bank of low mismatched couches arranged near the vending machines and beneath a cracked skylight that filtered in the last blue light of day.

Zane was sprawled like a prince returning from war, one leg hooked over the arm of the sofa. "I swear," he groaned, "if Herzog makes us draw our childhood traumas in magenta again, I'm switching to architecture."

Maribel smirked over her bag of trail mix. "You'd last five minutes in architecture. You'd draw a church shaped like a scrotum and call it a critique of colonialism."

"I'd get published," Zane replied, without missing a beat.

Emma was quieter than usual, her fingers absently tracing condensation rings on her iced tea glass. The world around her felt slightly diffused, like the afterimage of a flashbulb. She hadn't come fully down from whatever had happened in the drawing studio. Her body was here, but her mind kept drifting sideways.

James, legs crossed at the knee, leaned back in the battered club chair like he owned the building. "Color theory with Herzog's not so bad. Just... abstract something real, strip it to emotion, and find your own palette for it. Easy."

Zane turned to him, incredulous. "You're saying that like it's simple algebra. I still don't know how to *feel a glacier.*"

James shrugged. "Then don't. Paint it like fire. The point isn't what it is, it's what it *feels like.* Push contrast. Or invert. Bend the thing until it screams back."

Emma looked up at him, half-curious.

"But," James added, grinning, "you could also just say 'bollocks to that' and draw whatever the hell you want. Rules are suggestions. Paint a feeling, paint a frog, paint your landlord. As long as it's true to *something,* it counts."

Zane snorted. "Uh, I'm trying to *pass,* you maniac. Have a transcript that doesn't look like it was run over by a flaming shopping cart. I want a grade. I want Herzog to nod. I want the word 'competent' on my resume."

"Details," James said, waving a hand. "Things to deal with later."

Zane sat up, stretching dramatically. "Easy for you to say, mate. Some of us live in a cooperative state with the world. Or God. Pick one."

James chuckled and leaned his head back, looking at the skylight as if something interesting might drop through it. "Rules... schmules," he said lightly.

That made Emma flinch, just slightly. The words were tossed off casually, but something in the delivery—something amused and untethered—sent a ripple through her calm.

Maribel didn't miss it. She cocked her head and said, flatly, "You're joking, right?"

James looked back at them, blinking as if surprised they'd taken him seriously.

Or surprised that maybe... they should.

"Of course," he said. "Mostly."

They all sat with that for a moment. Then someone at a nearby table sneezed loudly and broke the spell. Zane began rummaging in his bag for the pastel set he'd probably spill, and Maribel snapped the rubber band on her wrist to keep herself from saying what she was thinking.

Emma took another sip of tea.

She didn't know what to say either.

But she was starting to understand the shape of the risk.

And it didn't always come with warning signs.

* * *

The air in the classroom had settled into a reverent stillness—more chapel than critique room. Students shifted only to ease a cramped leg or to see Herzog better as he moved down the line of pastel works pinned in deliberate symmetry across the studio wall.

The assignment: abstract a single aspect of the natural world into feeling. No objects. No references. Only color and form, pulsing with internal truth.

Professor Herzog stood before Emma's piece longer than he had most. A bloom of ochre in the lower left flared into a sensual sweep of crimson, countered by a trembling line of pale blue that bisected the field—barely there, like a breath you didn't know you were holding.

He studied it. Tilted his head. Then, to the room:

"This," he said, "is a study in vulnerability."

A flicker of something passed across Emma's chest. She held her body still.

Herzog stepped closer. "What we see here is not the object of desire, but the sensation of it—something just beyond reach. The ochre, yes, it grounds us. But the line..." He gestured to the trembling blue, "...that is the ache. The contrast is what makes this honest. Sensual curves pressed against restraint. This is not a perfect piece, but it is... revealing. It tells us where the artist is willing to meet herself."

He paused. "Art should not flatter us. Not at first. It should humble us—show us what we're carrying that we haven't named."

Emma's face stayed neutral, but a faint warmth had risen along her neck. She heard the echo of her own thoughts from the night before, the way the sky had looked just before the sun dropped. She had meant it. That piece. Every line.

Herzog moved on.

Two panels later, he stopped. A soft green spread over the square, touched with blue sky in broad confident strokes. Balanced. Beautiful. Tame.

Herzog frowned slightly. "Whose piece is this?"

James raised his hand.

Herzog didn't speak for a moment. Then: "And what was your intention here?"

James hesitated. "I was going for a sense of... calm. Like serenity, you know? Simplicity."

Herzog nodded slowly. "Yes. I see that. But Mr. Watson—calm is a difficult thing to render truthfully. What you've created is pleasant. Controlled. Beautiful, in its way. But it is not felt."

He turned toward the class, and the energy shifted. Everyone leaned in.

"I want to be clear: this is a well-composed piece. But it is not the assignment. The challenge was to abstract—to locate a sensation deep inside your relationship to the natural world and communicate that sensation, not its image."

He looked directly at James.

"You are a talented young man. That's not in question. You were approved by the committee, myself included, because we believed you could grow. Not because your work was finished."

James nodded slightly, his gaze fixed on the floor.

Herzog's voice softened, not in volume, but in charge. "Being in school is a sacred opportunity. Out in the world, you'll be tempted to create what sells, what pleases, what gets picked up by a gallery or applauded at an opening. But *here*—here, you are expected to break yourself open. Take risks. Follow the exercise not to obey, but to *discover*."

He stepped back. "You aimed for calm. But you avoided the vulnerability it requires. In doing so, you've created a replica of calm—not the feeling itself."

A long pause.

"You may continue this pattern. It may even serve you. But if you do, you may find yourself forever the dweller on the threshold—hovering just outside the door. Not only in art, Mr. Watson... but in all matters of life."

He let the silence deepen, then moved on.

James said nothing.

Emma, still sitting cross-legged a few feet away, kept her eyes on Herzog. She didn't look at James. But she heard it. All of it. And, inside her chest, something aligned. Not in judgment. In recognition.

He had been holding back. And not just today.

She knew the feeling.

Professor Herzog had put them all on the hot seat at one time or another, but this was the first time to date, she'd witnessed a Prof calling James out and naming that very slim thread she could now see as true. Now. What would James do with it?

* * *

The class let out in a quiet swirl of backpack zippers and soft murmurs. Emma moved to leave, feeling the last of Herzog's words echoing in her chest, when she heard James fall into step beside her. Neither of them said anything in the stairwell.

Once outside, the winter air cut clean between them. They walked for a while in silence, their boots scuffing the icy sidewalk, breath fogging slightly in the cold.

Finally, James spoke, his voice casual but edged with something searching. "So…" he said, glancing at her. "What did you think of Herzog's little sermon?"

Emma glanced ahead, pausing to dodge a patch of black ice. She gave a short breath of air that might've been a laugh. "Which one?"

"You know," he said. "The bit about… leaning on love and not hiding behind skill. Or whatever the hell that was."

Emma looked at him then, slowly. "I think he was talking to you."

James chuckled softly, rubbing the back of his neck. "Yeah, that's the vibe I got too." He squinted at the sky. "But… I mean, it was a good piece. My lines were clean. Color palette held together. It wasn't phoning it in."

"No," she agreed. "It wasn't phoning it in." She didn't say more.

They reached the corner. A gust of wind rustled a wrapper along the curb. James stopped and looked at her. "But you think he's right."

Emma hesitated, her fingers tightening around the strap of her bag. "I think… sometimes we're so good at sketching the surface that we forget how to risk the messy stuff underneath. I think you're really good, James. But sometimes being good makes it harder to listen."

He took that in, his eyes flicking down the street.

Then, after a pause, he said, "Yours was good today." Emma turned to him, caught off guard. "That piece. Yours. It was…" He searched for the word. "Real."

She smiled faintly. "Thanks."

He shrugged. "Anyway. Just thought you should know."

Another gust of wind pushed past them, scattering old leaves. James looked like he might say more, but then just nodded. "See you tomorrow," he said, stepping off the curb.

Emma watched him go. He didn't look back.

A man with all the tools—still not sure which door he was standing in front of.

* * *

Union Square Open Mic Night— *Feb. 11, 1988 — 8:40 p.m.*

The café was a former shoemaker's shop, all exposed brick and hanging Edison bulbs. Folding chairs lined the back, but the real crowd clustered up front—students in coats too long or too short, sipping bitter coffee and waiting for their turn at the mic.

James, Emma, Zane, and Maribel had scored a booth near the side wall, close enough to hear without being in the splash zone of earnest slam poets.

Zane leaned back, legs sprawled under the table like he was guarding the territory. "If someone does another poem about sloths on speed being a metaphor for capitalism, I'm jumping onto the third rail."

"Have a little faith," Maribel said, unwrapping a menthol lemon cough drop from her coat pocket. "One of these kids might actually say something new tonight."

James snorted, distractedly sketching shapes on a napkin. He hadn't said much since Herzog's critique, but he hadn't disappeared either. He was thinking, turning something over in his mind.

Emma was nursing a lukewarm chai, her eyes soft as she watched James move his pen—circles, diagonals, strange layering. Something was still being processed.

The mic hissed. A lanky boy with oversized glasses stepped up and mumbled something about heartbreak in the Ohio valley swallowing him whole. Zane's eyes grew wide, wider widest but before he could open his mouth to heckle Maribel kicked him under the table.

Then—of course—Sophie appeared.

She was wearing a dramatic velvet coat and holding a cigarette she hadn't lit, somehow managing to look both tragic and glamorous under the yellow glow.

"Oh my God," she said, slipping in beside James like she was expected. "That critique today? Herzog is such a—God, what's the word—*snob*. Honestly, James, I think he's threatened by you."

James blinked. "You think?"

"Absolutely." She swirled her unlit cigarette like an audition for a Betty Davis biopic. "You're too charming. Too composed. You make it look easy. They hate that."

Zane stared at her. "You know he was talking about how James *didn't* take a risk, right?"

Sophie waved him off. "It's just academic hazing. They push the ones they envy harder. It's a compliment, really."

Emma didn't say anything. She met Maribel's eyes for a flicker of a second, and then looked back at her cup.

"Anyway," Sophie continued, blissfully unaware of the group's quiet protest, "I think you're brave. The calm in that piece? It was *soothing*. Not everyone wants to scream their soul onto the paper. Some of us just want to feel okay."

Maribel stood up abruptly. "I'm getting something sweet. Anybody want anything?"

Emma stood too. "I'll come."

They escaped toward the pastry case while Zane lobbed dry questions at Sophie about whether she believed in reincarnation or just showed up dressed like someone who did.

At the counter, Emma rested her hand on the glass display. "I swear if one more person tells James what he wants to hear, I'm going to lose it—like a pebble on Pluto—maybe never to be found again."

Maribel glanced back at the booth. "He needs the truth more than praise right now."

Emma nodded. "Herzog wasn't wrong."

"Nope," Maribel said, already choosing a lemon bar. "But James heard it. You saw him. He's stewing. He's got something cooking."

They returned just as the next poet was launching into a breathless rant about lightbulbs and lamb chops and why did they both begin with an 'L'? Was it a conspiracy? The group leaned in to listen, or at least pretend to.

As the poet wrapped up, Emma tuned to James. "Hey."

He looked at her.

She hesitated, then added, "I liked your piece. It was beautiful."

James gave her a slow smile. "You mean... not revealing enough, but pleasant?"

Emma returned the smile, but said, "If you can whip something off that good, just like that... what would happen if you tried the task?"

James leaned forward to speak low just to her, "What if I did try the task and that was my... result?"

Emma drew in a breath and took a risk, "Try again."

Sophie was already eyeing the stage, clearly preparing for her turn.

Maribel passed around bites of lemon bar, and Zane stole James's napkin sketch of intersecting lines forming a geometric pattern to add his doodle of a cartoon sloth holding a megaphone.

"There. Done." Zane announced.

They laughed again, just like before. But underneath, something had shifted. A slow tightening of invisible strings. James looked down at his hands, at the pen, at the empty coffee cup. He was thinking.

Zane was still chuckling about the poet who rhymed "blisters" with "sisters" when James leaned forward suddenly, eyes locked on the stage. A beat passed. Then he turned back to the group, a glint in his eye.

"Who's got a large sketchpad on them?" he asked, low and urgent. "Zane? Your portfolio?"

Zane gave him a look. "Yeah, I've got it—but don't mess with my mess. What are you scheming in that jack-o-lantern head of yours?"

"I just need some blank pages," James said, already half-rising from the booth. "And a piece of vine charcoal—"

Emma was already reaching under the table. She popped open her battered tackle box, pulling free a handful of well-worn sticks.

Zane sighed, digging under the bench for his oversized sketch pad. "You owe me a new pad if you get all performance-art on it."

James flashed a grin. "Deal."

He took the tools like a surgeon receiving instruments. "Okay," he said, tucking the charcoal into his breast pocket. "Let's see who's not afraid to take a risk."

From the stage, Sophie was winding down—something about unwrapping tight minds and tulips in February. When she stepped off to light the cigarette she still wouldn't smoke, James lifted a finger and caught the emcee's eye.

Seconds later, he was on stage, sketchbook under one arm. The crowd looked at him, expectant. James simply stood there, smiling like he had a secret they didn't.

Zane leaned over to Maribel. "What's he on about?"

Maribel shrugged. Emma tilted forward, "Shhh. Just watch."

James leaned into the mic. "Evening all," he said with a deliberate southern drawl. "I'd like to try something a little impromptu tonight, if y'all are game."

The audience chuckled. He smiled then shifted to his own pattern of speech to say, "I propose... you give me your proposal. I'd like to know—what did you want to be when you were eight years old? And if you're brave enough to tell me... I'll document the moment for you. A quick sketch. One memory recorded."

A few hoots, some claps. James smiled.

"Right then. Who's first?"

The room hesitated, students glancing sideways, reluctant to step into the spotlight. Then, from the back: "I'll bite, you mad git." It was Zane of course, bailing out his buddy.

Laughter rippled as James grinned. "Good on you. What's your name me-lad?"

"Zane," he called.

James nodded. "Alright, Zane. Lay it on me—what did eight-year-old Zane dream of?"

He stood slowly, thinking back as he rose to crack, "I wanted to be a cosmonaut."

James paused, then laughed. "Not an astronaut?"

"No," Zane deadpanned. "Cosmonaut. Sounded more... cosmic. Bigger. Besides, I thought Russians were better at being stoic, that translates to 'cool' for those of you still managing their grasp of the English language."

The room laughed again, and James was already sketching, his hand moving with swift grace. Within a minute, he turned the pad around and held it up.

A boy with spiky hair and too-big boots stood wide-eyed on a cratered planet, a little Soviet flag in one hand and a half-deflated soccer ball in the other. The style was quick, gestural, but the essence—Zane's crooked smirk, his ironic longing and true heart too—was unmistakable.

Zane let out a breath, blinking. "Bloody brilliant," he murmured to Emma and Maribel. "Who is this guy? Our mate James?"

The audience applauded, and soon others were volunteering—an aspiring lion tamer, a boy who'd wanted to be a weather balloon, a girl who'd dreamt of building houses from candy and wood. With each story, James sketched quickly, fluidly, coaxing essence from paper.

By the end of it, the room was on its feet. Someone shouted, "You should charge for these!" James laughed, waved it off.

He returned to the table flushed with energy, dropping the pad with the image of boy-Zane in front of his friend.

"Yours to keep," he said.

Zane looked at it for a long moment. "You didn't keep the others?"

James shook his head. "Gave 'em away."

"Of course you did," Maribel murmured.

James missed the tone—still riding the wave. He reached for Emma's tea, took a sip, then leaned back like a king among friends.

But Emma was quiet. She hadn't applauded. She hadn't volunteered. Maribel's hand brushed against hers beneath the table in quiet recognition.

What James had just done was remarkable. Charismatic. Clever. Brilliant, even. But it was exactly the opposite of what Herzog had challenged him to do. He had read everyone in the room—but offered no glimpse of himself.

Zane sat back, eyes still on the drawing. "It's mad," he said softly. "He's made the moment... sing."

"Or maybe," Maribel added, "he made the moment dominate the memory."

Emma didn't say anything.

James tapped the charcoal dust off his fingers and smiled like he'd won a stuffed panda at a circuit fair for tossing a dime onto a slim clear glass plate.

No one else said it—but everyone at the table knew:

He had dazzled the room. And once again, told them nothing, a bait and switch maybe or a magicians trick. Maybe.

* * *

Chapter 6

Red Lakes, MN — Hawkins Residence — *April 13, 2002 — 11:45 a.m. — The Gauntlet*

The van pulled up to the Hawkins family home, gravel crunching under the tires. James stepped out first, his posture straight and confident despite the weight of the journey. Emma followed, her eyes darting between James and the three figures standing like sentinels on the porch.

"Hello Dad," Emma called out, her voice a mix of warmth and apprehension, "we're here."

George Hawkins nodded, his eyes never leaving James. Flanking him were two younger men, unmistakably Emma's brothers. Their faces were impassive, but their eyes were sharp and assessing.

James approached the porch, Emma at his side. Behind them, Alfred and Gerardo emerged from the van, hanging back slightly.

"Mr. Hawkins," James said, his voice steady as he extended his hand, "thank you for having us. I'm James Watson."

George's handshake was firm, his calloused palm a testament to years of hard work. "Welcome to Red Lake, James," he said, his tone neutral but not unkind, and then, "I know of you of course, but good to finally meet."

James nodded, looked down for a moment, but instead of answering directly to that interesting comment, he gestured to his companions, "This is Alfred Worthington, a dear friend, and Gerardo Jimenez, a colleague and friend."

George acknowledged them with a nod before turning his attention back to James. There was a moment of silent appraisal, each man taking the measure of the other.

James met George's gaze unflinchingly. There was depth in Emma's father's eyes, but also an unmistakable strength. This was a man who had faced his own share of trials and came out the other side, not unscathed, but unbroken.

Emma's mother appeared in the doorway. "Emma, come help me in the kitchen," she called out, her tone brooking no argument.

Emma hesitated, looking at James. He gave her a small nod, his eyes conveying reassurance. As she walked past her father and brothers, she tapped James's arm briefly before disappearing into the house.

"The sweat lodge is prepared," George said, his voice low, "we'll begin at sundown."

Gerardo stepped forward. "Mr. Hawkins, I was hoping to learn more about the ceremony before deciding if I'll participate."

George's eldest son, John, spoke up. "I'll explain everything," he said, gesturing for Gerardo to follow him, and then turned and invited Alfred to come with them so they would all have the same understanding of what was involved.

As they walked away, George turned his attention back to James. "You," he said, "come with me. We have things to discuss."

As they walked into the house, James could feel the eyes of Emma's younger brother, Michael, on his back, but he didn't falter. In the living room, George gestured to a chair. James sat, his posture relaxed but alert. George studied him for a long moment, his expression unreadable.

"The elder," George finally said, "he had a feeling about you—said you were a man on a journey."

James nodded slowly. "I suppose I am," he replied, "aren't we all?"

A ghost of a smile flickered across George's face. "Perhaps," he conceded, "but not all journeys lead to a sweat lodge on an Ojibwa reservation."

"No," James agreed, "they don't."

There was another moment of silence, but this time it felt less like a standoff and more like a mutual assessment.

"Tell me, James Watson," George said, leaning forward slightly, "what are you really looking for here?"

James met his gaze steadily and then drew in a breath and looked inside himself for the honest answer, he waited for a few moments and then said slowly, "Things can't go on the way they have, in this world, or with myself either. I'm here because of our deal, that's a fact, but I also discovered that I want this sweat lodge too, for myself." James said simply, "something has to change and I'm willing to try an old, true way. I'm grateful for it."

George's eyebrows rose slightly, a flicker of surprise and perhaps approval in his eyes. "Big words," he said. "Let's see if you can back them up in the lodge."

* * *

Michael gestured to James. "Come with me. There's something you should see."

Michael didn't speak at first. Just walked. James rose from the chair and followed Michael from the living room and out of the house without a word. Once outside the house, Michael paused and pointed down the slope toward the trees that framed the acreage. Michael took a moment to explain. "John took your friends to view the sweat lodge and probably walk the property, getting a feel for the place, the land. We're heading there."

They walked in silence and so James looked about the property, it looked to be about ten acres with the back section cloaked in trees, he assumed the lodge was kept out of direct view from prying eyes. The sun was climbing high into the sky to warm the day and James took in a deep breath and let it slowly flow back into the world and it's working parts.

Michael smiled and offered "That sounds close to a sigh, you gonna faint on me?"

James looked around the landscape and chuckled "Not quite yet, but I didn't bring my smelling salts, so let's hope not."

Michael actually laughed and so James expounded "It actually feels...good to...be in the flow and let someone else do the driving for a while."

Michael, cocked his head to look directly at him, his lean face and dark eyes were similar in cast and color to Emma—James noted in his private perpetually running analysis, and he said something rather interesting. "That sounds... almost reasonable."

James looked down and said nothing more, but it suggested that the family did indeed hold a private collective view of the role he'd played in Emma's life. Of course they would take 'her side' but it is one thing to be holding the image of a monster in your mind and quite another to actually meet the man and ever so gently begin separate him from the myth.

And then after walking into a clearing in the woods, Michael stopped and pointed out, "This lodge was built the old way. Cedar frame. Willow poles. The door faces east."

The sweat lodge was set low into a bowl of earth, stones ringed neatly nearby, waiting for fire. There was no grandeur to it—just the economy of purpose and impression of long standing intention.

Michael pointed toward the stones. "Those are the grandfathers. The oldest spirits. They hold heat. They remember."

James stood with his hands in his jacket pockets, listening.

Michael tilted his head slightly. "Have you ever done one of these before?"

James shook his head. "No."

Michael gave a slow nod. "For me, it's about what you're willing to release. Or face. Of course it will become a private matter for every human being."

There was quiet again. The wind moved gently through the branches high in the trees.

"You spoke well with my dad, I'm not going to say anything more, this is the time to quiet down. Sit still and prepare the way... as best you can." And then he smiled and offered "Good luck."

Just then, Albert appeared behind them, walking softly. "Mind if I join?"

Michael turned, smiled. "Not at all. You're welcome, Albert."

Albert stood beside James. "I don't think I can go through the full lodge this time," he admitted. "Body's not quite where it used to be."

Michael nodded. "The ones who witness with respect are present in the ceremony. Presence counts."

Albert exhaled. "Then I'll be present. That I can do."

They were quiet a while, the three of them.

Soon, Gerardo jogged down the path to join them. "Sorry," he said, slightly out of breath. "Didn't want to miss the walk."

Michael nodded. "Perfect timing."

Michael looked at the three men. "There are rules here. Not written down, but real. Silence is honored. So is laughter, when it comes from truth. If you need to leave, wait for the cycle of drumming to end, then you can leave. But if you stay... you stay with respect. My dad will explain more when we sit in the circle."

James and Gerardo both nodded.

Gerardo added, "I've read a bit about the traditions. I'll be quiet and follow your lead."

James said nothing, but his jaw had tightened with focus. Michael noted the change.

"Humility is the doorway," Michael said. "No one expects you to be perfect. Just... not make it about you."

That made sense, the men nodded in tandem, but said nothing.

They stood together, looking at the lodge, a silent witness to their conversation, waiting for them

* * *

Emma stood in the back yard of her family home and watched the group of men emerge from the woods and stand as an ensemble in a tight circle. It was Michael, James, Albert, Gerardo and as she watched, her eldest brother John, carrying his drum strode to meet them. As she watched she could see Gerardo point to the drum and from the groups body language it was clear the focus was shifting to John as he held the drum and spoke. She assumed she was speaking about the drum as the heartbeat to the earth, becoming one with the heartbeat of the earth.

She didn't notice her mother until she appeared beside her, hands wiping off on a faded dish towel.

"They look serious," her mom said softly, following her gaze.

"They are," Emma murmured. "I think they're talking about the heart of the drum."

"Hmm," her mother said, a small sound that covered a lot of wisdom. Then, glancing sideways: "You want to go down there, don't you."

Emma huffed gently. "I'm not dying to crash the boy's club or anything. I just... I don't know. I'm curious. It's natural."

Her mother didn't respond right away. The breeze played with the corners of her hair.

After a moment, she said, "Men are men and women are women, Em. We're made different. And so tests and training are different. Sometimes our paths cross..."

Emma arched a brow. "Like playing golf?"

Her mom chuckled. "If you like. But it's okay when they don't. Doesn't mean you're missing out. Sometimes being on the outside lets you see more."

Emma smiled faintly. "You always say that when I'm getting ready to bust a move."

"I'm not sure what that means, but yes, I suppose so." And here she gently touched her daughters elbow "I'm not trying to...inhibit you, but there are rules for good reasons. There is a time and a place."

Emma drew in a deep breath but chose to remain silent, what was the point? It was a repeated and sometimes tired conversation between them. Instead Emma leaned slightly against the porch post. "I wonder if James is ready for this."

Her mom's eyes narrowed as she studied the group again. "Well, he may have outgrown the young man you remember."

Emma turned toward her. "What do you mean?"

"I mean, he looks to be a full man steady on his feet... and as you know, the lodge doesn't require readiness. Only willingness. It meets you where you are."

Emma nodded slowly, considering.

Her mother bumped her shoulder lightly. "Come help me set up the benches, would you? If the weather stays good, we might as well eat outside. The light's too pretty to waste."

Emma followed her down the steps, glancing back once more at the men. James had crouched to the ground to peer at something in the dirt. Albert was speaking, quietly. Gerardo's face looked unusually thoughtful.

She turned forward again, hands sliding into her sleeves.

"I'll grab the tablecloths," she said.

Her mom smiled. "That's my girl."

The wind picked up a bit as they walked together toward the shed, skirts and jackets flapping lightly like flags flying and cracking in the wind.

* * *

James crouched in the dirt near the firepit, dragging the tip of a twig in looping arcs as Michael spoke about the structure of the lodge and the care taken in its placement. Gerardo was listening intently. Albert, hands in his coat pockets, had nodded in quiet approval.

James half-heard it all. His body was there. But his eyes drifted.

Up the hill, near the house, he caught sight of movement—a flicker of motion through the pine-filtered light. Emma.

Just walking.

She moved like she always had, like a human woman translated into a musical phrase. That smooth, unhurried slide-swing gait, as natural as breath and just as intimate. He had never seen another woman walk like that. He didn't know if any other man noticed. He hoped not.

His heart gave a small, absurd flutter.

There was his woman—*his*; now, where on earth had that buried treasure of a Cro-Magnon man notion come from? It had risen like a spring from a hidden source deep inside himself. Unbidden and possibly unwelcome, but there it was. Somehow, even after everything—there she was walking the earth, loose, without a tether to him. Just a month ago, she'd been as far away as the moon, a name in his past and behind a locked door in his chest. And now he was watching her walk up there, beside her mother, laughing, sharing the quiet humor of a common connection in a close knit family.

God, life was strange.

He blinked, plucked a twig from the ground, looked at it, put it in his pocket and then stood.

"Alright then," Michael said, glancing up. "Let's go to lodge, yeah?"

James looked back up the hill, then toward the lodge, drawing in a breath to calm... always to calm.

"Yeah," he said quietly.

* * *

Chapter 7

N.Y.C. – Cooper Union Campus – *Feb. 3, 1989 – 6:15 p.m. –*
Trembling

Emma sat on a worn leather couch in the corner of a bustling
coffee shop near campus, her sketchbook open on her lap but
her pencil motionless in her hand. Her eyes were steadfast on a
scene unfolding at the counter.

James stood there, leaning casually against the polished wood,
his gracious smile on ramped up to seven on the charm scale
as he chatted with Sophia, a stunning art history major who
had transferred in this semester. Emma watched as James ran
a hand through his tousled hair, a gesture she knew, as his place
to pause, ponder, then pounce with a particularly enlightened
and slightly disarming comment.

Sophia laughed, the sound carrying across the room, and Emma
felt a pang in her chest. It wasn't jealousy, well, yes it was, but
it was also stirred gently with... sadness, loss and a kind of small
death. Every time he flirted with a girl in this way was another
step further away from her. She'd seen this scene play out before,
with different faces, different laughs, but always with James at
the center, effortlessly drawing people into his orbit and away
from her. Oh yes, he would float back to her and hover and soak
in her flow of love...and then bing, bang away into another orbit
around another celestial body. And Emma was loathe to admit
that Sophia, indeed, was a fine figure of celestial body.

"Earth to Emma," Zane's voice cut through her reverie. He plopped down beside her, following her gaze to the counter. "Ah, I see. Watching the James Show, are we?"

Emma forced a smile. "Just... observing. For artistic purposes, you know."

Zane snorted. "Right. And I'm here for the excellent coffee, not because Maribel works the evening shift."

They sat in companionable silence for a moment, both watching as James said something that made Sophia throw her head back in laughter.

"He's good, isn't he?" Zane mused. "I swear, the guy could peel the paint off a canvas with a persuasive 'come hither'"

Emma nodded, her throat suddenly tight. "Yeah, he's special."

Zane turned to her, his expression uncharacteristically serious. "You know, Em, if you want to stake your claim, you should probably do it soon. James may be oblivious, but he won't be forever. And there are plenty of Sophias' out there who are very clear with him about what they want."

Emma's pencil snapped in her grip, the sharp crack making Zane jump. "Sorry," she murmured, staring at the broken pieces in her hand. "I just... I don't think it's like that. With James and me."

"No?" Zane raised an eyebrow. "Could've fooled me. And half the department."

Emma shook her head, her eyes drifting back to James. He was now showing Sophia something on his small flip phone, their heads bent close together over the small screen. "It's not what most people think or do... what you're suggesting is too small...what I feel can't fit into something that small, that casual. I know I'm special to him, just not special enough."

"Emma, come on—"

"No, listen," Emma cut him off, the words tumbling out now that the dam had broken. "James is like this with everyone. He makes everyone feel special, feel seen. It's part of what makes him so... whatever. But for me..." She trailed off, struggling to articulate the realization that was crystallizing in her mind.

"For you, it's different," Zane finished softly.

Emma nodded, feeling tears prick at the corners of her eyes. "I'm pretty sure I love him, I don't know, I've never been in love before, I can't explain... it," she whispered, the words both a revelation and a confirmation of something she'd known for a long time. "I love him, and somehow I feel that I won't love anyone else... like this, but for James... well, the world is wide, I'm just one of many. And so maybe he's out shopping... but I'm not. And I think I might go crazy if I have to watch it."

Zane opened his mouth to protest, but Emma shook her head. "It's okay. It's who he is. I don't want to change him. Really, really don't and I know what he does is none of my business, but I just... I can't be like Sophia; I'm just not made that way, I wouldn't know how. And... I don't want to be one of many. Not when he may be my only one. I don't know how people do it... break themselves up into different pieces to be with different people. What would be left?"

As if sensing their gaze, James looked up from the counter. His face broke into a wide smile when he saw Emma, and he waved enthusiastically, gesturing for her to join them.

Emma waved back, coughing up a small smile that didn't quite clear her throat to curl her lips. In that moment, watching James's attention immediately shift back to Sophia, Emma knew what she had to do. She couldn't stay and watch herself become just another face in James's ever-expanding circle. She might become bitter... or crazy.

"I think," Emma said quietly, closing her sketchbook with a sense of finality, "it might be time for me to consider that study abroad program in Florence."

Zane's eyes widened in understanding. "Emma, are you sure?"

Emma nodded, her resolve strengthening even as her heart ached. "I'm sure. It's better this way. For both of us."

As she gathered her things to leave, Emma took one last look at James. He was in his element, surrounded by admirers, his talent and charisma drawing people to him like moths to a flame. Well, moths get zapped. She wasn't kidding herself, she knew who she was and her mental limit. The party was over.

With a deep breath, Emma stepped out of the warmth of the coffee shop and into the cool evening.

* * *

James leaned against the coffee shop counter, basking in the warmth of Sophia's admiring gaze. The new art history transfer was hanging on his every word, and he had to admit it made him feel like one of the royals.

"So, James," Sophia said, leaning in closer, her perfume wafting over him, "I'd love to hear more about your latest project. Maybe over dinner sometime?"

James grinned, running a hand through his hair. "Well, it's a bit complex, but I could give it a go. You see, I'm working with different textures to create a sort of visual rhythm..."

As he launched into an explanation, his eyes darted around the coffee shop, almost unconsciously seeking out Emma. He spotted her in the corner, head bent over her sketchbook.

Something in him wanted her to look up, to see him here, to... what? He wasn't quite sure.

"That sounds fascinating," Sophia gushed, touching his arm lightly. "You're so talented, James."

He laughed, his Geordie accent thickening as it always did when he was pleased. "Ah, it's nothing special. Just mucking about with paint, really."

Another glance at Emma. Still not looking. Why wasn't she looking?

Without really thinking about it, James raised his voice slightly, making sure his next joke carried across the room. Sophia's laughter rang out, clear and bright. There. That ought to do it.

But when he looked again, Emma was still absorbed in her sketching. A flicker of annoyance passed through him, though he couldn't quite place why.

"Oh, you must show me some of your work," Sophia was saying, leaning in even closer.

"Right, 'course," James mumbled, pulling out his phone. As he scrolled through his gallery to find pictures of his latest pieces, he found himself pausing on a candid shot of Emma. Her face was lit up with laughter at something off-camera, and for a moment, James felt a strange tug in his chest. He quickly swiped past it.

He angled the phone so Sophia could see, their heads close together over the small screen. As he pointed out details of his work, he couldn't resist another glance at Emma. This time, she was looking right at him.

Perfect. Now she'd come over, and... and what? James wasn't sure, but he felt a sudden urge to have her join them. He waved enthusiastically, grinning at her.

Emma waved back, but made no move to join them. James felt his smile falter. What was her problem? Couldn't she see he wanted her to come over?

"James?" Sophia's voice broke through his thoughts. "Are you okay?"

"Yeah, sorry," he said, forcing his attention back to her. "Just saw a friend. Where were we?"

As he continued chatting with Sophia, James felt a growing sense of irritation. Every now and then, he'd glance at Emma, expecting her to have finally gotten the hint and come over. But she remained stubbornly in her corner.

Fine, he thought petulantly. If that's how she wants to be.

He turned his full attention to Sophia, laughing a bit too loudly at her jokes, leaning in a bit too close as they looked at his phone. He was vaguely aware that he was showing off, but he pushed the thought aside. He was just being friendly, wasn't he? That's what he did. Made people feel welcome, included.

So why did he feel so... off?

When he next looked up, Emma was gone, the coffee shop door swinging shut behind her. James stared at the empty space where she'd been, a confused jumble of emotions swirling in his chest.

"Everything alright?" Sophia asked, touching his arm again.

"Yeah," James said, though he wasn't sure if it was true. "Yeah, everything's fine."

But as he turned back to Sophia, plastering on another smile, James couldn't shake the feeling that something important had just slipped through his fingers. He just had no idea what it was, or why it mattered so much.

* * *

Zane watched the spectacle unfold at the counter, his eyes darting between James's animated performance with Sophia and Emma's increasingly withdrawn posture in the corner. He shook his head, muttering under his breath, "Bloody hell, James. You're mucking it up, mate."

As Emma gathered her things and left, a quiet determination settled over Zane. He'd been dancing around his feelings for Maribel for months, but watching James potentially throw away something special with Emma lit a fire under him. Life was too short for missed chances.

The door jingled as Maribel entered for her shift, her pixie cut slightly windswept. Zane's heart did a little flip as she tied on her apron.

"Oi, Maribel," he called out, surprised by the steadiness in his voice.

She looked up, eyebrows perking up. "What's up, Zane? The usual?"

"Actually," he said, leaning on the counter, "I was wondering if you'd like to go out sometime. With me, that is."

Maribel laughed, the sound both thrilling and terrifying to Zane. "Good one, Zane. You almost had me there."

But Zane didn't laugh along. Instead, he took a deep breath and launched into a rapid-fire list. "Right, then. How about the zoo? We could see the zebras. No? Okay, a walk down 5th Avenue? Feed the pigeons under the statue of Alexander Hamilton. Still no? What about—"

"Zane," Maribel cut in, her eyes wide. "Are you... are you serious?"

He nodded, his face flushing. "Dead serious. I can keep going, you know. Like the wheel of fortune. Just stop me when something catches your fancy."

Maribel bit her lip, a blush creeping up her cheeks. "Um... the walk. The one down 5th Avenue. That sounds nice."

Zane's face split into a grin. "Yeah?"

"Yeah," Maribel replied softly, a shy smile playing on her lips.

"Well, then," Zane said, settling onto a bar-stool, "I'll have a pint while I wait for the time to tick."

As Maribel moved to pour his beer, Zane couldn't wipe the goofy grin off his face. He was so lost in his happiness that he didn't notice James approaching until he was right beside him.

"What's got you grinning like a loon, mate?" James asked, clapping him on the shoulder.

Zane turned to him, his eyes bright. "All cuz of you, you great lunk of dumb git. If it wasn't for your thick as a brick bottled brain, I'd be over in the corner crying... instead... I have a DATE!"

James blinked, clearly taken aback. "A date? With who?"

Just then, Maribel returned with Zane's pint. She set it down gently, her fingers brushing against Zane's hand. Their eyes met, and she gave a small nod before hurrying off to serve another customer.

James's jaw dropped. "Maribel? You and Maribel? When did this happen?"

Zane took a long swig of his beer, savoring both the taste and the moment. "Just now, mate. Sometimes you've got to seize the moment, you know? Can't always wait for it to come to you."

As James stood there, looking thoroughly gobsmacked, Zane couldn't help but chuckle. He raised his glass in a mock toast. "Here's to taking chances, eh? You might want to think about doing the same."

With that, he turned back to his beer, leaving James to ponder his words and the unexpected turn of events. The coffee shop hummed with activity around them, but for Zane, the world had suddenly become a much brighter place.

* * *

The atrium outside the professors' offices was a study in contrasts: black and white tiles stretched across the floor, leading up to soaring arched ceilings that seemed to capture and hold every whisper. Usually a hub of activity, today it was quiet, save for the soft sound of Emma methodically deconstructing a bagel.

James spotted her from the hallway, his heart skipping a beat. Zane's words echoed in his mind: "Sometimes you've got to seize the moment." Without hesitation, he approached and sat down next to Emma, not waiting for an invitation.

Emma didn't look at him, continuing her careful dissection of the bagel. The silence between them stretched, but it wasn't uncomfortable. Instead, it felt like a living thing, wrapping around them, softening the edges of the world until only they existed.

James felt it building, that inexplicable connection that always seemed to hum between them when they were alone. He took a deep breath, gathering his courage.

"Em..." he began, his voice barely above a whisper, "can you feel this... between us? I know, I mean I think, I hope you do... right now, always, it's there. I don't know how to say it..."

His voice trailed off, the words feeling inadequate to describe the current flowing between them. Emma was still for a moment, then turned to face him.

"Yes," she said simply, nodding for emphasis.

Their eyes met, and James felt as if he were falling. Slowly, carefully, as if handling something infinitely precious, he reached out and took her hand.

The touch seemed to amplify everything—the softness in the air, the beating of his heart, the electricity crackling between them. "God, Em…" James murmured, at a loss for words. He bowed his head slightly, holding onto her hand like a lifeline.

Emma raised her free hand, about to run her fingers through his hair, when a commotion from the hallway shattered the moment.

"James! James!" Tonya's voice echoed through the atrium as she rounded the corner with Tim and Nell in tow. She was waving an envelope, her face flushed with excitement.

James looked up, nodding slightly, his attention still largely focused on Emma.

"Sorry, James, sorry," Tonya panted as she reached them, "but I had to bring this. It was in the box, and I know you've been waiting."

Emma looked at Tonya, confusion evident on her face. James, noticing her expression, quickly explained, "Tonya is Paul's girlfriend's flatmate. Our next-door neighbor."

Emma's brow furrowed slightly, wondering how this girl had access to James's mail, but before she could voice her question, James was already tearing into the envelope.

The atrium fell silent once more as James read the letter, the tension palpable. He finished reading and carefully tucked the letter back into the envelope.

"Well?" Tonya demanded, practically vibrating with anticipation.

James looked at Emma, a mix of emotions playing across his face. "Yes," he said softly, "they're taking both pieces."

The small group erupted in cheers and congratulations, their voices bouncing off the high ceilings. Emma sat stunned, trying to process this new information.

"You... you entered a curated show?" she asked, her voice barely audible over the celebratory din. "Where? How... when?"

But James was being swept up in the excitement, Tonya planting a kiss on his cheek as Tim and Nell thumped him on the back. As the group started to pull him away, James resisted for a moment, turning back to Emma.

"I'll explain everything tonight," he promised, his eyes bright with excitement. "I'll see you at your place and tell all. No, wait—let's meet later, I'll see you later, right? God, Em, I'm in a show!"

And then he was gone, whisked away by his jubilant friends, leaving Emma sitting alone in the suddenly quiet atrium. She realized her hand was still poised in mid-air, frozen in the act of reaching for James.

As the sound of celebration faded down the hallway, Emma lowered her hand slowly, a complex mix of emotions washing over her. Pride, confusion, and a lingering sense of something lost warred within her as she stared at the half-eaten bagel in her lap, wondering how a moment that had felt so perfect could be wiped out as if nothing.

* * *

Emma paced her small apartment, her footsteps echoing in the quiet space. Every few minutes, she glanced at the phone, willing it to ring. The excitement of James's success mingled with a growing unease in her stomach as the hours ticked by without a word from him.

"He said he'd explain everything," she murmured to herself, running a hand through her hair. "He promised."

As midnight approached with still no sign of James, Emma's worry overtook her pride. She dialed Zane's number, her fingers trembling slightly.

"'Lo?" Zane's groggy voice answered.

"Zane, it's Emma. Have you heard from James? He was supposed to come over, but..."

There was a rustling sound as Zane seemed to wake up more fully. "Oh, yeah, I heard about his big news. Haven't seen him though. Wait—" He paused, still waking up "When I called Maribel, she said he was there at the bar... celebrating pretty hard. Sorry Em, might've passed out somewhere?"

Emma's heart sank. "Oh. Okay. Thanks, Zane."

She hung up, fighting the urge to go out searching for James. But New York at night was no place for a young woman alone, even one worried sick about her... friend? Almost-boyfriend? Emma wasn't even sure what to call him anymore. Sleep eluded her that night, and she rose early the next morning, exhausted but determined.

Emma hurried down the hallway of the art center building, her footsteps echoing off the stark white walls. She'd barely slept, waiting for James's call that never came, but she couldn't cancel on Professor Herzog. The kindly older man had become a mentor to her, and his time was too valuable to waste.

As she rounded the corner towards Herzog's office, she froze. There, strolling towards the gallery where the spring show would be held, were James and Tonya.

James looked disheveled, his clothes rumpled as if he'd slept in them. Tonya had her arm linked through his, supporting him slightly as they walked. Emma's heart clenched at the intimacy of the gesture.

She wanted to turn away, to pretend she hadn't seen them, but her feet seemed rooted to the spot. James and Tonya stopped just outside the gallery doors. James turned to Tonya, a soft smile on his face that Emma had once thought was reserved only for her.

"Thanks for everything, Tonya," James said, his voice carrying in the quiet hallway. "Don't know what I'd have done without you last night."

Tonya reached up and smoothed James's tousled hair. "Anytime, James. That's what friends are for, right?"

Friends. The word echoed in Emma's mind. Is that all they were? The gesture seemed far too intimate for mere friendship.

As if sensing her presence, James looked up. His eyes met Emma's, and for a moment, she saw a flicker of... something, but no, and then he smiled, polite and distant, making a vague gesture that seemed to say he'd call her later.

Emma watched as James turned back to Tonya, placing a hand on the small of her back as he guided her into the gallery. The door closed behind them, leaving Emma alone in the suddenly too-quiet hallway. Stunned.

She stood there for a long moment, her mind stunned into silence. The floor beneath her feet felt like it was opening up and she was sinking, and as an internal aside she thought, 'Oh god, is this why people faint?' But she didn't faint, she made it to the wood paneled wall and placed a hand to steady herself.

The excitement she'd felt for James's success, the hurt of his forgotten promise, the confusion of seeing him with Tonya—it all swirled together into a nauseating mix of emotions.

A gentle voice broke through her thoughts. "Miss Hawkins? Are you alright?"

Emma turned to see Professor Herzog looking at her with concern. She forced a smile, but it felt brittle on her face. "Yes, Professor. I'm fine. Shall we begin our meeting?"

As she followed Herzog into his office, Emma made a decision. She couldn't keep doing this, couldn't keep waiting for James to remember she existed. She was wrong, whatever happened on the bench of the lobby, didn't happen at all. Or not in a way it would stick them together,

Little did she know that this moment in the hallway would be the last time she'd see James in person for over a decade. The next time their paths would cross would be in 2002, in circumstances neither of them could have predicted.

As Emma settled into the chair across from Herzog's desk, she took a deep breath, and waited for the world to come back into focus.

"Now, Miss Hawkins," Herzog said, his kind eyes twinkling, "let's discuss your latest project, shall we?"

Emma nodded, and opened her portfolio.

* * *

James stumbled slightly as he and Tonya made their way down the hallway of the art center building. His head throbbed, a reminder of last night's celebrations, but he couldn't keep the grin off his face. He was going to be in the spring show. Him. James bloody Watson from Newcastle.

"Easy there, superstar," Tonya laughed, tightening her grip on his arm. "Let's get you to the gallery in one piece, yeah?"

James chuckled, leaning into her support. "Thanks, Tonya. You're a real mate, you know that?"

As they approached the gallery doors, James's mind wandered to the previous night. The excitement, the drinks, the laughter. And the notable absence of Emma. A flicker of annoyance passed through him. Wasn't she supposed to be happy for him? Wasn't she supposed to join him at the bar? Where was she?

"Penny for your thoughts?" Tonya's voice broke through his musings.

James shook his head, forcing a smile. "Just thinking about the show. Can't believe it's really happening."

Tonya beamed at him, reaching up to smooth his disheveled hair. "Believe it, James. You deserve this. I'm so proud of you."

Her words warmed him, soothing the hurt he'd been trying to ignore. Here was someone who could genuinely celebrate his success, no strings attached. Unlike Emma, who always seemed to be competing with him, even when she was supporting him.

As Tonya's fingers ran through his hair, James caught sight of a familiar figure down the hallway. Emma stood there, staring at them, her face a mix of emotions he couldn't quite decipher.

For a moment, James felt a twinge of... something. Not quite guilt, but a vague sense of unease. But then he remembered her absence last night, the way she always held back just a little, and the feeling faded.

He offered her a polite smile and a vague gesture that could mean anything. Maybe he'd call her later, maybe he wouldn't. Right now, he had his success to focus on, and Tonya's unwavering support to bask in.

"Shall we?" James said to Tonya, placing a hand on the small of her back as he guided her towards the gallery doors.

As they entered the gallery, leaving Emma behind in the hallway, James felt a sense of moving forward. Emma had made her choice last night by not showing up. Now he was making his.

"So, where do you think they'll hang your pieces?" Tonya asked excitedly, her eyes shining with admiration.

James grinned, his arm still around her waist. "Let's find out, shall we?"

As they explored the gallery, discussing potential spots for his work, James felt lighter than he had in months. Here was someone who could appreciate his talent without making it a competition, who could be genuinely happy for his success. Who wouldn't stand him up on a big night.

If a small voice in the back of his mind whispered that something important had just slipped away, James ignored it. He was young, talented, and on the cusp of recognition. The world was opening up before him, and he had come ready to play.

Little did he know that the brief moment in the hallway would be the last time he'd see Emma in person for over a decade.

* * *

The office of Professor Herzog was a study in organized chaos, a reflection of the man himself. Emma sank into one of the two visitor chairs, her fingers absently tracing the cracks in the green leather. The chair, like its owner, had seen better days, but there was an undeniable strength in its craftsmanship, a sense of history that Emma found oddly comforting.

Her eyes wandered over the crowded bookshelves, each tome seemingly placed with deliberate care. A shaft of late afternoon sunlight cut through the dusty air, illuminating a collection of small ceramics on Herzog's desk. Time seemed to slow, each mote of dust dancing in the golden light of a universe unto itself.

"Miss Hawkins?" Herzog's gentle voice drew her back to the present. "You seemed a million miles away."

Emma blinked, forcing herself to focus on the professor's kind eyes. "Sorry, sir. It's been… a challenging day."

Herzog nodded, a knowing look crossing his weathered features. "Yes, I imagine it has. But let's set that aside for now. I wanted to discuss your work, particularly your glazing techniques. There's something exceptional about them. Almost supernatural, if you'll forgive an old man's fancy."

As Herzog spoke, Emma felt a weight lift from her shoulders. Here, in this cluttered sanctuary of art and wisdom, James's dismissive words seemed to fade away. She leaned forward, her passion for her craft overriding her usual shyness.

"It's… it's hard to explain," she began, her voice gaining strength. "It's like a kind of color theory, but more intuitive. The colors, they have personalities, souls even. Each one has its own mood, its own desires."

Herzog's eyebrows rose, but he remained silent, encouraging her to continue.

"When I'm working, I can feel which colors want to play together on the clay. It's almost like… like I'm having a conversation with them." Emma's cheeks flushed, realizing how strange it must sound. But Herzog's expression remained open, curious.

"Go on," he urged gently.

"Sometimes, I'll be working with a deep cobalt blue, and I can feel it yearning for a touch of copper red. Not a lot, just a whisper. And when I add it, it's like... watching old friends reunite."

Herzog's eyes widened, a spark of excitement lighting them. "Fascinating. Truly fascinating. And this communication with the colors, have you always experienced it?"

Emma nodded, surprised to find tears pricking at the corners of her eyes. She'd never shared this with anyone, not even James. "As long as I can remember. I thought everyone could feel it."

The professor reached for one of Emma's pieces, a simple cup that sat on his desk. As he held it, a shiver seemed to run through him. "Yes, yes, I see. When I hold this... I feel a pleasant shiver up my arm. You have the old ways about you, Miss Hawkins. The ancient way and something new too. Some earth trait."

He set the cup down carefully, his expression turning serious. "I would like to say something to you, something I would say to no one else. I would like you to consider my old school in Dresden, the capital of porcelain, as you know."

Emma's heart began to race. "Dresden? But... that would mean leaving Cooper Union."

Herzog nodded solemnly. "Yes, it would. But I don't think Cooper can teach you what Dresden can. And I believe you can help them too. You're nearly halfway through your junior year in credits. I would not want you to lose your standing as an alum of Cooper Union. I could arrange an almost full scholarship to Dresden Academy of Fine Arts."

He paused, his eyes searching Emma's face. "But there would be challenges. It's in Germany, as you know, now part of West Germany. But there are problems there, the language is formidable. The professors speak English, but you would feel alone, most certainly. It takes months and months to learn even rudimentary German and adjust."

Emma listened, her mind whirling with possibilities and fears.

Herzog continued, his voice softening. "I'm not painting a happy picture, but they are the ones who I think can help you best. And...are you aware of the bombing of Dresden during World War II?"

Emma nodded, her voice barely above a whisper. "Yes."

"Well, you can imagine there are still some bad feelings toward Americans..."

Emma looked down at her hands, twisting in her lap. "I'm not American... exactly." She looked up, meeting Herzog's curious gaze. "Well, I am, but I come from a Native American Nation, the Ojibwa from Red Lake."

Herzog's brows furrowed as he studied her. Emma felt compelled to explain further. "My mother is half Chippewa, half white, and my dad is Ojibwa. But, that's me."

A smile of understanding crossed Herzog's face. "Yes, that seems to explain your connection to earth tones, without being stereotypical."

Emma returned his smile. "No offense taken. We're all the same human family, just from different houses."

Herzog leaned back in his chair, his fingers steepled beneath his chin. "I know it's a lot to take in, to think about—"

"I know I need to think about it," Emma interrupted, surprising herself with her boldness. "But yes, I'm very interested. You see, my grandpa, my mother's father, is German. This may not be so strange, after all."

Herzog stared at her for a long moment, then took a deep breath. "I'll make some calls today." he paused, his eyes searching her face. "May I ask, Miss Hawkins... why are you so ready to leave? Is it just an opportunity, or is there something else?"

Emma felt a lump form in her throat. The memory of James's dismissive words, of feeling invisible and undervalued, threatened to overwhelm her. But here in this moment of decision, she found the truth was up front and clear.

"I... I need to find my way," she said finally, her voice steady despite the tears that threatened. "To see where this work can take me. And maybe find a place where people think like me."

Herzog nodded, understanding dawning in his eyes. "Then let us begin this journey, Emma. The world of color awaits you."

As Emma left Helmut's office and stepped into the lobby, she paused. The day's last light filtered through the beveled glass windows of the main door, casting a path that was fading fast. No time to lose, she looked straight ahead and stepped out—not looking left to the water fountain nor glancing right to the bench where James had held her hand. No, she simply walked out the door and went on her way.

* * *

The moonlight filtered through the high windows of the Cooper Union art studio, casting long shadows across the floor. Emma's footsteps echoed in the empty space, each sound a reminder of her solitude. She paused at her locker, her hand hovering over the combination lock.

For a moment, she closed her eyes, inhaling the familiar scent of linseed oil and clay. When she opened them again, her fingers moved with practiced ease, spinning the dial. The lock clicked open, loud in the stillness of the night.

Emma's hands shook as she began to empty the locker. Brushes, paints, half-finished sketches—each item a memory, a piece of herself she was leaving behind. She gripped the edge of the locker door, willing her hands to steady. "Not yet," she whispered to herself. "Don't fall apart yet."

With her locker emptied, Emma turned to survey the room. Her eyes lingered on her desk, the surface scarred with years of creative endeavors. She walked over, running her fingers along the worn wood, remembering late nights and breakthrough moments.

Her gaze drifted to James's spot. The stool where he'd perch, his long legs folded awkwardly, as he brought worlds to life on canvas. Emma approached it slowly, as if it might disappear if she moved too quickly. She rested her hand on the back of the stool, feeling the phantom warmth of his presence.

"Goodbye," she whispered, her voice barely audible.

Emma moved to the window, looking out at the New York skyline. The city lights twinkled, a reminder of all the dreams and ambitions that had brought her here. It had taken so much to get into Cooper Union—countless hours of work, sleepless nights, the constant push to be better. And it wasn't so much the reputation of the school that had pulled her here, it was the fact that it was free. And now, thanks to Professor Herzog, she'd still graduate, albeit through a satellite program in Dresden.

Dresden. The word felt foreign on her tongue. It wasn't free like Cooper, but the scholarship and housing funding made it possible. Still, as she stood there, Emma felt the weight of her decision. She had climbed to the top of this mountain only to jump off.

With a deep breath, Emma turned away from the window. It was time to go through another door for the last time.

* * *

Zane's apartment was a cluttered haven of artistic chaos. Maribel opened the door, her eyes widening at the sight of Emma laden with bags and boxes.

"Em? What's all this?" Maribel asked, ushering her in.

Emma forced a smile. "Just some things I thought you guys could use."

Zane emerged from the bedroom, his red hair tousled. "Bloody hell, Em. You robbing an art supply store?"

As Emma unpacked, explaining her impending departure, the room grew quiet. She handed Maribel a delicate ceramic vase, its surface a swirl of blues and greens. "I made this for you," she said softly.

For Zane, there was a sculptural piece, abstract yet somehow capturing his essence. He took it, his usual joviality subdued. "Em, I don't know what to say—you really going through with this?"

Emma nodded as she continued to unpack, Zane and Maribel exchanged a look. Finally, Maribel spoke up, her voice gentle but probing. "Em… we've kept quiet like you asked, but are you absolutely sure about not telling James?"

Emma's hands stilled on a stack of sketch pads. She didn't look up, couldn't bear to see the concern in her friends' eyes.

Zane leaned against the wall, his arms crossed. "Yeah, mate. Don't you think he deserves to know?"

Emma took a deep breath, still not meeting their gaze. "No," she said softly, then added, "He might try to get me to stay. I don't know what will happen to me if I have to watch him... be with women like Tonya, and I wouldn't want to stop him. Plus, there's other reasons, this is about me."

The words hung in the air, heavy with unspoken implications. Maribel and Zane shared another look, understanding dawning in their eyes.

Emma's hand hovered over the rock, her masterpiece. Its surface was a testament to her unique glazing technique, layers of color that seemed to shift and change in the light.

"You should keep that," Maribel said, her voice gentle. "or give it to James. He loves that piece."

Emma's breath caught. "James," she whispered, the name heavy with unspoken emotions.

Zane cleared his throat. "Yeah, mate. He'd treasure it."

Emma's fingers curled around the rock. "Maybe I'll give it to him later. I'll take it with me for now. It's heavy, but maybe it'll bring me luck."

The weight of the moment settled over them. Maribel's eyes glistened with unshed tears. Zane shuffled his feet, uncharacteristically lost for words.

"I guess this is it," Emma said, her voice barely above a whisper.

Maribel surged forward, enveloping Emma in a fierce hug. "You better write, you hear me?"

Zane joined the embrace, his lanky arms encircling both women. "We'll miss you, Em. It won't be the same without you."

As Emma pulled away, she felt something inside her shift. This was more than just leaving school; it was the end of an era, the closing of a chapter. She looked at her friends, memorizing their faces, knowing that no matter what came next, she would hold this moment in her mind forever.

"I'll miss you too," she said, her voice thick with emotion. "More than you know."

They both were looking at her, with almost the same exact expression, hovering between bewilderment and deep sorrow. Maribel was openly crying now, Ted put his arm around her.

"Yours is the hardest door." Emma said quietly, no need to explain what she meant, they knew.

With one last look at the dear friends she was leaving behind, Emma stepped out into nighttime New York and the door closed behind her with a soft click. Just like that.

Done.

* * *

Chapter 8

Red Lake, MN — Hawkins Residence — *Apr. 13, 2002 — 2:18 p.m. — Talk it Out*

The Hawkins family kitchen was warm and inviting, sunlight streaming through the gingham-curtained windows. The aroma of fresh herbs and simmering broth filled the air. Emma's mother, Gerte, moved with practiced efficiency, her silver-streaked black hair pulled back in a neat braid. Her weathered hands, testament to years of hard work, deftly chopped vegetables on the worn wooden cutting board.

Emma stood awkwardly by the counter, feeling vaguely out of place in this familiar setting. The kitchen clock ticked steadily, marking the passage of time until the sweat lodge ceremony would begin.

Gerte began listing off ideas for the post-ceremony meal, her voice steady and sure. "We'll need protein, fluids, something bitter with a small kick. Maybe the corn relish?"

She glanced at Emma, her dark eyes expectant. "What do you think, dear? Any ideas?"

Emma shrugged, avoiding her mother's gaze. "You'd know best, Mom."

Gerte paused, setting down her knife. She turned to face Emma fully, her expression serious, her voice calm, almost kind. "You think it's a small thing I do? A small service women do, feeding the family?"

Gerte's voice was gentle but firm. "Food is everything. It can be infused with love, just as you work with clay. That love moves into the body of the family. It helps—no, it keeps everyone alive and healthy. For the men to work, for the children to learn and play and come home to be refreshed. It's the circle, Emma."

Emma's voice was barely above a whisper. "I know, Mom. I know. I could never do what you do."

Gerte's next words were soft, but they hit Emma like a physical blow. "And that's why you lost him."

Emma turned away, looking out the window towards where the sweat lodge stood in the clearing. Tears welled up in her eyes, and she blinked rapidly, trying to hold them back.

"I just wanted... to learn for myself too," she murmured and then "there were other reasons I never told you, he wasn't focused on me, he had..." Emma couldn't finish the thought.

Gerte moved behind Emma, wrapping her arms around her daughter. The scent of sage and sweet-grass clung to her, comforting and familiar.

"Shh... shh," Gerte soothed. "You think I don't know? You think every woman isn't afraid of the very same thing? 'Who will I be if I surrender to this man I love? What will be left of me? My dreams?'"

Gerte stepped back, her hands resting on Emma's shoulders. "I know it's impossible to believe without experiencing it, but your father's dreams not only became my dreams, I discovered they were mine all along."

A wistful smile crossed Gerte's face. "This may be silly to quote, but it came to mind the other day. Remember that sad love movie from years ago? 'Love Story'? The girl is dying, and her husband feels so sad, like he's taken from her and not given back. And the girl says: 'Screw Paris.'"

Emma's eyes widened at hearing her mother swear, even in quotation. Gerte chuckled at her daughter's expression.

"What she meant was that her husband had taken nothing from her. No dream was left to her but him. It's how God builds families. And a good man will never, ever let his woman not have a voice in the family, because he knows in his soul, she is the family. She is the reason his life is worthwhile."

Emma's voice was small, vulnerable. "He may not even want me anymore. He hurt me, and so I hurt him back. A kind of tit for tat, I thought. But I think the wound I made was deeper than the scratch he gave me. He hasn't forgiven me, may not want me at all."

Gerte nodded thoughtfully. "He might not. If that's the case, make sure you stay out of his way—don't get in his head. I believe you were called to help him and maybe make up for the past. And you will, I know you love him, but if you're not for him anymore, and the path has split, don't make it harder on him or yourself. Grandfather wouldn't have agreed to this without very good reason, I think he sees something in him."

Emma looked down at her hands as she sliced cucumbers, tears falling silently. Gerte crossed to her and briefly wrapped an arm around her daughter's shoulders to give a quick comforting squeeze. The old floorboards creaked beneath their feet, a familiar sound in the well-loved kitchen.

"I'd like to tell you something now," Gerte continued, her voice taking on a conspiratorial tone. "Something your dad and I talked about years ago, something we swore we would never say."

When she didn't continue, Emma looked up from her chopping. The paring knife lay forgotten on the cutting board as she gave her full attention to this moment.

Gerte settled onto a kitchen stool, its legs scraping softly against the floor. "When you were a little girl, you were always drawing pictures on every surface you could find, even making shapes in the sand and dirt, digging in the ground to find the clay and shapes as if you were looking for something... always looking..."

As her mom spoke, Emma's mind drifted to those childhood memories—the feel of cool clay between her fingers, the search for the right feeling. "Yes, I remember doing that."

Gerte laughed "At first we thought it cute, then we saw nothing could satisfy you, there was no clay pot you could make or picture you could draw that really made you happy... we knew you would be a beautiful woman, we thought you would have so many suitors, but no, they all seemed to bounce off you, as if there were, what do you call it? A fence around you."

She took Emma's hand, her skin cool from handling the vegetables. "We both knew you were unusual, and you would require an unusual man, so when the information about your school came in such a way, we didn't try to convince you to stay. What did we know about art? Nothing, we never cared about all that... what we cared about was you finding your man, and if he wasn't here, he could only be out there."

Emma absently placed the cucumber slices in a nearby bowl, the sharp scent of onions from earlier preparation stinging her eyes—or perhaps it was just the emotions of the moment. "He may not want me, mom. I'm not even sure he ever did."

"Well if that's the case then do your best to help him and stay out of his way, as I said," Gerte replied, her voice gentle but firm. She glanced out the window at the gathering dusk, then back at her daughter. "But tell me, when was the last time you said your prayers?"

"It's been a while," Emma admitted, her voice barely above a whisper.

Her mom nodded her head and looked down, and said, her voice low, "If you really feel you can be good to each other, and last, why not humble yourself a bit with some prayers? I don't know what kind of answers you'll get, maybe it will just be support on how you can survive helping him and then saying goodbye again. You're not in an ordinary situation so the help coming your way won't be ordinary. But there's always the chance something extra-ordinary might happen."

Emma couldn't seem to stop the tears that were flowing again. The kitchen suddenly felt too small, too warm, the weight of her mother's words pressing in on her.

"Shh... shh now. You're strong, a very strong woman," Gerte reassured her, reaching for a clean dish towel to dab at Emma's cheeks. "You can do this. I wouldn't have said all that if you couldn't take it. Now, drink some water too. Don't want you dehydrating on me."

Gerte's tone lightened, bringing them back to the task at hand. She moved to the sink, filling a glass with cool water from the tap. "Come on now, we have a lot to do. Where should we eat, inside or outside?"

Emma took a deep breath, steadying herself as she accepted the glass. She took a long sip, the water soothing her throat. "Outside. It will be cooler, and that will help balance the temperature."

Gerte nodded approvingly, already reaching for serving platters. "Outside it is."

As they continued preparing the meal, the kitchen filled with the sounds of chopping and simmering. The afternoon sun dipped lower, casting long shadows across the floor and painting the sky outside in brilliant hues of orange and pink—a fitting backdrop for the ceremony to come. It looked a little like fire.

* * *

The afternoon sun hung low in the sky as Michael led James across the yard towards the sweat lodge. The scent of wood smoke drifted on the breeze, and James could see the fire pit in the distance, flames licking at a pile of large stones.

Michael, his stride purposeful, broke the silence. "I'll be drumming during the ceremony," he said, his voice gruff but not unfriendly. "Along with another friend. John and Dad will be singing."

James nodded, matching Michael's pace. "And you don't sing?"

A hint of a smile crossed Michael's face. "Can't sing worth a lick. But I can drum."

They walked in silence for a moment before Michael continued. "Some young men from the Res are coming too. It'll be an event." he cast a sidelong glance at James. "I'm sure they want a look at you—some strange white man participating."

James met Michael's gaze steadily. "I imagine so."

Michael's next words carried a hint of challenge. "You can imagine they're also placing bets on how long you'll last."

They reached the edge of the clearing where the sweat lodge stood. James's eyes were drawn to the fire pit, where the grandfather stones glowed with intense heat. Even from this distance, he could feel a blast like the heart of a furnace.

Michael turned to face James full on, "But I bet against the odds that you'll make it all the way." his tone was serious, almost warning. "Not because I like you or anything… but because my sister brought you all here. So people are going to be looking at *her*, wondering why she would bring men who fail. You get my meaning?"

James held Michael's gaze, understanding the unspoken message. "I do," he said quietly.

Michael nodded, seemingly satisfied. As they stood there, Gerardo approached, his usual jovial demeanor subdued.

"I've decided to participate," Gerardo announced, his voice a mix of nervousness and determination.

James nodded and took a deep breath and said, "Good man."

Michael's eyebrows rose slightly as he looked between James and Gerardo. "Interesting," he said simply, a hint of curiosity in his tone.

As the three men stood there, watching the flames dance around the stones, James felt a sense of calm settling over him. The chatter of his mind began to quiet, replaced by a growing awareness of the power of this place, these people, this moment.

Michael observed James's demeanor and nodded almost imperceptibly. Maybe, just maybe, his sister hadn't made a complete mistake in bringing these men here.

* * *

The sun was below the horizon now, taking cover for the night, but there was still residual color painted across the sky, some soft pink and purple, a trace of memory fading fast of a good day. The air was thick with smoke rising from the fire pit and the scent of sage and sweet-grass and the sacred offering of tobacco.

Around the fire pit, the men sat in a loose circle, the flames casting flickering shadows across their faces.

James turned to Gerardo, his voice low. "I'm not sure if you heard what Emma said in the car, but if it gets where you can't take it, reach into the cool earth in your mind, or even your hands. But don't peel up the side of the canvas, there is no opening after the door closes."

Gerardo nodded, his usual jovial expression replaced by one of determination.

Alfred, his silver hair glowing in the firelight, sat to the right of George's empty place, a position of respect befitting his age and status. The other men, a mix of ages and backgrounds, sat in respectful silence, the only sound was the crackling of the fire and the distant call of a night bird.

As if by some unspoken signal, the men fell completely silent, their attention turning to George as he stood. His weathered face was solemn, yet there was a warmth in his eyes as he addressed the group.

"I'm pleased to be here," he began, his deep voice carrying easily in the still night air. "Pleased that you are all here, let's take a moment and greet each other."

And so the men nodded to each other, James made certain he looked every man in the eye in turn and said hello. This simple exercise raised the energy and relaxed the group, they were not strangers anymore.

George was speaking now, this time his voice more amiable, "You were instructed ahead of time, that we will wear shorts in the lodge, you may bring a towel, but no water, there is an altar next to the lodge door for offerings of tobacco. The fire-keeper will smudge you at the doorway before we enter the lodge.

He went on to explain the procedure, his words clearly meant more for James and his group than the others.

"When we first enter, we will get down on our knees and as we cross the threshold we say 'all my relations' there is no need to raise your voice, they can hear you."

There was a small chuckle at this bit of welcome levity, George continued: "Once inside, we will crawl clockwise around the interior perimeter of the lodge until we are in place. In our lodge ceremonies, we prefer that the stone carriers will bring the seven grandfather stones after we are in place."

His gaze swept the circle, lingering on James and Gerardo. "If you think you cannot continue and must leave, don't. Stay until the break, the door will open after each round, you may excuse yourself then."

He paused, letting his words sink in. "Don't bring in water, it will not be comfortable, but that is the point, there will be cold water after. No talking. Remove your jackets, and leave them here by the fire along with the fresh clothes you've brought for after. You take your t-shirt off or leave it on with your shorts. There will be no teaching at this time, usually, it's reserved for after the close of the four rounds."

"And most important... you may bring the troubles you carry with you... and you may leave them there inside. We leave all our problems, our burdens in there with the Grandfather Stone, for the Great Spirit Grandfather to deal with for the good of all."

A hint of a smile crossed George's face. "My Gerte is a great cook. I recommend you stay until the end so you can get fed. We will certainly have a feast."

The men chuckled softly, the tension easing slightly.

George bowed his head, and the others followed suit as he said a prayer. When he finished, a chorus of "Ho" rose from the group.

George stripped off most of his clothes except a pair of long khaki shorts, placed a towel around his neck and walked to the birch-bark sweat lodge opening.

That was the cue for the other men to follow suit, James was wearing his jogging shorts under his exercise slacks which he stripped off along with his t-shirt and Gerardo followed suit. The evening air already felt cool on his skin, but James reminded himself this would not be the case for long.

Without another word, George turned and approached the sweat lodge, he placed an offering of tobacco on the altar, paused while he prayed and turned to face the fire-keeper, an older man, perhaps in his seventies who smudged him with smoke cedar.

George bowed low, pushing back the flap, and got down on his hands and knees. James could hear him say 'all my relations,'

The other men looked to James, who, realizing he was next to enter, followed George's example, laid the tobacco Emma had given him for the offering on the altar, waited for the smudge clearing, then got on his knees to humble himself and crawled inside.

One by one, the men entered the lodge, the air inside already thick and warm. John and Michael brought in the grandfather stones, glowing red-hot in the dim light, and placed them in the central hearth. When the last stone was in place, John closed the door flap to the lodge. Water was poured on the stones, there was an immediate hiss as steam began to rise.

As John and Michael took their places beside their father, a sense of anticipation built. Michael began a steady drum beat, the rhythm growing more complex as the moments passed. Then, the singing began, low and haunting.

James closed his eyes, feeling the heat begin to build. He was ready. He wanted this. As the ceremony began in earnest, he found himself becoming more aware of his breathing and the drumbeat that calmed his troubled heart.

He recalled George's advice, '*We leave all our problems, our burdens in there with the Grandfather Stone...*'

This is what James wanted, what he needed.

The lodge was filled with the sound of drums, singing, and the hiss of steam, the outside world fading away as the first round of the sweat lodge ceremony began.

* * *

Chapter 9

N.Y.C.– Cooper Union Campus—*Feb. 6, 1989 – 11:55 a.m. – Losing It*

James Watson bounded through the Cooper Union courtyard, fairly bouncing as best a human being can do when on top of the world but still bound by gravity. His portfolio was tucked under one arm, a grin plastered across his face. He'd just sold another piece, his third this month, and couldn't wait to share the news with Emma. Her quiet pride in his successes almost meant more to him than the money in the bank. Almost. Well, call it a tie and be done with the contest.

He burst into the studio, his eyes scanning the familiar chaos for her slight figure. "Oi, Em! You'll never guess what—" The words died on his lips as he realized the space that had been hers for the past two years was eerily empty. No canvases propped against the wall, no jars of brushes, no half-finished ceramics waiting for the kiln.

James felt a chill creep up his spine, his earlier elation evaporating. He turned to the nearest student, a lanky boy with paint-splattered glasses. "Oi, mate. Where's Emma?"

The boy shrugged, barely looking up from his sketchpad. "Dunno. Haven't seen her in days."

James's heart began to race, a dull roar filling his ears. He stumbled out of the studio, his feet carrying him automatically towards Zane and Maribel's usual haunt in the student lounge.

They'd know. They always knew everything that happened in the tight-knit Cooper Union community.

He found them huddled over a textbook, heads close together. "Zane, Maribel," he panted, the words tumbling out in a rush. "Emma's gone. Her studio's empty. What happened?"

Zane and Maribel exchanged a look, a silent conversation passing between them that made James's stomach clench. Maribel spoke first, her voice unnaturally even. "She's gone, James. Left for some fancy program in Germany."

The world tilted on its axis. James gripped the back of a nearby chair, his knuckles turning white. "Germany? What are you on about? She never said..."

"Course she didn't," Zane muttered, not quite meeting James's eyes. "Didn't want a fuss, did she?"

James felt as if he'd been punched in the gut. Emma, gone? Without a word, without a goodbye? It didn't make sense. They were... well, he wasn't sure what they were exactly, but they were something. Weren't they?

"But... why?" he managed, his voice sounding so small to his own ears.

Maribel's eyes flashed with something—anger? Disappointment? Before softening, "Oh, James. Do you really not know?"

The silence stretched between them, heavy with unspoken words. James's mind raced, replaying every interaction, every shared laugh, every quiet moment. Had he missed something? Said something? Done something?

"She needed to find her own way," Zane said finally, his usual jovial tone replaced by something more somber. "Away from... well, everything here."

James staggered back, the implications of Zane's words hitting him like a physical blow. Away from everything here. Away from him.

The world around him suddenly seemed alien, unfamiliar. He stumbled out of the student lounge, his feet moving of their own accord. The hallways of Cooper Union, once so familiar, now seemed twisted with odd turns; he had to look around to find the door leading outside.

Where was he supposed to be? A class? A meeting? The thoughts slipped through his mind like water through cupped hands. He found himself on the street, the cacophony of New York City a dull roar in his ears. People brushed past him, their faces a blur.

Panic began to rise in his chest, a tightness that made it hard to breathe. Who was he? What was he doing here? He stopped abruptly, causing a businessman to curse as he swerved to avoid collision. James barely noticed.

He screwed his eyes shut, pressing his palms against his temples. Think. Think. What's your name? The question echoed in the sudden, terrifying emptiness of his mind. For a heart-stopping moment, he couldn't remember.

Then, like a drowning man breaking the surface, it came to him. James. James Watson. The relief was short-lived as memories began to flood back, each one a sharp-edged fragment.

Sleeping in abandoned buildings when he first arrived in New York, the chill seeping through his bones. Scrounging for art supplies, choosing between food and a new set of brushes. The gradual climb from desperation to hope as his talent began to be recognized.

And through it all, Emma. Emma with her quiet strength, her brilliant mind, her gift for color that seemed almost magical.

Emma, who had been his anchor in the chaos of New York, of art school, of life itself.

Emma, who had left without a word.

The realization hit him anew, a physical pain that radiated from his chest. He found himself on a bench, though he had no memory of sitting down. The hard knot in his chest grew, expanding until it felt like it might burst through his rib cage. He pressed his fist against it, as if he could physically push the pain away, but it persisted, a dull, throbbing ache.

James looked up, suddenly aware of his surroundings. He was sitting on the boulevard in front of the Cooper Union admissions building. The very place where he'd first met Emma, where she'd captured his essence in a few deft strokes of her pencil.

His hand twitched towards his ever-present sketchbook, but he stopped short. The thought of drawing, of creating anything, suddenly felt hollow.

As he sat there, the initial shock began to curdle into something darker. She left without saying goodbye. The thought repeated, a relentless drumbeat in his mind. After everything they'd shared, everything they'd been through together, she'd just... gone.

As if he were nothing to her.

Nothing.

The pain in his chest began to transmute and morph into the hard edges of a sharper emotion and a darker state of mind—anger seeping in like poison. How could she do this? How could she just leave, without a word, without an explanation?

The anger felt good, in a twisted way. It was something to hold onto, something to fill the sudden, yawning emptiness Emma had left behind. James clenched his fists, embracing the fury that was rapidly replacing the hurt.

Emma had left without a goodbye. Fine. If that's how she wanted it, that's how it would be. He didn't need her. He didn't need anyone.

As the late afternoon sun cast long shadows across the boulevard, James sat alone, his heart hardening with each passing moment. The boy who had arrived in New York full of wide-eyed wonder was gone, replaced by a young man whose trust had been shattered, whose innocence had been lost.

And in that moment, James Watson made a silent vow. He would never allow himself to be hurt like this again. Never.

* * *

Dresden Academy — *Mar. 29, 1989 — 2:55 p.m.*

The kiln room at Dresden Academy of Fine Arts hummed with anticipation, the air thick with the scent of heated clay and possibility. Emma stood among her classmates, her heart racing as the professor slowly lifted the kiln lid. She'd poured her soul into this piece, infusing it with all the loneliness, hope, and determination that had filled her first two months in this strange new world.

A collective gasp rippled through the room as the lid came fully open. Emma craned her neck, trying to see past the bodies pressed around her. Had something gone wrong? An air bubble not pressed out? The clay not thoroughly dried?

"Mein Gott," the professor breathed, his voice filled with wonder.

The students surged forward, their excited German too rapid for Emma to follow. But as they parted, she saw it – her vase, sitting proudly atop the kiln shelf, its colors singing in the fluorescent light.

Soft purple swirled and danced with pure white, teasing into a gentle yellow at the base. It was as if she'd captured twilight itself, that magical moment when day surrenders to night, full of whispered promises and bittersweet farewells.

"Was ist das?" one student asked, his voice hushed.

"Wer hat das gemacht?" another chimed in.

Emma coughed softly, slipping through the crowd. Her fingers trembled as she reached for the vase, its warmth seeping into her palms. She looked up, meeting the awed gazes of her classmates, and in that moment, something shifted. The wariness in their eyes melted away, replaced by genuine curiosity and respect.

"Wie hast du das gemacht?" One young man asked, his German slow and clear for her benefit. How did you do that?

Emma looked at him, she thought his name was Wolfgang, but she wasn't completely sure. She opened her mouth to explain, to share the secret conversation she'd had with the colors as she mixed them. But the words caught in her throat as she turned, instinctively seeking out a familiar pair of warm brown eyes.

James.

His absence hit her like a physical blow. Where she expected to find his proud smile, his playful wink, there was only empty space. The realization was shocking. What did she expect? He was on the other side of the world.

"Oh my God," she whispered, her voice lost in the excited chatter around her. "What did I do?"

The vase suddenly felt heavy in her hands, a reminder that beauty is only realized when shared.

She wasn't sorry she'd come to Dresden. The growth she'd experienced, the way her art had flourished, confirmed she'd made the right choice for her future. But the way she'd left... the memory of slipping away without a word, of swearing Zane and Maribel to secrecy, now felt small. Petty, even. And cruel. How much time had passed? How could she possibly reach out now? What would she even say?

Emma's fingers traced the swirls of color on the vase, each shade a reflection of her tumultuous emotions. The purple of passion, the white of purity, the yellow of hope—and underneath it all, the unspoken truth she'd been too afraid to face.

She had wanted to marry him.

The realization hit her with startling clarity. All those times James had called her "too intense," when he'd spent time with other women, when he'd put her on some metaphorical back burner—had he sensed her deeper feelings? Had he been scared off by the weight of her unspoken expectations?

And so, to protect herself, to get "a bit of her own back," she'd left without a goodbye. In doing so, she might have sealed their fate forever.

Emma's vision blurred, unshed tears making the colors on her vase swim. If there had been another way, some perfect words to bridge the gap between them, she still couldn't find them. But as the ache in her chest mingled with the pride of her artistic achievement, she knew one thing with certainty.

She had been wrong.

The chatter of her classmates faded to a dull roar as Emma stood there, cradling her creation. In that moment, surrounded by newfound acceptance yet achingly alone, she silently vowed to do better. To be braver. To face her feelings head-on, no matter how terrifying. It had to begin with an apology.

* * *

The shrill ring of the telephone cut through the quiet of Emma's small Dresden apartment, startling her from her reverie as she looked out the window to the city street below. For a wild, heart-stopping moment, she thought it might be James. They'd always had that uncanny connection, sensing each other's thoughts, anticipating needs before they were voiced.

Her hand trembled as she lifted the receiver. "Hello?"

"Emma, sweetheart?" Her mother's voice, warm and familiar, flooded the line. Emma's shoulders relaxed, tension she hadn't realized she was carrying melting away.

"Mom," she breathed, a smile tugging at her lips. "I was just thinking about home."

There was a click, and her father's deep voice joined the conversation. "Hello, little one. How's our artist in residence?"

Emma laughed softly, the sound catching in her throat. "I'm good, Dad. Really good, actually. I had a breakthrough with my work today."

As she described the scene at the kiln, the awe in her classmates' eyes, Emma felt the earlier tumult of emotions rising again. Her mother, ever attuned to the nuances in her daughter's voice, picked up on the undercurrent.

"Emma, honey, what is it? You sound... different."

Emma took a deep breath, wondering how to put into words the complex swirl of feelings inside her. "I just... I realized something today. About James. About how I left."

There was a moment of silence on the line. Then her father spoke, his voice gentle but firm. "You did what you needed to do, Emma. Sometimes the path forward isn't clear until we're already walking it."

"Your father's right," her mother added. "But it's okay to feel conflicted. Growth often comes with growing pains."

Emma nodded, forgetting for a moment that they couldn't see her. "I know. I don't regret coming here. It's just..."

"You wish you'd handled things differently," her father finished for her.

"Yeah," Emma whispered.

Her mother cleared her throat. "Well, speaking of family and connections, your grandfather had an idea. Now that the wall is down and Germany is reunified, he thinks you should try to contact his brother—your great-uncle."

Emma blinked, surprised by the sudden change in topic. "I didn't even know I had a great-uncle in Germany."

Her father chuckled. "Old wounds, old stories. But maybe it's time to rebuild those bridges. What do you think, Emma? Could you look him up?"

As Emma considered the request, she felt a spark of excitement kindle in her chest. Here was a chance to connect with her roots, to weave together the disparate threads of her heritage—Native American, German, American.

"I'd love to," she said, her voice growing stronger. "Do you have any information about him?"

As her parents shared what little they knew—a name, a possible city—Emma felt a sense of purpose settling over her. This quest to find her great-uncle could be a way to honor her past. And perhaps, see a portion of the countryside too. Imagine traveling into East Germany, going through the mountains.

"Emma," her mother said softly as the conversation wound down, "we're so proud of you. You're carrying our stories, our colors, into a new world. Remember that, okay?"

"We love you, little one," her father added. "Stay strong, stay true."

As Emma hung up the phone, she felt centered in a way she hadn't since arriving in Dresden. The conversation with her parents was exactly what she needed to remind her how vital family was and is.

She turned to her desk, pulling out a fresh sheet of paper. There were two letters she needed to write—one to seek out her great-uncle, and another, perhaps, to begin bridging the ocean-wide gap between her and James. As her pen touched the paper, she paused and thought, no—don't think, or plan it out, just write.

* * *

N.Y.C. - Cooper Union— *Mar. 3, 1989 — 4:15 p.m.*

The clatter of dishes and the hiss of the espresso machine provided a chaotic backdrop to the hushed conversation taking place in the corner of the bustling café. Zane leaned across the counter, his red hair falling into his eyes as he stared at Maribel in disbelief.

"She's doing what? She went where?" his voice cracked with incredulity.

Maribel sighed, wiping her hands on her apron as she glanced around to ensure no customers needed her immediate attention. "I told you, Zane. Emma's gone to Geisa, Thuringia. Near the Rhön Mountains."

"Mountains?" Zane's eyebrows shot up. "Like, 'Sound of Music' mountains?"

Maribel rolled her eyes, a fond smile playing at her lips despite her exasperation. "Different mountains, luv, but yes, mountains."

The bell above the door jingled, and James sauntered in, his portfolio tucked under his arm. He caught the tail end of their conversation as he approached the counter.

"Who's gone to the mountains?" he asked, a hint of curiosity coloring his voice. "I've always wanted to paint mountains."

The air seemed to thicken, tension crackling between Zane and Maribel as they exchanged a loaded glance. Maribel bit her lip, hesitating for a moment before speaking.

"It's… it's Emma," she said softly, her eyes never leaving James's face.

James froze, his hand halfway to the coffee mug Maribel had instinctively started preparing for him. "Emma?" he repeated, his voice suddenly hoarse. "What about Emma?"

Zane cleared his throat, shifting uncomfortably on his stool. "She's, uh, she's gone to some place called Geisa. In Germany. To meet a great-uncle or something."

The color drained from James's face, replaced almost instantly by a flush of anger. "She's bloody well done what?" he exploded, his Geordie accent thickening with emotion. "An almost communist country? To meet some 'maybe' family she's never even met before?"

Maribel flinched at the vehemence in his voice. "James, calm down. It's not—"

"Calm down?" James cut her off, his eyes flashing. "How the bloody hell am I supposed to calm down? Who's taking her there? Don't tell me she's going alone. Christ on a bike, she doesn't even speak German!"

Zane reached out, placing a hand on James's arm. "Mate, take a breath. Emma's a big girl. She can handle—"

James shrugged off Zane's touch, pacing the small space in front of the counter like a caged animal. "Handle herself? In a foreign country where she doesn't know the language or the customs? Where the bloody *Wall* just came down? Is she out of her sodding mind?"

Customers were beginning to stare, drawn by the commotion. Maribel shot them apologetic looks as she tried to defuse the situation.

"James, please," she begged, "you're making a scene."

But James was too far gone, his fear for Emma manifesting as anger. "I can't believe I'm hearing this. I can't believe you two knew about this and didn't say anything. What if something happens to her? What if—"

He broke off, running a hand through his hair in frustration. The unspoken words hung heavy in the air: What if I never see her again?

Zane stood, moving to stand in front of James, "Listen, mate," he said, his voice low and steady. "I know you're worried. We all are. But Emma's smart. She's resourceful. And she's following her heart, doing what she needs to do."

James deflated slightly, the fight going out of him as quickly as it had come. He slumped against the counter, suddenly looking very young and very lost.

"But why?" he whispered, more to himself than to his friends. "Why didn't she tell me?"

The question lingered, unanswered, in the suddenly quiet café. Maribel and Zane exchanged helpless glances, the weight of unspoken truths and missed opportunities hanging between them all.

As the regular buzz of conversation slowly resumed around them, James stared unseeing at the coffee mug before him.

* * *

Dresden – Emma's Aprtment– *Mar. 13, 1989 – 7:30 p.m.*

The small desk in Emma's Dresden apartment was bathed in the warm glow of a single lamp, casting long shadows across the room. Outside, the city had settled into its night time rhythm, a distant hum of traffic and occasional laughter from late-night revelers floating through the partially open window.

Emma sat hunched over a sheet of creamy stationery, her pen hovering uncertainly above the paper. She'd been sitting there for what felt like hours, trying to find the right words to bridge the chasm she'd created. Finally, taking a deep breath, she began to write:

"Dear James,

I don't know if you'll read this. I'm not sure I would, if our positions were reversed. But I have to try. I owe you that much, and so much more.

I've just returned from Geisa, a small town near the Rhön Mountains. It's where I met my great-uncle Heinrich, my Grandpa Ernst's brother. James, it was like stepping into a living history book..."

Emma's pen flew across the page as she recounted her journey. She described the rolling hills of Thuringia, so different from the flat prairies of her childhood. She wrote of Heinrich's weathered face, how his eyes – so like her grandfather's – had lit up when she introduced herself in halting German.

"He told me stories, James. Stories of the war, of the brothers separated by an ocean and ideology. Of survival and loss and hope. And as I listened, I felt pieces of myself clicking into place. Like I was a mosaic, and I'd finally found some of the missing tiles."

Her hand cramped, but she pushed on, determined to get it all down.

"I thought of you, sitting there in Heinrich's tiny kitchen. I imagined your pencil flying across your sketchpad, capturing the lines on his face, the way the light hit the old photographs on his wall. I missed you so much that in that moment it has become a hurt that hasn't gone away.

James, I'm so sorry. Sorry for leaving the way I did, without a word. It was cowardly and cruel, and you deserved better. I was hurt and scared and so sure I knew what was best. I thought I was protecting myself, but all I did was cause more pain.

I don't regret coming to Dresden. The work I'm doing here, the things I'm learning about art and about myself – it's all been incredible. But the way I left... I regret that with every beat of my heart."

Emma paused, blinking back tears that threatened to smudge the ink. She took a shaky breath before continuing.

"I miss you. I miss your laugh, your terrible jokes, the way you'd scrunch up your nose when you were concentrating on a particularly tricky bit of shading. I miss our late-night talks about art and life and everything in between. I miss our friendship.

I don't know if you can forgive me. I'm not sure I deserve it. But I hope, someday, we might find a way to be friends again. Or at least to talk.

There's so much I want to tell you, so much I want to hear about your life.

I hope you're well, James. I hope your art is going the way you want. And I hope, maybe, you think of me sometimes too.

Always,

Emma"

She sat back, flexing her cramped fingers. The letter stared up at her, a jumble of emotions and memories poured out onto paper. It wasn't perfect. It probably wasn't even enough. But it was honest, and it was a start.

With trembling hands, Emma folded the letter and slipped it into an envelope. She addressed it carefully, using the information Maribel had reluctantly provided. For a moment, she held the sealed envelope to her chest, closing her eyes and allowing herself to imagine James reading her words, understanding, forgiving.

Then, before she could lose her nerve, she grabbed her coat and headed out into the cool Dresden night. The walk to the post office was short, but with each step, Emma felt as though she were crossing a vast distance.

As she dropped the letter into the mailbox, hearing it thump softly against the metal bottom, a mix of relief and anxiety washed over her. It was done. For better or worse, her words were on their way to James.

* * *

N.Y.C. – James's Apartment — *Mar. 27, 1989 — 8:20 p.m.*

The letter came too late—approximately twelve days too late. No, not approximately, it was exactly twelve days since he'd had sex with Tonya and the next morning he had felt so... so wrong, so defiled, he'd thrown up in the waste bin near her bedside.

She'd heard the sound, poked her head around the corner, and mused, "Too much to drink last night?"

"Oh...aye..." James had finally managed to say, and then to himself, all, too much. Too much wine, too much, what was that? Reefer? Had it been laced with something? The scent of her perfume and all. The music, and whatnot, whatever he had ended up in a tumble, jumble of bodies merging to his own shock, but not hers. Oh no, she had known from get to go exactly what she was doing, but he had not.

And so he didn't feel half bad about deciding to make some excuse and bound from the place... and dear God, had they used protection? Yes. Yes. He remembered that too. But it was ghastly.

He was not feeling at all what a man should be feeling after such a supposed night, what men said they felt, oh no, he felt... he felt... wronged, betrayed. And not by Tonya... but of course, by Emma.

It should have been her.

She was the one he really wanted, his skin fairly sang within four feet of Em; he shook his head. It should have been her. But she had left him.

Same old song.

He made up some excuse, he had to make it to class, which was true of course, and scrambled to find his clothes and beat a hasty footpath to the door... after he found it of course. He had some dim recollection of Tonya calling after him, laughing a little maybe?

Didn't matter, he was outside now and breathed deep, it was raining just a wee bit, and didn't that feel like himself too? Inside, he shook his head, it's not that the sex had been so, so terrible, it was because now, he felt so... ghastly. That was the word, like he had picked up some kind of slime from Tonya and wouldn't feel right until he could wash it off.

As soon as he got to his flat, or apartment as they say on this side of the big water, he peeled off the clothes, "gonna burn those," he said out loud to the sketches pinned to walls and ran the water and didn't wait for it to cool, no he wanted it hot, screaming hot from the spout to spray him good and douse the louse from him. He was sure Tonya didn't have lice, it wasn't that, it was... because it wasn't Emma.

Her purity, her light, the stream of love, yes, love coming from her would never have put this bitter taste in his mouth and now he felt forever changed because she had left him.

It all came back to that, over and over.

So often, he would stumble across Maribel regaling Zane with some latest tid bit biting her noggin about the goings on of dearest Emma in farthest parts of the world and always she would tame the tales down a bit when he came close, for fear of setting him off, but too late he had heard the name "Wolfgang... dear God, who would call their bairen Wolfie? Serves the bloke right" and there were other names Berta something and others, but of course the man's name had stuck in his mind—could mean nothing just one name among many, but it had stuck and so of course he had convinced himself he had to move on too. Thas' what folks did, right?

Move on, move away.

An' there was Tonya, always there it seemed now, oh well, didn't matter now, he was done with her... and he suspected she was done with him as well. Last night was what Tonya had wanted and got it in spades and clover. Dear god, James hoped the protection worked. There were diseases going around too, can't be too careful in the village.

It seemed the shower couldn't get him clean enough, it seemed his apartment couldn't be tidied up enough... and after seven days of trying he decided to move. He'd actually made enough money from some recent sales... and after he'd sent some money home for Sarah, he put a deposit down on a better place, with high windows, good light and he told no one the new address; two could play, two could play.

And so it was on the twelfth day and taking the last bits out the door and taking one last look about, he spotted some mail in a small pile by the door, something he had kicked aside for later, well, later is now. He picked up the envelopes, a couple of utility bills, oh, that looks interesting a note from a bloke and his wife about the blue painting they had bought at an east village gallery, Alfred somebody, best hang onto that... and then there, a small envelope with several bright stamps and post office marks suggesting a rough path halfway around the world, a letter from home probably, he didn't want to read his mom's words at the moment, and so without a second glance he stuffed all the mail into the lower pocket of his backpack; no he didn't want to read a letter from his mom or any woman at the moment.

He was afraid of course, that his mom would be able to read his mind in that uncanny way of hers just through the telegraph of reading her writing, and best table that. Oh aye, for a while. He took a deep breath.

Emma, luv...

He had thought about calling Emma, he had, he admitted it—just force her number from Zane, he would crack before Maribel. Just suck it up and call her, track her down and bellow at her or cajole her or beg her to come back... or, or stay in touch, anything, any crumb. But too, too late he thought, twelve days too late.

Something terrible had happened with Tonya and it was all because of Emma's pride, because of her over-reacting. Well, he had pride too, maybe now more than ever, maybe because he had lost a private part of himself twelve days ago, pride was all he had. There was no such thing as a one night stand, it lasted. The effect lasted and it was a pollution.

And he was convinced more than ever that men actually felt these matters deeper than women. Everyone thought it was the other way around, but no, that was for show. Men showing off to cover... what? He didn't know exactly, but maybe it was feeling like this. Hollow... hollowed out and desperately missing his rib. His good girl. His Em.

Didn't matter, move on, move along, nothing to see here, move along...

* * *

Newscastle – Watson Home – *Mar. 31, 1989 – 4:35 p.m.*

The taxi pulled up to the modest row house, and James felt a wave of nostalgia wash over him. He paid the driver and stood on the sidewalk for a moment, taking in the familiar sight. The front garden, small but well-tended, his mum's pride and joy. The faded blue paint on the door, chipping slightly at the edges.

James stood on the sidewalk, staring at the familiar row house. He took a deep breath, steeling himself before pushing open the gate.

With a deep breath, he walked up the short path. Before he could knock, the door swung open, and there was Sarah, her face lighting up with joy.

"James!" she cried, throwing her arms around him. The force of her embrace nearly knocked him off balance, and he marveled at how much she'd grown.

"Hello, pet," he said softly, hugging her back just as fiercely. He stumbled slightly, surprised by her strength. "Hello, pet," he murmured again, hugging her tightly.

His mum appeared in the doorway, wiping her hands on her apron. Her eyes were red-rimmed, betraying recent tears. "Come in, love. You must be exhausted." And then in a soft aside, "thanks for coming, Sarah's been distraught, can't stop crying... ta lad, for coming so quick."

He nodded but said nothing.

James stepped into the house, the familiar scents washing over him—his mum's cooking, the faint mustiness of old carpets, the lavender air freshener she'd always favored. His eyes swept the living room, taking in every detail.

The old couch, its cushions slightly sunken from years of use, sat against the wall. A ball of yarn and knitting needles rested on the arm, a half-finished scarf trailing onto the floor. James recognized the soft blue wool—the same color as the gloves and hat he'd received for Christmas.

"That's the color of my Christmas gloves," he said softly.

His mum smiled. "Good eye. I'm making you a matching scarf."

On the mantelpiece, a row of framed photos caught his attention. School pictures of Sarah, family holidays, and there—the photo he'd sent of himself with Emma, Zane, and Maribel. His throat tightened as he looked at Emma's smiling face.

Sarah came up behind him, wrapping her arms around his waist. "I'm so glad you're home," she murmured.

James patted her hands, soaking in the unconditional love radiating from his sister. "Me too, pet. Me too."

His da appeared from the kitchen, nodding gruffly. "Son," he said by way of greeting, his eyes searching James's face.

Sarah took his arm to get his attention again. "I'm so glad you're home," she murmured. "I was so scared."

James turned, he was concerned now, she had his full attention. "Scared? Why, pet?"

They settled in the living room, James perched on the edge of the couch. Sarah curled up next to him, her eyes wide and serious.

"I had dreams, James. Terrible dreams," she began. "There were monsters chasing you and you couldn't see them, but they were catching up."

James felt a chill run down his spine. He glanced at his parents, noting their worried expressions.

"It's just dreams, luv," his mum said gently. "James is fine, see?"

But Sarah shook her head vehemently. "No, it was real. I could feel it. And there was a girl, surrounded by bright colors, trying to help. But you couldn't see her either, James."

James's heart clenched, knowing instinctively she was talking about Emma. He forced a smile. "Well, I'm here now, aren't I? No monsters in sight."

His da cleared his throat. "Aye, and scaring us all half to death with your fancy art school and New York living. Couldn't you have found something closer to home?"

The rebuke was gentle, but James felt the sting of it nonetheless. "Da, I—"

"Never mind that now," his mum interrupted. "Dinner's ready. Come on, all of you."

* * *

The family gathered around the kitchen table, steam rising from the shepherd's pie in the center. James inhaled deeply, memories of countless family dinners washing over him.

"Smells great, Mum," he said, forcing enthusiasm into his voice.

His mum beamed, spooning a generous portion onto his plate. "Eat up, love. You're too thin."

As they began to eat, Sarah launched into an excited description of her new school. "And I've made a new friend, James! Her name's Lucy, and she loves to draw too. Not as good as you, of course, but we have so much fun!"

James smiled, genuinely warmed by his sister's enthusiasm. "That's brilliant, pet. You'll have to show me your drawings later."

"Oh, I will! And guess what?" Sarah's eyes were wide, "We're learning to use computers now. Can you believe it?"

His da grunted. "Computers. In my day, we learned with pencil and paper, and we turned out just fine."

"Now, George," his mum chided gently. "The world's changing. Our Sarah needs to keep up."

James pushed his food around his plate, his appetite waning. "The art world's going digital too. Lot of mixed media stuff now."

"Is that what you're doing these days, son?" his da asked, a hint of challenge in his voice.

James shook his head. "No, I'm still... traditional, I suppose. Oils, mostly."

"James painted a beautiful picture of Central Park," his mum interjected. "You sent us a photo, remember love?"

James nodded, not meeting anyone's eyes. "Yeah, sold that one actually."

"Good money in art these days, is there?" his da pressed.

James shrugged. "It's... up and down. Some months are better than others."

A moment of awkward silence fell over the table. Sarah, sensing the tension, piped up again. "Oh! I forgot to tell you about our class trip to the museum!"

As Sarah chattered on, James caught his parents exchanging worried glances. He knew they could see the shadows under his eyes, the slight tremor in his hands as he lifted his fork. He tried to focus on Sarah's story, but his mind kept drifting.

"James?" Sarah's voice cut through his thoughts. "Are you listening?"

He blinked, forcing a smile. "Sorry, pet. Jet lag, you know. Tell me again about the dinosaur exhibit?"

As Sarah launched back into her tale, James felt his mum's hand on his arm, a gentle, comforting squeeze. He met her eyes, seeing the unspoken question there. 'Are you really okay?'

He patted her hand, trying to convey reassurance he didn't feel. 'I'm fine, Mum. Don't worry.'

But as the dinner continued, with Sarah's excited chatter, his mum's gentle prodding to eat more, and his da's gruff inquiries about life in New York, James felt the weight of everything he wasn't saying pressing down on him. The struggles, the loneliness, the mistakes he'd made—all of it simmered just beneath the surface of their mundane conversation, unspoken but palpable in every hesitation, every forced smile.

* * *

As James helped his mum clear the table, Sarah bounced on her toes, eager to share more. "I've taken your bags up, James. Don't worry about a thing!"

His mum smiled fondly. "That's very thoughtful, luv."

Sarah's eyes sparkled with mischief. "I'll even unpack and lay out your pajamas. The ones with the little paint brushes on them?"

James felt a genuine laugh bubble up, the first since he'd arrived. "Oi, those are my lucky jammies. Handle with care, yeah?"

Everyone chuckled, the tension from dinner easing slightly. Sarah hugged James tightly, then her parents. "G'night, everyone. I'm so glad you're home, James."

As Sarah's footsteps faded upstairs, James's mum pulled out a thick photo album. "Come, sit down. I want to show you something."

They settled in the living room, James perched on the edge of the sofa, his parents in their usual chairs. His mum opened the album, revealing a mix of familiar and new images.

"Here's that Central Park painting you sent us," she said, pointing to a glossy photo. "And look, I've kept the newspaper clippings of your gallery showings."

James leaned in, surprised. There were more clippings than he remembered sending. His mum must have been scouring the international art sections.

"And here," she continued, turning the page, "are some of Sarah's school photos. Look how happy she is with her friends."

James studied the images of his sister, surrounded by smiling faces, engaged in various activities. "She really is thriving, isn't she?"

His mum nodded, her eyes misty. "She is. And it's all thanks to you, luv. Your support has made such a difference."

James felt a lump form in his throat. He turned the page quickly, coming across photos of Zane, Maribel, and... Emma. His fingers traced her face unconsciously.

"Such lovely friends you've made," his mum said softly. "Do you still see them often?"

James withdrew his hand as if burned. "Ah, well, you know how it is. Everyone's busy."

His mum's brow furrowed slightly, but she pressed on, showing more photos - Sarah's art projects, James's sold paintings, family gatherings he'd missed. With each turn of the page, James felt the weight of his absence, of all the things unsaid.

As his mum chatted, filling him in on family gossip and neighborhood news, James caught his da watching him intently. The older man's eyes narrowed, taking in James's forced smiles, his shaking hands, the dark circles under his eyes.

"Look," his ma said, opening another album to reveal pictures of Sarah at her new school. "She's doing so well, James. Learning things we never thought possible."

James leaned in, studying the photos of his sister surrounded by friends, her face alight with happiness. "That's brilliant," he said softly.

"The doctors think she might even be able to hold a small job someday," his mum continued. "Of course, she'll never be fully independent, but—"

"I'll take care of her, Ma," James interrupted. "I've promised, haven't I? I'll always—" His voice cracked, and he couldn't finish.

Finally, as James's mum paused to refill their tea, his da stood up. "Right then. Think it's time for a bit of fresh air. Come on, son. Let's have a pint out back."

James looked up, a mix of relief and apprehension on his face. His mum glanced between them, understanding passing unspoken. She nodded, closing the photo album.

"Go on, then. I'll just tidy up here." she assured them.

As James followed his da towards the back door, he felt a flutter of nervous energy. The time for small talk was over. Out on that back porch, under the stars of his childhood, he knew he'd have to face some home truths.

* * *

The night air was cool as James and his da settled onto the small back porch, each nursing a bottle of beer. For a while, they sat in companionable silence, listening to the distant hum of the city.

Finally, his da cleared his throat. "Right, lad. I want you to tell me what it's really been like for you. No sugar-coating. I've worked the docks, seen my share of rough times. I can take it."

James looked at his father, really looked at him, and saw the genuine concern behind the gruff exterior. He took a deep breath and began.

"It was... hard, at first. Harder than I let on in my letters," James admitted. "When I first got to New York, I was... well, I was homeless for a bit. Squatting in abandoned buildings with other artists and vagrants."

His da's eyebrows shot up, but he remained silent, letting James continue.

"Felt like ages, though it was probably just a few months. Eventually got work at a garage. Small stuff, you know? Changing oil, tires. Enough to eat and eventually rent a tiny room." James took a swig of beer. "Then I landed a TA position at the school. That was a big step up."

His da nodded slowly. "And the rest we know. School going well, selling your art, getting into shows."

"Yeah," James agreed. "That's the glossy version, I suppose."

His da fixed him with a penetrating stare. "But that's not all, is it? You're tough, son, always have been. That kind of life might break your toe, but not your heart. What's really eating at you?"

James felt something crack inside him. Tears welled up, silent and hot, rolling down his cheeks. He tried to shake them off, embarrassed, grateful for the dark of night, and the cover it provided, but still, he hung his head.

"I've made mistakes, Da," he whispered, "maybe big ones."

His da was quiet for a moment, then asked softly, "Was the bonny lass a mistake? The one in the pics, the one Sarah goes on about?"

James looked up, surprised. "Em? No, she… she wasn't a mistake."

"Is she a good lass?" his da pressed. "I'm not asking if you're pissed at her, I can see plain as day you are. I'm asking if she's a good lass, at her core. I'm asking if she's a good lass for you."

James nodded, unable to speak.

His da took a long pull of his beer, then said simply, "Well then," as if that settled everything.

They lapsed into silence again, but it was a comfortable one. After a while, his da began talking about the latest Newcastle United match, giving James time to compose himself.

As they sat there, the night deepening around them, James felt closer to his father than he had since he was a child. The unspoken understanding between them was a balm to his battered spirit.

When they finally stood to go back inside, his da clapped him on the shoulder. "You'll sort it out, son. You've got a good head on your shoulders, and a strong heart. Just… don't be afraid to come home, be with people who love you. You can't buy that with silver or gold."

James nodded, a lump in his throat. "Ta, Da," he managed.

As they stepped back into the warm light of the kitchen, James held the door open for his da, and then of all the unfathomable events to happen, he hugged his da right there on the threshold.

* * *

The sky was overcast, what else was new in England? And so the sun struggled to penetrate the lace curtains of James's childhood bedroom. He sat on the edge of his bed, fingers tracing the familiar pattern of the worn quilt. Two days had passed in a blur of shared meals, long talks, and rediscovered connections. Now, the weight of imminent departure pressed upon him.

A soft knock at the door. "James? Breakfast's ready, luv."

His mum's voice tinged with a forced cheerfulness that didn't quite mask her sadness. James swallowed hard. "Be right down, Mum."

In the kitchen, the scent of fried eggs and toast mingled with the ever-present aroma of his mum's lavender soap. James settled at the table, noting how his da hid behind his newspaper, how Sarah's eyes were red-rimmed from crying.

His mum set a plate before him, then hesitated. "I've got something for you, luv."

She produced a small package, wrapped in tissue paper. James unwrapped it carefully, revealing a knitted pencil holder in shades of blue and gray.

"It's not much," his mum said, wringing her hands. "The scarf isn't ready yet, but I thought... for your sketches..."

James stared at the simple gift, his throat tight. It was so thoughtful, so perfectly his mum. He looked up, really seeing her for the first time in years. The new lines around her eyes, the gray at her temples, the love and worry etched in every feature.

"It's perfect, Mum," he managed, his voice hoarse, "thank you."

His mum's face crumpled for a moment before she quickly turned away, busying herself at the sink. James stood, crossing the small kitchen in two strides. He wrapped his arms around her from behind, feeling her slight frame shake with suppressed sobs.

"I'm sorry," he whispered into her hair. "I'm so sorry I stayed away so long."

She turned in his embrace, her hands coming up to cup his face. Her eyes roamed about his face as if trying to memorize every detail. "My boy," she murmured. "My sweet son."

For a moment, James felt like a child again, safe in his mother's arms. All the struggles of New York, the disappointments, the loneliness—they all fell away with just a wee drop of love.

* * *

All too soon, the taxi arrived. James stood at the door, his bag at his feet, the knitted pencil holder tucked safely inside. Sarah clung to him, her arms wrapped tightly around his waist.

"I'll take care of you, James," she insisted, her voice muffled against his chest. "Don't worry. I'll never let you forget who loves you."

James stroked her hair, his voice gentle. "I know, pet. I know. Thank you."

Sarah continued, words tumbling out. "I'll watch your things at the house. Won't let Mum or Dad throw anything away. Promise."

Gradually, her grip loosened. As she stepped back, James saw tears in her eyes, mirroring those on his parents' faces.

His mum pulled him into a fierce hug. "You call us as soon as you land, you hear?" Her voice was stern, but her hands trembled as they smoothed his jacket.

"I will, Mum. Promise."

His da stepped forward, gruffly clearing his throat. He pulled James into a quick, tight embrace, then pressed something into his palm. James looked down to see a 50-pound note.

"Da, I can't—"

"You can and you will," his father interrupted. "It's what fathers do."

James nodded, understanding the gesture for what it was—not charity, but love.

"You'll all have to come visit me next," James said, surprised to find he meant it. "I've got a show coming up. Big deal in the East Village."

"Oi, 'A big deal' he says..." And this quip was from his mum—just a wee snark, but so uncharacteristic, they all laughed, the sound tinged with both joy and sadness.

With final hugs and promises to call, James climbed into the waiting taxi. As it pulled away, he watched his family in the rear view mirror—his mum waving, his da's arm around her shoulders, Sarah jumping up and down.

The image blurred as tears filled his eyes. James blinked them away, his fingers absently tracing the outline of the knitted pencil holder in his pocket. A piece of home to carry with him, back to the challenges and opportunities of New York.

* * *

The plane cruised at an altitude far above the realm of ordinary day-trippers. James pressed his forehead against the cool glass of the window, gazing out at the vast expanse of sky. Great billowing clouds stretched out below, like a landscape of cotton and dreams.

In that moment, suspended between earth and heaven, James felt a sense of peace wash over him. The warmth of Sarah's final hug, the love in his mum's eyes, the gruff tenderness of his da—it all swirled together, a balm to his battered spirit.

He closed his eyes, breathing deeply. For the first time in months, perhaps years, he felt... better. Truly, absolutely better. Family is what mattered, his family is what saved... well, his mind, probably.

And then, like a bolt from the blue, a memory struck him. The letter. Ma's letter. Where had he put it?

James's eyes snapped open, his heart suddenly racing. He fumbled for his backpack, tucked under the seat in front of him. Unzipping it with shaking hands, he began to rummage through its contents.

Nothing.

A cold sweat broke out on his forehead as he emptied the bag completely, searching every pocket, every crease. The letter was nowhere to be found.

He leaned back in his seat, mind whirling. Customs. They'd gone through everything, hadn't they? Pulled it all out, spread it all across the counter. Had they put everything back? He couldn't remember now.

Or had he... James swallowed hard. Had he been so angry, so hurt, that he'd "accidentally" thrown it away? He had a vague memory of holding the envelope, feeling the weight of unspoken words. But after that... nothing.

A flight attendant paused by his seat. "Everything alright, sir?"

James looked up, suddenly aware of the mess he'd made. "I... I've lost something. A letter."

The attendant's face softened with sympathy. "I'm so sorry. Would you like me to help you look?"

James shook his head, already knowing it was futile. "No, thank you. I'm sure it'll turn up."

But even as he said the words, a strange feeling settled over him. Had the letter existed for him? Or had it been a dream, a figment of his imagination and desire for connection to love born from those very rough weeks when he'd teetered on the edge of breakdown?

He gazed back out at the clouds, his father's voice echoing in his mind. Press on, son.

James took a deep breath, slowly repacking his bag. The letter was gone—if it had ever truly been there. But ahead lay his senior year, a big show to prepare for, the first steps into a future bright with possibility.

Press on.

The clouds below began to thin, revealing glimpses of the vast ocean. Somewhere out there, beyond the horizon, lay New York.

James settled back in his seat, the knitted pencil holder from his mum a comforting weight in his pocket. For now, he closed his eyes, letting the hum of the engines lull him into a peaceful sleep. The last chapter of his youth was closing, it was childhood's end.

* * *

Chapter 10

Red Lakes, MN — Hawkins Residence — *April 13, 2002 — 9:05 p.m. — After*

The night air was cool against their sweat-drenched skin as the men gathered around the fire once more. The flames licked at the twilight, dancing and poking at the coming night, casting flickering shadows across their faces, each bearing the marks of their experience in the sweat lodge.

Gerardo and two other men sat slightly apart, having made it through the third round, but not the fourth. George nodded at them approvingly, respecting their effort. A young man, no more than 16, sat with them, having only managed the first round but proud to have tried.

The remaining group—George, Michael, John, Bert, Young Thomas, Freddo, and James—formed a tight circle around the fire. George's eyes lingered on James, recalling how Michael had to prod him at the end of the fourth round. It wasn't that James had been asleep, rather, it seemed as if he'd journeyed to some far-off place and was slowly finding his way back.

When James had finally opened his eyes, he felt calm, not drastically different, but calmer than this morning. Despite the sweat that covered him, his gaze was steady, centered. He nodded to Michael, signaling he was alright, then they left the lodge with the same protocol as when they'd entered - clockwise and on hands and knees. Born anew.

* * *

After the men changed into their fresh clothes, they settled around the fire. There was no idle conversation, there seemed to be nothing to say. Now, as the men gazed into the fire, George rose to address them. His voice was low but carried easily in the quiet night.

"I'm going to keep this brief for now," he began, "but this seems to be a teaching for all men. Women."

The men didn't laugh. There was a gravity to George's words that demanded attention.

"The energy from creating comes through man to the woman, reinforcing the bind and trust men have to protect her, provide for her. But if that great work is disrespected, you are better off by yourself. Better to be alone than to be used, then divorced, lose your house, and still be sued to provide for her and children that you never get to see day to day and so lose your mind."

George's gaze swept the circle, meeting each man's eyes in turn. "This is not a small issue. It is a brick in the machine thrown by the evil one. And so tread carefully, make sure she is your friend and will stand by you."

The fire crackled, sending sparks dancing into the night sky. George's voice carried over the soft whisper of wind through the trees, each word seeming to settle into the men's bones.

George continued, his voice carrying weight and wisdom. "This experience here tonight can become in your life what you allow. It can be the great washing you were hoping for in your hearts, washed clean from the imprints from past actions, past activity. It is a call to God for just that blessing: clean my eyes so I can see, clean my heart so I can love, clean my mind so I can think what to do, clean my body from the past, impure un-sanctified activity."

The men listened intently, some nodding in agreement, others with eyes closed in deep reflection.

"I'm talking about what people call casual sex," George said, his tone serious. "There is no such thing as casually uniting your body with a woman in an act that can pave the way for life. There is nothing casual in the cosmos, when a star or a planet or some cosmic body is born, it is the same both large and small."

As George spoke about this very personal topic, James noticed a subtle shift in the group. Some men straightened their backs, muscles tensing beneath their fresh, post-sweat lodge clothes. Others lowered their gazes, suddenly finding the dancing flames intensely interesting. The air seemed to thicken with unspoken admissions and regrets, mingling with the lingering scent of sage and sweat.

"You think you need sex?" George continued, his voice carrying over the soft crackle of the fire. "I will give you a surprise, as much as you think you do, what if women need it more?"

James's mind flashed to Tonya, but it seemed a far off memory now, an event he could look at clinically from a distance or discard. He chose to discard it, taking a sip of water from a bottle, the cool liquid was a stark contrast to the heat they'd endured in the lodge.

George paused, letting his words sink in. The fire cast long shadows across his weathered face as he continued, "When woman was extended from man, the Creator put the human to sleep and reached in to extend half out and into a separate form. And so women became the holders of the lower bodies' three areas: the solar plexus, the womb or creation area, and the root for family. So you see, family is the primary force in their design. They are compelled to create, to unite with a good man, to settle down."

James glanced around the circle, noting the tightened jaws and general unease of his fellow men. Gerardo, sitting slightly apart with those who'd made it through the third round, nodded slowly, his usual jovial expression replaced by one of deep contemplation. The 16-year-old young man listened with wide-eyed concentration.

George's words took on a cautionary tone as he continued, "But the evil one enjoys throwing bricks in God's work, and a big one is fear. Women may become afraid of losing power, afraid of men, and so some women, the ones who don't love men, try to find ways to have their cake and eat it too. If being a woman feels like surrendering to service, of course that could be frightening and so many women are tempted to take the role of the opposite. To be free, like men, or so they think."

A cool breeze swept through the gathering, causing the fire to dance wildly for a moment. Michael, sitting to James's right, shivered slightly, pulling his blanket tighter around his shoulders.

"But let me ask you this in truth, how many of you men feel as if you are free?" George paused, his eyes scanning the group. It was a rhetorical question, but still, there was no hint of a response. Only the soft pop of burning wood broke the silence. George nodded, "You are here tonight, we are here together, because you feel compelled to get your ass on the highest path, to be of service as well, but in a better way than you have imagined to date. You have the Great Spirit in your ear all the time, nagging you, prompting you to be a good man, take care of your woman and children and to do that task, you need to take care of the entire world too. It is a long list."

The men seemed to lean forward, eager to catch every word. James felt the energy shift, a collective recognition settling over the group.

George continued, his voice carrying weight and wisdom, "So take care in your choice of a life partner, if you are married already, do your best to heal your own fear first, in knowing you are not crazy, there is an order that has been disrupted, and stay as calm as you can. You men, who are not yet married, do nothing. You live your lives, enjoy the world, do your work, reap your financial reward for it. No casual sex. You wait, you hold yourself away from women... they will eventually feel the lack of your presence in their lives. And come to you. The recognition and need must be mutual or in today's world I don't know how it will work."

George took in a deep breath, his gaze distant as if looking beyond the circle of firelight. Finally, he said, "We are at the back end of this situation, for both men and women, there are forces at play that are so subterranean, it is beyond my ability to tell you about, because I cannot see them either. And so we deal with where we are now and how to live well, and let that ripple around the world."

The fire crackled, sending sparks dancing into the night sky. George's voice carried over the soft whisper of wind through the trees, each word seeming to settle into the men's bones.

"I will tell you a truth now—men can live without women. Adam lived for a long time without Eve. You may think it's just a story, but read it again carefully. Most stories that survive time do so because there are elements of truth. Adam lived for a long time without Eve... externalized beside him, that is."

James found his thoughts drifting to Emma. Could he live without her? Hadn't he been living without her all these years? The questions were hard in his mind and hurt to think about them. George continued, his words hanging heavy in the night air.

"Adam was not fully happy or complete and yearned for her, but he could do it. Here is the other side: it is challenging for women to live without men. This is what women are really afraid of, the fear the evil one stokes daily."

George's words carried the weight of ancient wisdom. "Men build the buildings, the roads, the emergency services, all the heroic care-taking tasks that require strength of the body... and a specific kind of directed intelligence. There are women who can do all those activities too, but you will find they are all women who love men. There are reasons in cosmic law why this is so, but that is not the discussion for tonight. For now, we need to know that the drive to protect the woman and family comes from man—it is not an easy job, not at all. You have God breathing down your neck ALL the time to do the right thing, to set an example."

And here George smiled just a little as he thought about what he was to say next, "The women have the heroic task of carrying a baby, a baby for goodness sakes—their bodies changing, a pull on their energy and health, having a baby is a matter of life and death, and then caring for the infant and child and family too. The women who don't have children are always of service in a different way, and does any man imagine this is easy? No. Both men and women have heroic tasks, what I am suggesting is that respect be given to both in a way that makes common sense."

George's tone shifted, becoming more hopeful. "The Dark Ages are over, the days of Babylonia are over. The time and age for light is coming soon. Many cultures have talked about it, and it is coming. The sun is coming, growing brighter every day, burning off the dross."

As he spoke of the coming age of light, James noticed a change in the atmosphere. The tension seemed to ease, replaced by a sense of hope. He saw Gerardo sit up straighter, a small smile playing at the corners of his mouth.

"By the year, oh, around 2025, we will have obvious evidence of the effect of light and love on the world. It may appear to be chaos itself, but that is what happens when you clean out the garage. It is a mess of sorting and discerning what to keep and what to let go. We all need the light of God to clean out the dark basement or garage."

James felt a warmth spread through his chest, a glimmer of hope sparking his mind.

George paused, his gaze sweeping across the circle of men. "Those in the dark simply will not be able to handle the light. This is between those concerned and God, and none of your business. You do what you feel directed to do and keep yourself clean. You all worked hard today, you choose to walk the beauty way, if you want."

The fire had died down to glowing embers, mirroring the quiet intensity of the moment. George's voice softened as he acknowledged their efforts.

George's voice softened, filled with pride and respect. "I want you to look around at your fellows now. All of you have done well—one round, three, or four. Only you know how hard this was," how many grandfather stones were placed in the hearth."

James met the eyes of the men around him, seeing his own mixture of exhaustion and exhilaration reflected back. A nod here, a slight smile there—silent communications of shared experience and newfound respect. George was continuing now:

"Your willingness is what God sees. Of course, following all the way through is the goal, but how do you complete that journey if you don't even take the first step?"

He acknowledged the diverse group before him. "There are those in our tribe who feel we should reserve this ceremony only for our people, but there are also those among us who have been feeling the tap from the Holy Spirit to open the circle to all the people who are willing to respect our ways, men and women—not some watered-down version, but this, the correct use of this ceremony. And so this may be the beginning, and we can acknowledge our brothers who came to join the circle of human beings tonight."

George settled back, his words coming to a close. "We will be quiet for a while and see if anyone has something they need to say. Good job, men."

As he sat, a profound silence fell over the group. Each man seemed lost in his own thoughts, reflecting on George's words and their own experiences in the lodge.

James sat quietly, his eyes fixed on the fire. He'd hung onto the cool earth, as Emma had suggested and then after a while he didn't need to anymore. Towards the end of the ceremony, he'd begun to feel lighter in his body and mind, almost floating along the surface of a flowing river. In that gentle place, he had begun to imagine what he might see around the next bend.

As George finished speaking, a profound silence fell over the group. James closed his eyes, savoring the quiet in his mind.

The snapping of a twig broke the silence. James opened his eyes to see Emma approaching from the house, her figure silhouetted against the warm light spilling from the windows. Their eyes met for a brief moment before James looked away, not yet ready to bridge that gap.

George noticed Emma's arrival and nodded to her. "Food's ready, men," he announced. "Let's head back to the house."

As they stood, stretching sore muscles and exchanging quiet words, there was a sense that something had shifted. Each man carried with him the experience of the sweat lodge, and the wisdom of George's words.

James lagged behind as they walked towards the house. He could feel Emma's gaze turned in his direction, but he wasn't ready to face her yet. He needed time to process, to understand the changes within himself. He wanted to be quiet.

* * *

There were two long picnic tables placed thirty feet from the house, the first one was laden with food—from corn biscuits and fried chicken to potato salad and beef steaks. The second was a blank slate and open invitation for the men to sit around and share goodwill and easy conversation over a well earned meal.

James caught Alfred's eye at the far end, seated beside George, and nodded. As he settled between Gerardo and Michael, he noted John chose to sit directly in front of him—Em's family had him corralled good and proper.

James smiled at the thought, they were either putting forth an effort to make him welcome, or still giving him the once over. Maybe both. But any conversation to explore either road was set aside as they focused on the food. James admitted to feeling lightheaded and this hearty repast would certainly help ground him.

After consuming the first chicken leg, James risked a glance around the back yard, he spotted Emma and her mom by the food table, refilling empty trays. She looked over her shoulder at him, and nodded in his direction. A small tip of the hat, perhaps? Or just relieved he'd survived four rounds without sinking the ship? James decided not to linger long near that question, returned the nod and then leaned forward to catch what John was asking.

"So, this was your first sweat lodge?" John asked, looking James in the eye.

"Yes..." James replied, his tone light and self-deprecating. "I may have sat through a sauna or two, but those don't exactly measure sweat and tears on the same scale do they then?"

For some reason, the men near him found this to be funny indeed and a round of laughter rippled around the table.

"No, no." John agreed, "not *exactly* on the same scale."

And with that opening salvo, conversation flowed easily. The men enjoyed the food, each other's company and the blissfully cool evening under the rising silver moon.

* * *

The sun rose softly, almost sweetly, first peeking over the tops of the trees on the Hawkins property, then gathering itself to commit to the climb into day. There was a soft haze dispelling the morning mist and the blessing the edges of the porch railings. Emma stood out front, arms loosely crossed, watching James, Albert and Gerardo walk slowly toward the car. The three men moved in a kind of tandem synchronicity, there was no music track, no idle joking. Just the quiet communion of shared a destination. To the car we go, home, here we come.

Perhaps it was part of the afterglow from the sweat lodge—perhaps a more mundane form of bonding from a mutual experience. Seeing Emma, herself had participated in a sweat lodge ceremony years ago, she would opt for the former over the latter.

Her mother stepped outside behind her, adjusting the edge of her shawl, and pulled Emma into a brief hug. "Whatever shape this becomes, trust yourself. You are an honest person, you will know what to do."

Emma nodded. "Yes."

Then her father joined them, coffee in hand, letting the screen door whisper shut behind him.

He stood beside her on the porch for a while, watching the men in the distance without speaking. Then, with quiet clarity, he said, "You'll be walking with a man who carries light and shadow in equal weight. The light is obvious to see, the shadows... are subterranean, what he works to clean in quiet. As a father I believe you were correct to be cautious, as an elder, I can see potential if he can stay on the beauty way."

Emma didn't answer.

"The red clay will become a blessing only by loving hands." George took a sip of coffee and then completed his thought, "If there is no love, there is no agreement, doesn't matter how clever the hands are."

She looked at him directly. "I know."

He raised an eyebrow. "You sure?"

She smiled softly. "Okay... getting there."

He nodded, then leaned forward to kiss her forehead. "Go do good work."

And then—sensing the gap at the close for an epilogue—Gert stepped forward holding a small cooler.

Emma blinked. "What is that?"

Her mother opened the lid with a conspiratorial smile. Inside were at least a dozen and a half thickly layered turkey sandwiches, wrapped in parchment and stacked with military precision. There may also have been homemade pickles; Emma caught the distinct waft of the vinegar aroma.

Emma's eyes widened. "Really, Mom? Where's the football team?"

Gert chuckled. "Everyone loves turkey sandwiches. They'll munch away and be asleep in an hour. Guaranteed peaceful car ride. Won't even know what hit them."

Emma shook her head, laughing. "That's a wee bit on the Machiavellian side."

Gert added, lifting the lid halfway closed, "Not completely sure what that means, but if that cooler's empty when you get home, you're coming back for the next pow wow. If not—"

"Don't finish that wager," Emma said, hugging her again. "I'll be back."

Behind them, her father chuckled and slipped an arm around Gert's waist, kissing the side of her head. From the porch swing, Michael called out, "Bring James and your crew!"

Emma didn't answer. She just lifted the cooler and headed toward the car.

Gerardo stepped forward to meet her halfway, taking the cooler from her with a low whistle. "What is this, a family care package?"

"Turkey sandwiches for the road," Emma said, brushing her hair behind her ear. "From my mom. Everybody say thank you."

From the open car doors, the voices chimed in unison like schoolboys:
"Thank you, Mrs. Hawkins!"

Gerardo peered into the cooler with exaggerated reverence. "With mayo? Lettuce?"

Emma lifted an eyebrow. "I would not be surprised."

They shared a smile, and Emma climbed into the passenger seat and closed the door. When she looked up, James was already watching her—his eyes open, kind, without pressure. Her heart fluttered, just a little. Just a wee flutter of wings finding the space to practice a bit.

She gave him a small nod.

He smiled, then tapped the horn twice—lightly. A farewell.

Then they pulled away from the house and into the long curve of road ahead.

* * *

Later that day, in the early evening, Emma sat at her small kitchen table, one foot tucked under her, hands curled around a mug of tea. The light outside had softened to gold in that turn of the day where things looked better, kinder. Even that dark blue dumpster pressed up against the red and brown brick wall had something positive to say about its place in the color wheel.

Her apartment wasn't much—one tall window with a view of a different brick wall and a wide restaurant pie slice size view of sky—but the sun was doing its best to make something of it. The shadows were long now, stretched across the linoleum and into the hidden places in the wood grain of the chair opposite her.

On the table sat the last of the turkey sandwiches, half-wrapped in wax paper. She picked at the corner but hadn't committed to eating it yet.

Her flip phone buzzed on the counter.

She got up, thumbed it open, squinted.

James:
Got a message from Maribel (Zane too—now goes by Ted). They

. They want to see us Saturday.
Won't take no.

Another buzz.

James:
Evanston. Heads up.

She smiled at the lack of punctuation. The low-key urgency of it.

She typed back slowly—she was still getting used to the small keys and time it took to send a message on the flip phone—texting was a three-press affair on each button.

Emma:
Yes. I know they're in Evanston.
And yes. I'd like to go.

A pause.

James:
Ok. I'll pick you up high noon on Sat. (?)

She thought a moment and took a risk to send something slightly, ever so slightly more... emotional. She sent a colon next to a single right parenthesis; the ode to a smile face in 2002.

:)

She watched the screen a second longer, no response from J. Watson, then closed the phone with a click that felt louder than it needed to.

She looked back at the sandwich.

Emma could, if she wanted to, find fault in the fact that he hadn't called in person. Or that he hadn't asked her while they were still in the car. Or failing to respond to her simple smiley. Or a dozen other small slights she used to cut into her mind to bleed emotion.

Or... she could let it go.

Buy the ticket. Take the ride.

Emma shook her head, smiling to herself, and unwrapped the rest of the sandwich. The bread was a little soft now, the turkey cold, but it still tasted... almost sweet. It tasted like... victory. She nodded and then laughed out loud.

She took a sip of tea, leaned back, and enjoyed the last of the light as the sun settled down for the night.

So did she.

* * *

Chapter 11

Evanston, IL — Thomason House — *May 4, 2002 — 2:16 p.m. — Old Friends, New Day*

The late afternoon sun bathed the quiet Evanston street in a warm, golden light as James pulled the car to a stop in front of Ted, formerly known as 'Zane,' and Maribel's modest two-story house. The faded yellow paint and white trim spoke of bygone eras, but the carefully tended flower boxes beneath each window hinted at the love and care of its current occupants.

James glanced at Emma in the passenger seat, noticing the slight tension in her shoulders. "Ready for this?" he asked, his voice genuinely curious. "You haven't seen them for a while."

Emma nodded, brushing a strand of hair behind her ear. "I really am, Maribel and I have stayed in touch, it's gonna be good." she replied with a small smile.

They climbed out of the car, James balancing two six-packs of craft beer while Emma cradled a carefully wrapped dessert—Maribel's favorite, sans sugar. As they approached the front door, it swung open, revealing Ted—the man they'd once known as Zane. His trademark red hair was shorter now, peppered with gray at the temples, but his eyes still held that mischievous glint.

"Well, if it isn't the dynamic duo, together again..." Ted grinned, punched James's arm before turning to Emma. "Em, luv, it's been way too long."

Before Emma could respond, Maribel appeared behind Ted, her pregnant womb leading the way. Without hesitation, she enveloped Emma in a warm embrace. "Oh, Em, Oh Em... it's so good to finally see you in person! Emails and letters just aren't enough."

Maribel finally released Emma, then she kissed James perfunctorily on the cheek and led the way into the foyer of the house. The rich scent of lemon oil and furniture polish enveloped them. The entryway opened into a living room where every surface seemed to glow with a warm, golden light. Maribel had clearly been hard at work, stripping away layers of old paint to reveal the natural beauty of the woodwork beneath.

"Maribel's on a mission to resurrect every bit of wood in this place," Ted explained, noticing their wandering gazes. "Reckon we'll be living in a forest by the time she's done."

Maribel beamed. "You know me, I can't resist a good project."

As they handed over their offerings, James couldn't help but notice the slight changes in his old friends since he'd seen them last. Ted seemed more grounded, the restless energy of his youth channeled into a quiet confidence. Maribel glowed with maternal pride, her artistic spirit evident in every corner of their home.

Emma, too, was taking it all in, her eyes lingering on the mantelpiece where the ceramic pieces she'd gifted them years ago held places of honor. "You kept them," she said softly, a mix of surprise and gratitude in her voice.

"Of course we did," Maribel replied, squeezing Emma's hand. "They're part of our history. Part of us."

The patter of small feet announced the arrival of Ted and Maribel's daughters. Theodora, the elder at six, had her father's red hair and a look of steadfast determination that seemed beyond her years. Four-year-old Minnie, a whirlwind of energy, had her mother's artistic flair evident in her paint-splattered overalls.

"Uncle James!" they chorused, launching themselves at him. James caught them both, spinning them around as they giggled.

"Hello, my little daisies," he laughed, setting them down. "Have you been good for your mum and dad?"

"Always," Theodora said solemnly, while Minnie nodded enthusiastically.

Emma watched this interaction with a mix of surprise and warmth. This was a side of James she hadn't seen before—comfortable, at ease with children. It stirred something in her she wasn't quite ready to examine.

"Do you like your new plate?" Minnie asked, hopping up and down in hearty expectation of enthusiastic gratitude from her favorite uncle ever.

"Oh my goodness! It's…" and here James provided a quick substitution for 'bloody brilliant' with "off the charts amazing and so beautiful it knocked me socks right off. See? I still haven't been able to keep them on." And here James pointed to his bare ankles for proof. "I got me loafers, but the socks won't stick."

Minnie thought that so hilarious, she fell right down on the floor, rolling in peals of laughter.

"I helped too!" insisted Theodora, "Mom! Tell Uncle James I helped too. It was my idea, you can put your keys on it, like dad."

"I think he can hear you honey." Bel responded, her tone, kind but instructive. "Let's bring it down a couple notches, okay? You're gonna wake the baby."

This intrigued Emma. "Seriously? You can feel when the baby is sleeping?"

Maribel smiled and nodded, "I really think so."

And with that request from his wife Ted took over. "All right you lot, outside, plenty of backyard to run around in, me and Uncle James will be right out, let's calm things a bit for the baby, right?" And here he placed a finger over his lips, the universal signal for 'Shhh' and remarkably, the girls did the same. They 'shushed' and tiptoed through the dining room and out back holding their mirth until they were well outside.

"Ah the little dears," Maribel sighed.

"They really are." Em agreed softly.

Instead of replying Maribel hooked her arm through Em's and laid her head on her shoulder and whispered, "So, so glad to see you... and seeing you looking so well too. You're beautiful Em, well, you always were, but, you've grown into your cheekbones or something, Don't you think our Em is bonnier than ever, James? Ted?"

When James said nothing, Ted began singing to fill the void, "Oh her eyes they shine like the diamonds, you'd think she was queen o' the land, and her hair hung over her shoulder, hung up with a black velvet band.."

Maribel had joined in with singing the Irish Rover's tune and they rounded out in laughter. James hadn't joined in the song but he was smiling now, his eyes bright as he enjoyed his friends enjoying themselves. It felt like coming home.

Emma walked to Bel and hugged her, there was nothing like the love and friendship of people, friends and family that 'knew you when.' "Maribel, Ted you are really over the top kind—you're looking beautiful too."

"Well then," Ted announced, clapping his hands together. "Now that we've settled that, who's ready for a proper catch-up? I've got the grill fired up out back, and these beers won't drink themselves."

Maribel led the way into the kitchen, her voice animated as she pointed out various features of the house. "We had to redo the entire plumbing system when we moved in," she said, opening a cupboard to retrieve some bowls. "You wouldn't believe the state of it. But it's coming along nicely now."

Emma nodded, taking in the warm, lived-in feel of the kitchen. Crayon drawings adorned the refrigerator, and a row of herbs growing in small pots on the windowsill. "It's lovely, Maribel, really homey."

Emma turned her gaze to Bel, studying her for a moment, her finger lightly patting her upper lip and then the light bulb went 'bing'. "I know what's different, the tattoos on your arms are gone, the piercings have faded or at least you're not wearing jewelry."

"Oh yeah, that had to go right away, babies like to grab... and what's more, I didn't feel like it anymore... I didn't want them around the baby, I'm talking about Theadora, I think they made her cry. Anyway, Ted supported me through it all, we found a good way to remove the tats safely and I. Could. Not. Be. Happier."

"Well, you look great... you all do and happy too, I'm glad for you all." Emma's voice was soft.

"Thanks," Maribel smiled, handing Emma a bowl. "Could you fill this with those chips? The girls will devour them in no time."

As Emma poured the chips, Maribel continued, "The move from New York was challenging, but Evanston has grown on us. It's a good place for the girls. Ted loves his job, he can be creative, get really outside the box thinking going, but structure his ideas too. It was a scary jump, but it's working."

Emma hummed in agreement, her eyes drifting to the backyard where James was now chasing the giggling girls around the lawn. Maribel followed her gaze, a thoughtful expression crossing her face.

"Em," she said softly, setting down the tray she was holding. "How are you doing? Really?"

Emma's hands stilled on the chip bowl. She was quiet for a moment before asking, "Has he ever asked after me? All these years, or talked about me?"

Maribel took a deep breath, her honesty evident in her eyes. "Well, not really. Not in an obvious way."

Emma nodded, a sad smile tugging at her lips. "Then that explains how I'm doing in a... nutshell."

Maribel reached out, squeezing Emma's arm gently. Then, in an attempt to lift the mood, she asked, "So, tell me about this big project you're working on together. How did it all come about?"

As Emma began to explain, Maribel busied herself with preparing the steaks. "Do you want these pre-seasoned?" she interjected, holding up a bottle of marinade.

Emma nodded, grateful for the momentary distraction. "Yeah, Ted likes them that way, doesn't he?"

As Maribel worked on the steaks, Emma continued her story. "It was a series of coincidences, really. I overheard a conversation at a gallery opening in L.A. about a community art project in Chicago—didn't think much of it at the time."

She paused to help Maribel arrange some vegetables on a platter. "Then, a few weeks later, a friend of a friend mentioned they were looking for artists with experience in large-scale mosaics. Asked if I'd be interested in having my name put forward. I'd had a small gallery showing at the Art Institute that did well, and they knew me, I had contacts in the city, so... there was a path."

Maribel looked up from her task, curiosity evident in her expression. "And you had no idea James was involved?"

Emma shook her head, a wry smile on her face. "None whatsoever at first. Then of course I wanted to know who I'd be working with, and after I found out... well, it was a shock, but there are no such things as accidents, mom and dad drilled that into me early on... so I thought it was time. And something more, Bel... I'd been having dreams of him, more than one, so I knew it wasn't a fluke... that he was in trouble and I could help. So I decided to go with the flow of events, and maybe make things up with him too."

"And you've never spoken with him? All these years?" Bel asked, her tone, soft but pointed.

"No."

When Maribel cocked her head to look at her friend, Emma explained, "I did reach out to him a few months after I left to apologize... but I guess he'd already moved past it... or wasn't interested. So that was that, his silence was his answer. I had to really suck up my pride to come take this job, lemme' tell you."

There was quiet for a long moment, Bel focused on making hamburger patties, once the patty was nice and round she placed it in the pan and said simply, "I see. I didn't know that."

Emma shrugged, "It was years ago." her voice softened as she continued, "don't worry, it's just work between us, I'll stay out of his way. As my mom has told me, if the path is split, let it be the way. But I can, well maybe correct my own karma or something."

Maribel grimaced and whispered, "Come here, stand next to me for a minute. I want to say something."

Emma looked puzzled but she did as Bel bid, she came close, then picked up Bel's task and pushed hamburger into the press and listened.

Maribel thought for a moment then picked up the thread of what she'd been itching to say for years. "What you did wasn't all wrong you know. You all are forgetting, but I haven't—James was getting to be full of himself... back then. So let's face things square on... James was a genius, we all knew it. There was and is this light coming out of him, we all knew he was going places, but maybe he knew it too and maybe, what was needed was a swift blow to the noggin to jolt him back to mortal-land. Because a person can be a genius, but that doesn't make them *elevated*. Doing art is the same as... toting a barge, or..."

"Lifting a bale?" Em offered.

Bel laughed, "Yeah, guess so, but my point is, a job's a job that's all it is, and he's right grounded now, but back then, maybe not so much. An' so maybe what you did was no accident cuz you're kinda genius too, and dang stubborn, so maybe you did him a favor."

And here Bel paused to catch her breath and gather steam to say the tough part, "But it was a blow Em, one he never saw coming, an' that's the truth too. James fell hard and fast down to mere mud—might have had a nervous breakdown too, happens to some people, and no one knows why this one and not that. But he came back, more distant, more reserved, but more grounded too. More normal, more human and humane. I guess I've been holding all that in for years, I've never breathed a word of it to Ted—James is his best mate and brother. So all that to give you the whole picture and also say maybe you weren't all wrong."

Long pause and Emma took it in, she was arranging cheese on a plate and for a moment Maribel thought she had stepped too far but then Emma said:

"Thanks for that, Bel... and no, it wasn't all wrong, I hear what you say and even agree with a lot of it, but I could have done better. Way batter. That's always the point, of course."

Maribel studied her friend for a moment, clearly wanting to say more but respecting Emma's boundaries. Instead, she asked, "Could you grab that serving dish from the top shelf? The blue one?"

As Emma reached for the dish, Maribel added, "Save some of the mosaic project details for Ted to hear too. You know how he loves a good story."

Emma laughed, some of the tension easing from her shoulders. "Oh, I remember. Some things never change, do they?"

"No," Maribel agreed, her eyes warm as she looked at her old friend. "Some things don't. But others..." she trailed off, glancing meaningfully towards the backyard where James was now helping Ted with the grill.

Emma followed her gaze, a mix of emotions playing across her face. "Yeah," she said softly. "Others do."

They worked in companionable silence for a few moments, the sounds of laughter and conversation drifting in from outside. As they finished preparing the food, Maribel turned to Emma one last time.

"Em," she said, her voice gentle but firm. "Whatever happened in the past, whatever's happening now... just know that Ted and I are here for you; we saw it all, we know it all, we'll always be here for you... and him too of course."

"Of course." Emma's eyes shimmered with unshed tears as she pulled Maribel into a tight hug. "I know," she whispered. "Thank you."

"Okay, enough about me, so tell me about this wee one you're carrying." Em asked brightly.

"Oh well! I'm eating like a... well a pregnant woman, I suppose, which is a LOT and guess who else has a huge appetite and low metabolism?"

"Ah...Zane? I mean Ted?"

"Yup! So I think this 'un's is a boy taking after his Dad. I'm pretending not to know, but I think he is a boy. Ted loves his little girls and will welcome another, but a boy could be fun too."

"I'm so happy for you all," Emma said simply.

"Ta..."

"Bel! Bel! Hey you lot in there, where's some food? Even snacks, whatever—the girls are starting to graze on the grass!" It was Ted's low voice raised loud enough to carry to where they worked in the kitchen.

"Speaking of, there's the call." Maribel said and then, "Grab a couple of fruit juice boxes from the fridge, right? Thanks Em, here we go, round one."

They are laughing as they exited stage left to enter downstage center carrying bowls of crisps or chips, as they say, stepping down onto the small stone paved patio, that Ted lay himself, he did. Bel was so proud of Ted in all these ways large and small, Emma smiled, she just had to.

* * *

Evanston, IL — Thomason House — *Meanwhile in the back yard.*

The late afternoon sun cast long shadows across the small backyard as James and Ted stood near the grill, the aroma of charcoal and marinating meat filling the air. James's eyes wandered over the newly laid patio, his foot nudging one of the stones.

"These are new," he observed, glancing up at Ted.

Ted shrugged, a hint of pride in his voice. "Not as grand as 'some people when they're at home' mosaic walls, but it'll do."

James chuckled, accepting the beer Ted offered him. They both took a long swig, the cool liquid a welcome relief in the warm afternoon air. The distant sound of traffic mingled with the chirping of birds settling in for the back-side of the day.

Ted leaned against the grill, his eyes studying James. "Okay, so... Em, Emma... dear mad, brilliant, beautiful Emma—what's going on with that?"

"Stop," James said, his tone light despite the sudden tension in his shoulders.

Ted grinned, unable to resist ribbing his friend. "Stop what? Stop the presses? Stop pouring the coffee you're overflowing my cup? STOP! Icarus! Ouch! Too close to the sun!"

James laughed, shaking his head. "You should be making me mad, but you're just too cute."

The mood shifted as Ted leaned in, his voice taking on a more serious note. "James, mate, you're my brother, and that's not the booze talking—I've only had one. Seriously, Em's a good girl, brilliant—"

"Bloody brilliant," James interrupted, his eyes lighting up. "She's already helped move this project ahead to light speed with some well-placed suggestions and sharp skills, and that's just for starters."

Ted looked at him expectantly. "Well then?"

James sighed, taking another sip of his beer. The sound of a lawnmower started up in a neighboring yard, filling the momentary silence. "Okay, since you laid down 'the brother' card, I'll play..."

He paused, his gaze distant as he collected his thoughts. The minute stretched on, marked by the gentle swaying of the trees and the sizzle of the heating grill.

Finally, James spoke. "I don't know, I really don't. I'm not pretending or skirting, I just don't know. It seems like she and me... we were doing this slow dance around each other back then, always sizing each other up. And we moved from instant friends to close friends to best mates, and always just there, the next day maybe we'll get closer, only we didn't, something always seemed to put us off track, until the road split quite in two as you know."

He took another swig of beer before continuing. "And now here we are working well together—that has never been an issue. The plans are moving forward like bloody clockwork, and stuff is bound to come up like on any project, but we'll holler our way past it, we both have a stiff upper lip... as for the other... maybe it's a case of bad timing or being stuck in that old pattern and we both got hurt and who knows what's on the other side of that wall."

And here James stopped and looked his dear friend in the eye, Ted said nothing, but he was listening closely so James continued, his voice soft, "You know, in the time she's been here on this project, meetings, drinking coffee, working, whatever, not once has she ever even hinted that she was sorry she left me cold as a stone. She hasn't even come close to explaining, and who does that? What kind of person is she really? Is she so busy with *her work*, she can't see me as a person in front of her?"

And here Ted looked down and they both sipped beer in silence for a moment and then James finished his thought.

"I'm trying me best to let it go, I really am, Zane, er, Ted... and I know how I feel about her, I'm not fooling myself... I look at her 'an... god, she is beautiful, a full blown flower..."

James shook his head, couldn't voice it out loud, so instead he said, "but I am now forewarned about the likes of her, of people who put work first, cut people off cold, her own da warned me, Ted, her *own da*, mate."

"No," Ted objected, 'I don't believe it, I don't know the man, but—"

"—Yes, it was after the sweat lodge, it was indirect-like, but he did." James said firmly and shook his head, "I know I have a long list of promises to meet before I leave this earth, God has given me a lot, an' looked after me family and Sarah—don't tell me her change isn't a miracle and I'm no squelcher, I pay me debts. But I cannot do it with a broken heart."

James sighed, looking down at the stones cobbled together as the patio floor, at three slim blades of grass struggling to grow through one small crack, gasping for sunlight and air.

When he spoke again, his voice was frank, almost casual but rang true, "I know myself well enough to know that I can't go through a grind like that again. So there's a wall between us, but I'm not sure I want to climb it. Fair?"

Ted considered this, nodding slowly, "Fair enough."

They clinked their bottles together in a silent toast, the glass ringing out in the quiet yard.

Suddenly, the peaceful moment was shattered as Minnie and Theodora came tearing across the lawn, screaming with glee.

They tumbled onto the grass, giggling as they pretended to be cats.

Ted shook his head, laughing. "I'm telling you straight up, you can't buy moments like these," he said, gesturing towards his daughters.

James watched the girls with a mixture of amusement and something close to reverence.

"One more word and then I'm done for a spell," Ted said, turning back to James.

James met his friend's gaze. "Okay, shoot straight, don't miss."

Ted took a deep breath. "Here it is… back then, see, me and Maribel remember better than you two, 'cuz we were watching. We had no stake in the game, so we're not biased. So… could it also be that you fell in love with our Em on the spot, and it all felt too real, too intense, too permanent at the tender age of 18? 'Cuz we were that young… and maybe you wanted to have some fun, kick up your heels and THEN come around to our Em, sitting patiently, pining in the corner? An' now you're holdin' back, 'cuz…you're just ole fashioned stubborn?"

James felt a flare of anger, but he breathed through it, waiting for Ted to finish. When James spoke, his voice was calm. "Is that what Maribel thinks?"

Ted looked surprised, his brow furrowing. "I don't know, I swear we never talked that open about it. I'm sure she has her own thoughts, but she's so happy I have you for my brother, she would never put a bug in my ear. But you're about to piss me off if you're suggesting I don't know me own mind."

James shook his head, regret clear in his expression. "Sorry, sorry. No one likes being talked about, and I know you won't beat this up after today… but to answer your question, truly, I really don't know. It is as you say, memory gets mixed up with the... motion from back then and now I think it's best to just... well, let it go."

Ted nodded, satisfaction evident in his stance. "okay, thanks. I know you're an honest man."

"Boy...that was a straight shot, though," James admitted, a hint of admiration in his voice.

"One of me best," Ted grinned, then turned his attention to his daughters. "Oi, girls, what are you doing now?"

"We're horsies, daddy..." came the giggled response from Minnie.

"Well, stop munching on the greenery..." Ted called back to them, then turned towards the kitchen window. "Bel! Bel! Hey you lot in there, where's some food? Even snacks, whatever—the girls are starting to graze on the grass!"

As the sun dipped lower in the sky, casting a golden glow over the yard, James found himself pondering Ted's words. The weight of the past, the complexity of the present, and the uncertainty of the future all seemed to hang in the air, like a balloon that could only stay aloft for an undetermined amount of time.

Yeah, one day it was gonna pop. But not today.

* * *

As the afternoon progressed, they all migrated to the backyard where Ted took the stage as Prometheus unbound and lit the grill. There might have been applause. The space was small but tenderly tended, a vegetable patch was anchored in one corner but gaining ground with the vibrant mural painted in broad, bright strokes along the fence—undoubtedly Maribel's handiwork.

Bel led Emma on a grand tour of her garden, pointing out the peas plotting a coupe vs. the green tomatoes gearing toward greatness. As Em 'ooohed and awed' with the gravitas of a seasoned art critic, the girls latched onto each of her hands. Suddenly, the trio transformed into a single, large untamed butterfly hop-skipping into lift-off.

Bel was laughing so hard the dang camera wouldn't shoot straight, but managed to capture the essence of the impromptu avant garde dance of 'The Jumbo Butterfly 'Ore The Velvet Valley.' She even caught a few of James and Ted snapping their fingers as applause and homage to their Beatnik ancestors—which meant they had to put their beers down—and of course the kids—always the kids.

James watched as Emma frolicked with the girls, she jumped full tilt into the momentum of pure play. He knew this aspect of her nature, he knew *this Em*, it was the girl he'd met on the steps of Cooper now making a triumphant return. This part of herself, reserved for her inner circle, was Emma right on time as her naked heart and best self. James shook his head. Emma Hawkins was a mystery all right.

Catching Ted's puzzled look, James could only shrug and shake his head, as if to say, 'Don't ask, mate. I'm as lost as you are.' He'd already spilled his guts about Em, but it didn't change a thing. What could he do? She was the beautiful woman he loved, and so every little thing she did was, indeed, magic.

But someday that balloon was going to pop, oh yes. And when it did, James knew it would be the beginning or the end of them.

And so, like a man dearly in need of a visit to the dentist for the decree of healing remedy vs extraction, he voted for neither—just didn't want to know right now.

* * *

The afternoon sun slanted lower, painting Ted's lawn in stripes of gold and shadow. James and Ted huddled by the grill, their banter punctuated by the sizzle and pop of burgers hitting the grate. A bark of laughter from Ted coincided with a particularly dramatic burger flip, as if choreographed by some cosmic comedy director. Flip, splat and follow through with a combo punch.

Maribel and Emma lounged nearby, the picture of sun-soaked contentment, looking way too comfortable for words, such as 'indolent' or 'in repose', Their drinks left wet rings on the side table, like tiny crop circles marking the mystery of time.

"Come on, Em," Maribel prodded, her eyes sparkling with curiosity. "Dresden couldn't have been all schnitzel and strudel. I loved your letters and emails, but it's not the same as hearing it live—spill all the stuff you couldn't spell."

Emma grinned, launching into tales of mountain adventures and linguistic mishaps, the comedy of learning the German language, and how she came to rely on a kind of universal sign language.

"You know what I mean, Bel," she said, gesturing broadly for comic emphasis. "waving for 'hello,' rubbing my tummy for 'I'm hungry' and picture this," she said, "me, in my version of lederhosen, trying to order bratwurst using nothing but charades—"

"Stop, stop it, don't dare demonstrate *that*—" Bel was laughing.

"—*And so* I had a great native accent, everyone understood me, no problem." Emma finished landing her routine with a solid finish.

Bel laughed and this time she heard Ted and James laugh too, 'ah, so they were listening were they'?

Emma couldn't help but notice James would glance her way occasionally, his smile polite but guarded. He laughed easily with Ted, all relaxed charm. But when he looked her way, that ease vanished. His smile turned polite, careful. It was like watching a door slowly close, again and again. It was unnerving when she remembered how it used to be so easy between them.

Well, how could she expect otherwise? He had never forgiven her.

* * *

The patio lights flickered to life as twilight deepened, casting a warm glow over the flower print tablecloth on the table. Daisies they were, bright white little daises strewn across the table as musical underscore. Empty plates bore testament to a meal thoroughly enjoyed, while condensation-beaded bottles stood like sentinels among the debris. A gentle breeze carried the heady scent of Maribel's prized jasmine, mingling with the lingering aroma of grilled meat—a sensory snapshot of early summer perfection.

As they lounged in various states of post-meal bliss, the conversation flowed in a natural expected way, one idea flowing to another, touching on shared memories and filling in the gaps of the years they'd been apart. Ted regaled them with stories of his transition from struggling artist to successful graphic designer.

"You know," he said, eyeing James with a mixture of gratitude and suspicion, "I've always wondered if you had a hand in landing me this gig in Chicago. Greased some wheels, did you?"

James shrugged, a smile playing at the corners of his mouth. "Might've put in a good word or two," he admitted, raising his beer in a mock salute. "You did the rest yourself, mate."

"Ted." Emma interjected, trying out the name again, 'Ted…"

"Thas' me an all." Ted replied, just waiting, waiting for *the* question.

"Speaking of good *words*," Emma chimed in, leaning forward with the eagerness of a bloodhound on a scent, "I've been dying to ask—why the name change? When did Zane become Ted?"

Ted's eyes twinkled with mischief as he took a swig of his beer, before answering, "Ah, now that's a tale and a half. You lot remember what a pretentious git I was back in the day, yeah?"

The others nodded, smiling at the memory of the wild-haired, poetry-spouting youth they'd known. Maribel patted her husband's arm consolingly. "We remember, luv, but you were *our* pretentious git."

"Well," Ted continued, "turns out the corporate world isn't too keen on hiring a 'Zane' but Theodore? Now that's a name you can trust with your ad campaign and robust salary. Having Maribel with me and the kids, well that informed the direction too... and I'm glad, I'm having a ball. I love shocking the suits and they hired me for it. The 'out of the box' wildcard element, 'thas me. Ted."

Ted's eyes then darted around the backyard with exaggerated caution, like a secret agent in a low-budget spy flick. He leaned forward, elbows planted firmly on the table, eyes twinkling with mischief. The others, as if pulled by an invisible thread, instinctively drew closer by the promise of a good story. Even the patio lights seemed to dim, conspiring to set the stage for Ted's grand reveal.

"Go on..." Emma encouraged, her fingers absently tracing the rim of her wine glass, leaving a faint, high-pitched hum in the air.

Ted took a deep breath, milking the moment for all it was worth. "Okay, brace yourselves," he said, his voice dropping to a conspiratorial whisper that could probably be heard three blocks away. "My real name is Theodore."

"Get out of town!" James exclaimed, nearly knocking over his beer in surprise, the bottle wobbled precariously before settling, "Well, I lost my old bet. I was thinking more along the lines of 'Pluto' or 'Steadfast Landing'."

Emma's laughter rang out, clear and melodious in the night air. "What?" she shrugged, noticing the others' amused glances. "That's funny."

Ted grinned, warming to his tale like a stand-up comedian hitting his stride. "It's my real name, see, and I had to show this 'un," he gestured to Maribel, who was already shaking her head in anticipation, "my birth certificate just to prove it. But once known, well, oh my God, guess what name was saved for that moment when a wife wants her man to listen up and pay attention? 'Theodore,' she'd say or 'Theodore Zane' when she was on the border of being really pissed, and dang if it didn't work."

Ted's voice dropped even lower, a hint of pride coloring his words. "An' there's more..."

Both Emma and James leaned in, their chairs scraping slightly on the patio stones. Maribel, guessing what was coming, covered her face with her hands, her wedding ring catching the light.

Ted continued, his voice taking on a husky quality, "When a woman, a real woman, is in the throes of passion, shall we say, an' things are going very well indeed... and getting right close to that sweet spot."

"Oh dear God..." Maribel muttered, her face flushing a deep pink visible even in the dim light. She looked like she was contemplating diving under the table, she even raised the edge of the table cloth to check for clearance. "Oh dear God…" she repeated.

"No, not him," Ted corrected his wife, "but on second billing and batter up… yours truly as 'Ted'."

Emma and James burst into laughter, the sound rich and full, startling a nearby cat that had been prowling along the fence. The feline shot off into the night like its tail was on fire, clearly not appreciating the subtler points of human humor. Ted raised his voice slightly to be heard over their mirth, determined to land his final punchline.

"An' when a man hears his name called that… enough times, well, there's no going back to buffoonery, is there?" Ted looked at his audience all innocence—the necessary transition to 'Ted' was all too obvious.

Emma wiped tears from her eyes, her cheeks flushed from laughter and wine. She looked like she'd just run a marathon, but instead of exhaustion, her face radiated pure joy. "You are a work of nature, a pure work of nature," she managed between giggles. "Sorry, Bel, but that is just so sweet…"

James nodded, still chuckling. His eyes crinkled at the corners, years melting away in the face of genuine mirth. "What's worse is I can never say his name again… I'll have to make some kind of change. Theo? Is that okay? 'Cuz I can't say—"

"—Don't! Don't say it!" Emma exclaimed, setting off another round of laughter.

For a while, it was like the old days, but better. The years melted away, replaced by the warmth of friendship and shared humor. The patio echoed with their joy, a bubble of happiness in the quiet evening.

Finally, Maribel spoke up, her voice tinged with amusement despite her attempt at seriousness. "Hush now, shh. The neighbors are closer than we think." But she was smiling, unable to hide her delight at the scene before her. What could she say? It *was* funny. Her man had these 'genius artist-world-known types' rolling on the floor. He *was* a work of nature and he was hers. She smiled.

Ted stood, moving behind Maribel's chair. "See?" he said, his voice soft with affection. "She doesn't mind when it's true. She just doesn't like tall tales." He leaned down, and placed a sweet kiss on her cheek.

The night had deepened, the patio lights casting a warm glow over the group. The remnants of their meal lay forgotten on the table, replaced by fresh drinks and the comfortable silence of old friends reunited. In that moment, surrounded by laughter and love, it was clear that some things—like true friendship—only get better with age.

Maribel, seeking to divert attention from herself, pointed at James. Her eyes sparkled with mischief, a look that reminded Emma of their college days when Maribel would concoct some wild scheme. "You! You never did tell us how you actually got to be on this project, let alone the lead—"

"—Co-lead," James corrected with a nod to Emma. His lips quivered in that half-smile that always made Emma's heart do a little flip.

"Co-lead designer," Maribel amended, waving her hand to include Emma. "How did that actually happen?"

James leaned back in his chair, the wood creaking slightly under his weight. The late afternoon sun slanted through the windows, casting a golden glow on his profile. Emma found herself mesmerized by the play of light on his features, the way it highlighted the top of his hair.

"Well, my old friends and mentors, Alfred and Mabel, always kept tabs on me, never really let me far out of their sight." James began to unravel the sequence of events, "so after I came to visit you both here in Chicago, after what happened in New York in September, and you moved here for that new job—"

"—That I suspect you set up," Ted interjected, a knowing smirk on his face.

"—And check on the bairns," James continued, ignoring the interruption with the ease of long practice. "I... well, I really connected to this place, put me in mind of Newcastle upon Tyne, working class kind of town, but upscale. So Alfred and Mabel knew I was here, they hear the Eco Building is looking for something fresh, so bingo, now the Epoch Alliance is involved and arms twisted puts me at the driver's seat."

Maribel shook her head, unconvinced. She leaned forward, in her lawn chair, hand touching her chin, making little 'thinking' taps to keep her mind moving in the right direction. "Nope, nothing is ever that simple. There must have been an interview, or something. 'Coz why would they give a project so important in Chicago to a Brit? Emma's got connections to the Art Institute, they did a showing of her work, she had her own section on special display. So what did you, a Brit, say to get this gig?"

James chuckled, running a hand through his hair. The gesture was so familiar, so quintessentially James, that Emma felt a wave of nostalgia wash over her.

"I can see you're just like your spouse and won't let this go, holy hello." James observed and they all laughed good-naturedly. The sound filled the patio, wrapping around them like a comfort quilt. "Okay, let's see if I can remember..."

He paused, his eyes distant as he thought back. The chirping of crickets filled the silence, accompanied by the soft rustle of leaves in the breeze. A car horn honked in the distance, a reminder of the bustling city beyond their cozy gathering.

"A Brit, eh? Well, that's just it, isn't it? James was thinking out loud as he worked his way through to his goal line, "I wasn't a Brit anymore, was I? I've been a U.S. citizen since 2000, took the pledge 'an all and I admit to more than a few tears when I did. This country's been so good to me, and in extension my family. Sarah got the care she needed and me family never could afford—"

"—But you wouldn't have told them that. Come on, you're fudging—" Maribel pressed, her eyes narrowing playfully.

James held up his hands in mock surrender. "No, no, I'm getting there," he insisted. His voice took on a passionate tone as he continued, his eyes lighting up with that fire Emma knew so well. It was the same look he'd get when an idea was about to take over his mind.

"It's this: I'm an immigrant, a classic case of an American immigrant, come here with 'nought in my pocket 'cuz Cooper Union says if you pass our bars we'll let you study here for free. And who does that? Anderson Cooper, some bloke with bloody perfect vision to see the future and the way it will be. An' that's what happens in America. Who was Tesla before he came here? Nought... and Einstein only really became Einstein here in the States."

As James spoke, Emma found herself leaning in, caught up in the rhythm of his words. She glanced around the table, seeing the same rapt attention on everyone's faces. Even Ted, who'd heard most of James's stories a hundred times, looked enthralled.

James paused, reaching for his glass, he had switched from beer to water and the ice clinked softly as he took a sip, the sound oddly amplified in the hushed space. When he continued, his voice was softer, more reflective.

"I proposed a wall with tiles, clay from the earth that would carry the blessing of that intention, the best part of being an American. And where better than a building devoted to changing Ecosystems for the long haul? Had no idea of the nuts and bolts and bits that Emma brilliantly added to make it work in real time… but being a new immigrant, well, what was more American than that? I might have pitched the ball like that."

As James finished speaking, a comfortable silence fell over the group. Emma found herself blinking back unexpected tears. She wasn't really sure why his words had reached into her for this reaction, it seemed there was something else he wasn't telling yet.

Silence fell over the group as they absorbed James's words. The distant sound of traffic and the gentle clinking of ice in their glasses were the only sounds for a moment.

"Well, you did ask," James said, breaking the silence.

Maribel nodded, impressed. "I'd hire you."

"In a heartbeat," Emma added softly.

"Ditto," Ted offered, raising his glass in a small salute.

James grinned, relieved. "Well, I'm glad I have the home team sorted, but it's going to be tough. You all are coming to make tiles, right? And the wee girls too, can't forget this is for them."

The conversation shifted to the logistics of the project. Emma leaned forward, her eyes bright with enthusiasm. "We're setting up two large tents near the Field Museum, round picnic table tile making stations on both sides and a storage shed in the middle, to keep some clay out of the summer sun."

James nodded, his knee brushing against Emma's under the table. The brief contact sent a spark through them both, a reminder of the connection that had always simmered beneath the surface. They both pulled back a little, adding some space between them, Mirabel and Ted exchanged a look.

James cleared his throat and added, "We'll have wood plates prepped with a layer of clay. People can choose which clay tile they want, square or round and carve their designs directly onto the clay."

Maribel, ever the practical one, leaned in. Her brow furrowed slightly as she asked, "How long will people have to work on their tiles?" She was already thinking about how to manage the girls during the process, her mind whirring with the logistics of wrangling two excited children through an art project.

"We're aiming for about 30 minutes per person," Emma explained, her voice soft but confident. She met Maribel's eyes, understanding the unspoken concern. "It's enough time to create something meaningful."

Ted chimed in, "And the girls can really participate? You'll use their tiles too?" His voice held a note of hope, as if he was already imagining the proud papa moment of seeing his daughters' creations immortalized in the mosaic.

"Absolutely," James affirmed. "We want all ages involved, it's about everybody, of course, everyone. No one will be turned away, but we won't accept any negative themes, of say, war, battles or hurting whatnot. And no words, all images, drawings, you get the idea."

* * *

As the night wore on, the conversation took a turn towards deeper waters. Emma, her cheeks flushed from wine and good company, found herself speaking of her ongoing correspondence with Professor Herzog. Her eyes lit up as she described how his influence had shaped her work over the years.

Ted, sprawled comfortably in his chair, raised his beer in a mock toast. His eyes twinkled with mischief as he declared, "He's still kicking, then? To old Herzog, may his critiques be as cutting and his praise rare as ever."

"To Helmut..." Em agreed, clinking her glass against Ted's bottle with a soft chime.

James's eyebrows shot up, a grin tugging at the corners of his mouth. "Ah, are we first names, then?" He turned to the group, his voice taking on a nostalgic tone. "Didn't you love that about college? All of a sudden you can call the professor by their first name, except Professor Herzog. Well, I'm glad he had you as a friend Em."

"Boy, he sure gave you a rough time James," Ted observed, his words slightly slurred from the beer.

James leaned back, his chair creaking slightly under his weight. He ran a hand through his hair, "Well, I don't know if it was rough," he mused, his eyes distant with memory. "We certainly had our discussions. He did his job; he was pretty hard on everyone, even Em. What do you say, Em?"

Emma's lips curved into a soft smile. "He was hard... if I didn't listen," she said, her tone thoughtful. Her fingers traced the rim of her wineglass as she spoke. "If I let what he was instructing bounce off my emotions, it would have been hard... and I don't know how he did it, but when I took his advice I always improved."

Maribel, who had been listening intently, chimed in with a laugh. "He had laser vision. Like a superhero."

Their laughter filled the warm night air, a joyous sound that seemed to make the stars shine brighter.

As the night deepened and the wine flowed freely, Ted turned to James, a mischievous glint in his eye. "So, James, you became a Pat too. Never thought you'd give up the crown."

James chuckled, shaking his head. "Ah, well, times change, don't they? Besides, as I said, this country's been good to me. Felt right to make it official."

There was a moment of silence, heavy with unspoken thoughts. Then James, his voice softer now, began to speak about what had led him to this decision. He told them about that day near Trinity Church, looking at the empty space where the World Trade Center had once stood.

"It was like being punched in the gut," he said, his eyes distant. "All that sorrow, that loss, it wasn't a thing of the mind, it was something I felt, right here in my gut. I actually doubled over, right there in the open lot... it didn't matter that I wasn't a citizen yet, nationality meant nothing... my brothers and sisters were taken violently from me, from our family, I felt the... empty space where they had been... I had to lean over, I think to keep my balance, keep from fainting maybe... then... anger started, and then... it was the strangest thing. I felt like I was being held, like great, great mile high arms were around me. And slowly, I don't know how God did it, but that anger was...dissolved completely and it has never come back. I'm not saying I don't get angry about other things, or petty or, but that particular anger is gone.

And that doesn't mean I don't want justice, I do, but that's a different kettle of fish from..."

"Revenge?" Asked Em softly.

They looked at each other and James nodded, "Yeah."

Maribel and Ted looked at each other, it was clear they didn't want to speak a word to break the possibility of a peace treaty between two beloved friends.

And so they were all quiet, listening to the sounds of the wee creatures living in the dark places of night taking their turn to come out and get a meal and go about the daily work of surviving and thriving.

As the night drew to a close, Ted and Maribel shared their own news—Maribel's budding career as a children's book author was moving forward, slowly but with certainty. The soft glow of the porch light cast warm shadows across her face, highlighting the sparkle in her eyes as she spoke.

"Started making up stories for the girls," Maribel explained, her voice tinged with a mixture of pride and amusement. "I self-published using some online services so the girls could see the pictures and stories in print." She chuckled, shaking her head slightly. "Turns out other kids like them too. I'm not selling a whole lot, but it feels right...and fun. Who knew my late-night extempore 'once upon a time' speeches would click with other families too?"

James nodded, a thoughtful expression on his face. He leaned back in his porch chair, the old wood creaking as an afterthought beneath him. "It suits you, Bel, you've grown into it."

"Speaking of growing," Emma interjected, turning to Maribel with a mischievous glint in her eye "How are you feeling? You look absolutely radiant, like you've swallowed the sun."

Maribel brightened, her hand instinctively resting on her rounded womb. The soft cotton of her flower print dress stretched taut over the curve. "Exhausted, but happy," she admitted with a rueful smile. "This little one does like to kick. Practices football moves at all hours of the night—and when I say football I mean soccer, I swear, the 'z's coming from Ted is the only thing that quiets the baby—must think it's the roar of a crowd or something."

"Oi!" Ted protested good-naturedly, his voice carrying from the kitchen where he was rummaging for more snacks. "I do not snore. I am a dedicated breather. When I commit to something like breathing, I'm in for life."

The group on the patio chuckled, this was fun, just good, good, fun.

As they continued to munch on leftovers, dessert snacks and chat, the conversation meandered through various topics—from Maribel's budding career as a children's book author to the challenges of raising kids in the city. The ease of their interaction belied the years they'd spent apart, as if they were simply picking up threads of conversation they'd left hanging years ago.

James found himself observing more than participating, his eyes often drawn to Emma like a peaceful resting place. He noticed the way her eyes lit up first before she smiled and then she laughed at Ted's jokes, like some internal chain reaction, how she leaned in to catch every drop of every word when Maribel was speaking, The gentle way Emma interacted with the girls, her voice softening as she complimented their crayon masterpieces.

It felt so familiar, so perfectly natural. He wanted to reach out, to take her hand in his, to feel the warmth of her skin against his palm. The urge to pull her close, to have her come and sit close next to his side was almost overwhelming. James realized, with a start, that having Emma near felt like nourishment, like some essential nutrient his soul had been craving all these years.

There it was—that was truth laid bare in his mind. It was what he wanted, craved even, but not what he would do. The chasm of years and misunderstandings still stretched between them, a grand canyon he wasn't sure how to bridge.

As the evening wore on and the last crumbs were licked from plates, Ted stood up with the rolling thunder of a Shakespearean actor preparing for a soliloquy. He stretched, his joints popping audibly, and declared, "Right then, who's for a nightcap? I've got a bottle of the good stuff I've been saving for a special occasion."

"And this qualifies, does it?" James teased, arching an eyebrow. "What happened to saving it for when you completed the Chicago Marathon?"

Ted grinned, the force of it crinkling the corners of his eyes. He clapped James on the shoulder, nearly knocking him off his chair. "Old friends, new beginnings—what could be more special than that? Besides," he added with a wink, "at the rate my knees are aging, that bottle might turn to vinegar before I make it."

As Ted shuffled off to fetch the drinks, muttering something about 'ungrateful Brits' and 'no appreciation for the effort to partake in fine American sports', Maribel herded the girls inside. Their protests about not being tired were undermined by jaw-cracking yawns and drooping eyelids.

Suddenly, James and Emma found themselves alone in the backyard. The silence between them was comfortable, filled with the ambient symphony of a city settling into night. A distant siren wailed, a cat yowled its objections to some unseen slight, and somewhere, a car alarm briefly shattered the peace before giving up with a petulant chirp.

"It's good, this," Emma said softly, gesturing vaguely at the house, the remnants of their meal, the whole evening.

James nodded, his own voice equally hushed, "Yeah, it is," he agreed, a small smile tugging at the corners of his mouth. "Feels like… coming home."

Their eyes met in a social way, as a mutual neutral agreement, but then stuck, quite locked together now, and for a moment, it was as if all the years between them took a weekend holiday. But before either could speak, Ted's voice boomed from the house, breaking the spell.

"Alright, you two! Get in here and let's make a proper toast!"

* * *

As they were preparing to leave, Maribel, ever perceptive, pulled Emma aside for a final hug. The warmth of her embrace lingered, a cocoon of friendship and understanding. "Give him time," she whispered, "He's been through a lot, but he's here with you, that says something."

Maribel paused, pressed her lips together as if weighing her next words carefully. Then, with a mischievous glint in her eye, she leaned in close again, her voice dropping to a conspiratorial murmur meant only for Emma. "Em… there's always this: when the time is right, you can always jump him, I don't think he'll kick up too much of a fuss, because Em… men need to be needed, almost more than being loved." And then she kissed her stunned friend on the cheek and smiled, looking entirely too pleased with herself.

Emma's eyes widened, a blush creeping up her neck. "I can't believe you said that."

Maribel shrugged, the picture of unrepentant sass. "Well I can't take it back now, oops. Plus, I have two kids, and one in the waiting room, so I think I know what I'm talking about."

Emma laughed lightly, the sound tinged with affection and just a hint of nerves. "I love you, you know," and then louder so Ted could hear, "I love you guys."

"Uh oh, somebody cut her off, she's not driving is she?" he asked James, his words only slightly slurred.

"Not bloody likely." James replied, his tone dry as Arizona in August.

* * *

As Maribel pulled Emma aside to offer advice about the benefits of conjugal bliss, Ted was doing the same with James in another corner of the room. The two couples, unaware of the parallel conversations taking place, were about to receive some well-intentioned, if slightly inebriated, marital wisdom.

Ted, swaying slightly as he stood, fixed James with an earnest gaze. His eyes, slightly unfocused, nonetheless burned with the intensity of a man on a mission. "Now, mate, now... this actually might be the drink talking coz I'm gonna give you some advice—"

James sighed, rolling his eyes. "Oh lord, not more—"

"Noooo... no, you're going to like this advice," Ted insisted, waving a finger that seemed to have a mind of its own. "Now I'm not saying or suggesting you don't know what to do when the time comes with a woman, I'm sure you 'all know what goes where and why-"

"Ted, you are drunk—" James interjected, a mix of amusement and exasperation in his voice. He couldn't quite decide whether to laugh or to gag his old friend with the nearest throw pillow.

Ted nodded sagely. "Quite probably, yes, but lemme finish. You've been living like a... in a desert or monk... and I'm not saying thas' bad, I think thas' good, because nothing will keep you from her, so thas' brilliant, but James, Jimmy, knowing women and living with your wife, are two entirely different creatures... when your woman, feels safe, really safe.... wooooo, watch out... she will open in a way you literally cannot imagine and take you somewhere... that's not in this world. But that can only happen if she knows you will receive her child, her baby too and you all will be safe. Get me drift?"

James shifted uncomfortably, but couldn't help a small smile. "Impossible not to... but yeah, I do."

Ted swayed a bit more noticeably. "Ok, Am I still standing up?"

James chuckled, reaching out to steady his friend. "Sorta, the armchair is a considerable help."

Indeed, the armchair behind Ted was doing most of the heavy lifting in keeping him vertical.

Undeterred, Ted pressed on. "What I'm saying Jimmy, is I know you need to climb the wall, I know you have reasons, I also know life isn't perfect, so if you find yourself getting at all close to real, she'll know, she'll feel it and watch out; nature will take over guaranteed, kablammy! There is no halfway with you two. So if you really don't want her, please figure it out fast, before you make an explosion you can't deal with."

James nodded, a mix of emotions playing across his face—amusement, affection, and a hint of something deeper. "Okay... ah thanks?"

Ted beamed, patting James on the shoulder. "You're very welcome."

* * *

As they drove back toward the city later that night, the Chicago skyline glittered before them like a constellation of earthbound stars. Lake Michigan stretched out to their left, a vast expanse of inky darkness occasionally broken by the distant lights of boats. James and Emma sat in comfortable silence, the hum of the car's engine providing a soothing backdrop to their thoughts.

It had been a wonderful day, and rather than risk breaking the bubble, they sat quietly and enjoyed the ride southbound down Lake Shore Drive.

However, unbeknownst to each other, they both had sex on their minds, thanks to the 'advice' from their well-meaning friends. Consequently, they didn't really look at each other much for the entire drive, each lost in their own thoughts and the implications of the conversations they'd had earlier.

Emma found herself fascinated by the play of streetlights across the dashboard, while James suddenly developed an intense interest in the proper positioning of his hands on the steering wheel. Both equally import tasks to be conducted to ensure a safe trip home.

As they neared the Lawrence Ave turn off toward Emma's place, both James and Emma found themselves simultaneously dreading and longing for the moment when the drive would end. The unspoken desires simmered between them like a pot of Maribel's famous five-alarm salsa—tempting, potentially dangerous, and impossible to ignore.

* * *

Chapter 12

Chicago — Outside Field Museum *— Jun. 15, 2002 — 8:55 a.m. — For the People*

The morning sun committed itself to climb higher in the Chicago sky, faithfully adhering to its mission statement: to illuminate the molecular structure from the inside out—of all creations large and small, of all creatures sentient or not. And so the pristine white tents, erected on the grounds of the Field Museum, fairly sang out a clarion call to all and sundry as a beckoning hand extended to come hither from yon. Come join us, come join us...

Emma stood at the entrance of the larger tent, her eyes tracing the vibrant sashes that draped elegantly from each corner. Deep purple, orange, yellow, sky blue, and light green fabrics billowed gently in the passing breeze—colors chosen by James's assistant, Val, for no particular reason other than they looked "pretty" and "flowy." The soft whir of the museum's air conditioning provided a steady backdrop to the growing hum of excited voices as people began to queue up outside.

Her gaze drifted to James and Gerardo, deep in conversation near the small shed that housed the precious clay. James took a long swig from the water bottle Rhonda Morrison had given them all as a 'good luck launching gift,' the crystals of condensation catching the light as he lowered it. His brow furrowed slightly as he listened to Gerardo, no doubt discussing last-minute logistics.

Taking a deep breath, Emma smoothed down her clay-stained apron and stepped forward to greet the first group of participants. Their eager faces turned towards her, a mix of excitement and nervousness palpable in the air.

"Welcome, everyone," Emma began, her voice warm and inviting. "We're so glad you've come to be part of this incredible project. Before we begin, I'd like to go over a few guidelines to ensure your tiles can be included in our final mosaic."

She gestured to the round picnic tables inside the tent, each adorned with a wicker basket overflowing with carving tools. "If you'd all sit down at this first table, I'll walk you through the process."

As the participants took their seats, Emma settled at one of the tables with a group of five. She looked around at their smiling faces, each one appeared more than willing to 'dig in' when she blew the whistle. The scent of clay was mingling with the earthy aroma from the nearby gardens and in the distance, a seagull cried out over Lake Michigan, a reminder of the vast world beyond their creative bubble.

Emma picked up a smooth slab of clay, its cool surface a comfort against her palms. "First and foremost," she said, her fingers tracing invisible patterns on the clay, 'we're focusing on positive images and themes. This mosaic is a celebration of our community, so let your creativity flow in an uplifting direction."

A young girl with pigtails raised her hand tentatively. "Can I make a butterfly?"

Emma's face lit up with a smile. "A butterfly would be perfect. Just remember, we're avoiding specific numbers, letters, or names. We want these tiles to represent images everyone can relate to in some way."

She reached into the basket, pulling out a wooden block and a selection of carving tools. "Now, as you work, be mindful of the depth of your carving. We don't want to weaken the clay, so try not to go too deep. This wooden block is your guide for height—feel free to build up on the clay, but stay within this limit."

Emma demonstrated, her hands moving with practiced ease as she began to shape the clay. The group leaned in, captivated by her fluid movements. The very soft scrape of a tool against clay could be heard, oddly comforting in its simplicity.

"See?" Emma offered, "the clay is moist enough to be moved, yet firm enough to hold a shape. Lots of fun."

An older man wearing a Buccaneers T-shirt sitting across from her laughed. "Well, we'll see what kind of shape it'll be after I mess with it for a while."

The other adults at the table chuckled, but the little girl with pigtails piped up, "No, don't worry, teacher tells us we can't make a mistake. Isn't that right?"

Emma nodded in agreement. "That is exactly right. And if you want to attach separate pieces," she continued, her voice taking on a rhythmic cadence that matched her actions, "carve small lines in both the base clay and the piece you're attaching. Then, use this mixture—we call it slip—of clay and water. Paint it on with a brush, like so, and gently press the pieces together."

She held up the finished piece, a simple but elegant flower emerging from the clay. A soft chorus of "oohs" and "aahs" rippled through the group.

"Don't be afraid to experiment," Emma encouraged, gesturing to the lace doilies and mesh pieces laid out on the table. "These can create beautiful patterns and textures. And remember, your tile is part of something larger. Each piece will contribute to telling our community's story."

The little girl with pigtails reached for a doily, her eyes wide with wonder. "Ooh, it's so pretty! Can I press it into my butterfly?"

Emma nodded enthusiastically. "Absolutely! That's a wonderful idea. It'll give your butterfly beautiful, delicate wings."

As Emma finished her explanation, she noticed James approaching, his eyes twinkling with approval. She felt a flutter in her chest, that quick-silver migrated to her nether-regions, *gotta suppress that.* Dang, that sex bug Maribel had put in her ear was turning her body into an amusement park ride. Up and down, in and out—stop. Seriously? Focus, she reminded herself.

"Any questions before we begin?" She asked, scanning the eager faces before her.

A middle-aged man with salt-and-pepper hair spoke up. "How long do we have to work on our tiles?"

Emma smiled. "We've allotted about 30 minutes per person. It's enough time to create something meaningful without getting too complex."

The man in the Buccaneers T-shirt chuckled. "Thirty minutes? I might need thirty hours to make something half recognizable."

"You'll be surprised how much fun it is once you begin," James chimed in, his voice warm and encouraging. "Let your imagination run wild and watch out, it'll be great."

Emma felt that sweet softness in her heart welcome the sound of his voice again, and just when had that begun? She didn't recall the timber of his tone being able to move like this years ago. Time to shift gears. She drew in a deep breath and exhaled, "Shall we begin? Feel free to go up to the cutting table and get a clay tile from Jasmine or Roberto. And there's Mark over there... they can also answer any questions you have."

As the group began to disperse, Emma called out softly but clearly above the growing murmur of conversation, "So, who would like to share what they're thinking of creating?"

The little girl with pigtails bounced in her seat. "I'm going to make a butterfly with lace wings!"

The older man and football fan, scratched his chin thoughtfully. "I was thinking about the old oak tree in my backyard. Been there longer than I have."

James nodded approvingly. "Both sound wonderful. Remember, it's all about what you are in the mood to do right now, trust that... and have fun."

As the participants began to work, the tent filled with a buzz of creativity and conversation. Emma caught James's eye, sharing a moment of quiet satisfaction before they turned in tandem to assist their eager artists.

* * *

As the morning progressed, the hum of activity in the tent grew. The air filled with the earthy scent of clay and the gentle scraping of carving tools. Emma moved from table to table, offering encouragement and guidance. Her eyes darted occasionally to the large clock hanging at the front of the tent, a seed of concern growing in her mind.

At one table, a middle-aged woman with graying hair pulled into a messy bun was meticulously carving an intricate tree of life design. Her brow furrowed in concentration, she seemed oblivious to the world around her.

"That's beautiful," Emma said, leaning in for a closer look. "You've captured so much detail."

The woman looked up, startled. "Oh! Thank you. I just… I want to get it right, you know?"

Emma glanced at her watch, then back at the woman's tile. It had been nearly 45 minutes, and the design was only half complete. "Take your time," she said softly, patting the woman's shoulder.

Across the tent, James was deep in conversation with an elderly Japanese man who was carefully etching a scene from his childhood neighborhood. The man's gnarled hands moved slowly but deliberately, each line a testament to a lifetime of memories.

"And this here," the man was saying, pointing to a small building in his design, "that was old Mrs. Johnson's candy store. Had penny candy back then, candy bars for five cents, we'd collect old pop bottles in the alley and turn them in for a refund and then fly on licorice for hours…"

James chuckled, his eyes crinkling at the corners. "Sounds like the way to live."

Emma made her way to James, considered which part of his anatomy would be the most innocuous to touch and eventually settled on his elbow, "James," she said softly, "can I have a word?",

They stepped away from the tables, moving closer to the tent's entrance where the fluttering purple sashes provided a semblance of privacy.

"What is it, Em?" James asked, his eyes still scanning the area, watching the interns interact with the public. He didn't seem to be really listening to her.

"James, seriously, I need your attention,"

"Sorry Em, what is it?" James was looking at her in the eyes now, well that didn't help, but Emma took a deep breath and soldiered on.

"It's taking longer than we anticipated. Most people aren't finishing in 30 minutes. Not even close."

James's brow furrowed. "How much longer?"

"Some are taking up to an hour," Emma replied. "But James, you should see what they're creating. It's…it's amazing. The detail, the emotion they're putting into these tiles. I don't think we should rush them."

James ran a hand through his hair, a habit Emma recognized as a sign of his internal struggle. "We have a schedule to keep, Em. If we let everyone take twice as long, we'll fall behind. We can't afford that."

Emma nodded, understanding his concern. But she couldn't shake the feeling that something important was happening here, something that shouldn't be curtailed for the sake of a schedule.

"I know," she said softly. "But I think the quality will be more important than quantity. There's nothing worse than hearing a bell ring when you're not ready to go. These people, they're pouring their hearts into these tiles. It feels wrong to cut them off."

James's eyes met hers, and for a moment, Emma saw a flicker of the connection they once shared. He understood. Of course he did. This was about expression. About doing justice to the vision they'd had for this project.

"You drawing a line in the sand, pet?" He asked, his tone half-serious, half-teasing.

Emma straightened her spine, feeling a rush of both nervousness and determination. "Yes, I think I am. Quality will be more important than quantity. Let's give them the time they need."

James was quiet for a moment, his eyes roaming over the tent full of absorbed, creative people. Emma held her breath, watching the emotions play across his face. Finally, he nodded, a slow smile spreading across his features.

"Alright, I agree with you too, by the way," he said, his voice warm with admiration. "But you're gonna work late, right? 'Coz, I'm already in."

Emma felt a smile spread across her face, relief and excitement mingling in her chest. "Of course. Whatever it takes."

As they turned back to the room, their shoulders brushing slightly, Emma felt a renewed sense of purpose. This was why they were here. Not just to create a mosaic, but to give people the space and time to express themselves, to be part of something larger.

The day stretched ahead of them, longer now, but full of possibility. Emma rolled up her sleeves and dove back in, ready to guide, encourage, and witness the birth of each unique tile. The mosaic might take longer to complete, but it would be better for it.

* * *

As the morning wore on, the initial flurry of activity settled into a steady rhythm. The soft scraping of carving tools and murmur of conversation created a soothing backdrop, punctuated occasionally by exclamations of delight or frustration from the participants. Emma found herself with a moment to breathe, and she seized the opportunity to get to know the interns better.

She approached Jasmine, who was carefully cutting clay circles at one of the preparation tables. The young woman's dark curls were pulled back in a messy bun, a smudge of clay adorning her left cheek like a badge of honor.

"How are you holding up, Jasmine?" Emma asked, leaning against the table.

Jasmine looked up, her brown eyes sparkling with enthusiasm. "It's amazing, Ms. Hawkins. I never thought I'd be part of something like this." She gestured around the tent with a clay-covered hand. "It's like… like we're all creating a piece of history together."

Emma smiled warmly, touched by the young woman's excitement. "Please, call me Emma. Tell me, what drew you to this project?"

As Jasmine began to speak about her interest in community art and her studies at the Art Institute, Emma found herself genuinely engaged. The young woman's passion was infectious, reminding Emma of her own early days at Cooper Union.

"I've always believed art should be accessible to everyone," Jasmine was saying, her hands moving animatedly as she spoke. "Not just something you see in museums, but something you can be part of, you know?"

Emma nodded, about to respond when her eyes drifted across the tent, landing on James. He was deep in discussion with Clara, a young blonde intern from Gerardo's hand picked staff.

They were bent over a particularly intricate tile, James pointing to a specific place as he explained something. Clara's face was a picture of rapt attention, her eyes fixed on James as if he were revealing the secrets of the inter galactic time travel.

Emma felt an odd pang in her chest, like that 'wobbly' reverberating discordant sound when a cartoon character walks into a wall—'wonnng!' Dang it—a feeling she understood all too well. Little green about the gills are we? She asked herself, the inner voice dripping with sarcasm.

Quickly, she averted her gaze, her mother's words echoing in her mind: *stay out of his way.* The advice felt like the cold splash of a water balloon on an unsuspecting aunt bringing her best raspberry Jell-O mold—with marshmallows—to the family barbecue. In short: didn't quite see that coming.

"Emma? Are you okay?" Jasmine's concerned voice broke through her thoughts.

Emma shook her head slightly, forcing a smile. "Yes, sorry. I just remembered something I need to check on later." She took a deep breath, centering herself. "You were talking about community art?"

As Jasmine resumed her enthusiastic explanation, Emma made a conscious effort to focus. She was here to work, to add her specific skills to create a timeless work. There was no time for small thinking. Nothing else mattered. Nothing.

'Grow up!' She advised herself sternly. 'You're a professional, act like one.'

But even as she nodded along to Jasmine's words, a small part of her couldn't help but wonder what James was saying to Clara that had the young intern so captivated. The thought nagged at her, a persistent itch she couldn't quite scratch.

Emma squared her shoulders, pushing the feeling aside. She had a job to do, a vision to bring to life. And if that meant ignoring the way James's eyes crinkled when he smiled at Clara, well...that's exactly what she'd do. No matter how much it stung.

* * *

As the lunch hour approached, James's voice cut through the general hubbub. "Alright, everyone! I think we've all earned a break. We'll do lunch in shifts, how about it? I'm buying."

A chorus of agreement rose from the tired but satisfied staff. James grinned, that wide, bright smile like he had energy to burn. Everyone was feeling the fade, but no, he still had a celestial event in the tank with a starburst to spare. Emma shook her head at the thought, he continued, "I know a great sandwich place nearby. My treat for all your hard work."

Well that brightened the halfway mark on their first day.

James's assistant, Val, began making rounds, jotting down orders on a notepad. When she reached Emma, Val raised an eyebrow expectantly.

"I'll have the steak and cheese sandwich," Emma said, then added after a moment's hesitation, "and cheese fries, please, lots of cheese." She felt a twinge of guilt at the indulgence, but pushed it aside. After all, she'd be working late, gonna need those carbs, kinda.

James, who had drifted closer, overheard and chuckled. "Ever steak and potatoes, eh our Em?"

Emma felt a flush creep up her neck but managed a casual shrug. "Gotta love the classics," she bantered back, proud of how steady her voice sounded. Inside, her heart was doing a sweet swing at the use of his pet name for her.

James nodded approvingly before moving on to the next group. Emma let out a breath she hadn't realized she'd been holding. See? She could do this. She could be the coolest of the cool, all professional and detached, and she had been doing so, holding the course, but ever since Bel had put that idea into her head, the one she would not repeat even inside the private space of her own mind—she was blushing whenever she got within ten feet of him.

But thank god, he seemed clueless to what was going on. He was friendly toward her, even kind, but he was the same with everyone. The very same. Emma watched as he joked with Clara, the young intern hanging on his every word. She felt that familiar pang again but quickly squashed it.

As the lunch orders were being finalized, Emma took a moment to survey the morning's work. The quality of the tiles was exceptional. Each piece told a story, captured a memory, or expressed a hope for the future. It was more than she could have imagined.

Gerardo sidled up next to her, his eyes also roaming over the tables. "It's something else, isn't it?" He murmured.

Emma nodded, a lump forming in her throat. "It really is. I think we made the right call, giving them more time."

Gerardo squeezed her shoulder gently. "Definitely. Quality over quantity, always."

And if, in quiet moments, her eyes still drifted to James, consider those small glances as mini respites to enjoy, ah...the scenery. Emma sighed, life was so strange.

"You okay there, Em?" Gerardo asked, his voice laced with concern.

Emma startled, realizing she'd been staring. "Oh, yes. Just... taking it all in."

Gerardo's eyes twinkled knowingly. "Uh-huh. Well, just remember, we've got a long afternoon ahead. Pace yourself."

Emma nodded, grateful for Gerardo's gentle reminder. For now, there was work to be done, a community to engage, and a mosaic to build. One tile at a time. And if her heart did a little gymnastic flip every time James smiled in her direction, well... that was just part of the job, wasn't it? Who could she talk to for hazard pay? She chuckled, at the thought, thank goodness for levity.

* * *

As the afternoon sun began its descent, casting long shadows across the Field Museum grounds, the energy in the tent remained high. The extended time for each tile had indeed slowed their progress, but the quality of work was undeniable. Emma found herself lost in admiration of a particularly intricate piece—a delicately carved cityscape that seemed to capture the very essence of Chicago, its skyscrapers reaching for the heavens while the gentle curves of Lake Michigan embraced the shore.

James appeared at her side, his presence both comforting and unsettling. The aroma cast from clay and his familiar scent mingled in the air between them. "It's getting late, Em," he said softly, his eyes on the clock that now read 7:30 PM. A hint of weariness weighing down his voice, betraying the long day's journey into dusk.

Emma nodded, a mix of pride and concern washing over her. She brushed a stray lock of hair from her face, leaving a smudge of clay on her cheek. "I know. But look at what they're making, it's beyond what we could have hoped for, there's literal drawings, and abstract too, detailed complex and simple gesture carvings." Her eyes were sparkling, despite the fatigue attempting to persuade her to sit, no, lay down flat on the grass next to the tent pavilion.

As if on cue, Mark's voice carried across the tent, tinged with regret. "I'm sorry, but we're going to have to start packing up. We can't give out any more tiles today."

Emma's head snapped up, her eyes landing on two middle-aged women who had just arrived, disappointment etched on their faces. Before she could move, James was already striding towards them, his voice warm and reassuring.

"You forgot, mate," he said to Mark, as he passed. "I'm staying the night, so these ladies can get their clay and carve while we watch the sun go down." And then as an aside to Mark, "You lot can start packing up around them, Em and I will stay to finish up."

The women's faces lit up, one of them clasping James's hand. "Thank you, thank you," she said, her voice thick with emotion. "My sister's husband passed away a few months ago, and she wants to carve their image in a tile. Bless you, young man."

James coughed, clearing his throat to hide his own surge of emotion. He guided them to an empty picnic table, his hand gentle on the grieving woman's back. "Let's get you started, shall we? Did you bring a photo?"

Emma watched as he gave them a personal tour of the process, his patience seemingly endless despite the long day. She marveled at his ability to connect with people, to make each person feel seen and heard.

When he caught her eye, he winked. "In for a penny, in for a pound, eh Em?"

Emma felt a smile tugging at her lips. This was the James she remembered—kind, generous, always going the extra mile for the work and for others. "You never could resist a damsel in distress," she teased gently.

"Or two," James quipped back, his warm hazel eyes shifted with the light, as they always did.

As the night deepened, the last participants finally left, most of the trays of the precious completed clay tiles were packed in the van to take to the office work space, where they would be set out to dry, at an even rate. The interns, exhausted but exhilarated, began the process of cleaning up. The soft clink of tools being put away and the rustle of tarps being folded filled the air.

Emma approached James, who was studying the last few trays of finished work with a mixture of pride and contemplation. The warm glow of the setting sun cast a golden hue over the tiles, making them seem almost alive. "You were right," she said softly, coming to stand beside him.

He turned, an eyebrow raised. "About?"

"About running late. Very late. It's 9 PM, James. We're three hours behind schedule." She gestured to the clock, its hands seeming to mock their best-laid plans.

To her surprise, James chuckled. "Ah, well. What's that saying? 'Life is what happens while you're busy making other plans'? Or in our case, while we're busy making tiles." His laugh lines deepened, the man did know how to laugh.

"You didn't complain once. Even when those ladies showed up at the last minute." Emma deliberately bumped his shoulder gently with her own, an old familiar gesture from their shared past. She did it without thinking, but he took it in stride, the day seemed constructed to reassemble a working way to be together.

James's eyes softened. "How could I? Did you see their faces? That's what this is all about, Em. Not schedules or numbers, but people. Their stories, their lives." He paused, running a hand through his hair. "My concern about the schedule is for the long view, this is our first day and everybody is energized, but I know how it'll be even after a week, all day in sun, the interns are gonna get tired. We—you and I have extra energy coz we're driven, not everybody has that."

Emma nodded, understanding dawning. "So the schedule was for long-term success."

"Exactly," James agreed. "But if you and I both get here early and work late—and Gerardo when he can, and maybe Val too—we can do this. I'm saying I would love for everybody to take their time. That's what I want too." He chuckled self-deprecatingly. "Sorry I made a speech. I promised myself I wouldn't make another for at least four weeks."

Emma laughed and said without thinking, "Well, thank goodness you're not the only one who loves the sound of your voice."

He looked at her, smile widening as he cocked his head. "You what? You like my speeches?"

"I didn't say that, exactly." Emma stuttered, looking for a way out, her cheeks flushing.

"I'm pretty sure you did," James insisted, thoroughly enjoying this new level of play with his best sparring partner ever.

"Didn't."

"Did."

They looked at each other to see who would hit the ball back. After a moment, they both laughed, the sound reverberating into the birds, the bees, and the trees. God, it was good having your best friend back, they thought almost simultaneously.

"We should probably start packing up," Emma said finally, reluctant to break the moment. She glanced around at the scattered remains. The interns had packed most of the long tables and tools from the round picnic tables, but it would still take at least a half hour to wrap up what was left—pack the rest of the tiles in the van and lock the shed. She drew in a sigh at the work ahead.

James nodded. "Aye, we should. But first..." He reached into a cooler and pulled out two bottles of water. Condensation beaded on the plastic, a welcome sight after the long, dusty day. Handing one to Emma, he raised his in a toast. "To a successful first day—running late, but right on time."

Emma bumped her plastic bottle against his, a laugh bubbling up from deep within her. "Running late, but okay," she echoed.

The cool water was a balm to her parched throat as she took a long drink.

Emma took another sip, savoring its relief to her system. She glanced around at the remnants of the day's work—scattered tools, half-folded tarps, and the last few trays of tiles waiting to be packed. There was still much to do, but the weight of it felt lighter somehow.

"Right then," James said, carefully recapping the empty water bottle. "Let's get this sorted."

As they set about their tasks, Emma found herself humming softly. To her own surprise it was an old folk ditty, a tune that worked especially well in three- or four-part harmony. But now that it was moving in her mind, it had to flow into the air to be shared. Sotto voce, of course—her own private serenade to the stars just beginning to spark on the horizon.

"If I had a hammer, I'd hammer in the morning, I'd hammer in the evening... all over this land... I'd hammer out danger, I'd hammer out warning... I'd hammer out love between my brothers and my sisters..."

To her surprise, the intern Jasmine—who was working alongside—sang a bit with her. She turned, eyebrows raised. "Jasmine... I wouldn't have pegged you for American folk circa 1964."

She shrugged. "Some tunes are timeless."

And then, not to be outdone, James picked up the thread. Under his breath he announced, "If I had a bell... I'd ring it in the morning..."

"I'd ring it in the evening..." Jasmine countered, matter-of-fact.

"Well, it is the bell of freedom..." Emma reminded them, all the schoolmarm now.

"Okay, just nobody start with a hundred bottles of beer on the wall..." James said to the group in general—and to Emma in specific. "I most sincerely beg you."

They all shared a laugh. It wasn't really that funny as such, but they were exhausted after a long, exacting day, and sharing like this was as good as a grand meal.

When Emma resumed her tasks, she buttoned her lip just a bit for the sake of group sanity—but she was smiling.

* * *

Chapter 13

Chicago W. Loop — Office Work Space — *Jun. 17, 2002 — 10:15 a.m. — Distance Unresolved*

James pushed open the door to the first-floor workspace, inhaling deeply as the familiar scent of clay and possibility washed over him. The large room, once an unused office space, now hummed with the energy of artistic creation. His eyes swept the area, searching for Emma. She was the co-lead designer, after all, and he felt a nagging need to check in with her. But her station stood empty, though her tote bag on the floor suggested she was somewhere about. The supply room, perhaps?

"Right then," James said, turning to Clara and Roberto, who hovered expectantly behind him like eager puppies waiting for a treat. "Let's start with a quick tour, shall we?"

As they moved through the room, James expertly explained each stage of the process, from the drying carved tiles to the smoothing and glazing. Clara, the young blonde intern, hung on his every word, her eyes bright with curiosity. James couldn't help but notice how she leaned in close as he pointed out details, unconsciously mirroring his movements. It reminded him of his own early days at Cooper Union, that burning desire to absorb every scrap of knowledge.

Emma, having returned from the supply room, watched this interaction from her workstation. James watched her place four canisters of glaze on the surface of her station and waited until she looked up to him to nod hello, but she didn't, instead her attention shifted to her clipboard to study the figures and her own private code.

James drew in a breath, looked at the two interns waiting for the next drop and continued, "Once these tiles are dry," James continued, "we'll move them to the Lill Street studio. That's where the Monster kiln is—big enough to handle our volume efficiently."

Roberto's eyebrows shot up. "Monster kiln?"

James chuckled, and switched to a soft Scottish brogue to emphasize, "Aye, it's a beast, Laddie, but necessary for a project this size." and then back to his normal speaking voice to add, "You'll love it Roberto, makes your average kiln look like a toaster oven dreaming of glory."

As he led the interns to the far end of the room, James found his attention divided. Half of him focused on explaining the intricacies of clay preparation, while the other half puzzled over Emma's distracted behavior. She still hadn't said 'hello' she seemed oddly distant, focused intently on her task as if determined not to look his way. He noticed the tension in her shoulders, the way she seemed to be avoiding eye contact. A part of him wanted to go to her, to understand what had shifted, just yesterday they had gotten along so well at the Field Museum, but the presence of the interns kept him rooted in place. Professional boundaries, he reminded himself, were a necessary evil.

A little odd, but she was busy arranging glaze pots, labeling each with meticulous care—probably having fun from her point of view, probably her version of Silas Marner counting coin—so he let it go.

"But who decides how they all fit together?" Clara's voice cut through his musings, high and clear as a bell. "I mean, who's designing the overall mosaic?"

"Well, now," he began, injecting a note of self-deprecating humor into his voice, "that's where things get interesting. You see, we've got this brilliant co-lead designer—that's Emma over there—who's got an eye for color that'd make a rainbow hard pressed to call itself pretty. And then there's yours truly, muddling along and hoping not to mess it all up."

He grinned, but his eyes strayed back to Emma. Still no response. Now he knew something was wrong, how could she resist an easy lob like that? What was going on in that clever head of hers?

"But again... 'cause you didn't really answer my question—who decides how they all fit together?" Clara asked, her voice carrying across the room with the petulance of a persistent seagull. "I mean, who's designing the overall mosaic?"

James's eyes flickered briefly towards Emma before answering, still hoping to include her in the conversation. "Well," he said, his tone carefully measured, "the design will flow from the group mind, so to speak. It's amazing how people drawn together will find ideas in common. Once we see what emerges, we can begin to visualize a design."

"We? Or... you?" Clara pressed, leaning in slightly. "Aren't you the design element?"

James smiled, a hint of something unreadable in his eyes. "I'll help guide the process, yes. He paused, then called out, "Anything to add, Em?"

Emma looked up, her expression carefully neutral. "Not right now, maybe later," she replied, before turning back to her task. She missed the brief look of concern that crossed James's face.

But he nodded, as if her response was exactly what he'd expected or hoped for. "Right then, shall we move on?"

As James continued the tour, he found his gaze drawn back to Emma. He noticed the tension in her shoulders, the way she seemed to be avoiding eye contact. At one point she *may* have nodded—there *may* have been a small smile—but when she said nothing, James shrugged and herded the group to the far end of the room.

"Now," James said, clapping his hands together as they reached the large work tables, "who's ready to get their hands dirty?"

Clara, her blonde hair pulled back in a messy bun, nodded eagerly. Roberto, more reserved, offered a small smile.

"Follow me," James instructed, leading them towards the work tables. As they walked, he began his explanation. "Now, what we're about to do is the foundation of our entire project. Without this, we'd have no tiles for people to carve, no canvas for their creativity. So pay attention, yeah?"

They reached the first table, where a large, square mass of red clay sat waiting. James ran his hand over its surface, feeling the cool, smooth texture beneath his palm. "This, he said, his voice taking on a reverent tone, is our raw material. Shipped straight from the earth, waiting to be shaped by our hands."

He reached for a tool that looked like a wire stretched between two wooden handles. "This here is our cutting wire. Simple, but effective. Like me," he added with a twist of self-deprecating and a side of wink.

With practiced ease, James positioned the wire at the edge of the clay block. "Watch closely," he instructed. With a smooth, controlled motion, he drew the wire through the clay, slicing off a layer about two inches thick.

"Beautiful," he murmured, lifting the slice and laying it on the table. "Now, we'll need three of these for each slab. Think of it like making a clay sandwich, only less tasty and more artistic."

Clara stepped in to catch the small details and Roberto watched intently as James cut two more slices, laying them out side by side on a sturdy canvas cloth. Emma glanced over occasionally, clearly admiring James's technique while simultaneously trying to focus on her own work. James nodded and smiled and she nodded but went back to her own work.

James shook it off for the moment and focused on the training at hand, "Here's where it gets a bit physical," James grinned, rolling up his sleeves. "We need to join these pieces together, create one seamless slab. Watch."

Using the heel of his hand, James began to press firmly along the edges where the clay pieces met. His movements were strong yet controlled, the muscles in his forearms flexing with each press. Clara was watching him closely, cocking her head to one side to see from a different angle.

"You want to really work it," he explained, his voice slightly strained with effort. "We're creating a makeshift seam here. It needs to be strong, or the whole slab will fall apart when we lift it. Bit like life, that," he added more to himself than to the interns.

Once he'd worked his way along both seams, James stepped back, wiping his brow. "Right, now for the fun part."

He gestured to a large roller at the end of the table. "This beauty here is going to do the hard work for us. But first, we need to get our joined pieces onto it."

With careful movements, James lifted the canvas cloth, transferring the clay onto the roller's surface. "Now, watch this, " he said, a hint of excitement in his voice."

Grasping the large hand wheel on the side of the roller, James began to turn it. The heavy weight pressed down onto the clay, smoothing out the seams and creating an even surface.

"And there you have it," James announced proudly, lifting the now-smooth slab. "One perfect clay slab, ready for carving. Almost as smooth as my dance moves—wait, I take that back. Probably not a good comparison—one of you might ask me for a floor show to prove the point, and I'll be left attempting to explain the meaning of the word *hyperbole*."

There was the expected round of gentle chuckles, which also drew a direct look from Emma. Undeterred by the reviews, James pressed on.

He set the slab back on the table, covering it with a sheet of plastic. "We'll keep it covered like this to hold in the moisture. These are what we'll be taking to the tents at the Field Museum."

James turned to Clara and Roberto, his eyes bright with enthusiasm. "Now—who wants to give it a go?"

Clara stepped forward eagerly. "I'd love to try, she said, reaching for the cutting wire."

James nodded approvingly. "Excellent. Remember, slow and steady does it. We want even slices."

As Clara began to cut, James moved closer, his hand hovering near hers, ready to guide if needed. "That's it, "he encouraged. Feel the wire moving through the clay. Let it do the work."

Roberto watched intently, his brow furrowed in concentration as he observed every move. James noticed his focus and smiled. "You'll be up next, Roberto. Each of you will need to master this. We've got a lot of clay to process, and not much time to do it in."

As Clara finished her third slice, James nodded appreciatively. "Well done. Now, let's see you join them."

Clara began to press the edges together, her smaller hands struggling slightly with the force needed. James stepped in, demonstrating again. "Like this, he said, his hands moving confidently. You've got to really put your weight into it."

Clara tried again, this time with more success. "That's it." James exclaimed. "You're getting it now."

Excited by her success, Clara impulsively put her hand on James's arm. "Thank you, James, I think I've got it now."

Emma, happening to look up at that moment, saw the contact between James and Clara. She quickly averted her gaze, her posture stiffening noticeably. More importantly, James caught the tail end of it. The causal factor hadn't been connected yet, but it was half-logged in his noggin now.

As they worked, Emma's voice drifted over from her glaze station, a gentle reminder of her presence. "Don't overdo it, James. We've got a long day ahead." Her voice carried a mix of concern and coolness that was another clue.

James looked up, offering a quick, if somewhat puzzled smile in Emma's direction before turning back to his students. "Right, Roberto, your turn on the roller. Remember, slow and steady. We want even pressure across the whole slab."

As Roberto began to turn the wheel, James continued his instruction. "This process, it's not just about making clay slabs. It's about creating a foundation. Every tile that comes out of this project starts right here, with what we're doing now."

He paused, looking at Clara and Roberto in turn. "You're not just interns here. You're craftsmen, artists in your own right. Every step of this process matters, and you're an integral part of it. Never forget that. Especially when your arms feel like they're about to fall off from all this rolling."

The interns nodded, their faces serious as they absorbed James's words. Guess they couldn't see the funny side...yet.

As the afternoon wore on, James began to notice Clara's increasing proximity and frequent glances. A slow realization dawned on him—dang it, she was flirting. When did that start? Had he done something to initiate that? Feeling a bit uncomfortable, he subtly increased the distance between them, making sure to give equal attention to both interns.

As the pile of finished slabs grew, James worked alongside the interns, his hands never idle, his voice a constant stream of encouragement and instruction. This was fun—creating, teaching, bringing old fashioned arts and crafts into the world one piece at a time, taking care now, to keep a professional distance... and even tone, too.

James stepped back, watching as Clara found her rhythm. She seemed to be doing all right now—he could have overreacted. It could be nothing. Probably was nothing. Just enthusiasm. But still. Better to draw the line clear and solid now, before...

Well—before anybody got any ideas.

James glanced at Clara, then at Emma—who looked away quickly before he could catch her eye. But he caught her. She'd been checking in on him.

Hmm... interesting, that. Very.

Towards the end of the session, he shifted focus from the training and gave Emma his undivided attention. He crossed his arms and observed her, absorbed in her own work. There was something slightly withdrawn in her demeanor—and yes, it was adding up.

An unbidden thought slipped into his mind, and it was this: *Was our Emma jealous?*

Was a wee blonde girl attempting to cross the line into Em's staked-out territory?

James cocked his head. *Could be. Could be.* It wasn't an aspect of her nature it would be wise to dwell on. Better to pretend he hadn't noticed—and maintain an aura of obtuseness. If that was a word.

But as he turned back to his work, a tiny smile played at the corners of his mouth. The day had been productive in more ways than one, and the rhythm of their shared work felt just a bit sweeter.

* * *

Emma squinted at the test tiles, comparing light sky blue mixed with sea green moss to aqua-blue mixed with medium forest green. The subtle differences were giving her a headache, or maybe that was just the fumes from the glaze.

She looked up, intending to check the actual sky for reference, and instead found herself eye-to-eye with James. He was standing right in front of her, arms crossed, considering her carefully.

"Oh god," Emma gasped, her hand flying to her chest. "You scared me. Don't sneak up on people like that."

James's lips quivered in a half-smile, he seemed merry enough, as if he had gotten the joke she missed. "I'm wearing my jogging shoes," he explained, tapping his foot lightly on the floor. "They're feather-light. I can walk right quiet when I want."

Emma's brow furrowed, unsure how to respond. "Okay well...I'm happy for you?" she offered, then asked, "what can I do for you?"

"Well, for starters, good morning," James said, his voice quiet but carrying an undercurrent of something that sounded vaguely like a test... or potential social reprimand. "Or good afternoon by now, I suppose."

She knew what he meant, Emma looked down, suddenly finding the grain of the wooden table fascinating. "Good morning," she murmured. After a beat, she added, "Looks like your training went well. Those two seem to be cranking out what we'll need." She paused, then rushed to explain, "I... I didn't want to interrupt your flow."

As Emma watched James's face, she saw his expression shift from pleasant to something closer to disappointment, tinged with a sadness that made her chest tighten. The light in his eyes dimmed, and Emma felt a pang of regret.

"What?" she asked, her voice barely above a whisper. "What is it?"

James's eyebrows rose, his voice tinged with disbelief. "That's why you've been ignoring me? That's your pitch? You know, Em it's okay to admit you misunderstood how I can handle the interns. The earth won't blow up."

Before Emma could formulate a response, James turned and walked away, leaving her staring after him.

What had she misunderstood? Was... this about Clara?

She had been careful not to interfere. Then why did it feel like she'd just made a clumsy gaffe? Had she implied that he lacked the ability to be in charge... or to train impressionable young minds?

She glanced at the test tiles, their carefully mixed colors suddenly seeming trivial in comparison to this *professional space* growing between her and James. With a sigh, she picked up her brush, determined to lose herself in her work.

But the nagging feeling that she'd been a coward at an important moment refused to leave her alone.

* * *

Chapter 14

Chicago — L Train Brown Line — *Jun. 19, 2002 — 3:20 p.m. — The Documentary*

The L train rumbled along the tracks, its rhythmic clatter a soothing backdrop to Emma's thoughts. She gazed out the window, watching as the Chicago skyline melted into a blur of brick buildings and leafy streets. The familiar route to her Lincoln Square apartment usually allowed her mind to wander, to process the day's events and plan for tomorrow. Today, however, her thoughts kept circling back to one persistent issue.

James.

Since the sweat lodge, he'd been different, that was number one. Not unkind, exactly, but distant. He would still play with her, with verbal sparring and fun one-upmanship and she'd get glimmers of how good it could be between them, they would come closer, actually enjoy and look forward to being with each other, but then some misunderstanding would happen or small grievance get blown up and back they would go to opposite sides of the room to cry in a respective corner. At least that's how she was feeling. Alone and frustrated.

So now, in a Herculean effort to keep the project running smoothly, James had become professional to a fault. Emma had even noticed a shift in how he interacted with the interns. That old flutter of silly worry in her stomach had quickly dissipated, replaced by a dull ache. He was professional with them... which meant he was equally professional with her.

It didn't matter that he was doing exactly what she'd expected him to do, and what he ought to do to keep the project on track, all it really did was highlight how much she wanted him.

Or rather, how she wanted her friend back, she had loved that first weekend at the Field Museum, when the wall between them had seemed to dissolve like the vapor it was.

Emma realized, with a start that made her seatmate glance over in concern, that she wanted James to be professional with the interns, but not with her. Despite her own confusing behavior and mixed signals that would baffle even the most skilled traffic cop. She could be honest about that, at least with herself. It really was an impossible standard they both had to meet, but there it was, sitting in her mind like a rhino in a cunning jumpsuit.

She was acting, at least in her mind, like a possessive woman and she really was not. She wasn't possessive, she was confused. Two totally different things. Right?

She smiled ruefully. Well, it was funny, in a 'laugh or you'll cry' sort of way.

It was as if James had erected an invisible wall between them, one that Emma couldn't quite figure out how to scale. She'd tried logic, emotion, and was seriously considering a grappling hook. She sighed, her breath fogging the window slightly. The project was going well, that was the important thing. She'd just have to find a way to adjust to this new 'normal', even if it felt about as comfortable as high heels on a tightrope.

Because here was the other thing, if she did manage to scale the wall or bring it down or otherwise-whatever and found herself face to face with James... what would she do then?

Who was she prepared to be with him?

And while she couldn't answer that question without his input, she could only admit that whatever it was between them now, felt stifled, suffocating on the vine and... not the way it should be.

* * *

As the train rattled on, Emma's eyes drifted to her fellow passengers, seeking distraction. A woman sat engrossed in a book, probably wishing she could crawl inside its pages and escape the mundane world of public transport. A man in a suit tapped away at his phone, his furrowed brow suggesting he was attempting to calculate Pi to the last decimal or read through the new service agreement of his phone contract. A group of students chatted excitedly, their enthusiasm for life not quelled by the crush of commutes and overpriced coffee.

And then, her gaze landed on a man she hadn't noticed before. Dark hair, gray eyes partially hidden behind stylish glasses that probably cost more than Emma's monthly rent. He was fiddling with a sleek video camera, his brow furrowed in concentration as if the grand reveal of Pluto's planetary status was officially revealed in its viewfinder. Planet or dwarf planet? Emma almost leaned forward to take a look for herself.

Suddenly, as if feeling her gaze, he looked up. Their eyes met, and he offered a friendly smile, Emma felt herself smiling back, almost involuntarily.

"Heading to Belmont?" he asked, his voice carrying easily over the train's cacophony of squeals and groans.

Emma nodded, "Yes, in that direction. You too?"

"Yes, that's me." he replied, his smile widening to reveal teeth so perfect, Emma half-expected to see a toothpaste product placement stitched onto his jacket. He seemed a pleasant enough young man, perhaps around twenty six years old or so.

She nodded back, finding herself intrigued despite her usual reserve with strangers.

Sam's brows pulled together in concentration, "Do I know you? You look familiar or remind me—wait, wait just one minute, maybe two."

He pulled open the Chicago Reader and peeled back a few pages and then: "Ah. Yes, see?"

He got up from his seat, crossed to where she was sitting and without so much as a 'by your leave' plunked down in the empty seat beside her. He opened the paper and there, in grainy black and white image, was Emma herself, helping a Hispanic girl and her mom carve a clay tile.

"That's you or I'll eat my camera bag." The man challenged, as if offering to consume expensive electronics was a normal way to complete a thought.

Emma chuckled, partly from amusement and partly from the sheer absurdity of the situation. "Yeah, that's me, Rhonda must be hard at work getting the news into every corner of Chicago… yes, that's our project."

"Emma Hawkins on that massive mosaic project? The man insisted she claim it all, feathers, froo-ha-ha and all.

"Well, me and thousands of others." Emma's voice was dry. "So you've heard of it?"

"Heard of it?" The man chuckled, and mused, "this has to be kismet, or synchronicity or whatever but yeah, I'm a documentary videographer, he added, gesturing to his camera, like it was a newborn… goat, it was a little too large for kitten and too impersonal for a baby, so yes, baby goat, it was.

"Well, just starting out, really," He explained, " but I've got a great Sony prosumer camera and I've got a good feeling about your project. I'm Sam, by the way, Sam Petosky."

As the train pulled into the Belmont station, Emma found herself caught between curiosity and caution. "Hello Sam, I'm Emma..."

"Yeah you are." Sam confirmed happily. "Congratulations!"

She laughed, thought for a moment, "That's... interesting, she said carefully. But we're not really set up for taping..."

Sam's face fell slightly, but he rallied quicker than Tom Brady at three and ten. "No pressure, of course. But hey, why don't we grab a coffee? I'd love to hear more about the project, even if taping it isn't on the table. There's a great place just off the station—Leona's. What do you say? Lunch is on me, a working lunch."

Emma hesitated for a moment. James's face flashed in her mind, his distant professionalism a stark contrast to Sam's open friendliness. Maybe a bit of outside perspective wouldn't be such a bad thing.

"You know what?" she said, surprising herself. "Why not? Lead the way, Sam."

As they exited the train together, Emma felt a small thrill of excitement. This unexpected encounter might just be the breath of fresh air she needed. And who knew? Maybe Sam's documentary idea wasn't so far-fetched after all.

* * *

The bustle of Belmont Avenue enveloped them as they made their way to Leona's. The late afternoon sun cast long shadows, but still provided enough light to energize Emma's steps as she embraced this unexpected break from her routine. She found herself relaxing, drawn into easy conversation with Sam about his background in theatre and his transition to videography.

"So," Sam said as they settled into a cozy booth at Leona's, "tell me more about this mosaic project. It sounds unique, like a once in a lifetime event."

Emma took a sip of her coffee, savoring the rich flavor as she gathered her thoughts. "Well, it's a community-driven piece. We're inviting people from all walks of life to create tiles that represent their experiences, their hopes, their connection to Chicago and more importantly to address the question, how do you want to live your life?"

Sam leaned forward, his eyes alight with interest. "That resonates with me, I like that. The stories you must be hearing..."

"Oh, you have no idea," Emma laughed, warming up to her topic. "There's this one woman who made a tile depicting her journey from Poland to Chicago. The detail she put into it, she used the symbol of winding road with touchpoints and all on a five by five round clay tile. People do amazing things when motivated. I will never forget these tiles, I'll always have them in my mind."

As Emma continued to share anecdotes from the project, she found herself relaxing and enjoying the conversation. Sam's enthusiasm was infectious, and he had a habit of pushing his glasses up higher on his nose when she made a particularly interesting point. Her earlier melancholy faded into the background.

"Tell me about some of the other tiles," Sam prompted. "What's been the most surprising one you've seen?"

Emma's eyes lit up. "Oh, there was this little boy, couldn't have been more than seven. He created this intricate design of a city skyline, but instead of buildings, it was made up of books. When

I asked him about it, he said it was his dream for Chicago—a city built with time to read."

Sam whistled, impressed. "That's profound for a seven-year-old."

"Exactly," Emma nodded. "That's what makes this project so special. It's not just about art, it's about hopes and dreams and the human spirit."

"You know," Sam said thoughtfully, "I really think this would make an amazing documentary. I'm sorry but I'm going to push a little more. The process, the people, the final reveal... it's a videographer's dream."

Emma bit her lip, considering. "It does sound compelling when you put it that way. But I'd have to discuss it with the team, especially James. He's... particular about how the project is presented. This is really his brainchild."

Sam nodded understandingly. "Wow, I'd love to meet him, but of course, of course. No pressure, I take the pressure back... but, if you're interested, I'd love to at least show you some previous work. My roommate could bring over a tape of a doc I just finished, I don't live far from here and he'll bring it over. How does that sound? It'll be here before we finish our ravioli."

Emma glanced at her watch, surprised to find that over an hour had passed. She should be heading home, and should be focusing on tomorrow's tasks. But something about Sam's enthusiasm, his genuine interest in the project, made her hesitate.

"You know what? Why not," she found herself saying. "I'd love to see your work."

As Sam called his roommate, Emma felt a mix of excitement and trepidation. This wasn't how she'd expected her evening to go, but maybe that was a good thing. After all, the mosaic project was all about embracing unexpected connections, wasn't it?

"So, while we wait," Emma said, "tell me about your theatre background. How did that lead you to documentary filmmaking?"

Sam's face lit up. "Oh, that's a story. It all started with a disastrous production of 'Waiting for Godot' where the lead actor actually did wait... in the wrong theatre."

"No, you're putting me on–"

"Only a little, the lead, whose name I will never mention, was so blind drunk he gave the cab driver the address of the previous show he'd done, so he ended up at the wrong theatre. So he walks on set, sans costume, to a production of 'The Rainmaker' quite a different kind of play you know, deaf, dumb and blind to where he is and begins his opening scene, but he was so good, none of the actors wanted to stop him—stage manager had to shut it down."

"Stop it, no, and you were on stage? NO! You were the lead?" Emma asked.

"No, no to both—too bad, that would have been even more fun—no, I was in the audience, but I had a wake up, this 'real life' episode as accidental art was more honest and true and closer to what I wanted than any play. I laughed for three days solid, no kidding, I was worried about my gizzard. Jostled it so much."

As Sam launched further into his tale, Emma found herself genuinely laughing for the first time in days. Little did she know that this chance encounter on the L, this impromptu coffee at Leona's, would set in motion events that would shape not just the documentary, but the entire trajectory of the mosaic project.

* * *

The soft glow of Emma's desk lamp cast long shadows across her small apartment. Outside, the Chicago night hummed with distant traffic and the occasional rattle of the L train. Emma sat cross-legged on her worn leather couch, her eyes fixed on the television screen before her, where Sam's documentary played out its final moments.

As the credits began to roll, Emma realized she'd been holding her breath. She exhaled slowly, feeling a mix of emotions wash over her. Sam's work was raw, undoubtedly, but there was something undeniably powerful about it. The documentary wasn't just a straightforward narrative; it was a patchwork of moments, each one a small revelation. The way he'd captured those everyday moments, transforming them into something profound and moving, it was unlike anything she'd seen before

Sam had asked his friends to recall moments when they had over reacted negatively to something, instances they could now look back on and laugh about. But he hadn't stopped there. In a stroke of brilliance, he'd revisited the scenes of these events, creating a visual counterpoint to the stories. The juxtaposition of present-day calm with remembered chaos was striking, almost poetic.

Emma reached for the remote, pausing on a frame that showed a young woman laughing, her eyes bright with a joy that seemed to leap off the screen. Behind her, a busy street corner where she'd once had a meltdown over a missed bus now seemed peaceful, almost mundane. The contrast was beautiful. This was what art was supposed to do, wasn't it? Revisit reality, honor truth.

"James would absolutely love this." Emma murmured to herself. Despite their recent professional distance, she knew his artistic soul would appreciate the unconventional approach, the way Sam had turned everyday moments into something profound.

Before she could second-guess herself, Emma reached for her phone. Her fingers hovered over the keypad for a moment before she punched in the numbers Sam had scrawled on a napkin at Leona's.

The phone rang once, twice. On the third ring, Sam's voice came through, a mix of surprise and pleasure evident in his tone. Hello?

"Sam? It's Emma. Emma Hawkins."

"Emma, I wasn't expecting to hear from you so soon. Did you get a chance to watch the doc?"

Emma smiled, despite herself. "I did, actually. Just finished it."

There was a pause on the other end of the line. When Sam spoke again, his voice was softer, almost hesitant. "And… what did you think?"

Emma took a deep breath. "I loved it, Sam. It was beautiful. The way you juxtaposed those past moments with the present was inspired. And that last story, the one about the missed proposal? I'll admit, it made me cry. Happy tears, though. It's raw, yes, but so honest, it's exactly what our project needs."

She could almost hear Sam's grin through the phone. "Really? I'm so glad you connected with it. I was worried it might be too experimental."

"No, not at all," Emma assured him. "If anything, that's what makes it special. It's exactly the kind of fresh perspective our project needs."

"You mean…"

"Yes,' Emma said, surprising herself with the firmness in her voice. "I haven't spoken with James yet, but I think he'd appreciate your approach. He's always pushing for new ways to look at art and life, but since there will be no charge, right?"

"Right, of course," Sam quickly assured her. "This is about the art, the stories. I'd be honored just to be part of it. All pro bono or bust."

Emma felt more than a little relief, "Then I'd love to have you onboard. Do you have a pencil handy? I'll give you our schedule."

As Emma rattled off dates and locations, she found herself opening up more than she had in weeks. "You have two weekends left to shoot the carving of the tiles at the Field Museum, " she explained. And I'll give you the locations of our working office area, where we cut the clay, dry and clean the tiles for first firing, the Lill Street studio for the Monster kiln firing, and of course the large working loft where it will be assembled for design when that's available, lots of other details, but you'll see. You know, James has this way of seeing connections that others miss. I think he'd be fascinated by how you linked past and present in your documentary."

"He sounds like an interesting guy," Sam said. "I'd appreciate meeting him."

"He is, but he can be intense sometimes, just letting you know up-front." Emma clarified.

"Got it," Sam said, the excitement evident in his voice. "Emma, this is... thank you. This is going to be great."

They chatted for a few more minutes, the conversation flowing easily from project logistics to artistic philosophies. It felt good.

As she hung up the phone, Emma felt a mix of exhilaration and nerves. She'd made a command decision, one that could change the course of the project. James might not be happy at first, but she was confident he'd see the value once he watched Sam's work.

She glanced back at the frozen frame on her TV, at the joy captured in that single moment. This was bigger than her, bigger than James. This was about preserving the spirit of what they were creating, about finding new ways to tell the mosaic's story.

"Welcome aboard, Sam," she murmured to herself, a smile playing at her lips. Whatever came next, she knew she'd made the right choice. The mosaic project was about to take on a whole new dimension. She couldn't wait to share this with James, to see his eyes light up with a new toy to play with. The mosaic project was evolving, and that was good, right?

* * *

Chapter 15

Chicago — Outside Field Museum — *Jun. 22, 2002 — 8:35 a.m. —*
Synergy

The early morning sun cast long shadows across the Field
Museum grounds as Emma arrived, her arms laden with
supplies for the day ahead. The familiar sight of the white tents
and the bustle of interns setting up brought a smile to her face.
But today was different. Today, Sam will be joining them.

As if summoned by her thoughts, Sam appeared, his Sony
DCR-VX2000 cradled in his arms like well, the aforementioned
baby goat. He was fiddling with the flip-out screen, his brow
furrowed in concentration.

'Wowsa," Clara's voice drifted over from nearby.

"Double wowsa," Jasmine echoed, her eyes wide as she took in
Sam's tall frame, focused expression, and well, let's face it, movie
star good looks.

Emma felt a tap on her shoulder and turned to find Jasmine
leaning in close. "Psst, hey Emma, come here," she whispered,
her voice barely audible. "I don't want him to hear me. How
come you didn't tell us the videographer is a double yumm?"

Emma glanced back at Sam, who was now attaching a
microphone to his camera. "Is he? Well, he did have cute glasses.
He's not wearing them now."

"Oh, well that explains it," Clara chimed in, her tone as dry as the Arizona heat.

"Ladies," Emma chided gently, trying to keep a straight face, "let's try to maintain some semblance of professional decorum, shall we?"

Jasmine grinned unrepentantly. "Oh, come on, Emma. You can't tell me you haven't noticed. He's like a walking Greek statue!"

"Musta' skipped that particular art history class." Emma ventured, still amused.

"Oh don't mind her, she's set her cap for James." Jasmine observed.

"Her cap? What is this, 1885?" Bette asked.

Emma's eyebrows shot up but before she could confirm or deny, she caught sight of James striding towards them, his face unreadable. Her stomach clenched involuntarily. Despite his initial acceptance of Sam's involvement, she still worried about how he'd react to the reality of a camera documenting their process.

To her surprise, James's face broke into a genuine smile as he approached Sam. "So, you must be our documentarian," he said, extending a hand. "James Watson. Welcome aboard."

Sam looked up, a grin spreading across his face. "James It's great to meet you. I can't tell you how excited I am to be here."

As the two men fell into easy conversation, Emma felt a weight lift from her shoulders. She'd been so worried about James's reaction, imagining scenarios where he bristled at Sam's presence or resented her decision. But here he was, animated and engaged, pointing out different areas of the setup to Sam with evident enthusiasm.

Emma shook her head, marveling at her own misconceptions. When had she started thinking of James as mercurial? He'd always been passionate, yes, but not unpredictable. It was this new, all-business approach with her that had thrown her off balance. A side of him she'd never seen before.

It was an interesting visual image of contrast and similarity, they both were of a like height, charismatic, with that inner light leaking out, but where James had defined cheekbones, a hawk like profile and keen expression, Sam's visage was more pliant, more poetic perhaps, They both had brown hair, but where Sam's was dark, almost brunet, James's shade of brown had lightened and been burnt brighter by the summer sun.

As she watched James and Sam discuss camera angles and lighting, Emma felt a familiar warmth in her chest. This was the James she knew—open, creative, always eager to explore new perspectives. As she watched the two men get to know each other A.K.A. sizing each other up, she turned and saw that Clara, Jasmine and the new one, Bette were standing beside her also looking in the men's direction.

At Emma's inquiring expression, Clara shrugged and asked "Emma, hon, what were you thinking? With that kind of double distraction, we're not going to get anything done."

Emma looked incredulous, "What? Modern gals like you? Chin up, soldier on, take one for the team—"

"—Would love to." Slipped in Bette

"Shhh, they'll hear you" Jasmine hushed her fellow interns. "Professional."

Bette giggled, then quickly composed herself. "Sorry, Emma. It's just... well, it's not every day we get to work with such... inspiring individuals."

Emma rolled her eyes, but couldn't help the small smile that tugged at her lips. "Inspiring, huh? Well, let's see if you find clay cutting and mixing clay slip as inspiring. Come on, ladies, we've got work to do."

Before they could wander any further down that sidetrack, James sounded the morning trumpet.

"Alright, everyone," James called out, his voice carrying across the grounds. "Let's get started. We got tiles to cut, tools to sort, stories to encourage, Val's put plenty of water in the cooler and she'll be coming by for your lunch order, have fun, work up an appetite, lunch is on me."

James nodded to Emma... and she winked at him, well, that was new, that sparked his attention. He smiled, shook his head slightly, took a second look over his shoulder at her, his expression puzzled, then grinned as they moved in tandem to their respective stations.

As the first participants began to arrive, Emma caught Sam's eye. He gave her a thumbs up, already blending into the background as he began to film. This second Saturday was beginning very well, indeed, the word was getting out now, so they were expecting a crush of folks, and indeed there was already a line forming along the low stone wall in front of the two tents. Thank goodness Val had thought to place additional chairs.

Good on her, what a gal-Friday; Emma would have to put aside some time and get to know her better. But not right now, they were busy as all-get-out.

* * *

The day unfolded like a flower in time-lapse, each moment a petal unfurling to reveal new colors, new textures. Sam moved through the space with the grace of a dancer, his camera an extension of his being. He'd started slowly, feeling out the rhythm of the place, the ebb and flow of creativity that pulsed through the air like a heartbeat.

A young woman with pale blond hair caught his eye. She was bent over her tile, her tongue poking out slightly in concentration as she carved intricate swirls into the clay. Sam approached, his footsteps soft on the grass.

"That's some camera you've got there," she said, looking up with a grin. "Planning on making us famous?"

Sam laughed, a warm, rich sound that seemed to put everyone at ease. It was the kind of laugh that made you want to share secrets over coffee—he seemed to put everyone at ease. Sam adjusted the strap of his camera, the familiar weight a comfort against his chest. "Well, that depends. Got any hidden talents you want to share with the world?"

The woman held up her tile, a complex pattern of waves and stars emerging from the clay. The afternoon sun caught the damp surface, making it gleam like a precious gem. "Does this count?"

"It absolutely does," Sam said, his eyes lighting up. He crouched down, bringing himself to eye level with the tile. "Mind if I ask you about it? Did you come here today with this idea in mind, or is it just coming alive in your hands?"

The woman's face softened, her eyes taking on a faraway look. "You know, it's the strangest thing. I came here thinking I'd make something for my mom—she loves the lake, you see. But as soon as I started working, it was like the clay had its own ideas."

Sam nodded encouragingly, his camera capturing the play of emotions across her face. "Tell me more about that. What do you think the clay is trying to say?"

As the woman began to speak, her words flowing as freely, spontaneous but without hesitation, Emma watched from across the tent. There was something almost magical about the way Sam drew people out, how he made them forget about the camera and simply...be.

James appeared at elbow, his voice low. "He's good, isn't he?" a mix of admiration and amusement playing across his face.

Emma nodded, a smile tugging at her lips. "He really is. Look at how relaxed everyone is around him." She gestured towards the tables, where people were laughing and chatting as they worked, any earlier nervousness completely forgotten.

Indeed, as Sam moved from table to table, the initial curiosity about the camera gave way to genuine engagement. People began to open up, sharing stories about their tiles, their lives, their connection to the community. The tent buzzed with conversation, punctuated by the occasional scrape of a carving tool or burst of laughter.

"Did you come here planning to carve your life story, or is that just what happened when you picked up the tools?" Sam asked an elderly man, his eyes twinkling with mirth.

The man burst out laughing, his wrinkled face creasing with joy. "Son, I came here planning to make a nice, simple flower for my granddaughter. But somehow, I've ended up with the entire family tree." He held up his tile, which indeed seemed to be sprouting branches and leaves in all directions.

Laughter rippled through the nearby tables, the sound mingling with the scrape of carving tools and the soft murmur of conversation. It was a symphony of creation, and Sam was conducting it masterfully.

As the day wore on, Emma found herself drawn more and more into Sam's orbit. She watched as he captured not just the finished tiles, but the process itself—the hesitation before the first cut, the moment of inspiration that lit up a face, the quiet pride as a participant held up their completed work.

"This is more than just documentation," James murmured, once again appearing at Emma's side. He ran a hand through his hair, leaving it slightly mussed. "He's becoming part of the art itself."

Emma pursed her lips, considering, "Well, I guess that makes sense, he told me he had a background in the theater."

James nodded at that, a mischievous glint in his eye. "Interesting, an old skill blending with a new one maybe. Looks like he'll do okay as long as he remembers where he is and doesn't start swinging from the sashes."

"Doesn't seem likely," Emma deadpanned, fighting a smile. "I don't think they'll hold his weight, but I'll keep an eye on him—"

"—Not too close an eye..." James remarked, his tone unreadable. Before Emma could decipher his meaning, Alberto's voice rang out, summoning James away.

Emma watched him go, mulling over his parting words. What in the world did that mean? She'd made an impulsive decision to bring Sam on board, a risk that could have upset the group dynamic. But it was working out beautifully.

She felt proud that Sam was demonstrating not only a videographer's technical skills but also a keen awareness of who he could joke with and who required a quiet space to create.

It was sometime well past high noon when Sam finally lowered his camera. His face was flushed with excitement, his eyes bright. He looked around the tent, taking in the scene of creative chaos with a sense of wonder. He walked to stand beside Emma, looked around the area and then turned is attention to her.

"This is incredible," he said, his voice filled with awe. "The stories these people are telling, the way they're pouring their hearts into these tiles... it's not general, not an emotional wash, these are specific reasons, and stories and intent is powerful."

"Welcome to the winding road," James said as he approached the pair and then to Sam he offered, "Did you get some lunch when we ordered? I got a feeling you worked straight through most of the day."

"I didn't want to miss anything." Sam confessed.

"Wait a second Sam..." James turned and called out to his ever-ready rock 'em sock 'em assistant, "Hey Val!" and then back to Sam, "Sam, I think Val put some sandwiches in the cooler."

James turned, spotted Val and waved her over, she started over on a quick trot but slowed down to a full stop when she got a good look at Sam Petosky.

"Val... are there sandwiches left?" James asked and then as he walked by his assistant he advised in sotto voce, "Val... your mouth is hanging open."

Val closed her mouth, swallowed and finally asked, "So... would you like ham and cheese on a submarine... ah bun, or maybe... chicken?" Val asked, her voice... was soft now and was that actually a *sweet* tone?

Emma observed the exchange from afar. Sam was watching a replay on the camera viewer screen, so he didn't respond right away, but then looked up and said "Oh... uh... ham and cheese would be great thanks."

When Val didn't leave right away, Sam looked at her and she stammered "It's okay, coz I put the sandwiches in a cooler, not a cheap cooler, a good cooler, so you know... we don't get food poisoning of something... coz... ah, that's my job."

"Sam looked puzzled, "Not to poison people?"

"Yeah... well, I better go." And with that Val spun on her heel and went for said sandwich and a seltzer.

Oh boy, Emma thought. "Uh oh..." Was Sam really that good-looking? Good enough to turn Val's knees to jelly and her usual razor-sharp wit to mush? Emma felt a pang of sympathy for Val, who was brilliant, steadfast, sharp as an exacto blade and funny as a stand-up comic... but not pretty in the conventional sense. Her mind was a masterpiece, but how many men would take the time to appreciate that particular work of art?

Emma shook her head, determined to pretend she hadn't witnessed Val's momentary meltdown. It was like watching a usually unflappable chess master suddenly forget the dimensional function of the Knight. It wasn't her business. Still, she couldn't help but wonder if she'd inadvertently introduced a new dynamic to their carefully balanced team. Only time would tell if the resulting changes would be positive... or something a bit more complicated.

Sam was going to break for the day soon, anyway, he'd already told Emma his camera battery and the backup were just about drained. His plan was to run his car engine and recharge a battery via a portable AC/DC charger hooked to the cigarette lighter. He had planned ahead, but still, as everyone knew, crap happens.

Emma watched Sam methodically packing his gear, each movement precise and economical. The click of camera cases closing punctuated the ambient hum of creativity filling the tent. She made a mental note to ask him about his battery setup later—in this heat, every bit of technical knowledge could be the difference between success and a day's work lost.

She had other things to worry about, the heat for one. The tent provided excellent shelter from direct sunlight, but she found herself going around to the tables to advise folks that they could dampen the clay with water as they worked to keep it pliant. The air under the canopy was thick with the earthy scent of clay and the collective breath of concentration.

"Just a touch of water," Emma reminded a young woman whose brow was furrowed in frustration. "It'll bring the clay right back to life." The woman's face relaxed, her fingers once again moving confidently across her tile's surface.

James had gone to get more clay slabs. They had seen pretty early that they might run out and would have to rotate the completed clay tiles out of the shed with the fresh clay slabs and then transport the finished tiles to the converted office studio to lay out and dry properly. Emma glanced at her watch, a knot of worry tightening in her stomach. He should have been back by now.

And there were still hours left in the day. Hours. A lot of *bad* can happen in the hours and hours stretching ahead, there is always the possibility of disasters and triumphs in equal measure. Emma could feel the weight of responsibility pressing down on her shoulders, no kidding, she was getting a stiff neck indeed. She rolled her head, trying to ease the tension, but the knot of worry remained stubbornly in place.

All their plans could still work, there was no reason to dwell on potential negative outcomes... unless some people didn't come through as they were supposed to. She knew, plans got broken by unexpected water pipes bursting in your face that no one saw coming. Emma's eyes darted to the corner of the tent where the water main was located, half-expecting to see a telltale puddle forming.

Or in this case, perhaps a sudden downpour, or a clay slab dropped and shattered on the unforgiving ground. Emma's imagination conjured the sound of clay meeting concrete, a sickening thud followed by the tinkling of shards. And nowhere to protect the finished tiles because they had run out of space in the shed and just where was James with the van?

She found herself glancing at her watch again, then towards the entrance of the tent. The absence of James and the van was becoming more noticeable with each passing minute. Emma tried to focus on the participants still working diligently at their tables, but her mind kept wandering to worst-case scenarios. The day wasn't over yet, and there was still so much that could go wrong.

* * *

The sun beat down mercilessly on the Field Museum grounds, the heat shimmering in waves off the pavement. Emma wiped her brow, her shirt sticking uncomfortably to her back. She'd been rotating between the tents and the shed all morning, checking on the drying tiles, fretting over their condition in this oppressive heat. The air was thick, heavy with the scent of baking clay and rising tension.

Gerardo approached, concern etched on his face. "Emma, we're out of room in the shed. What should we do with these new tiles?" His voice carried a hint of urgency that matched the quickening of Emma's pulse.

Emma looked to the clay cutting stations, where people had brought their completed work back to the long tables. The tiles were transferred to plywood planks, bricks placed carefully in the corners to prevent crushing. But the stacks themselves were growing...higher and higher. A precarious tower of creativity and potential disaster.

Emma bit her lip, considering their options. "Maybe we should rotate the trays? Take some from the shed and switch them with the ones starting to bake in the sun." The words sounded hollow even to her own ears, a desperate grasping at straws.

Gerardo shook his head. "No, waste of energy. James should be here any minute with the van." The doubt in his voice belied his attempt at reassurance.

Emma nodded, her eyes scanning the rows of clay creations. "I know. But he should have been back with fresh slabs an hour ago." She glanced at her watch, frowning. "No, make that two hours ago. I forgot my phone at home, did you ever get one?"

"No... not yet," Gerardo admitted. "Should I run out and get some tarps or something? We can double layer shelter over the tiles on the tables, over the stacks." The doubt in his voice was clear, a mirror of Emma's own uncertainty.

Emma considered the weight of the decision pressing down on her. "That would definitely help, but where's the nearest hardware store? Ace over on Clark? In this Saturday traffic it could mean almost an hour before you get back." She bit her lip again, tasting the metallic tang of worry.

"Let's give him another fifteen minutes. If he's not back, we'll have to figure something out. Maybe there's something the Field Museum can give us, even big trash bags would help."

"Okay, fifteen minutes and I'll go ask," Gerardo offered. "We promised the Field Museum not to be a problem, but this isn't a big ask." Emma nodded, grateful for his initiative.

The minutes ticked by, agonizingly slow. Emma found herself touching the edges of the drying clay tiles, fretting over their condition. She had a strategy to save every tile if one broke during drying or firing—but why create more trouble? Each second felt like a small eternity, filled with the potential for disaster.

Just as Gerardo was about to go for help—and Emma was nearly ready to take the shirt off her back to give the stacks extra cover—the familiar rumble of the van's engine cut through the air. Relief washed over her, quickly followed by a wave of irritation as she saw James pull up to the side entrance, laughing and smiling with a very cheerful Clara.

Well, if that didn't beat all.

Emma felt her jaw clench, a mix of emotions swirling in her chest—relief, anger, and a spark that ignited a storehouse of dry kindling in her secret stash of emotions.

Without thinking, she strode toward them, her face set in a tight, tight mask—stretched just far enough to flatten her features. She was dangerously close to demanding *Where have you been?* but before she could speak, James held up a hand, reading her mood with clinical precision.

"Wait now, wait..." he said, his voice low, a yellow-light warning. The words hung in the air between them, a fragile barrier against the storm brewing in Emma's eyes.

"Don't tell me to calm down," she snapped, the heat and stress of the day boiling over. Her words crackled with tension, sharp enough to cut.

"I didn't say that," James replied carefully, his jaw tightening. The muscle in his cheek twitched—a silent testament to his own fraying nerves.

Clara, picking up on the obvious, quickly excused herself and hurried off to find Gerardo to run interference. This situation was way over her pay grade. Her blonde hair bounced as she retreated, a flash of sunlight against the gathering clouds of conflict.

Emma took a deep breath, trying to modulate her tone. The air felt thick in her lungs, heavy with unspoken accusations. "We've got trays and trays of tiles getting baked in the sun. They should have been moved an hour ago. We needed that van."

James looked down, his voice barely above a whisper. "I see. All about the business. All about your work. All about you."

The words fell like stones between them, each one widening the chasm.

The coolness in his tone caught Emma off guard. She opened her mouth to retort, but James had already turned and was walking briskly toward the tents without another word. His retreating back was a wall—impenetrable and unyielding.

Emma stood there, stunned, as Gerardo approached cautiously. "Em," he said gently, "Clara just told me what happened. They nearly got hit head-on. James had to pull onto the sidewalk to avoid it. Clara's still shaking. Val had put a medkit in the van, so James stayed until emergency services arrived—to talk to the police."

The blood drained from Emma's face as the implications sank in. "Oh God," she murmured, her earlier frustration evaporating. "Oh my God..." The world seemed to tilt to twirl, to shift beneath her feet.

She found James by the van, pulling out the cool slabs and placing them on the pavement to make room for the finished trays. His movements were sharp and agitated as he began loading tiles into the vehicle.

Emma approached slowly, each footfall a tentative tap on the sidewalk, as if James were a wounded animal she didn't want to startle. "James," she began, her voice soft. "I'm so sorry. I didn't know—"

He cut her off, eyes not meeting hers. "It's fine, Emma. Let's just get these tiles moved, yeah?" His words were clipped, each one a small barrier erected between them.

Emma nodded, words failing her. They worked in silence, the tension between them palpable.

As they loaded the last of the tiles into the van, Emma tried again, her voice barely above a whisper. "James, please. Can we talk about this?"

He paused, his hand on the van door. For a moment, Emma thought he might refuse. Then, slowly, he turned to face her. The look in his eyes made her heart hurt.

"What's there to talk about?" he asked, his voice tired. "You made your priorities clear. The work comes first. Always has, hasn't it?"

The hurt in his eyes landed like a blow. Emma reached out, her hand stopping just short of his arm. "That's not fair," she said softly. "You know how much this project means to me. To both of us."

James sighed, running a hand through his hair. "Do I? Well... there's dedication... and there's *driven*. And you do the driving, *all* the time."

"I don't... that's not fair..." Emma finally managed, but her voice had no power. No get-up and gotcha. The words felt hollow—even to her own ears.

"Isn't it? Have you even checked if Clara is okay? Asked after her? She was on the passenger side, you know. Would've gotten it square on. Never mind. It's useless talking to you when you're like this."

They stood there, the afternoon sun casting long shadows around them. The unspoken words were useless weapons—it all felt pointless.

Moot medieval clubs in the atomic age.

Without another word, James climbed into the van, leaving Emma standing on the pavement, staring after him. The slam of the van door echoed in the space between them—a final punctuation to a conversation left to drift out to open sea, for the waves to toss... and the sharks to snack.

* * *

Chapter 16

Chicago — Outside Field Museum — *Jun. 23, 2002* — *10:26 a.m.* — *Personal Conflicts*

The late morning sun glinted off the bronze lions guarding the Field Museum's entrance. James stood at the main tent, his eyes scanning the approaching crowd. In the distance, he spotted Sam, his Sony DCR-VX2000 raised as he captured B-roll shots of the museum's Beaux-Arts facade.

James's attention was drawn to a familiar shock of red hair bobbing through the crowd. Ted and Maribel approached, their daughters Theodora and Minnie skipping ahead, their excitement obvious and electrifying the air.

"Uncle James!" The girls' shrieks pierced the air as they raced towards him, a burst of energy in the already bustling scene.

James knelt down, arms open wide. "Hello, my little roses," he laughed, the scent of sunscreen and cotton candy enveloping him as the girls crashed into his embrace.

As Ted and Maribel reached them, Maribel's eyes searched the area. "Where's Emma?" she asked, shielding her eyes from the sun, her voice carrying a hint of concern.

James straightened up, his smile faltering slightly. His gaze swept the grounds, finally landing on a familiar figure. Emma stood near a cluster of oak trees, engaged in conversation with Sam. She was pointing toward a group of people gathered around a picnic table; her face lit with enthusiasm as Sam nodded, listening intently, occasionally adjusting his camera.

"Oh, she's over there," James said, his voice carefully neutral, though a muscle in his jaw twitched almost imperceptibly. "Probably discussing some documentary details with Sam."

Maribel and Ted exchanged a quick glance, picking up on the undercurrent in James's tone. There were obvious questions front and center but nothing they wanted to broach at the moment.

As James led them through the tent, the air thick with the earthy scent of clay, Ted couldn't help but notice the stiffness in his friend's posture. It only seemed to increase each time James's gaze drifted to where Emma and Sam were now interviewing one of the interns, their heads close together as they reviewed something on the camera's flip-out screen.

"So, how's it been going?" Ted asked casually as the girls ran ahead to examine a table full of carving tools. "Working with Emma again, I mean."

James's hand paused mid-gesture, hovering over a particularly intricate tile. "It's... fine, he said after a moment, each word measured and deliberate. "We're professionals, after all."

Just then, Emma looked up, finally noticing the new arrivals. Her eyes lit up at the sight of Maribel and the girls, but when her gaze met James's, there was a flicker of something—guilt? Uncertainty? Before she quickly looked away from him. She focused her attention on her old friends that just arrived.

"Maribel! Ted!" Emma called out, her voice carrying over the hum of conversation in the tent. "I'm so glad you could make it."

As the women embraced, Maribel shot a questioning look at Ted over Emma's shoulder. Ted gave a small shrug in response, his eyes darting meaningfully towards handsome Sam, who was now filming some of the tile-making process nearby.

* * *

The next hour passed in a flurry of activity. The rhythmic scrape of carving tools mingled with laughter and excited chatter as Ted, Maribel, and the girls set about creating their tiles. James and Emma moved around the tent, offering guidance and encouragement, but always seeming to orbit on opposite sides of the space, like planets with misaligned gravitational pulls.

Sam weaved through the crowd, his camera capturing the creative process. He was careful not to film Ted and Maribel's family directly, instead focusing on the interns and the general atmosphere. His presence, however, was a constant reminder of the project's growing scope, and of the unspoken tension between James and Emma.

Theodora, her tongue poking out in concentration, looked up from her tile. "Uncle James, can you help me make this flower prettier?"

James knelt beside her, his voice softening as he guided her small hands. "That's it, petal. Nice and gentle with the carving tool." For a moment, the world narrowed to just this interaction, a brief respite from the underlying strain.

Across the table, Emma was showing Minnie how to create texture using a piece of lace. The little girl giggled as she pressed the delicate pattern into the clay, leaving behind a perfect imprint of flowers and swirls.

For a moment, as James and Emma's eyes met over the children's heads, there was a flash of their old connection. But just as quickly, it was gone, replaced by the now-familiar tension.

Emma's gaze drifted to Sam, who was filming nearby, and James, witnessing the exchange, felt a tightness in his chest that said, 'hell no.'

As the girls became engrossed in their work, Ted pulled James aside while Maribel engaged Emma in conversation. Sam, noticing the pairs breaking off, discreetly moved his filming to a different area of the tent, focusing on a group of students creating a collaborative tile.

"Alright, spill it," Ted said, his voice low as they stood near a table of glazing samples. "What's going on with you two? And who's the blockbuster bloke with the camera?"

James sighed, running a hand through his hair. "It's nothing, Ted. Just… professional differences. And that's Sam, the documentary videographer Emma brought on board."

Ted snorted. "Bollocks. I've seen you two have 'professional differences' before. This is something else, and Emma brought him on? Without consulting you?"

Across the tent, Maribel was having a similar conversation with Emma.

"Em, honey," Maribel said gently, helping Minnie clean clay off her hands, "last time we saw you, things seemed to be going so well between you and James. What happened? And how does this new guy fit in?"

Emma's shoulders slumped slightly. "I don't know, Bel. It's like… we've forgotten how to talk to each other. And Sam… he's here to document the project. It was my idea to bring him in, but James… he's been… on and off… and we had words yesterday."

Mirabel raised one eyebrow. "Must have been some words."

* * *

As the day wound down and the girls proudly displayed their finished tiles, the tension between James and Emma had become impossible to ignore. Even Theodora, perceptive beyond her years, tugged on her mother's sleeve as they packed up their belongings.

"Mommy," she whispered, her eyes wide, "why are Uncle James and Aunt Emma sad?"

Maribel's heart clenched at the innocence of the question. "Sometimes, sweetie, even grown-ups have trouble figuring out how to be friends."

Sam, who had been nearby capturing some final shots of the sunset gleaming off the museum's windows, lowered his camera. His brow furrowed as he observed the interaction between James and Emma, noting the careful distance they maintained,

As they prepared to leave, Ted pulled James into a tight hug. "Listen, mate," he said, his voice serious. "Whatever is going on between you two, sort it out. And don't let your pride get in the way."

Maribel, meanwhile, embraced Emma. "Remember what I told you last time?" she murmured. "Give him time. But don't wait too long. And be honest with yourself about what you want."

As Ted, Maribel, and the girls drove away, their car kicking up dust on the gravel path, James and Emma stood side by side, waving goodbye. For a moment, the façade of professionalism slipped, and they were just two people, lost and uncertain.

"They're good kids," James said softly, his voice barely audible over the distant rumble of traffic.

Emma nodded. "They are. Ted and Maribel are lucky."

A beat of silence passed between them, heavy with unspoken words. Sam approached, his camera now packed away in its case.

"That's a wrap for today," he said, his tone professional but friendly. "You've got a great community here. It's been amazing to capture."

James and Emma murmured their thanks, both acutely aware of the other's presence, like two notes in a chord that didn't quite harmonize.

"I'll see you both tomorrow at the office studio? And Emma? Tomorrow morning for a Monster kiln lighting?" Sam asked, glancing between them.

They nodded, and Sam headed off towards the parking lot, leaving James and Emma alone in the growing twilight.

Emma took a deep breath, the scent of night-blooming jasmine from a nearby garden filling the air. "James, I think... we need to talk, really talk. About everything."

James nodded slowly. "Aye, I think we do."

The sun was dipping low now, prepping for a final bow, but not yet, there were still folks here playing with the clay, still working and wrapping up after a very long day.

The balloon James had dreaded and expected had finally popped.

Em and he were going to have a conversation.

* * *

Chapter 17

Chicago — The Green Mill — *Jun. 23, 2002 — 9:20 p.m. — In the Mill*

The day's work at the Field Museum had wound down, the last of the participants trickling away into the warm Chicago evening. James found Emma packing up her supplies, their movements slow with fatigue, bruised and emotionally battered from the events of the past few days. But it wasn't over yet.

James Watson stood near the entrance of the tent, his eyes scanning the area, watching the interns pack up the loose ends until they landed on Emma. She was bent over a table, methodically packing up her supplies, her movements slow with the fatigue that comes from an exhausting day.

Screwing his courage 'to the sticking place,' as the phrase goes, James approached, the keys to his Prius jingling in his hand. "Need a lift home?" he asked, his voice carrying a forced casualness that didn't quite mask the underlying tension.

Emma looked up, surprise flickering across her face. For a moment, she seemed to hesitate, weighing her options. "Oh. Um, sure. Thanks, James," she finally replied, her voice a mixture of gratitude and uncertainty. And then understanding—he wanted to talk. Tonight. Now. No more delay. She drew in a deep breath.

As they made their way to James's car, the silence between them was a mutual agreement. It was an armistice to bring them into physical proximity for the interim until they found a place to land, park and probably bark at each other. It was filled with years of unspoken words and missed opportunities and at the very same time, that familiar physical electric current flowed too. That connection they felt within five feet of the other. It would drive them mad if they didn't sort this out.

One way or the other.

And so the distant sounds of the city—car horns, snippets of conversation, the faint melody of a street musician—seemed amplified in contrast to their quiet.

Once in the car, navigating through Chicago's evening traffic, the silence grew even more oppressive. The physical proximity is even more challenging to ignore. James fiddled with the radio, his fingers dancing across the buttons as if they held the key to dispelling the awkwardness. Emma stared out the window, her reflection in the glass a study in contemplation. Both were acutely aware of the other's presence, the small space of the car magnifying every breath, every shift in posture.

James, feeling the weight of the silence pressing down on him, decided to break it with the first thing that came to mind. "So," he began, then faltered, realizing too late how inadequate his opener was. "Hot weather we're having."

Emma turned to him, a small smile tugging at the corners of her lips despite herself. Her eyes, warm with a mixture of amusement and fondness, met his. "Really? Weather, James?"

He chuckled, the tension easing slightly. The sound of his laughter, rich and genuine, seemed to fill the car, pushing back the awkwardness. "Suppose that wasn't my best opener," he admitted, his eyes crinkling at the corners, in that way she liked.

As they approached Lawrence Avenue, a neon sign caught James's eye. The Green Mill, its vintage lettering a beacon in the growing dusk, seemed to call out to him. It was a place out of time, a refuge from the complexities of their shared history. "The Green Mill," he read aloud, an idea forming. "Fancy a drink? Might be easier to talk somewhere that's not... well, moving."

Emma hesitated for a moment, her eyes flicking between James and the inviting glow of the club's sign. She weighed the proposition, considering the implications of prolonging their time together. He was right, it had to be done and now, or she wouldn't sleep tonight. All too much on the mind. Finally, she nodded, a decision made. "Why not?"

The Green Mill was indeed a time capsule, its Art Deco interior transporting them to another era the moment they stepped through the door. The soft strains of jazz filled the air, wrapping around them like a comforting blanket. The low lighting cast everything in a warm, amber glow, softening the edges of reality and making everything seem just a little bit magical.

They found a small booth in the corner, the worn leather seats cradling them as they sat. A waiter, his demeanor suggesting he might have been there since the prohibition era, took their drink orders with a nod of quiet understanding.

Emma's eyes roamed the space, taking in the vintage posters, the small stage where a jazz trio was setting up, the patrons who seemed as much a part of the décor as the furnishings. "This place is amazing," she breathed, her voice filled with wonder.

James nodded, a small smile playing on his lips as he watched Emma's reaction. "It's got character, that's for sure," he agreed, his own gaze sweeping the room before settling back on her face.

As their drinks arrived, just beer on tap, the silence that had plagued them in the car threatened to return. Emma traced the condensation on her glass, her finger leaving intricate patterns that mirrored the complexity of her thoughts. James sat quietly, his own mind a whirlwind of memories and questions.

Finally, Emma spoke, her voice barely audible over the music. "So," she began, her eyes meeting James's with a mixture of trepidation and determination. "I guess we should talk."

James nodded, his expression serious as he leaned in slightly. "Aye, I suppose we should."

What happened next caught them both by surprise. As if orchestrated by some unseen force, they both blurted out, "I'm sorry," simultaneously. The synchronicity of the moment hung in the air for a beat before they both chuckled, the tension breaking slightly.

"You go first," James said, gesturing to Emma with a gentlemanly wave of his hand.

Emma took a deep breath, her fingers tightening around her glass and gathered her thoughts, of everything on the list she could apologize for and went for the big one: "I'm sorry for leaving the way I did, all those years ago," her voice soft but steady, "it was... cowardly."

Stunned silence.

James pulled his hand away from his beer mug, his hand resting on the table top. The admission seemed to stall his engine for the moment and hung in the air between them, so heavy, so honest and true, he asked, "Why did you, Em?" His voice is a mixture of hurt and genuine curiosity. "Was it something I did?"

Emma shook her head, her eyes dropping to the table as she searched for the right words. "No. Yes. I don't know," she admitted, her voice barely above a whisper. "I was scared."

James leaned forward, his elbows resting on the table, his eyes searching Emma's face. "Of what? Of me?" His voice was low, barely audible above the music, but Emma could hear the undercurrent of hurt and confusion.

Emma's gaze darted around the room, taking in the vintage posters on the walls, the couples swaying gently to the music, anything to avoid meeting James's intense stare. The weight of the past seemed to press down on her, making the air feel suddenly oppressive, finding no escape, she forced herself to look at him.

"Yes."

James leaned back in the booth, the leather creaking softly under his weight. His eyes never left Emma's face as he considered her, his expression thoughtful. Emma could almost see the gears turning in his mind, revisiting their shared history, analyzing key moments from their past. After a moment, he shook his head slightly, as if clearing away the cobwebs.

"You are one of the bravest souls I know," his voice tinged with a mixture of admiration and bewilderment. "Brave should be your middle name. Do you know what you were scared of?"

Emma's fingers traced the condensation on her glass, leaving intricate patterns that mirrored the complexity of her thoughts. "I...think... I felt I would disappear in you," she began, her voice barely a whisper. "If I had been the center of your world, that would have been all right, I think... but I wasn't." She paused, taking a shaky breath before continuing, "James, I thought you didn't want me."

As the jazz trio launched into a new song, its melancholic notes seeming to underscore the weight of Emma's confession, James's jaw dropped open in shock. His eyes widened, disbelief written clearly across his features.

"Not want you?" He echoed, his voice a mixture of incredulity and amazement. "Em, I was head over heels for you. I just... I don't think I knew how to show it."

Emma kept her head down as she spoke, unable to meet James's gaze. The soft light caught the auburn highlights in her hair, creating a halo effect that made her look almost ethereal. "I know you cared for me... I could feel... I think we both could feel the... softness between us. I know that was true... but did you *want me*?"

When James remained silent, Emma finally looked up. She found him studying her intently, his brow furrowed in concentration as he processed her words. Seeing his contemplative expression, she decided to clarify further.

"One time, you called me intense," she said, her voice gaining strength as she pushed through her vulnerability. "You said 'you are so intense.' I wasn't sure what you meant at the time. But later I think you meant I should be more casual about how I felt about you. Did you mean not committed to you? So you could not be committed to me?"

The truth now lay exposed between them, raw and unvarnished. Emma's voice dropped to a whisper, "Please be my friend, James, and tell me the truth."

James drew in a deep breath, the sound audible even over the gentle murmur of conversation and music that filled the club. His fingers stroked the wooden table top as he gathered his thoughts.

"I don't know if it's that simple or clear," he began, his voice low and measured. "You were the best friend I ever had. I am more myself with you than anyone. I wanted you around me all the time... but if you're asking me if I knew what that meant... I didn't."

He paused, running a hand through his hair in a gesture that Emma recognized from their college days. It was a habit he fell into when grappling with difficult thoughts or emotions.

"I don't think I got that far in my mind," James continued, his words coming faster now as if a dam had broken. "I was immature. I don't mean that as an insult to myself, I was literally not mature enough to understand what was happening. I was living several lives at the same time—mine with you, mine with classes, and mine with...success."

The jazz trio transitioned into a new song, its tempo slightly faster but still tinged with melancholy. The change in rhythm seemed to mirror the shift in James's demeanor as he delved deeper into his past mindset.

"I don't think I made a conscious choice of one over another or... felt I had to," he admitted, his eyes fixed on a point just past Emma's shoulder, as if he were looking into the past. "I'm thinking back now, working at remembering how it was for me... I guess I thought it could all be together. I guess that means I thought I could do whatever I wanted... so I wanted you, but maybe I wanted it all too."

The Green Mill seemed to hold its breath, the jazz music fading into the background as James and Emma's conversation intensified. The soft amber light that had once felt comforting now seemed to spotlight their every expression, every micro-movement, as they navigated the treacherous waters of their shared past.

Emma's voice was barely above a whisper as she asked, "And... and do you want it all now? Do whatever you want?" Her eyes, wide and vulnerable, searched James's face for any hint of his answer before he spoke.

James's response came quickly, his voice tinged with a weariness that spoke of hard-earned lessons. "No... no that's been burned out of me good and proper."

Emma nodded, her silence prompting James to look down, his fingers tracing the rim of his glass. When he looked up again, his eyes held a mix of pain and curiosity that had been simmering for years.

"But why didn't you tell me?" He asked, his voice low and intense. "If you wanted to go, have this opportunity, in Dresden, I wouldn't have liked it... but I wouldn't have tried to hold you back... not even then, you're bloody brilliant. You flattened me when you left like that... why didn't you tell me?"

Emma's voice was soft, almost fragile, as she asked, "The truth?"

"Nothing but," James replied, his tone leaving no room for evasion.

Emma's admission came like a thunderclap in the quiet booth. "I'm sorry, but I think I wanted to hurt you." She kept her eyes downcast as she spoke, unable to meet his gaze. When she finally looked up, she saw the shock written plainly across his face.

James's voice was strained, barely controlled, as he responded. "Well, you succeeded in rubies and diamonds, but why?"

Emma covered her face with her hands, drawing in a deep breath. The sounds of the jazz club seemed to fade away, leaving them in a bubble of their own making. When she lowered her hands, there was a new determination in her eyes.

"James, are you seriously telling me you don't remember us sitting on the bench holding hands and finally coming so close and the very next day I see you climbing all over that... that... girl, that terrible girl. You seriously don't remember giving me the brush off big time there in the lobby of the Hewitt Building?"

James's face transformed as if he'd been physically struck. His eyes widened, memories clearly flooding back. "I remember, on the bench, so clear, then I got the letter about the show... and you didn't come out to meet me that night, you wouldn't celebrate with me... so I remember being a little pissed at that, but... that... girl, was nothing..."

A heavy silence fell between them, broken only by the distant clinking of glasses and the muted conversations of other patrons. Emma's voice was steady when she finally spoke again.

"It didn't look that way, it didn't feel that way to me. I take full responsibility for being cruel, but you asked me why and so I'm telling why—I felt so hurt... I wanted to hit back, I needed to stop you from being in my life."

"Because of that girl? That, that...*nutcase*?" James's voice rose slightly, disbelief coloring his words.

Emma's response was measured, but there was an undercurrent of frustration. "I can't really talk to you about it if you don't remember or if we remember it differently."

James leaned forward, his voice taking on an intensity that matched the emotions cooking between them. "Oh, we're going to talk about it, we opened this can of worms, so we're gonna pull it all out. For months, as I started to sell my work, I'd get the feeling, you were happy for me, but holding back too—we were always competing and I see now it wasn't healthy, but admit it, back then, you were old fashioned jealous."

Emma swallowed hard, her gaze dropping to the table. She felt tears welling up, unbidden and unstoppable. As she wiped at her eyes, trying to clear her vision, James's voice softened slightly.

"Ah Em, don't cry... but we gotta get through this part..."

"I'm not crying..." Emma's voice was thick with emotion. "It's just, you never yelled at me before."

"I've yelled plenty."

"Hollered, but not yelled like you meant it."

Their heated exchange was interrupted by the arrival of a waitress, a middle-aged woman with kind eyes and a no-nonsense demeanor. She looked between them, concern evident in her voice as she asked, "Is everything all right here? You okay, miss?"

James turned to the waitress, exasperation clear on his face. He seemed on the verge of saying 'piss off' when Emma intervened, her voice shaky but sincere.

"I'm okay, we're okay, just some stuff."

The waitress nodded, but added a gentle warning before leaving. "Well, all right, just keep it down a bit."

James handed Emma a napkin from the table, watching as she blew her nose. The brief interruption seemed to have taken some of the heat out of their exchange. When James spoke again, his voice was softer, but still insistent.

"Were you jealous?"

Emma finished wiping her nose, then nodded slowly. "I think I was... but maybe not in the ordinary way, like people think. I felt myself disappearing."

James's expression softened, regret and understanding warring in his eyes. "I can't believe I made you feel that way, if I did, I am really sorry."

The Green Mill seemed to hold its breath, the soft jazz melodies weaving through the air, providing a melancholic backdrop to the windup and big reveal.

Emma's voice was soft but steady as she continued, her eyes never leaving James's face. "That's just it, you didn't do it on purpose, you were just being you. I never wanted you to be less, still don't. You...are a gift, James, to a lot of people."

James leaned forward, his brow furrowed in concentration. "But I made you feel invisible?"

"No... that's not it," Emma replied, shaking her head slightly. Her fingers traced the rim of her glass, a nervous habit she'd never quite shaken. "I think I felt myself disappearing not from the earth, but... into you. I loved you so much James."

The admission hung in the air between them, James's face softened, his eyes growing moist. He reached for a napkin himself now and wiped his eyes dry.

Encouraged by his reaction, Emma pressed on, her words coming faster now, as if a dam had broken. "I... I had an experience once, in class, remember that interview we did once? It happened then, this white light came out of you, all white, then the air went white, then the whole world went white, everything dissolved and me too... and I know now it was love. This is how love really is, no borders or anything."

James listened intently, his eyes never leaving Emma's face as she described her experience. The jazz band transitioned into a softer melody, the gentle snare drum and mournful saxophone seeming to underscore the weight of Emma's words.

"And I knew then I would have given up every dream I had to be your wife," Emma continued, her voice barely above a whisper. "But after what happened that day, in the lobby, I did not believe you would ask me, or ask me soon enough before I went crazy. And..."

She paused, listening to the music for a moment, gathering her thoughts. The soft rift of the snare drum and saxophone filled the silence, a momentary melancholic interlude and resting place.

"And... I didn't want to be stopped either," Emma resumed, her voice stronger now. "I felt you outpacing me, and if I couldn't be your wife, I had to be myself, but better than I could imagine. It seemed you could do everything you put your hand to—"

James interrupted, his voice tinged with frustration. "I worked and still work very hard... what in the world makes you think it's easy?"

Emma held up her hand, a placating gesture. "I know you do, but you asked and I'm not saying it made sense, it's how I felt—you could do everything so well and maybe I could do just this one thing, my ability with color... and I wanted to be better than you with that one thing."

"Em..." James began, but Emma pressed on, determined to lay everything bare.

"No, let me get it out, you deserve to hear it all," she insisted. The words tumbled out now, "I don't believe you were trying to hurt me, with that girl... I believe you were oblivious to how it would affect me... and that scared me even more."

Emma's voice quavered slightly, but she pushed through. "I really felt I would go crazy if you put me on the back burner and I had to watch you having fun with those girls, it would have ended me, that's the truth. You could be free of me to do what you wanted, but I couldn't be free of you. If that's not jealousy, I don't know what is."

The jazz band had taken a break, the room was quieter now, the Green Mill continued its nightly dance of patrons and performers, somewhere a group of people started singing 'Happy Birthday to you...' but it was distant, a far away song as if from childhood. It pulled at their attention but only for a moment, Emma drew in a breath and continued, her voice soft, so soft, but still he heard every word,

"And so when a way came to save myself, with the one thing I could do better than you, I took it," Emma concluded, her voice soft but firm. "But I decided not to tell you, because I knew it would hurt you. I could never have found a boy or man to 'get even' that would have been impossible for me, unthinkable, so the only way I could hurt you enough to stop you, was to leave as if you were nothing to me."

The weight of Emma's words hung between them, James sat motionless, absorbing the full impact of Emma's confession, his face a canvas of conflicting emotions—shock, pain, and a dawning understanding that threatened to overwhelm him.

After what felt like an eternity, James took a deep breath, his chest rising and falling visibly. When he spoke, his voice was barely above a whisper, tender and tinged with a hint of sadness.

"Well, it took a lot to tell me... see? You *are* brave." But the attempt at levity fell flat, and neither of them could muster a smile.

James ventured further, his voice steady but subdued. "I guess I imagined it was something like that."

Emma's eyes, which had been fixed on the table, slowly lifted to meet James's gaze. Her voice, when she spoke, was small and vulnerable, a stark contrast to her usual confidence. "Can I ask you one thing?"

James held her gaze, a whisper of understanding passing between them. He had a feeling he knew what was coming, but he nodded, bracing himself for the question.

"Would you have married me back then?"

The question hung in the air; right there in the air like a cartoon thought balloon. James swallowed hard, the muscles in his throat working visibly. Emma's bravery demanded honesty in return, and so, with a heavy heart, he slowly shook his head. His words came out measured, each one carefully chosen, but slipping into the idiom of his youth, as he did when emotionally moved.

"It wasn't anywhere in me mind, the word, 'marry'... I was homeless for months, when I first got to New York, I never told you, I didn't want you to worry. An' there was looking after Sarah's schoolin,' helping her in any way I could, getting my career going, balancing it all... no, I don't think I ever thought about it. So maybe, I did have some kind of 'brake' on, maybe thas' why we stayed friends for years in school, without anything else, you know what I mean, respecting you—not wanting to lose my friend. I wanted to have you in me life, always, but I never made it to that word: 'marry.' I really, really don't know why."

A flicker of pain passed through her eyes, but her face remained composed. Her voice was steady as she replied, "I believe you, thank you for telling me."

James nodded, his gaze distant as he continued softly, "God, life's a puzzle, so strange, what happens when God gives a gift like that to children? Coz, that's what we were, weren't we? Children, not so much in age, eighteen is old enough to understand the rules of life...but in... playing with this thing called 'art' or 'career.' I'm getting the oddest thought... if I'd been a chicken farmer, say, we'd have a passel of kids by now, right?"

A small smile tugged at Emma's lips, a brief moment of lightness in the taxing conversation. "You, a chicken farmer?"

"Damn straight great chicken farmer, don't know why thas' so funny. But you didn't answer my question," James pressed, his eyes searching her face.

"Yes, we would have a passel of kids by now," Emma said simply.

"Thought so," James replied, his voice soft and contemplative.

Their moment of introspection was interrupted by the waitress, who approached their table with a knowing look. "Last call, this one's on me for the road," she offered, her voice warm with understanding.

James glanced at Emma, reluctant to end their conversation. "Coffee?" He suggested, his tone hopeful.

"Decaf will be okay," Emma agreed, her voice matching his lighter note.

As the waitress left to fetch their drinks, they both turned their attention to the jazz trio on stage. The musicians were winding down for the evening, their long notes stretching out like a collective sigh at the end of a long day.

The soft thump of sturdy ceramic on wood punctuated the air as the waitress set down two thick, white mugs of coffee. These were the unbreakable kind, totally dishwasher safe... what? Thirty years old? Emma felt the thickness of the handle, now that was great ceramic built for the long haul.

The waitress placed the tab on the table with a gentle rustle, then paused, her eyes softening as she regarded James and Emma.

"Glad to see you working it out," she offered, her voice carrying the weight of wisdom gained through years of observing life's dramas, "I see plenty of folks in here... all I gotta say is, life is short, and the older you get, the faster time goes, it's all way too fast—that's it, have a nice evening folks."

As she retreated, James turned to Emma, a hint of sheepishness in his voice. "She's getting a big tip; you got a twenty in your purse? I tapped out me cash to get lunch."

Emma's laughter, bright and genuine, a breath of fresh air. "Yes, I think I can spot you a 'Jackson.'"

"Ta, would hate to look a chump," James replied, his own smile ghosting hers.

The bar gradually emptied around them, the last patrons filtering out into the night. In the newfound quiet, James and Emma found themselves at a crossroads, with the inevitable question coming fast on hot wheels.

"So, where do we go from here?" Emma asked, her eyes searching James's face in the soft, dimmed light.

James ran a hand through his hair, "I don't know, Em. We've got a project to finish, a community counting on us. Maybe... maybe we take it one day at a time?"

Emma nodded, a small twinkle of hope lighting her eyes, "One day at a time. I can do that."

James nodded, breathed deep and slowly exhaled.

* * *

After they settled their tab, they stepped out into the cool night air. Lawrence Avenue was quiet now. It was late on a Sunday night with virtually no traffic up or down the street.

"I'll drive you home, okay?" James offered softly, his keys jingling in his hand.

Emma nodded, a small smile playing on her lips. "Thanks. For everything... well, except for the drinks, cuz, I kinda picked up the tab."

"Only the cash for the tip, I put the rest on my card," James muttered, a hint of amusement in his tone. "Boy I'm not going to hear the end of that."

"Not likely," Emma agreed, then added after a moment's pause, "James... we just had our first fight."

He turned to look at her, his brow furrowing slightly as he caught on a particular word. "First? Does that mean there'll be others?"

Emma's eyes widened, but she remained silent, the question hanging suspended in the air between them like a prop dropped from the scaffolding in a matinee melodrama. *Will there be others?*

The car was nearby, right off Lawrence, so it was a brief walk to the sanctuary of the Prius.

As they drove through the quiet streets, the silence in the car was no longer oppressive. It felt softer, yielding and open to the words: m*aybe we aren't crazy.*

* * *

Chapter 18

Chicago West Loop — Office Work Space — *Jun. 27, 2002 — 8:30 a.m. — Shifting Sands*

Emma pushed open the heavy door to the first-floor office space, the familiar scent of clay and glaze welcoming her like an old friend. The late afternoon sun slanted through the windows, casting long shadows across the room and illuminating the busy scene before her. Interns moved with purpose, their hands stained with clay as they carefully prepped tiles for firing. The small kiln she was utilizing for testing glazing samples in the corner hummed steadily, its red-hot interior visible through the peephole like a dragon's eye winking in the dim light.

Her gaze was drawn to the empty holding rack near the far wall, its metal shelves gleaming accusingly in the fading sunlight. A small smile tugged at her lips, equal parts pride and longing. The empty rack meant James and Gerardo had been here late last night, moving the day's work to the Monster kiln on Lill Street. It was a testament to their dedication, working in the quiet hours when the rest of the world slept.

"Burning the midnight oil again, I see," Emma murmured to herself, running her fingers along the cool metal of the rack. She felt a pang of guilt for not being there to help, but they were all juggling the growing demands of the project as best they could. It was a testament to their dedication, working in the quiet hours when the rest of the world slept. She knew James was working through the day too, hunting for a large loft space for the next phase and working on the final design to boot.

But his absence during the day was becoming more noticeable, his creative process requiring more solitude than usual. She understood the need for focused time, but she couldn't help feeling the weight of his absence in the shared space. The air seemed thinner somehow, lacking the spark of energy that always accompanied James's presence. His energy filled so much space there was a definite and obvious void.

Emma sighed, her breath stirring a small pile of clay dust on the nearby workbench. "And I miss you, you great massive lunk," she whispered, half-annoyed at herself for the admission. She missed him sneaking those sidelong looks at her, oh yes, she knew about that. It was like he'd gone off on a sailing ship to fish the waters while she held the house together, she knew he was working to fortify 'the family' and she would do her part, but—

She missed him.

She drew in a deep breath, that conversation at the Green Mill had taken courage for both of them, perhaps they even rated superhero status of some kind in an ordinary way. But the real benefit of such a heart-to-heart was what could happen in the quiet moments afterward, in the time spent together after the storm to assess if your new old friend was in 1989 or living as they were now in 2002.

In brief, had they both truly changed?

Emma knew she was watching him for signs and she was sure it was mutual. Now that he needed this time on his own to dive deep into problem-solving and designing, she absolutely needed to give it to him and back him up. What's more, she wanted to. But that didn't make the waiting any easier.

And... Emma wanted him to succeed.

The sharp click of heels against the linoleum floor pulled Emma from her thoughts, she looked up to see Rhonda Morrison striding towards her, impeccably dressed as always in a charcoal gray suit that seemed to absorb the very light around her. A portfolio was tucked under one arm, clutched like a shield against an unseen enemy.

She didn't miss the slight furrow in Rhonda's brow, the tightness around her eyes that spoke of mounting pressure. It was a look she'd seen more and more frequently lately, like storm clouds gathering on the horizon.

"Emma," Rhonda called out, her voice carrying over the low hum of activity in the room. "Do you have a moment?"

Sge nodded, straightening her posture instinctively. "Of course, Rhonda. What can I do for you?"

As Rhonda approached, Emma noticed a small clay smudge on the cuff of her otherwise pristine white blouse. It was such an incongruous detail that Emma almost laughed. Even Rhonda, it seemed, couldn't escape the all-pervasive nature of their work.

"Is everything alright?" Emma asked, her tone carefully neutral. "You look like you're carrying the weight of the world in that portfolio."

Rhonda's eyes scanned the room, taking in the busy interns and the conspicuous absence of James. Emma watched as Rhonda's gaze lingered on the empty holding rack, a flicker of confusion passing over her face before she schooled her features back into professional neutrality.

Rhonda's lips twitched in what might have been an attempt at a smile. "Maybe not the world," she replied, "but certainly a good chunk of Chicago's art scene. Is there somewhere we can talk, Emma?" and then added her voice low, "privately."

Emma felt a flutter of apprehension in her stomach. Private conversations with Rhonda rarely bode well these days. But she squared her shoulders and nodded, gesturing towards the small office in the corner. "In the office there," she said, hoping her voice sounded steadier than she felt.

Emma led her to a small office in the corner of the workspace, as they moved across the workspace, Emma caught the curious glances of the interns. Clara, her blonde hair pulled back in a messy bun, raised an eyebrow in silent question, Jasmine was looking their way as well. Emma gave a small shrug in response, mouthing "Later" as she followed Rhonda into the office.

Once inside the small room, Emma closed the door behind them. The room was cramped but quiet, offering a respite from the creative bustle outside. Emma leaned against the desk, her fingers absently tracing the worn wood grain as she waited for Rhonda to speak. Whatever was coming, she had a feeling it was going to change the delicate balance they'd all been maintaining.

"Emma," Rhonda began, her tone measured but with an undercurrent of urgency, "I've been watching you work. You're clearly the driving force behind this project right now."

Emma felt a flicker of defensiveness rise in her chest. She knew how it must look from the outside—her constant presence in the workspace while James was notably absent. But she also knew the unseen hours he poured into the project, the midnight trips to the Lill Street kiln, the constant coordination with suppliers. The scent of fresh clay and glaze hung in the air, a tangible reminder of the work that never seemed to cease.

CHAPTER 18   313

"We're all working hard, Rhonda," Emma said, careful to keep her voice neutral. She absently traced the edge of a nearby tile, its surface cool and smooth under her fingertips. "James is—"

"James seems to be absent more often than not," Rhonda interrupted, her eyes softening with what Emma recognized as genuine concern. A strand of Rhonda's usually immaculate hair had come loose, betraying the stress she was under. "I'm worried about the project's timeline. The Epoch Alliance board is getting nervous."

Emma took a deep breath, weighing her words carefully. She could see the tension in Rhonda's shoulders, the way her fingers tightened almost imperceptibly on her portfolio. The late afternoon sun slanted through the windows, and into the small office area, highlighting the worry lines on Rhonda's face.

She took a deep breath, weighing her words carefully. Emma could see the tension in Rhonda's shoulders, the way her fingers tightened almost imperceptibly on her portfolio. Rhonda was under pressure, caught between the demands of the board and the realities of the creative process.

"I understand your worries, I even get it," Emma said, her voice gentle but firm. She gestured to the bustling workspace around them, where interns moved with purpose, their hands stained with clay and activity. "But James has trained the interns, very, very well, they are all hand picked by Gerardo and are doing better than great—I'm saying there's more happening than what you see during office hours. James and Gerardo have also been working late nights, taking the prepped tiles to the Monster kiln on Lill Street. That's why the holding rack is empty every morning."

Surprise flickered across Rhonda's face, followed quickly by a mix of relief and frustration. "I... I didn't know that," she admitted. "But Emma, the board needs to see tangible progress.

I'm talking about the final design, they need to see that design before handing it over as their submission to Max at Epoch United. They're asking questions I can't answer."

Emma nodded, understanding the difficult position Rhonda was in. "I know it's not easy to quantify creative work, especially when so much is happening behind the scenes. What can we do to ease the board's concerns?"

Rhonda's posture relaxed slightly, but Emma could still see the worry lingering in her eyes. "Have you considered taking a more prominent role in the design aspect?" Rhonda suggested, her voice careful. "If James is needing this much solitude—"

"He's not blocked," Emma interjected, perhaps too quickly. She took a breath, centering herself before continuing. "James is doing the work. His process might not be visible day-to-day, but it's essential to the project. He's deep in the creative zone, it's what happens, if he's taking longer than other people might, that just means he's deeper."

Rhonda nodded, but Emma could see she wasn't entirely convinced. "I understand, Emma. But it doesn't change the fact we're running out of time. The board needs to see progress on the actual design, not just prepped tiles."

As Rhonda's words hung in the air, Emma felt the weight of expectation settling on her shoulders. She knew the pressure Rhonda was under, and could see the genuine concern beneath the professional exterior. But she also felt a fierce loyalty to James, to their shared vision. The memory of their conversation at the Green Mill floated back to her, testing the depth of their connection.

"I hear you, Rhonda I really do," Emma said finally, her voice steady. She met Rhonda's gaze directly, her chin lifted slightly in determination. "But James and I are a team. We'll deliver the design on schedule. I promise. We have one last weekend of clay tile construction coming up. I'll be able to check in with him this weekend, and we're still a good two weeks away from the final deadline, we'll make it. He's doing the work."

Rhonda held Emma's gaze for a long moment, searching for reassurance. Finally, she nodded, a small smile softening her features. "I hope so, Emma. For all our sakes."

As Rhonda turned to leave, Emma felt a complex mix of emotions. She understood Rhonda's position, the need for tangible progress. But she also knew the depth of James's commitment to the project, the unseen hours he poured into their shared vision.

Emma watched as Rhonda made her way back through the workspace, pausing to observe the interns at work. She could see the appreciation in Rhonda's eyes for their dedication, but also the underlying concern about the project's direction.

As the door closed behind Rhonda, Emma let out a long breath. The pressure was mounting, the delicate balance between creativity and deadlines becoming more precarious by the day. She knew she needed to talk to James, to find a way to bridge the gap between his process and the board's expectations.

Plus, it would be old fashioned nice just to sit next to him too.

* * *

Chicago – Montrose Harbor – *Jun. 27, 2002 – 2:48 p.m.*

James, for his part, was watching grass grow. Literally.

The great lunk of a man sat cross-legged on the verdant expanse of Montrose Harbor Park, his eyes fixed on the swaying blades before him with the intensity of a child discovering the world anew. Watching the grass grow.

He'd been on his way to the library when his plan was derailed, deterred or otherwise upended and he found himself parked on the turf. He had a notion about the spark sitting inside him, the incessant nagging wee spark of an idea that would flame just so high, high enough to show him a glimpse of what was needed, but couldn't be sustained long enough to find the center. The frustration of almost-but-not-quite understanding prickled at the edges of his mind like a faulty lighter, it kept sputtering out just as he thought he'd caught hold of it.

It couldn't grow full blown until he found the center of every great idea that was personal. The high stakes personal part that could fire him up in such a way to hold the flame forever... regardless. He wasn't blocked, mind you. No, our James was looking for the medium to fan the flame, the kindling that would turn this spark into a bloody inferno.

He had a vague idea of an old sci-fi film he should revisit, 'The Incredible Shrinking Man' was the title, if memory served—he'd seen as a child and it had fired him up good and proper, but there were gaps in his memory, like missing pieces in a jigsaw puzzle of the mind. And so he was on his way to the library branch in uptown, his research indicated there might be a VHS copy on the shelf there, a relic holding the key to his creative conundrum.

And on the way, as he turned off Lake Shore Drive onto Montrose, the wide expanse of green grass of Montrose Harbor Park had looked so... real. He pulled off a side street on the way to the harbor, found a place to park, and now, for the past few hours he's been watching the grass grow, while the city of Chicago hummed a tune and throttled the citizenry around him, oblivious to the epic journey taking place in the mind of one James Watson.

It felt so good to sit on the grass and relax, just think nothing and watch the grass as he had when he was a child. When he was a young boy, he would lay on his back for hours at a time watching the clouds, the grass, infinitely entertained by both the grandeur of the sky and the minutia of all the small things walking and growing. He revisited the memory now, as he 'communed' with nature. 'Om Mani Padme HUM' indeed.

He used to look into the grass, between the blades of grass and imagine himself down there, small in the grass, working his way through the tall blades of the grass, brave in his hard work to stay alive, cutting down blades of grass as if in a jungle, then, looking up at the clouds, infinitely changing as if they were always watching him and having a conversation about his epic journey, and then he'd—

James straightened up, his back ramrod straight, as if someone had stuck him with a cattle prod right in the 'patoot.' He stopped breathing for a moment, no distraction in the mind nor body to get in the way of the idea... it was coming together, slowly, slowly...

James smiled, he had it. The spark was on fire and nothing could blow it out now. Not even a warning from Noah about a deluge could douse it now.

He found it, he knew where the idea began. Now, the challenge would be how in the world to articulate it and in time, oh yes, he knew the clock was ticking. The pressure of the deadline loomed, but it was a welcome challenge now that he had his direction. Ha! 'The game was afoot, Watson.'

James looked at his phone, no message from Em yet today... okay good, good, she wasn't banging on the door yet, she would hold them off and buy him time, he knew it. Good lass, holding down the fort while he gallivanted about in the grass.

He would see her this weekend for the final tile building sessions and he missed her too, Christ, he missed her. Missed her steady hands and keen eye, the way she could pluck his half-formed ideas from the nebulous shape between them and shape them into something magnificent.

Well, just hold that thought Em, until I get it up and running on a good track. James thought and then, 'God bless our Em,' his heart swelling with a peculiar mix of gratitude and longing that left him feeling both buoyant and grounded.

James heaved himself to his feet, brushing grass from his jeans like a man emerging from a fever dream. Time to get cracking. He had a vision to bring to life, a deadline breathing down his neck like an asthmatic dragon, and a partner in creative crime to dazzle.

Her sense of color would be absolutely critical, he knew that already, and if anyone could pull off this mad scheme, it was them. Of that, James was certain.

God bless our Em.

* * *

Chapter 19

Chicago — Sheffield St. — *Jul. 3, 2002 — 8:15 p.m. — Through the Lens*

The fading sunlight filtered through the dusty blinds of Sam's cramped apartment, casting long shadows across the piles of camera equipment and stacks of hard drives. The room smelled of stale coffee and the faint ozone scent of overworked electronics. Sam hunched over his editing station, his eyes bloodshot from hours of staring at the screen. The low hum of the computer's fan provided a steady backdrop to the click-click-click of his mouse as he scrolled through footage.

On the screen, images of the final tile-making session flickered by, a kaleidoscope of colors and faces that blurred into a montage when he pressed the 'fast forward' hotkey. Sam's finger hovered over the spacebar now, pausing on a frame that caught his eye. Emma stood by one of the purple sashes at the tent pole, her hand raised in a beckoning gesture, a fem la femme 'come hither' if ever he saw one. And he had seen one or two and counting.

Sam leaned in, his nose almost touching the screen. He'd misplaced his glasses and had to make do with his natural set sans artificial alignment, but per one of his favorite Shakespeare quotes: *twas enough 'twould do.* "Well, hello there," he murmured, hitting the spacebar to play the next sequence.

James appeared in the frame, striding purposefully towards Emma. There was something different about his gait, a lightness to his step that hadn't been there before, as if he'd lost ten pounds and the world was better for it. He reached Emma, and Sam's eyebrows shot up as he watched James lean down, his head tilted at an intimate angle to catch Emma's words.

Sam rubbed his chin thoughtfully, "Now that's interesting." Funny, the personal moments a camera picks up that go unnoticed in real time.

He navigated to footage from the previous weekend, pulling up a similar scene. James and Emma stood side by side, professional and polite, but with a palpable distance between them that could have housed a family of bears, well, small bears. Sam flicked back and forth between the two clips, his eyes narrowing as he cataloged the differences.

James's shoulders were tense, his movements slightly stiff, as if he were still recovering from an 'iron man triathlon' completed the previous weekend." Emma's smile, while warm, didn't quite reach her eyes. But in the new footage, there was a fluidity to their interactions, a comfortable synchronicity that spoke volumes, each movement a word in a language only they understood. It was a private moment in public.

"Well, well, well," Sam whistled, leaning back in his chair, "we do have a story inside a story after all. I think I deserve a Bavarian crème donut."

He wasn't kidding, he'd been saving one as a personal reward for finding 'a golden moment,' as he worked through the tedium of logging footage.

Table that treat for now, though, because he was greedy for more proof in print. He began to scroll through more recent footage, his eyes darting across the screen catching moments he'd missed before. James's hand lingering on Emma's shoulder as they examined a tile, just a tad bit longer than what was required to get her attention. Emma's laughter, bright and unguarded, at something James had said—really? Was James really that funny *all the time*? No, Sam was watching ole fashioned 'girl giddy.'

And especially the way they gravitated towards each other in group settings, like planets locked in orbit, their movements a dance choreographed by the universe itself.

Whew, good stuff.

Sam's mind raced with the possibilities. This wasn't just about the mosaic project anymore. It was about connection, about two people finding their way to each other amidst the chaos of creation.

"Now that's a narrative arc," Sam mused, already mentally rearranging his storyboard. "Love among the Ruins.' Oops, that one's been taken, still, who'd have thought?"

* * *

A sharp rap at the door startled Sam from his reverie. He blinked, momentarily disoriented as he shifted his focus from the screen to the real world. Glancing at his watch, he frowned. He wasn't expecting anyone, especially not at this hour when most folks were settling in for TV dinners and mindless sitcoms.

Sam opened the door to find Val standing there, a small thumb drive clutched in her hand. Her usual efficient demeanor seemed slightly off-kilter, a faint blush coloring her cheeks.

"Val? What brings you here?" Sam asked, running a hand through his disheveled hair, suddenly aware that he probably looked like he'd been dragged backward through a hedge.

Val thrust the thumb drive towards him. "I, um, took some photos during the last tile-making session. Thought they might be useful for your doc."

Sam's eyebrows rose in surprise. "That's… incredibly thoughtful. You know, I noticed your camera, it's a good one, thanks so much—come in." He stepped aside, gesturing her into his lair of cinematic creation.

As Val stepped inside, her eyes widened at the organized chaos of Sam's workspace. A half-eaten slice of pizza sat congealing on a paper plate next to a cold cup of coffee, the iconoclastic bachelor's apocalypse. The walls were plastered with post-it notes and index cards, a spider's web of ideas and connections.

Val's professional instincts kicked in, overriding her initial nervousness. "You know, a good file management system could really streamline your workflow here." she said, her tone suggesting she was already mentally reorganizing.

Sam chuckled, inserting the thumb drive into his computer. "Probably. But there's a method to my madness, I swear."

Val perched on the edge of the couch, her eyes drawn to the screen. "What were you working on when I arrived?"

"Actually, I'm glad you're here," Sam said, pulling up a clip. "I'd love your opinion on something. You work closely with James, right?"

Val nodded, her curiosity piqued. "Jimmy the James? Yes, why?" Her use of James's nickname was casual, but there was a hint of fondness in her voice that didn't escape Sam's notice.

Sam played the clip, showing James and Emma in conversation by the tent. "Notice anything different about their interaction here?" His tone suggested he knew something she didn't.

Val leaned forward, studying the footage intently. After a moment, she asked, "Is there sound? Do you have what they were saying?"

"Good catch," Sam said, impressed. He fiddled with the audio settings, isolating the conversation and cleaning up the background noise. As Sam played the clip with enhanced audio, they both leaned in, absorbed in the unfolding interaction between James and Emma. The conversation, seemingly innocuous on the surface, took on new meaning with their shared context.

Sam turned up the volume, Emma's voice came through first: "Not pushing or anything..."

James's reply was quick, tinged with amusement: "Which means you are—"

"Which means I am—" Emma finished, both of them chuckling. Then, her tone shifted slightly, "But how's the design going, really?"

James's voice softened. "You mean am I watching the ticking clock?"

Emma made a sound that could only be described as a vocal grimace. "I'm not worried... but *some* people are... sitting on a wire waiting to see which way the wind will blow."

"What's your favorite expression... from, what, the second meeting?" James asked, a smile evident in his voice.

Emma's surprise was palpable. "You were listening to me?"

"Always... your voice does... pierce."

"Does not."

"Does..." Emma stares at him, James sighs dramatically, "right, you win, it does not."

Sam paused the playback, a grin spreading across his face. "Here, watch this," he said, rewinding slightly and slowing down the footage. In slow motion, they watched as James casually picked a small chunk of clay off Emma's shoulder.

"There, see that?" Sam asked, his voice tinged with excitement.

Val swallowed hard. "Wow, for anyone else, that's a nit-picking nut, but for James... Sam, that's second base."

"Wow." Sam agreed, feeling like he'd just witnessed a rare celestial event. A white nebula blushing pink perhaps.

"What's her favorite phrase, does she say?" Val asked, leaning in closer. They both leaned in, watching intently as the scene continued to unfold in slow motion, then Sam played the clip at regular speed.

Emma's voice, "You can't speed the plow."

Val's eyes widened. "Oh my God, for them, at the slow pace they've been moving, that's almost a blue movie."

Sam shook his head, chuckling. "No, it's not."

"Well, not for ordinary people," Val conceded, "but for them? Okay, I'm exaggerating, but you get my point."

They shared a laugh, the absurdity of the situation hitting them both. But then Val grew quiet, a crease forming between her brows. "Wait a minute, I'm not sure if you can use that. Is that too personal?"

Sam leaned back in his chair, his expression turning thoughtful. He ran a hand through his hair, considering Val's words. "You might be right," he said slowly. "It's a beautiful moment, but..."

"But it's private," Val finished for him. "It's not just about the project anymore, is it?"

Sam shook his head. "No, it's not. And that's where things get tricky. Where do we draw the line between documenting the project and intruding on personal lives?"

Sam nodded, a mix of disappointment and respect in his eyes. "You're right. This stays between us, okay? It's not for the doc."

Then Val's hand shot out, stopping Sam before he could delete the clip. "No, don't delete it," she said urgently. "It's too funny, in a good way, and beautiful. Hang onto it, see where the project goes, and maybe just ask them. Show them the clip, the progression, and ask them. In context of the whole project, it will look more normal except to those of us that know them. I'm saying, who knows."

They shared a small laugh, the tension in the room easing. Val's eyes lit up suddenly, and she tapped Sam's shoulder without thinking, her focus entirely on the video timeline. "Oooh, can I see that moment of the little girl with her hand in the water bucket washing the clay and tools?"

Sam felt a sudden, unexpected frisson of energy coursing down his arm from that light contact. He blinked, surprised by his own reaction. Val, however, remained oblivious, her attention fixed on the screen.

"Uh, sure," Sam managed, his voice slightly rougher than usual. He scrolled through the timeline, trying to ignore the lingering warmth where Val's hand had been. "Here it is."

As the new clip began to play, showing a young girl gleefully splashing in a water bucket, Sam found himself hyper-aware of Val's presence beside him. Well that's… interesting. He stole a quick look at her profile, but she was looking at the computer screen completely engrossed in the footage, her eyes sparkling as she watched the child's joy unfold on screen.

"This is perfect," she murmured. "It captures the spirit of play, don't you think?"

Sam nodded, not trusting himself to speak just yet. He watched Val's face, animated now... and beautiful. Funny he didn't notice before.

"Hey," Val said, turning to him with a smile, "What other gems have you got hidden in here?"

Sam cleared his throat, "Let's find out," he said, returning her smile. "So," Sam said, turning back to Val with a renewed energy, "want to help me go through the rest of the footage for that hour? Promise there's nothing else quite so scandalous."

Val laughed, settling in more comfortably on the couch. "Bring it on," she said, ready to lose herself in the work and the company.

* * *

The digital clock on Sam's microwave blinked 11:47 p.m., its red glow casting a faint crimson sheen across the now-cluttered coffee table. Empty pizza boxes mingled with half-eaten cartons of lo Mein, a testament to the hours that had slipped by unnoticed.

Val sprawled comfortably on the couch, her shoes kicked off and her legs tucked under her. Sam hunched over his laptop, his eyes alight with the fervor of discovery. The air hummed with the electricity of shared creativity.

"Oh, oh, oh!" Sam exclaimed, his fingers flying across the keyboard. "I think I've found it—the perfect closing montage for the tile-making phase."

Val leaned in, her shoulder brushing against Sam's as she peered at the screen. "Show me," she demanded, her voice husky with fatigue and excitement.

Sam hit play, and the screen came alive with a kaleidoscope of images and sounds: a time-lapse of the sun setting on the final day, shadows lengthening across the field of tents.

Gerardo's booming laugh as he twirled the intern, Jasmine in an impromptu dance. "We did it, bambina! We made art with a thousand hands!"

Quick cuts of hands—young, old, smooth, calloused—all pressing designs into clay.

Val's own voice, caught on camera as she joked with Gerardo: "If I find clay in my hair one more time, I'm shaving my head and blaming you."

Gerardo's retort: "Ah, but you'd be the most bellissima bald eagle in all of Chicago!"

A slow-motion shot of Emma, her head thrown back in laughter as James 'took the stage' full tilt into his Will Rogers-esque storytelling mode.

Rhonda, her usual stern demeanor softened, addressing the group: "I've overseen a lot of projects in my time, but this... this is special."

Close-up of male hands carving a tile next to female hands carving a tile, camera pulling back to reveal it's James and Emma carving their own tiles.

A montage of participants sharing their stories:

"I put my grandmother's favorite flower in this tile. She's gone now, but this way, she's part of something lasting."

"I've never thought of myself as an artist, but today... today I feel like Edward Hopper meets Frederic Remington."

"My kid made this one. Can you believe it? My little guy, part of a real art installation!"

James and Emma, standing side by side as they watched the last participants leave. James turns to Emma, leans in as if he's going to kiss her then asks, "Ok, who gets to roll up the sign?"

Emma's reply, her eyes gleaming: "Race ya—'"

They exchanged a look, then bolted for the long sign advertising the clay tile sessions on the low stone wall. Each grabbed an end, rolling to meet in the middle. Their laughter echoed across the now-empty space as they jostled each other playfully. James caught Emma in his arms, spinning her around in a moment of pure joy.

Gerardo's cheerful voice over: "Ok, knock it off. You'll set a bad example. "

Final shot: James set Emma down gently, his eyes never leaving hers. "No, that's it, got it out of our systems, we're ready for phase two, right?"

Emma's response was immediate and confident: "Born ready."

The screen faded to black, leaving Sam and Val in stunned silence.

"Well," Val finally managed, her voice thick with emotion, "if that doesn't capture the essence of this whole crazy project, I don't know what does."

Sam nodded, a grin spreading across his face. "It's perfect, isn't it? The joy, the creativity, the sense of community—and that bittersweet feeling of an ending that's really a beginning."

Val punched his arm lightly. "Look at you, Mr. Poet. But you're right. It's all there."

They sat in comfortable silence, absorbing the weight of what they'd witnessed.

"You know," Sam said, breaking the quiet, "I came into this thinking it was something special... I could feel it... but you never really know how it's going to work."

Val nodded, her eyes distant. "It's about connection. About creating something beautiful together. About..."

"Love?" Sam finished, his voice barely above a whisper.

Their eyes met, and for a moment, the air felt soft... or maybe it was the afterglow of Chinese hot and sour soup. Sam smiled.

Val cleared her throat, breaking the spell. "Well, um, it's getting late. I should probably head out."

"You have a car? You gonna be alright?"

"Oh yeah, I'm a Chicago native, I know the drill, and still never take it for granted, I'll be okay, I have a good apartment, safe building."

As she gathered her things, Sam felt a reluctance to see her go. "Hey, Val?" he called as she reached the door.

She turned, one eyebrow raised in question.

"Thanks for... for everything. Your insight, your photos. You're an inspiration."

"Huh. You mean like a 'muse'?

"Sure." Sam smiled again, he couldn't think of what else to say.

"Huh." Val ventured "I've never been a muse before, 'amused' all the time, 'amusing' quite often or so I've been told, but... never..." and here she continued her soliloquy as she walked down the hall leaving Sam to watch after her stunned and maybe a little gobsmacked.

"Who was that masked woman?" Sam asked

"I heard that," Val called from down the hall and when she turned, Val's smile was soft, almost shy. "Anytime, Sam. See you tomorrow?"

He nodded and waved, watching her disappear around the corner to the elevator.

As the door closed, Sam walked back to his computer, the montage still frozen on the screen. He studied the image of James and Emma, standing on the cusp of something new.

"Next phase indeed," he murmured, settling in to work. The night stretched before him; plenty of time to get work done.

* * *

Chapter 20

Chicago West Loop — Office Workspace — *Jul. 5, 2002 — 11:20 a.m. — Pressure*

Emma stood in the first-floor workspace, surrounded by rows of drying tiles. The air was thick with the earthy scent of clay and the faint tang of glazes, a familiar aroma that always made her feel at home. Sunlight streamed through the tall windows, catching the subtle textures and colors of the community's creations, bringing each piece to life in its own unique way.

As she heard Alfred's familiar footsteps approaching, Emma felt a mixture of warmth and unease. His visits were always welcome, but lately, there had been an undercurrent of concern in his demeanor and she was fairly certain of the causal factor. The soft tap of his well-worn loafers on the concrete floor echoed slightly in the quiet space.

"Emma, my dear," Alfred called out, his voice carrying its usual warmth. The sunlight glinted off his silver hair as he entered. "How are our little masterpieces coming along?"

Emma smiled, gesturing to the rows of tiles. "They're incredible, Alfred. Come, let me show you some of my favorites." She led him to a nearby table, pointing out a tile with an intricate tree design. "This one's by a woman who just moved here from Thailand. She told me it represents putting down new roots while honoring where she came from."

Alfred nodded appreciatively, his eyes crinkling at the corners. Beautiful. It's amazing how much people can express themselves in such a small space."

As they moved along the rows, Emma shared more stories—a tile made by a cancer survivor, another by a child dreaming of becoming an astronaut. Each piece seemed to radiate with personal strength and hope.

After a while, Alfred's expression grew thoughtful, his brow furrowing slightly as he turned to Emma. "Emma," he began, his voice softer now, carrying a hint of concern that made her stomach tighten, "I hope you don't mind me asking, but... have you noticed anything different about James lately?"

Emma felt a flicker of unease. "Different how?" she asked, trying to keep her voice steady.

Alfred sighed, running a hand through his silver hair, a gesture that seemed to age him momentarily. "He seems withdrawn. I've known him for years, and I've never seen him like this. I'm worried something might be troubling him."

Emma paused, her mind drifting back to the countless times she'd watched James work at Cooper Union. His process had always been unpredictable, like trying to predict the pattern of leaves in the wind. Sometimes he'd be a whirlwind of activity, other times he'd retreat into long periods of quiet contemplation, as still as Mount Rushmore.

"You know, Alfred," she began slowly, "James has never really had a consistent work style. He adapts to each project differently, at least that is what I remember. Wasn't there a mural he did for a children's hospital? I heard he disappeared for days and came back with a fully formed concept."

Alfred nodded, a small smile tugging at his lips, the worry lines around his eyes softening slightly. "That's true. He certainly keeps us on our toes."

Emma continued, her voice growing more confident. "And think about it—if James thought he was in trouble, if he couldn't deliver, do you really believe he'd put the project in danger for the sake of his own pride?"

Alfred's eyes widened slightly, considering her words. "You're right," he said after a moment. "He is not a megalomaniac. He's always put the work first."

"Exactly," Emma agreed, feeling a wave of relief wash over her. "If he was really in trouble, he'd let us know. He'd let me know. I spent this past weekend with him during the final tile making. He seemed in good spirits, happy about the work done and looking forward. I don't know if someone put a bug in your ear or something, but from what I saw, he's taking the time he needs. You simply cannot speed the plow. I know I keep coming back to that, but it's true."

Alfred's shoulders relaxed visibly. "You're absolutely right, my dear. I suppose I've been letting my worries get the better of me. Thank you for reminding me of what I already know."

As Alfred left, his footsteps fading into the distance, Emma felt a renewed sense of confidence. She still wanted to talk to James, to reassure herself, but the gnawing doubt had eased.

She retreated to the private office, the soft click of the door closing behind her like a punctuation mark. She retreated to the private office and dialed James's number. The phone rang once, twice, three times before going to voicemail. Emma's heart sank a little as she heard James's familiar greeting.

"James, it's me," she said, her voice steady and warm, "I hope everything's going well with your part of the project. I'd love to catch up when you have a moment." She paused, weighing her next words carefully. "No rush, which means of course, there is, here's a heads up—Alfred's getting nervous, and I think he told me, so I would tell you. I think... I think we need to talk about the design. Soon, and..." her voice softened, a hint of vulnerability creeping in, "I miss you. Call me when you can."

As she hung up, Emma gazed out the window at the bustling city. She thought about James, wherever he was, working in his own way. She imagined him hunched over sketches or lost in thought, piecing together a pattern for them all to play with. Whatever he was doing, she trusted him. That said, she would sure like to hear from him. It had only been four days since the final day at the Field Museum, but admittedly, she was feeling the pressure too.

* * *

Chicago – Emma's Apartment— *Jul. 10, 2002 – 9:35 p.m.*

Emma sat in her small apartment, her phone clutched in her hand like she had forgotten how to let go. She slowly peeled her fingers back from her grip on the flip-phone to reveal the small screen that glowed with a single message from James: "At the loft. Working on it." And then, as an afterthought, a wee 'smiley face' image.

It had been four hours since Emma called him—not that she was counting, but, yeah, she was counting, she'd been able to count since the first grade. It was a lesson that had stuck and it sure came in handy now, because even if James didn't know the time of day, she did.

She sighed, running a hand through her thick dark hair, the bright shine of glowing good health catching the soft lamplight. She drew in a deep breath and looked at the flip-phone screen again. The brevity of the message would do little to calm the gathering bellowing crowd banging on her door and even less to assuage her growing concerns.

"A smiley face? Really James?" She muttered, her index finger poised over the keypad. After a moment's hesitation, she sent back a 'thinking face' emoji with a straight line instead of a smile. Then, softening, she added a little heart—a digital olive branch.

The apartment felt too quiet, too still and then a strange thought: *this is what it sounds like on the moon*—unearthly quiet. Emma was half tempted to go to the window to have a look at the state of the silver orb for sake of comparison. But instead, her gaze drifted to the half-finished sketches scattered across her desk, each one an ode to a long days journey into sleepless nights. She was about to lose herself in her work again when a sharp knock at the door startled her from her thoughts.

Emma walked with care down the narrow hallway to the front door, careful to keep on the soft carpet to cushion her footfall. Wait, could it be James? She stepped a little quicker and peered through the peephole, and saw Rhonda's familiar face, all business even at this late hour.

Emma opened the door, taking in Rhonda's appearance, she wasn't exactly disheveled, but she wasn't in her usual impeccable dress code. Her clothes sagged a bit, as if they'd given up the work day and surrendered to gravity at 7:15 p.m. while their owner definitely had not. No, Rhonda's dark brown eyes were as bold and direct as ever.

And...she had a bulging brown accordion file folder wedged under her arm that looked like it had swallowed a small filing cabinet.

"Rhonda? Kinda late, isn't it?" Emma said, her voice a mixture of surprise and wariness.

Rhonda's smile was all business. "We need to talk, Emma. May I come in?"

"Of course." Emma opened the door wide and led the way back into her small apartment. "There's not much room, but the couch is comfortable."

"Thanks." Rhonda removed her coat and settled on Emma's couch, taking a moment to look at the flower print tapestry, worn with care, but an excellent weave, soft pink peonies on an abstract garden vine, it was vintage, but excellent taste. Rhonda nodded almost imperceptibly and then without a word spread the contents of her folder across the coffee table.

Emma's eyes widened as she recognized her own work—sketches, designs, and reviews from her time in Dresden and beyond.

Emma walked slowly to the armchair adjacent to the couch, buying time as she thought hard and fast, once settled in the chair she observed, "You've been busy." Emma said, her voice carefully neutral, cautiously Swiss.

Rhonda nodded. "I've done my research, Emma. Your work is exceptional. The board would have no reservations about you taking the lead on this project."

Emma's brow furrowed, she took a breath and tried to keep an even tone, but yes, a bit of a bite crept in too, a hint of sharpness like a cat's claw peeking out from a velvet paw. "The board? *The board*? Have you *spoken* with the board? Or are you guessing what they'd think?"

Instead of answering directly Rhonda pointed to one particularly intricate design. "Look at this," she said, her voice softening with admiration. "Your understanding of color theory, your ability to balance complex elements—it's exactly what this project needs."

Emma felt a flush of odd pleasure, quickly followed by a warning bell. "Rhonda, I appreciate the compliment, but—"

Rhonda's expression hardened, "Emma, we're running out of time. The board needs to see progress. Real, tangible progress. Not vague promises of a design in the works."

Emma crossed her arms and said nothing, she let her silence do all the talking and simply stared at Rhonda.

Rhonda leaned back on the couch and studied the talented woman sitting in the chair opposite her. She took a cleansing breath, looked down at the pictures spread on the coffee table, lowered her head and said, "I'm not loving being the bad guy, I don't want to be typecast as the villain and contrary to what it may look like at the moment, I don't wake up in the morning and throw darts at photos of James in-between sips of my morning coffee. "

Emma's eyebrows shot up, but she kept her lips sealed tighter than Silas Marner's wallet.

Rhonda leaned forward, her voice softening. "I'm not asking you to push James aside. I'm asking you to step up if he can't deliver."

Emma remained quiet in her chair, with nary nod nor twitch and took a moment to think out what Rhonda was trying to say. Of course she had an understanding that she was very good at what she did, and perhaps pride was a part of that assessment too and of course she was loyal to James. But the larger issue was, you don't trample the other side of yourself. It would do more harm than good in the long run.

Finally Emma said slowly, carefully, "I understand your concerns, Rhonda, I do. But James and I are a team. We made an agreement, more than that, either of us would be less without the other. Do you understand? I'm not short-selling myself, I'm not underselling myself, but our combined vision is what this project needs. Everyone involved deserves our best effort and that's it."

Rhonda sighed, her frustration evident. "Emma, be honest with yourself. You're carrying this project right now, I see you as Atlas holding up the whole thing. Your skills, your vision—they're what we need. And if you want to work together, great, but maybe he is the one who can assist you with *your* design and not the other way around. Maybe it's time for you to be the super hero and he can play Robin to your Batman."

Emma's face turned to stone, as if Rhonda had become Medusa in front of her eyes—it was hard to breathe, "What are you thinking?"

Rhonda held up a placating hand, as if warding off Emma's rising indignation. "I admit I wanted a lead designer to reflect more diversity. I can own that, having a woman take the lead may play a tiny part in my thinking. And yes, James is brilliant—you both have brought us to this point. But what good is brilliance if we're still fumbling in the dark?"

Emma rose from her chair and paced her vibrant Navajo rug, its geometric patterns providing a running board to gather steam. She turned to face Rhonda, her voice steady but charged with emotion. "You're right. I am good, very good, even. But James has..." she paused, searching for the right words. "He has a way of seeing invisible threads and connections.

She continued to move as she spoke, to get a feeling of the right words to say, "He can read not only how a work can be balanced, but the effect of it, the ripple effect. I've seen this, even back at Cooper Union. It's not ordinary. Rhonda, I'm not belittling myself, but James is the kind of person who's the starting point for ideas, like an inception point."

Emma studied Rhonda, she remained quiet on the couch, her body language a bit tense from the long day, but it seemed she was listening. Emma turned away from her for a moment and tried to imagine another more literal way to express what she was trying to communicate.

"I remember this one project," Emma said, her voice softening. "James had rearranged a seemingly perfect wire sculpture. At first, his changes looked like chaos incarnate, but as people interacted with it, the genius of his design became clear. It wasn't just about looking good, or to deliberately un-create—it was about feeling what the wire itself was feeling, all twisted up like that. Who has empathy like that?"

Emma looked at Rhonda again to note her response, Rhonda's face impassive now, as if she'd swapped it for a poker player's mask. Emma tried again, simplifying her point to its bare bones. "James doesn't just create art, he creates experiences."

Rhonda's gaze locked onto Emma's, "And why can't it be you to create that experience? How will you ever step up if you don't try?"

The question hit Emma hard, it reverberated in her bones like a tuning fork in her body, it was a notion that had haunted her for years, one of the seeds of doubt that had fueled her escape to Dresden a decade ago. Now here it was again, wrapped in a tempting package of professional advancement.

Emma sank back onto the couch beside Rhonda, the closeness turning their conversation into a hushed exchange between two women navigating the choppy waters of ambition and collaboration.

"I've asked myself the same for years," Emma admitted, her voice soft. "But maybe it's not the right question." She paused, gathering her thoughts. "When I was in Germany, I made some good friends. Wolfe and Berte loved taking me to football games."

Rhonda raised an eyebrow. "Football? I didn't peg you as a sports fan."

Emma chuckled. "I wasn't. But Wolfe was passionate about it. He explained how the game worked, how the players on the team would work together, passing the ball to the exact right player at the perfect moment to move it down the field and score."

"Sounds like basic teamwork to me," Rhonda interjected.

"That's just it," Emma nodded. "Wolfe said there was no ego about it. It was all about finding your role, playing your part, and winning together."

Rhonda leaned in, intrigued. "And you see a parallel with your work with James?"

"I do," Emma said. "Rhonda, I admit I deal with my ego. I think all women in business do. There's jealousy amongst ourselves and with men. Men have had practice with this concept in sports and other group activities, but for women, not so much, plus, I think we're afraid there aren't enough resources for us all, which can be true."

"But?" Rhonda prompted.

"But that can't blind me to what it means to be on a team," Emma continued. "If I want the ball to go to James, it's because I know he can do it. Just as I'm completely sure he'll pass it to me when it comes to color schemes and how they'll work—areas where he might not see as clearly."

Rhonda's brow furrowed. "So you're content to play second fiddle?"

Emma shook her head emphatically. "It's not about being second fiddle. It's about recognizing our value to each other and to the project. In truth, it's about creating something greater than either of us could alone."

Rhonda sat back, absorbing Emma's words. After a moment, she spoke, her tone thoughtful. "It's an admirable perspective, Emma. But in this cutthroat world, are you sure it's not just... naïve?"

Emma thought for a moment, a smile playing at the corners of her mouth. "Naïve or...nouveau? Maybe everything old is new again. Who built this apartment building? Men. And the roads? And every building you'll see on your way home? Men. It's not because women can't or are being denied that opportunity... it's because we don't want to."

She leaned forward, her eyes bright with conviction. "All I'm suggesting is that I find what I'm called to do, be honest about it, and help out in the best way I can. Perhaps on another project, it will be me in the lead. On this one, it's James and me together."

Rhonda listened, her expression thoughtful. After a moment, she nodded slowly. "I see your point, Emma, you're making yourself clear, but I have to ask—are you sure this isn't just about your feelings for James?"

Emma's cheeks flushed, momentarily stunned by Rhonda's perceptiveness.

Rhonda leaned forward, her eyes softening with understanding. "Emma, I've noticed how you look after him, even dote on him a little. Women have a way of putting ourselves aside for the men we care about, the ones we want to see succeed. You keep bringing this conversation back to James, and I admit, that's part of my motivation for pushing you. But I also refuse to see

Alfred and Mabel fail. That's my bottom line. I'm asking you to think about yours and be clear about it."

Emma sat quiet, her eyes drawn to the window and into the deep night, the moon was in view now. From her second-floor perch, she had a front-row seat to the night's unfolding drama as the moon inched across the sky determined in its mission, yet always alone.

She ran a hand through her hair. "My bottom line? Creating something beyond wonderful, but I won't do it by pushing James aside."

Rhonda nodded slowly, a mix of admiration and frustration playing across her face. "You're loyal, almost good-dog-loyal, which isn't entirely as bad as it just sounded, I'll give you that. But loyalty won't solve every issue we're facing."

"No," Emma agreed, "but it might just create something truly remarkable."

The two women sat in silence for a moment, the weight of their conversation hanging between them. Finally, Rhonda stood, gathering her papers.

"I see," she said, her voice softer now, Rhonda paused and looked down as if considering how much to reveal, "It seems I have to play my final card, it's an Ace and it's this: there are other groups who want the opportunity to design the lobby wall space at Eco United. I've heard rumors, and some gossip, but Alfred knows about it, which means I do too. Max from Eco is being pressured to present a competing concept. There it is in bold type billboard size font, everyone has worked too hard, I want us to succeed. I am trying to save this project."

Rhonda paused to observe Emma's reaction to this particular thunderbolt and lighting strike. Emma rose from the couch to look her in the eye, she watched the color drain from Emma's face and then nodded.

"So you see how it is," Rhonda stated, her tone clear, and even kind, "please keep the space open to submit your design. Do it. At this point, I'll settle for 'very, very good' rather than M.I.A."

And without another word Rhonda left, with a little less bounce in her step now, this evening and the late hour had taken a toll on them both. Emma followed her out, locked the door behind her and then slowly walked back to rest on the couch, her head in her hands. The weight of the project, her loyalty to James, her own ambition too, and now this new dark cloud.

No wonder Rhonda had paid her a late night visit. It was pressing down on all of them.

After a long moment, she reached for her phone again. No new messages from James. Her finger hovered over his number, then, almost of its own accord, picked up her large sketch pad instead.

"I believe in you, James," she murmured as she began to draw. "But just in case..."

The soft scratch of her pencil on the paper filled the quiet apartment. Emma worked late into the night, her face illuminated by the soft glow of her desk lamp, creating a design that honored both her vision and what she knew of James's. It wasn't a betrayal, she told herself. It was a safety net. For the project. For the community. For James.

As the first light of dawn crept through her windows, Emma looked at what she'd created. It was good. Very good, even. There was something missing, it was a first draft, and could be pulled together later, but still, it lacked that spark, that intention. That was because she had been mimicking James, anticipating what he might do. If she was to do this in earnest, it would have to come from herself, be her vision.

She flipped the cover shut on her rendering to protect the first draft and then set her phone aside. Her eyes felt gritty from lack of sleep, but her mind was clear.

Today, she decided she would go to James's loft. Whatever was happening, whatever he was struggling with, like it or not, ready or not, it was showtime... or showdown. The mosaic project was their shared vision, and Emma was determined to see it through—hopefully, with James by her side, even if she had to force an ebony pencil into his hand and threaten to call his mum.

As she stood, stretching her stiff muscles, Emma caught sight of herself in the mirror. Her dark hair was a mess, her eyes shadowed with fatigue, but there was a determination in her gaze that looked like she knew where she was going and why.

"I don't want to replace him," she said to her reflection. "I want to work with him. Now, will he work with me?"

The looming competing threat would bring whatever happened later today into sharp focus, they could make it work if they stuck together. And maybe... maybe this had been the source of those dreams she'd had months ago of James being in trouble. Well, those nightmares had brought her here, and today that meant it *was* showtime or showdown.

She could help him, it could still work.

With that thought, Emma headed to the shower. Time to *freshify* herself, maybe even smell pretty, and get ready to face whatever the day might bring. Plus, she was going to see James.

Pink heart on the plus side of the column.

* * *

Chapter 21

Chicago — Fulton St. Loft *— Jul. 11, 2002 — 7:59 a.m. — The Design Unveiled*

The early morning sun crept over the Chicago skyline like it had nothing better to do, so why not visit Shy Town and take a look around? It was peeking around the John Hancock Building illuminating a golden path for one Emma Hawkeye to walk. And so she did. Despite the long night or maybe because of it, she felt light on her feet all the way from the corner restaurant to James's loft, a bag of his favorite croissants and deli delights in one hand, a tray of steaming coffee and tea balanced precariously in the other. It felt good to be finally moving forward.

She caught a whiff from the coffee and checked the beverage tray, it was holding steady as she steamed ahead. She had a momentary flash of Rhonda's observation, what was it again? "Doting" and "good-dog loyalty" and shrugged. Oh well, maybe it was a matter of perception. People had to eat, didn't they? And James... well, James needed feeding more than most. He simply did not stop to eat when 'in the zone.' And so bringing him food was a civil service.

Emma saw his building just up ahead, and drew in a breath, in fact the closer she got, the more her imagination wandered further afield as to how she might find him. Her mind conjured absurd images of James locked away, reenacting Melville's Bartleby the Scrivener, preferring not to do anything but count the hairs on the backs of his hands.

"Artists," she muttered to herself, pausing at the edge of a wide puddle left over from last night's rain... but Noah was not in sight, so Emma solved it the old fashioned way—*she walked around.* See? Easy. "Artists... and geniuses have a knack for losing their marbles at the worst possible moment—don't know how to problem solve the easy stuff."

Not that she truly believed James had gone off the deep end. Still, a knot of worry tightened in her stomach.

The elevator groaned its way up to James's floor, protesting each level passed as if it were being dragged to a proctologist appointment. When it finally deposited her in the hallway, Emma found herself hesitating before his door. Her hand, poised to knock, hovered in midair as she searched for the new doorbell Val was supposed to have installed.

"No chime yet," she sighed. "Oops. Nothing like a gentle 'ding-dong' to soften the blow of a wake-up call. Oh well..."

Taking a deep breath that did little to calm her nerves, she rapped her knuckles against the worn wood. One Mississippi, two Mississippi... Emma counted in her head, waiting for a response. At precisely six Mississippis, the door swung open.

The sight that greeted her was not at all what she'd been bracing for. Instead of a disheveled, wild-eyed madman, there stood James—disheveled, yes, but with eyes that shone brighter than pretty pearls. His hair stood on end as if he'd been slow dancing with an electrical socket, true, but there was an unmistakable aura of triumph about him. Emma recognized that look all too well. He'd had a breakthrough.

"Em!" James exclaimed, his voice warm and welcoming. "Perfect timing. Come in, I've got something to show you." Without waiting for a response, he turned on his heel and disappeared back into the depths of the loft.

Emma stood there for a moment, blinking in surprise. Where was the man she'd come to rescue? The tormented artist in need of sustenance and sanity? This James looked as content as a kitten on a pink pillow, and if she was being honest with herself, and because she did have a detailed list of some human-esque emotions, it pissed her off just a little bit.

She stepped inside, momentarily stunned by the transformation. Every surface was covered with white paper, drawings, and magazine cutouts. The air thrummed with creative energy, the scent of coffee and graphite mingling with the fresh morning breeze from an open window.

She called out to his retreating form, "Just like that? No 'hello,' no, 'I've been burning the midnight oil,' just 'come on in'?" Emma's tone was light, but she let some frustration creep into her voice too.

James turned back to her, his smile softening as he took in her slightly frazzled state. "Sorry luv, hello, I've definitely been burning the midnight oil—ooooh, is that food?"

Emma couldn't help but laugh, the tension in her shoulders easing just a fraction. "Yeah, but you don't get a lick until I see what in the world you've been making," she retorted, setting the bag down on a rare clear spot on his kitchen island. "You have no idea what's been going on out there. There are wolves at my door, James. Wolves!"

She wheeled on her heel to hammer the point home, "You won't believe the conversations I've been fielding. 'Where's James? What's up with James? Is his passport updated? Has he left for Sri Lanka?' What?"

Emma was making jokes, but there was a kernel of real frustration beneath the humor. The past few days had been a whirlwind of worry and speculation, and here was James, looking like he'd just stepped out of a particularly invigorating yoga retreat, sans the mud mask. But there was plenty of clay around here... somewhere, she could fix that oversight right quick if he needed a good slap... of mud.

Before she could get to the really funny stuff to bring the house down. James closed the distance between them and planted a light kiss on her cheek. A sweet frisson of calm radiated from the point of contact, spreading through her body like it had all the time in the world to warm her bones... and other parts. Emma blinked, her hand halfway to her cheek before she caught herself. She took a deep breath, trying to regain her composure.

"Thanks pet for holding down the fort," James said softly, his breath warm against her skin. "Gerardo and I were still working, which you saw, I'm sure and I've got lots of news for the next stage—for the large warehouse space we need, but... Em... I'm so glad you're here, I think I have it."

Emma stepped further into the loft, taking her coat off slowly, turning in a circle to take in the controlled chaos. Sketches and diagrams covered every available surface, transforming the space into a cocoon of creativity. The morning light streamed through the windows, illuminating the scene with a fresh, energizing glow.

"Where?" She asked, still stunned at the chaos, her eyes darting from one paper-covered surface to another. "You sure you remember where you left it? It's like a tornado hit a stationery store here."

James chuckled, running a hand through his already disheveled hair. "That's funny, I like that. You may continue to amuse me nonstop, I'm sure, but seeing as I'm a tad hungry, and food's off limits til I bare all—"

"—Please, not all..." Emma cautioned, a mischievous glint in her eye. "Mixed company here—"

"Indeed, not all," James wisely corrected himself, his lips twitching with suppressed laughter. "but enough..." His face grew quiet as he looked into her eyes, a sudden intensity replacing the playful banter. "It's done, Em, well, except for the final color rendering, but enough to get it. It's laid out on the conference table—needed the extra space for the full view."

Emma's heart skipped a beat, the weight of his words bringing her right down to earth. This was it—showtime.

James led the way to the long folding table set up now in the center of the studio area of the loft. As they walked toward it, he began to explain, his words slow, as if measuring each word for its idiosyncratic value before weaving the sentence together. "Watching you, watching everyone make their tiles provided the general way. Who we are, who we all are, flexes, moves, and lives as individuals under the umbrella... of the larger image of ourselves... what we call society. Micro to the macro."

James pointed to the far right end, "It begins there, as you would walk into the lobby of the Eco United Building."

As James narrated, Emma stood back to get a visual grasp of the long view and then leaned in, studying the intricate design spread out before her. Her eyes widened as she began to grasp the scope of James's vision. He had created a blueprint to represent small tiles as the beginning point of the concept, the micro-image expanding out to the macro. Utilizing the concept of pointillism or impressionism, up close you would be able to identify all the individual tiles and details and as you stepped back to view the whole mosaic, the single tile would become part of a larger different image.

Emma's fingertips hovered just above the surface, tracing the intricate patterns without touching, as if afraid to disturb the paper, lest it evaporate before her eyes. The design seemed to have a pulse, she could feel a shiver run up her arm as she followed the lines, getting a grasp of how it would be.

"It's like a plant growing from a seed, Em," James continued, his voice steady with calm conviction. "The final plant doesn't resemble the seed, but the energy of the intent extends to the creation and final effect."

Emma nodded, understanding dawning. She saw how the design moved from individual tiles inside larger themes—forests, rivers, continents, sky, and beyond. Her finger traced the lines, following the flow of the design, marveling at its complexity and elegance.

"But it doesn't stop there, does it then?," James asked, guiding Emma's gaze across the design. "See how it moves to the next wall? Into the cosmos, planets in orbit... all from one seed, one tile. Nothing is lost, no one is small, ultimately, we are all connected."

The loft fell silent as Emma absorbed the magnitude of James's vision. Emma's breath caught in her throat, the enormity of James's vision moving toward her like an unstoppable tsunami. "I... I can feel it James... and almost see it... see where you're going... it's like... it's like the entire universe in miniature," she whispered, her voice filled with awe. "Each tile is a star, a world unto itself, but... humble too, playing a part in... something larger than we can understand."

Outside, the city was coming to life, the sounds of early morning traffic and birdsong filtering through the open window. The morning light fills the loft to overflowing—illuminating the space, seeping into every corner to glow it from the inside out.

In that moment, surrounded by the physical manifestation of James's creativity, Emma felt a surge of pride and awe. She absolutely loved his mind, his ability to see connections, to weave individual stories into a grand tapestry of human experience, never ceased to amaze her.

As they stood there, side by side, the air seemed to hum with possibility. The mosaic project had evolved into something far greater than either of them had initially imagined. It was no longer just about art or community engagement—it was a visual representation of the interconnectedness of all things, a reminder of the profound impact even the smallest action could have.

Emma's breath caught as she took in the grandeur of the vision. The early morning light streamed through the windows, illuminating the intricate design spread across the table. It was not only about reaching out to God, she realized, but about being connected in the family of God, from the smallest child and detail to the infinite expanse of the universe.

"It's like... it's like we're building a cathedral of the human spirit," Emma murmured, her fingers tracing the outline of a particularly intricate section. "But instead of stone and stained glass, we're using clay and color."

James nodded, a soft smile playing at his lips. "And every person who contributed a tile is a master craftsman in this cathedral," he added, his voice warm with appreciation of her understanding.

As Emma studied the design, her eyes tracing the complex patterns, she could visualize how the tiles, glazed in complementary and contrasting colors, would fill the shapes. The colors seemed to shimmer in her mind's eye, bringing the design to life. Themes of brown tiles for forests, their earthy tones rich and varied, blended into shades of blue for rivers flowing into vast waters. Her gaze caught on abstract shapes too—a large wheel like a mandala, its intricate patterns driving the whole work, seeming to pulse with energy even in its static form.

"James," she breathed, her voice barely above a whisper, "this is… wonderful."

James's excitement finally bubbled over as he heard her approval and awe, he explained further, his right hand pointing the way as he spoke. "The small tiles holding certain feelings, like happy faces and hearts, will be arranged in a larger image of a similar mood or intent—a family house, or wild forest. We'll sort them using intuition, putting them into 'families' which could be literal families, or themes like owning a business, growing a garden, living with nature, science, ecology."

Emma's eyes traveled along the length of the table, taking in how the smaller sections connected to larger themes. The morning light, nature's own highlighter, emphasized the details. "And then it all connects," she murmured, her finger tracing the lines, "to the continent, the earth, the sky, space…"

"And God," James finished, his voice soft with reverence. "The Great Spirit, as you call him."

Overwhelmed by the beauty and complexity of the design, Emma turned to him. The rising sun cast a warm glow on James's face, highlighting the passion in his eyes. "James… Jimmy the James…" Without thinking, she wrapped her arms around him, hugging him tightly. The scent of coffee and graphite clung to his shirt, familiar and comforting. "Thank you for doing justice for the clay, I think the people will be so pleased… and honored."

When she finally let go, James looked at her, a hint of amusement in his eyes. A stray lock of hair had fallen across his forehead, giving him a boyish appearance despite the intensity of his gaze. "So you like it then? Think you can light this up?"

Emma nodded, wiping away tears of joy. The early morning light caught the moisture on her cheeks, making them glisten. "Yes... I already have a lot of these colors ready... as if I knew somehow." She paused, a mischievous glint in her eye. "Though I might need to invent new layers of blue just for that bit there," she added, pointing to a particularly large section of sky.

James continued, his excitement building again. He moved around the table, gesturing to different sections of the design. "As we assemble the smaller tiles into the larger sections, there's room for improvisation. Everyone can make command decisions over the smaller details. We are a community, and the energy of many hands will be in the actual assembly too."

Emma smiled, she felt just fine—fine overflowing. She could almost see the finished mosaic in her mind's eye, a living, breathing tapestry from everyone who came to play. "Yes, I can see that... and just to be fair..." she paused dramatically, "I'll even let you play with some colors."

James did a double take, his eyebrows shooting up in mock surprise. "You what? Em Hawkeye is giving up a wee space for me to play with me crayons? Has the world gone mad?"

She playfully pushed at him, laughing. "Don't get too excited. I said *some colors*. And I'll be supervising, of course. Can't have you going rogue with the fuchsia."

James laughed, "Uh oh, you know me too well. Should I be flattered or terrified?"

"It's a tough job but someone has to do it," Emma observed and then clarified, her eyes twinkling with mischief. "I know what happens to your mind when you discover a new color, it just explodes and you gotta find every tonal variation. I remember your lime-green period in 1987—the studio at the Hewitt Building looked like a radioactive organic garden. And your amber period—that was a nice one. 1988 I think? Everything glowed like sunlight trapped in a bottle, we had to wear sunglasses—"

And this time it was James who spontaneously hugged Emma and breathed in her ear these simple words: 'Thanks Em."

* * *

It wasn't until about ten minutes later while they were enjoying breakfast, did Emma realize that earlier today had been the first time she'd hugged James in twelve years. It was the first time she'd held him close. It brought a bittersweet smile to her face, but noting how contented James seemed as he munched his bacon and cheese egg biscuit, and that he had just hugged her back—maybe he hadn't minded her forward move at all. Maybe Mirabel was right, and he wouldn't put up too much of a fuss if she tackled him.

She shook her head, and lowered her gaze as a warm flush swept through her body to pink her cheeks. The memory of his arms around her, his particular warm, earthy scent sent a shiver... well, all around her everywhere.

"What?" James asked, a bit of egg clinging to his growing stubble of a beard.

"Nothing, I'm just happy." Emma replied, resisting the urge to reach out and brush away the crumb... and maybe touch his face, feel the spiky threads of his five o'clock shadow at nine a.m.

He thought about it, and then: "I'll accept that. Plenty of work ahead for you. We're going to have to buckle down to fill in the colors for a full size complete rendering so everyone can get the full picture."

"I'm loving it already." Was Emma's simple reply.

James nodded, he seemed to accept that too.

As the sun rose outside, and really, truly committed itself to a good wake up and Rouse! Rouse!

Emma and James sat side by side, next to the conference table, drinking tea and coffee respectively, and glancing at the design occasionally, the city was waking up around them, the distant sounds of traffic and birdsong filtering through the open window as if reiterating that this would be a good day. No, wait, double down on that missive and make this a wonderfully fantastic day. And somewhere in the middle of it all were a man and a woman finding their way to each other.

* * *

Fulton Street Loft — *Jul. 17, 2002 — 8:45 a.m.*

The morning sun crept through the tall windows of James's loft, casting long fingers of light across the hardwood floor. The clock on the wall showed 8:45 a.m.—unusually early for visitors, but this was no ordinary day. James stood motionless, his eyes tracing the intricate design that now stretched the entire length of the wall adjacent to the windows. The colors, carefully selected in collaboration with Emma over countless late nights and heated debates, breathed life into the complex shapes and patterns.

He took a step back, then forward again, his artist's eye catching every nuance, every subtle shift in hue. The scent of fresh coffee wafted from the kitchen, mingling with the lingering aroma of clay and paint. The browns of the forest section undulated like a living thing, each shade carefully chosen to complement its neighbors while maintaining its own distinct identity. Blues flowed from cerulean to navy in the river and ocean sections, creating a sense of depth and movement that seemed to ripple before his eyes.

James's fingers twitched, itching to make one last adjustment. "Steady on, mate," he muttered to himself. "It's done. Let it breathe."

The sound of footsteps on the stairs outside broke James's reverie. There was a solid knock and he called out, "It's open, come on in." And then turned as the door swung open, revealing Rhonda, her usual businesslike demeanor softened by an expression of curiosity. Her crisp light green suit contrasted sharply with the artistic chaos of the loft, like a perfectly manicured lawn in the midst of a wildflower meadow.

"Good morning, James," she said, her eyes immediately drawn to the long stretch of paper attached to the far wall facing the front door. "This is the design." Rhonda confirmed as she slowly approached the full color rendering,

James nodded, a small smile as he studied her reaction. "Aye, it is."

Rhonda stepped further into the room, her heels clicking on the hardwood floor, softer now, as she stepped onto a vibrant rug in the center of his living space. She stood silent for a long moment, her eyes roving over the expanse of color and form. When she spoke, her voice was barely above a whisper. "I've never seen anything quite like it. Ever, anywhere. It's humbling, we're small in the clockwork... but not. We're all included... and loved."

James felt a warmth spread through his chest at her words. He came and stood next to her, not sure what to say, so opted for nothing as they considered her very good words. Finally he said, "Thanks for working so hard. Couldn't have done it without you holding the line."

Rhonda turned to look at him, really look at him, maybe for the first time in months and then shook her head slightly, "You had me spinning, James, you really did, not sure where you were going to land. I feel like I just dropped ten tons of 'worry'."

After a moment, he offered in his sweetest, tenderest tone "I may have a homeopathic remedy for stress relief in the medicine chest, if you'd like. Guaranteed to soften the edges... or make them clearer, depending on your preference."

She laughed, bright now, more relaxed, "Is that how you survive dealing with yourself?"

"Doesn't hurt at all, sometimes I feel like I'm just along for the ride." James shared and she chuckled.

Instead of responding directly Rhonda asked "How long did this take you?" She had moved closer now, her fingers hovering near the rendering, as if afraid to touch it, as if human contact might cause it to dissolve or reveal it as a glamor, gone with snap of the fingers.

"Weeks for the design, as you know, waiting for the carvings people were making to accumulate enough so I could get a grasp of what people were praying for, then breakthroughs, here and there to keep me sane and on track." James replied, running a hand through his disheveled hair. "Emma was a blessing as you know, running interference and holding the line, and she and I lost track of time on the rendering more than once. We went days into nights, when one of us needed sleep, we worked in shifts—maybe that was about four days. But we're still a solid week ahead of Eco's deadline."

"Yes we are." Rhonda confirmed, a hint of victory song queuing up in her tone. "Speaking of Emma, where is she?"

James's eyes softened at the mention of Emma's name. "Sleeping, I hope. She deserves it after the trek around the world we've been through—move over Magellan. Gerardo's picking her up later."

The door opened again, admitting Alfred and Mabel this time. Alfred's eyes widened as he took in the scene, while Mabel let out a soft gasp. The couple, usually so composed, seemed momentarily stunned by the sight before them. Without saying a word they came and stood in front of the expanse of the design, James and Rhonda cleared the way for them to get close.

"Oh, James," Mabel breathed, her hand reaching out to grasp Alfred's arm. "It's beautiful."

Alfred's keen eyes taking in every detail. "The scope of it... it's everything we all spoke about, my boy, everything we wanted."

James nodded but said nothing in response except, "Would you like a closer look?" He offered, gesturing towards the wall.

As they moved nearer, the intricate details became even more apparent. Tiny figures and symbols were woven throughout the design, symbolizing how the tiles might lie within the templates, each telling its own story within the larger narrative.

"Is that... is that symbolizing the Chicago skyline?" Mabel asked, pointing to a section near the top right corner over the 'reeds and onion field template.'

James nodded. "Good eye. We wanted to incorporate elements of the city, to give a specific nod to the time and place where it all began."

Alfred ran his hand along the edge of the wall, careful not to touch the design itself. "The texture on the design to raise the surface, to add the feeling of how it might look in real time... how did you achieve this?"

As James launched into an explanation of their techniques, the loft buzzed with energy. The morning light continued to shift, bringing new aspects of the design to life. It was clear to all present that they were witnessing a work from the heart—a vision brought to life through passion, skill, and collaboration and no small amount of the collective group soul.

Alfred stepped closer to the wall, his keen eyes examining the details. The morning light caught the silver in his hair as he leaned in, squinting slightly to take in the intricate patterns. "The way you've integrated the individual elements into the larger whole... it's masterful, my boy, I can better visualize now what we were talking about." he said, his voice filled with wonder.

"I couldn't have done it without Emma," James said, his voice soft and certain. He cleared his throat before continuing, "Her understanding of color... our ability to... almost read each other's mind, I guess helped bring the whole thing to life. There were moments when we'd both reach for the same color at the same time—bit Twilight Zone, really."

Rhonda turned to James, her professional mask slipping to reveal genuine admiration. Her usually stern features softened as she looked around the loft. "You said Emma is coming? She should be here for this."

James chuckled, "Yes... she's on her way I'm sure—unless Gerardo got lost, there are a lot of streets that run in a diagonal in Chicago, it can get confusing. " James chuckled and then when Rhonda didn't join in, he patted her arm "No, seriously, it's okay. She had to check her message machine—she'd been camping out here while we worked—should be here any minute."

"Good, good," Mabel said, her motherly instincts kicking in, "in fact I'd like to get some breakfast going for us all, you are looking too thin James, I admit it makes me nervous."

James laughed, a low, warm, rich sound that filled the loft. "I wouldn't say no, there's ham and eggs, and I'll join to help, actually...you go sit, relax and enjoy the view, I'll make breakfast—I know where everything is. Val stocked the fridge for me and Em, and left food out for us like we were feral cats, but we didn't eat much, you know how it is when you're in the flow."

The clock on the wall ticked loudly in the ensuing silence, marking the seconds until, as if on cue, the door opened once more. Emma stepped in, her large tote swung across her body with Gerardo close behind. She froze just inside the threshold, her eyes locked on the design.

James watched as a myriad of emotions played across her face; "You have it on the wall... ah James, it looks... oh my goodness... it looks even better when we can look at it in this way."

"Well your eyes are probably clear now, thas' a help," remarked James from the kitchen as he put pans on the stove and pulled food from the fridge.

She moved to stand beside Mabel who had left the kitchen to greet her, they hugged briefly then Emma walked closer to the design and now Alfred hugged her tight and Rhonda as well.

No one spoke, just one grand hugging 'fest' until the cycle of greeting and gratitude was completed.

Gerardo still stood close to the door, he'd shut it behind him, but remained firmly planted from afar to get the whole view, the grand vista and sweet supplication to God.

"Gerardo! How'd you like your eggs?" James called from the kitchen, his voice cutting through the contemplative silence.

"Ah... I'm having a moment here, just... hold that thought..." Gerardo's voice was soft, some of the cheer and bravado definitely on the back burner for the moment.

Slowly he stepped into the center of the living room area and the folks down front shifted so he could get a clear view as everyone present turned to observe his reaction and his subdued expression.

"Gerardo?" Emma's voice was tentative, searching for what he might be feeling without trying to prompt a specific response.

Without responding Gerardo stepped closer, and then paused, looked at his arms, and ran one hand up his left arm. "See that? Goose bumps, those shivers I get when faced with something... connected. James... Emma, what did you do?"

James came from the kitchen to get a closer look at his dear friend and saw he was close to weeping and asked softy "What is it mate? We're all friends here in the same boat, you can tell us, we can take it."

Gerardo looked at Emma, then James and said "It's beautiful... so beautiful it is profound. I can almost hear the voices of the wonderful people too, but my friends... what happens to a work that is so beyond the pale, it might... frighten the ungodly. Some people are known to tear down holy places... this must be built and we are the team to do it, I feel that so solid in my bones... but now we must protect it too. Don't you feel it?"

James nodded. "I do." A solemn understanding passed between them.

"That will be my job." Alfred said quietly, "Mabel and I will take care of that, I think we all agree that respect for this work will be a high priority at the installation and beyond."

Gerardo nodded, and then after wiping his eyes and clearing his throat he said to James, "I feel like I should hug you, but seeing you're wearing an apron—"

"A chef's apron—" James corrected smoothly, a glint of humor in his eyes.

"Whatever... in that case I'll have my eggs over easy on hash browns and don't dare break the yolk... but I will hug Emma, come 'ere chickita."

And so Emma was the beneficiary of one of Gerardo's big bear hugs he reserved for special people on special occasions.

"Okay, okay, everybody relax, you too Gerardo, put the lady down, please, " James suggested, his tone a mix of amusement and mock exasperation. "Still need her somewhat operational. Can't have you squeezing all the go-to juice out of her."

"Uh oh... touchy about your turf?" Gerardo smiled and winked at Alfred and Mabel in the living room, but placed Emma carefully back down, then kissed the top of her head for good measure. She patted his arm and hugged him back, a quick minny 'Emma' hug.

"Oh... dry up." James advised, but they were having pure fun now, all in good humor, James continued, "Anyway, this will be a buffet serve-yourself spread, Emma and I will sling out the hash and if you're lucky or quick you can catch it with your teeth."

General round of laughter filled the loft, the joy of creation and friendship, an ordinary but precious blessing radiating the very air.

Mabel stepped forward, her eyes glistening. "It's like watching a dream come to life," she murmured, reaching out to squeeze Emma's hand. Emma hugged her once more before going to join James in the kitchen to 'get food ready for this lot.'

The room remained silent for a long moment, save for the rattle, bang and banter of Emma and James in the kitchen. Each person was lost in their own thoughts as they absorbed the magnitude of what lay before them. The distant sound of traffic and the gentle hum of the loft's heating system provided a subtle backdrop to their contemplation.

It was Rhonda who finally broke the spell, her voice filled with a mixture of awe and determination. She unbuttoned her jacket, took it off, and placed it on the back of the couch, as she thought ahead. "Well," she said, her tone regaining some of its usual briskness, "James, Emma... you've outdone yourselves."

"Wait... hold that blue ribbon, you haven't seen me eggs yet." James warned, a mischievous glint in his eye. "I've been practicing my egg juggling. Who's brave enough for an omelet à la cirque du soleil?"

"Oh stop... I know you were a short order cook in Newcastle, you can't fool me, I can spot a 'ringer.'" Rhonda was wry, everyone laughed.

"Did you crack a joke, our Rhonda?" James loved it, "All right, the sucker-bets are off, but let me have some fun and make you all breakfast, right?"

"Gerardo!" It was Emma calling from the side table, where she was placing sides of ham, cheese and fruit, "Would you put some music on, please? Whatever you like."

"My pleasure." Gerardo was already on his way, humming as he went. "Let's see what the maestro has in his collection."

After spinning through James's collection of CDs, and then to everyone's surprise, they heard the opening melodic chords of George Frederick Handel's 'Messiah' begin earthbound and float upwards, ever upwards.

Alfred smiled as he and Mabel sat in overstuffed easy chairs and watched Emma bring them fresh squeezed orange juice. As she handed the tall glasses to them, she said, softly, privately, "Thank you. For everything."

The loft hummed with the energy of creation and friendship, the morning light now fully illuminating the masterpiece on the wall. As they gathered for breakfast, there was a sense that something monumental had begun, a journey that would change not just their lives, but the very fabric of the community they sought to serve.

James caught Emma's eye across the room, a silent understanding passing between them. No words needed at the moment. Whatever challenges lay ahead, they would face them together, buoyed by the strength of their shared vision and the support of their friends. The design on the wall was more than just a beautiful image; it was a promise, a declaration of hope and possibility. And as the smell of cooking breakfast filled the air and Handel's music soared, they all knew that this was just the beginning.

* * *

Breaking fast wound down, but still the group wanted to stay together, after such massive effort en masse, they yearned to linger and enjoy each other's company, like a pride of lions lying sprawled on the savannah, they were reluctant to leave their best happy place in the sun.

Val had joined them by now, but James refused to let her into the kitchen to clean even one spot on one plate, today was 'on him' his treat. So she stood in front of the vast design munching from a bunch of grapes. She would study the work, step in close for a look at the rendering, then step back, cock her head to alter her perception, and then repeat the process.

James was currently on maintenance duty in the kitchen, and it's possible he was humming a mixed version several Beatles tunes, "Two of Us' and the improbable "I Dig a Pony" or maybe he was just making it all up as he went along like a two year old taking the English language for a spin. In any case, he noticed his assistant's 'chicken dance' and so he called out to his valiant Val:

"What is it, pet? What's cookin' in that noggin? Are you trying to decode the Dead Sea Scrolls with 'naught but pert grapes for a mile marker?"

Val did a quick double take to her boss, shook her head a little, "I'm ignoring that for the moment and instead gotta say, I'm absolutely blown away by the design details, just blown away" She took a quick breath to refuel her lungs, then, "James, you're leaving no room for doubt, you laid out a road map, I've mentioned that before, but I'm also... struck dumb- "

"—You?" Gerardo cut in from his vantage point on the couch "at a loss for words? Rhonda, write down the date and time." There was a mild round of laughter as a quarter hour medication, but let's face it, they were all so giddy, everything was funny now.

"Ha, ha..." Val said in her best mock-offended autocratic tone and then continued, "but what I'm looking at now are the layers of color, James... I didn't really notice what you and Emma were doing up close when I came to throw food at you, didn't want to break your flow, so seeing it complete like this—at the layers and layers of color. It's like a super close up of the transitions of a rainbow, something you don't notice from the ground. But the design takes that proposal and inserts it into a kaleidoscope. My mind is boggled, I'm assuming the tiles will have a similar aesthetic, but can you talk about that, Emma?"

"Sure." Emma stepped forward, her fingertips lightly brushing the surface of the design, getting a feel of the paper, just for the fun of it. The early afternoon light streaming through the loft windows caught the auburn highlights in her dark hair, creating a halo effect around her head.

James stopped his humming/singing-background-filler-whatever and came around the kitchen island to get a good view of Emma as she moved into high gear. He crossed his arms and smiled.

"If you all come a bit closer," Emma said, her voice soft but carrying easily in the hushed room, like a private conversation across still water, "I'd like to show you how we've approached the color palette."

The group rose as an ensemble from their scattered positions around the living room, and shuffled forward, their shoes scuffing softly on the hardwood floor. The scent of fresh coffee and pastries from the nearby kitchen mingled with the earthy smell of clay and paint, creating an olfactory backdrop as rich as the visual one before them.

Rhonda had her notebook handy now, her pen poised to mark the moment. The leather cover cracked slightly as she opened it to a fresh page.

"Now, prepare to have your socks knocked off," Emma said with a grin, her enthusiasm infectious. "And I mean that literally. You might want to check your feet after this; I can't be held responsible for any missing footwear."

Emma gestured to a section of the design representing a sprawling forest. The greens and browns seemed to shimmer in the light, creating an almost three-dimensional effect that made Gerardo blink rapidly, as if trying to clear his vision.

"We've used complementary and analogous colors to create balance and harmony," she explained, her eyes alight with passion. "Much as you'd see in nature itself. Mother Nature has set the gold standard—we just took a page from her playbook."

Her finger traced the outline of a tree, following the subtle shifts in brown hues. The movement was graceful, almost like a dance—*a mudra in motion,* James thought, watching the fluid arc of her hand.

She was speaking now, so James shifted his attention to the subtitles: "Notice how the browns vary here," she continued. "We're not using a single, flat color. Instead, we have a range—from rich, deep umber to lighter, almost golden tans. It's as if the forest put on its Sunday best for us."

Her hand moved again, the fingers of her hand parting like petals blooming—less instructional now, more evocative. A dance still, but different this time. Something older.

Polynesian storytelling, perhaps.

James watched the full arc of her arm as she spoke, stepping away from the kitchen to catch every word—and enjoy the show.

Emma continued "Notice how the browns vary here..." she continued. "We're not using a single, flat color. Instead, we have a range—from rich, deep umbers to lighter, almost golden tans... and we have amber, the highs and lows of amber—James just loves his amber." And here she stole a glance at him and they both laughed. Everyone else looked puzzled.

"I don't get it." Val said

"Never mind, private joke," James broke in and then pointed the way back to Emma, "Back on track now, Em's just warming up."

Emma thought for a moment getting back into her slipstream, "Think of it like this, it's like seeing the forest at the golden hour, you know just before the sun sets, when all the colors of nature are highlighted to reveal different tonal values but are still all together at the same Sunday picnic."

Mabel leaned in, her glasses perched on the end of her nose. A strand of her silver hair fell forward, and Alfred gently tucked it behind her ear, with the tenderness of a lifetime of love. "It's remarkable," she murmured. "It's as if the trees are alive, shifting in an afternoon breeze. I half expect to see a squirrel pop out and start chattering at us."

Emma beamed, pleased by the observation. "Exactly. We want to create depth and texture, just as you'd see in a real landscape. The eye naturally picks up these variations, even if we're not consciously aware of it. It's a kind of nature-magic."

She moved along the wall, coming to a section where the forest gave way to a winding river. The transition was so smooth, it was almost impossible to see where one ended and the other began, like the seamless blend of sea into sky.

"Now, watch how we transition from the earth tones to the blues of the water," Emma said, her voice taking on an instructional tone, adding her own personal emphasis to what she wanted to highlight.

Alfred stepped closer, his eyes narrowing as he studied the subtle shift. His fingers twitched, as if longing to touch the design. "Fascinating," he muttered. "You've used some greens in there, haven't you? As a bridge between the browns and blues? It's like... like the forest is dipping its toes in the water."

Emma nodded enthusiastically, a strand of hair falling across her face. She brushed it away absently, leaving a small smudge of color on her cheek that James found, well, just old fashioned sweet, but he remained where he was—didn't want to break the spell Emma was weaving.

"Good eye, Alfred." Emma encouraged, " Yes, we've incorporated some muted greens—think of the mossy banks of a river. It helps the transition feel natural, not abrupt. We don't want the eye to work harder than it has too. James's design has excellent control of focus, so we don't fight against that flow, we use that for harmonious color transitions and high contrast too, just as there is in nature. When there is contrast, it is deliberate. A pleasant shock to the senses."

"You must absolutely give a clinic on this at the Art Institute School..." Gerardo broke in, fascinated and then amended, "okay we'll talk later, sorry to interrupt."

"Thanks, and that's all right..." Emma assured him. "Maybe this is a good time for questions."

Rhonda, who had been furiously scribbling notes, looked up. Her normally stern expression had softened, replaced by genuine curiosity. "And this approach... is it consistent throughout the entire design? It's not just a one-hit wonder?""

Emma chuckled, "Funny and yes," she confirmed, her voice filled with quiet confidence. "We've applied this principle of natural color transition throughout. From land to sea, from earth to sky, even into the more abstract cosmic sections. It's like a grand color journey from the ground beneath our feet to the stars above our heads."

She led them to a portion of the design representing the night sky. The deep blues and purples seemed to glow, even in the bright morning light, as if they had captured a piece of the midnight sky and pasted it onto the wall.

"Here, see how we've used deep purples and midnight blues, with hints of silver and gold for stars? It's still harmonious with the overall palette, but it creates a distinct mood and atmosphere. It's like we've bottled up the feeling you get when you look up at a clear night sky and realize how vast and beautiful the universe is.""

James, who had been quietly observing, stepped forward, unable to contain himself any longer. "Em's got a knack for this," he said, his voice warm with admiration. "She can see connections between colors I'd never even thought of. It's like she's got some sort of telepathic color super power."

Emma chuckled, glanced quickly in his direction, then said softly, addressing the group, "It's a collaborative effort, James's vision gives the colors a purpose, a story to tell." She glanced back at him for a moment, but looking into each other's eyes felt so good, they couldn't break away, as a current of understanding passed between them and mutual approval.

Val saved the day with a short sarcastic replay of their mutual admiration society, she turned to Gerardo, pretended to tip her imaginary hat, and quipped "Oh sir, you are too, too grand, do go first—"

Gerardo immediately picked up his cue, shook his head vehemently and insisted "Oh *no*, senorita, you must oblige me, you are grander than all grand and must proceed, ever upward."

Alfred laughed out loud, a full hearty Santa Claus sound, he was thinking. of course, of James' private conversation with him at that first meeting. But instead of mentioning *that* he said this: "Well, I'll take it, glad to hear you both are getting along."

Mabel was chuckling too and Emma blushed a full peony pink, but what of it? They were among friends, after all, and she did look pretty in pink.

All James could come up with was. "Oh... dry up, you lot." but he was smiling,

As the general mirth subsided, Emma breathed deep and retook the driver's wheel and steered the talk back on track and toward, well, the icing on the cake, the bread in the basket... the cosmos.

"As we move into the actual mosaic creation," Emma continued, her voice regaining its professional tone, "we'll be using these color guidelines to inform our glaze choices. Each tile will be a small part of this larger color story. It's like we're writing a novel, but instead of words, we're using colors and shapes.""

Alfred nodded approvingly, his hand resting on Mabel's shoulder. "It's more than just aesthetically pleasing," he mused. "It's... emotionally resonant. The colors evoke feelings, memories. It's looking at a life well-lived"

"That's the hope," Emma said, her voice tinged with excitement. She pointed to various parts of the design as she spoke. "We want people to connect with this on a visceral level... here... and here, note how the color pauses to rest; we want to see ourselves metaphorically actualized in colors and shapes."

James smiled and offered in best 'upper crust Brit,' "I could listen to her for hours."

He was sitting in his favorite easy chair now, enjoying the show for a change, instead of you know, *being* the show. It was a relief. He even kicked off his shoes.

There was a general wash of amused laughter, and a lighthearted giddiness in the room. They had climbed a mountain and could see the mountain range ahead, but oh what a view. Anything and everything felt possible... and just where do we begin?

"Winner, winner, chicken dinner," Gerardo announced, his eyes sparkling, "Or should I say, winner, winner, color *spinner*? Either way, we've hit the jackpot, I'm itching like a cat on a new couch."

The room erupted in laughter once more, a joyous crescendo to mark the moment. As the mirth subsided, James caught Emma's eye across the room. In that moment, in this way, they were friends again, as if the years of separation had been nothing more than a long commercial break in their favorite TV show. What might happen between them, he still couldn't say, but he was so very pleased to have his friend again and from the way she was smiling at him, perhaps she felt the same.

James looked once more at the design attached to the wall, shook his head... and then realized that Emma was now standing by his side.

"What is it?" She asked.

James shook his head, and spoke in a subdued voice, "You know, people keep looking to us, thanking us 'an all, but really it's Alfred and Mabel who made this happen. Em, if this gets accepted by Eco United, we need to make this the best possible product we possibly can, right?"

Em was already nodding at the halfway mark of his closing soliloquy. "Right. Shake on it?"

That was it, they agreed, shook hands... and then found it hard to let go. Their fingers seemed to have a mind of their own, intertwining for a good weave and lockdown.

"Do you have some kind of SuperGlue on your hands?" Emma asked, her voice very, very quiet barely above a whisper.

"Pretty sure I don't." James observed equally subdued. "Unless they've started putting it in hand sanitizer as a practical joke... or cautionary tale."

"Okay on the count of three, we let go." Emma said, her voice trembling now, "One, two... three..."

* * *

Chapter 22

Chicago — Fulton Street Loft — Assembly — *Jul. 22, 2002 — 3:10 p.m. — While We Wait*

The late July sun hung low on the horizon, painting the Chicago skyline in hues of gold and amber. From their perch atop James's loft building, the city sprawled before them with the dadaistic brilliance of a playroom aftermath—like the work of a four-year-old who'd spent the better half of the morning hurling building blocks across a best-blankey. Some called it city planning.

Emma, James, Gerardo, and Val lounged on mismatched lawn chairs—a hodgepodge collection that fairly screamed *Americana yard sale, circa 1985—ka-ching!* In the center of their circle sat a low patio deck table, and in the middle of that, Val's and James's cell phones were placed front and center, in full view and easy reach.

It was several days after the big reveal. Val had made photocopies of the fully rendered design for the team at Eco United to either accept or reject. Alfred had passed them along to Max, who was presenting the materials as they waited.

And wait they did—perched atop the roof like birds on a wire. Sometimes they glanced at the two little phones side by side. Sometimes they gazed out at the view in silence. More often, they bantered, joked, and launched full-throttle entertainment-mode to distract each other from the fact that it was now four p.m. and fading fast—and still, no call.

Like two little hot-wired eggs waiting for a *peep*—or a beep, depending on the ringtone—James and Val's phones sat center stage, ready to announce 'yea' or 'nay' from the Eco United selection committee. But the phones were silent.

Maybe they were duds.

A small portable grill sizzled nearby, the aroma of roasting hot dogs mingling with the ever-present scent of possibility that defined the Windy City. Val, self-appointed queen of the grill, wielded her tongs with the precision of a surgeon.

"Alright, listen up, yous' guys," Val said in full native Chicagoan-ese. "You uncultured... polecats—"

"What's a polecat?" James wanted to know.

"—Don't interrupt and don't know—" Val tried to continue.

"Sounds unpleasant," Emma murmured. "Like a cat stuck up a pole?" She paused. "Or is it a slur? About Polish cats?"

"I would *never* say something like that!" Val protested. "Everybody stop interrupting me! Okay—back on track. You, you... group of sad sacks—"

When Gerardo looked like he was going to chime in, Val aimed her pincers at him. "I'm warning yous' guys—I know how to use these. In a *pinch.*" She clicked them together like castanets.

Gerardo laughed. "Withdrawn, withdrawn. We are indeed sad sacks."

"But not for long," Val declared, with the flair of someone about to change lives. "Because I'm about to introduce you to the art of the Chicago-style hot dog."

Gerardo leaned forward, eyes wide with mock reverence. "Educate us, O Wise One of the Wieners."

Val rolled her eyes but couldn't suppress a grin. "First," she said, holding up a perfectly charred dog, "we start with an all-beef frank. None of that mystery meat nonsense."

"Wouldn't dream of it," James said, raising his beer in salute.

Val continued her master class, layering each hot dog with practiced efficiency. "Mustard. Never ketchup. Chopped onions. Neon-green relish—don't ask, no one really knows where it comes from, it's tradition. Sport peppers. Tomato slices. And—*critical*—a pickle spear. Personally? I prefer two. And a sprinkle of celery salt."

She stepped back from the grill and held one aloft. "Alas! A Chicago dog in all its glory... for yous' guys."

Val handed the dogs on paper plates out to each person present, first to Gerardo then in tandem to James and Emma, then sat in the remaining lawn chair to enjoy her meal.

As they bit into their loaded hot dogs, making appropriately appreciative noises, Val's phone trilled. She fumbled to answer, nearly dropping her culinary masterpiece.

James, Emma and Gerardo stopped consuming their dog simultaneously, as if someone had hit the 'pause' button on the playback, Val was aware of all eyes and ears on her as she placed her hot dog down on the patio table and picked up the phone from the center of the deck table.

"Hello? Oh, hi Sam!" James and Emma resumed eating their meal, Gerardo took a sip of beer and Val's voice lifted almost a full octave. "Oh no, that's okay you can call anytime..." Val's voice took on a breathy quality that made Emma and James exchange knowing glances.

"No, no, we haven't heard anything yet," Val continued, twirling a strand of hair around her finger. "James's phone is right here, too, primed and ready for action."

James leaned towards Emma, his voice a low murmur. "I've seen less devoted Tibetan monks doing their prayer pujas than our Val on that phone at the moment."

Emma stifled a chortle, elbowing him gently. "Shh, you'll make her self-conscious."

"What's that? Oh, the lighting was perfect?" Val's cheeks flushed a delicate pink. "I'm so glad you got some good shots to use."

Gerardo, catching on to the situation, grinned mischievously. "Hey Val," he called out, loud enough for Sam to hear, "ask your boyfriend if he got my good side!"

Val's eyes widened in horror. "He's not my—I mean, Sam's not—oh, ignore him, Sam. Gerardo's just being… Gerardo."

James chuckled, shaking his head. "Smooth, Ger, real smooth."

"What? I'm just trying to help the course of true love," Gerardo defended, his hands raised in supplication to the sweet Chi sky.

Val, her face now resembling a ripe tomato, turned away from the group. "Sorry about that, Sam. You were saying about the footage?"

As Val continued her conversation, her voice dropping to a near-whisper, Emma leaned into James. "Should we rescue her?"

James considered for a moment, then shook his head. "Nah, let her have this. Lord knows we could all use a bit of joyful distraction right now."

Val's conversation wrapped up, her "Goodbye, Sam" soft and tinged with reluctance. As she rejoined the group, her eyes dared them to comment.

Gerardo, never one to back down from a challenge, opened his mouth, but James cut him off with a sharp look. "So," James said, his voice deliberately casual, "any news from our intrepid documentarian?"

Val shook her head, some of her usual composure returning. "No, just checking in. He's got some great footage from the tile-making sessions. Says it's really coming together."

"That's great," Emma said warmly, hoping to ease Val's discomfort. "We can't wait to see it."

As Val's voice wound down, Gerardo placed his empty plate down, and thanked Val for the meal. There was a sound of siren from the street below so Gerardo got up and walked to the edge of the rooftop, to check it out. The siren was distant now, another mournful cry among many, echoing off the concrete canyons. He tracked the ambulance's progress, watching as it drove far down the street now, turning right now, its lights a frantic dance of red and white and now suddenly gone from view.

He said a soft prayer under his breath for people at risk, for the family in fear for their loved one.

The interruption put their current wait into perspective. He looked back to where James's cell phone sat on the rickety patio table in front of the small group still feasting on their respective meals. Its presence is both unassuming and loaded with anticipation. The device seemed to mock them with its silence, a high-tech monolith stubbornly refusing to bridge the gap between uncertainty and revelation.

To break the monotony of no news Gerardo took the reins again.

"Hey, Val!" Gerardo called over his shoulder, his eyes still fixed on the horizon. "Tell your boyfriend there's a killer view of the skyline up here. Perfect for his doc."

Val's cheeks flushed pink again. "He's not my—" she started, then sighed in defeat. "I'll let him know."

Gerardo turned back to the group, his gaze landing on James. "Or better yet, James should paint this. You did some classic cityscape style back in the day, right? All purple shadows and glowing windows?"

James leaned back in his chair, a wistful smile playing at his lips. "Once upon a time," he replied, "I had my hand in." His voice is soft with exaggerated emotional memory recall.

"More than a little..." Gerardo observed, his tone dry, "Your paintings are still circulating, still selling, and prices going up in auctions, 'course Val will know better than me your business and net worth—"

"Don't look at me, I'll never tell..." Val interjected in a mock-huff and then as a comic's solemn resolve, "besides I'm not talking to you right now."

As twilight deepened around them, and the first stars peeked out from the darkening sky, a contemplative silence fell over the group. The fading light seemed to invite confidences, as if the approaching night granted permission for exploration into the quiet nooks secreted away from ordinary view.

Gerardo walked from the edge of the building back to his chair, thinking out loud along the way, "You know, James, I've always wondered something..."

James raised an eyebrow, curiosity piqued. "Oh? What's on your mind, Ger?"

Gerardo gave him a contemplative look, thought for a moment then forged ahead, "okay here it is, you're still making money off the paintings that are out there circulating, so demand hasn't fallen off. And you haven't lost your touch, that's clear... so what made you switch from painting to clay? And now mosaics? It's quite a journey, isn't it?"

The question hung in the air, in the way big questions do, like a billboard posing a rhetorical question: 'Is Smoking Bad For You?' And then waiting to see if he'd drive by with a flip of a phrase to laugh it off or pause and really answer the question.

Emma and Val exchanged glances, sensing the shift in atmosphere. The city sounds below seemed to fade away, leaving only the soft whisper of the evening breeze.

James took a long swig of his beer, his eyes distant as he gazed at the emerging stars. He took a deep breath, as if preparing to dive into deep waters. When he spoke, his voice was low and thoughtful, carrying the weight of years of reflection.

"Well," he began, "it had been on my mind for a while, creeping in inches..."

Val made a last minute adjustment, placing her phone back on the table and straightening James's phone, setting the necessary props before James dove deep into his tale. When she was settled, James took a drink of his beer and continued.

"I saw, or felt that most paintings weren't really helping the artist or anyone... and maybe there was a reason a lot of artists go nuts. Em, remember back at Cooper, we used to talk about the energy of the artist, their intent moves into the work?"

Emma nodded, her eyes never leaving James's face.

"Well... what if that isn't a very nice person, or a crazy person, or the most terrible kind of person?" James continued, his voice growing softer. "Then the painting would be poisonous, wouldn't it?"

"Interesting." Gerardo observed.

"Isn't it?" Confirmed James and then continued, his voice growing softer. " There's a story about the painting 'The Scream'..." his gaze turned inward as he recalled the details, "Some people stole that painting, but then found they couldn't fence it. They couldn't get rid of it. Nobody wanted it... and it brought them such bad luck, such dark dreams... they actually gave it back."

A murmur rippled through the group. Emma watched as understanding dawned on their faces, one by one.

"I was finding more and more that most paintings I was seeing, even from friends, not you Gerardo, your work is a blessing..." James added as an aside then continued, "I'd get headaches after going to a gallery opening, feel like I wanted to climb in a hot shower and stay there, even got physically ill sometimes. I used to think maybe it was bad cheese at these gallery openings, but no. No."

James paused, his eyes finding Emma's. She nodded encouragingly, understanding the weight of what he was sharing.

"And then my family came to visit, sweethearts, one and all, especially Sarah. Well, they came to a gallery opening—a respected place, to see my work. I was doing a green valley golden light abstraction—so they came to see mine, but unfortunately they had to walk through the gallery to get there... yeah, can you imagine Sarah as sensitive as she is to nuance and energy walking through that? What was I thinking? I had become a little numb to it, but this next event woke me up good."

The rooftop was quiet, the small troupe present was hanging on every word. Even the distant hum of traffic from the street seemed to fade away.

"One man, one... creep, I can't even say his name, crawled up next to our Sarah, stood there getting close and closer... Ma and Da had told her to stay quiet, soft as a kitten, so she was afraid to shout for me, but thank God, thank God I was on the second level and saw this...demon... pulling Sarah away and toward an exit."

Emma gasped softly, her hand flying to her mouth. Gerardo leaned forward in his chair; fists clenched, his knuckles white.

"I don't even know how I got down there so fast," James voice was so soft, "Sarah told me later that I flew, maybe I did, I swear... if me da hadn't pulled me off that demon... I might have ended him... I might have, I was that determined to stop his crimes."

James's voice trailed off, the emotion of the memory evident in his face. The room was so quiet, they could hear the tick of the clock on the wall.

After a moment, James seemed to gather himself. "But that was the end for me, that world... and what did that leave? Well I remembered how much fun we used to have in pottery class, well, Em didn't at first, right? The clay talked back in those days. Anyway, I remembered from art history and my own common sense, about people doing wonderful art and craft at its best... all unsigned, and brilliant. Who made all those beautiful pots and mosaics found in ancient ruins engraved on the wall? No one knows, I liked it. With no ego, less chance of attracting some kind of monster to your work, more chance of being an actual blessing."

James paused, his eyes scanning the faces around him. "Well I still needed to make money... for the family, and myself too, I admit it, so I'm still signing my stuff, but I dream of the day when I do not. That will be a wonderful day."

Long pause.

"Thanks, James, for telling that. The truth is important, there are those kinds of people in the art world especially." Gerardo said quietly. "I know it, we all do."

James nodded in response, but said nothing more, the group remained silent as well. The afternoon light was gone now, and what light remained was shifting rapidly past twilight and heading straight into night as they waited.

There was nothing more to say, en masse, they were ready to know, one way or the other.

James's phone rang once, Val looked at him, he nodded, she let it ring once again for good measure, and then picked it up.

"Hello Alfred, yes it's Val, yes, we're all here..." She listened for about fifteen seconds and then smiled. She looked around the small group, nodded her head and smiled again, even broader.

Stunned silence then Gerardo 'whooped.'

That just about said it all.

* * *

Chapter 23

Chicago — Warehouse Loft — Assembly — *Jul. 24, 2002 — 7:30 a.m. — The Move*

The early morning sun streamed through the tall windows of the new warehouse loft, casting long shadows across the concrete floor. James was already hard at work, his sleeves turned up as he methodically rolled out thin cushioned cardboard along the length of the space. His movements were careful, precise—he would go to one end of the loft, place the large spindle of cardboard in place and, well, kick it down the length of the room, unrolling the cushioned cardboard as a safety measure against potential accidents. Dropping a precious tile, for example, or some as yet, unforeseen dilemma.

The heavy metal door slid open with a soft groan, and Emma stepped in, her arms laden with bags of food. Her eyes immediately sought James, finding him at the far end of the open warehouse. She watched him for a moment at work, kick rolling his way down the field. A smile bloomed on her face as she called out, "Good morning kick-start... you have a tryout coming up for Newcastle United? Getting those knees and legs in shape?"

James looked up, fairly glowing in this early light, his face breaking into a grin when he saw her. He called back "I'm past my prime for that dream, sorry to say, still, it's good to keep in shape."

She nodded appreciatively at him as he trotted over to greet her. "Oh, I don't know, you're still getting around pretty good, you look like a jack rabbit out there, or something equally energetic—I have treats for you."

When he saw the bag from his favorite restaurant, his eyes lit up another full notch. If that was possible, "Ooo our Em, ta... luv thank you," he said, his voice warm with appreciation. And then gave her a quick 'thank you' peck on the cheek as if it was the most natural act to consummate in the wee morning hours.

Emma felt the kiss land like a sweet plumb line testing her true north, she turned to the table so he wouldn't notice her blush. "Sorry if the carbs ruin your workout," she said, setting the bags down. "But... can you show me around first? Before we eat?"

Her smile was earnest, a little shy. "I really can't wait to see it all."

James nodded. "Oh aye, I'll show you 'round and 'round, m'lady."

Slip-tripping, he moved into tour guide mode, he pointed to the area just right of the main entrance. "As you come in the door, you'll see the tall, wide windows—for your viewing pleasure, literally. I'm thinking we can set up long tables down the length of the wall beneath them, and get the benefit of natural light for your color glaze testing."

"Nice," Emma endorsed succinctly and stamped it 'approved.'

"And along this adjacent wall..." James led the way. "We have a freight elevator centrally located, so we can get up and down—"

"With the greatest of ease," Emma supplied.

"On the flying trapeze... you got it in one, Miss!" James grinned. "And center ring..."

His excitement was riding high on the Big-Top, but he was so darn cute Emma wouldn't coax him down from lion to kitty cat.

"An' here's the best part—come on, you're too slow, move your butt, come see…" James practically bounced as they entered the main open area. "Lots of open windows, lots of light, and look—"

Emma's eyes widened as she followed his gaze upward. "Oh James… there's a second floor overlooking the main area," she breathed. "We'll be able to see the whole design come together at a distance—to make sure it's flowing and working."

James beamed. "Cupie doll for the young Miss! Exactly. No more climbing up and down scaffolds. And what's more, there's 220 electricity throughout—as you can imagine—but we have the space now—"

"—To have our own kiln," Emma finished, her mind already working the logistics.

James nodded enthusiastically. "Maybe two. We'll still need the Monster, of course—we're talking thousands of tiles and multiple firings. But with a couple of extra kilns, we can handle the small work. We'll design and carve some of the abstract pieces ourselves—the connecting visual elements—and fire them here."

His excitement was infectious as he continued, leading her around a corner. "AND… there's a grand, solid white wall so Gerardo and I can use the light-tracing projector to project designs onto paper templates, trace them on brown paper, and lay it all on the floor. Removes any guesswork or error when hand-drawing. This has to be drawn to spec—so it fits perfectly on the Eco lobby wall. No mistakes."

Emma stepped into the open area, her eyes roaming the space, already seeing the process unfold. She turned slowly to look at him, her face soft with admiration.

"James…"

"Yes, pet?" he replied, his voice gentle now—almost casual—as if it were the most natural endearment in the world while he waited for her professional verdict.

"I think you deserve a double-chunk chocolate cookie. Maybe two." She sounded so specific, there must certainly be a supply afoot. Or at least in a nearby bakery bag.

"Ooooh," James exclaimed, his eyes lighting up like a child. Without hesitation, he dashed for the food bags Emma had left on the long conference table by the door.

* * *

As they shared their impromptu breakfast, Emma's mind was already mapping out the workflow. By the time the interns started to arrive, she had a clear vision of how the space would function.

Roberto and Jasmine arrived first with Emma's entire collection of glazes, while Mark and his buddy brought in the long work tables. Everything fit neatly into the freight elevator, a testament to James's foresight in choosing the space.

As each sub-team arrived, James and Emma took them on a tour, allowing everyone to get a feel for the place. They all gathered at the main entrance, clustering around the conference table as James and Emma talked them through the workflow.

James had put up the color version of the design along the length of the wall to the left of the conference table, serving both as reference and inspiration. After a light breakfast, the air was filled with excited chatter as everyone present discussed the myriad details of the project ahead.

Emma watched the team begin their work, she felt a sense of awe at how far they'd come. She glanced at James, often catching his eye, to share a moment of silent thanksgiving. This was it—the next phase was about to begin.

* * *

The mid morning sun slanted through the windows of the warehouse loft, illuminating a high white path of light across the expanse of brown paper templates that covered the floor. Emma stood in the center of the 'continent' section, her eyes roaming over the tiles already laid out. The air was thick with the earthy scent of clay and the faint tang of wet glaze.

And so Emma was on pause at the moment, studying the pattern of the tiles laid thus far on 'the continent.' The template was laid before her on the cardboard, true to spec and bit by bit, she and James had been laying tiles in place, looking for the pattern and sense of energetic cohesion. In brief, what was the story?

Emma moved slowly, her steps careful and measured, as if moving in time to a subterranean sound. Her fingers traced the edge of the tile she was currently holding in her hand, it was a detailed carving of a person's bare back and head, a wonderful piece. She'd been feeling into the energy of the piece looking for where it might fit in the whole.

Emma stepped back, her brow furrowing as she took in the bigger picture. Something wasn't quite right, but she couldn't put her finger on it. The flow was there, but it felt...incomplete.

Where was James when she needed him?

He was at the far end of the room laying out more of the templates. The plan was to put down all the brown paper placeholders while the interns were pulling the tiles from their storage boxes to see what they actually had. These particular tiles had the benefit of a first firing and after each one had been housed into their place in the pattern, the glaze would be applied.

It would be a long, glorious process, but they were focusing on completing the continent first, so they could have a section ready for the community outreach party in less than one month. One month. They could do it, but a little James 'help' at the moment might, well...help.

"James," Emma called, her voice carrying across the vast space. "Can you come look at this?"

Lickety-split, James was at her side, his presence a comforting warmth. He stood silent for a moment, his eyes scanning the layout, taking in the internal flow of the lines, the way the tiles 'talked' to each other.

"You're close," he murmured, his voice low and thoughtful. "Try this..."

With careful movements, he made four or five adjustments, his hands moving with the confidence of a master technician. Then to cap it, he picked up a tile with a swirling, abstract mandala carved into its surface. Emma watched, fascinated, as he placed it slightly off-center, towards the right and next to an abstract carving of a human face.

"There," James said, stepping back. "See how it acts as a kind of wheel or heart spark? It's turning the whole, moving the land towards water, but in subconscious agreement with that human face... with humanity, a quiet level of accepted responsibility."

He made a few more subtle changes, then turned to Emma, his eyes alight with pleasure. "See how the eye is now subtly directed toward the water? As you walk into the Eco Building, the person will be moved into the lobby, in flow toward the water and ultimately cosmos and infinite possibility. You see?"

Emma stood transfixed, her eyes wide as she took in the transformation. It was as if James had unlocked a secret code, revealing a hidden harmony in the design. She felt a surge of emotions—gratitude, admiration, and something deeper impossible to name.

When she didn't respond, James turned to her, a hint of uncertainty in his voice. "What? You would have found it. You had the face tile carved right there, you were close..."

Emma smiled, a warmth spreading through her chest. "Yes, but ta for speeding it along. Saved me from taking up knitting as I sat in contemplation for a month."

James's face broke into a grin, his eyes twinkling. "You said 'ta.'"

Emma turned back to her color coding, her hands moving with renewed purpose. Over her shoulder, she called, "I did indeed."

She looked over the whole section. "James, I think that's it, we're ready to start assigning colors."

"Really?" He stood by her side, studied the continent section with her and finally nodded, "You're right, I agree," He looked up, thought for a moment and then quoted:" 'nothing can come of nothing.'

As if no further comment or footnote was needed.

"If that's Shakespeare talk for, 'if you sit on your butt it won't get done,' we agree *Sir James*." Emma lobbed the birdie back. It was a reference to a conversation from years ago, she waited to see if he remembered.

James eyes opened a tad wider, "'Though she be but little, she is fierce!'"

"Go to! You are a saucy boy! " She shot right back and now he laughed outright.

"Where in time and space did you pick up that obscure quote?" He considered her with respect anew.

"I remembered it from a high school reading of Romeo and Juliet, we all thought it was the best line in the whole mess." Emma was walking away from him now talking over her shoulder, on her way to the glaze station, she couldn't wait one more minute to get started on her color scheme.

"And you've been saving it up all this time for the right shot." James called after her retreating form.

Emma spun on her heel as an answer, a sweet pirouette, capped off with a matador stance. Jasmine and Bette applauded.

Indeed, they were having a wonderful time, it was an excellent way to begin the actual work, and Emma in particular was moving into her spotlight and tour de force. She'd been prepping color tiles for a month, and felt ready to begin the super extra fun part.

As she immersed herself in her work, Emma felt a sense of rightness settle over her. This was where she belonged, among the colors and shapes, bringing life to their shared vision. The tiles before her seemed to hum with potential, each one a tiny universe of infinite expansion, but no worries here, color was the key to the cosmos.

Emma had the codes already written down on a clipboard which she now carried along with a roll of masking tape and a black waterproof marker back to the continent template.

She moved among the baked clay carvings, her fingers gently touching the surface of each one, then looked over her clipboard with adjacent color samples, chose the match made in heaven, wrote the code on a piece of masking tape and then firmly affixed the tape on top of the tile.

And in this way, blues flowed into greens, earthy browns gave way to fiery reds, each transition as natural as the changing seasons.

As the sun reached midpoint, the light cranked up to demonstrate its intention to illuminate the works. It meant business about getting this day up and running, but Emma, lost in the rhythm of her work, barely noted the shift.

She felt suspended in a bubble of time stretching long past the literal clock and into the void of space, the morning hours had slipped by unnoticed. She was in the zone, this was her turf and color heaven, where every shade and hue were always singing if only one paused to listen.

It couldn't be explained, only lived.

And if, every now and then, her eyes drifted to where James worked at the other end of the loft, well... that was just under-painting the canvas to get the mood going in the groove, wasn't it?

* * *

After the lunch break they began with renewed vigor, the warehouse fairly hummed with the expectation of the upcoming hands-on training. Emma gathered the interns around a large work table. Sunlight came through the high windows as it was bound to do, a fairly unstoppable force determined to light up every nuance of every sample color tile Emma had tested to date. It was merciless in its effort to highlight every tonal quality of similarity and high contrast. Emma didn't mind, she'd made friends with the sun long ago and so she welcomed the foresight, so to speak, to catch any flaw now, before a glaze was laid.

She looked at Roberto, Jasmine, Mark, Bette and even Clara were her dear comrades now and so she introduced them to their new best friend, the sunlight coming through the window.

"The very first order of business when you to come to the glazing station," Emma instructed, "is hold the sample glazed tile up to the light—check the hue and cross check the code number that I've written on the tile, make sure it matches... and make sure that match makes sense. Let's say you're working on section of a river and your code directs you to a green/yellow glaze combo, double check my handwriting and if it still doesn't make sense bring it to me first, James second, I'm not saying he's color blind or anything—"

There was general laughter at the thought, Emma was chuckling too. "I'm saying he and Gerardo have their hands full and need to focus...but do not guess. If you're not sure and can't find one of us, or Gerardo, don't guess."

Emma caught movement in the corner of her eye, it was Sam taping at a distance with a shotgun mic attached to his camera. She smiled and nodded a 'hello' to Sam, his camera a familiar presence now, but discreet as well. He had placed himself quietly in the background and was now moving among them, capturing the moment with practiced ease.

His trusty Sony caught Emma's eyes as they sparkled with excitement, as she began to explain her system. "Alright, everyone, listen up. This is important." She held up a sample tile, its surface a subtle blend of blues and greens. "Almost every tile will have two glaze firings, or two layers of glaze, depending on the placement in the wall. For two layers of glaze, we paint one layer, let it dry then overpaint the other half or the raised part of a tile. That decision will be made ahead of time, but how the tile is actually painted with the glaze will be up to you. You have all been recommended by Gerardo, so you know more than the basics, but bear with me as we cover it all anyway."

Jasmine, Bette and Clara leaned in close, Roberto and Mark peeked over the other's heads, their faces a mix of curiosity and concentration. Emma continued, her voice bright, her enthusiasm a catchy thing, "It's going to be a lot of work, but trust me, it'll be worth it. Take a look at these sample tiles." She gestured to a row of finished pieces, each one a small masterpiece of color transition.

"See how one color moves into another? That's what we're aiming for. It's not just aesthetically pleasing—it emulates nature." Emma's hands pointed to one in particular "See how these two colors are different shades of blue? This will suggest undulation in the wave, you see? We'll use the color design as our guide. Any questions?"

Bette, pushed her red hair away from her face and raised her hand. "How do we know which colors to use for each tile? Can you cover the coding system a little slower?"

Emma smiled, pleased by the question. "Excellent. That's where our coding system comes in. Let me show you." She demonstrated, in writing a code AF-071 on a piece of masking tape and affixing it to the top of the tile. "So the code shows the first glaze 'AF' you come over here to the row, look for 'AF' double check the code, check the color in the sunlight, and that's the first glaze. The second code is the second glaze '071' now you put the masking tape on the bottom, as you well know, we never glaze the bottom, it will stick to the shelf of the kiln, that's your security blanket and brake. It might seem complicated at first, but you'll get the hang of it."

Mark, usually so laid-back, raised his hand. "How long does each glaze firing take?"

Emma smiled, appreciating his practical question. "Thanks for the question, Mark. Each firing takes about 8 to 10 hours, depending on the kiln's size and the specific glaze we're using. And remember, we're doing this twice for almost half the tiles."

Bette, the newest addition to their team, looked slightly overwhelmed. "So, for each tile, we're looking at... what, almost a full day of work?"

"Technically, correct; we've laid out tiles in some of the templates to be completed by the January preview party. So we'll focus on those, painting the glaze, then transporting the tiles from that template to the Monster kiln and after the firing, brought back here to be reassembled, then glued to the green web backing, and is now prepped for installation. At least," Emma nodded. "That's not counting the time it takes to apply the glazes, which is where our hands-on craftsmanship comes in. Let me show you."

She picked up a brush, dipping it into a chalky light blue glaze. "As you know, the color of the glaze before will look different than after, so, again, always check the codes on the masking tape to compare with the bottle to make sure you have the right glaze. With practiced strokes, she began to apply it to a bisque-fired tile.

"The first layer is all about creating a base. We want to cover the entire surface, but we're not aiming for perfection here. In fact, a bit of unevenness can add character to the final piece. Heavier coatings in some places, for example."

Roberto leaned in, his eyes fixed on Emma's hands. "And the second glaze?"

"That's where the magic happens," Emma grinned. She picked up another brush, this time choosing a soft green glaze. "We apply the second color while the first is still wet. See how they blend at the edges? That's what gives us that depth we're looking for."

As Emma demonstrated, Sam slipped into the background, with his ever-present camera. He moved quietly among them, capturing the moment with practiced ease. The soft whir of his camera seemed to underscore the weight of Emma's words.

When she had a free moment and the interns were intent on the test task in front of them, Sam approached the table, his eyes scanning the array of glazed tiles. "These are incredible, Emma. Can you tell me about this one?" He pointed to a tile with swirls of deep purple and gold.

Emma's face lit up. "Ah, that one. It's inspired by a sunset I saw in Minnesota as a child. The way the colors bled into each other... I've been trying to recreate that moment ever since."

Sam nodded appreciatively, his hand resting briefly on Emma's forearm. "It's beautiful. You've really captured the glow—it looks alive."

Across the room, James looked up from his work, his eyes narrowing slightly at Sam's casual touch on Emma's arm. He turned back to his templates, but his movements were less fluid now, his concentration just a bit broken.

Gerardo, working quietly nearby, leaned in. "You know," he murmured, his voice pitched low for James's ears only, "Sam used to be in theatre. Those theatre types are always hugging and touching. People like that probably didn't get enough attention as kids or something."

James rolled his eyes at his friend's rather transparent attempt at reassurance but said nothing. He focused on his work, trying to ignore the laughter drifting over from Emma's table.

Back at the glaze station, Jasmine was carefully applying a first layer to her tile. Her hand shook slightly, leaving an uneven streak across the surface. "Oh no," she groaned. "I've ruined it."

Emma was at her side in an instant. "Not at all," she said softly. "Look." She took the brush, adding a few more uneven strokes. "Now it's intentional. When we add the second color, these imperfections will create a beautiful, organic pattern. Sometimes our mistakes lead to the most interesting results."

* * *

Within an hour, the interns transitioned from live training to utilizing their skills on the main floor and with the templates. Jasmine and Bette began to work independently, each applying Emma's system to their assigned tiles, sitting near the continent template. While Roberto, Mark and Clara were unpacking boxes and boxes of tiles to be laid on the cardboard cushioned floor for future sorting. In a few hours they would switch tasks, so they would receive the benefit of all around training.

The air filled with the sounds of the gentle clink of tiles being sorted and the room was quiet for the most part, everyone preferring to focus on integrating the training, rather than chat or listen to music in the open space just yet. There would be a time for that later.

Emma moved among them, offering guidance and encouragement, her eyes lighting up with each successful application of her technique.

As Emma continued her explanation, Sam moved around the group, his camera capturing the rapt expressions on the interns' faces. He paused occasionally, asking Emma a question when she had a free moment. Her answers were always thoughtful, her passion for the project evident in every word.

Sam lowered his camera, taking in the scene before him. The warehouse had transformed into a hive of focused creativity. Emma, surrounded by her eager students, seemed to glow with an inner light. James, in his solitary corner, radiated an intense concentration that could slice a sturdy plank.

The sun moved lower on the horizon, casting long shadows across the floor, Sam couldn't help but feel incredibly fortunate. There had been moments during the long day, when he'd simply rested his camera at his side to enjoy the view and witness the developing comradery amongst the crew.

He would study the long view and get a feeling of what might work visually—the breeze from an open window billowing a section of plastic back from a slab of clay Gerardo had been cutting to reveal the form of a billowing cloud. The puffed cloud would now be set aside to dry for a small kiln upstairs.

It all took time, step by step.

He raised his camera once more, capturing Emma's smile as she praised Mark's work, the determined set of James's shoulders as he adjusted a projection. Sam knew he'd back-assed-stumbled into perhaps the most important project of his life and so the responsibility to secure these moments on HD tape as best he could and place it all, metaphorically, under glass for future reference was paramount in his mind.

This event felt larger than a community installation, it was hard to explain, but more and more Sam had the impression he was documenting an historical event in real time, in all its beautiful, messy glory.

* * *

The afternoon progressed and so did the work flow as the activity in the warehouse kicked up into a higher gear. The air filled with the soft scratch of brushes on clay, the occasional clink of glaze jars, and the constant, reassuring presence of Emma's guidance.

Sam moved through the space, his camera capturing it all. He paused by James's station, taking in the intricate templates spread across the table. "This is quite the undertaking," he observed. "How do you keep track of where each tile will go?"

James looked up, his face a mask of professional courtesy. "It's all in the coding system," he explained, pointing to a series of numbers and letters on the template. "Each of these particular tiles have a unique identifier that corresponds to its place in the overall design. Gerardo and I are working on what we call the filler tiles, these are the specific visual cues we are making ourselves to help tie it all together."

Sam nodded, impressed. "And how many tiles are we talking about in total?"

"Well, for this purpose perhaps, only a couple of hundred, some large and some very small, if you're talking the hand carved tiles from the public, that's thousands, close to four thousand is our best guess." James said, a hint of awe underscoring his tone.

"But the pieces for these particular tiles in the templates you're making now will be fired in the kilns onsite, right?" Sam pursued the point.

James looked up, impressed at the younger man's ability for recall and to make logical deductions. When he spoke his tone was more relaxed. "Yes, and no, all of the elements, Em, Ger and I are adding, that is, drawn with our hands via some of these templates, the so called 'filler tiles,' will be fired with kilns onsite. The larger template sections Gerardo and I are projecting and tracing will house the four thousand tiles. What you currently see on the floor represents only about a third of the design. Would you say, Ger?" James asked.

"More or less." Gerardo confirmed as he continued tracing the outline on the brown paper taped to the wall.

"And those tiles, due to the volume, will be fired in what we call the Monster kiln at the studio on Lill street. It will help make short work, well... shorter work of the whole thing." James smiled, "Our own time travel machine, maybe, gets to the future a bit faster."

And with that small display of James's natural charm, finally showing through to get on tape, Sam thanked them both, it was challenging at times to get responses from either man, which was typical of artists in general and a lot of men in particular who preferred doing vs. what they considered unnecessary talking. Taken in that context, Sam felt he had just struck gold.

As Sam stepped away, Gerardo called after him, "James and Emma will be opening the small kiln later for the first firing if you want to take a look."

Sam's eyes lit up, "Yes, thank you, I'll be ready... if that's all right."

"Sure... sure, por nada..." After he stepped away, James pointed his gaze at Gerardo, who grinned. "Can't help it, I like the poor guy, probably didn't get enough attention when he was a kid."

"Well, he's making up for it now." James observed dryly and inclined his head to where Bette and Jasmine were cheerfully, or shall we say, enthusiastically greeting Sam as he rejoined the activity on the main floor.

Gerardo laughed, "Sorry, it's funny, it really is."

* * *

The late afternoon sun slanted through the high windows of the warehouse, casting long shadows across the bustling workspace. James stood at the far end, ostensibly focused on projecting images onto the paper templates, but his gaze kept drifting towards Emma.

She moved among the interns with the grace of a woman who knew who she was. James found himself captivated by the smallest details—the way a stray lock of hair fell across her forehead, the slight furrow of her brow as she concentrated, the gentle curve of her smile as she praised a particularly well-executed glaze application.

A gentle breeze from a nearby fan ruffled the papers on his workstation, drawing his attention momentarily. He noticed an oddly shaped paper clip holding together a stack of notes—it looked almost like a tiny, metallic swan. He wondered idly if Emma had bent it into that shape during one of their planning sessions. It seemed like something she would do, creating beauty in the most mundane of objects.

James's eyes drifted back to Emma. She was kneeling beside Mark now, her finger tracing the edge of a tile as she explained something. The sunlight caught the tile at just the right angle, sending a prism of colors dancing across Emma's face. For a moment, she looked like a living legend of herself.

He watched as she stood, brushing clay dust from her jeans. Her hand left a smudge on her thigh, a perfect hand print in powdery white—even that was visually riveting to him. A playful swat from the project itself.

Oh Christ in a cup.

"James!" Gerardo's voice broke through his reverie. "Are you planning on projecting that image, or are you just gonna stare at the wall all day?"

James blinked, realizing he'd been holding the projector remote without activating it. "Right, sorry mate. Got lost in thought for a moment there."

Gerardo followed James's previous line of sight, a knowing smirk playing on his lips. "Thought, eh? Is that what we're calling it now?"

James felt a warmth creep up his neck. "Oh, belt up," he muttered, but there was no real annoyance in his tone.

The mechanical whir of the projector, the soft murmur of voices, the occasional clink of tiles—it all blended into a symphony of creative energy. It felt good and correct, and left him feeling more centered in himself and more at peace than he had in years.

* * *

The day was ticking down now, running lower on natural light and James looked up from his work to find Emma's eyes on him. For a moment, the bustling warehouse faded away, leaving just the two of them in a bubble of *hello you*.

Emma's smile was soft, almost shy. She raised her hand in a small wave, a gesture so familiar, so sweet, without conscious thought, James found himself returning the wave, like kids greeting each other from a distance, the universal language of *so good to see you, my waving hand must clear the way*.

A clatter of falling tiles broke the moment, drawing Emma's attention away. James watched as she hurried to help, her hands gentle as she gathered the scattered pieces. As Emma knelt to retrieve a tile that had rolled under a table, she glanced once more at James. Their eyes met again, and this time, James felt a spark, *that spark*.

He hadn't felt quite like this before, a bright spark that ignored his mind went right through his heart and straight to his loins. It wasn't a flamethrower, it was only a spark, but still, it left him unsettled, exhilarated and yes, maybe terrified too. It was like the beep of an early warning system alerting him to what lay ahead if they continued down a particular path.

He stood still, practicing breathing for a good solid sixty seconds.

* * *

The day was dwindling down to a full stop, and most of the interns had left, scheduled to resume their work early tomorrow, but it was approaching the golden hour now and so Sam lingered, waiting for the moment the sun would go liquid yellow and saturate the tiles and warehouse loft with the sweet final rays of the day. The loving long goodbye, is how Sam liked to think of it and so who better to tape and interview in this golden moment, than Emma herself, the woman who had brought him onboard.

Emma sat cross-legged next to a template of a sun, of all celestial objects, deliberately placed in a patch of golden light from a near tall window facing the west. The irony wasn't lost on her either, she loved the inside joke, and smiled as she picked up each tile to carefully apply the first coat of glaze with steady, practiced strokes.

Sam adjusted his camera, zooming in on Emma's hands as she worked. "So, how long have you been doing this?" he asked, his voice casual.

Emma glanced up, a small smile playing at her lips. "Glazing, or art in general?"

"Both, I guess," Sam replied, lowering the camera to meet her eyes.

Emma considered for a moment, her brush pausing mid-stroke. "Well, I've been making art since I could hold a crayon. But glazing… that came later, at Cooper Union. It was like discovering a whole new language."

Sam nodded, his interest piqued. "What drew you to it?"

"The unpredictability," Emma said, her eyes lighting up. "You put all this work into a piece, and then the kiln transforms it into something... unexpected. I'm collaborating with the elements."

Sam lowered his camera, his eyes curious. "But... Cooper Union - that's where you met James, right?"

Emma's brush paused mid-stroke. She looked up, a fleeting expression crossing her face. "Yeah, that's right. First day, actually. I sketched him standing on the corner looking up at the sky."

"Must've been quite a sketch," Sam probed gently.

Emma chuckled, resuming her work. "It was... adequate. James thought it was better than it was."

Sam nodded, sensing her reluctance to elaborate. "And you've been friends ever since?"

"More or less," Emma replied, her tone neutral. She picked up another tile, examining it closely. "It's complicated, you know? Life takes you in different directions."

Sam opened his mouth to ask another question, but Emma beat him to it. "How about you? Any long-lost art school friends in your past? No wait, you told me you have a background in the theatre."

"Yes, that's right, decades, really, college then here to Chicago," Sam explained, "which has a highly respected regional theatre community—"

"Steppenwolf Theatre... The Remains, wait, let me think," Emma paused to remember, "and New Crime Productions, though I don't think they're here anymore."

"Yes, that's right, some great work, plus more..." Sam began but then the usual verve in his voice seemed to sputter and slow.

"But you've left?" Emma pursued, she really wanted to know more about him,

"It wasn't working for me any more, I wasn't getting close to what I wanted," Sam leaned against a workbench, his camera momentarily forgotten. "You know, this space reminds me of a rehearsal space we used to use, we had this actress in our ensemble, Olivia Reeves—you might've heard of her, she's doing pretty well now—anyway, she had this incredible way of bending a scene... extending a moment..."

Val stepped into the warehouse, her footsteps masked by Sam's avid storytelling. She paused in the shadows, listening.

"She had or still has, incredible stage presence..." Sam was saying, his eyes bright with the memory. "Olivia nailed it, every single time. I've never seen anyone work with her kind of energy before or since really."

Emma looked up from her glazing, a knowing smile playing on her lips. "Sounds like you were—I think the word is 'smitten.' Do you still see her?"

Sam shrugged, his expression suddenly guarded. "Now and again, when she's in town. But that's not really interesting..."

Val felt a tightness in her chest, it was a little hard to breathe. She cleared her throat, stepping into the patch of sunlight. "Emma? James was asking about the glaze schedules."

Emma started to explain, then paused. "Actually, I'll take it to him. I need to ask him something anyway." She hurried off, leaving Sam and Val alone.

Val stood awkwardly, her eyes darting to the mirror by the office area, her practical ponytail and comfortable clothes self defining and appropriate for her, she would never complain about herself, she deeply appreciated the many gifts she'd been given since birth, but was now more aware of how she lived in a different sphere than the one Sam seemed to know so well.

"So," Val said, trying for casualness, "I couldn't help overhearing. You really know Olivia Reeves?"

Sam ran a hand through his hair, looking slightly uncomfortable. "Yeah, I did, I do… hadn't really intended to let that slip, to be honest. Mind keeping it under wraps?"

Val nodded, feeling chasm between them widening now into a canyon, it never really struck her before, but he was from an entirely different world, after another beat, she assured him. "Of course. I should probably get back to work."

As she turned to leave, Sam spoke up. "Hey, Val? I was thinking about that conversation we had the other day, about documentary ethics. I'd love to get your take on something I'm working on."

Val hesitated, torn between her resolution for professional distance and the warmth in Sam's voice. "I… I'm not sure I'm the best person to ask about that."

Sam's brow furrowed. "Why not? You always have interesting insights, and you've been working with James for a couple of years. I understand, he comes into contact with a lot of issues, I'll bet."

Val shrugged, not meeting his eyes. "I'm sure there are more qualified people you could talk to."

"Val," Sam said, his voice gentle. "Your perspective is valuable, I don't know of anyone who thinks sideways like you do, absolutely no one."

Val looked up, surprised by the sincerity in his tone. For a moment, the world destroying asteroid size crater between them seemed to narrow.

"I... I suppose I could spare a few minutes," she said cautiously.

Sam's face lit up. "Great! So, I've been thinking about this sequence..."

As they fell into conversation, Val felt her earlier resolve wavering. Maybe, maybe they could be friends, maybe that would be enough. And... she could soak in moments like these, kinda absorb him into her mind and memory and maybe that would be enough to last her the rest of her life.

Maybe.

* * *

Emma paused, glancing back from the front office area to sneak a peek at Sam and Val deep in discussion, their heads bent close together over Sam's camera. She picked up the glaze schedule, a small smile played on her lips as she continued on her way to find James.

Speaking of, she barely went five feet when she heard him holler.

"Em! Our Em!" It was James, of course, practicing his best base yodel from the summit of the Alps.

"What? I'm right here, on my way—" Emma called back

"I'm about to open the kiln upstairs. Wanna come see if our birds survived the firing?"

Emma's face lit up with excitement and a hint of nervous anticipation. "Wouldn't miss it for a rerun of Martha Stewart baking white clay in her oven," she replied, already moving in a quick trot across the warehouse floor.

"Sam!" Gerardo called out "the kiln is being opened, get your 'arse upstairs right quick!"

James and Emma climbed the stairs together, a palpable tension building between them. The small kiln sat in the corner of the upper floor, its presence looming large with possibility and potential disappointment. Cue the suspense soundtrack.

Sam and Val appeared close on their heels, slightly out of breath, Sam had his Sony open and already taping, Val was pulling her camera from her bag, both kept a respectful distance and were forearmed to preserve the moment, but hey, no pressure.

James reached for the kiln door, then paused, looking at Emma. "Care to do the honors?"

Emma took a deep breath, her hand hovering over the handle. "I feel like I should be singing 'Ode to a Grecian Urn'," she murmured, and slowly opened the lid door.

A wave of heat washed over them as they peered inside. For a moment, neither dared to speak, both holding their breath as they scanned the contents.

Then, Emma let out a soft gasp of delight. "James, look! They made it!"

Sure enough, nestled safely inside were the template versions of flying birds, their wings outstretched as if ready to take flight. The glaze had settled beautifully, creating an iridescent effect that seemed to shimmer in the kiln's residual heat.

James felt a grin spread across his face. "Well, I'll be a loose goose," he chuckled. "Not a single one lost its way. The top layer looks great, a good sign."

As they stood there, admiring their creations, James became acutely aware of Emma's presence beside him. The warmth from the kiln, the thrill of success, and the closeness of her body all combined to create a heady mix of emotions.

Emma turned to him, her eyes shining with joy and pleasure—he had pleased her, what is it about making a woman happy men found absolutely intoxicating? James's heart skipped a beat.

"We did it," she said softly.

"We did," James agreed, his voice equally soft. For a moment, they just stood there, basking in their shared accomplishment and the sheer fun of play.

And if their hands occasionally brushed together as they carefully removed the birds from the kiln, what of that? Maybe they should opt in for hazard pay.

Wonderful, wonderful, it was a good sign.

* * *

Chapter 24

Chicago — Warehouse Loft — Party — *Jan. 17, 2003 — 6:30 p.m. — Community Impact*

The mid-January sun hung low in the Chicago sky, casting a pale golden light through the tall windows of the large work space loft. James stood at the entrance, his eyes sweeping across the room, taking in the fruits of their labor. Sections of the completed mosaic lay spread out on the floor, a vibrant tapestry of color and form that seemed to pulse with life. It was a kind of pay-off day and show and tell to a select audience of family, friends, donors, patrons, Epoch and of course Eco United, to demonstrate the project was on track and proceeding as planned.

He noticed an odd detail—a small, dark brown tile near the edge of one section. It was slightly askew, its placement just a touch off from its neighbors. James felt an inexplicable urge to adjust it, but resisted. The Navajo, he knew, have a tradition of deliberate imperfection, of placing an error in a completed work to remind ourselves that human beings are not perfect and the work itself is not an idol, but an aspiration, a love letter to God. That same imperfection could work as a 'spirit line' or pathway and the part of the craftsmen's being that entered into the mosaic wall could now safely exit. And so all that to say, the work on this particular section of the wall as a demo, was complete, it would do.

There was a hum in the air, the pleasant buzz of background conversation as human voices talking in concert with each other. The guests had begun to arrive and were producing a sound like none other found in nature, a pure human sound. A wonderful thrum and constant power chord to underscore tonight's party, and celebration of their progress to date. This was also a photo-op night for Epoch Alliance to shake their tail feathers, some hands too, and offer thanks to the world at large and small.

James Watson knew well how the system worked and the importance of this mile marker and still he tugged at the collar of his more formal shirt, feeling slightly out of place in the 'dressed-up' attire. He much preferred his T shirt and khaki slacks, but tonight called for a traditional presentation.

James's eyes caught on a smudge of blue glaze on his crisp white cuff. He'd missed it while getting dressed, and now it stood out like a tiny beacon against the fabric. James smiled to himself, oddly comforted by this small reminder of the work that had brought them here. It was a testament to the hours spent hunched over tiles, hands coated in clay and glaze, bringing their vision to life. And it was still only a third complete.

The warehouse work space had been transformed for the evening. Soft lighting cast a warm glow over the exposed brick walls, and strategically placed spotlights illuminated the mosaic sections. The air hummed with conversation and the gentle clink of champagne glasses. James took in the eclectic mix of guests:

There was Mrs. Abernathy, her silver hair piled high in an elegant up-do, pearls gleaming at her throat. She'd been one of their first donors, believing in the project when it was nothing more than sketches and dreams. Now she stood before a completed section, her eyes misting with emotion.

Near the refreshment table, a group of young art students from the local university huddled together, chatting with the interns, Bette, Mark and Roberto, their excitement palpable. They spoke in hushed, reverent tones, pointing out intricate details and discussing techniques. Their youthful energy was a stark contrast to the more subdued appreciation of the older patrons.

James watched as they moved among the mosaic sections, their faces alight with wonder. He overheard snippets of conversation:

"Look, there's my tile!" exclaimed a portly man in a tweed jacket, his round face beaming with pride. "Right there, next to the river!"

"I never imagined it would look like this when it all came together," murmured a woman in a sleek black dress, her hand resting on her husband's arm as they gazed at the artwork.

"It's like the whole city is here, in color and shape," marveled an elderly gentleman, leaning on his cane as he peered closely at a section depicting the Chicago skyline.

James nodded and felt a sense of confirmation of what they all had hoped for. This was what they wanted—a true community project, where every person could see themselves represented, front and center in the world.

As he moved through the crowd, greeting people and answering questions, James kept an eye on the door. His family would be arriving soon, and the thought filled him with a mixture of excitement and joy. It had been so long since they'd seen his work in person. He imagined his mother's proud smile, his father's quiet nod of approval, and Sarah's wide-eyed wonder. Their presence would make this night complete.

The guest list was a tapestry of Chicago's diverse community. City officials mingled with local business owners. Art critics engaged in passionate debates with community organizers. Even a few celebrities had turned up, drawn by the buzz surrounding the project. James spotted a well-known Chicago Bears player admiring a section that depicted the city's sports culture.

And there was a comedian, James recognized in an animated discussion with Sam Petoskey, James vaguely wondered if Sam knew him personally. James hadn't spotted his assistant Val yet, but she would be here, he was certain of that.

People were arriving in a steady flow, and the warehouse seemed to pulse with energy. The mosaic sections, bathed in the warm light, appeared to come alive. The one completed continent section was placed closest to the general reception area, where people could sit at small tables and relax, and where the speeches would be made later. The incomplete templates were stretched out down the length of the warehouse space, so folks could observe the different stages of work in progress.

The warehouse work space had plenty of room for people to mill about and people felt welcome to walk around and look at the completed sections and parts in progress. Everything seemed to be working well. Famous last words. Knock on wood. James smiled, it was a grand evening.

And speaking of the topper, just where was Em? There was a main staging area set up to his immediate left where slides would be shown and speeches made, and ah... there she was standing next to Rhonda pointing to the clay station they'd set up for people present at the party to contribute their tile to the project. Even now, they were still welcoming the tiles people could make.

And while that was interesting and would certainly pull his attention in an ordinary way, on an ordinary day, the dress she was wearing stopped his mind from considering anything else at the moment.

When was the last time he'd seen her in a dress? What was it about a woman wearing a dress, the flow and ease and sway of the material that accentuated her movements, her dip and thrust as she moved through space that could undo a man where he stood.

It was a rhetorical question and one he might ponder later, for now, he simply enjoyed the stiff satin texture of the dark cranberry color dress that fit snug around her bosom, cut low enough to show her neckline, but not so low he'd have to hand her a shawl. Her dark hair hung down her back with some loose locks landing on shoulders and shimmered with glowing good health.

She looked stunning, but there was something more, something about how she looked tonight that reached deep inside to wake a snoozing lion and touch his elemental nature and now James was acutely aware he had to look away and soon, or he wasn't quite sure what he would do. It was an odd feeling to suspect his body could outvote his mind.

"Em…" he breathed, turning his back on her to focus on the templates stretched before him. But it was no use. He could feel her gaze on him now, like a warm caress across his skin.

Was Emma trying to seduce him? The thought seemed stunning, but once it slipped into his mind, it refused to budge. Em understood color better than anyone on earth. She would know exactly the right shade to… to get to him on a night like tonight. She knew the effect of color. It was her superpower.

James ran a hand through his hair, loosening his tie. 'Get it together, Watson,' he chided himself. 'You're a grown man, not some hormone-addled teenager, take a little responsibility.' He took a deep breath, willing his heart rate to slow. It stubbornly refused. Well, if she was going to all that trouble to get his attention... and she was willing... what would be the harm?

And then, unbidden, and absolutely the last message he expected slipped into his mind in bold caps: 'No casual sex.' They were the words from Emma's father, George, of all people, and acted now like a bucket of cold water, to dampen some heat.

To put him on pause long enough to study Emma more closely. There was no overt flirtation, no clichéd batting of eyelashes. And yet... there was something. A heat in her gaze when their eyes met, a gentle parting of her lips as if already imagining what he might taste like.

But there was no Machiavellian machination going on here. He knew what it felt like to be seduced, he remembered it well. No, Emma had simply picked out a great dress she knew he'd like and was being her natural self vying for his attention. It was nature, just old fashioned nature making a power move.

Now, being self aware might help calm him... somewhat... but how now to calm Em? How to help her without hurting her feelings? How to comfort her without falling off the cliff together in an explosive roll before they were truly ready?

"James! Jimmy!" Sarah's voice cut through the fog of desire. His family's presence effectively snipped the fuse line leading to an untimely explosion with Em. Assuming Em had wanted to.

Thank God, for this distraction.

Suddenly, there they were. His mum and da, looking slightly overwhelmed by the bustling crowd, and Sarah, her eyes wide with wonder as she took in the colorful scene. James felt his focus softly shift from Emma and their close encounter to his family unit, his heart swelled at the sight of them.

"Jimmy!" Sarah's voice rang out above the crowd as she spotted him. She rushed forward, enveloping him in a tight hug. "Oh, Jimmy, it's so beautiful!"

James hugged her back, feeling the tension he'd been carrying melt away. "Thanks, pet," he murmured. "I'm so glad you could come."

* * *

As James led his family around the loft, explaining the project and showing them the sections of the mosaic, Emma watched from across the room. She'd been watching James, of course, she'd felt the fire deep inside him turn his attention toward her... and she had welcomed it, but once again... something happened to come between them.

She'd been talking with Rhonda in the midst of discussing glaze techniques alongside a group of interested guests, when she had turned to look at him, but he was looking away. Had she imagined it? Maybe these were her feelings welling up and not mutual. Then Emma spotted his family arrive.

The change in James was immediately apparent to her. His whole demeanor softened, the slight stiffness he'd been carrying in his shoulders all evening disappearing as he interacted with his family. Emma found herself captivated by the gentle way he guided Sarah through the space, his hand on her shoulders, leaning down to explain details of the mosaic to her.

There was a moment when Sarah bent down to examine a particular section of tiles, and James crouched beside her. Emma watched as he pointed out different elements, his face animated as he described the process. Sarah listened with rapt attention, her hand reaching out to gently touch a tile, then quickly pulling back as if remembering she wasn't supposed to.

James laughed, a warm, rich sound that carried across the room. "It's alright, pet," Emma heard him say. "These ones are all set. You can touch them."

The joy on Sarah's face as she carefully ran her fingers over the mosaic was beautiful to behold. Emma felt a lump form in her throat at the tenderness of the scene.

She was so absorbed in watching James and his family that she almost didn't notice Sam approaching, his camera held at the ready. He'd been moving through the crowd all evening, capturing moments just like this one.

"Beautiful, isn't it?" Sam said softly, nodding towards James and Sarah.

Emma nodded, not trusting her voice for a moment. When she did speak, her words were quiet, meant only for Sam. "He's so different with them. So... open."

Sam adjusted his camera, zooming in on James as he helped Sarah to her feet. "It's like watching someone come alive," he mused.

As they watched, James looked up, his eyes finally, finally meeting Emma's from across the room. For a moment, everything else seemed to fade away. James's smile softened, becoming something more intimate, rather serious, but more real than the polite expression he'd worn for most of the evening.

Emma felt her breath catch in her throat. She raised her hand in a small wave, a gesture that felt both familiar and new, it seemed to be their personal greeting now. James's smile widened in response, she watched him stand up from his crouched position, take in a deep breath as if to brace himself to face her and then beckoned her over.

As Emma made her way across the room, weaving through clusters of chatting guests, she felt like she was in the flow, in the groove, whatever... it felt correct and good to be sharing what they had all done so far with such tender hearted people. Speaking of, her little personal cruise boat finally made a soft landing at his dock.

She reached James and his family, exchanged warm greetings with his parents and received an enthusiastic hug from Sarah. She loved how Sarah hung onto her, until she felt well and truly loved. She kissed the top of Sarah's head and she finally let go. She shook hands with James' mum, Dora and da, Joe, but that didn't seem to be enough for them either, because his mum also hugged her hard.

"So happy to see you lass, so happy." Dora was almost weeping.

James finally turned to look her straight in her eye and Emma felt the edges of her world soften and then fade. The power of what he kept buried deep inside himself seemed naked in his gaze now, he was showing a secret side of himself to her as private in public. There was a perpetual fire burning in James that could consume her and he let her see it. He wanted her, in the way she hoped, but couldn't imagine and he let her see that too. Her knees went weak, and for a moment, she wondered if he might have to catch her.

"James..." His name escaped her lips like a prayer.

"That is some dress you chose for tonight," he said quietly, his voice a low but steady rumble that seemed to bypass her ears and go straight to her core.

It was true, she had chosen this dress with him in mind, to shock his senses, but had no idea it would actually work. She watched his face closely, realizing he seemed to be taking charge of the situation and she might just be along for the ride. It was like she'd lit a match and was now stunned to find it might actually burn the house down.

"Not now, not tonight, but we need to have a talk," James said, his voice serious as a cat four hurricane.

"Another talk?" her voice aimed for lightness but overshot the moon. Seeing his unwavering gaze, she sobered. "What is it, James? You can tell me... or talk in code. I can still read your mind pretty well."

"That won't be hard at the moment, luv," he said, a wry smile tugging at his lips. "I'm running a little hot here, Em. I need to know, did you wear this dress for me tonight?"

Emma felt her cheeks flush, the heat rivaling the warmth of the cranberry satin against her skin. "I... yes," she admitted, her voice barely above a whisper. "But... I didn't think it would affect you like this."

James's eyes softened, a mix of desire and tenderness swirling in their depths. "Oh, Em," he sighed, "you have no idea the effect you have on me. But we can't... not here, not now. We need to talk about this, about us, before we do something we can't take back."

Emma felt a wave of emotions wash over her—relief, frustration, and more than a touch of embarrassment. She'd wanted to provoke a reaction, sure, but now she realized she'd been playing with fire without fully understanding the consequences. The dress suddenly felt too tight, too revealing, like she'd put on someone else's skin for the evening.

She took a deep breath, gathering her courage. Honesty had always been their strength, even when it was difficult. "I'm sorry," she said softly, her eyes meeting his. "I guess I don't know how to talk to you sometimes, how to reach you." She paused, her heart thundering in her chest. "Can you tell me, because now I need to understand, what do you need from me? Do you know?"

The question was a good one, and the answer should be the truth. James seemed to consider it carefully, his brow furrowing slightly as he searched for the right words. The party continued around them, but at that moment, they might as well have been alone in the universe.

James took a deep breath, his eyes never leaving Emma's. When he spoke, his voice was low and intense, barely audible above the hum of the party.

"What I need from you, Em?" he paused, running a hand through his hair. "I need... I need to know that this isn't just about the project, or the heat of the moment, or pushed into each other's lives. I need to know that you see me—not just the artist, not just your old friend from Cooper, but the man I am now. You wore this dress to show me your desire, and a few moments ago, I showed you who I am too, something I'll never share with anyone but my wife..."

He took a step closer, close enough that Emma could feel the warmth radiating from his body. "I need to know that you want all of me, Em. The good, the bad, the bloody stubborn Geordie who's probably going to drive you half mad half the time." A wry smile tugged at his lips. "And I need to know that you're ready for that, for us, for everything it means."

James's hand twitched at his side, as if he wanted to reach out and touch her but was holding himself back. "Because once we cross that line, luv, there's no going back for me. You're it, Em. You always have been. In return I'll give you everything I have, with my heart front and center on a plate."

He let out a shaky breath, vulnerability clear in his eyes. "So I guess what I'm asking is... are you sure? Are you ready for all of that? Because I need you to be sure, Em. I need you to be as all-in as I am."

The weight of his words hung between them, the noise of the party fading into the background as they stood on the precipice of a cliff.

* * *

Emma opened her mouth to respond, her heart racing with the weight of James's words, when a familiar voice cut through the tension.

"Oi! There's our dynamic duo!"

Ted's booming greeting startled them both, breaking the intimate bubble they'd been wrapped in. James and Emma turned to see Ted and a very pregnant Maribel making their way through the crowd, Ted's arm protectively around his wife's expanded waistline.

"Bloody hell, Ted," James muttered, a mix of frustration and relief coloring his tone. "Your timing is impeccable as always."

Emma let out a shaky laugh, grateful for the interruption even as part of her mourned the lost moment. She smoothed down her dress, suddenly aware of how flushed she must look.

"Emma!" Maribel exclaimed, waddling forward to embrace her friend. "You look absolutely stunning. That dress is a knockout."

"Thanks, Bel," Emma replied, returning the hug awkwardly around Maribel's prominent bump. "You're looking pretty radiant yourself. How much longer now?"

"Three weeks, give or take," Maribel said, rubbing her belly. "Though this little football player feels like he might decide to make an early appearance."

Ted beamed proudly, his hand resting on the small of Maribel's back. "Right then, where's this masterpiece we've been hearing so much about? I hope it lives up to all the hype, I even bought a new digital camera to take pictures," he added, clapping James on the shoulder.

James, still a bit dazed from his intense conversation with Emma, took a moment to switch gears. "Right, yes, the mosaic. It's just over here. Come on, I'll give you the grand tour."

As they moved towards the displayed sections of the mosaic, James and Ted led the way, their heads bent close in conversation. Emma fell into step beside Maribel, grateful for the distraction of the lower key kind of grilling known as girl talk.

"So," Maribel said, her voice low and conspiratorial, "what exactly did we interrupt? The air between you two is still thick."

Emma felt her cheeks flush again. "Nothing," she said quickly, then sighed. "Everything. I don't know, Bel, I don't know what to do."

"Wait one minute…" Maribel stopped walking and took her friend's elbow, touching the satin material, "This dress… did you pounce? Are you pouncing?"

"Fat chance, he saw me coming from a mile off, I'm telling you Bel, the man is uncanny, not ordinary." Emma chuckled, but lowered her head to hide her expression. "He set me straight, Bel… and he's not wrong."

"Ah hon… I'm so sorry if I steered you wrong, so sorry." Bel looked like she was going to cry.

"Shh... shh... don't cry, you'll upset Ted... shhh... shhh" Emma consoled her by wrapping an arm around her to hold her close.

"It's the hormones... I'm okay really, I just would like to see you both happy, that's all, like Ted and me, I'm so happy..." Bel said with tears flowing down her cheeks.

Emma hugged her again until she calmed, then stepped back to look at her. "I know, Bel, I know... and it worked out, in a way... we... we cleared the air, I asked him what he really needed from me, and he told me."

'So, it'll work out?" Maribel's voice was hopeful as pulled a tissue from her bag and blew her nose.

Emma didn't want to dash her hopes, but wanted to be truthful too, so she said in the kindest way she could, "I don't know, of all the things he said he needed, I feel I gave him years ago, and he turned me down." Emma turned to look at Bel, but she was watching and listening closely so Emma continued, "I don't know what else to do, there are no guarantees in life, how can I promise to never hurt him again? No one can promise that."

Maribel's knowing smile was both comforting and slightly unnerving. "You can promise to try. Don't worry, honey. You'll figure it out."

Emma chuckled, she had to, Mirabel was just too sweet, so kind and so certain love would indeed find a way, and then Mirabel said something unexpected that caught her ear.

"And you can always pray your butt off... I mean, you're dealing with James, so consider it mandatory." Bel laughed at her own great family in-joke.

They were approaching Ted and James again as they stood over the mosaic, and Emma felt some of the tension drain from her shoulders. Here, surrounded by the fruits of their labor and the warmth of old friends, she could breathe again.

She caught James's eye over Ted's enthusiastic examination of a particularly intricate section. And he gave her a small, private, wry smile that seemed to say: 'I see you, I haven't forgotten about you and maybe even: *'I love you.'*

Can someone say 'I love you' with their eyes? Maybe. Maybe it was time to take her mom's advice that she'd almost forgotten and now Bel too and stand under the stars and pray.

* * *

The party continued around them, a swirl of color and conversation. Sam moved through the crowd, his camera capturing moment after moment—a child excitedly pointing out their tile to a grandparent, a couple standing hand in hand before a particularly beautiful section of the mosaic,

And James and Emma moving together in a semi-comfortable, almost-manageable truce now.

It seemed to be a mutual silent pact to table their trouble until after. And so they often walked in tandem talking with guests, or their heads bent close as they explained some detail of the project to an interested guest.

Sam was careful how he tracked their progress, staying out of range of the shotgun mic. They would be the heroes of the doc, the touch point characters and so of course he had to track them, but give them space too... because something was definitely happening tonight. He also kept an eye out because he wasn't completely sure if they were going to have a knock down fight or drag each other off to a quiet cave to copulate. No one else seemed to notice though, and he would say nothing, but he kept an eye out, just in case, just in case.

Whew. It felt like a close one, though. Maybe he picked up on it, because he was the observer, or his energy training in the theatre, or his need to develop his instincts as a child to protect himself, in any case he had very good radar and trusted it. But they seemed better now, more at peace and more themselves and so Sam turned his attention to other sites to shoot

Life went on, every person present sharing the air and walking the floor had a host of trouble they set aside to come to the party. Everyone had the opportunity to lighten up, have a snack, chat with old friends and meet new ones too. It could be a wonderful evening, if one was open to the possibilities, and could see the funny side of falling down. It was called a pratfall.

Pratfalls were funny, not because someone fell down but because it was unexpected. It was the comic law of contrast. Sam Petosky knew that law, and so he looked for contrast, the unexpected moment that might mean visual levity gold.

The buffet table could be a funny place, there was a wide variety of appetizers, and treats laid on a long table for folks to try, Epoch had spared no expense and Rhonda had outdone herself in the eclectic array.

Sam began the evening with establishing shots, getting the long view of the buffet area, the full color rendering of the design on the wall and a 3D scale model of the design on the Eco United Lobby Wall. Then he switched his attention to capturing key personnel, of course getting footage of James and Emma at the outskirts of the party, in discussion so deep there was an impenetrable wall around them. No need to mention more about that.

Sam switched to tracking Rhonda, he adjusted the focus on his camera, zooming in on Rhonda as she sat at the tile-making station. It was an unexpected sight—the usually composed and businesslike woman was hunched over a small square of clay, her face a study in concentration and childlike wonder.

As he filmed, Sam noticed the subtle changes in Rhonda's demeanor. The furrows in her brow, ever-present during project meetings, had smoothed out. Her lips, often pressed into a thin line of determination, were now curved in a soft smile. She seemed years younger, unburdened by the weight of responsibility she usually carried.

James's family approached the station, Sarah leading the way with an enthusiasm that was infectious. Sam panned the camera to capture the moment as they settled around Rhonda, James's mother Dora, offering gentle encouragement while his father Joe Watson watched with amused interest.

"What are you making, dear?" Dora asked Rhonda, her voice warm and curious.

Rhonda looked up, a flash of self-consciousness crossing her face before melting into a genuine smile. "I'm not entirely sure," she admitted with a laugh. "I think it's meant to be a tree, but it's starting to look more like a lopsided umbrella."

Sarah leaned in, her eyes bright with interest. "I like it," she declared. "It looks like a magic tree. The kind that might grant wishes."

Rhonda's laugh was full and rich, a sound Sam realized he'd never heard before. He zoomed in, capturing the crinkles around her eyes, the way her shoulders shook with mirth. This, he thought, was Rhonda in her true light—not just the driven project manager, but a woman with a heart full of passion for the work she did.

As the family engaged Rhonda in conversation, drawing her out of her shell, Sam let his camera wander. He caught sight of the interns huddled around a table laden with food. Oh good, more food and fun moments. There were Roberto, Clara, Jasmine, Mark and Bette. Their laughter carried across the room, a testament to the bonds formed over long hours of work and shared purpose.

One of the interns, it was Bette, was in the middle of an animated story, her hair a vibrant chestnut color tonight, reflecting the light, Sam, noting that would look great on camera, came close to pick up the story; "And then," she said, "James walks in, covered head to toe in this ridiculous orange glaze. He looks at us all serious-like and says, 'I meant to do that.'"

The group erupted into laughter, and Sam couldn't help but smile behind his camera. These were the moments that truly made a project come alive—the shared jokes, the camaraderie, the human connections forged in the crucible of creativity.

Sam paused filming for a moment, he pulled the camera up close to his chest, and scanned the room, but where was Val?

A tap on a microphone drew Sam's attention to the makeshift stage area. Alfred stood there, his silver hair catching the light, a glass of champagne in his hand. Sam moved closer, adjusting his shotgun mic to catch the speech clearly.

"Friends, colleagues, artists," Alfred began, his voice rich with emotion. "What we see around us tonight is nothing short of miraculous. Not just because of its beauty, though that is undeniable, but because of what it represents."

Sam panned across the room, capturing the rapt faces of the audience. He lingered on James and Emma, standing side by side, about two feet apart, together, but not touching, their expressions a mix of awe and humility.

Alfred continued, his words painting a picture of community and shared vision. As he finished, Rhonda took the stage, her speech a perfect complement to Alfred's—where he had spoken of art and beauty, she spoke of logistics and teamwork, of the countless hours and tireless effort that had gone into bringing this project to life.

As other members of the Epoch Alliance took their turns at the microphone, Sam found his attention drawn to a group standing slightly apart from the main crowd. They were dressed in sharp suits, their postures stiff and formal amidst the relaxed atmosphere of the party. With a start, Sam realized these must be representatives from the Eco Building where the mosaic was to be installed.

He zoomed in, noting their frozen smiles and tight expressions. Something about their demeanor set off a warning bell in Sam's mind. Another warning bell. Hmm...

"Something *is* rotting in Denmark..." It was Val.

He heard her before he saw her, and turned toward the voice at his right side to say "Val! Where have you—" the rest of the words dried up in his mind—he found himself looking at a beautiful young woman, her dark brown hair falling in a shining waterfall from the crown of her head far down her back, wearing a stylish 50's vintage dark blue cocktail dress, bringing out her soft, dark green eyes, that right now, were and sparkling with amusement.

"Didn't recognize me, did you?" She asked, all innocence, but resisted the temptation to bat her eyes, she simply drew a few lines and that was a big one. She was no flirt.

"Well, sure I do, your dead-on accurate observation was a giveaway." Sam smiled, "you look great.

"You look great too." Val stuttered, then recovered the fumble. "I mean you clean up good."

"That is a great, great dress." Sam nodded

"Thanks, again." Val thought about revealing that Emma had told her to pull over to the consignment shop on Lincoln to get the dress in the window, but maybe some things were better left unsaid.

'Maybe you'll let me tape you later?" Sam asked, looking at the dress and cocking his head slightly for a different angle. "That dress will look great on tape... but just in casual conversation, not posed or anything." Sam ventured.

Slight pause, this wasn't exactly the reaction she was hoping for, but Val agreed "okay, I don't see why not. Now, why'd you look so funny a few moments ago? Do you have a bad angle? You wanna set up somewhere else?"

"No, I'm moving around using the steady-cam, I'm getting great, great shots, this party will provide a good resting place in the doc, a chance to pause and reset to climb the last mountain." Sam paused to look around the room, to look at the group from Eco United, "But maybe sometimes I see moments I shouldn't see, and best forget."

"That was a mouthful and a mystery." Val cocked her head to look at him better.

Sam shrugged, he would say no more, but he made a mental note to keep an eye on this group, filing away the observation for later consideration and review.

"Did you get some food?" Val asked, "I've got extra cheese puffs in my purse."

Sam laughed "Now, that is exactly what an actor would do. And great food comedy, lemme take a shot of that."

Val laughed, and opened her clutch bag to reveal, yes, she did indeed, have cheese puffs on top of red napkins inside her purse. Sam was laughing so hard the camera shook.

Val looked at him and observed, "You are a strange, strange man."

"Said the kettle to the pot..." Sam smiled and then reached in and took two of her treasured cheese puffs and popped them in his mouth. At her stunned expression he proclaimed, "What? You said I could."

"Well, I'm glad you feel at home," Val chuckled, smiled then looked around the surrounding area at the people milling about, everyone wearing their 'besties' as her gran would say, even the interns over there by the clay station, were in their respective versions of high gear. It was a homecoming for the project thus far.

She turned to Sam and spoke from her heart. "I'm... so glad to have you onboard Sam, I'm not sure I said that yet." Val was suddenly a little shy.

"Well, I'm glad to be here, I owe Emma Hawkins big-time–wait... I gotta go grab that shot, don't leave without saying good night." And with that Sam turned on his heel and was off toward three small children dancing alongside the stretch of clay tiles.

"Yeah, that is a great shot," Val remarked to the empty air, but he was already gone. She sighed a half-sigh.

* * *

After the speeches concluded, the party began to wind down. Sam captured some final moments—guests lingering over particularly beautiful sections of the mosaic, James and Emma thanking people as they left, Jasmine, Clara and Roberto pitching in to help with clean-up despite protests that they should enjoy the party.

As the last guests trickled out, Sam found a quiet corner to review some of his footage. The evening played back on his small screen—a kaleidoscope of joy, creativity, and community. Yet that nagging feeling about the Eco Building representatives lingered.

He glanced up, catching sight of James and Emma standing amid the remnants of the party. They weren't speaking, just standing close, surveying the room with matching expressions of tired satisfaction. Sam raised his camera one last time, capturing this quiet moment of shared triumph. So glad there were no bruises or torn clothes. Whew. Maybe he was the only one who noticed. He hoped so.

The loft slowly emptied, the buzz of conversation fading to silence. The mosaic sections lay quiet, it was a good day—wait, what happened to Val? Sam thought, did she leave already?

* * *

The crisp night air nipped at Emma's cheeks as she stepped outside the building, leaving Maribel sheltered behind the glass doors. Ted had gone to fetch the car, not wanting his very pregnant wife to walk too far in the cold.

Emma tilted her face up to the sky, drinking in the vast expanse of stars overhead. The city lights dimmed their brilliance somewhat, but still they twinkled, silent witnesses to the dramas unfolding below. She drew in a deep breath, feeling the chill settle in her lungs.

"Alright, God," she whispered, her breath forming small clouds in the frigid air. "I know I'm not exactly on your speed dial, but... I could use a little guidance here."

She paused, gathering her thoughts. A gust of wind rustled through nearby trees, as if urging her on.

"Look, you know how sorry I am for what happened with James all those years ago," Emma continued, her voice barely audible. "You know all the reasons—I don't need to list them or even dwell, but time's gone by, and now..."

She trailed off, her eyes fixed on a particularly bright star. "Now that I see him every day, work with him, I just... I can't imagine my life without him in it. Not anymore."

Emma wrapped her arms around herself, suddenly feeling very small beneath the vast night sky. "I'm not asking for a magic wand or anything. I know that's not how this works. But I promise you, I'll try my absolute best not to hurt him again. Not like before. Not with intention."

A car horn honked in the distance, reminding Emma of the bustling world beyond this quiet moment. "I know he's one of your precious children, God. I know we all are, I get that now, in a way I didn't before. So I guess... I'm asking for a miracle. If you're not too busy."

She chuckled softly, shaking her head at her own audacity. "Oh and... while I'm at it, thank you for bringing me to this project. No regrets, whatever happens."

Emma fell silent, listening to the whisper of the wind and the distant hum of the city. The night air seemed to soften around her, as if cradling her in a gentle embrace. She closed her eyes, feeling a warmth spread through her chest despite the chill.

"I suppose...I'm willing to be corrected," she murmured, "but I don't know what else to do."

As the words left her lips, something inside Emma shifted. The carefully constructed walls she'd built around her heart began to crumble, and she felt a wave of emotion wash over her. Her next words came out in a whisper, thick with unshed tears.

"Oh God, I've made such a mess of things," she confessed, her voice trembling. "I thought I was protecting myself, but all I did was hurt us both. I've been proud, stubborn, but I can't go back or beat myself up anymore either, I know you don't want that, and I did apologize—with my whole heart—in that dang letter I sent years ago, but he... never mind.

She sighed "Am I waxing long? But I wanna add, there's no point in looking back, is there? So... is it really over between James and me?"

A single tear slipped down her cheek, quickly followed by another. Emma didn't bother to wipe them away.

"I love him, I guess you know that" she breathed, the words feeling both terrifying and freeing. "Help me be the woman he needs, help us find our way to be with each other...and... if not... if he doesn't want me, please help me find a way to leave him alone and not hurt anymore."

As her tears subsided, Emma took a deep, shuddering breath. The night air filled her lungs, crisp and clean, it felt good.

"Thank you," she said softly, "Thank you for listening."

She glanced up at the stars again.

"Oh and... thank you for my mom and dad and family too. I probably don't say that enough."

Another pause. Then: "I miss you, God. Sorry I haven't stayed in touch. I'll... do better."

Through the glass doors, Maribel was watching her curiously. Emma waved and tried a small smile, hoping the shimmer in her eyes wasn't visible.

Her hand brushed the cold metal of the door handle, but she lingered just a second longer.

"Oh and God? If you could maybe give James a little nudge too... that might not be off base."

She stepped back inside, the warmth enveloping her like a hug. Whatever came next, she'd faced her fears and was open to try in a way she hadn't before. What else can a person who'd made a mistake do?

She stopped and turned. "Oh and God..." then she chuckled "skip it...talk later..."

* * *

Chapter 25

Chicago — Fulton Street Loft — *Jan. 17, 2003 — 9:45 p.m. —*
Unfinished Business

James was relaxing on his living room couch after the party, all had gone very well, there was an excellent reception for the work done—and the design itself too, Rhonda had done an outstanding job orchestrating the whole event from top to bottom. His family had a great time and best of all they could stay for a week before heading back. His own private heaven.

Including the vision of Emma in that dark cranberry colored dress that he will never erase from his mind. James sighed, he was glad she wore it—because it had become the catalyst for that brief but life-changing conversation. He couldn't recall exactly all of what he'd said; it came out in a stream unbroken and ready to wear—like it or not ready or not.

They didn't get a chance to speak again before the evening wound completely down. Emma had stayed by Maribel's side as her protector for the rest of the evening, so Ted could walk freely around the warehouse as James gave him the deluxe grand tour. And then their old friends had taken Emma home.

And... and maybe Emma had wanted it that way.

James sighed again, but Emma had been a vision, and Sarah and his family seemed to approve of her too. Ah well. But something was going to change—and soon, for both their sakes, it would be all in or all out, before they went half-mad in tandem.

The soft glow of the lamp cast long shadows across James's living room. The distant hum of Chicago traffic filtered through the windows—a stark contrast to the quiet intimacy of the moment. James sat on the worn leather couch, his sister Sarah beside him, her eyes bright with excitement.

"I've got something for you, James," Sarah said, her voice filled with pride as she handed him a plastic-sealed bag. "Been keeping it safe, I have."

James took the bag, feeling its unexpected weight. "What's all this then, pet?"

His mother's voice drifted from the kitchen. "Just some mail that came for you, luv. Sarah's been ever so diligent about saving it."

James upended the bag, letting its contents spill onto the coffee table—a cascade of envelopes, fliers, and postcards spread before him, a paper trail of the life he'd left behind in Newcastle.

"Well, look at you, Sarah. Quite the guardian of correspondence, aren't you?" James said, ruffling her hair affectionately.

Sarah beamed, clearly pleased with herself. "I take good care of you, don't I?"

James began sifting through the pile, his movements casual, unhurried. A utility bill here, a flier for a local art show there. His fingers paused on a thick envelope, the paper high-quality and cream-colored. Better save that and take a look later.

And then—buried beneath a colorful postcard, James saw it. A small envelope, adorned with several bright stamps, its edges slightly worn from its long journey. His heart skipped a beat as he reached for it, assuming it was the long-lost letter from his mum.

But as his fingers closed around the envelope, time seemed to slow. The room faded away, leaving only James and this unexpected piece of the past. He turned it over, his breath catching in his chest as he recognized the handwriting—not his mother's familiar scrawl, but the elegant curves of Emma's script.

James felt as though he knew what it was like to be at the bottom of the Mariana Trench—suddenly plunged into pressure so extreme he could spontaneously implode. His hands began to tremble slightly as he stared at the return address, confirmation of what his heart already knew.

"Sarah," he managed, his voice barely above a whisper. "Where... how... did you get this?"

Sarah looked at him, confusion clouding her features. "I told you, James. I save your mail. I look after you. I kept it all together." Her voice took on a hint of worry. "The stamps are very pretty, so that means it's important, right? I did okay, James, right?"

James swallowed hard, trying to find his voice. "Yes, pet. You did brilliantly. Absolutely brilliantly."

Sarah's face lit up with relief, but James barely noticed. His world had narrowed to the envelope in his hands—to the letter he'd never known existed. A letter from Emma, sent all those years ago, that had somehow found its way to him now.

With shaking fingers, James carefully opened the envelope. As he unfolded the paper inside, he could almost smell the faint scent of jasmine that always seemed to cling to Emma. The first words swam before his eyes:

"Dear James, I don't know if you'll read this. I'm not sure I would, if our positions were reversed. But I have to try. I owe you that much, and so much more."

James closed his eyes, overwhelmed by the flood of emotions. When he opened them again, he saw Sarah watching him with concern.

"Are you okay, James?" she asked softly.

James managed a small smile. "I'm alright, pet. Just... just remembering something I'd forgotten."

As he settled back to read the letter, James felt as though he was standing on the edge of a precipice. Whatever words Emma had written all those years ago, he knew that reading them now would change everything. With a deep breath, he began to read, stepping off that edge.

After reading through the letter, once, he read it through again—and then third time's the charm, gave it yet another go. Em had opened her heart to him in this letter, put pride aside and humbled herself. All these years. All these years. What must she have thought? That he'd received her heartfelt confession and couldn't be bothered to reply? And yet, despite believing he had callously ignored her olive branch, she had still come when he needed her—answering the call to help with the project.

Amazing woman.

The lamp's warm glow caught the slight tremor in his hands as he carefully folded the letter, his fingers lingering on the creases as if trying to smooth away the time that had passed.

"Amazing woman," he murmured, his voice barely audible above the muffled sounds of the city beyond the windows.

The sudden clatter of dishes from the kitchen startled James from his reverie. His mother's voice drifted in, warm and familiar. "Time for bed, luvs. Sarah, do you remember where your room is?"

"Of course, Ma. What do you think?" Sarah's indignant reply brought a small smile to James's face—a moment of normalcy in this sea of emotional turbulence.

"Goodnight, then," his mother called. "Your Da's already fast asleep. See you in the morning, lad."

James mumbled a response, his eyes drawn to the phone on the side table. Should he call her now? His fingers itched to dial the number—to hear Emma's voice, to begin unraveling this tangle of misunderstanding. But no, he thought, this wasn't a conversation for the impersonal distance of a phone call. This needed to be face to face—where he could see her eyes, read the emotions that words alone couldn't convey.

First thing in the morning, then. He knew Emma would be at the work loft by 6 AM, always the early bird, pouring over the pieces of their mosaic puzzle before anyone else arrived. The image of her, bathed in the soft light of dawn, brow furrowed in concentration as she studied their creation, warmed his hurting mind.

"Ma," he called out, his voice stronger now, decision made. "I'm going to the work loft first thing in the morning, but call if you need me, right?"

His mother's affirmative reply was almost lost in the sound of Sarah's giggles as she prepared for bed. James sat back on the couch, the letter still clutched in his hand. The night stretched before him, sleep a distant possibility as his mind raced with all the things he needed to say—and what had to be set right.

Outside, the city hummed on, oblivious to the seismic shift that had just occurred in James's world. But in the quiet of his living room, surrounded by the ephemera of his past and the promise of a future suddenly bright with possibility...

What was it he'd just told her this evening that he needed from her? Wasn't this letter—written years ago—a testament to him of the woman she was? And still is.

Tomorrow morning they would both find out.

James felt as though he was standing on the edge of a blade—the razor's edge. Morning couldn't come soon enough.

* * *

Chapter 26

Chicago — Warehouse Work Loft — Assembly *— Jan. 18, 2003 —*
6:50 a.m. — Rise and Shine

The early morning light filtered through the loft's high windows, casting long shadows across the floor strewn with clay tiles. The air was thick with the scent of dried clay and the faint drift of percolating coffee. Emma sat cross-legged on the floor, her back to the door, dark hair cascading down her shoulders. She was so absorbed in her work, carefully arranging tiles into intricate patterns, that she didn't hear James enter.

James paused in the doorway, the letter clutched in his hand like a lifeline. He watched Emma work, the sunlight catching the chestnut highlights in her hair, and felt a familiar warmth glow in his chest from the inside out. Sensing his presence, Emma turned, her eyes meeting his, immediately lighting up with a spontaneous warmth that seemed reserved just for him. James realized, with a start, that it had always been this way—her face brightening at the sight of him, not out of training or habit, or some social suggestion on how to behave, but from a genuine, unguarded joy.

Even after last night's conversation, she was first and foremost her natural self—always shining through. She was watching him carefully now, studying his mood this morning, her mouth opened as if to ask about last night, then stopped.

Her brow furrowed as she took in his expression. "What? What's happened? Is Sarah okay?"

James crossed the room, his footsteps soft in the cavernous space. He stopped in front of her, adopting a casual tone that belied the storm brewing within. "What? You never heard of a phone? Alexander Graham Bell goes to all the sodding trouble to invent the bloody thing—changes all the world and moon travel too—and you put your trust in stamps and the post?"

Confusion clouded Emma's features for a moment before her eyes landed on the envelope in his hand. Recognition dawned, and her face paled. "Oh God..." she breathed, the words barely audible.

"Yeah... God indeed..." James said, lowering himself to sit beside her. He placed the letter on the floor between them like a woebegone puppy. The weight of unspoken words and lost years seemed to press down on them, making the air feel thick and heavy. Almost—*almost* un-breathable.

"Oh God..." Emma repeated, her voice a mixture of disbelief and dawning horror.

James tried to keep his tone light, but emotion crept in despite his best efforts. "It seems I thought this was from Ma when I was moving out of me old place. Stuffed it in me bag and once back in Newcastle, Sarah is looking after all my letters, you see, to keep them safe...and... brings it back to me now... along with a pile of others—twelve years later. So she didn't single you out special to pick on you, just to let you know."

Emma's voice was small, vulnerable. "So you read it?"

"Oh aye, I did last night. Several times plus. Makes good reading." James's attempt at humor fell flat in the face of the magnitude of the moment.

"Just last night... for the first time?" The hope and terror in Emma's voice were mixed in equal measure.

James nodded, and they lapsed into silence, the now-read letter looming large between them, a physical manifestation of lost time and missed connections.

"Em... why didn't you call? When you figured it out. I would have come running." The words were out before James could stop them, raw and honest.

Emma paused, her gaze distant as she searched her memories. "Would you? I wasn't so sure... I wanted to give you room to say 'no' if you wanted. I was never really sure what we were to each other. I don't think either of us knew... back then, how deep it went. When I didn't hear from you, I thought you said 'no.'"

"Ah, Em..." James's voice was thick with regret and growing understanding.

They sat in silence for a moment, both lost in thoughts of what might have been. The loft seemed to hold its breath, the only sound the distant hum of the awakening city.

James broke the silence, his voice hesitant. "I have to tell you something too. It came to me in the sweat lodge, cleaning things out... people out." He trailed off, deciding some things were better left unsaid. "Watching you with Petoskey..." He held up a hand to stop her protest. "Let me get this out... watching you talk with him, even if it's just you being kind to all... and curious about people, made me think about what you might have felt... back then in school. I knew girls liked me, well, maybe I knew you didn't like it when I chatted... I know we covered some of this at the Green Mill, but I've been wondering... what if it was the other way around? What if I was forced to see it in me face? I'm saying I understand. There were times watching you with

Petosky, I had to leave the area, just couldn't watch that shit show, sorry."

Emma's eyes widened at his confession, a mix of surprise and understanding crossing her face. She spoke softly, her words measured. "Best not to think about 'what if.' We might go nuts, but... I've been thinking... all these years, I have this theory that's helped me make peace with how it was."

James couldn't help but interject, a hint of his humor returning. "Oh God, please do tell. Don't keep that treasure to yourself."

Emma smiled, the tension easing slightly. She continued, her voice gaining confidence. "I've heard that love, real love, begins up here, at the crown chakra, with the mind, the eyes, then down to the speech center, getting to know someone, then the heart, then the solar plexus for emotions, then down here, for sex, then the root for family, home, and kids..."

James's brow furrowed in confusion, and he shook his head. Emma clarified, her words painting a picture of their shared past. "I'm saying that in the years in between, I've often wondered why when I knew I loved you—I even had that white light experience I told you about—but I could never call you my boyfriend or something like that. I wasn't even sure I had the desire to kiss you, but still, I loved you. And I think that's because where we were, at least for me, was still up here in the head area and just reaching the heart. I don't think we knew what to do with each other. We simply were moving at our own... rate. Maybe what happened for us is how love really is."

James smiled, her words moving slowly into the quiet places of his mind. "I'd like to read up on that. That feels like it could be true."

Emma shrugged, a gesture so familiar it made James smile.

"Huh... well, I wonder where we are on that scale." James mused, he couldn't take his eyes off her, in an odd way, he felt free to look his fill now, to drink her into himself.

"Let's say... last night was a... miscue, from frustrations boiling over from both of us, I can own my reaction, so what say we write that off... right off the books... but keep that dress safe in the closet, mind you..."

Emma smiled a little, the humor of the situation finally reaching her natural wit, she looked at him and nodded very slowly, her eyes wide and vulnerable as she asked, "and start over?"

"Well, not completely over, wouldn't want to go back to scratch and day one..."

"How about now, right now?' Emma said as soft as he could make it, she was already looking at his mouth, already leaning ever so slightly toward him.

"Yeah..." his voice was low, soft, sweet to hear, "so... should we kiss and find out where we are?" The words were out before James could second-guess them.

Emma smiled, now the idea was out and hanging suspended in the air for God and all and sundry to see, it wasn't outlandish. At all. They leaned towards each other, movements slow and careful, as if approaching a skittish wild pony with a promise of safe haven. Their lips met, and the world slowly, slowly fell away. Frissons of light and energy radiated from the point of contact, flowing through blood cells and bone, sweetening tissue and sinew to settle low in their bellies igniting a sweet single flame that would now never go out. It was done.

"Definitely felt that," James managed, his voice husky.

Emma lowered her head, fingers touching her lips lightly, her hair falling forward to hide her face. James gently tucked her hair behind her ears, revealing the tears that had begun to fall.

"Shh... ah Em... sorry I was such a fool," he murmured, his own eyes suspiciously bright. "I'm sorry too, you know. I don't think I knew what I felt until you'd gone. I fell apart, quite apart."

Emma looked up at him, her eyes searching his face. James repeated, his voice thick with emotion, "I did 'an all. Twas Sarah and me folks that pulled me back from the brink... so to speak."

He turned to look at the mosaic pieces spread out before them, thousands of tiles waiting to be placed, then glazed. "Look at 'em all, Em... are we mad? What are we doing?"

Emma didn't reply immediately, her gaze following his to the sea of clay before them. When she spoke, her voice was soft but sure. "Something wonderful."

James felt a smile tugging at his lips. "I'll take it. Buy the ticket, take the ride, eh, ole girl?"

Emma poked him, a flash of her bright spirit shining through. "Hey, speak for yourself."

"No, I got it straight. We're like a couple of ole marrieds been through the ringer 'an all and still working at it."

"I'll take it," Emma said, then rested her head on his shoulder, as they looked out over the tiles spread before them like a sonnet carved in clay.

As the world outside began to wake, and the sounds of the city filtered in through the windows, James had one last thought. "Thank you for the letter."

Emma's reply was simple, but sincere, "You're welcome."

And just like that, one handwritten letter on a single sheet of paper changed everything.

A miracle.

* * *

Chapter 27

Chicago — Epoch Alliance Office *— Jan. 24, 2003 — 10:30 a.m. — Look Out*

Alfred leaned back in his leather chair, a contented smile playing on his lips as he gazed out at the Chicago skyline. The past week had been nothing short of triumphant—the party a resounding success, the project humming along smoothly, everything falling perfectly into place.

He reached for his cup of tea, savoring the aroma of Earl Grey that wafted up. As he took a sip, his eyes fell on a small potted plant on the windowsill—a gift from Emma, thriving under his care. Its vibrant green leaves seemed to embody the vitality and promise of their mosaic project.

A gentle knock at the door interrupted his reverie. Margaret, his secretary, poked her head in, her silver-rimmed glasses perched precariously on the tip of her nose.

"Mr. Worthington? Max Hollister from the Eco United selection committee is here. He doesn't have an appointment, but..."

Alfred's face lit up. "Max? Wonderful! Send him in, send him in," he said, setting down his teacup and straightening his tie. He stood, ready to greet his visitor with the warmth of shared success.

However, as Max entered the room, Alfred's smile faltered. Alfred expected Max was coming in person to congratulate them all and to request an updated timeline, instead Max's expression was quite serious—and a little sad, as if he pitied Alfred. It seemed to Alfred the exact look Dr. Avery had when he'd come to say his mother might not last the night.

Alfred gestured to the chair across from his desk, his voice measured and calm as he said, "Sit down, Max. Something on your mind?"

As Max sank into the chair, looking as if he carried the weight of the world on his shoulders, Alfred felt a sense of foreboding settle over him. The electric hum from his desk computer suddenly seemed louder, underscoring the moment with a suspense-thrum undertone.

"The board has decided to go in a different direction," Max explained, his words, cherry-picked with care, crafted for a corporate pink slip. "They feel that the mosaic, while beautiful and meaningful, doesn't align with their new vision for the space."

For a moment, Alfred sat in stunned silence, the electric thrum from his computer deafening in the quiet room. Then, there was a spark in Alfred's eyes and he pointed it at Max, as his preferred weapon in the upcoming duel. Disbelief vs anger.

"Bullshit," Alfred said, his voice low but intense. Max flinched at the unexpected vehemence. "That design is hope itself—for the world to be better, to realize its divine perfection in form and humans are all a part of it. It's exactly Eco's credo."

He leaned forward, his gaze boring into Max. "Don't bullshit me, Max, don't do it. Someone's moved in and made a power play, right? Anderson's younger brother. Oh I know the talk and what goes on." His voice took on a hint of bitter amusement. "And you don't want to take the heat and bad PR for dropping out after we've delivered in spades and clover."

Max looked down, unable to meet Alfred's gaze. His silence was all the confirmation Alfred needed.

"Exactly," Alfred murmured, more to himself than to Max. He placed his hand over his heart, as if trying to physically hold back the tide of emotions threatening to overwhelm him. For a long moment, he sat there, his mind racing through implications and possibilities.

Then, with a calmness that belied the turmoil within, Alfred reached for the intercom. "Margaret," he said, his voice steady, "please call 911 for an emergency. I think I might be having a problem."

As Max jumped to his feet, panic replacing the guilt in his eyes, Alfred closed his eyes. The electric hum faded away, replaced by the sound of his own breathing. In this suspended moment, as his world tilted on its axis, a single thought crystallized in his mind: he couldn't let this be the end. Somehow, someway, he had to find a way to save the project, to honor the vision and hard work of so many precious people.

He would not die, please God, not yet...

The last thing Alfred saw before the paramedics burst into the room was the small bronze Thinker on his desk, its pensive pose now seeming like a challenge. 'Think,' it seemed to say.

Think and find a way.

Then darkness engulfed him, the weight of responsibility and the shock of the news finally overwhelming his senses.

* * *

James was behind the wheel of his Prius, driving down 90/94, from O'Hare International Airport back to Chicago, his hands resting comfortably on the steering wheel. The late afternoon sun hung low on the horizon, there was still hours of daylight left, but the sky was overcast and so made it seem later than it was, The familiar scent of leather seats mingled with the lingering aroma of his mother's perfume, a bittersweet reminder of the family he'd just bid farewell.

Sarah had clung to Emma, James was afraid he'd have to oh so gently, peel her away—something he dreaded to do. His mum had signaled him to let it run its course and sure enough Sarah finally let go. Em had whispered something to Sarah, that was clearly a secret between sisters, but of course James wanted to know.

"What did you say to our Sarah that helped her let go?" When Emma didn't respond, James turned to look at her and asked, "Well?"

Emma shrugged and smiled. "I'm thinking if I should tell you or not, it might be private."

"Huh. Sarah's never had a secret from me before, not sure if I like it." James remarked in a mock huff and quite put-out. "She was my sister first, you know."

Instead of answering directly she was looking out the window and said thoughtfully, "She loves you so much James—she wants someone looking after you all the time... I mean all the time."

After a moment James said softly, "I'm not sure what I can do about that, I can't live in a box."

"No, you can't and shouldn't." Emma looked down at her gloves lying in her lap. I told her I would help take care of you... I hope that's all right, but it's what she wanted to hear."

James cocked his head and looked at her, but Emma was gazing out the window when she said, "I meant it..."

Long pause, and finally Emma looked at him, waiting for his response.

"Well?" she asked.

"Oh, do I get a say in this stakeout?" But his eyes were fairly dancing with pleasure, he reached over and took her hand, "I think that's very kind... all right then, I like my lawn mowed at five inches high please."

"You don't have a lawn," Emma knocked back.

"Yeah, but now I can get one," he emphasized, "now I'll have one less thing to worry about."

Emma chuckled and adjusted her weight in the passenger seat, her gaze fixed on the passing scenery. A comfortable silence had settled between them, born of shared experiences and the emotional weight of goodbyes. The rhythmic hum of tires on asphalt provided a soothing backdrop to their thoughts.

A discordant chirp shattered the quiet. James's phone, nestled in the cup holder, lit up with an incoming call. The name on the screen made James's brow furrow—Mabel. His mentor's wife rarely called him directly.

"Em," James said, his voice tinged with a hint of concern, "could you get that? It's Mabel."

Emma nodded, reaching for the phone. As she answered, James noticed a small clay smudge on her wrist, a tiny reminder of her daily work.

"Hello, Mabel?" Emma's voice was warm—he watched from the corner of his eye as Emma's expression shifted, her face paling slightly.

After a moment that seemed to stretch and stretch until it would break his patience, Emma turned to James. "You better pull over on the next turn, James," she said, her voice carefully controlled.

James felt his stomach drop. He guided the car up the next ramp and into the nearest haven, a roadside convenience store—'Stop 'N Shop' the sign advised—the gravel crunching beneath the tires as they came to a halt. The setting sun cast long shadows across the dashboard, creating an otherworldly atmosphere within the confined space of the car.

"I'm putting this on speaker so Emma can hear," James said, his voice sounding strange to his own ears. He took the phone from Emma, their fingers brushing momentarily, a fleeting point of contact in the face of whatever news was coming.

Mabel's voice filled the car, tinny through the phone's speaker but unmistakably strained. "James, dear, I'm afraid I have some bad news. Alfred's in the hospital."

James felt as if all the air had been sucked out of the car. "What? How?" he managed to ask, his mind reeling.

"He had an episode," Mabel continued, her voice wavering slightly. "He's under observation now. The doctors think he'll be okay—he recognized the signs quickly, thank goodness."

James shook his head in disbelief. "But... Alfred's healthy. He exercises three times a week, eats a high-protein diet. How could this happen?"

There was a pause on the other end of the line, filled only by the soft sound of Mabel's breathing. When she spoke again, her voice was heavy with the weight of what she had to say.

"James, Emma... you need to prepare yourselves. Alfred had a shock today. The installation at the Eco Building has been canceled. They're going with someone else. Everything... everything has been canceled."

The words hung in the air, each one a blow to the mind; James felt Emma's hand on his arm, a silent gesture of support and shared disbelief.

Outside the car, life continued its relentless pace. Cars were driving past at blinding speeds, oblivious to the shift occurring within the parked vehicle. A plastic bag danced on the breeze, its erratic movements a stark contrast to the stillness that had settled over James and Emma.

James stared at the phone in his hand, as if it might suddenly reveal this all to be some elaborate misunderstanding. But Mabel's heavy breathing on the other end of the line was all too real, a testament to the gravity of the situation.

"Mabel," Emma said, her voice steady despite the tremor in her hand, "we're on our way. Which hospital is Alfred in?"

As Mabel provided the details, James found his gaze drawn to the mosaic of city lights beginning to twinkle in the deepening twilight. Each light represented a story, a life, a dream—and he wondered: what happened when a dream died? Where did it go? Could a dying dream take his dear friend Alfred with it? He simply could not wrap his head around the sudden changes in their world.

James turned to Emma, his eyes searching her face. In that moment, he saw not just his partner in this project, but the woman who had stood by him through countless challenges. The woman who, despite everything, was still here, ready to face whatever came next.

"Em," he said, his voice barely above a whisper, "what are we going to do? It's Alfred."

Emma reached out, her hand finding his. The warmth of her touch seemed to anchor him, a reminder that he had someone with him now.

"First," she said, her voice soft but determined, "we're going to the hospital. Are you all right to drive? I have my license."

"No, I'm all right... I am..." James reassured her, "I just need to focus on this next task."

"We'll be there for Alfred and Mabel, that's what we'll do. And then..." She paused, her eyes meeting his with a fierce intensity. "We'll think about the project later."

James nodded, he started the car, the engine humming low, smooth and ready to connect a pathway to Alfred and Mabel.

* * *

The late afternoon sun cast long shadows across the parking lot of Northwestern Memorial Hospital. James guided the car into a space, the tires crunching over a discarded soda can. As he turned off the engine, he took a deep breath, the familiar scent of leather seats mingling with the faint aroma of Emma's natural scent.

James turned to Emma, "okay, here's the deal," he began, his voice low but steady. "Nobody, not one person on earth is going to die on our project, I mean for our project. It's not that important, it's little pieces of baked clay for God's sake."

Emma nodded, her eyes meeting his with silent agreement, she waited.

"He had an 'episode' because he cared so much," James continued, the words tumbling out now. "Well, I think it's time we all dialed it down a hundred notches. So Em, please let's not talk about the project while we're there, how we're going to keep going? All that rot?" He paused, catching himself. "I mean it's not rot, but no wheels spinning in the mud, until we find some real solutions, right? I don't want his brain spinning trying to dial in a golden answer."

Emma's face softened, "I know what you mean. We play it cool, no worries. None."

James felt a wave of relief, "Yes, yes… thanks."

* * *

They made their way through the hospital corridors, the antiseptic smell mingling with the faint aroma of cafeteria food. James noticed a child's crayon drawing taped to a wall, its bright colors a stark contrast to the muted hospital tones.

The light in Alfred's room was subdued, it was still overcast outside and so what little light could squeak through the clouds leaked into his room to spread minimal cheer. James was relieved to see Alfred sitting up in bed, his complexion closer to its usual ruddy hue than he'd feared. Mabel rose to greet them, her embrace warm and comforting.

After some bright banter, James noticed Alfred's gaze sharpening, focusing on him and Emma standing side by side. "Wait just one minute," Alfred said, his voice stronger than James had expected. "Something's changed between you two."

James felt a flutter in his stomach, like the moment before revealing a new piece of art. He feigned a puzzled look, but Alfred wasn't fooled. "Take Emma's hand," he commanded, a hint of his old authority creeping back into his voice. "Go on, hold her hand. I want to see something."

James glanced at Emma, a mixture of amusement and anticipation in his chest. As their hands joined, he felt that familiar soft frisson of energy, like a current flowing between them.

Mabel's face broke into a gentle smile, mirrored by Alfred's own expression. "Do you see that Mabel?" Alfred said, his voice filled with a quiet joy that made James's heart smile. "Finally, our boy has found someone."

"I see," Mabel replied, her eyes glistening.

Alfred sighed contentedly, and James noticed the tension in his mentor's shoulders easing. "That's all I ever wanted for you, son. For you to be happy. From the first painting we bought, that blue one, remember? We knew... well, we won't say now, doesn't matter. Now I can die happy."

"Whoa, hold on there," James interjected, his voice tinged with mock alarm, relieved to see the twinkle in Alfred's eye. "I'm dropping Em's hand like a hot biscuit, see? You're not going anywhere, right?"

"Just joking," Alfred chuckled, the sound warming James from the inside out. Then Alfred's face grew serious. "But I want to talk about the wall—"

"No, no talking about the wall," Emma interrupted, her voice impossibly calm and reassuring. James marveled at her ability to soothe, to bring peace to a room with just her words.

"You have a plan, James?" Alfred asked, his eyes searching James's face.

James hesitated, unable to lie to the man who'd guided him for so long. "Not exactly," he admitted, "but, I did have a thought, there are these Tibetan monks that make these insane intricate sand mandalas. Takes months and months to complete and once done, you know what they do?"

Alfred nodded, "They wipe them away. Everything is impermanent."

"That's right," James said, his voice growing stronger, "which means, we'll be okay whatever happens. If it works out in some way, great, if not, thank you dear God for the ride." And here without thinking he picked up Em's hand again.

The small action didn't go unnoticed and Alfred's face softened, a peace settling over his features that made James realize how much tension his mentor had been carrying. "Thank you, son. That was well said. I think I need a nap now."

James leaned down, pressing a gentle kiss to Alfred's forehead. He noticed a few new lines there, but also the familiar scent that was uniquely Alfred—a mix of aftershave and well-worn books.

"See you tomorrow," James promised.

As James and Emma made their way out of the room, they heard Alfred's voice, soft but clear, speaking to Mabel. "Everything is going to be alright."

In the hallway, James and Emma paused. A nurse walked by, her squeaky shoes providing a counterpoint to the steady beep of monitors. Through a nearby window, James could see the sun beginning to set, behind the clouds, painting the sky in brilliant oranges and pinks. They both paused for a moment to look at it.

James turned to Emma, taking in every detail of her face—the flecks of gold in her eyes, the small smile lines that spoke of joy and laughter. In that moment, surrounded by the stark reality of the hospital, the mosaic project seemed both important and insignificant.

As they made their way back to the car, their hands found each other again of their own accord.

* * *

Chapter 28

Chicago — Fulton Street Loft — *Jan. 24, 2003 — 9:00 p.m. — The Mod Squad*

Without talking about it, they drove in silent agreement back to James's loft, rode the elevator up to his floor and once in the final stretch to his front door, James's eyes fell upon Gerardo, sitting cross-legged on the floor outside his door. The sight was both amusing and touching—Gerardo's large frame folded up like an over-sized origami creation, his back against the wall, a patient sentinel.

"You really gotta get a cell phone," James quipped, his voice tinged with affection and exasperation in equal measure.

Gerardo unfolded himself, rising with surprising grace for a man of his size. His eyes—dark and questioning—settled on James and Emma. "Been to see Alfred?" he asked, cutting straight to the chase—and heart of the matter—as was his way.

Emma nodded as James fumbled with his keys. The lock finally clicked open—a sound that seemed unnaturally loud in the close quarters of the hallway and the charged atmosphere.

As they filed into the loft, James's gaze was immediately drawn to the wall where their design hung—a vibrant tapestry of color and form that now seemed impossibly beautiful and tragically fragile. He stood before it, silent, seeking answers in the intricate patterns.

Emma, slipping easily into the role of hostess, gestured for Gerardo to sit. "Come in, sit down," she said, her voice gentle but firm.

Gerardo sank into his favorite easy chair, the leather creaking softly under his weight.

"The doctors said he had an episode," Emma explained, moving towards the kitchen.

There was a pause as they all contemplated those words—ran them forward and backward in their group mind—until the pinball finally landed with a bing: episode.

"He caught the signs early, and it was more from emotional shock than a physical issue. They say the signs look promising, they'll watch him carefully tonight."

Gerardo's sigh of relief was audible, a gust of wind in the quiet room. "Gracias a Dios," he murmured, his accent thickening with emotion.

Emma returned with beers, the bottles leaving rings of condensation on the coffee table as she set them down. She didn't even pretend to look for coasters or proxy coasters, such as that last months edition of Scientific American lying on the couch. The soft hiss as she twisted the caps was the only sound for a long moment.

James remained at the wall, his back to them—a solitary figure against the riot of color. The silence stretched, elastic and taut with unspoken questions.

Finally, Gerardo broke it, his voice hesitant. "Do you have any ideas?"

James drew in a deep breath and shook his head, not turning around. "Not at the moment," he admitted. "Lots of 'fake ideas' like maybe this or maybe that... but nothing with a spark. Really too early, I vowed not to think about it for at least fifteen minutes."

"Then come sit down," Gerardo urged, his tone gentle but insistent.

James sighed, a sound that seemed to carry the weight of the world, and turned away from the wall. He sank into his chair, the familiar contours holding him close like an old friend.

The three of them sat in silence, their gazes fixed on the design that now loomed over them like a beautiful, impossible dream. The only sound was the soft ticking of the clock on the kitchen shelf, marking the passage of time that now felt both, too fast and too slow.

The shrill ring of the doorbell cut through the silence like a Siren's shriek—they all jumped approximately a quarter of an inch.

"Well, that was on cue," James quipped, a ghost of a smile flitting across his face.

"I'll get it," Emma offered, rising from her seat. Her footsteps echoed softly as she crossed the room. "Val had the doorbell installed."

"Might want to test out a few more rings, James—say Darth Vader's theme? Might be more welcoming."

As the door swung open, Rhonda Morrison stood framed in the doorway, her usual composure noticeably cracked. Her eyes were rimmed with red, evidence of recent tears, and her normally impeccable suit was rumpled, as if she'd been sitting with her head in her hands.

"I didn't know where else to go," she said simply, her voice hoarse and vulnerable.

464   NOTHING LOST COPY KDP VERSION

The moment hung in the air, fragile as spun glass. Emma's hand, still on the doorknob, tightened imperceptibly. In the living room, James and Gerardo exchanged a glance, a whole conversation passing between them in that single look.

Then, almost in unison, they all seemed to take a collective breath. Emma stepped back, opening the door wider in silent invitation. Rhonda hesitated for a heartbeat, then stepped over the threshold, into the warmth and light of the loft.

As Emma closed the door behind her, the soft click seemed to signal the start of something new. As Rhonda joined them in the living room, her presence adding a new color to their palette, there was after all, strength in numbers.

* * *

The night had settled over James's loft like a drawn curtain, one moment there was ambient light and the next only the artificial glow from the lamps and light fixtures. It muffled the usual city sounds and shielded the inhabitants from public concerns so they could focus on private ones. The clock on the kitchen shelf did what it did, its steady rhythm a constant reminder of the passage of time, each minute without news from the hospital—a small victory.

As the hands swept past nine, then ten, James found himself studying the faces of his unexpected guests. Rhonda, usually so composed, had curled up in an armchair, her stocking feet tucked beneath her, wrapped in his Da's old sweater. The garment, with its worn elbows and faint scent of pipe tobacco, seemed to have lent her a vulnerability he'd never seen before.

Gerardo sprawled on the couch, his large frame somehow making the furniture seem smaller. His fingers absently traced the pattern on a throw pillow, over and over, as if the repetitive motion could soothe his worried mind.

Emma moved about the space with a quiet grace, refilling water glasses, and tea mugs adjusting a crooked picture frame, her presence a balm to the unspoken anxiety that hung in the air.

When James announced the sleeping arrangements, his friends drew in a collective sigh of relief and resignation. No one really wanted to head out in the frigid cold night. "There's two rooms upstairs that I dressed out for my folks and Sarah," he said, his tone matter-of-fact, as if hosting an impromptu slumber party was the most natural thing in the world. "Em, you and Rhonda can flip a coin for whichever one you want. Gerardo, you get the couch, but it's plenty wide and long and there's pillows and a quilt. You'll make it through the night all right, you can always cuddle up to the radiator behind you."

The gentle laughter that followed was like a collective exhale, a release of pent-up emotion. James caught Emma's eye, noticing the way the corners of her mouth turned up in that special smile she seemed to reserve just for him. It made him feel natural, a natural man. Hard to describe it better than that.

As midnight approached without a call from Mabel or the hospital, they all seemed to relax somewhat, it was still too soon to celebrate, but maybe they could all sleep tonight. The worst news always seemed to happen around midnight and having past this mile marker without a nod from the reaper, they retreated to their designated sleeping spots, and the loft settled into a different kind of quiet.

* * *

Rhonda stirred just before dawn, beating the sun's first crack at the day in a photo finish. She padded into the kitchen, her bare feet making soft sounds against the cool floor. The oversized white shirt she wore—borrowed from the closet in the room where she was sleeping—swished around her thighs as she moved, a stark contrast to her usual tailored suits.

The coffee maker gurgled to life under her practiced hands, its aroma soon filling the space. Rhonda inhaled deeply, her eyes closed, savoring the moment of peace before the day truly began.

Gerardo stirred on the couch, his eyes opening to an unexpected vision. Rhonda stood in the kitchen, backlit by the early morning light, her legs seeming to go on forever beneath the hem of the white shirt. He blinked, wondering if he was still dreaming.

Rhonda felt his gaze and turned, a self-conscious smile playing on her lips. "Sorry if I woke you," she said, her voice still husky with sleep. "I really need my morning cup pretty quick."

Gerardo shrugged, his usual eloquence deserting him in the face of this new, softer version of Rhonda. "Por nada... no worries," he managed, then, before he could stop himself, "You look good in the morning Ms. Morrison... I mean without your clothes... well, that didn't come out right either."

A chuckle escaped Rhonda's lips, a sound so unexpected and delightful that Gerardo smiled. For a moment, he caught a glimpse of the girl she must have been, before life and Alfred Worthington had sculpted her into the formidable woman she was now.

"I think that's a compliment," she said, her eyes twinkling. Then, sobering slightly, "So... no phone call?"

Gerardo shook his head, sitting up and running a hand through his sleep-mussed hair. "Not that I know of."

Rhonda picked up her coffee cup, the porcelain warm against her palms, and moved to sit in the easy chair next to Gerardo. There was a moment of comfortable silence as they both sipped their coffee, the city outside slowly coming to life.

Then, with a hint of conspiracy in her voice, Rhonda leaned in slightly. "So... James and Emma?"

The way she said it, the raised eyebrow, the knowing look—it was clear she'd noticed the subtle shift, the way Emma had seamlessly stepped into the role of 'woman of the house' the night before.

Gerardo matched her posture, leaning in as if sharing a secret. "I don't think yet," he whispered, his eyes darting towards the stairs. "But close, very close."

A smile spread across Rhonda's face, genuine and warm. "Good," she said, surprise and approval mingling in her tone. "I'm surprised, but good."

They sat back, each lost in their own thoughts, the morning light growing stronger around them. Rhonda's mind drifted back to another dawn, years ago, when Alfred had first spotted her. She'd been a scrappy kid from Cabrini Green, all elbows and attitude, but he'd seen something in her that she hadn't even recognized in herself.

"You know," Rhonda said softly, her voice tinged with wonder, "sometimes I still can't believe how I got here."

Gerardo tilted his head, curiosity piqued. "What do you mean?"

Rhonda's eyes grew distant, focusing on some point beyond the loft's walls. "Alfred... he gave me my first real break. Recruited me when I was young, still living in Cabrini Green. I'd just graduated from Northwestern, up north of Chicago."

Gerardo's eyebrows shot up. "Northwestern? That's a tough school to get into."

Rhonda nodded, a hint of pride in her voice. "Scholarships, loans, grants—you name it, I pieced it together. Graduated with a mountain of debt, but I had my degree." She chuckled softly, lost in the memory. "Epoch Alliance was doing a recruitment call. My mama, bless her heart, kept pushing this lime green suit on me. Said it'd make me stand out."

Gerardo snorted, trying to picture Rhonda in lime green. She shot him a mock glare before continuing.

"I had to explain to her how it worked. Couldn't walk in there dressed for Sunday service. Needed to look like I already belonged, you know?" Rhonda's voice softened. "Once she understood, my whole family got in on it, all the Morrisons and Jacksons on my mama's side—sending me pictures of outfits they saw in stores, magazines—anything they thought might work."

She paused, her fingers tracing the rim of her coffee mug. "Finally found it at Marshall Fields. Dark blue, but with a cut that said, 'Yeah, I'll play by some of your rules, but I'm still me.' Cost two months' rent, even on sale."

Rhonda's voice caught slightly. "My mama took out a payday loan to help me buy that suit."

Gerardo leaned forward, caught up in the story. "And that's what sealed the deal with Alfred?"

Rhonda laughed, a rich, warm sound. "That's the funny part. Alfred told me later he'd already made up his mind about me. Said he'd seen me organizing a community cleanup in Cabrini Green the week before—watched me corralling volunteers, negotiating with city officials for dumpsters, he said I was running the whole show like a seasoned pro."

She shook her head, a mix of amusement and disbelief on her face. "But I've never told my mama that. As far as she knows, that blue suit clinched it. And you know what? In a way, it did. I felt invincible in that suit, like I could take on the world."

Gerardo sat back, his eyes wide with newfound respect. "Rhonda, thank you for sharing that."

Rhonda shrugged, a hint of her usual no-nonsense demeanor returning. "It's not something I advertise. But this project, what we're doing here—it's a chance to create those kinds of opportunities for others. To be Alfred to someone else's Rhonda, you know?"

Gerardo nodded slowly, understanding dawning in his eyes. "That's why you push so hard, why every detail matters so much to you."

"Exactly," Rhonda said, her voice soft but intense. "Because sometimes, all it takes is one person paying attention, one chance, to change a life. And that change? It ripples out, affects whole families, whole communities."

They sat in silence for a moment, the weight of Rhonda's words settling around them. The loft was quiet save for the soft bubbling of the coffee maker and the distant sounds of the city waking up. Rhonda's eyes grew misty, her gaze unfocused as she stared into her coffee cup.

"Gerardo," she began, her voice barely above a whisper, "Alfred and Mabel... they don't just take a person under their wings. They take you in and sit on you until you're good and hatched and ready to fly." She paused, swallowing hard. "The thought of Alfred... of him not being here..."

Her voice trailed off, the words catching in her throat. Rhonda shook her head, as if trying to physically dislodge the idea. "I can't... I can't even imagine it. He's always been there, you know?

Gerardo leaned forward, his face etched with concern. "They're family," he supplied softly.

Rhonda nodded, a single tear escaping down her cheek. She wiped it away quickly, almost angrily. "I'm not ready for him to go... it's not fair."

Gerardo didn't know what to say, it was true, it wasn't fair and so he reached out, gently squeezing Rhonda's hand.

Rhonda managed a watery smile. "Thanks, Gerardo. I just... sorry I got weepy."

Gerardo nodded, his eyes serious. "I get it, and I can take a little rain—always loved the rain."

Rhonda took a deep breath, squaring her shoulders and smiled a small smile."

Gerardo reached out, placing his hand over Rhonda's for a brief moment. "Thank you," he said simply. "For reminding me why we're doing this."

As they waited for the others to wake, Rhonda and Gerardo found themselves settling into a comfortable silence, the kind shared by old friends rather than colleagues thrown together by circumstance. It seemed, well, a kind way to start the day.

* * *

The loft windows, usually a portal to the bustling Chicago skyline, now framed a world of muted grays and a determined low hanging fog. Empty plates bore the remnants of a hastily prepared but heartily consumed meal—a smear of jam here, a crumb of toast there, telltale signs of appetites returning after a night of worry.

The low murmur of the weather station provided a soothing backdrop, the meteorologist's steady voice a counterpoint to the group's subdued conversation. On the screen, swirling patterns of blue and white heralded the approach of a snowstorm, nature's own contribution to the growing list of concerns.

The shrill ring of James's cell phone cut through the air at precisely 10:18 AM, the digital clock on the microwave marking the moment with unfeeling accuracy. James's eyes flicked to the cell phone screen, his hand reaching out its own accord.

"Hello, Mabel," he answered, his voice carefully neutral.

Rhonda's finger found the mute button on the remote, silencing the weatherman mid-sentence. All eyes turned to James, watching his face for any hint of news.

At first, James's expression was a mask of stoicism, each muscle carefully controlled. Then, almost imperceptibly, a change—his fingers moving to pinch the bridge of his nose, a gesture so small yet so telling. It was as if he was trying to physically hold back the tide of emotion threatening to overwhelm him.

Emma was at his side in an instant, her presence a silent support. Rhonda reached out and took Gerardo's hand, barely breathing, as James nodded, his voice rough with suppressed feeling.

"No, no, thas' good, Mabel, thas' good. Sounds like he's doing very well."

A collective exhale seemed to sweep through the room. James nodded to the group, a small smile tugging at the corners of his mouth. "Alfred is doing well... and, wait, he wants to talk to me..."

The silence deepened as James listened, the others leaning forward unconsciously, straining to hear. When James spoke again, his voice held a note of bemused disbelief. "Is that a fact? Really? I know you're in great shape an' all, but I don't think you can kick Max's ass and all of Eco to boot in one round..."

Laughter erupted, the sound startling in its suddenness and intensity. Rhonda threw her arms around Emma, their shared relief palpable. Gerardo's deep chuckle rumbled through the room like a quadraphonic sound system.

James turned away slightly, but not before they caught a glimpse of the tears in his eyes—happy, relieved tears that he tried to hide even now. His voice, when he spoke again, was thick with emotion. "Okay, well, we'll talk about that particular disaster later. Oh... there are people here for you—Rhonda, Ger, and Em, of course."

He turned the phone outward, and a chorus of "Hello!" and "Get better soon!" Rang out, their voices overlapping in eagerness to be heard.

James brought the phone back to his ear. "There, that's your Mod Squad. Okay, I'll let them know, but I'm telling you—I'm tabling it for a while. An answer will rise to the surface. Absolutely no worries. None."

He paused, listening. "Okay, I'll tell her."

And here James turned to Emma, nodded to her with a weak smile, then continued, "See you later, Alfred... oh—well, see you at your home then. But mind, there's a snowstorm coming, so maybe stay another day, right? Okay. I love you too. Bye."

As James ended the call, Emma stepped forward. Their eyes met.

The world went soft underfoot, and in a movement that seemed both inevitable and surprising, James pulled her into an embrace. His arms wrapped around her tightly, as if he could pull her into himself—pouring all his relief and gratitude into that one gesture.

Emma melted into the hug, resting her head on his shoulder, her hands coming up to press on his back. They stood like that for a long moment, the world around them fading away.

Rhonda and Gerardo exchanged a glance, eyebrows raised. Rhonda's lips quirked in a small smile, while Gerardo's eyes twinkled with knowing amusement. The air in the room seemed to shift, charged with a new energy—relief for Alfred, yes, but also the sense that some long—awaited celestial event was finally taking place and the heavens would now be open to view visions of bunnies hopping and rainbows spouting—okay you get the idea. A good step.

As James and Emma slowly separated, their hands lingering on each other's arms, the others tactfully looked away, busying themselves with clearing the breakfast dishes. Outside, the first snowflakes began to fall, dusting the windowsill with white. A storm was coming, but they were forewarned—and what's more, the group was still together.

* * *

Chapter 29

Chicago — Sheffield Apt. — *Jan. 25, 2003 — 10:31 a.m. — Wrong Room*

Val jolted awake, her heart racing. For a disorienting moment, she couldn't remember where she was or why her pillow felt damp. Then the events of the previous day crashed over her. Alfred. The hospital. The project—their beautiful, doomed project— canceled with all the ceremony of a sneeze in a crowded elevator.

She stared at the ceiling where a stubborn cobweb clung to the corner, waving gently in the draft from her ancient radiator. The alarm clock on her nightstand blinked an accusatory 9:00 a.m. Three hours until her meeting with Sam. The thought of him brought her temperature up enough to take some chill out of the room—seemingly. He'd become her touchstone in this chaos, a human security blanket.

Val hauled herself out of bed, her feet hitting the cold floor with a shock that jolted her fully awake. A quick shower, she decided. No sense in marinating in her own misery any longer than necessary.

She thought about washing her hair, but knew it would take a long time to dry in the cold air of her apartment, even with the blow dryer going full throttle, you just couldn't go outside with even slightly damp hair in Chicago—in January—no. That was an engraved invitation to a two week chest cold. Val found her thoughts drifting back to Sam. The idea of sitting in her apartment for the next three hours, watching the clock, was unbearable. Sam was an early bird, probably already working on his latest project.

Emerging from the shower, Val threw on the first clean clothes her hands touched—a sweater that was more holes than wool at this point, and jeans that had seen better days, possibly during the Clinton administration. Fashion be damned. This was a day for comfort, not couture. She peered out the window where fat snowflakes were descending steadily. Great. Because what this day really needed was a side of treacherous road conditions.

Val bundled up in her warmest coat, a puffy monstrosity that made her resemble a perambulating sleeping bag and jangled her keys nervously. "Please," she muttered to her car, "just start."

Miraculously, the engine sputtered to life on the first try. Val patted the dashboard affectionately. "Good boy," she cooed. "There's a quart of oil in your future if you get me there in one piece."

The streets were a slushy mess, cars inching along slowly. By some miracle of urban planning—or more likely, sheer dumb luck—she found herself outside Sam's apartment building at 10:30 AM, a full hour and a half early.

She sat in the car for a moment, suddenly hesitant. What if he wasn't up? What if he was in the middle of some critical work and she ruined it with her unannounced arrival?

Well, it was freezing out here and no doubt warmer in there, and he wouldn't want her to freeze, would he? Solid no. Sam would understand, and right now understanding was what she needed.

Within minutes she was walking down his hallway and once outside his door, she paused to listen and see if she could hear the sound of the t.v. or some other indication that he was up and moving around and...

Val's fingers hovered over Sam's apartment door, poised to knock. The muffled sounds filtering through the wood made her pause, her brow furrowing in confusion. Then, unmistakably, a woman's voice rose in passion, accompanied by rhythmic thumps and creaks that left little to the imagination.

Val's eyes widened, her cheeks flushing scarlet. She backed away from the door as if it had suddenly transformed into a portal to Hades, her heart pounding an erratic tattoo against her ribs. The sounds continued, oblivious to her presence in the hallway, like some bizarre avant-garde performance art that ran on with or without an audience.

"Oh… oh my," Val whispered, her voice barely audible over the blood rushing in her ears. She turned and fled, her winter boots leaving a wet imprint on the linoleum floor, each puddle a mute reminder of her intrusion.

Outside, the crisp morning air did little to cool her burning cheeks. Val glanced up and down the street, feeling oddly exposed, as if everyone passing by could somehow read the embarrassment written across her face. Her eyes landed on the familiar neon sign of Manny's Diner just down the block. Without conscious thought, her feet carried her towards its promise of coffee and anonymity.

The bell above the door jingled as Val entered, drawing a few curious glances from the sparse morning crowd. She slid into a corner booth, its cracked vinyl seat cool against her legs, a stark contrast to her flushed skin. She half-expected to see "Val was here, mortified beyond belief" etched into the tabletop.

"Coffee, hon?" a waitress asked, appearing at her elbow with a well-worn pot, the aroma of fresh brew momentarily grounding Val in the present.

Val nodded, not trusting her voice. As the steaming liquid filled her cup, she blurted out, "And biscuits and gravy, please." Comfort food seemed necessary in the face of her emotional turmoil. Maybe she could drown her embarrassment in gravy.

Forty-five minutes ticked by with excruciating slowness. Val nursed her coffee, glancing frequently at her watch, her mind conjuring unwanted images with each passing minute. She'd allowed ample time, she reasoned, for... activities... to conclude. The thought made her cheeks burn anew.

Finally, with a shaky hand, she pulled out her phone. It took three attempts to dial Sam's number correctly, her fingers refusing to cooperate. Each ring felt like an eternity, her imagination running wild with possibilities of what—or who—might be delaying his answer.

"Hello?" Sam's voice, slightly breathless, came through the line.

Val swallowed hard, her throat suddenly dry. "Sam, it's Val. I... I have some news. It's confidential. Can you come to Manny's? I'm in the corner booth."

A pause, heavy with unspoken questions. "Sure, I'll be there in ten."

True to his word, Sam appeared exactly ten minutes later. His hair was slightly damp, as if freshly showered—he stepped out in the Chi-town with a wet head in the coldest week of the year, she noted and then dropped it from her mind—but otherwise, he looked remarkably composed. Val couldn't help but stare, searching for some sign of his recent... activities. She half-expected to see a neon sign above his head flashing "Just had a wild morning!" But he looked frustratingly composed.

"Hey, Val," Sam said, sliding into the booth across from her, he looked as put-together as a mannequin in a department store window. Val couldn't decide if she was impressed or irritated by his composure. His eyes flicked to her plate, taking in the congealed gravy and barely-touched biscuits. "Been here a while?"

Val nodded, pushing the cold food away. It now resembled a culinary crime scene more than breakfast. "Sam, I... there's no easy way to say this. Alfred had a heart episode last night."

Sam's face fell, genuine concern etching lines around his eyes. "Is he okay?"

"We're waiting on word," Val said, her voice low. "But there's more, and this part is strictly confidential." She leaned in, her words barely above a whisper, as if sharing nuclear launch codes. "The project's been canceled. Eco backed out and gave it to someone else."

Sam blinked, processing the information. "Canceled? But... all that work, all those stories..." He trailed off, his brow furrowed in thought. looking like a puppy trying to divide twenty-two by seven.

Before either could speak further, Val's phone buzzed insistently. She glanced at the screen, her eyes widening. "It's from James," she said, her voice tight with anticipation.

Sam held his breath, watching Val's face intently as she answered. He saw the play of emotions across her features—concern, relief, a hint of tears gathering at the corners of her eyes.

"Good, that's good," Val said into the phone, nodding. "I'm so glad to hear that." She looked up at Sam, a small smile breaking through her worry. "James says it looks like Alfred is going to be okay. He's doing much better this morning."

Her attention returned to the call. "Yes, I'm with Sam, now. Yes, I told him. I will... thanks, James, for letting me know so soon."

As she hung up, Val fixed Sam with an intense gaze. "You can't tell anyone about Eco canceling. There's to be no criticism coming from us about it. James wants no gossip to get back and upset Alfred. So. No one, Sam. I mean it."

Sam nodded solemnly. "I understand. Not a word."

Val's voice dropped, her words sharp and pointed. "No. One. Not even an old friend you've known for years, especially a world-famous actress."

Sam's eyes widened slightly at her words. He glanced down at her plate, the pieces finally clicking into place. "You came by my apartment earlier," he said, his voice barely above a whisper.

Val's composure crumbled at his words. Tears welled up in her eyes, threatening to spill over. Sam felt a sharp pain in the center of his chest, an inexplicable urge to cry rising within him. He wasn't sure why—they'd only known each other a few months—but the sight of Val's distress cut him deeply.

He reached out instinctively to comfort her, but Val shrank from his touch. That small retreat reached deep into Sam's psyche and he felt the need to explain he wasn't the bad guy.

Sam swallowed hard, trying to find the words to clarify. "Val, I... Olivia and I, we've known each other a long time. It's hard to explain—"

"You don't have to," Val cut him off, her voice trembling. "It's none of my business—"

"Because I knew her when," Sam interrupted, his words tumbling out in a rush. "She comes back to see me now and again to feel real, I suppose, and... and she's helped me too."

Val raised a hand, her eyes pleading. "Really, Sam. You don't owe me any explanation. I'm just a little overwhelmed—well, it's been an intense couple of days, and you know..."

Sam nodded, reaching for the napkin dispenser. He pulled out a few and offered them to Val, who accepted them with a watery smile. As she dabbed at her eyes, Sam sat in helpless silence, acutely aware of the Grand Canyon gap between them now.

The diner's ambient noise seemed to grow louder, filling the awkward silence that stretched between them. Val blew her nose softly, the sound muffled by the paper napkin. Sam's fingers absently touched the edge of the table, his eyes darting between Val's face and the window, as if searching for the right words in the passing traffic outside.

"I'm sorry," Sam finally said, his voice low and sincere. "About everything. The project, Alfred, this..." He gestured vaguely between them.

Val nodded, crumpling the used napkin in her fist. "Me too," she whispered, her eyes meeting his for a brief moment before flicking away.

They sat there, the remnants of Val's cold breakfast between them, both acutely aware that something had shifted. The easy camaraderie they'd built over the past few months, the potential for something more that had been slowly blooming, now felt as congealed and unappetizing as the abandoned biscuits and gravy.

* * *

Sam trudged up the stairs to his apartment, each step feeling like a personal Everest. He fumbled with his keys, the metal cold against his fingers, before finally managing to unlock the door. The warmth of his apartment hit him like a wall, a stark contrast to the frigid Chicago winter and the even colder atmosphere he'd left behind at the diner.

Olivia was perched on the arm of his well-worn couch, reading messages on her flip phone. She looked up as he entered, her face breaking into a smile that could melt glaciers. "Hey, you. I was thinking about ordering in. It's colder than a witch's... well, you know." She wiggled her eyebrows suggestively, a reminder of their shared history of terrible jokes and worse puns.

Sam couldn't help but smile back. Olivia had that effect on people—it was part of what made her such a captivating actress. Her beauty was undeniable, but it was her vibrant energy that truly set her apart. She could make a DMV waiting room feel like the most exciting place on earth.

"Food sounds good," Sam replied, shrugging off his coat. "I'm not sure I could face the outside world again today."

Olivia's brow furrowed slightly, picking up on the undercurrent in his voice. "Rough meeting?" she asked, patting the spot next to her on the couch.

Sam sank into the cushions with a sigh. "You could say that. Some... unfortunate news." He rubbed his face, then back of his neck and finally rounded down to rolling his shoulders.

"Want to talk about it?" Olivia asked, her voice gentle.

Sam shook his head. "Can't really. Confidentiality and all that." He paused, debating whether to share the next bit. "But that's not the worst of it. Val... she was here earlier. She overheard us."

Olivia's eyes widened, but to her credit, she didn't laugh. Instead, she slid off the arm of the couch to sit next to Sam, her shoulder bumping his companionably. "Oh, Sam," she said, her voice a mixture of sympathy and something else. "You like this girl, don't you?"

Sam stared at his hands, flexing his fingers now, rubbing his hands to warm them. "Damn cold outside—"

"—Sam."

Pause, and then he looked at the floor, "I think I do," he admitted, the words feeling both terrifying and liberating as they left his mouth.

Olivia leaned back, studying him with the intensity she usually reserved for perusing the craft service table on a new shoot. "Well," she said finally, a small smile playing at the corners of her mouth, "isn't that something."

"Yeah," Sam agreed, running a hand through his hair. "Something alright. Something I've managed to royally screw up, apparently."

Olivia nudged him with her elbow. "Hey, none of that. We've known each other too long for you to start with the self-pity now. Besides," she added, her eyes twinkling with mischief, "if she likes you half as much as you clearly like her, a little misunderstanding isn't going to derail things."

Sam snorted, a sound halfway between amusement and despair. "A little misunderstanding, huh. If it happened to you, something you overheard, how little of a misunderstanding would it be? On a scale of 1 to 10, ten being 'oh god, I'm screaming'?"

Olivia cocked an eyebrow. "Was I screaming?"

"You were, but back on topic. How'd you score it?"

"Well, how long have I known this guy?"

"About seven months."

"And have we... you know?"

Sam rolled his eyes. "No."

"Kissed?"

"No."

"Anything?"

"Come on, you're stalling."

Olivia grinned. "No, I'm getting into character."

Sam couldn't help but chuckle. "We caught on fast. She's funny, brilliant, thinks fast, her mind spins on a dime. I feel..."

"Safe?" Olivia supplied softly.

"Yeah."

Olivia's face grew serious. She moved to sit across from him on the coffee table, leaning in to look him in the face. "You like this girl. Really like her."

Sam said nothing, his silence more telling than any words could be.

"How much does she know about you?" Olivia probed gently.

"Not much," Sam admitted, his voice barely above a whisper.

Olivia nodded, her expression changing subtly as she slipped into character. Sam watched in amazement as she became Val before his eyes—the tilt of her head, the quirk of her smile, even the cadence of her laugh. He shook his head, always a little stunned by her abilities.

"So, Ooops." Olivia-as-Val said, her voice tinged with a mixture of hurt and confusion that made Sam's heart clench.

"I'm sorry, Sam," Olivia continued, her own voice returning. "The score is going to be eleven. Off the charts. There is no way she will understand. She's not made that way, doesn't compartmentalize. Not sophisticated from your world—well, your old world. She's a good girl, holds herself apart, may be pure."

Sam's eyes widened. "You sure?"

Olivia nodded solemnly.

Sam leaned back, running a hand through his hair. The weight of the situation seemed to press down on him, making the couch feel like quicksand. He looked at Olivia, his oldest friend, the one person who knew him better than anyone else in the world. Her ability to read people, to understand motivations and emotions, was uncanny. If she said eleven, it was eleven.

"What do I do?" he asked, his voice small and uncertain. "I can't... I don't want to lose her, Liv. Not over this. Not when we haven't even had a chance to start."

Olivia reached out, squeezing his hand. "You tell her the truth, Sam. All of it. About us, about your past, about why you left the theater. Everything."

Sam blanched. "Everything? But what if..."

"What if she can't handle it?" Olivia finished for him. "Then she's not the right person for you. But Sam," she leaned in, her eyes intense, "if she is who you think she is, who I think she might be based on how you talk about her... maybe I'm wrong and it isn't off the charts at eleven. I'm saying you have a good, good heart and there's a reason why you like her. So, maybe she'll understand. What do you have to lose?"

Sam nodded slowly, the enormity of the task ahead of him settling in. "And if she doesn't?"

Olivia smiled softly. "Then you'll still have me. And pizza. Speaking of which..." She reached for her phone, already calling their favorite place.

As Olivia ordered, Sam sat back, his mind whirling, the thought of laying himself bare was daunting, Would it be worth it? Revealing parts of his life he'd kept hidden from view. Then the memory of her soft pats on his arm, the sweet thrill of his body's response. As if his body and soul recognized her well before his mind did.

He'd been around long enough to know that kind response wasn't ordinary. He'd often cringed when a certain kind of person touched him, it had happened all too often. He called it the 'vampire touch' when he felt energy being drawn from him against his will. Small little vampire hands taking from him, not giving.

Sam just hoped she'd give him the chance to explain.

The aroma of melted cheese and spicy pepperoni filled the apartment as Sam and Olivia ate in companionable silence. The quiet was broken only by the occasional crunch of crust and the muffled sounds of the city beyond the windows.

Suddenly, Sam's voice cut through the quiet. "You have someone, don't you?"

Olivia froze mid-bite, her eyes snapping up to meet his. She set her slice down slowly, a rueful smile playing at the corners of her mouth. "I keep forgetting about that radar of yours."

Sam's eyebrows rose slightly. "How's it going?"

Olivia shrugged, her gaze dropping to her plate. "Oh, you know."

"I'm gonna give you some free advice," Sam started, his tone gentle but firm.

Olivia groaned dramatically. "Can I stop you?"

"Don't torture him, Liv," Sam continued, ignoring her protest. "You don't have to get back at every single man you know."

"Except you," Olivia said quietly, her eyes meeting his again.

Sam said nothing, his silence hanging heavy between them.

"Except you, right?" Olivia pressed, a hint of desperation creeping into her voice.

Sam sighed, running a hand through his hair. "Not anymore, Liv. Not for a long time. Because I get you now. I understand." He leaned forward, his gaze intense. "So give this guy a chance, and put down the sledgehammer."

Olivia looked down, her fingers tracing the edge of her plate. "I'm not that bad," she mumbled, but there was no real conviction in her words.

"Does he know you're here?" Sam asked softly.

Olivia shook her head. "No, not yet." She looked up at Sam, her eyes suddenly shimmering with unshed tears. "You're saying goodbye, aren't you?"

Sam didn't answer immediately. He stood up, moving to sit next to Olivia on the couch. Gently, he took her hand in his. "Liv," he began, his voice thick with emotion, "you're my oldest friend. You've been there for me through... well, everything. But this thing with Val... it's different. And if I have any chance of making it work, I can't..."

"You can't have me popping in and out of your life," Olivia finished for him, a sad smile on her face.

Sam nodded. "It's not fair to her. Or to you, really."

Olivia squeezed his hand. "Or to you," she added softly.

They sat in silence for a moment, the weight of years of history and complicated emotions settling around them, ever-present and ever-ready to suck them back into inertia too. It was a caution.

Finally, Olivia spoke. "You really love her, don't you?"

Sam's breath caught in his throat. "I... I think I could," he admitted, the words feeling both terrifying and exhilarating as they left his mouth.

Olivia nodded, a single tear escaping to trail down her cheek. She brushed it away quickly. "Then you have to try, Sam. You have to give it everything you've got."

Sam pulled her into a tight hug. "Thank you," he whispered into her hair.

As they pulled apart, Olivia's trademark mischievous grin suddenly reappeared. "Just promise me one thing?"

"What's that?"

"When you two crazy kids finally work it out, and you're disgustingly happy together, you'll let me play her in the movie version of your love story."

Sam burst out laughing, the tension of the moment shattering. "Deal," he said, his eyes twinkling. "But only if I get final approval on the script."

As their laughter filled the apartment, Sam felt a weight lift from his shoulders. The road ahead wouldn't be easy, it never was, but as Olivia had observed, 'what did he have to lose?'

* * *

Chapter 30

Chicago — Warehouse Loft — Assembly — *Feb. 12, 2003 — 9:30 a.m. — Whispers and Waiting*

The harsh fluorescent light flickered overhead as James stood in the empty warehouse, his breath visible in the cold air. He ran his fingers over a half-finished tile in his left hand, the clay rough against his skin, its texture reminiscent of a cat's tongue.

"You're brooding again," Emma's voice echoed from the doorway, a hint of amusement coloring her words.

James turned, a wry smile tugging at his lips. "Just thinking," he replied, his eyes crinkling at the corners.

"Uh oh. *Danger Will Robinson*," Emma quipped, crossing the room to stand beside him. She pulled her coat tighter around her body, adjusted the soft blue woolen scarf wrapped twice around her neck, shivering slightly. "Especially when it's cold enough to freeze-dry the thoughts right inside your head."

"It *is* cold here." James observed, noticing how the tip of Emma's nose had turned a delightful shade of pink. "And we are rather Lost in Space at the moment—thank you for the odd sequitur—let's head back to my place. There's nothing to do here—the water's off, just enough heat to keep the pipes from freezing... the rent's paid up until the end of next month, might as well let things be for now. The others will be at my loft soon."

"They've worked hard, they're just taking a nap," Emma said, and then inclined her head toward the tiles for emphasis. "Unlike some people we know who live in perpetual motion."

James chuckled softly. "Are you implying something, Ms. Hawkins?"

"Me? Never," Emma replied with mock innocence. "I'm just saying, if thinking was an Olympic sport, you'd be a gold medalist."

James nodded and then linked his arm with hers as they watched 'the kids' have a nice lie down. The tiles, spread out before them like sleeping children, seemed to shimmer slightly in the cold light, each one holding a piece of their shared dream.

* * *

As they stepped outside, the bitter Chicago wind whipped around them, nipping relentlessly at their exposed skin. James fumbled with his key, his fingers stiff from the cold.

"Electric buttons not working, must've gotten wet—and froze—and I can't get the manual key out," he muttered, his breath forming small clouds in the frigid air.

"Here, let me," Emma said, taking the fob. With the steady hand of a seasoned diamond cutter, she popped the manual key out using the edge of her fingernail and unlocked the car.

They sighed as they climbed in, relieved to find shelter and relative warmth from the arctic blast.

The drive home was quiet. Both lost in thought, the only sound the soft purr of the Prius engine.

As they pulled up to James's building, Emma broke the silence. "Have you heard from Alfred?" she asked, her voice walking on tiptoe.

James shook his head, his eyes still fixed ahead. "Mabel says he's resting. Doctor's orders. They're minimizing phone calls so he's forced to actually rest."

Once safe inside the old converted warehouse, the elevator gave a familiar groan—as if in disbelief it had to carry these two up to the third floor *yet again.*

Emma set the pace at a quick trot to his door. James was ready with key in hand this time, going a personal best for fastest entry and direct dash to the thermostat. He cranked the dial toward *tropical ambiance,* aiming for something close to the island of St. Croix—birthplace of Alexander Hamilton. Fun fact.

"Tea?" he asked, already halfway to the kitchen, his movements automatic.

"You Englanders and your tea as the perpetual emotional poultice for every situation."

"So that's a yes?"

"Please," Emma replied, flashing a bright smile as she wrapped her arms around herself, keeping her coat snug until she was certain of a safer haven.

She paused by the window, looking out at the gray skyline—a canvas of concrete and steel. "Twelve days," she murmured.

"What's that?" James called from the kitchen, his voice barely audible over the clatter of mugs.

"It's been twelve days since we made that pact. We promised each other three weeks of calm, remember?" Emma's voice carried a hint of wistfulness.

The kettle whistled, suddenly demanding immediate attention: *Now! Now! Now!* James pulled the kettle from the fire and the screaming slowly subsided to a whimpering complaint. He poured the hot water over the peppermint bags, prepping the beverages in the American way and returned with two steaming mugs. The sweet tang proceeded him into the main room. "Some calm," he said, handing one to Emma, his tone a mixture of irony and resignation.

The dulcet sound of the *new doorbell* interrupted them, a melodic intruder in their moment of quiet contemplation.

"I gotta say, I love your new doorbell—" Emma observed. "Sounds more like... flowers trying to grow or something."

"Really? I kind of miss people knocking down my door." James said on his way to the door. "And that's Val's sense of humor I suppose—after the Siren scream, she went for contrast."

"Well, you could have taken Ger's suggestion and gone for Darth Vader's power chords... or the windup from Rocky. Might be a legitimate compromise between the two. Emma's tone was contemplative.

"God, no." James was laughing now as he opened the door to discover Rhonda and Gerardo huddled close together in the hallway.

"Oh, sorry mates," he said drawing a long face, and oh so woebegone, "Earnest Shackleton's second expedition to the south pole is that way."

He pointed south and began to close the door amidst yowls of protest and cries for help.

"Emma! Em, tackle this madman, let us in—" It was Rhonda and she meant business.

"I'd love to... James! Don't make me audition for a linebacker—" Emma warned getting up from her chair.

Laughing, James opened the door all the way, "Sorry you lot, it was just too funny, had to be done."

'Yeah, it'll be really funny… in about twenty minutes after I warm up and can feel my toes again." Rhonda whispered as she stepped past him.

"Christ, it's cold out there," Gerardo exclaimed, rubbing his hands together as he entered.

Rhonda was moving toward the nearest radiator in the living area, her usually impeccable appearance slightly disheveled, as if she'd wrestled with the wind and lost. "We need to talk," she said without preamble, without debate—simply the way it is.

"I've got tea going, there's coffee too, will be ready in a sec." James's voice was low, not quite his usual 'in the top ten' self,' but working ever-upward. "You can put your coats anywhere."

Rhonda reluctantly began taking off her coat, testing each button to let in more of the heated air before committing to sans outer-wear for the inner-weather of the loft. She slowly placed her thick wool coat on the back of the couch near the source of heat, Gerardo followed suit removing his arctic parka gear, layer by layer.

They gathered in the living room, the tension was sucking a considerable amount of breathing air out of the immediate space, the cold air still clinging to their clothes. Gerardo settled in his favorite leather arm chair, Rhonda in her soft easy chair and James and Emma sat on the couch, their bodies angled towards each other like magnets.

After they were settled, Gerardo pulled out a deck of cards from his pocket with the flourish of a master magician's finale and grand reveal.

"Really? Now?" Rhonda asked, exasperation coloring her voice.

"Humor me," Gerardo replied, shuffling the deck with a skill that suggested he'd done this before at least once, maybe twice. "Let's cut to the chase, high card goes first. We list what we want and don't want for the new installation."

They drew: Rhonda, Queen of Diamonds. Emma, Ten of Hearts. Gerardo, Jack of Diamonds. James, Ace of Hearts.

"Of course," Gerardo chuckled. "Why am I not surprised? If this was a poker game in the old west, we'd all have our eye on you."

James chuckled and sighed, leaning back in his chair. "Alright, here goes. "Believe it or not, I can boil it down. Absolutely number one: the Ojibwa's clay offering bound us to a promise. Anything less in scope and intent than our original vision would be disrespectful, that is what they agreed to, that is what we should deliver, this is one treaty we will not break."

He took a pause to look around to his friends to see if they were with him, when he was satisfied they were together on this salient point, he progressed. "Number two: The design took weeks because it had to encompass every prayer from every tile, we can't disregard the effort people put into those tiles. Each one is a personal mountain. They came together with one purpose, as one family, we need a space large enough to see the whole family as an... entity... and the individual as well. We can't break that up."

"But we can't use them all, the Eco lobby wall is rare." Rhonda interjected, her voice cutting through the matter to make her point, "not in their current form."

"Exactly," James nodded. "Which leaves us one option: go bigger."

Pause. The silence that followed was so thick you could have spread it like apple-butter on your mum's flax-seed waffles—if you were so inclined.

"Bigger than Eco?" Emma asked, her eyebrows raised.

"Why not?" James leaned forward, his eyes brightening just a bit. "We dreamed big once. Why stop now?"

The room fell silent, each lost in thought. The clock on the shelf in the kitchen ticked loudly, marking the passage of time—a metronome to bring their disparate thoughts in sync. A burst of the winter wind whipped past the windows rattling the frames.

They all turned to look at the windows startled out of their reverie.

"Ah… is that a sign?" Gerardo asked lightly, his attempt at humor falling a little flat in the tense atmosphere.

"Let's say that's the hoped for beginning place." And here Rhonda inclined her head to James, "There's something else," Rhonda said hesitantly. "The rumors… they're getting worse."

James's jaw tightened. "About me, you mean."

Gerardo nodded grimly, his usual jovial demeanor replaced by a somber gravity. "They're saying you're difficult, unreliable. That you're the reason Eco pulled out."

"That's ridiculous," Emma said, her voice sharp. "That's absolutely… I can't even find the words—" She trailed off, her indignation rendering her momentarily speechless.

"Is it?" James asked quietly. He stood, moving to the window to check to see if they were secure and firmly closed, when he continued, his voice was calm, even a little amused. "I am difficult, from a certain point of view, I am exacting." And then he went to the kitchen without saying another word, pulling mugs from the cupboard, "Tea?"

"James," Emma started, but he held up a hand, poured a cup of tea, and continued.

"No, hear me out. I've been thinking..." He completed his task, pouring four steaming mugs of tea into four wildly different ceramic mugs, each one a character in its own right. placed them on a tray and carried his offering to his friends, placing it on the coffee table in front of where Emma sat on the couch, the steam rising like an offering to the ethers from each cup.

"Maybe it's time I step back. Let you all move forward without... extremity."

His compatriots erupted in protests, their voices blending like a discordant symphony. Emma was on her feet in an instant, her eyes flashing.

"Don't you dare, James Watson. Don't think it, take it back. We're in this together."

"Em's right," Gerardo added. "We're a team. The 'mod squad', remember?"

Rhonda nodded, a rare smile softening her features. "Besides, who else is going to drive me crazy, what did you say—difficult and exacting? You forget, you're *our* difficult and exacting."

James made no rebuttal, he simply handed out the warm tea, first to Rhonda, then Gerardo, his movements as precise as a tea ceremony master.

"Sorry for the station break, I may be a U.S citizen now, but tea is still the English remedy for all... Drink your tea and think about it, just consider it." he advised.

He handed the last mug, a soft pink creation with white swirls on the side to Emma, momentarily touching her fingers in the exchange. A soft current to help calm them both.

James returned to the couch, sat down, and seemed more relaxed now that it was out and fermenting in the groups respective noggins. He had a sip of tea himself, then draped his right arm on the top of the couch behind his Em.

There was a pause as they did what he suggested, they thought about it, they imagined what it would mean going forward. The silence was thick, but not uncomfortable, each person lost in their own thoughts, the tea warming their hands and their souls.

Gerardo was the first to break the spell, when he spoke his words were slow and precise.

"Difficulty is measured by people who won't even consider trying, did we, any of us, ever think this was difficult? Exciting challenges, yes," and here he nodded to Rhonda "working hard to find the best possible outcome given our time frame, yes. But did any one of us *ever* consider, this was beyond our grasp or ability if we worked together?"

"No." Emma said simply, her voice as firm as bedrock.

The room fell silent, each lost in thought. The clock in the kitchen is still doing its job—marking the moments, measuring the abstract concept of time like a metronome keeping tempo for their collective contemplation.

It was Rhonda's turn this time her voice rising like a preacher at the pulpit.

"I'll be damned... literally damned in church by my mom, family and congregation too—if I allow some... *gossip*... direct my thoughts, my life and what I choose to do. Gossip is the lowest way of communicating, it is based on exaggeration, cherry picking extraction... lies and you all know who is the king of lies. So, hell no."

Once Rhonda had taken the stage in such a way no one dast break in a sideways remark and now Emma took a sip of her tea, nodded and said, "Thanks Rhonda, for that, I don't think anybody could have said it better, I know, it may seem I'm biased, because..."

And here Emma's voice softened as she looked at James, "You may have noticed, things have gotten better between us—"

"You think?" Gerardo interrupted, his voice dripping with playful sarcasm. There was a light round of chuckles and general amusement at her understatement.

Emma flushed a sweet pink, a precious strawberry blossoming, in the sun. Gerardo softened his voice, "Sorry, Em... go ahead..."

"You made me lose my train of thought," she ribbed Gerardo, thinking for a moment, "no you haven't—because it's right there in my mind, it's always there... Who are we if we sacrifice a member of our group to gossip? That is the ancient, ancient mistake—that sacrificing people into the volcano, it's a ritual that never works. In truth it probably achieves the opposite. That's not a solution—that's giving in to fear and desperation. And gossip goads people into it. We are together as a group or we are not. Our choice. On our time."

"James, do you have something to say?" Rhonda asked her voice was firm, insistent—a teacher calling on a recalcitrant student.

He thought about it and looked at Emma, his eyes twinkling with affection. "Boy, she doesn't give speeches much, but when she does they're ringers." He looked to each of his friends and said, "I agree with you all, and would only add—we need to do this for Alfred and Mabel, and in order for that to happen we need each other at full speed. I agree with you all."

They all sipped their peppermint tea allowing the beverage to invigorate the senses and stimulate the group mind.

Gerardo broke the silence again, a mischievous glint in his eye—like a child about to suggest a daring two a.m. raid on the cookie jar.

"All right then, you know what we need? A proper pact."

"What did you have in mind?" Rhonda asked, eyebrows raised.

"A pinky swear," Gerardo declared, holding out his hand. "Old school—but binding."

James chuckled, shaking his head. "Back to eight years old are we?"

Emma nudged him gently. "Sometimes a child's promise is exactly what we need."

And so they placed their mugs down, leaned forward to be in physical range, formed a circle, and linked pinkies in a chain of friendship and commitment. The late afternoon light bathed them in a warm glow, casting long shadows across the room.

"To the mod squad," Gerardo intoned solemnly. "May we always swim in uncharted waters."

"To find something better," Rhonda added.

"To honor every prayer, every tile," Emma said softly.

James looked around at his friends, feeling a swell of emotion. "To us," he said and added, we search for a better situation, inside and outside the box, bring it back and we vote. Including Alfred and Mabel of course. Sounds good? We pinky swear it?"

They looked around at each other, smiling now—perhaps euphoric—took a collective breath as their pinkies tightened around each other.

They broke apart, laughing at the absurdity and sincerity of the moment, their merriment a binding pact and ode to friendship and shared purpose.

* * *

As Gerardo and Rhonda gathered their things to leave, Emma saw them to the door, hugging each in turn. James found himself lingering by the window, lost in thought, his reflection a dream-like presence in the darkening glass.

Emma approached and rested a hand on his arm, her touch a butterfly landing. "Penny for your thoughts?"

James turned, a wry smile on his face. "Just thinking about uncharted waters."

"Scary stuff," Emma said, though she didn't sound frightened at all. No—it sounded more like she was getting ready to hop on a roller coaster at Six Flags America.

"Terrifying," James agreed, but he was smiling too.

Emma laughed. "Admit it. Let me hear you admit it—you kinda love an impossible dream."

Instead of answering, James went to sit on the couch and patted the cushion next to him—the universal gesture for "please come sit next to me." When she was settled and both were relaxed, he sighed, leaning his head back against the cushion.

"I suppose I do," he said, his voice thoughtful. "I was just thinking about how much I love this country. I love the group mind and democracy. We'll find something, I'm sure. We may not all agree, but we've agreed to the majority. Maybe that's the best any group can do."

Emma nodded, feeling a flutter of nervousness in her stomach. "You're not worried about... well—"

"—Ever working again?" James finished for her, a hint of amusement in his voice.

To her surprise, James laughed, the sound rich and genuine.

"Luv, I was halfway out the door already," he said, his accent thickening slightly as it often did when he was relaxed, the words rolling off his tongue like honey. "I've got my own rules for my own reasons. No one needs to follow mine."

Then, almost to himself, he added, "My reputation may be done. No prospects. Naught up the pike... so what say we get married? Sailing off the edge of the world sounds like the perfect time to get married."

He paused, a grin spreading across his face. "Also—big plus—I'm a U.S. citizen now, so you don't have to worry that I'm marrying you for your... um... can't quite think of the word. Not benefits... um..."

"So you don't get kicked out of the country?" Emma supplied, her heart racing despite her calm exterior.

"That's it," James agreed, nodding wisely.

There was a moment of silence as Emma looked at him, trying to read the truth behind his words. The very furniture in the room seemed to lean imperceptibly forward to catch her answer.

"I can't tell if you're serious," she said finally, her voice barely above a whisper.

Something in her tone seemed to sober James. He straightened up, taking her hands in his. His eyes dropped for a moment, as if gathering courage and momentum again, before meeting hers.

"Sorry, luv, if I'm mucking it up," he said, his voice low and sincere. "It just kinda came out that way, but it's what I always wanted under everything. Sorry if I never said it. I love you, Em—"

Before he could finish, Emma silenced him with a kiss. It was soft and sweet and opened the flower of herself to reveal all she had to give him.

When they finally parted, both were breathless. The room seemed to have shifted somehow, as if the very air around them had rearranged itself to accommodate this new pinky swear.

They sat there, hands still clasped, foreheads lightly touching. The fading light painted them in soft hues—two figures on the precipice of a new adventure.

And as night fell over Chicago, wrapping the city in a blanket of twinkling lights, James and Emma remained on the couch, talking softly of free-range chickens and new beginnings, of art and love and the infinite possibilities that lay ahead. The future was uncertain, but in that moment, it was also filled with promise—one as old as humans on earth.

* * *

Chapter 31

Chicago to Janesville, WI — *Feb. 15, 2003 — 8:30 a.m. — Road Trip*

The winter sun hung low in the Chicago sky, casting long shadows across the snow-covered streets as James maneuvered his car through the quiet neighborhood. A restlessness had been building in him for days—an inexplicable urge to escape the confines of the city and breathe in the crisp country air. When he'd mentioned it to Emma, her eyes had lit up with an excitement that thrilled his inner man. Let's face it, men have this *thing* about making their woman happy.

"I know just where we should go," she'd said, her voice filled with a childlike enthusiasm that made James smile even wider—from ear to ear. Cheshire cat, go get a new job.

Now, as he pulled up to Emma's apartment, he couldn't help but smile at the sight of her waiting on the stoop, a small overnight bag at her feet and a thermos of what he assumed was her signature blend of chai tea clutched in her gloved hands—as if she couldn't stay in her apartment one minute more and couldn't wait to get on the road with him. She looked like a character from a winter fairy tale: her cheeks flushed with cold, her eyes bright with anticipation.

"Ready for an adventure, luv?" James called out as he got out and popped the trunk.

Emma's laugh was like music as she hurried to the car. "You have no idea," she said, her breath forming small clouds in the frigid air.

He put her small bag in the hatchback trunk of the Prius, rubbing his hands together to warm them, and got behind the driver's seat.

As they settled into the warmth of the car, Emma began to explain their destination.

"In 1994, a female white buffalo was born on a farm in Janesville, Wisconsin," she said, her voice taking on a reverent tone. "My grandfather, father, and mother made a pilgrimage to see her when she was still a calf. But I'd like to see her now. Her name is Miracle, and she's nine years old."

James listened, fascinated, as Emma explained the prophecy of the Lakota Sioux—how Miracle's coat had changed color over the years, from white to red/brown, to black, to yellow/tan, and now back to white.

"It probably means she won't be here much longer," Emma said softly. "I'd like to see her while I can."

"Done," James said without hesitation. "Let's go for a few days or more—really get away."

"Oh, James, thanks. Sounds great—I'll pay for gas." She leaned over and kissed his cheek, marking the spot for future landings.

"Wait—you what?" James protested. "Oooh, I like that. Remember that move."

"All right, I'll get the road snacks," Emma said, drawing a line, "but you can't stop me from getting road food. It has to be a particular vintage and variety."

"Okay, oh sommelier!" James deferred.

"Smelly what?" Emma's expression was blank.

"A sommelier is—" James began his clinic dissertation on the role and purpose of a sommelier in modern society, as the ultra wine connoisseur, but was brought to a dead stop. "Wait a minute, is that a setup? You set me up?"

Emma couldn't keep her face straight. Her control broke, and she began laughing. She was having such a good time already it was hard to fasten her seatbelt.

"Sorry, sorry—it was just too easy—"

James leaned in, drawing her close, and kissed her lips. When he finally pulled away, Emma's knees were weak, her body tingling as if spun into liquid gold.

"Good morning, luv," he said, his voice low and husky. "I think... this is going to be some holiday." He couldn't help but add, "You know, Em, I think this might be our first proper getaway together. Bit backwards, aren't we?"

She touched the side of his face, and then laughed—a low love sound. "Backwards, forwards, spinning sideways—as long as I'm not driving right now, onward ho!"

He chuckled, then kissed the palm of her hand as a kind of keepsake she could cash in later.

* * *

Before they set off, they made a series of phone calls to the "mod squad," including Alfred and Mabel. They agreed to start looking in earnest for new project possibilities, planning to reconvene in three to four weeks unless something big came up sooner.

With directions to the Heider farm in Janesville safely stored in James's Wi-Fi navigator, they set off on their impromptu road trip. The best way to Wisconsin and Janesville was north on 94, and once on the highway, it stretched out before them, a ribbon of black cutting through the snow-covered landscape. They took their time, stopping at roadside diners for what Emma declared was "terrible but necessary" road trip food.

"Chicken nuggets are an American tradition," Emma insisted as they pulled away from a drive-thru, the scent of fried food filling the car. "You've gotta start earning your stripes."

James laughed, popping a nugget into his mouth. "If this is what earning my stripes tastes like, I might have to reconsider my citizenship."

As they drove, the city gave way to rolling countryside, blanketed in a thick layer of pristine white snow. When the road stretched out straight and clear before them, they'd reach for each other's hands, fingers intertwining like love-struck teenagers.

"Tell me more about the Lakota legend," James said, glancing at Emma. "About Miracle's changing coat."

Emma smiled, her eyes bright with enthusiasm. "Did I tell you already?"

"Doesn't matter," James replied softly. "I love to hear your voice."

Emma's laughter filled the car. "Well, then I should probably sing..."

"Oh God," James muttered, but his eyes crinkled with amusement.

"No, I have a CD I've been meaning to play at the warehouse studio," Emma said, rummaging in her bag. "I thought you and Gerardo would get a kick out of it."

She pulled out a CD case, and James raised an eyebrow at the band name. "Average White Band? What kind of name is that?"

"Shh," Emma admonished playfully. "Terrible name, but *great* jazz-funk-type song that rocked the '70s. Mom and Dad loved it."

As she slipped the CD into the player, the opening notes of "Pick Up the Pieces" filled the car. James found himself bobbing his head to the infectious rhythm.

"Great layers of sound," he observed appreciatively.

Emma nodded excitedly. "Just wait... wait for it... here it comes!" She began to sing along with the band: "Pick up the pieces... uh huh, pick up the pieces, that's right, pick up the pieces..."

When the saxophone solo kicked in, James's eyes widened in amazement. He glanced at Emma, watching her 'get down' in the passenger seat, her body moving to the music, her face alight with joy.

"Wow," he murmured, a rush of love and certainty washing over him. "I'm gonna marry that."

"Ah... sing with me, it comes around again!" Emma urged, nudging him with her elbow.

James shrugged, a grin spreading across his face. "Why not?" And so he did, their voices blending together in a surprisingly harmonious duet.

As they drove on through the winter landscape, the car filled with music and laughter, James felt joy... good old-fashioned, new-fangled joy. This was what he wanted—what he'd always wanted. Don't think about the past, or even the future—just ride the wave and enjoy the view.

The road stretched out before them, full of promise and possibility. And as Emma launched into yet another enthusiastic rendition of the chorus, James joined in wholeheartedly, his voice mingling with hers, harmonizing with the music, zipping down a snow-lined highway with the woman he loved.

* * *

The late afternoon sun hung low in the sky, casting long shadows across the snow-covered fields as James and Emma turned onto the final stretch of country road leading to the farm. The car's tires crunched softly on the gravel, a rhythmic sound that seemed to underscore the growing sense of anticipation in the air.

James glanced at Emma, noting the way her eyes scanned the horizon, as if searching for something beyond the ordinary. "Tell me about Miracle's coat changing color again," he said softly, breaking the comfortable silence that had settled between them. "You thought you told me, only you didn't—and then got distracted."

Emma blinked, coming back to the present moment. "Oh, right. Sorry," she said, a small smile playing at the corners of her mouth. "This is an old legend. White Buffalo Calf Woman is the sacred being that holds the place for this energy. When the white calf is born, it signifies that the time has come for the races to come together—for hope, to start again... and unify and... come together."

James couldn't resist a gentle tease. "You're not going to break out in another song, are you? 'Cause I gotta warn you, I know that one."

Emma's voice softened, taking on an almost reverential tone. "No, no more singing now—unless it is the ancient songs. We're getting close. We should stop talking and show respect with silence."

James nodded in agreement, feeling a shift in the atmosphere. Whether it was from being in close proximity to the woman he loved, with snow falling gently outside the car windows, or something more ineffable, he felt a kind of cushion envelop them. The air seemed to thicken with expectation—and a touch of the sacred.

As they pulled up to the farm, James was struck by its ordinariness. It looked like any other buffalo farm, with no garish signs or tourist traps. A small area near the farmhouse offered postcards for sale—a humble way to support the upkeep of the place.

A young man greeted them, his breath visible in the cold air. "Not sure if Miracle will come down to the fence today," he said, his voice carrying a hint of apology. "She's getting kinda tired. But stay as long as you like. Oh—and no photographs, sorry."

James and Emma nodded their understanding before setting off down the path toward a wooded area enclosed by a fence. As they drew closer, James noticed an array of objects adorning the fence—colorful scarves, dreamcatchers, and small bells, some showing signs of weathering.

"This is a kata," James murmured, gently touching the red silk end of one of the scarves. "Buddhism. They're usually white, but can have colors too."

Emma nodded silently, her eyes taking in the eclectic mix of offerings. The dreamcatchers swayed gently in the breeze, their feathers rustling softly, while the occasional tinkling of a bell punctuated the winter stillness.

They stood side by side at the fence, waiting. The minutes ticked by, marked only by the soft crunch of snow beneath their feet as they shifted to keep warm. Then, after what felt like an eternity—but was probably closer to twenty minutes—they heard it: the soft crackle of twigs and the muffled sound of hooves on snow.

Miracle emerged from the underbrush, her white coat a tonal match with the muted colors of the winter landscape. She moved with a slow, deliberate grace toward the trough by the fence, seemingly unaware of her audience.

James held his breath, afraid that even the slightest sound might startle her. He watched as Miracle lowered her head to the trough, the sound of her chewing oddly comforting—as a common, day-to-day activity.

Then, after feeding for about five minutes, Miracle raised her head to look them over. She stopped chewing and turned her gaze directly toward the man and woman watching her. James felt Emma's body tremble beside him, and he instinctively wrapped his arm around her, pulling her close.

The moment stretched—elastic and surreal. Miracle's eyes, dark and unfathomable, seemed to look not just at them, but into them. James felt a curious sensation, like a soft touch on his mind—a feather-light caress, perhaps even a gentle kiss on his temple.

They stood there, frozen in that moment of connection, until Miracle, having apparently seen all she cared to, turned and ambled back the way she had come. The spell broken, James became aware of the cold air biting at his cheeks, the warmth of Emma pressed against his side, and the steady beat of his own heart.

As Miracle disappeared into the woods, James looked down at Emma. A single tear had traced its way down her cheek. He reached up, his gloved thumb gently brushing it away.

"Well," he said softly, his voice rough with emotion, "I think I understand now why they call her Miracle."

Emma nodded, words seemingly beyond her for the moment. She leaned into James, her head resting on his shoulder, and they stood there for a long while, watching the empty space where Miracle had been, each lost in their own thoughts about what they'd just experienced.

* * *

As the sun dipped lower, painting the snow-covered landscape in hues of pink and gold, James and Emma finally turned to leave.

"Wait, I almost forgot..." Emma reached into her winter jacket pocket and pulled out a white ceramic bell. She held it up by the strong braided twine for James to see.

"Beautiful," he observed.

"I made it years ago, years..." Emma said softly, and without saying more, she stepped up to the fence, found an open space, and fastened the end of the twine to the wire fence where the bell could swing free and sing when it wanted.

They waited about ten minutes more, watching the bell, listening to the sweet tinkle as the wind lifted it now and then. They turned to leave, their footsteps crunching in the snow, creating a duet trail with the gentle tinkling of the bells on the fence.

James opened the car door for Emma, then paused, looking back at the path they had walked. The falling snow was already beginning to erase their footprints, but the memory of what they had experienced would remain indelible. With a small smile, he walked around the car and got into the driver's seat.

* * *

When they reached the main road, James surprised Emma by turning right at the stop sign, heading into Janesville rather than back toward the highway. Emma didn't question his decision, content to go with the flow of this unexpected journey. She watched the small town unfold before them, its streets dusted with snow, holiday lights still twinkling in shop windows despite the lateness of the season.

On the outskirts of town, James pulled into the parking lot of a quaint, upscale motel. Emma's brows furrowed slightly, a silent question in her eyes.

James's voice was soft, almost apologetic, as he explained, "Nothing funny, just a place to sleep tonight. Don't think it's a good idea to drive back right now—neither of us are... grounded."

Emma nodded, finally breaking her silence. "And it would be nice to stay in the area... near her, for a little while."

James felt a rush of affection, realizing they'd had the same thought. The peace they'd found with Miracle wasn't a blessing to walk away from lightly.

He returned from the office with a key, jingling it lightly. "Number 10... should be right around the corner. The clerk told me there were restaurants nearby, but we can order delivery too, if we just want to camp in."

"That sounds nice," Emma murmured, then added with a hint of shyness, "cozy."

"Sorry, I got one room." James's voice was hesitant. "I'd like to stay by you, if that's okay. Nothing funny or anything."

Emma's smile was soft, tinged with amusement. "Well, no one ever accused you of being funny."

"Not sure how to take that," James chuckled, but his eyes were warm as he gathered their bags.

The room was cozy and surprisingly upscale, with plush carpets and tasteful artwork adorning the walls. The desire for quiet contemplation still hung in the air, so Emma wordlessly headed for the shower while James settled in.

As steam filled the bathroom, Emma let the hot water wash over her, feeling as though it was carrying away more than just the chill of the day. When she emerged, wrapped in soft flannel pajamas, she found James was ready to take his turn in the shower.

Using the room phone, she ordered delivery from a nearby Italian place. The menu items seemed to call to her—ravioli, spaghetti with meatballs, and even steak. It was more food than they usually ate, but tonight felt different. Special.

James, fresh from his shower, answered the door when their food arrived. He laid out the spread on the small round table in the corner, steam rising from the containers and filling the room with the rich aroma of garlic and tomato sauce.

They ate in reverent silence, savoring each bite as if it were a sacrament. The clinking of forks against plates and the soft rustle of napkins were the only sounds that broke the quiet.

As they finished their meal, a deep weariness settled over them both. Without a word, James settled into the bed closest to the door, while Emma curled up in the other. The soft whir of the heating system and the distant sounds of the town fading into night lulled them both into a deep sleep.

It was in those quiet hours that James began to dream…

* * *

The dreamscape unfolded like a watercolor painting, colors bleeding and blending at the edges. James found himself standing in a vast, snow-covered field, the sky above a canvas of swirling purples and deep blues. In the distance, he could make out the silhouette of a buffalo, its white coat gleaming under an unseen moon.

As he watched, the buffalo began to change. Its coat shifted from white to a vibrant yellow, to a rich, earthy red-brown, then to the deepest black he'd ever seen. The transformations continued, each color more vibrant than the last, until the buffalo's coat settled back into a pristine white.

Suddenly, James was no longer an observer but found himself running alongside the magnificent creature. The snow beneath his feet felt warm, almost alive, and with each step, flowers of every hue burst forth, creating a rainbow path in their wake.

The scene shifted, and James was standing before a great council fire. Faces both familiar and strange surrounded him—he recognized Emma, Gerardo, and Rhonda, but also men from the sweat lodge ceremony, alongside ancient people from different cultures. Some he recognized; some he didn't. There were traditional garb of various Native American tribes. An elderly woman, her face etched with the wisdom of ages, approached him.

"You are looking for a home for your children," she said, her voice carrying the weight of mountains and the whisper of prairie grass. "Don't look at the buildings men make. What good are they going to do you? Look at the earth."

Before James could ask what she meant, the dream dissolved, reforming into a new vision. He was standing on a hill, overlooking a vast expanse of land. In the valley below, he saw the mosaic they had created—but it was no longer confined to a wall. Instead, it flowed across the landscape, following the contours of the earth, rising and falling with each hill and valley.

People from all walks of life wandered the paths of this living mosaic, their faces alight with wonder and joy. As James watched, he felt a hand slip into his. He turned to see Emma beside him, her eyes reflecting the beauty of the scene before them.

"Hello," she whispered. "Good to see you again."

* * *

Chapter 32

Janesville, WI — *Feb. 16, 2003 — 9:10 a.m. — I'm Only Dreaming*

There was a small stain on the ceiling that resembled a lopsided heart. At least, that's what it looked like as consciousness returned to one James Watson. It was morning; he could see soft white shards of light peek through the gap in the dark blue curtains—but he was momentarily disoriented, not sure where he was, what was happening. He turned and saw Em, half dressed (which could also be described as half-naked), by the coffee pot and smiled. If he'd just woken up in an alternate universe, he'd take it.

No... wait, this was his world now—and she was in it. Hallelujah.

Emma stood by the kitchenette, pouring steaming liquid into two mugs. The coffee maker gurgled its final notes, a discordant symphony accompanied by the distant scrape of a snowplow outside. James sat up slowly, his equilibrium momentarily askew.

"Whoa," he muttered, pressing a hand to his temple.

Emma turned. "You okay there, sleepy-head?" She crossed the room, settling beside him on the bed. An errant spring creaked in protest.

James accepted the offered mug. "Yeah, just... I had this dream. It was wonderful, but now it's gone."

"A dream?" Emma took a sip of her coffee, her interest piqued, her mind flashing to the spiritual encounters of recent days. "After your track record this past half year... I'd love to hear that dream."

James furrowed his brow, concentrating. "There was... a buffalo, I think. And colors. So many colors." He shook his head, frustrated. "It's all liquid now—I can't hold onto it."

Emma nodded, her gaze drawn to a small ladybug crawling along the windowsill, its red shell a stark contrast to the winter landscape outside. *What in the world? How is it coming out of hibernation now?* A mischievous thought struck her. "Maybe... if I withhold your coffee and use some kind of rewards system, it'll jog your memory."

James clutched his mug protectively. "You wouldn't dare, Hawkins."

Their laughter was light, playful—a sense of rediscovering a long-forgotten rhythm together.

"You know," James said slowly, tracing the chip in his mug, "I'm rather enjoying this little adventure of ours."

Emma's smile widened. "Me too. It feels like..."—and here she looked down—"like we're us again... only better."

A comfortable silence followed as they simply enjoyed the moment without edit—except for, you know, the backup alarm of the snowplow outside sounding *beep, beep, beep* as it cleared the parking lot. They looked at each other and smiled. See? Every little thing was funny.

James's gaze wandered to a faded tourist brochure on the nightstand, its corner curled with age. "Say, aren't there some Indian mounds around here in Wisconsin?"

Emma nodded, her mind already thinking ahead. "Oh yes, quite a few actually. There's a cluster not far from here that's open to the public—and a great park, not too far away, a couple of hours maybe, though I've never been."

James set his mug down on the nightstand, inadvertently aligning it perfectly with a circular water stain. "What do you say we extend our trip? Take in some history, do a walking tour? Would you like that, luv?"

Emma's eyes lit up. "I'd love that. I've got my camera with me... I'd love that."

"Right then," James confirmed. "We're officially on vacation."

As they finished their coffee, Emma materialized four blueberry scones from a baker's bag for him to choose from. He let out a sound that could be described as an "eeep!"

She laughed. "I guess that translates to *yum* in some cities."

James took out two scones, considered taking a third, looked at Emma's slim form and muttered, "You're too thin by half. Please eat—these two, plus let's stop for a meal."

Emma looked at him. "I think there was a compliment in there somewhere... uh, thanks?"

They chuckled and began to pack for their extended adventure. James couldn't help but marvel at how easy it all felt. Here they were, in a tiny motel room in the middle of Wisconsin, planning a walking tour in the snow—and he'd never felt more at home.

* * *

The late morning sun hung low in the winter sky as James and Emma pulled into the parking lot of Aztalan State Park, about 50 miles west of Milwaukee. The air was crisp and still—the kind of cold that nips at exposed skin but invigorates the soul.

As they stepped out of the car, the crunch of snow beneath their boots seemed unnaturally loud in the quiet surroundings. James reached back into the vehicle, pulling out a thermos of hot tea Emma had thoughtfully prepared before they left the motel.

"Okay, now you're on my turf," she said with a smile, her breath forming small clouds in the frigid air as she adjusted the shoulder strap of an insulated camera bag around her body.

James nodded, his eyes bright with anticipation. "'Lead on, McDuff,'" he replied, zipping up his coat and pulling on a pair of thick gloves. When she looked at him questioningly, he rephrased: "Ah... westward ho, Sacagawea?"

She kissed his cheek for an answer—and then liked it so much, she kissed his mouth too.

They looked at each other, smiled, and Emma asked, "You like that?"

"I do," James agreed.

With another smile, she took his hand and they set off down the marked trail, the packed snow squeaking softly under their feet. The path led them through an open, snow-covered field, the Crawfish River visible in the distance, its waters partially frozen. The stark beauty of the winter landscape seemed to heighten the sense of ancient mystery that permeated the site.

As they walked, James found himself hyper-aware of the small details around them. A red-tailed hawk circled overhead, its cry piercing the silence. Animal tracks crisscrossed the snow, telling stories of nocturnal wanderings.

Rounding a bend in the trail, they came upon the first of the large pyramidal mounds. It rose before them, an imposing earthwork that stood in stark contrast to the flat surrounding terrain. James and Emma approached slowly, almost reverently.

"It's larger than I expected," James murmured, his voice hushed with awe.

Emma nodded, her eyes tracing the stepped contours of the mound. "And so precisely constructed," she replied. "Can you imagine the work that went into this?"

They stood in silence for a moment, taking in the sight. Then, as if drawn by an unseen force, they both moved to place their hands on the earth at the base of the mound. Even through their gloves, James fancied he could feel a warmth—a vibration, of sorts—emanating from the ground.

"Can you feel that?" he whispered, turning to Emma.

Her eyes met his, wide with wonder. "Yes," she breathed. "The earth is alive. We can feel it more here, I think."

As they stood there, hands pressed to the ancient earth, James felt a sudden rush of... something. Images flashed through his mind—people gathering, singing, building. He was aware it could be his imagination, a projection of an expectation, but that might be all right too... or maybe he was remembering something else.

"Em," he said, straightening to stand fully upright. His voice was cautious, careful. "I think I'm remembering my dream."

"Can you tell me?"

And so, standing there in the winter sunshine, their breath mingling in the cold air, James began to recount his dream. He spoke of the changing buffalo, the rainbow path, the council fire, and the vision of their mosaic spread across the land.

As he talked, Emma listened intently, her eyes never leaving his face. When he finished, a comfortable silence fell between them, broken only by the occasional call of a bird or the soft whisper of wind across the open field.

Finally, Emma spoke, her voice filled with awe and a touch of excitement. "James, I think your dream may be a vision."

James nodded slowly, the truth of her words resonating within him. "But what does it mean?" he asked, more to himself than to Emma.

She smiled and looked around at their surroundings. "Maybe we'll find out soon."

They stood there a while longer, hands still pressed to the ancient earth, each lost in thought. The sun climbed higher in the sky, casting long shadows from the mound across the snow-covered ground.

As they finally turned to continue their tour of the site, James felt a sense of anticipation building within him. This journey, he realized, was becoming about much more than just seeing historical sites. It was a journey of discovery, of connection—to the land, to the past, and to each other.

He reached for Emma's hand as they walked toward the next mound. Their fingers struggled a bit to intertwine while wearing gloves, but they did it. Success.

* * *

The winter sun was lower in the sky now, but the sky was still clear—a great day for taking photos—so Emma had wandered afield, using her camera as best she could to capture the feeling of the day, the quality of the construction of the main mound, and the general landscape and wildlife to boot. She was having fun.

James sat on a small public bench, his breath forming small clouds in the frigid air. His eyes followed Emma's diminishing figure as she walked toward the distant mound, her bright blue coat a vibrant splash of color against the shocking white snow.

He studied the mound, its soft contours gentle to the eye and senses. Was that a crow sitting on top? Its black feathers were a stark contrast to the pristine place, as if nature itself was placing a marker on this round ancient structure. The sight put James in mind of something he'd seen before... what was it?

Igloos, of course. Igloos had an economical shape that allowed wind to whip around while the people inside stayed safe. The igloo had no corner to grab to break apart the whole; it was invisible to profound gales. James chuckled to himself, watching as a loose leaf tumbled across the snow, dancing on the breeze—not like that little guy.

That's a funny thought, he mused. The round shape wasn't exactly found in nature—not like that—it was made by man... but nature gave it a pass. He watched as Emma lined up a long shot with her camera. What was she aiming at? Oh—a rabbit, a jackrabbit. It darted across the field of snow. Gone now.

He looked at the mound again. There was something else tugging at the edges of his memory. A flash of color caught his eye—a red cardinal perched on a bare branch, its vibrant plumage reminiscent of the kata he'd seen yesterday, attached to Miracle's fence. Katas were most often white, but that one had been red. What else did he know? Well, katas were made of silk, a pure natural fiber to hold the blessings of masters for their devoted students—for prayer and pilgrimage to places such as the Boudhanath Stupa.

And then it hit him. Stupas. That's what the mounds reminded him of—the sacred round Buddhist structures built to last millennia. Built round to be accepted by the earth as one of its own, with sacred artifacts and blessed items placed inside to carry the resonance for millennia, to bless the earth. A perpetual prayer.

His breath quickened, forming rapid little clouds in the cold air. He stood up abruptly, startling a nearby squirrel that had been cautiously approaching.

"Oh my God," he whispered. "Oh dear God."

It was mad... a mad idea... but once it took hold of an inch of his mind, it doubled and trebled until it consumed him. Build a stupa for the mosaic tiles. Build a permanent home that people could come see—and walk around—and inside, too.

A gust of wind swept across the park, carrying with it the faint sound of distant chimes. James tilted his head, listening. There was a reason why sacred sites were set aside on the ley lines of the earth, a reason why he and Emma had chosen to be still and quiet these past few days.

Because in the quiet, in the calm, you can hear your own heartbeat... and hope to hold hands with God.

He remembered the feather-light touch in his mind yesterday, the kiss on his brow. It hadn't come from Miracle, exactly... he believed now it had been a sweet angelic touch and blessing because he and Emma had shown respect, kindness, and reverence.

A hawk soared overhead, its wings outstretched. James shielded his eyes with his hand as he watched the bird catch an updraft and float, suspended for a few moments between heaven and earth.

Nice. Hope Emma caught that on camera.

James began walking toward Emma, his footsteps crunching in the snow. Each step seemed to accentuate and mark the pattern of his thoughts. The landscape and all around was quiet, except for that. When the work loft was quiet, with no music playing, he could sit by the tiles lying on the template and feel a sweet shiver sometimes up his arm. He knew Emma could feel it too. There was that time he showed her the letter, their first kiss—they both had felt it in the stillness.

If the mosaic wall had been placed in the Eco building, how many people would have truly felt it? Or discovered it in the clang and bang of day-to-day living? A rare sensitive person like his Sarah, maybe—and Emma, and maybe even himself—but he ventured to say few others. People would enjoy the beauty and complexity and color, but how many would actually *feel* it?

By the time he reached Emma, standing like a wildflower on the white landscape in her bright blue coat, his mind was made up. It was mad—he was starkers, absolutely no doubt about that. He was either decades ahead of time or centuries behind. But he wanted to follow this through—to either raise it up or place it to rest.

He had research to do first: How large could a stupa be? How many people could it hold? It would need to have four cardinal directions, and it would have to be done in the ancient sacred way of alignment... so many details.

As Emma turned to face him, her cheeks flushed with cold and eyes bright with curiosity, James hesitated. Should he mention this to Emma while it was still one-tenth baked?

A flock of geese flew overhead in perfect V-formation, their honks echoing across the park. They both turned to watch, and after the flock had passed, James took a deep breath and began to speak—his words forming misty patterns in the cold air between them.

"Em, I've had an idea..."

* * *

The late afternoon sun cast long shadows across the undulating landscape of the Nicholls Mound. They had progressed to the next stop on their walking trail, and now James and Emma meandered along its base, their footsteps leaving temporary indentations in the damp snow. A gentle breeze carried the scent of wild grass, bark, earth and distant water, nature's own perfume.

James paused, his hand brushing against a patch of dried grass standing up through the snow, "You know," he mused, his voice thoughtful, "a Stupa wouldn't need to be enormous. Maybe just 40 yards by 40 yards. That would give us enough wall space for the design."

Emma nodded, her expression a mixture of amusement and growing intrigue. When James had first mentioned his Stupa idea, she'd listened with the indulgent smile one might give a child describing a castle in the clouds. But as their mound tour had progressed, his dreamy notion had begun to take on more substance to fire the imagination.

"And where would this marvel stand?" She asked, a playful lilt in her voice.

James's eyes lit up, encouraged by her engagement. "Somewhere quiet, away from the city bustle. A place where you can hear your own thoughts, right?" They began their ascent up the mound, the incline gentle but persistent. A red-winged blackbird trilled from a nearby shrub, its song a counterpoint to their conversation.

"It would need space around it," Emma found herself saying, surprising herself with her contribution to this fanciful plan. "For a community garden, perhaps. To remind people that animals, food, everything comes from the land."

James nodded, his pace quickening as their thoughts built one upon the other. "Yes. And at the center, we'd have the Stupa itself, built with red clay from the Ojibwa people. Their gift, helping to hold the line."

They reached the summit, slightly out of breath but exhilarated. The view stretched out before them, the Mississippi a silver ribbon in the distance. James turned to Emma, his eyes shining with more than just the reflection of the setting sun.

"Yes." He said softly, just that direct affirmative, then, with a hint of mischief, "I think I want to make love with you right now, is that too forward?"

Emma laughed, the sound carrying across the open space.

"She thinks I'm kidding," James said, addressing the mound beneath their feet as if confiding in an old friend. "I'm not kidding. What was it you said about love moving down through the chakras? First the crown, then eyes—'better to see you with'—then speech, throat, talking, getting to know each other, becoming friends. Then heart, then emotions, then, well, the hot parts, and then taking root, right?"

He stepped closer to Emma, his voice dropping to a husky whisper. "Well, I'm feeling a little toasty right now. Think I'm getting near the hot parts—"

"I love you," Emma interrupted, her voice filled with a certainty that took them both by surprise. "It seems I have all my life, and maybe past lives too…"

Don't forget the future," James murmured, pulling her into a kiss that threatened to melt the snow around them.

As they stood there, entwined atop the ancient mound, the setting sun painted the sky in hues of lavender and gold.

When they finally parted, both slightly breathless, Emma rested her forehead against James's. "You know," she said softly, "this crazy Stupa idea of yours might not be so crazy after all."

James chuckled, the sound rumbling through his chest. "High praise indeed, coming from you." He looked around the landscape, as if searching for something, "I feel like I should pick you up and carry you off... but it's a long hike back to the car."

Emma laughed.

As darkness began to settle around them, they made their way back down the mound, hand in hand. The first stars winked into existence above, silent witnesses to the changes one day can bring.

They reached their car just as the last light faded from the sky. Before getting in, James paused, looking back at the shadowy form of the mound. "Thank you," he whispered, though whether to the ancient builders, the land itself, some greater cosmic force, or the coming evening with his wife-to-be, he couldn't say.

* * *

Chapter 33

Chicago — Epoch Alliance Office — *Feb. 20, 2003 — 11:14 a.m. —*
The Art of Compromise

Rhonda had been anchored to her desk since the crack of
dawn, her bottom left drawer a treasure trove of flaxseed
muffins—her secret weapon against the gnawing hunger that
came with marathon workdays. The mini-fridge behind her,
stocked with enough seltzer water to fizz up a small pond,
stood as a silent sentinel to her dedication. She'd been rooted
to this spot since 7:30 a.m., showing no signs of uprooting
anytime soon.

The late afternoon sun slanted through the Venetian blinds
in Rhonda's office, casting striped shadows across her
meticulously organized desk. The air hummed with the soft
whir of her computer fan and the distant sounds of city life
filtering through the partially open window.

Rhonda sat, phone pressed to her ear, her free hand hovering
over a series of manila folders spread before her. Each folder
was topped with a glossy photograph—potential sites for
the mosaic installation—and adorned with colorful sticky
notes bearing her neat handwriting. Her eyes flicked between
the folders as she spoke, her voice a practiced blend of
enthusiasm and professionalism.

"Yes, that's right," she said, her fingers drumming lightly on the
folder marked with a hopeful question mark. "Did you receive

the images of the completed glazed tiles? The colors are quite stunning in person."

She listened intently, her gaze drifting to the other folders. One, marked with a bold *SOLID NO* in red ink, seemed to mockingly remind her of past rejections. Another, labeled *POSSIBLE* in cautious green, offered a glimmer of hope. But it was the folder currently open before her—the best candidate so far—that held her attention.

The voice on the other end of the line shifted the conversation. "And who did you say the lead designers were?"

Rhonda's spine straightened imperceptibly. "Both from Cooper Union. James—"

She was cut off mid-sentence, the interruption sharp and unexpected. "No, no, I've heard the gossip, and it may be gossip, but it's hard to believe Eco would bail on Alfred. There might be something to it... and we don't have that kind of space. You've seen the wall we have—it's not that grand."

Rhonda's mind raced, her eyes darting to the photo of the library's entrance hall in Lincoln Square. This was the best potential site yet, promising to reach a diverse array of cultural groups. She couldn't let it slip away so easily.

Taking a steadying breath, she replied, "We also have a woman lead designer. Emma Hawkins."

The pause on the other end of the line was palpable. Then: "Em Hawkeye? I know her work—saw the exhibit at the Art Institute... plus, a woman, right? That might be nice for a change. Do you have any designs on hand? I mean, the one I'm looking at blows me away, but won't be right for our space."

Rhonda's hand moved with practiced efficiency to the back of the folder, extracting a black ink drawing—Emma's backup design, created in case James had hit a creative block.

"Yes, in fact, I do," she replied, a note of triumph in her voice. "This one is a little downsized and streamlined in theme, but that might be exactly what you're looking for."

The voice on the line brightened considerably. "Well, send it over. You're getting me interested."

As Rhonda concluded the call, promising to send the design ASAP, she felt a mixture of exhilaration and unease wash in equal measure. She clasped her hands together, noticing with some surprise that they were trembling slightly.

"You're not betraying them," she murmured to herself, the words barely audible above the ambient noise of her office. "This is what we agreed to—search out the possibilities, take the side roads too."

She took a deep breath, her eyes falling on a small potted succulent on the corner of her desk—a gift from Emma, pert and resilient.

With a shake of her head, as if to dispel her doubts physically, Rhonda reached for her phone once more. Her finger hovered over Emma's contact for a moment before she pressed *call*.

As the phone began to ring, Rhonda's gaze drifted to the window. A pigeon had landed on the sill, its iridescent feathers catching the late afternoon light. It cocked its head, seeming to regard her with a mixture of curiosity and judgment.

Rhonda turned away from the window, focusing on the task at hand. Whatever came of this call—whatever path the project took from here—she knew one thing for certain:

The mosaic of their shared dream was shifting once again, each piece falling into a new and unexpected pattern.

* * *

The shrill ring of her cell phone cut through the quiet of Emma's apartment, its tinny melody incongruous with the peaceful atmosphere. Emma fumbled in her pocket, her fingers finding the familiar shape of her flip phone. Assuming it was James, a smile played on her lips as she snapped it open.

"Hey, you..." she laughed, her voice warm with affection.

"Hey yourself," Rhonda's voice replied, catching Emma off guard. "Gone for what seems like... well, days and days. Glad you guys got back before the snow falls again. Have a good time?"

Emma sank onto the couch. "Oh God, yes. The best—saw wonderful sites, and ideas are percolating too."

"Speaking of which..." Rhonda's tone shifted.

"Oh, this is a business call."

"Little bit of both... Em, are you sitting down?"

Emma glanced down at her position on the couch, a wry smile tugging at her lips. "I am now."

Rhonda took a deep breath. "I've got a solid bite. The entrance lobby of the Lincoln Square Library is interested in your wave design."

"It's smaller than the design," Emma frowned. "Remember what James said about that? I agree with him. That design has to breathe to be able to be seen."

"Yes, yes, about that," Rhonda hesitated. "Here's the straight shot—no cushion for the fall. They love your color schemes, they love your design... but they don't love James attached."

Emma sat up straight. "Wait, wait... back up the pony. They love the color, they love the design, but how can they love the design and not want James? *He is* the design."

"Sorry, I wasn't clear," Rhonda explained. "I sent them your design—your backup design—when we—"

"*You*," Emma interrupted. "When you were afraid he was blocked."

"Well, you wouldn't have done a design unless you were kinda afraid too," Rhonda countered. "But that's not the point. They love that design. It would work well in that space. You won't be able to use all the tiles, obviously, but the tiles that aren't glazed yet could be fired to suit your design, couldn't they? So it would be specific to their site and your design?"

Emma's head was spinning. "Hold on... how did they get that design, Rhonda? That was for your eyes only."

Rhonda thought about saying she forgot, but they were the mod squad; no place to hide for any of them. There was a pause before Rhonda admitted, "I know, I know... I admit I was scared. Nothing else seemed to be a fit, and they perked up so much at your name. They are interested and love it, but they understand as well that I'm fishing. I was clear that we're on a fishing expedition. I will take it back right now, I will call them and remove that design. Maybe you can do another one... or not. Maybe we can forget them. But Em... this could be real."

The line went quiet.

"Em? Are you there? I'm so sorry. The last thing I want is to hurt either of you—the last."

Emma took a deep breath. "It's okay, Rhonda. It's alright. But I thought one of the points was to help save James's reputation."

Silence hung between them. Emma's gaze drifted to a small clay figurine on her bookshelf, a whimsical piece James had made for her years ago. Its misshapen form seemed to take on a questioning tilt as Emma processed Rhonda's words.

Rhonda finally spoke. "Em, that's one of *your* goals. James said—and I quote—'I don't care two flying figs fighting over a rat's arse about me rep, do what's right for the work.' I know 'cause I wrote it down."

Emma couldn't help but smile. "Yeah, that sounds like both of you." She sighed. "It *sounds* amazing. I know that the library has high walls and depth. If it's the wall I'm thinking of, the design I drew could work there in a natural way. It's a universal concept."

"Exactly," Rhonda agreed, relief evident in her voice.

"I'm going to have to tell James," Emma said, her voice heavy with the weight of the decision.

Better you than me, thought Rhonda, but what she said was: "Thank you." Then she added, "Wait—you said something about percolation? You got something?"

"James had a lightbulb blink on, but it's off-the-charts wild. Very Cooper Union sideways, and it's in the baby stage. Well... an embryo. Not as developed as this."

"Well, I'd still like to hear his idea," Rhonda pressed.

"I think we'll be meeting in about three weeks, maybe four. That'll give everyone time to lock down their proposal so it feels real."

"But come by my office tomorrow," Rhonda insisted. "We gotta talk."

Emma hesitated before agreeing. "Okay. And thanks, Rhonda."

As the call wound down, Emma found herself agreeing to meet Rhonda at her office the next day. The weight of the conversation settled around her as she ended the call, the silence in the apartment suddenly oppressive.

She stood, moving to the window. Outside, a pair of pigeons were squabbling over a discarded piece of bread in a petty conflict. The sun dipped lower, casting long shadows across the street below.

Emma's phone buzzed again—a text from James, confirming their dinner plans at Ann Sather's. She typed a quick reply, her fingers hesitating for a moment before hitting send. Ah—cinnamon rolls and comfort food might help. And true, James *said* he wanted the work to come first. But saying something and living the reality of being left behind—

Wait. NO.
God, no.
She was *not* leaving him behind. Not ever.

She needed to talk to him now. She would splurge and take a taxi.

Emma got her heavy winter coat back on, grabbed her tote bag, locked the door behind her, and stepped out into the fading light. The city hummed around her, oblivious to the twists and turns as she tried to think of a way to have her cake and eat it too.

She walked to Lawrence, where she stood a better chance of hailing a taxi. Within minutes, a yellow cab stopped—just as the first stars began to twinkle in the twilight sky.

* * *

Chapter 34

Chicago — Ann Sather's Restaurant — *Feb. 20, 2003 — 7:05 p.m.*
— Dinner Deliberations

The warm glow of Ann Sather's embraced Emma as she stepped through the door, shaking off the evening chill. Her eyes scanned the cozy interior, landing on James, who was already seated in a booth, his face lighting up as he waved her over. He was clearly happy to see her, his love flowing to her as if from a perpetual spring.

What's that poem? "The more I give to thee, the more I have..." That could be James's theme song.

For a fleeting moment, she was transported back to their Cooper Union days, a bittersweet nostalgia washing over her. Maybe he'd always been this way.

As Emma approached, James stood, greeting her with a quick 'fire-us-up' kiss that left her slightly breathless. They slid into opposite sides of the booth, the vinyl seats creaking softly beneath them.

Emma began peeling off her coat, ready to launch into Rhonda's proposal, but James was already talking—his words tumbling out in an unstoppable scrolling roll, like movie credits at the end of a film.

"You won't believe this, Em. I just got a call from Gerardo. He's had some kind of breakthrough with a couple of different ideas and places."

Emma paused, her coat half-off. "Tell, please tell." She urged, while internally conflicted—hoping for a clear choice while simultaneously feeling a twinge of disappointment at the potential loss of the library opportunity.

James leaned forward, his elbows on the table. "Well, here's the thing—he starts telling me idea number one, and I realize, damn, this is good. Gerardo is brilliant, so expect no less. But as he's talking about tunnels or something, I realized I had to stop him."

"No, no, why?" Emma interjected, shrugging off her coat completely. "There's something I need to tell you too—"

James held up his hand, just as their waiter approached with menus and a friendly smile.

"Good evening, folks. Can I start you off with some drinks?"

"Just water for me, thanks," Emma said, her eyes never leaving James's face.

"I'll have a beer. Whatever's on tap," James added.

As the waiter nodded and retreated, James continued, "I don't think I want to hear it, and here's why. I think it would turn this into a kind of competition. If one of us thinks, 'Oh man, that idea is so good,' maybe we stop looking or researching. And then if that 'other' idea falls through, we could be short. Or maybe I would drop the Stupa idea because it's so far-fetched—if something scaled down is closer in reach."

Emma's brow furrowed. "So we all research and work in a vacuum? Couldn't that also mean we get so attached to our own idea, we only vote for our own and become deadlocked in that way?"

James paused, considering. The waiter returned with their drinks, setting them down quietly.

"Are you ready to order, or do you need a few more minutes?"

"Oh, um—" Emma glanced at the menu, suddenly realizing she hadn't even opened it. "Can we have a few more minutes?"

"Of course," the waiter smiled, retreating once more.

James took a sip of his beer before responding. "That's a good point. I hadn't thought of that... you're right, that could happen. Maybe that's the risk we have to take." He thought a moment more and then offered, "Of course, you all can talk amongst yourselves, but for myself, I don't want to know yet. I'm heading into uncharted waters, and I don't want to rock my own boat while this idea is still on a raft and clinging to one good review among thousands."

Emma absently stirred her water with the straw. "So you think... you might change your mind? Try another angle, or space?"

James leaned back, taking a moment to look at the little amber bubbles floating up in his beer stein. "Look at that, Em," he said, pointing. "Kinda fetching..."

They looked at the bubbles, and Emma smiled. "Where's my camera when I need one."

"Yeah..." James agreed. Where she had been half-joking, he was not—and for a moment, she was frightened for him. He was a strong man, very strong—he could carry this whole project on his back without blinking—but the one thing he could not do well was survive personal heartbreak.

She took his hand and waited for that connection between them. When it opened and was flowing, he looked at her and smiled.

"You're worried about me..." James said. He shook his head a bit. "Don't be. This idea, this notion, seeped into my mind like it had a will of its own, and it feels close to that dream I told you about. And when I struggle to get a handle on where this scary idea is heading... I don't know how to say it, but that particular worry seems to fade away. And the world feels more real—or bright—to me. The colors are cleaner... like looking at you now."

His gaze softened as he studied her face. "I see these sparks of amber where the light touches your hair. How did I miss that before?" He wove his fingers with hers and held tight so she could feel it. "I'm not losing it, luv... I think I'm finding it."

Emma looked down, a blush creeping up her cheeks.

"I believe you. And I want to respect your way of doing this—but I feel I should tell you that Rhonda called me. She has a lead."

James shrugged, his attention momentarily caught by the waiter's return.

"Have you had a chance to decide?"

"Oh—yes," Emma said, grateful for the interruption. "I'll have the meatloaf with mashed potatoes, please."

"Excellent choice. And for you, sir?"

James glanced at the menu. "I'll go with the Swedish meatballs. When in Rome, right?" He grinned, handing back the menu.

As the waiter left, James turned back to Emma. "To what end? I want you to do whatever you need to... I mean it. I'll go with the group vote—whatever it is. Now, if you want to work with me on developing the idea of the Stupa, that's different."

They fell into a thoughtful silence, broken only by the clinking of cutlery and the low murmur of conversations around them.

Emma spoke first. "I feel I'd get in the way of your freestyle gymnastic floor exercise or something. Imagine me trying to 'spot' you when I have no idea which way you'll flip next."

They both chuckled at this. She thought for a moment, then added, "I know I'm a problem solver and ask questions—that's me—but dealing with my list of questions consumes energy when you don't have the answers yet. But you *did* get me thinking, and I like the idea of the Stupa being connected to related community activities. I'd like to help you with that—when or if the time comes."

James nodded, a smile playing at his lips. "Done and done. I like that too. But you're right—I have to nail down the logistics first... mind-boggling issues." He paused, studying Emma's face. "Rhonda hooked you with an idea, right?"

Their eyes met, a silent understanding passing between them.

"Maybe..." Emma admitted. "There are a lot of positives about it—and some really downer negatives."

James shrugged, his response interrupted by the arrival of their food. The aroma of home-cooked comfort filled the air as the waiter set down their plates.

"Enjoy your meal," the waiter suggested with a smile before leaving them to their conversation.

James cut into a meatball, steam rising from the plate. "We're in an odd situation. If Alfred hadn't had that episode, we might've left this to him. The tiles belong to Epoch Alliance, but we stepped in to help keep the momentum going. Alfred agreed to a democratic vote, and sometimes democracy is messy—but whatever the group wants... it will float."

Emma took a bite of her meatloaf, savoring the familiar taste as she mulled over James's words. She wasn't at all sure about those rose-colored glasses he was wearing, though. Dream or not.

James watched her face, reading her doubt. He shrugged, spearing another meatball. "We all want the happy ending—the interns, Val and Sam Petosky too. The five of us will make the decision because of that group effort. I don't know what else to say, Em."

As they continued their meal, the weight of unspoken words hung between them. The clink of forks against plates and the gentle hum of the restaurant around them seemed to underscore the complexity of their situation. Emma found herself stealing glances at James, marveling at his optimism even as she grappled with her own doubts—and the knowledge of Rhonda's proposal.

There was one more thing Emma wanted to say, and seeing no opening had been made, she had to carve one herself.

"I... I had a good time during our vacation, James. Thank you," she said softly, and looked at her plate—trying to decide whether to take the last bite of meatloaf or potatoes.

When he didn't respond, she looked up sharply—but his expression was open, soft, and sweet. Once he had her full attention, he asked:

"Do you mean, in general—or were there certain days in particular you found the most... enjoyable?"

Emma flushed and blushed. *Damn,* he knew exactly what she meant. But if he could joke about it, so could she.

"Well, there were certain days—"

"When you say *days,* do you mean *nights*?" he asked, all innocence itself.

She considered his question carefully. "Sometimes days, sometimes nights... sometimes days *and* nights."

"Well, that just confuses me," James looked perplexed. "Because, you know, sometimes a day can be very nice indeed, and then night is good too—but if you really practice, the next day can blow your wheels off—"

Emma put her face in her hands. "Oh my God..." she said and wouldn't look at him.

He took her right hand away from her face, held it for a moment as he looked into her eyes, and then kissed the open palm of her hand. He said quietly, only for her ears:

"Thank you, Em. This is absolutely the wrong place to have this conversation—but I don't want another moment to go by either. I've been walking on pillows for days. I am so happy—never knew it was possible to feel like this. I joke, but... I hope you're happy too."

She nodded, but glanced up only briefly before looking back down.

"'Cuz I can make you happier," James revisited the idea. "Maybe with a little practice. I'm more than willing—"

Now she did laugh. "I was *plenty* happy. In fact, just the sound of your voice saying these things, and your eyes looking at me like that, is making me on the verge of being 'happy' right now."

His eyes widened—then he called for the waiter.

"Check please."

Emma actually smiled. She finally got the last word.
Almost.

* * *

Chapter 35

Chicago — Epoch Alliance Office — *Feb. 12, 2003 — 10:20 a.m. —
Conspiracies and Conundrums*

Rhonda had her favorite writing pen in hand, and she used the tip of it now to tap the top folder away to reveal the blueprint beneath. Her desk was cluttered with photographs and sketches. Emma leaned forward, her brow furrowed in concentration as she scribbled notes, while Rhonda pointed out potential adjustments to the library wall's scale.

The sudden burst of energy that accompanied Gerardo's entrance was like a gust of wind in a still room. He breezed through the open door, his satchel swinging wildly at his side, words already tumbling from his mouth.

"Rhonda, you won't believe what I've—" He stopped short, his eyes landing on Emma. A grin spread across his face. "Em! Delighted. Deee-lighted. I'm going to come tousle your hair because I can't hug you while you're sitting down. Ready?"

Emma braced herself, but instead of the expected tousle, Gerardo gave her a soft pat on the head.

"Enjoy your northern sojourn through the hills and plains?" he asked, his voice taking on a playful British tone.

Emma, picking up on his cue, replied, "Absolutely. The views would knock you silly."

A knowing glance passed between Gerardo and Rhonda—quick, but not quick enough to escape Emma's notice.

"You what! I saw that look," Emma said, eyes narrowing.

Gerardo sighed dramatically. "God, she's beginning to sound like him."

They all laughed, the sound warm and familiar in the small office. But as the laughter faded, Gerardo's expression sobered.

"Seriously—I'm glad you found each other. Or more to the point, that *he's* found you," he said, his voice soft. "I love the guy like my brother... anyway, I'm glad he has you."

Emma studied him closely. "What's going on, Ger?"

Gerardo pulled up a chair, then placed his file folder on Rhonda's desk. He leaned in, his voice dropping to a near-whisper. "Have you guys noticed—even *mentioning* his name brings the big-time cold shoulder?"

Rhonda and Emma exchanged a glance, and Gerardo nodded, reading their silent confirmation as permission to continue. "It's not right or fair, and it's making my blood boil more than a little, but what's really strange to me is that word was circulated so fast—Eco obviously has connections, but that kind of speed speaks to intention... that they had a plan, maybe in the background, but, yeah. Planned. It is just so cold blooded."

The women remained silent as they all considered the chain of events, then Rhonda offered softly "I don't want to talk out of turn either, so maybe we can just agree that it was best we found out now."

Gerardo nodded, then took a breath to continue, "Okay, setting that aside, I've found some options—some pretty good possibilities—that frankly could be made even better with him on board. Maybe we ghost him as a designer, include him, and then in the unveiling say: 'Ha, ha! Fooled you.'"

Emma nodded, her voice dripping with sarcasm. "Oh, that would be special. Gotta get Sam's camera on that golden moment."

"He *did* say to do this for the work," Rhonda reminded them, her fingers absently adjusting the folders on top of her desk.

Gerardo agreed. "He did... anyway, I have some options. James won't even hear my ideas—says he wants the whole picture when it's ready—and I want to bounce off *somebody*, and me best mate won't play with me."

"See?" Emma said, a hint of a smile on her lips. "You pick up his phrases too."

"Like fly paper, though." Gerardo grinned, before opening his file folder with a flourish. "Now, let me present three ideas that might just knock your socks off."

He spread out three sets of drawings on the desk, each one more intriguing than the last.

"First up," Gerardo began, "we have the *Multi-Building Urban Canvas*. Picture this: the mosaic split across multiple buildings throughout Chicago. It's like a city-wide scavenger hunt of art. We could include the Art Institute, other museums—even get some corporate buildings on board."

Rhonda leaned in, her eyes scanning the proposal. "Interesting... it would certainly increase visibility and engagement."

Emma nodded thoughtfully. "It's ambitious. I like how it weaves the art into the fabric of the city."

Gerardo grinned, clearly pleased with their reactions. "Now, for something a bit more... contained. What about an *Underground Art Tunnel?*"

He unveiled the second set of drawings, revealing plans for a transformed underground space. "We take an unused tunnel—maybe an old section of the 'L' or a decommissioned pedestrian walkway—and turn it into an immersive art installation. The mosaic could cover the walls and ceiling, creating a journey through the artwork."

Emma's eyes lit up. "That's... that's actually quite brilliant, Ger. It solves the space issue and creates a unique experience."

Rhonda nodded, but her brow furrowed slightly. "It's certainly creative, but the logistics of working underground... that could be challenging."

"Ah, but wait until you see the *pièce de résistance,*" Gerardo said, his eyes twinkling with excitement. He dramatically revealed the final set of drawings. "I present to you... the *Floating Art Island on Lake Michigan.*"

The room fell silent as Rhonda and Emma leaned in, their eyes wide with a mixture of awe and disbelief.

"Inspired by Christo's *The Floating Piers,*" Gerardo explained, his voice filled with enthusiasm, "we create a temporary floating island on Lake Michigan. The mosaic could be installed on the surface, allowing visitors to literally walk *on* the art."

Emma let out a low whistle. "Now *that's* thinking outside the box. Or should I say, off the shore?"

Rhonda shook her head, but there was a hint of a smile on her face. "It's certainly... unique. But the permits alone..."

As they continued to discuss the merits and challenges of each proposal, the energy in the room was palpable. Ideas bounced back and forth, each one sparking new possibilities and potential solutions.

The morning light shifted, casting new patterns across the desk cluttered with possibilities. As Gerardo launched into a detailed explanation of the floating island's structure, Emma caught Rhonda's eye. They shared a small smile, both thinking the same thing:

This was going to be one hell of a Mod Squad meeting.

* * *

Chapter 36

Wilmette, IL — Worthington Residence — *Feb. 21, 2003 — 12:00 p.m. — Breakfast and Banter*

Alfred was stirring his cup of decaf coffee, mainly from habit. There was no sugar—Mabel had cut that out for the meantime—and he wasn't fond of cream, so that left only the comforting ritual of swirling the coffee with a sterling silver spoon while thinking.

Mabel broke the silence. "James, dear, you look like you haven't been eating properly. Have some more toast. I've made that blackberry jam you're so fond of."

James smiled gratefully, reaching for a slice. "Thanks, Mabel. Your cooking could lure me anywhere, you know that."

Alfred cleared his throat. "Now, James, you know I don't have a glass jaw. What's making me nervous is hearing nothing. We've known each other for a decade and counting. Why don't you tell me about this idea you're percolating?"

James shifted in his seat, his vague answers doing little to satisfy Alfred's curiosity. Finally, Alfred leaned back.

"Well, all right, I'll tell you some of my ideas."

As Alfred began to outline his proposals, James listened intently, his mind racing. The first idea involved transforming a large, abandoned industrial complex on the outskirts of Chicago into a contemporary art space, with the mosaic as its centerpiece. The second suggested creating a new sculpture garden along Chicago's lakefront, with the mosaic as its crowning jewel. The third—perhaps the most ambitious—proposed a floating art barge on the Chicago River, a mobile gallery that could showcase the mosaic at different locations.

When Alfred finished, James asked simply, "And with me on board as lead designer? They'll accept me working on site?"

Alfred paused. "So you're hearing something leak through the mill?"

James shrugged. "I'm guessing, but yes. Em won't look at me when we talk just about it. Or Gerard—they can't hide worth a lick. Probably terrible at Texas Hold 'Em."

Alfred's voice took on a steely tone. "I will never do this project without you. They all want your design. They love it. I'm just an inquiring mind, with no commitment."

"If I'm a deal breaker, you'll have to drop me," James said softly.

Alfred's response was immediate and forceful. "It's not that easy. I can't stand to let them win. It would be admitting to a lie. I simply cannot do it. You will have to save us, my boy. Don't you have an idea by now—something to bail us out and keep our integrity in place? We are the Epoch Alliance, built for time. We don't have the heart or space for small minds and ways and politics—or retaliation either. I believe it would lower the energy of the wall you love, in being debased, dishonored, by agreeing to a kind of subterfuge to achieve an end. Since when do the ends justify the means? Don't think you're doing anyone a favor if you back out."

James nodded slowly. "No, I suppose you're right."

"Damn straight," Mabel interjected. Both men looked at her in tandem—and then chuckled.

Alfred took Mabel's hand. "You don't want to tell me your idea, fine. But please tell me you have one."

James met Alfred's gaze. "I do... but it's mad. So far out of the box, it would redefine—well... public installation of art."

Alfred's eyes lit up. "Then you're right—don't tell me. Don't tell anyone who'll point out the flaws while it's still tender. But find someone you can bounce ideas off of. Someone to test the borders, push the edges of 'what if,' so to speak. Someone who has no stake in the vote. Someone who isn't already invested creatively. People you trust implicitly."

James thought for a moment before answering, "Yes."

Alfred leaned forward. "Because I have to tell you—the others are humming along, and mine are good too. One is very good, and could satisfy most of the parameters. But I have a feeling about you. And Mabel had a dream. And we both would like you to reach for the stars and succeed. I don't mind admitting I would like to, well..."

"Careful..." Mabel warned, a smile playing at her lips.

Alfred grinned. "What I was going to say is dissolve 'the stones and arrows of outrageous fortune'—make something wonderful for the ages."

"But no pressure," James quipped, a hint of his humor coming up for a breath of air.

"None at all," Alfred agreed. "Well, except the clock. We will meet in about two and a half weeks."

James looked at them both, his eyes shining with affection. "I love you lot."

They both nodded, and Mabel said, "Now eat your porridge."

James laughed, and in his best Oliver Twist impression, pleaded, "Please, sir, can I have some more?"

His dear friends laughed, and Alfred chuckled, "I'd save room for course two and three—there are ham steaks and eggs in the warmer."

James smiled.

* * *

As they prepared to part, Mabel pulled James aside.

"You know, James," she said, "I had the strangest dream the other night. I was walking over rolling hills—maybe a prairie—looking for something. I had the feeling I would walk as far as I needed to get there... and as a kind of reward, a path of color rolled up to greet me. It wasn't solid—more like vapor. Strange but wonderful."

James felt a jolt of recognition. The image Mabel described resonated deeply with his Stupa concept—a sideways confirmation that he was on the right path.

"Mabel, that's perfect," he said. "It sounds like what I've been thinking about."

She smiled knowingly. "Does it now? Well, isn't that a lovely coincidence. Don't be afraid to dream big, dear. The world has room—it can take it."

Just as he was going out the door, a flash of color caught and held in the corner of his eye, refusing to let him move another step. He turned and saw a quilt spread out on the couch, a little rumpled as if waiting to be used.

"Wait," he said, moving like water toward the bright geometric forms splashed across the fabric. "Mabel," he asked softly, "is this one of yours?"

She came to stand beside him, but it was Alfred who answered. "It's her new get-well quilt—for me," he said, his voice soft. "Isn't it something?"

James moved around the end of the couch to get a better look at the whole. After a long moment, he said, "It truly is."

Mabel explained, "I took fabric pieces from a lot of old projects—and this is where it gets unique—I took photographs of friends and family, people Alfred has helped, dreams of the future too. Turned them into vector graphics, had them laser printed onto small cloth, then cut them up so you can still see the main image, and wove them together."

"Brilliant. Bloody brilliant," James breathed. "And look here—I recognize a scene from one of my paintings... and other artwork... and those buildings..."

"Yes. All things, places, people Al loves or that have inspired him," Mabel said. "And the pattern itself—it's sacred geometry. I got that idea from watching you, James. I used the Sri Yantra. The lines fit the layout I wanted. And really, the Sri Yantra is a kind of diamond-shaped quilt already, so it wasn't too hard to make the adjustments."

"It works," Alfred said simply. "I'm feeling great. You have to love my Mabel."

James nodded. "I do."

"Has this given you an idea, son?" Alfred asked.

James paused. "Not so much given me an idea... as provided the answer to a possible problem. Ta. Can I take a photo?"

"Of course," Mabel said. "I'd let you take the quilt, but Alfred is still using it."

James was already laying the quilt out on the floor to get a good view.

"Oh no, the photo will do well... very well."

Without saying another word, he kissed Mabel absently on the side of her head, patted Alfred's forearm, and called over his shoulder as an afterthought:

"I'm going to be out of touch for a few days—maybe more—but if you need me, don't hesitate. Call my cell. I'll have it on me."

"Sounds good," Alfred replied, as they both watched James leave, a man clearly in a world of his own.

After the door clicked shut, Alfred turned to Mabel and said, "Sounds very good."

* * *

The late morning sun glinted off the sleek curves of James's new 2003 Prius as he approached it, keys jingling in his hand. He paused for a moment, admiring the vehicle's understated elegance and aerodynamic lines. With a gentle pat on the hood, as if greeting an old friend, he murmured, "Ready for another adventure, are we?"

Just as he reached for the door handle, the shrill ring of his cell phone cut through the quiet street. Fishing it from his pocket, James glanced at the screen—and smiled. Recognizing the number, he leaned casually against the car.

"Dang if I wasn't just thinking of you lot," he said warmly. "How is Maribel? And the girls? And the new one, of course—William?"

As he listened, the smile deepened, his free hand absently tracing patterns on the Prius's smooth surface. The world around him dimmed, eclipsed by the familiar comfort of the voice on the other end.

Then, a slight shift—hesitation flickered across his features. "Say, are you both free for a couple of hours straight? Maybe during nap time, when the kids are on leave? I really need to bounce something off you both."

A pause. Then relief washed across his face.

"Ta, ta... Theo. Yes. Sunday lunch is perfect. Twelve, twelve-thirty. See you the day after tomorrow—and thanks."

As he ended the call, James looked up at the sky, a mix of hope and trepidation tightening his brow. "Hope you know what you're doing," he murmured, as if addressing God directly.

The gentle hum of the Prius's engine coming to life seemed to underscore the moment—a quiet affirmation of forward motion, of progress, even if the destination remained unknown.

The call with Ted had sparked something—something vital. Ted and Maribel were two of the few people who truly knew him, untangled from the current project's web of tension and diplomacy. Their clarity could be a lighthouse. And they would tell him the truth.

He'd already put Val to work, researching and printing the images and specs he'd need—she was sorting through the stacks now, categorizing the data so he could take it in at speed. Between the two of them, they could cover almost every angle. But Ted and Maribel? They'd raise the questions he wouldn't think to ask. The ones that mattered.

The Prius hummed along, its eco-friendly engine a quiet reminder of the balance James was trying to strike in his own work—between innovation and tradition, vision and grounding.

Saturday couldn't come soon enough.

Lunch with Ted and Maribel might be the spark that turned his wild, impossible idea into something tangible. Maybe even something world-changing. With a long breath and a silent prayer, James pressed forward, the city blurring past as he drove into the unfolding unknown.

* * *

Chicago – Lincoln Square – Val's Apartment – *Feb. 21, 2003 – 2:00 p.m.*

Val O'Rourke was loving this thing called the internet—L.U.V.—luving it. Of course, when James had detailed to her what, in essence, his concept was for the new installation for the mosaic wall, Val had listened closely, nodding her head in the appropriate places and absolutely left any personal thoughts and questions that might have spontaneously exploded into her skull in a small box in the corner of her mind that read: open only if going down the drain.

In brief, she was a scientist at heart and a professional to boot, and so she had done what any solid researcher with a deadline and a caffeine drip would do—she had headed to the Harold Washington Library and checked out a stack of actual books on sacred geometry, Stupas, early Buddhist temples, and ley lines of the Earth. Even a book about ancient hilltop temples in the Andes, just to cast the net wide. That part was fun. But not nearly as fun as listening to the patient whir of the HP tower as it dialed in—chirrrp, chkkk, shhhoooonnk—and navigating the magic that was this upstart engine called Google.

Yes, Google. That clean little bar at the top of the Netscape window, the one that actually brought you results without also throwing in a half-dozen pop-up ads for herbal Viagra or bootleg CDs.

God, she loved it. You just typed in, hit enter, and waited for the flowers to bloom. And bloom they did—thumbnails, PDF abstracts, grainy photos, even a Yahoo message board where a retired architect from New Mexico was debating the acoustics of Stupa domes with a infra red light healing practitioner in Sedona. It was glorious.

She was still slightly suspicious of it—this new start-up from California, all lowercase letters and cheery confidence—but every time she hit return and the screen responded from its fathoms-deep reservoir, she felt like she'd wandered into a reference librarian's utopia.

This morning alone she'd tracked down photographs of Sanchi, Borobudur, and Swayambhunath, compared them to diagrams of geodesic domes and aerials of crop circle formations, then cross-referenced them all against regional seismic charts and architectural case studies from the University of Tokyo.

Val clicked open another link and reached for her tea, only half aware of the snow still gently falling outside her window. She was already knee-deep in blueprints and sacred ratios, her mind leaping ahead to put herself in James's shoes... to imagine how he might try to pull this off...

...Crazy as all get out—oops, judgy thought just leaked through—but the process was glorious.

She was just about to print a comparison diagram of hemispheric domes when a sharp knock at the door made her jump. She frowned and glanced at the time. Two-oh-two.

James, probably. In full regalia, no doubt. Maybe even a backup band. He had that kind of timing when ideas were percolating—she wouldn't be surprised if he came in mid-sentence, already pitching a totally different idea, scrap it—we're going to Mars—the big tweak, as if she hadn't been elbows-deep in ancient temple specs for the past five hours.

Val stood and smoothed her oversized sweater, brushing muffin crumbs from the hem, and padded barefoot to the door. She opened it—

And froze.

Not James.

Sam.

Standing there in her hallway, backlit by the muted glow of the afternoon, was Sam.

"Sam?" she said, blinking as her professional composure scrambled to catch up. Her fingers gripped the edge of the door, inching subconsciously toward the deadbolt—her thoughts stuttering.

Crates of crap—didn't see that coming.

He looked like he'd rehearsed being there but hadn't expected the scene to begin quite so soon. He was wearing a wool cap pulled down low, which only seemed to emphasize his eyes—which were looking right at her. And the strangest thing was the look on his face—not casual, not cocky, not even especially nervous—but something direct... present, almost confrontational. He was also carrying a small ziplock plastic bag. Whatever was in it was safe from the elements.

Val blinked. "Sam?"

Her voice came out more puzzled than guarded. She reached for the inside latch on instinct but didn't fully open the door.

"Seems only fair I show up at your door," Sam said, offering a careful, maybe-too-light smile. "Just to even things up."

For a moment, they stood frozen in tableau, the absurdity of the situation hanging between them. Then, almost against her will, Val felt the corner of her mouth twitch upward. It wasn't quite a laugh, but it was something.

"Fair and square," she agreed, stepping back slightly to allow him past the doorway and into the small living room. "Did you need something?" She crossed her arms—more to steady herself than anything else.

Sam held out the small bag. "I came to return these. The thumb drives. All seven of them." He paused, then added with a hint of humor, "I counted twice, just to be sure."

Val accepted the bag, careful not to let their fingers brush. "Thanks," she said, her voice neutral. "I don't really have time right now for anything else. James is in the middle of something big, and I'm helping him with research."

Sam's eyes drifted past Val to her desk, curiosity getting the better of him. His gaze landed on her computer screen, where images of ancient round structures—mounds, but clearly man-made—were displayed. Beside them were pictures of modern monolithic domes, and there...

"Is that... a Stupa?" he asked, recognition dawning on his face.

Val tensed, quickly moving to block his view. "It's just research," she said evasively.

Turning back to Val, Sam nodded, his eyes searching her face. "Val," he said softly, "I had a conversation with Olivia. We're... not going to see each other anymore."

Val felt her heart skip a beat but kept her expression carefully blank. The computer humming on the desk seemed suddenly loud in the silence.

"I hope you didn't do that on my account. We hardly know each other."

He looked at her in a contemplative way, surprised by her observation, his brows drawn together as if considering whether to challenge that—and instead, decided on a different track.

Sam took a deep breath, as if steeling himself. "I'm only going to cover this once, and you'll never hear me mention it again," he began, his voice low and serious. "When I was a kid, maybe about eight years old, I thought up all kinds of ways to break my nose. Thank God my brother stopped me, wrestled me to the ground, and took the hammer away."

Val's eyes widened, her posture stiffening. "Why... why would you do that?"

Sam's gaze grew distant. "When a child—a boy—looks a certain way, it's like a magnet for creeps. Perverts come out of the closet at him. At me." His voice grew harder. "You would simply not believe, Val, how many of them there are in the world—in schools, clubs, sports, whatever, wherever."

Val listened intently, her earlier wariness replaced by a mix of concern and questions. "That must have been terrifying," she said softly.

Sam nodded. "Okay if I sit down?"

Val nodded and gestured toward the vintage green couch. Sam took a breath and sat down. After a moment, he continued. "Luckily, I was tall for my age and strong—able to run or hit—and never be trapped in any situation. But I thought if I broke my nose, I would look different and it would all stop."

He paused, swallowing hard. "My brother told on me, of course. My mom and dad didn't freak out too much. Instead, my dad took action. There was nothing to do really about contacting the police or the school—I hadn't actually been assaulted. So my dad taught me and my brother to box. To street fight. My mom sent me to martial arts—Aikido, to be precise."

Val leaned against the doorframe, her body language softening. "That was smart of your parents."

"Yeah," Sam agreed. "And my dad said something I'll never forget. He told me, 'Don't you ever, ever try to hurt yourself. People like those perverts go after boys who can't defend themselves, and hurting yourself is breaking your own spirit. Then you become a target. You're strong—they go after you regardless because of how you look, but you fight back. You do whatever you need to fight back, and everyone will know to leave you alone.'"

Val listened carefully, her voice gentle as she stepped forward to ask, "Why are you telling me this?"

Sam ran a hand through his hair, looking slightly lost. "I'm not quite sure. I just started talking and this came out. I think I'd like you to understand Olivia and me. See, some children—some little girls—aren't in a position to fight back. Olivia never told me specifically, but she's hinted, and her behavior isn't always normal. What I'm saying is, I was always suspicious of anyone who wanted to be near me. Olivia was the same. The only people I felt completely myself with, I can count on one hand. One was Olivia—we trusted each other, and sometimes she's so lonely she comes back, and I can't bear to turn her away."

He took a deep breath before continuing. "Anyway, you overheard something, so I'm telling you all this to kind of maybe... help you think of us as people trying to work out some ancient crap—and friendship too—and not become monsters in your mind haunting you. That things... people aren't always as they look on the surface. Sorry, but I hope it helps."

Val was quiet for a moment, processing everything she'd heard. Finally, she spoke, her voice soft but steady. "That's a lot to tell me, Sam. I'll keep it quiet, but... we hardly know each other."

He couldn't let it slide a second time. His eyebrows rose slightly. "Don't we?"

The question hung in the air between them, heavy with unspoken possibilities. Val swallowed hard, her throat suddenly dry. "I suppose... we know each other a little," she conceded. Then, after a moment's hesitation, she asked, "Can I ask you something?"

He nodded, his expression open. "Of course."

Val moved from her position in the doorframe to stand next to the easy chair adjacent to the couch so she could watch his face more closely.

Val's voice was barely above a whisper. "Do you feel bad or repulsed when... anyone touches you?"

Sam's eyes widened slightly, then softened with understanding. "No, no," he assured her quickly. "No, I've got great radar, and I love being with people. I learned to recognize vampire types long ago and stay away. No, I didn't say all that for sympathy. Every single person alive has something going on. I'm not shaking in my boots—that's life, for some reason—but there was no small way to explain me and Olivia, and so I had to tell the bigger picture. So, all that to say, I'm good."

Val nodded, relief washing over her face. "I'm glad," she said simply.

She stood behind her stuffed chair as he sat before her in silence for a moment, the air thick with the long list of things still left unsaid. Way too long for today. A neighbor's door slammed somewhere down the hall, making them both look toward the door.

Finally, because she couldn't think of what else to say, Val nodded and cleared her throat. "I should get back to work. Either Emma or I will be in touch when there's an update."

Sam took the obvious hint and rose from the couch to leave. He was at the door within seconds—it was a small apartment.

But as Val moved to close the door behind him, Sam spoke up. "Val? When there's news... could you be the one to call?"

Val paused, her hand on the doorknob. She met his gaze, seeing a glimmer of hope.

"We'll see," she said softly. "Maybe."

As the door closed, Val leaned against it, letting out a long breath. She looked down at the bag of thumb drives still in her hands, her expression a mix of wariness and something softer—something like: I wonder.

I wonder what I would have done if I was him... or her, for that matter.

"Well, that was unexpected," she murmured to herself, shaking her head with a wry smile.

She pushed off from the door, heading back to her desk where stacks of research materials awaited. James was under pressure—oh boy, was he. Her mind trembled for him sometimes, and this was one of those times. It wasn't often it seemed her boss was over his head, but still, it was wonderfully audacious—a Stupa to house the mosaic wall. Who in the world comes up with an idea like that?

Her boss, that's who.

Lots to do. She was already getting images from the other members of the mod squad and Alfred to turn into slides for the big showdown. So she had her poker face on, and no one would see or hear her opinion. She was the stage manager now and all about getting it done for everyone.

But boy, she sure hoped James wasn't going to fall on his face. There was a first time for everything, and she sure hoped this wasn't his "bridge too far."

She turned to look over her shoulder to call to Sam to come see the image of Swayambhunath Stupa—"Oooh. It's a good one..."—and stopped.

She looked around the empty room, her heart beating fast. Of course he was gone, but she had the feeling of him still in the room, the gentle impression of his tender heart still here with her.

And she knew then, deep in the core of herself, that she was in trouble. Big trouble. She really cared about him. She could feel it as a permanent resident in the core of herself, flowing effortlessly into the world as a steady stream, looking for him.

It changed nothing at all. They were from two completely different mindsets and worldviews. She liked who she was. She didn't want to be like other people. She didn't want to be changed. She did not want to be like Olivia—ever.

So where did that leave them, really?

Maybe she'd been daydreaming about him all along. And what was that line from some old film? "A bird can love a fish, but where would they live together?"

She couldn't think about it. She had work to do.

* * *

Chapter 37

Evanston, IL – Thomason Residence – *Feb. 23, 2003 – 12:00 p.m. – The Pitch*

It was high noon when James Watson came to call upon the noble Thomason estate—the highly esteemed Maribel and Ted, and new baby William. He arrived a little early so he could look at the new baby before he took his nap, to coo a bit and marvel at how he'd grown since he'd seen him brand new. Once down for his nap—which, for a baby, was pretty often—they tread carefully, softly, to the living room to relax and ready themselves for the pitch.

James would be pitching in this afternoon's sport, and Maribel and Ted would be catching.

The afternoon sun illuminated the cozy Evanston home, setting the stage for this romp. Ted lounged on the couch, one arm draped around Maribel, both watching with keen interest as James rummaged through his satchel. The rustle of papers and soft clink of metal clasps filled the air.

Finally, Ted broke the silence. "Okay, I'm not going to ask why you haven't brought Em—"

"I will," Maribel interjected, her eyes twinkling. "Where's our Em?"

James paused, his hand halfway out of the satchel. He ran his fingers through his hair. "She's hard at work on her own proposals," he explained, his voice tinged with a mixture of pride and guilt. "You know how things stand with the installation. We've got the mod squad meeting in less than two weeks, and I'd like her to stay focused. It's just... I was afraid..."

"That she'd give up time for her own ideas for you," Maribel finished for him, her voice soft with understanding.

"Something like that, yeah," James admitted, pulling out several folders and laying them on the coffee table. "Plus, she's bloody sharp, our Em. She'd spot the flaws in this mad idea before I could even finish explaining it." He chuckled, as he laid some photos face down on the coffee table. "And let's face it—she's got her own stake in this decision. Didn't feel right asking her to split herself in two. You both are neutral."

"Well, at least he didn't say 'neutered,'" Ted quipped, looking at his wife.

James laughed, some of the tension visibly easing from his shoulders. "I don't think anyone's gonna think that," he said, nodding toward the toys scattered across the floor.

Maribel leaned forward, her eyes bright with anticipation. The fading sunlight caught some of the silver strands in her dark hair, reminding James how long they'd all known each other.

"Alright, fly-boy," she said, using the old nickname from their college days. "The floor is yours. Give it to us."

James handed them each two folders, thick with papers. Ted whistled low as he took his. "Ooh, posh," he remarked, earning another gentle nudge from Maribel.

Taking a deep breath, James began. "Friends, what I'm about to propose might seem, at first glance, completely mad. But I ask you to hear me out—to imagine with me, if you will, a future where art transcends its traditional boundaries and becomes... a spiritual conduit."

Pause. That got their attention.

The room fell silent, save for the distant laughter of children playing outside. Ted and Maribel exchanged a glance, their expressions a mix of curiosity and concern. Whatever they had been expecting, this clearly wasn't it.

James began slowly, gathering his thoughts. "It's what every artist dreams of, but doesn't actually achieve. And why? Because we sign our art—we stamp our ego right on it. So subtly, eventually, the focus shifts from the art to the artist."

Ted leaned forward, his brow furrowed. "Alright, James. You've got our attention. Where are you going with this?"

James smiled, a spark of excitement lighting his eyes. "Bear with me. It all started when Em and I were in Wisconsin..."

As James launched into his explanation, Ted and Maribel settled in, ready to hear about the mad idea that had their old friend so fired up. Whatever it was, they knew it was going to be quite a ride.

"When Em and I were in Wisconsin, we visited ancient mounds—incredible earthworks that have stood for centuries—and it was clear to both of us that these mounds were resonant, held a tone, and were beautiful too. It was also unclear which ancient people built them or why. And of course, it's important—but it didn't really matter. Their ability to connect us to our past while still resonating in the present, as the rounded shape that harmonizes with the earth—that was their job, and they're still doing it."

Ted nodded, his expression thoughtful. "I've heard about those mounds. Never seen them myself, though."

"They're quite something," James affirmed. "You'll see in your folders—images of mounds, rounded earth domes. And pay attention to the igloo—a round form built for arctic conditions that high winds can whip around. It's man-made but flows in harmony with the earth. Harsh weather gives it a pass. That's the very nature and function of the sacred geometry of the circle... and so, as a natural extension and progression, the circle becomes the Stupa."

Maribel leaned forward, her eyes scanning the images in the folder. "These structures are fascinating, James. I can see why they captured your imagination."

James paused, allowing Ted and Maribel time to review the photocopies. Once he had their full attention again, he turned to face them fully.

"A Stupa, in its essence, is a sacred structure—a focal point for meditation and spiritual connection. The prana, or life force, that flows through the earth harmonizes, joins with the circle, and flows up through it. And if the interior holds the blessed relics of a master teacher, the resonance is amplified and broadcast—to sing in nature, into the very atomic structure of the cosmos. That's the science of osmosis. That's how blessing in sacred geometry works."

Ted's eyebrows raised, clearly intrigued. "That's quite a concept. How did you come across this idea of Stupas?"

"It's been a journey of discovery," James replied, his voice steady and confident. "The more I researched these ancient structures, the more I realized their potential for our project. The more I could feel it myself."

Maribel nodded, her expression thoughtful. "I can see why you're excited about this. It's a beautiful fusion of art, spirituality, and science. But how do you envision applying this to the mosaic project?"

"So, what if we could utilize this time-tested technology for our time and place? What if we could create a structure that houses not just relics, but the very essence of our community's hopes, dreams, and creativity?"

Ted leaned forward, his brow furrowed. "So you're talking about building a... modern Stupa?"

James nodded. "I am. Imagine a structure, circular in form, rising from the landscape like a beacon. Its exterior would be a work of art in itself—and inside? Ah, inside is where the good magic happens."

He gestured expansively. "The interior walls would house our mosaic. But not as a static installation. No, the mosaic would flow, telling a story as you move through the space. It would be a journey—a pilgrimage of sorts—through the heart of our community's collective imagination. We would use the same design for the eco building, but expanded even further."

Maribel tilted her head, considering. "I admit I'm a little in shock, still taking it in. But James... why a Stupa? Why not just a modern art gallery? Wouldn't that be simpler?"

James's eyes lit up at the question, as if he'd been waiting for someone to ask. He knelt down in front of Maribel, his voice passionate and earnest.

"Because a Stupa is more than just a building, Maribel. And more than a symbol or tradition—it's a literal bridge between earth and sky, between the mundane and the sacred. In a world that's increasingly fragmented, disconnected, we need spaces that not only remind us of our shared humanity, our connection to something greater than ourselves—but that actually *are* that living connection. Because we all need to feel that connection in a way that is real. There are people who think that God doesn't even exist. How in the world does that happen?"

Ted nodded slowly, his skepticism giving way to intrigue. "So what you're saying is... we desperately need these sites based on sacred geometry to help us feel our way back to God?"

James continued, his voice growing passionate. "And with that kind of connection, think about the form—circular, with no beginning and no end. It's the cyclical nature of life, of art, of community. As you walk through, you're not just observing art—you're participating in it, becoming part of the story. You're engaging with the divine in a way that's both ancient and utterly modern."

Ted leaned back, rubbing his chin thoughtfully. "I can see the appeal. I really can. But James, the logistics of this... it's not exactly a small undertaking. We're talking about a massive construction project, not to mention the challenges of maintenance, accessibility..."

James grinned. "Ah, but that's where it gets even more interesting. You see, I'm not proposing we build this in the city. No—I'm thinking bigger. And paradoxically, smaller."

He pulled out a map from one of the folders, spreading it out on the coffee table. Ted and Maribel leaned in, their curiosity piqued. James's finger traced a path to a spot marked with a red X.

"Imagine this structure set in nature. Perhaps on a hilltop overlooking the prairie. A destination, yes—but also a retreat. A place where the journey to get there is part of the experience."

Maribel's eyes widened as understanding dawned. "You're talking about creating a pilgrimage site," she breathed, her voice filled with awe.

"Exactly!" James exclaimed. "This would be a pilgrimage for the soul of our times—a journey to reconnect with nature, with prayer, with ourselves."

He paused, letting the idea sink in. "Think about it—in a world where everything is instant, accessible at the touch of a button, there's something powerful about creating a space that requires effort to reach. That demands presence and engagement. That delivers a profound connection to something greater than ourselves—not of the mind, but something we can feel."

Ted and Maribel exchanged a look, both clearly overwhelmed by the scope of James's vision. But there was also a spark of excitement in their eyes—a growing realization of the potential impact of such a project.

"It's ambitious," Ted said slowly. "Maybe even crazy. But I've got to admit, James, it's also... inspiring."

Maribel nodded in agreement. "It's like you're proposing to build a cathedral for the modern age," she mused. "A place where art, spirituality, and community can all come together."

James smiled, grateful for their understanding. "That's exactly it," he said softly. "A cathedral for our times—built not just of stone and clay, but of dreams and hopes and the collective spirit of humanity."

Ted leaned back, a thoughtful expression on his face. His fingers drummed a gentle rhythm on the arm of the couch as he processed James's ambitious proposal. "It's wild, but I've got to admit—it's compelling. How do you see this fitting with this particular project—the community engagement aspect?"

James nodded, having anticipated the question. He stood up with renewed energy. "That's the beauty of it, Ted. The community engagement doesn't end with the creation of the tiles. It becomes an ongoing process." His eyes lit up as he continued, gesturing passionately. "Imagine workshops held on-site, artists-in-residence programs, school trips that combine art education with nature experiences."

He paused, turning to face his friends. "Picture this: a group of schoolchildren, eyes wide with wonder, creating art inspired by the natural surroundings and the energy of the Stupa. It's not just about observing art anymore—it's about immersing themselves in the creative process."

James gestured to the folders spread out on the coffee table. "I've outlined some ideas for how we could make this a living, breathing space—one that evolves with the community, that continues to tell new stories even as it honors the old."

Maribel leaned forward, her curiosity piqued. She flipped through the papers, her expression a mix of awe and concern. Her eyes widened as she took in the scope of James's vision. "James, this is... it's breathtaking. But the scale of it, the cost..." She trailed off, her voice a mixture of excitement and apprehension.

James held up a hand, his voice gentle but firm. "I know. I know—it's not small. But think about the impact." He knelt again in front of Maribel, meeting her gaze. "Maribel, Ted—this wouldn't just be a one-time installation. It would be a legacy. Something that could inspire generations to come."

He took a deep breath, feeling the weight of his next words. "I believe this is what art needs to be in our time. Not just something we observe, but something we experience—something that changes us." James's voice grew more passionate as he continued. "This Stupa could be a catalyst for change. A reminder of our shared humanity in a world that so often seems bent on division."

His gaze drifted to the window where the sun was dipping lower in the sky, painting it pink, yellow, blue in vibrant hues. When he spoke again, his voice was softer, more introspective.

"And as for the unanswered question—why a Stupa for this particular project? The answer is personal, so I'm not sure if I can use it in a presentation. But I'll tell you both: I believe—no, I *know*—that all the good wishes, hopes, and prayers in those tiles that both Emma and I handled every day for months—thousands of them—saved us."

Ted and Maribel exchanged a glance, sensing the depth of emotion in James's words. He continued, his voice thick with feeling.

"Those prayers, that support, that faith in love gave us both the courage to forgive and let go—and to be what we already were: a man and a woman who love each other more than we were attached to pride."

After a moment of reflective silence, James added, "We both would feel shivers—pleasant currents of energy running up our arms. Sometimes she would call me over to look at one particular tile, sometimes I would call her. And these are just from ordinary people with ordinary hope—but hope is a powerful connection to God. And four thousand powerful prayers deserve a sacred space to house them... and hopefully amplify them, through the sacred form of the Stupa, to share with the world."

The room fell silent as Ted and Maribel absorbed the enormity of James's vision. Outside, the sun had begun to set, painting the sky in hues of orange and pink, as if nature itself were offering a canvas for their imagination.

Finally, Ted spoke, his voice quiet but firm. "It's mad, James. Absolutely bonkers." He paused, a slow smile spreading across his face. "And I think it's brilliant."

Maribel nodded, reaching for James's hand. Her eyes shimmered with unshed tears. "It's a beautiful dream, James. But how do we make it real?"

James squeezed her hand, feeling a surge of gratitude for his friends' open-heartedness.

"That, my dear Maribel, is where I need your help. We've got the vision. Now we need to figure out how to bring it down to earth—without losing its power to lift us up."

* * *

The living room of Ted and Maribel's Evanston home had transformed into a war room of creativity. Papers littered the floor, a sea of ideas and sketches that lapped at the edges of the furniture. The mantelpiece—usually adorned with family photos and knick-knacks—now served as a gallery of architectural wonders. Photos of stupas from around the world jostled for space with images of igloos and contemporary monolithic domes, a visual testament to the universality of the circular form.

James stood in the center of this chaos, his eyes alight with the fervor of inspiration. The setting sun cast long shadows across the room, lending an almost mystical quality to the scene. Ted and Maribel sat on the couch, leaning forward, completely engrossed in James's vision.

"How do you see the stupa being built?" Ted leaned forward, his voice soft but intent. "You hinted that the stupa would be built differently—not with poured concrete, not like the monolithic dome."

James nodded, grateful for the prompt. He took a deep breath, steeling himself for what he was about to propose. "The sprayed concrete for the monolithic domes is a brand-new technology and would work in a matter of days, and last for hundreds of years as well—and carry the sacred vibration. Put that as a safety thought on the back burner."

Maribel's eyes widened, a spark of excitement flickering in their depths. "Oooh, that part is good," she interjected, leaning forward. "Remember to use that part. It's a perfect blend of modern technology and ancient wisdom."

James paused, considering his next words carefully. "In the ideal, perfect world of the future," he said, his voice taking on a lighter quality, "I would love to learn and emulate how the stupas were made in the ancient way—without concrete at all, with close-fitting brick. That is truly a dream at the moment, so the sprayed concrete would be the most economical and long-lasting."

Ted's eyes lit up, a grin spreading across his face. "We want in," he said simply, his voice filled with determination. "I want in with that. I would love to learn how to do that too—all of that. I'm feeling... I've got this feeling that if you, me, and your friend Gerardo—and Emma too, and Maribel—well, all of us really, we could do that."

He paused, his expression growing more serious. "I want in. Can't give up me job—got the family and all—but whatever you need—"

"We're in," Maribel echoed, her hand finding Ted's and squeezing it tightly. Her eyes shone with a mixture of excitement and trepidation. "It's scary, but... it feels so right, doesn't it? Hard to explain. Like we're meant to be part of this."

"We're in," Maribel echoed again, just in case James hadn't heard them the first three times, her hand finding Ted's and squeezing it tightly.

"Thank you," James said, his voice rough with emotion.

He moved to the window to check the darkening sky. The first stars were beginning to appear—tiny pinpricks of light in the deepening blue. "You know, when I first had this idea, I thought I was going mad. But standing here now, with you both..." He turned back to them, a wry smile on his face. "I feel like we're all going mad together. Sorry—had to slip some levity in."

They laughed. Then Maribel stood, moving to stand beside James. She placed a gentle hand on his arm.

"It is extraordinary," she said softly, her voice filled with wonder. "And of course, terrifying. But isn't that what all great endeavors are? A little bit of madness, a lot of courage, and a whole lot of faith."

Ted joined them, clapping a hand on James's shoulder. His touch was warm, reassuring. "So, what's next, mate? Where do we go from here?" he asked, his voice brimming with anticipation.

James turned to face his friends, a smile spreading across his face. "Next, we plan. We figure out every detail, every challenge, every possibility, prepare for every potential problem—and see if the group will go for it."

"To the future," Ted said, raising an imaginary glass.

"To the past," Maribel added.

"To the eternal present," James finished. "Where all things are possible."

* * *

The house hummed with the quiet energy of a family winding down for the night. From the kitchen came the soft clatter of plates and the murmur of Ted's voice as he prepared a snack for the girls. The scent of chamomile tea wafted through the air, a soothing counterpoint to the electric excitement that still buzzed in James's veins.

Maribel stood at the door with James, her eyes soft with understanding and a hint of something more—a mixture of concern and encouragement that only a true friend could convey. The porch light cast a warm glow on her face, highlighting the slight furrow of her brow.

"The baby will be awake soon..." she began, her voice trailing off meaningfully.

James, his hand on the doorknob, nodded quickly. "Oh, I'm heading out..."

Maribel shook her head, her words coming faster now, as if racing against time. "No, what I mean is—I'll hafta say this fast. I know you love Em, it's clear as clear as clear, so you gotta tell her, James. Tell her now... or she may just blast you if you don't."

James sighed, his shoulders sagging slightly under the weight of unspoken words. "She is so good, Bel, so brilliant. I gotta let that breathe and grow. I have my reasons—I don't want her feeling like she's disappearing, or less than me, or anything like that. I can't hurt her."

Maribel's eyes flashed with a mixture of exasperation and affection. "'Cept she gets a choice too. She's brilliant—then bring her on. She will expand this, root it into nuts-and-bolts reality. It's what she's good at. It's time. You're ready. The idea, your designs—they're solid. Nothing small is going to blow them away. Now it's time to get real. You saw the effect on us. We went from... hmmm, great idea but... to true believers."

James met her gaze, the truth of her words sinking in. "You're right," he said softly. "I will."

A smile of relief spread across Maribel's face. "Good," she said, then called out over her shoulder, "Ted! James is leaving."

Ted appeared in the archway between the living and dining room, a dish towel slung over his shoulder. The warm light from the kitchen silhouetted him, giving him a glowing outline.

"You drive carefully," he said, his voice gruff with affection. "There's still weather kicking up a fuss."

James nodded, suddenly aware of the wind whistling outside. "See you later," he said. "I'll be in touch."

As he stepped out into the night, the cool air nipped at his cheeks, a stark contrast to the warmth he was leaving behind. The trees lining the street swayed in the wind, their leaves whispering secrets to the darkness. James paused for a moment, looking back at the house. Through the window, he could see Ted and Maribel, their heads close together—no doubt discussing the day's revelations.

The streetlights flickered on, one by one, as James wiped the light layer of snow from the driver's side window and got into his car to have a good think.

* * *

Chapter 38

Chicago – Lake Shore Drive — *Feb. 23, 2003 — 6:30 p.m. – Texting Then Driving*

The Prius hummed to life, its electric motor a gentle whisper in the snowy Chicago evening. James sat in the driver's seat, the warmth of Ted and Maribel's home still clinging to him like a comfortable sweater. He gazed out at the snow-dusted street, the streetlights casting a soft glow on the white-blanketed world outside.

His fingers, slightly chilled from the brief walk to the car, hovered over his phone. A bemused smile played on his lips as he composed the text to Emma: "Ok, if you show me yours, I'll show you mine."

As he hit send, James noticed a small crack in the corner of his phone screen. It reminded him of the first time he'd dropped it—right after Emma had returned to his life. A good omen, perhaps?

The car began to warm up, its dashboard lights casting a soft blue glow across James's face. He drummed his fingers on the steering wheel, an old habit from his days of driving beat-up vans to art shows.

A soft 'brrr' broke the silence.

"Well, that got her attention," James chuckled, reaching for his phone in the cup holder. The holder rattled slightly—he'd need to fix that soon.

Emma's response glowed on the screen: "What? :)"

James couldn't help but grin. He could almost hear her voice—that mix of surprise and amusement that was so uniquely Emma. His thumbs danced across the keys: "got your attention, let's update project status, if you want :)"

As he waited for her reply, James noticed a small thread hanging from his sleeve. He absently twirled it around his finger, thinking of the intricate patterns Emma could weave with just her hands and a lump of clay.

The phone buzzed again. Five smiley faces, an exclamation mark, and a single word: "Where?"

James felt a warmth spread through his chest that had nothing to do with the car's heating system. He typed back: "You still at university? I'll get you and go for a drive down Lake Shore Drive."

Her response was immediate and enthusiastic: "YES! I'll be out front."

James smiled, slipping the phone back into the cup holder. He put the Prius in gear, careful as he pulled out onto the snow-covered street. The tires crunched softly on the fresh powder, leaving twin tracks behind them.

As he navigated the quiet streets toward the university, James's mind wandered to Emma. He pictured her wrapping up her guest lecture, her eyes bright with passion as she shared her knowledge with Gerardo's students. He'd always loved watching her teach—the way she could make the most complex concepts accessible, the gentle patience she had for even the most struggling student.

The city passed by in a blur of twinkling lights and snow-capped buildings. James found himself looking forward to their drive along Lake Shore Drive. There was something magical about the city at night, especially in the snow. And with Emma by his side... well, that was a different kind of magic altogether.

As he approached the university, James felt a flutter of anticipation in his stomach. It was silly, really—they'd been working together for months now. But somehow, this felt different. More personal. More like... a date?

Well, they were beyond dating now, right?

They were so backwards.

He shook his head, chuckling at his own thoughts. But as he pulled up to the front of the building, seeing Emma's figure emerge from the doors, bundled up against the cold, that flutter returned in full force.

James reached across to open the passenger door, a grin spreading across his face. "Hello, Professor," he teased as Emma slid into the seat beside him. "Ready for that project update?"

Emma's cheeks were pink from the cold, snowflakes melting in her hair. She returned his grin, her eyes sparkling with a mixture of excitement and something else... something James couldn't quite name, but that made his heart skip a beat.

"Lead the way, Mr. Watson," she replied, settling into her seat. "I believe you have something to show me?"

"I do indeed. Let's get on the drive—maybe go to Montrose Harbor?"

"You just want a reason to keep driving your car," Emma observed.

"Well... yeah," James replied. "Notice I didn't say 'double duh.'"

She laughed, and once the traffic on Michigan Ave was clear, James pulled away from the curb, the Prius's tires leaving fresh tracks on the newly fallen snow.

* * *

The Prius sat like a warm cocoon against the frigid Chicago night, its windows slowly fogging from James and Emma's shared breaths. Outside, Lake Michigan stretched dark and vast, its waves a distant whisper against the shore. Inside, they huddled close, the scent of coffee and fish and chips mingling in the small space.

Emma's fingers, still cold from the outdoors, curled around her coffee cup. She took a moment to appreciate the warmth seeping into her hands, a small comfort against the weight of the conversation to come. "This has gotta be a first," she mused, a smile playing at the corners of her mouth. "Holding a meeting in the comfort of your car, just to play with the systems."

James grinned, his eyes crinkling at the corners. He loved these moments with Emma, the easy banter that flowed between them. "Well, gotta put her through the paces..." he replied, patting the dashboard affectionately. He'd chosen the Prius not just for its efficiency, but for moments like this—the ability to sit in comfort, protected from the elements, while they worked through the big ideas that seemed to constantly swirl around them.

"Ok," Emma said, her gaze sharpening with anticipation. She shifted in her seat, angling her body towards James. "I have warm coffee, you've got a bag of fish and chips. We're set, so spill."

James nodded, suddenly feeling a flutter of nervousness in his stomach. This was it—he gestured to the floor. "Grab that satchel at your feet. There's a folder in there."

"Ooh, visual aids," Emma teased, but her playful tone died as she opened the folder. Her breath caught audibly as she took in the image of the magnificent stone Stupa, her eyes tracing the tag: *The Great Stupa of Sanchi located in India.*

But it was the next image that truly stole her breath away. James's design was revealed before her, a masterpiece of simplicity and complexity intertwined. It was traditional, yes, adhering to the sacred geometry of a Stupa, but there was something uniquely James about it. Something fresh, contemporary, almost... joyful.

Emma's fingers hovered over the lines, afraid to touch, as if the drawing was too pristine for human hands. The design radiated a sense of unconditional love—not from any specific element, but from the essence of the form itself. It celebrated the complexity of cosmic structure through simplicity, reminding her of why children loved drawing circles and squares. It was pure, unadulterated fun.

As she studied the design, Emma felt a shift within herself. This wasn't just a building or an art piece—it was a statement, a declaration of hope and possibility. She could almost feel the energy radiating from the paper, the potential for change and growth.

She looked up at James, seeing the intensity in his gaze as he watched her reaction. He'd been holding his breath, she realized, waiting for her response.

"You're in it to win it," she said softly, her voice filled with a mixture of awe and trepidation.

"Yes," James replied, his voice barely above a whisper. He felt exposed, vulnerable, having laid his vision bare before her.

Emma nodded, a mix of admiration and concern washing over her face. She took a deep breath, organizing her thoughts.

"Well, I'm glad you're committed... but James, I mean it's brilliant, but where do I start with the issues?"

James had been anticipating this. Emma was brilliant, but she was also practical. He knew she wouldn't be easily swayed by the beauty of the vision alone. So, drawing from his recent discussion with Ted and Maribel, he began to explain his journey to this idea.

He spoke of the growing urgency he felt, the sense that the world was at a tipping point. He described how the mosaic project had opened his eyes to the power of community, of shared vision. As he talked, Emma listened intently, her brow furrowing as she absorbed his words.

When he finished, she spoke carefully, her voice laced with both awe and apprehension. "This is brilliant, no question about it... none. And in an ideal world, great, the mountains get moved and the road is paved. But there are so many ways this could fall apart—from the public, from peer pressure... and from jealousy too."

She paused, gathering her thoughts. "You having a breakthrough... like this, like... well, Andy Warhol's Soup Can for goodness' sakes—only the opposite of mundane—this is big and can change art installation overnight. But there are people who live to tear down beautiful ideas, sacred sites—believe me, I know. And I would hate to have everybody's heart at *Epoch* broken again if this gets torn apart before it even gets built."

James nodded, understanding her concerns. A month ago, her words might have stopped him in his tracks. The thought of hurting anyone with art was antithetical to his personal mission. But now, he was convinced this was the highest road.

He leaned in, his voice low and urgent. "Em... you're right, the road is hard. So many people would try to stop this on an instinctive level, because we are kind of addicted to the habit of our own pain, aren't we? And really don't want the world to be better—at least they think they don't... but Em... luv..."

He paused, meeting her eyes with an intensity that made her breath catch.

"The world is burning... it's burning, and people seem oblivious... but this is God's world, not ours. We're here on God's dime, and there is a clock... right now, with all those prayers from all those people, on all those tiles—we can try. Who are we if we don't try?"

Emma lowered her head, absorbing his words. She felt the weight of his conviction, the urgency in his voice. When she spoke, her voice was soft, almost reverent.

"During the sweat lodge... you had a vision? Something you haven't told anyone? Michael told me you were in a kind of trance or something at the end of round four, not exactly racing to get out."

James's eyes grew distant as he recounted his experience. "I did what you suggested, first," he began. "I reached my mind down into the earth, and that helped, but it wasn't enough. So then I reached back, parted the hides, and dug my hands right into the earth. That really helped, but it wasn't a vision as such."

He paused, gathering his thoughts. "It's what I have been imagining, seeing, feeling since then... and the feeling of the clock ticking and God's not fooling around. The feeling that evil only exists for the time God gives to us as an opportunity to use right will in action—to wake up. This can't go on forever, what's happening in the world... it's not right, not fair... and disrespectful in the extreme. What are we if we don't try to walk a little straighter? Who are we as humanity at all if we don't try to make an offering?"

As James finished speaking, silence filled the car, broken only by the soft hum of the heater. Emma felt the weight of his words, the urgency of his vision. She needed time to process, to reconcile her practical concerns with the undeniable power of what James was proposing.

"Let's go for a walk," she said suddenly, reaching for the door handle.

They stepped out into the crisp night air, their breaths forming small clouds in front of them. Emma took James's elbow as they walked in step to the edge of the breakwater, the Chicago skyline a glittering backdrop before them.

They stopped at a bench, the sound of waves crashing against the rocks below filling the silence between them. Emma studied the water intently, her mind churning with thoughts. The vastness of the lake before her seemed to mirror the enormity of what James was proposing.

"You're right," she said finally, her voice barely audible above the waves. "When we look at the water or sky like this, we might think we have all the time in the world, so we might get lulled into a kind of daydream... like 'maybe tomorrow, maybe next week'... I have to admit, I've had dreams too. When I was a little girl, I would have terrible dreams of waves crashing up against the house and rising water and nothing to do, nowhere to go... and not just that but other signs too."

James listened silently, his presence a steady anchor beside her. He could sense her working through something, approaching a decision.

There was a long pause, filled only by the rhythmic crash of waves. Then Emma spoke again, her voice stronger now, tinged with a new resolve.

"We would need to have a community garden, and an education center. People come out of the city to visit—there should be some kind of reward system, and a way to point them in a positive direction."

She turned to look at James, her eyes bright with a mix of excitement and trepidation.

"I thought I was making it up before, when we were walking the mounds... but maybe I wasn't. We would need space to grow... acres. How many? Have you worked it out yet?"

James said nothing. Instead, he gently took both her hands in his, removing her pink mittens with careful reverence. Then, his eyes never leaving hers, he brought her hands to his lips, placing a soft kiss on each one.

In that moment, with the city lights twinkling behind them and the vast lake stretching out before them, something shifted. Emma felt it deep in her bones—a certainty, a commitment to something larger than herself. She realized that this wasn't just about a project or an art installation. It was about answering a call, about stepping up to meet the challenges of their time.

The night deepened around them, but neither was in a hurry to leave. They had all the time in the world—and no time to waste.

* * *

Chapter 39

Chicago — Fulton Street Loft — *Mar. 1, 2003 — 10:33 p.m. —*
Connecting

The soft glow of the computer screen illuminated James's
face in the dimly lit loft, casting long shadows across the
worn hardwood floor. Outside, the Chicago skyline glittered
against the night sky, a testament to human ambition and
creativity. Inside, James sat hunched over his keyboard, his
fingers tapping a rhythmic staccato as he navigated the digital
landscape of sacred sites and ancient wisdom.

A half-empty mug of tea sat forgotten at his elbow, a thin film
forming on its surface. James absently reached for it, grimacing
slightly as the cold liquid touched his lips. He set it back down,
his eyes never leaving the screen.

The search had begun with Stupas, those ancient monuments
of enlightenment. James had pored over images of these
structures from across Asia, marveling at their intricate designs
and spiritual significance. But as the well of information on
Stupas began to run dry, his curiosity led him down new paths.

He found himself reading about White Buffalo Calf Woman,
the sacred figure of Native American lore. The story of the
four races resonated with him, echoing the universal themes
he sought to capture in his art. His mind whirled with
connections, drawing invisible lines between cultures and
beliefs.

A pop-up advertisement briefly interrupted his flow, advertising a sale on art supplies. James dismissed it with a quick click, barely registering the irony of commerce intruding on his spiritual quest.

His search led him to Angkor Wat, the magnificent temple complex in Cambodia. James leaned closer to the screen, his nose almost touching the glass as he examined the intricate carvings and imposing architecture. He marveled at how stone could be transformed into such a profound expression of faith and artistry.

As he scrolled through the information, a stray thought nagged at him. What was he really looking for? The question hung in the air, unanswered but insistent. Then, almost by accident, a new link caught his eye. It led him to an article about a living incarnation of the Buddha Maitreya, recognized by numerous Tibetan lineages as the reincarnation of Milarepa and other great masters. James's heartbeat quickened as he read, feeling as if he was on the verge of something significant.

The article detailed the Buddha Maitreya's involvement in financing and building The Great Namgyal Stupa in Dharamsala. James's eyes widened as he read about the project's unprecedented scope:

"A major project is underway to collect information about people affected by Tibet's fall. This includes gathering names, histories, and details about lost relatives, loved ones, and monasteries. Letters containing this information will be collected from Tibetan villages and placed in a large urn inside a Stupa. Prayers will be physically placed upon the urn containing these collected stories, to bring forgiveness and healing. This will facilitate the ability to forgive and forget all events that have happened to these people, and will bless and heal these individuals in their future reincarnations."

James pushed back from his desk, the chair wheels squeaking softly on the floor. He blinked rapidly, as if trying to clear his vision. Then, drawn by an irresistible force, he leaned in again, re-reading the passage.

"This," he whispered, his voice barely audible in the quiet loft. "This is wonderful... this is..." Words failed him, inadequate to express the magnitude of what he was feeling.

It was as if a missing puzzle piece had suddenly snapped into place in his mind. The gap that had been nagging at him, the sense that something was missing from their project, suddenly closed. In that moment, James felt his fate sealed with an audible click in the universe.

He stood abruptly, the chair rolling back and bumping against a nearby bookshelf. A small ceramic figurine—a gift from Emma years ago—wobbled precariously but didn't fall. James barely noticed as he strode to the wide window overlooking the city.

Chicago sprawled before him, a tapestry of lights and shadows. But James's gaze was turned inward, his mind racing with implications and possibilities. Everyone already thought him mad for proposing the Stupa project. But this... this was something else entirely.

James moved to his worn leather armchair, sinking into it with a soft sigh. He needed to think, to be quiet and let this new revelation settle into his consciousness. The ticking of the kitchen clock seemed unnaturally loud in the stillness of the loft.

As he sat there, staring unseeing at the city beyond his window, James felt the stirring of something monumental. What he and Emma, Ted, and Maribel had come together to work on was good—very good. It was potentially explosive in its impact on the art world and beyond.

But now, with this new information swirling in his mind, James understood with startling clarity that it wasn't enough. There was another step to be taken. No, not a step—a leap.

The night deepened around him, but James remained motionless in his chair, his mind on pause, waiting for the connection to illuminate what he was missing. Dawn was coming, but he felt no closer—just couldn't quite see the missing piece.

But it was there.

* * *

The cheerful chatter of friends and the earthy scent of clay filled James's loft, transforming the eclectic space into a hub of creative energy. In the studio workspace, James sat at a low table with Ted and Maribel's daughters, Theodora and Minnie, their small hands eagerly shaping gray porcelain clay into simple coil and pinch pots. The dear old friends had come to visit and spend at least half a day on Saturday, and of course James was thrilled—and the girls were even happier. Coming to play at Uncle James's loft was akin to play day at an amusement park, only better.

Emma leaned against the kitchen counter, absently stirring a mug of tea as she watched the scene before her. She couldn't help but smile at the sight of James, his brow furrowed in concentration as he guided Minnie's tiny fingers around a delicate coil of clay.

Maribel sat nearby, cradling her newborn son, his soft coos barely audible over the girls' excited chatter. Ted hovered at her shoulder, his eyes never straying far from his infant son's face.

The sudden shrill ring of the landline phone cut through the peaceful atmosphere. James looked up, his hands covered in clay. "Would you get that, luv? I'm deep in clay at the moment," he called out to Emma.

Emma set down her mug and trotted over to the phone, tucking a stray strand of hair behind her ear as she picked up the receiver. Her face immediately brightened as she recognized the voice on the other end.

"Hello... Sarah! How are you?" Emma's voice was warm with genuine affection. "Yes, I'm good. Yes, I'm taking care of James, I promise..." She laughed, a light, melodious sound that drew James's attention. "You're right, he does forget to eat sometimes. Your Ma is right... hang on, I'll get him..."

James was already making his way over, wiping his hands on a nearby towel. He nodded to Emma, taking the phone with a grateful smile. Turning to his friends at the table, he waved, signaling he'd be a few minutes before settling into his favorite easy chair.

"Hello, pet," James said, his voice softening as he spoke to his sister. "That sounds wonderful... that sounds great... yeah, I've got time, tell me..."

As James chatted with Sarah, Emma returned to the workspace, helping Theodora with her pot. She couldn't help but overhear snippets of James's conversation.

"Oh lass, that's beautiful," James was saying, his voice puffed a bit with pride. "And did you think of that? Your whole class? Well, that's brilliant... so what did you donate? I mean, give away... your doll? The one you've had since forever?"

There was a pause as James listened, his expression growing more tender by the moment. "Oh no, it was in good condition, sitting on your shelf and all. I thought you wanted her there so you could see her. Well, that's just the kindest thing I ever heard."

The conversation shifted, James's voice dropping slightly as he spoke with his mother. A squeal of laughter from Minnie, completing her new pinch clay pot, punctuated the quiet, causing James to chuckle.

"Oh... that's Minnie, Ted and Maribel's youngest girl... that's right, and they have a little boy too now. Yes, I will tell them. No, you're not bothering me, but I'll call you tonight. Ask Sarah for the news. Ta, bye Ma."

As James hung up the phone, shaking his head with a fond smile, he made his way back to the table. "That was our Sarah," he announced, his voice filled with a mixture of pride and wonder. "I gave her a beautiful doll, something she really wanted for ages, and once she got it, she put it up on a shelf so she could look at it... every day... and know it would never get lost or hurt."

He paused, his eyes misting slightly. "So she called me to ask if it was all right that she gave it away... just gave it away to the wee children in hospital. It was a class decision, something they all wanted to do. Give away something of theirs... can you imagine that? Sweetest thing I ever heard."

The group nodded and murmured in agreement, touched by Sarah's generosity. Maribel smiled softly, hugging her baby closer. "That's beautiful, James. Your sister has such a kind heart."

Ted nodded, ruffling Theodora's hair. "It's a good lesson for all of us, isn't it? The joy of giving."

Emma watched James closely, noting the way his eyes seemed to shine with unshed tears. She could almost see the wheels turning in his head, knowing that Sarah's act of kindness would resonate with him deeply.

As the conversation shifted back to their project, Emma found herself fielding questions about some of the logistical issues they'd been grappling with. She launched into an explanation of her ideas for community outreach and educational programs, her voice animated as she described her vision.

"I've been thinking," she said, spreading out some notes on the table, "we could partner with local schools, create workshops that blend art and environmental education. And what if we had a rotating exhibition space, showcasing work from community artists alongside our main installation?"

James listened intently, nodding along, but Emma could tell his mind was partly elsewhere. The call from Sarah had struck a chord, and she knew it would be percolating in his subconscious for a while.

As the evening wore on and their friends prepared to leave, Emma helped clean up the workspace, stealing glances at James. He seemed lost in thought, his movements automatic as he washed clay from his hands.

* * *

The next morning, James stood in front of the bathroom mirror, razor in hand, his face half-covered in shaving cream. As he drew the blade across his cheek, his mind wandered back to Sarah's call, her act of kindness replaying in his mind. Just the thought of her bright voice in his mind raised his spirits—he might start singing any moment now.

He paused mid-stroke, catching sight of his reflection—half clean-shaven, half masked in white foam. A chuckle bubbled up from his chest. "Well, aren't you a sight for sore eyes," he muttered to his bizarro doppelganger.

Did he know any tunes from *Phantom of the Opera*? Because that's the role he looked at the moment. He chuckled; no, none of those tunes were actually toe-tapping numbers to be yodeled in the early morning wake-up process. His own inner musings tickled him so, he laughed out loud—and then stopped.

A full stop at half-laugh.

James looked deep into the image staring back and thought about the Phantom of the Opera lurking in the shadows as half-man, half-monster, half mad.

Interesting.

Just why had he been so fascinated by that genre or storytelling line when he was young? He remembered that old sci-fi flick *The Fly*—the one with Vincent Price—had been a knee-rattler all right, a scientist's experiment that had gone so terribly, irrevocably wrong it had been heartbreaking to watch. And then as a young man—

His hand became still. When he was sixteen years old, he'd been fascinated by another literary creature: Gregor Samsa—Kafka's unfortunate hero, transformed into a monstrous vermin. That slim novel had held him spellbound when he was a teen... until...

His heart quickened, and James lowered himself onto the closed toilet lid, the cool porcelain a stark contrast to the heat flushing through his body, putting all systems on alert. He closed his eyes, willing himself to remember that particular day in the park. It had been a pivotal moment, one that had opened a window to God, and unconditional love itself. He remembered that day with his sister—Sarah, of course. It had become a touchstone for him, but it seemed important to recall it all, as best he could.

He concentrated, and slowly, the scene began to unfold in his mind's eye. The creak of swing chains. The rustle of leaves in the gentle breeze. The weight of Kafka's *Metamorphosis* in his lap, its pages dog-eared and well-worn. He'd been keeping an eye on Sarah while she played on the swing set at the local park, but passages from the book were pulling his mind away from her. She seemed to notice this void and so brought the mountain to him, so to speak.

Sarah's voice cut through the memory, clear as a bell. "Whatcha reading, Jimmy?"

James smiled, remembering how he'd tried to explain the complex story to his eight-year-old sister. "It's about a man who wakes up one day and finds he's turned into a giant bug," he'd said, watching her face scrunch up in confusion.

"You mean like a ladybug?" Sarah had been puzzled, trying to figure it out, imagine the picture.

"No, sorry to say, more like a cockroach, I suppose. The lad had a bad wake-up," James had replied—which turned out to be a regrettable choice of arthropod, for Sarah understood the meaning of that well enough.

"God would never do that!" she had fairly shouted, her voice rising with the righteous indignation only a child can muster. "God would not do that, James! That's a lie!" Her little hands balled into fists at her sides. "He wouldn't turn a person into a bug. Never!"

James had been caught off guard by her vehemence. He'd come up with an explanation about how some writers will make up stories that weren't meant to be taken literally—that is, like it really could happen in life—called a metaphor... like an example, he had tried to explain.

"—But why?" Her small hand had reached out to touch the book's cover. Sarah's eyes had widened in shock, then horror. An expression very seldom seen on her tender young face.

James had remembered fumbling at the goal line, trying to explain the concept of symbolism to a child who saw the world in black and white—good and evil, truth and lies. But Sarah had been adamant.

"Then the story is a lie," she'd declared, "because that would never happen."

And then... this was where his memory sharpened. This was the part he often played in his mind to keep it fresh and alive in his life.

Seeing how upset Sarah was, he knew he had to use a strategy that worked with her—that included her feelings—and so he set the book aside, giving Sarah his full attention. "Alright then, cute boots, if you were telling the story, how would you do it? Say you wanted to talk about someone who felt so bad about themselves—or society felt so bad about them—that they actually became as ugly as they thought they were?"

And this part he remembered very well indeed. Her answer had been simple, and went something like this: "I would say someone was sitting on a park bench crying because he was so sad, and then his sister came and gave him a hug, because you don't hug someone who is a bug or a monster, do you? So then they were both happy. The end."

Her simple words had the crack of thunder and verbal power to pierce his mind—to find his soul inside and waiting. The simplicity of her solution, the purity of her logic, found the eggshell encasing his soul and, with a simple tap, broke the crust to cast gold.

Before he could think one thought more, his sweet sister Sarah had launched herself at him, wrapping her arms around his middle in a fierce hug. And would not let go.

James felt his throat tighten, even now, remembering the simplicity of her solution. He'd felt it—a love so pure, so unconditional, it could only have come from God Himself.

From the Great Himself—no disrespect intended—through Sarah to him. It was as if He'd been trying for years to get James's attention and finally found the route to reach him through his questing mind, as his sister Sarah's fierce hug and specific laws of cosmic order.

And wasn't this her job on earth too? Yes. It was who she was born to be. Absolute.

Sarah is a different kind of human being. Someone as beautiful as our Sarah is never a coincidence or a crazy accident or any of those strange things that might be held in the public mind.

In that moment, sitting on the toilet lid with half his face covered in melted shaving cream, James felt the same rush of divine love flow through him from the inside out—which gave him the strength to stand up, meet his own gaze in the mirror, and give himself the best counsel of his life to date.

"Sarah is exactly what God intends her to be. Back in 1985 or yesterday on the phone. It's all a wake-up call." And then, as a playful aside and electric jolt, James added in direct address, "You silly double-wank of a dolt."

James splashed water onto his face and then wiped the residue of the shaving cream away. And by the time his ritual was complete and his face patted dry, he turned away from the mirror, placed the towel back on the rack, and said softly:

"There it is... I think I see it," he murmured.

The Stupa, and what would go inside, wasn't just about art, or community, or even spirituality. It was about love—pure, simple, unconditional love—and what love does. Love that can transform a monster into a man, a broken world into a place of hope and forgive.

Enough love to have the courage to make amends, offer hope, and try again.

James walked slowly into the kitchen—so slowly, his steps measured and deliberate. The table was still covered with plans and materials from the previous evening's discussion. James eased onto a stool, his eyes scanning the scattered papers until he found the scribbled note he was looking for.

As he read the hastily jotted words, everything clicked into its proper place in the picture. All of it—the Stupa, the mosaic, Sarah's gift to the hospital, the article about the gift of saving grace of the Great Namgyal Stupa—coalesced into a single, brilliant point of clarity. No accident. None of it.

All of it. Could make it work. If he considered all the pieces, and how these seemingly disparate elements might be placed side by side to land in the right place with the most powerful value to the most people—if he climbed to the absolute top of the mountain with the best intention, it would work.
All of it could make it work.

James moved to his favorite armchair, absently taking a pad of paper along the way. For hours, he sat there, scribbling furiously, working out the logistics of this enhancement. The sun climbed higher in the sky, the phone rang twice, but James barely noticed—lost in his thoughts.

Finally, he sat back, surveying his notes. "It could work," he repeated. It was his fav phrase of the day—and probably for the rest of his life. He smiled. He deserved a smile, and so he smiled again. His eyes drifted to the calendar on the wall. The meeting was only one week away.

One week.

They had all come so far. But this... this alteration would make it all come together.

James reached for the landline phone, then paused, his hand hovering over the receiver. No, he decided. This wasn't the time to share. The decision that would make it work relied on other people. There was no reason to upend everything for what might be a mad idea.

He set the phone down, his resolve strengthening. He would wait, refine his thoughts, contact the people who would be directly affected, and present them when the time was right. For now, this revelation would be his alone—a secret treasure to anchor the works into reality.

* * *

Chapter 40

Chicago — Epoch Alliance Office — *Mar. 9, 2003 — 9:40 a.m. — Showdown*

Emma's footsteps echoed in the empty conference room of the Epoch Alliance headquarters, the polished wood floors reflecting her solitary presence. Somewhere below, faint Sunday-morning city noise—the occasional bus groan, a delivery truck backing up with its mechanical beep—drifted up through the double-paned windows. Her lithe figure, clad in a soft, forest green wrap dress that complemented her Native American heritage, moved with grace. The dress hugged her curves in a way that spoke of confidence rather than vanity, its hem swishing gently against her calves as she walked. Her dark hair, usually pulled back in a practical ponytail, cascaded in loose waves around her shoulders, framing a face that seemed to glow from within.

Her fingers trailed along the smooth surface of the newly installed round table, tracing the grain in the wood, acknowledging the tree it once was. The faint, comforting scent of *something* fresh still clung to the air. She couldn't help but smile at Alfred's choice—a not-too-subtle nod to equality and open communication. The smile lingered, softening her features and hinting at the deep well of contentment she now carried.

Her eyes, bright and alert despite the early hour, swept the room, taking in the meticulously arranged details. The slide projector stood at attention, its lens aimed at a pristine white screen.

Nearby, a podium waited patiently, ready for anyone who felt the need for a more formal presentation. Poster boards with sturdy clamps lined one wall, blank canvases waiting to be filled with their vision. The faint hum of the building's heating system underscored the stillness.

Emma's gaze landed on the carafes arranged neatly on a side table—water and hot beverages, prepared for every preference. The aroma of strong coffee curled up from one of them, cutting through the faint tang of office carpet cleaner. She counted the seats around the table, her brow furrowing slightly, creating a small crease that James often found adorable. "Ten?" she murmured, mentally ticking off the expected attendees. "Rhonda, Gerardo, James, Alfred, Mabel, Val... that leaves three extra. Curious."

She glanced at the clock, its steady ticking a reminder of the impending meeting. Forty minutes until the general rundown, and then the main event at 10 AM, Sunday at the Epoch Alliance headquarters—Alfred's choice for a closed, secure meeting. There would be very little traffic in the building on a Sunday, and none in the Epoch office, save for the mod squad plus two... and Val. And the three empty seats.

As she pondered this puzzle, Emma absently smoothed back her hair, tucking it behind her ears. The light caught the delicate silver bracelet on her wrist—a gift from James—sitting alongside the silver and turquoise bracelet from her grandmother, sending tiny reflections dancing across the room. Despite the gravity of the upcoming meeting, there was an aura of calm about her, a quiet strength that seemed to radiate from her very being. It was as if the love she now shared with James had unlocked something within her, transforming her into a subtle yet powerful force of nature.

"Where is everyone?" Emma wondered aloud, her voice echoing slightly in the empty room. "Where's James?"

Emma strode out to the lobby. The sight of Rhonda and Gerardo chatting by the elaborate potted plant arrangement in the center brought a sense of the circle beginning to close around their group. The lobby smelled faintly of winter coats and the citrus cleaner the weekend janitorial crew favored. This was really happening.

Rhonda stood tall and poised, a vision of corporate elegance in her charcoal gray pantsuit. The jacket's sharp lines accentuated her confident posture, while a pop of color from a deep purple silk scarf at her neck softened the overall effect. Her dark hair was coiffed into a smooth cut, each strand perfectly in place as if held there by sheer force of will. Dainty pearl earrings, just a touch of sweetness, caught the light as she turned her head to smile at Emma.

Beside her, Gerardo provided a stark contrast. His usual exuberant energy seemed barely contained within his navy blue blazer, which strained slightly at the shoulders as he moved. He wore his light blue shirt with an open collar, and he had taken care to trim the edge of the beard he had begun to grow a few weeks ago. His warm brown skin seemed to glow with an inner enthusiasm that no amount of formal attire could suppress, but he looked good. Handsome.

"Well, you two are looking like a power couple. No kidding, you look great. Have you seen James or Alfred and Mabel?" Emma asked, approaching them. "Or even Val, for that matter?"

Rhonda shook her head, her perfectly styled hair barely moving. "They'll be here, believe it," she said, her tone leaving no room for doubt. Her manicured nails, a subtle shade of mauve, tapped rhythmically against her leather portfolio.

"Of course," Emma replied, "of course. This is going to be the best show in town, he's not going to miss it."

But Emma couldn't shake the feeling that James was up to something. His recent behavior—the 'hiding,' the furtive calls with Val, as if every single one was a response to a 911 cry. The way he'd avoid prolonged eye contact, as if in fear that she would read his mind or something—all pointed to a secret simmering beneath the surface. She'd given him space, knowing the pressure of the upcoming presentation, but today was showdown. No more hiding.

As if summoned by their conversation and Emma's will, James appeared, his presence immediately filling the space. He cut a striking figure in his crisp white shirt, the fabric smooth and bright, like a blank canvas. Over it, he wore a light brown blazer that seemed to capture and reflect the warm tones of his hazel eyes. The jacket's slightly rumpled appearance spoke of a man more concerned with ideas than ironing—a detail Emma found endearingly familiar.

His eyes lit up at her appearance, taking in her dress appreciatively, sans leering. "Morning, luv," he greeted, with a warm smile, leaning in to kiss her on the cheek, his stubble tickling her skin. "You look radiant."

Emma smiled, feeling a flutter despite her concerns. "Thanks. You're not looking too shabby yourself, Mr. Watson."

James chuckled, then turned to the others. "Rhonda, Ger, ready for the big reveal?"

Gerardo grinned. "Born ready, amigo. Though I wouldn't say no to some caffeine first."

Rhonda nodded in agreement. "Seconded. Where's Alfred with those pastries he promised?"

As if on cue, Alfred and Mabel arrived, their familiar dynamic bringing a sense of normalcy to the charged atmosphere. Alfred, dapper in a tweed jacket, carried a box of pastries whose warm, yeasty aroma instantly cut through the cool air. Mabel, elegant in a pale blue dress, followed close behind.

"Did someone mention sustenance?" Alfred asked, blue eyes twinkling.

"Let's go into the conference room, shall we?" he suggested, his voice carrying the weight of authority. "We need to cover several items before we begin."

As they filed in, Emma caught James's eye, searching for a clue to his hidden thoughts. But he simply smiled, gesturing for her to go ahead. Whatever he was planning, she'd find out soon enough.

* * *

They filed into the room, each person gravitating towards a seat. Emma couldn't help but note the three empty chairs again, their presence now seeming less like an oversight and more like an intentional gap. The faint hum of the building's old HVAC system filled the stillness, blending with the occasional muffled street noise from Madison Street below.

Alfred cleared his throat, drawing everyone's attention. "Sorry for any delay," he began, his eyes twinkling with a hint of mischief. "We're waiting on three more members of our group."

Rhonda's eyebrows shot up, but she remained silent, her curiosity evident in the tilt of her head.

Mabel settled into her chair, Alfred taking the seat beside her. "We decided," Mabel said, her voice warm but firm, "but feel you would all agree, to expand our group to include representatives of the group that made this tile construction possible."

Before anyone could respond, Alfred's face lit up. "Ah! They are here. Welcome!"

All eyes turned to the doorway, where Val stood, ensuring the double doors were wide open. Her face was a mask of professional neutrality, her role as stage manager evident in her composed demeanor. And there, framed by the entrance, stood three figures that seemed to bring with them the weight of history and tradition.

George Hawkins, his weathered face a map of wisdom and experience, stepped forward first. His silver hair caught the light, creating a halo effect that emphasized his dignified presence. Behind him, Joe Cloud and his wife Theresa entered, their presence commanding respect without a word spoken. Joe's posture was straight and proud, his eyes keen beneath bushy brows. Theresa moved with a quiet grace, her long silver braid swaying gently as she walked. A faint scent of cedar seemed to follow them into the room, grounding the moment.

Emma felt her breath catch in her throat. The elders from the Ojibwa nation, one of them her own father—here, now, part of this meeting. Her mind raced, trying to process this unexpected turn of events.

As the newcomers made their way to the empty seats, Emma's eyes met James's across the table. In that brief moment of connection, she saw a flicker of something in his gaze—there was a definite light burning there, but otherwise appeared calm... determined. That was game-face James, he was going for it. Whatever it was, would be full tilt.

As the newcomers settled into their seats, a tangible shift in the room's energy was palpable. Alfred rose, his presence commanding attention without a word spoken. He began the introductions, his voice warm and welcoming, as if this unexpected addition was the most natural thing in the world.

"Friends, colleagues," Alfred began, his eyes twinkling with barely contained excitement, "I'd like to introduce George

Hawkins, Joe Cloud, and Theresa Cloud, esteemed elders of the Ojibwa nation. They've graciously agreed to join us today."

Emma's gaze flicked between her father and the other elders, searching for any hint of recognition or acknowledgment. Their faces remained impassive, focused on Alfred with an intensity that spoke of the gravity of the situation. George's hands, weathered by years of work and wisdom, rested calmly on the table. Joe's eyes, deep and thoughtful, scanned the room, while Theresa sat with a quiet dignity that seemed to anchor the entire gathering.

As the introductions concluded, Alfred turned to Mabel, who straightened in her seat, her voice carrying a weight of responsibility. "There was a feeling earlier this week," she began, her words measured and deliberate, "that seemed to become clearer and clearer. These clay tiles would never have been completed, especially as powerful and special as we all know them to be, without the Ojibwa nation agreeing to offer the raw red clay to us under the belief and understanding of how it would be used. Now that those plans have been upended..."

She paused, turning to Alfred, who seamlessly continued the thought. "We believe, and know you all would agree, that it was never our intention to break or alter that agreement," he said, his eyes scanning the faces around the table. "And so, we asked the Ojibwa to send three representatives of their nation to ensure the clay is used in a way that is consistent with that agreement. They have agreed to vote with us, and as our number is now nine, will ensure there will be no brick wall, no tie."

Emma's mind raced, piecing together the implications of this revelation. Her eyes darted to James, noticing the slight tension in his shoulders. 'Had a feeling, my eye,' she thought, a mixture of admiration and frustration at war inside her. This has James Watson stamped all over it. He must have had one of those brainstorms and passed the torch to Alfred.

She watched as Alfred and Mabel exchanged a look of quiet understanding, confirming her suspicions. James had set this in motion, and they had wholeheartedly embraced it. As she glanced around the table, seeing the nods of agreement and the respectful gazes directed at her father, Joe, and Theresa, Emma felt a swell of pride and confusion.

Why hadn't he just told me? she wondered, her eyes lingering on James. It was a good idea. Why keep it a secret?

Mabel's voice drew Emma back to the present. "Good, very good," she was saying, her tone warm with gratitude. "We are very grateful they came all the way to vote with us. Alright, here are the ground rules."

As Mabel outlined the procedures for the day, Emma found her attention split between the words being spoken and the unspoken currents flowing through the room. She noticed the way her father's hands rested on the table, steady and sure, the intricate patterns of his turquoise ring catching the light. Joe and Theresa sat perfectly still as well, their presence a grounding force in the room's charged atmosphere. Val moved silently around the perimeter, her face an unreadable mask as she ensured everything was in order. The glow from the overhead halogen lights reflected faintly off the glossy projector screen, still blank and waiting.

"Any necessary tools you might need are here..." Mabel was saying, gesturing to the various presentation aids around the room—a couple of old easels, the slide projector, stacks of transparencies in plastic sleeves. "Everyone can speak for as long as they need to, no time constraints, but be prepared to take breaks. Please make notes for questions, which will be tabled. We suggest that after all is heard, we take another break, come back, see which ideas have risen to the top, and open the floor for questions at that time. Any questions?"

The room fell silent. Emma found herself holding her breath, her mind whirling with possibilities. Whatever James was about to present, it was clear that it would change everything. The presence of the Ojibwa elders, the careful orchestration of this meeting—it all pointed to an intention.

As she looked around the table one last time, Emma caught James's eye. For a brief moment, she saw the well of deep passion that had drawn her to him all those years ago. Whatever was coming, whatever secrets he'd been keeping, she knew it would be worth it. The Stupa project was about to take on a new dimension, one that would honor not just their artistic vision, but the deep, spiritual connection to the land and its people.

With a deep breath, Emma steeled herself to be amazed, challenged, and perhaps, fall in love with their shared vision all over again. And... she might want to knock him on the noggin too.

Why hadn't he told her?

* * *

The room settled into a focused quiet as Val, her face, with the still, infinite well of a Japanese Noh theatre mask itself, readied the slide projector. The machine gave a faint click as she adjusted the carousel, the warm smell of dust on the bulb just starting to rise in the air. James watched her, noting the slight furrow of concentration between her brows as she double-checked her cue sheet—a neatly typed page with penciled marginalia from earlier in the week. She looked up, meeting his gaze without a flicker of emotion, not a trace of revealing what she knew was coming, before returning to her task. *A professional, damn straight,* James thought, a mixture of pride and amusement washing over him. *Gonna give that lass a bonus.*

James felt a sense of calm settling over him, his body instinctively mirroring the stillness of the Ojibwa elders. He was ready, yet acutely aware that the outcome was not entirely in his hands. Life was a river, and they were all simply riding its current. He caught Emma's eye briefly, offering a small, reassuring smile.

Gerardo rose, his usual energetic presence tempered by his professional alter ego—this was the man with a respected position at the Art Institute School. The fabric of his suit jacket stretched slightly as he straightened, betraying the well of energy bubbling beneath his composed exterior. His leather shoes made a soft *thock* on the varnished floor as he approached the front of the room, nodding to Val as he took his position. Without preamble, he signaled for the first slide.

The image that filled the screen was a close-up of several clay tiles, their surfaces alive with the interplay of light and color. The double glaze technique that Emma had perfected created a depth that seemed to shimmer and dance, even in the static photograph. James noticed George Hawkins lean forward almost imperceptibly, his eyes fixed on the masterful work of his daughter. A small, proud smile tugged at James's lips, mirroring the subtle softening of George's weathered features.

The room seemed to collectively exhale, tension dissipating as they all absorbed the undeniable beauty before them. This wasn't a flight of fancy; it was something tangible, something worth fighting for. Rhonda's pen tapped softly against her yellow legal pad, the only sound breaking the reverent silence.

Gerardo's voice, rich and confident, broke the quiet. "Here's an example of four or five completed tiles with two color glazes already selected, and placed on a template as you can see," he began, his hand gesturing towards the screen. "The strongest value is how the tiles relate to each other. Take one away, and the flow might not be as strong."

He paused, allowing his words to sink in—the soft hum of the projector filled the momentary silence, the faint mechanical click of the fan steady in the background. "I've picked these tiles completely at random for a reason, to show how strong the work is on the micro level, to be reflected in the macro."

With a nod to Val, the slide changed, revealing a wider view of the same tiles within their template. Gerardo turned back to the group, his eyes scanning their faces. "You see? Strong, a good design, even though we all know this design pulls all the way back to the heavens and beyond. The templates as sections can and do stand on their own."

His voice took on a more serious tone. "I'm offering these proposals as a worst-case scenario... because, well, someone has to." A soft chuckle rippled through the room, breaking the tension further. Emma's laugh, though quiet, rang clear and true, drawing a warm glance from James.

"If we can't maintain the integrity of the whole, we can maintain it in the sections. Pull back further than this section, and it loses its way. Just this section, and it works."

As Gerardo continued, he outlined three potential scenarios. First, he described a plan to place sections of the mosaic in different areas around Chicago, creating a kind of artistic treasure map for the city. The slides showed potential locations—parks, public buildings, even unexpected nooks in bustling neighborhoods. Emma leaned forward, her eyes sparkling with interest, while Rhonda's pen flew across her notepad, capturing every detail.

Next, he presented a more daring proposal: a floating exhibition. The images depicted sections of the mosaic displayed on barges, moving along the Chicago River and Lake Michigan. It was a bold vision, one that would bring the art directly to the people in an ever-changing, dynamic way. Joe Cloud's eyebrows raised slightly, a flicker of intrigue crossing his usually stoic features.

Finally, Gerardo's voice took on a note of barely contained excitement as he revealed his personal favorite. "And now, the pièce de résistance," he said, a twinkle in his eye. The next slide showed a long, curving tunnel—a pedestrian passage between two subway stops. The dated, 1980s-style tilework in the reference photo made his point clear: transformation was possible. "Imagine," Gerardo said, his hands painting pictures in the air, "walking through this underground space, surrounded by our mosaic. It would be like stepping into another world, a journey through art and spirit with every step."

As his presentation came to a close, James found his gaze drawn to the faces around the table. He saw a mixture of emotions—excitement, skepticism, hope. But most importantly, he saw engagement. Every person in the room was fully present, fully invested in the possibilities before them. Theresa Cloud's hands were clasped tightly together, her knuckles white with tension or anticipation—it was hard to tell which.

* * *

As Gerardo settled back into his seat, a palpable shift in energy rippled through the room. Rhonda rose, her movements crisp and deliberate, a stark contrast to Gerardo's easy-going demeanor. Her tailored suit rustled softly as she took her place at the front, commanding attention without a word. She stood at the front of the room, her gaze sweeping across the assembled faces before simply stating, "Watch."

With a nod to Val, the first slide appeared on the screen. A wide-angle shot of the tents outside the museum filled the room, capturing a moment of pure joy and creativity. People of all ages hunched over tables, their faces alight with laughter and concentration as they worked on their tiles. George Hawkins leaned forward slightly, his weathered hands clasped tightly on the table.

Another nod, another slide. This time, a close-up of a young boy and his mother, their hands covered in clay, eyes sparkling with shared delight. The image was so intimate, so full of life, that it seemed to bring the scent of fresh clay and the sound of cheerful chatter into the room. Theresa Cloud's eyes softened, a ghost of a smile playing at the corners of her mouth.

Slide after slide followed, each one a window into the heart of their project. James caught glimpses of himself in some of the photos, surprised by the open joy on his face as he interacted with community members. There was Emma, her hands guiding an elderly woman's fingers over a tile's surface. Gerardo, surrounded by a group of teenagers, all of them laughing at some shared joke. The interns, their youthful enthusiasm infectious as they worked alongside seasoned artists.

Rhonda raised her hand, signaling Val to pause the slideshow. She turned to face the group, her eyes bright with passion. "Notice anything similar?" she asked, her voice carrying a hint of challenge. "People. All people, of all races, of all ages, come together to have fun and look forward. People in a community agreeing to make something simple, wonderful, intricate... but never mundane."

Her words hung in the air, heavy with meaning. James found himself nodding unconsciously, caught up in the power of her observation. Alfred's gaze was fixed on Rhonda, his expression thoughtful and engaged.

"The people came to give," Rhonda continued, her voice softening slightly, "and I believe we should do whatever we can to honor the promise to give back, to have the installation in an accessible, approachable setting to keep inspiring forward."

She paused, letting her words sink in. "Okay, we admit in life that sometimes we can't always have what we want, but what is life, if not being flexible?"

With another nod to Val, a new image appeared on the screen. It was the interior of a library, its walls vast and inviting. "I admit it's not the full scope for the design," Rhonda explained, "but it does indeed have breath and depth, natural light coming from above—an impossibly excellent situation for this."

The next slide elicited a collective intake of breath from the room. It was Emma's design, rendered in full color, a masterpiece of waves within waves within waves. Abstract yet evocative, it gave the unmistakable impression of cycles and expansion. James felt his breath catch in his throat. He'd known Emma and Rhonda were working on something, but this... this was beyond his wildest expectations. His eyes darted to Emma, who sat poised and calm, her gaze fixed on the screen.

Rhonda went on to explain the details of the library installation, her voice rising and falling like reciting from a passage of poetry, of Coleridge at his best. "The mosaic would cover the main wall of the central reading room, visible from multiple levels. The natural light from the skylight would play across the tiles throughout the day, bringing the piece to life in an ever-changing dance of color and shadow."

"But that's not all," Rhonda said, a hint of excitement creeping into her voice. She presented two more ideas, each one building on the concept of accessibility and community engagement, laying them out as a generous feast for the imagination.

The second proposal involved a series of smaller installations in community centers across the city, each one a piece of the larger design. "This way," Rhonda explained, "we bring the art directly to the people, making it a part of their daily lives."

Her final idea was perhaps the most ambitious—a plan to incorporate elements of the mosaic into a new public transportation hub. The slides showed sleek, modern spaces transformed by the vibrant tiles, turning an everyday commute into an artistic journey. "Imagine," Rhonda mused, "rush hour becoming hush hour as commuters pause to admire the beauty around them."

As Rhonda concluded her presentation, James found himself in awe of the scope and vision of her ideas. They honored the community aspect of the project while still maintaining the integrity of the design. He glanced around the room, noting the engaged expressions on everyone's faces. Even the Ojibwa elders seemed impressed, their usual stoic demeanor softening as they studied the images.

For a moment, James felt a flicker of doubt about his own plan, like a tiny pebble of uncertainty caught in his shoe. What Rhonda and Emma had created was beautiful, community-focused, and deeply meaningful. It aligned perfectly with their original vision for the project.

But then he thought of the Stupa, of the deeper spiritual significance it could bring. His resolve strengthened. Yes, Rhonda's ideas were wonderful, but there was still something more—something higher—they could reach for.

As the room buzzed with excited discussion, James caught Emma's eye. He saw the dedication and passion shining in her gaze, and he felt a flow of love leave his body and move across the expanse of the table to be with her. One amazing woman. She turned to look at him, of course, her eyes warming to overflowing as she absorbed every drop.

James took a deep breath, centering himself. His turn was coming, and with it, the moment that would change everything. The highest road was calling, and despite the beauty of what had just been presented, James knew he had to answer that call—even if it meant throwing a wrench into the works.

* * *

As Rhonda took her seat, a palpable sense of anticipation hung in the air. Alfred rose next, his movements deliberate and unhurried. The room fell into an expectant hush, all eyes drawn to the elder statesman of their group.

"I'll go with my personal favorite first," Alfred began, his voice carrying the weight of years of experience. "It's actually based on a conversation James and I had long ago—something we had brainstormed, and now I would like to revisit it."

James leaned forward slightly, his eyes sparking with recognition. He remembered that conversation—a late-night session fueled by coffee and wild dreams. To see it resurrected now, in this context, sent a thrill of excitement through him.

Alfred continued, his words measured and clear. "The actual construction from the color rendering of the design James and Emma have is just about half complete, but the finished color-rendered drawing is about as perfect as I've ever seen. It is how we began—it is what I, personally, believe we should complete."

He nodded to Val, who smoothly transitioned to the next slide. The image that filled the screen was of an abandoned sewing mill, its weathered brick façade telling a story of industrial past glory. "A garment facility just west of the city," Alfred explained, "as a lot of these structures are. But the foundation is good, the bones are good, and this is what I see."

Val advanced to the next slide, and a collective gasp rippled through the room. The image before them was a stunning reimagining of the old mill, transformed into a vibrant community center. James recognized his own handiwork—a sketch he'd done once on a whim—now brought to life in vivid detail.

"This is a redesign of that same building that James did one time as a lark," Alfred said, a hint of pride in his voice. "But I held onto it. I saw the possibilities of a community center for teaching, learning, and, most of all, the science of ecology—research and support for alternative energy systems."

As Alfred spoke, James found himself nodding, the potential of the idea unfurling in his mind. He could see it clearly now—the mosaic as the centerpiece of a living, breathing hub of community and innovation.

"The installation would need to be expanded to fill the first-level hall," Alfred continued, "but I've been assured that expanding the design could work, where contracting would not."

James's nod became more emphatic. This could work. This could really work. He glanced around the table, seeing the same realization dawning on the faces of his colleagues. Even the Ojibwa elders seemed intrigued—George Hawkins exchanged a meaningful look with Joe and Theresa Cloud, their stoic expressions softening slightly as they studied the image before them.

Everyone present in the room seemed to collectively exhale, a tension they hadn't fully acknowledged dissipating. Rhonda began scribbling notes furiously, her pen moving across the page with practiced efficiency. Val, ever the professional, maintained her composure, but a small smile played at the corners of her mouth.

Alfred, encouraged by the positive response, moved on to his next two ideas. The second proposal involved transforming an abandoned warehouse into a multi-level art installation, with the mosaic serving as the focal point of a larger exhibition

622   NOTHING LOST COPY KDP VERSION

space. The slides showed a cavernous interior, reimagined with walkways and platforms that would allow visitors to experience the mosaic from various angles and heights.

"Imagine," Alfred said, his voice taking on a dreamy quality, "being able to walk through the mosaic, to see it from above, below—to be truly immersed in its beauty and meaning."

His final proposal was perhaps the most ambitious—a plan to incorporate sections of the mosaic into a series of public parks across the city. The slides depicted green spaces dotted with curving walls and structures, each bearing a portion of the grand design.

"This way," Alfred explained, "the mosaic becomes a part of the city's fabric—accessible to all, a daily reminder of our shared vision and community spirit."

As Alfred concluded his presentation, James felt a surge of hope. These weren't just backup plans; they were viable, exciting possibilities in their own right. He caught Emma's eye across the table, seeing his own thoughts mirrored in her gaze.

The room buzzed with renewed energy. Rhonda was furiously scribbling notes, her earlier skepticism seemingly forgotten. Gerardo was nodding enthusiastically, already building on Alfred's ideas in his mind. Even George Hawkins and the other Ojibwa elders seemed more engaged, their earlier reserve giving way to genuine interest.

James sat back in his chair, a complex mix of emotions playing across his face. Alfred's presentation was undeniably impressive, and part of him thrilled at seeing his old sketch brought to life in such a grand vision. It was good—very good, in fact. He could see the excitement in the room, the way everyone seemed to lean into the possibility of it all.

But beneath that initial surge of enthusiasm, James felt a weight in his chest. The plan was good, yes, but was it the highest road? He thought of his own vision for the Stupa—the offering he wanted to make to the people. It was more than just an art installation or a community center; it was a spiritual beacon, a place of healing and transformation.

As he watched his colleagues scribbling notes and exchanging excited glances, James felt a growing sense of resolve. He knew what he had to do, even if it meant derailing a very, very good train. No one would love him for it, but it must be done. He sighed.

His eyes met Emma's across the table, and he offered her a small, almost apologetic smile. She knew him well enough to recognize that look—the one that meant he was about to change everything.

Apple cart—look out.

James took a deep breath, centering himself. He glanced at the Ojibwa elders, noting their attentive but still reserved expressions. They, perhaps more than anyone else in the room, would understand the importance of what he was about to propose. At least, that was the hope.

As the excited chatter began to die down and all eyes turned expectantly toward him, James felt a calm settle over him. With a slight nod to Val, signaling he was ready to begin his presentation, James leaned forward, and the room fell into an expectant hush.

However, as Alfred concluded his presentation, Mabel, ever attentive, noticed the slight slump in Alfred's shoulders—the faint lines of concentration deeper around his eyes.

Before James could rise to take his turn, Mabel stood—her movement graceful yet purposeful. "We've been going for hours now," she said, her voice cutting through the low murmur of conversation. "Let's take a 20-minute break or so, shall we? We'll come back for James and then Emma."

The suggestion was met with a collective nod of agreement. Bodies shifted in chairs that had grown uncomfortable with prolonged sitting. It was a good call to make.

James, who had been sitting with an air of serene composure throughout the presentations, rose smoothly from his chair. Unlike the others, who were quick to stretch or reach for their phones, he moved with a deliberate calmness toward the long windows at the far end of the room.

As Emma watched him standing there, framed by the window, a realization dawned on her. *He knows what he's doing,* she thought to herself. *Nobody is going to like it, because it will mean breaking every notion we have about public installation of art, and it would be hard—hard work on every conceivable level—but he's going to do it anyway.*

As the others filtered out of the conference room, seeking refreshment or a moment of solitude, James remained by the window. He was acutely aware of the challenge that lay ahead. His proposal would need to honor and include everyone's efforts and visions while simultaneously elevating the project to its highest potential. That was extremely important.

He was wrong about one thing—he wasn't throwing a wrench into the works, he was actually carving a way for them to have it all. Community engagement, extension into alternative sciences, hopefully, eventually in time if all went well... and finally, out-of-the-box conception. Like the mosaic wall itself, no one's heart desire could or would be left out.

He began to re-formulate his approach in his mind, stripping away all unnecessary language, honing in on the essential truth of his vision. The Stupa, as an offering with the highest intent, would be the core of his proposal. But it would need to be more than that—it would be a vessel to hold, even amplify, every single proposal brought to the table today. Because every single idea was brilliant in its own right, which meant they were all inspired... and there were no accidents. And seeing they were all inspired, that hotlink came from heaven; there was a reason to the rhythm of their group which included the elders of the Ojibwa nation too. One was not better than another... it was about timing to include them all. Something about the timing.

James knew that after his initial presentation, he would give the floor to Emma as planned. Her practical expertise would be crucial in grounding his vision in reality. And then, he would return to address the inevitable flood of questions and concerns, ready to reveal the solution.

As the minutes of the break ticked by, James remained still—still at the window and still—a pillar of calm in the midst of the bustling preparations for the meeting's continuation. He was not nervous, not restless. He was ready.

When the others began to file back into the room, they found James already seated, his posture relaxed yet alert. There was something different about him—an aura of quiet power that seemed to radiate from his very being. The Ojibwa elders exchanged knowing glances, recognizing the calm before the storm.

As Mabel called the meeting back to order, James took a deep breath... and then slowly exhaled.

* * *

The room fell into a hushed anticipation as James remained seated. All eyes were fixed on him, waiting for the grand reveal, the next big idea. But James, in his quiet wisdom, chose a different path.

"You're right," he began, his voice carrying easily across the room without the need for projection. "Every single one of you, my friends and colleagues, are absolutely brilliant and right to bring these proposals to the table. They all have merit, one and all, they are inspired."

A collective breath seemed to be held as James continued, his words taking an unexpected turn. "We got dubbed the 'mod squad' as a joke, but it sticks because it's true. We are contemporary visionaries of the modern era, and I suggest you hang onto that, because here we go. Don't be surprised by what you hear, because this is what we're really looking for."

The silence in the room deepened, if that were possible. This was not the presentation anyone had anticipated, but there was something in James's tone, a certainty that commanded attention. It was as if he possessed knowledge that was out of reach from them in an ordinary way, and they were all leaning in, desperate to grasp it.

James continued, his voice taking on a more contemplative tone. "In ordinary times, we would be enjoying ourselves and our creations as extensions of our hearts, respecting sacred form, to be reminded of sacred forms. But these are not ordinary times."

He paused, letting the weight of his words settle. "Nothing has been ordinary for about, what? The past couple thousand years or so? No, in these un-ordinary times, we see idol worship in all its negative aspects. A painting of a fart that sells for millions? Really?"

A few nervous chuckles rippled through the room, quickly stifled as James pressed on. "And then hanging onto that fart and bequeathing it from one generation to the next as a cursed work no one seems to let go of because we're caught on the idol. And it is extremely challenging to loosen the grip and reach for what we really want... God."

At this, James stood, his movement deliberate and unhurried. Emma found herself studying him intently, her mind moving ahead to imagine where he was going. This wasn't what they had planned, not by a long shot. She glanced around the room, noting the rapt attention on every face. Even her father, usually so stoic, had leaned forward slightly, his interest piqued.

James's gaze swept the room, lingering for a moment on George, Joe, and Theresa. The Ojibwa elders met his eyes unflinchingly, a silent understanding passing between them.

"The world is burning," James continued, his voice filled with a quiet intensity. "But because God loves us so much, our world is dressed with bright colors, green grass, noble trees, to be cushioned as best God can from the truth that this is not heaven, far from it. And anyone, anyone who attempts to straighten their life and get off a crooked road finds they come up against the evil one pretty darn quick."

With measured steps, James moved to the front of the room. Val stood ready at the projector, waiting for the signal that had not yet come. Everyone present was on the edge of their seats, waiting to see where this unconventional presentation would lead.

James stepped to the side, his movement fluid and purposeful, opening the view to the screen behind him. The room held its collective breath, the air thick with anticipation.

"Okay, Val," James said softly, his voice carrying easily in the hushed space.

The image that filled the screen elicited a collective intake of breath. It was not what anyone was expecting to see — an ancient city materialized before them, its stone structures so weathered they seemed to have grown from the earth itself. The intricacy of the carvings, despite their age, was breathtaking — a testament to human ambition and artistry.

"This," James began, his voice taking on a reverential tone, "is an image of Angkor Wat, built in the 12th century in the middle of a jungle in Cambodia. It sits on what many believe to be a ley line of the earth, the energetic grid holding the pulse points to radiate life force to the whole world."

His eyes scanned the room, noting the rapt attention on every face. Emma leaned forward unconsciously, to get a closer view.

"These people moved far away from the coast to the middle of a jungle to build this," James continued, gesturing to the towering structures on the screen. "You can see the effort in the towers, lifting up and up, earthbound but hopeful, looking up. It is not near a waterway, there were no super highways, that we know of, there is no commercial advantage for building a city in this location that archeologists can determine, and still you can see the massive amount of effort that went into this construction. There appears to be no other reason or purpose, except this: it was constructed to last millennia because it is placed on a ley line."

The room was silent, absorbing the weight of history and human endeavor captured in the image.

"Okay, Val," James said again, and the slide changed.

The Great Stupa of Sanchi filled the screen, its dome a perfect hemisphere against the sky. James's voice took on a scholarly tone, rich with respect for the subject.

"This was built around the 3rd century BC and enlarged in the 1st century BC—it is The Great Stupa of Sanchi, and is believed to contain some ashes of the Buddha. Emperor Ashoka is thought to have built this magnificent structure as a way to make amends for the conquest and subsequent slaughter he initiated on his neighboring nation."

George Hawkins shifted in his seat, his eyes narrowing slightly at the mention of conquest and amends. James noticed the movement and nodded slightly in acknowledgment before continuing.

"It was built for perpetual cycles of prayers to be transmitted through the intent and sacred geometric design. Here you can see what symbolizes the cosmic axis and supports a triple umbrella structure, chattra, which is held to represent the Three Jewels of Buddhism — the Buddha, the dharma (the doctrine), and the sangha (the community)."

The next slide appeared, showing a more contemporary structure. "And this is the Great Namgyal Stupa in Dharamsala, constructed, I believe, in 2001. A relatively small structure financed and built by the living incarnation of the Buddha Maitreya."

James's voice softened with reverence and respect. "In it, he had placed the names, information, history, and anything that could be found about all the people who have lost relatives, loved ones, and the monasteries too during the fall of Tibet. Prayers were placed on the urn to forgive and forget all the negative connections that had happened to those people so when they reincarnate, they will be blessed and healed."

The room was utterly still, the weight of history and spiritual significance palpable in the air. And then, with another nod to Val, James revealed his vision.

The gasp that filled the room was involuntary, a collective exhalation of awe. James's design of a large Stupa appeared on the screen — brilliant white, a half-dome shining with the soft undulating curves of a crest at the top reaching upward, fairly singing with love and sweetness and unconditional compassion.

Emma felt her heart skip a beat. The love, the soft feeling, wasn't coming from James per se, but from his understanding of how to draw sacred form... and keep his ego out of the way. It was a masterpiece of spiritual architecture, a beacon of hope rendered in clean, pure lines.

"And this," James said, his voice barely above a whisper, "could be built sometime in the upcoming summer of 2003."

He paused, allowing the image to sink in, to work its magic on the assembled group. Then, with a voice filled with quiet conviction, he continued.

"The round form is in harmony with the Earth. It is not found on Earth in nature, but nature, as I've been saying, gives it a pass. Hurricane winds whip around it, earthquakes flow under. Domes, and more recently geodesic domes, are constructed to last hundreds of years. And why? Because it is not a burden on the earth, but a blessing."

As James's words hung in the air, the room remained in stunned silence. The enormity of what he was proposing was slowly sinking in. This wasn't just an art installation or a community center — it was a spiritual beacon, a place of healing and transformation that could stand for generations.

Emma found herself blinking back tears, overwhelmed by the beauty and significance of James's vision. She glanced around the room, seeing similar expressions of awe and contemplation on the faces of her colleagues. Even the Ojibwa elders, usually so stoic, seemed moved by the presentation.

The air in the room felt charged, as if they were standing on the precipice of something monumental. James had taken them on a journey through time and spiritual tradition, only to bring them back to the present with a vision that could change everything. The question now hanging unspoken in the air was: were they ready to take this leap with him?

* * *

James looked down for a moment, his fingers tracing an invisible pattern on the table before him. The room held its breath, sensing that what was to come would be even more profound than what had already been shared.

When he looked up again, his eyes were filled with a mixture of sorrow and determination. "I could show you so many sacred sites placed almost strategically throughout history," he began, his voice low but carrying easily in the hushed room. "Always with the effort and intention to ask for forgiveness and bestow blessings for transgression and ignorance."

He paused, his gaze sweeping across the faces before him. "And many of them have been taken down — many in China, under communist rule, but in other places of the world as well. The land itself is alive, and the Native Americans, traditionally, have known that and lived it, and so mistreating the land itself is a form of tearing down a sacred site."

George Hawkins nodded almost imperceptibly, a flicker of recognition crossing his weathered features. James acknowledged him with a slight incline of his head before continuing.

"We are losing our sacred sites. Is there any wonder the world is burning?" The question hung in the air, heavy with implication. "So, what are we to do? Where is the contemporary equivalent of a sacred site?"

James leaned forward, his voice taking on an urgent tone. "Here, we have the roots of how it can be done, but it isn't easy to see because we have been blind for so long. We've never done it before, no one we know has any living knowledge... but something happened when we all came together to work on this project."

He turned to Emma, his eyes softening. "You, Emma, you told me you had a dream." She nodded, a small smile playing at the corners of her mouth as she remembered.

"Gerardo said yes before I was even finished asking," James continued, a note of fondness in his voice.

Alfred spoke up, his voice carrying a hint of pride. "Rhonda turned down a job on the East Coast that would have made her rich."

James nodded, a smile of acknowledgment crossing his face. "I believe it. We all felt it. The Ojibwa nation allowed us to use the raw red clay. We all could feel the hum of energy flowing through the clay, which was then amplified by the thousands and thousands of prayers people imprinted on the clay, traveling along the matrix and energy meridians in the clay to extend out, to radiate the new song, the earth song blended now with human prayer and this hope: 'If we can just love each other, it will be alright.'"

His voice took on a more personal tone, filled with wonder and reverence. "I, personally, could feel it clearest in the quiet of the room, after people had left, the music was turned off, and I would find myself studying the design. And as I did, I might feel a shiver run up my arm, just a pleasant shiver... sometimes more. There is no doubt for me that the tiles are singing all the time."

Emma found herself nodding, remembering similar moments of quiet communion with their creation. Around the room, others were doing the same, recalling instances when they had felt that inexplicable connection.

James's voice grew more intense, filled with conviction. "The challenge for us, if we can, is to place them in a location in such a way where anyone who visits and sits quietly can feel it too. If we place the mosaic wall as designed in a sacred form and seal it in an area of earth that welcomes it, it could stand for millennia. For people to visit, if we are fortunate in that way."

He paused, letting the weight of this possibility settle over the room. "It has been so long since humanity has built a sacred site as a regular practice... isn't it time to try again? We have the very rare opportunity for ordinary people like us to actually feel love and blessing come from the earth as the tiles. We're not monks or saints, and yet we feel this when we are quiet... that means other people will too."

James looked at Val and nodded, and she pressed the button to reveal the final slide.

A collective intake of breath filled the room as all present at the table beheld a full-color rendering — no, a painting — of how the design he and Emma had created would look in real time inside the Mosaic Stupa. The 'continent' section began to the immediate right as a flat wall, just as in the Eco Lobby design, then followed true to spec.

But at the end, it curved gently now to face the viewer, presenting planets spinning out into cosmic dust. James had employed his skill in classical painting style along with photorealism to illuminate the vision as it would appear on a sunny day. Natural light streamed in from high at the back of the Stupa, indicating windows placed as skylights, camouflaged to be unseen when approaching the structure from the front. It was a true-to-life version of how it would look — a breathtaking painting in its own right. And tellingly, unsigned.

The room was utterly still, each person grappling with the enormity of what James was proposing. It wasn't just about art anymore, or even community. This was about creating something that could change the world, one visitor at a time.

A collective hush fell over the group, broken only by the soft sound of indrawn breaths. Eyes widened, postures straightened, as the full impact of James's vision sank in. Emma's hand went to her throat. Alfred's eyes gleamed with a mixture of pride and awe, while the Ojibwa elders exchanged a look heavy with personal meaning.

The painting had transformed James's abstract concept into a tangible reality, one they could all envision and, perhaps, believe in. The unsigned nature of the work didn't go unnoticed, subtly underscoring the communal nature of the project.

"Because it boils down to this," James continued, his voice filled with quiet urgency. "If we don't find a way to share this in a way that amplifies the blessing in a respectful way, now, when we can actually feel into something that's real, then when? Who are we waiting for to come and save us?"

The question hung in the air, a challenge and an invitation. James looked around the room one last time, meeting each person's gaze with a mixture of hope and determination. Then, without another word, he went to sit in his chair and nodded to Emma.

* * *

Emma rose in a fluid motion to take her turn, the room remained in a state of stunned contemplation. James had not just presented an idea; he had laid bare a vision of hope, of healing, of re-connection with something greater than themselves. The air thrummed with possibility, with the weight of a decision that could alter not just their project, but potentially the course of history.

Emma took a deep breath, feeling the enormity of the moment. Whatever she was about to say, whatever plans she had prepared, would now be filtered through the lens of James's transformative proposal. As she began to speak, the room leaned in, ready to see how all the pieces might come together in this new, expansive vision of what their project could become.

She took a deep breath, centering herself before beginning.

"About a month ago," she started, her voice warm with memory, "James and I took a tour of the Native American mounds in Wisconsin. I'm thoroughly enjoying myself just walking along in the snow while James is sitting on a bench doing that thing he does, which is God knows what..."

A ripple of laughter spread through the room, breaking some of the tension that had built up during James's presentation.

James piped up, his voice tinged with mock indignation, "Oi! Still here, you know." This elicited more chuckles, but the attention quickly returned to Emma, everyone eager to see how her words would complement or challenge James's proposal.

Emma continued, her eyes twinkling with amusement, "And then he comes walking up to me with this bright light in his eye, and I think, 'Oh boy, I think he's going to kiss me'... but no, he pitches me a wild ball." She paused, her gaze softening as she looked at James. "But I caught it. It's a fun idea, a Stupa... okay, but it's catching. I think he's mostly kidding or imagining out loud, and so I join in. Why not? It's fun to play..."

Her voice took on a more serious tone. "And so I started describing how it could be, how it could work... and turns out I was playing true, but it was thought-form building... how any enterprise, especially a huge enterprise, begins."

She nodded to Val, who brought up the next slide. "This blueprint design is pretty close."

The image that filled the screen was breathtaking in its scope and detail. Emma's voice grew more animated as she described what they were seeing.

"This slide shows an image of the main Stupa in scale, about 50 yards by 50 yards. Large enough for our needs and community events, but small enough to be manageable and doable."

Her finger traced the lines on the screen. "Around the side, you'll see pathways to two geodesic domes, a learning center and another place to experience the effect of sacred geometric forms in person and a variety of alternative healing modalities, all vetted with clinical trials."

The room was silent, absorbing every detail. Emma's practical approach seemed to ground James's spiritual vision, making it feel more tangible, more possible.

"In the back," she continued, "you'll see some acres for a community garden or maybe even bison to raise and harvest for a stream of income and because meat, in particular, the protein in meat, has powerful healing potential."

As Emma spoke, the vision expanded, becoming more than just a spiritual beacon. It was a self-sustaining community, a place of learning, healing, and growth. She outlined plans for educational programs, research facilities, and sustainable agriculture practices that would support the Stupa and its surrounding community.

"We could partner with local universities," she suggested, her eyes bright with possibility. "Offer internships in sustainable agriculture, alternative energy, and holistic healing practices. The learning center could host workshops and retreats, bringing in experts from around the world."

She went on to describe how the geodesic domes could serve multiple purposes — as meditation spaces, classrooms, or even temporary housing for visiting scholars or retreat participants. The community garden would not only provide food for the center but could also be used as a teaching tool for sustainable farming practices.

"And the bison," she added, her voice filled with respect, "they're not just a source of income. They're a connection to the land, to the history of this continent. We could work with Native American communities to ensure we're honoring their traditions and knowledge."

As Emma continued to outline the practical aspects of this ambitious project, the room seemed to come alive with energy. People were leaning forward in their seats, eyes bright with excitement. Even the Ojibwa elders, who had remained stoic throughout much of the meeting, were nodding in approval.

James watched Emma with a mixture of pride and awe. She had taken his spiritual vision and given it roots, grounding it in the practical world without losing any of its transformative power. As she spoke, he could see the project coming to life, not just as a sacred site, but as a living, breathing community dedicated to healing and growth.

When Emma finally paused, the room was buzzing with potential. She looked around, meeting each person's gaze, before finally resting her eyes on James. In that moment, they were perfectly in sync, their individual strengths combining to create something truly extraordinary.

* * *

As Emma concluded her presentation, a palpable shift occurred in the room. The initial awe and excitement began to give way to a more pragmatic energy. James, ever attuned to the room's mood, noticed the subtle changes in posture, the furrowed brows, the pens poised over notepads.

He caught Rhonda's eye, noting the long list she had compiled during the presentations. Alfred, too, was studying his own notes with an intensity that spoke of concerns brewing beneath the surface. Even Gerardo, usually the most enthusiastic among them, was scribbling furiously, his face a mask of concentration.

James knew this moment was inevitable. Dreams, no matter how beautiful or inspiring, must eventually face the harsh light of reality. He decided to meet the challenge head-on, a quiet confidence buoying him as he held his secret close.

"We will take questions first," he announced, his voice calm and steady. "Ask your toughest question, one after the other. We'll write them down, not try to answer them just yet—just get the list first."

The room seemed to collectively inhale, preparing for the barrage of inquiries that would follow. James nodded to Gerardo, inviting him to begin.

Gerardo leaned forward, his usual jovial demeanor replaced by a serious expression. "Funding," he said simply. "This is a massive undertaking. Where's the money coming from, and how sustainable is it long-term?"

Emma jotted down the question, her pen moving swiftly across the page. Before she had finished, Mabel's soft voice chimed in.

"Community buy-in," she added, her tone gentle but firm. "How do we ensure this isn't seen as an imposition on the local area? We're talking about a significant change wherever we decide to build this."

James nodded, appreciating the thoughtfulness of the question. His eyes flickered briefly to George, Joe, and Theresa, the Ojibwa elders who sat in silent observation. A small smile played at the corners of George's mouth, invisible to all but the most discerning observer.

Alfred cleared his throat, his years of experience evident in the gravity of his voice. "Legal implications," he said. "We're not just dealing with art anymore. This is land use, potentially agriculture, maybe even animal husbandry. The legal complexities are... significant."

Rhonda, ever practical, jumped in next. "Logistics," she stated firmly. "Transportation of the tiles, preservation during construction, water and waste management for such a large facility. These are massive undertakings."

As each question was posed, James felt a mixture of appreciation for his colleagues' insight and a quiet assurance that his ultimate proposal would address many of these concerns. He knew the path ahead would be challenging, but he also knew he held a key that could unlock many doors.

Val, who had been quietly operating the slides, surprised everyone by speaking up. "Timeline," she said, her voice steady. "A project of this scale... how long are we realistically looking at from start to finish?"

James nodded, grateful for Val's practical insight. He glanced at Emma, seeing a mix of excitement and concern in her eyes. He wished he could reassure her, to share the weight of the secret he carried, but he knew the time wasn't right.

As the initial flurry of inquiries began to slow, James noticed Alfred shifting in his seat, a look of deep contemplation on his face. He knew what was coming would be one of the toughest challenges they'd face.

"Zoning," Alfred said, his voice carrying the weight of years of experience in navigating bureaucratic waters. "This isn't just an art installation anymore. We're talking about a multi-use facility with residential components, agricultural elements, possibly even livestock. How on earth do we get that approved, especially if we're looking at areas that are traditionally zoned for agriculture or low-density residential use?"

The room fell silent, the enormity of this particular hurdle sinking in. But before anyone could dwell on it too long, Rhonda cleared her throat, ready to pose the final—and perhaps most challenging—question of all.

"Cultural appropriation," she said, her voice steady but her eyes revealing the complexity of emotions behind the words. "We're drawing on traditions and practices from multiple cultures—Native American, Buddhist, and others. How do we ensure we're honoring these traditions rather than exploiting them? And who gets to make that decision?"

The question hung in the air, heavy with implications. James saw George Hawkins and the other Ojibwa elders exchange a meaningful glance. This, he knew, would be the crux of everything. Their answer to this question would determine not just the feasibility of the project, but its very soul.

As the room sat in contemplative silence, James took a deep breath. The list of questions before them was daunting, each one a potential roadblock to their vision. But as he looked around at the faces of his colleagues, he saw not defeat, but determination. They had dreamed big, and now it was time to work big.

"Thank you all," he said, his voice filled with genuine gratitude. "These are exactly the questions we need to be asking."

James paused, feeling the weight of the moment. "I think we all need some time to process these questions and gather our thoughts," he said, his voice calm and assured. "Let's take a 20-minute break. When we return, we'll start working on answers."

As the group began to stir, preparing to disperse for the break, James caught George's eye. The elder Ojibwa man held his gaze for a moment, a flicker of understanding passing between them. James felt a surge of hope. Perhaps, on some level, George sensed what was to come.

The room slowly emptied, filled with murmured conversations and the shuffle of papers. James waited until the room cleared, his mind relatively calm, given the landscape—but it was time to take a break from thinking, and right on time Emma was waiting for him at the open double doors.

* * *

Chapter 41

Chicago — Epoch Alliance Office — *Mar. 9, 2003 — 12:00 p.m. — Turn*

The conference room door swung shut behind them, the soft click echoing in the suddenly quiet hallway. James and Emma moved in tandem, their steps unconsciously synchronized as they made their way down the length of the lobby. They settled near a large window at the far end, the city skyline a silent witness to their conversation.

James lowered himself into a chair opposite Emma, his movements deliberate and controlled. The afternoon light caught the faint wisps of silver threads in his hair, a testament to the years and experiences that had brought them to this moment.

Emma leaned forward, her eyes searching James's face. "Why do I have the feeling you not only knew that was coming... but wanted it?" Her voice was low, a mixture of curiosity and concern coloring her words.

Before James could respond, a shadow fell across them. They looked up to see George Hawkins approaching, his presence commanding even in the spacious lobby.

"Dad..." Emma's voice held a note of surprise. She had been acutely aware of her father's silence towards her since his arrival, and this sudden approach sent a ripple of anticipation through her.

George's weathered face softened as he looked at his daughter. "Hello, little one," he said, his deep voice carrying a warmth that belied his previous reserve. "You did good in there."

Emma nodded, a small smile tugging at the corners of her mouth. The simple praise from her father felt like good medicine.

George then turned his attention to James, his dark eyes studying the younger man with an intensity that seemed to peer into his very soul. After a moment of charged silence, he spoke — his words more of a statement than a question. "You have another card to play."

James met George's gaze steadily. "Yes," he confirmed, his voice low but clear. "Two cards, actually. Do you know what they are?"

George paused, considering. The lobby was quiet, the distant sounds of the city that still filtered through the thick windows fading into insignificance. "We have an idea," he finally said, his words measured. "Play them and we'll see."

With that cryptic response, George turned and walked away, his steps sure and purposeful. He didn't look back, leaving James and Emma in a wake of questions and possibilities.

Emma turned to James, her eyes wide with a mixture of confusion and anticipation. "James?" His name was a question, an invitation, a plea for understanding.

James leaned in close, his voice barely above a whisper. "I'm going to tell you fast, but don't act surprised, don't say anything, just listen."

As James spoke, Emma's eyes grew wide, her breath catching in her throat. She listened intently, her mind racing to keep up with the implications of what he was saying. Slowly, as the full scope of his plan unfolded, her face relaxed, a look of understanding and resolve settling over her features.

When James finished, Emma took a deep breath, centering herself before responding. "I'm not sure if they will go for it," she said, her voice a mix of caution and hope, "but try with all your might... as you say, we gotta try. And James?"

"Yes, luv?"

"When you are near the end of what you want to say, toss me the ball. I think I have something that will help, I'll tell you as we walk back to the room."

James nodded, gratitude and determination shining in his eyes. In that moment, the bond between them strengthened to unbreakable.

The lobby began to stir as their colleagues started to filter back in, the break coming to an end. James and Emma exchanged one last look, a silent pact passing between them, and as they walked, Emma shared with him what she would like to say to the group.

* * *

James stood at the head of the table, his posture relaxed yet purposeful. The room fell into an expectant hush as he began to speak, his voice clear and steady.

"Val, last slide please," he said, nodding towards the projector.

The image that filled the screen drew a collective intake of breath from the room. An intricate American quilt in a diamond pattern sprawled across the white backdrop, its vibrant colors and diverse imagery immediately captivating.

James's eyes swept across the faces before him, noting the spark of interest that had ignited in even the most skeptical gazes. He allowed a moment for the image to sink in before continuing.

"What we're looking at," he began, his voice taking on a warm, storytelling quality, "is an exceptional example of the American quilt in a diamond pattern. If you look close, you'll see images of artwork—some famous paintings, some not so much. There are buildings, city-scapes… I even spy a favorite meal from a five-star restaurant."

He stepped closer to the screen, his hand gesturing towards different sections of the quilt. "People's faces, all kinds of people, different shapes and races… favorite cities from around the world, and their food."

James's voice softened, taking on a more personal tone. "My dear friend Mabel made this quilt for her husband Alfred. She took these images and turned them into vector graphics, had them laser-printed on material that she cut into a quilt pattern."

He turned back to face the room, his eyes finding Mabel and Alfred. A smile played at the corners of his mouth as he continued, "She gave these images of different cultures, people, places that he loved to him as a balm and blanket to help heal his heart."

The room was utterly silent, each person seemingly lost in their own thoughts as they absorbed the significance of the quilt and James's words.

"That," James said, his voice gaining strength, "is what cultural variety offers people—the ability to enjoy, relish, share and re-share that feeling of identification with another country."

He paused, his gaze sweeping the room once more before settling on the Ojibwa elders. George, Joe, and Theresa sat perfectly still, their faces impassive but their eyes intent on James.

"Now," he continued, a hint of challenge in his voice, "why would a person, any ordinary person, feel the desire to visit Greece, for example? Just some desire always there, and who knows why? If we could remember all our past, in the lives before this one, we would know why. The man lived and thrived in Greece, with wonderful memories impressed upon his soul, and so of course it is natural to rekindle the connection. Consider we all are made that way, on purpose, to help dissolve the borders."

James's words hung in the air, heavy with implication. He could see some of his colleagues shifting in their seats, processing this unexpected turn in the conversation.

"Reincarnation is real," he stated, his voice firm and unwavering. "Does anyone really imagine you can see the whole place in just one trip? Even Disneyland takes a week... so I've heard."

A few chuckles rippled through the people in the room, as a cushion and general invitation to continue, James pressed on.

"So, granted, we've all been here before and are drawn to the cultures that are imprinted upon us, then cultural appropriation is, in truth, a struggle to understand."

As James finished speaking, a palpable shift occurred in the room. The tension that had been building since the tough questions were raised seemed to dissipate, replaced by a thoughtful, almost contemplative atmosphere.

James's eyes remained fixed on the Ojibwa elders. George's expression had softened almost imperceptibly, a glimmer of interest visible in his dark eyes. Joe and Theresa exchanged a quick glance, a silent communication passing between them.

In this charged silence, the quilt on the screen seemed to take on a life of its own—its myriad images a testament to the complex tapestry of human experience and the interconnectedness of all cultures. As the group sat in quiet reflection, the stage was set for the next revelation, the next step in James's carefully orchestrated vision.

* * *

"In that spirit and with reverence," James began, his eyes scanning the room, "I would like to draw your attention to the oral teaching of White Buffalo Calf Woman." He turned to Emma, a soft smile playing on his lips. "Em, do you have those postcards? The ones of Miracle? Can you pass them around the table?"

Emma nodded, reaching into her bag to retrieve a stack of colorful postcards. As she began to distribute them, James continued, "In 1997, Miracle was born and immediately recognized as the first white buffalo in decades. This is not an albino; it is a legend alive on earth." His voice grew more animated as he explained, "The white buffalo is born with brown eyes, white fur that turns red/brown, then black, then yellow-tan, then back to white at the close of life."

As the postcards made their way around the table, James gestured to them. "There are postcard photos of every stage of Miracle's life so far. You can see the color changes, every element of prophecy fulfilled—specifically pointing at all the races in the world, specifically drawing our attention to all the race changes happening on one body, one being... all the races are one being."

The room was silent, each person studying the images before them with intense focus. James paused, allowing the weight of his words to sink in before continuing.

"Jesus teaches us, 'What you do for the least of them, you do for me'... both good and bad, every action directed back to one being, that is, in fact, all beings. There is no such thing in truth as 'yours, mine, not ours.'"

James's voice took on a more somber tone. "I can point out all the logic, all the reasons we know are true in our hearts, and still it might bounce off, still leaving a feeling of being offended... which leaves only the emotional response. And the emotional response is there because of hurt feelings, of having been cheated, or a lack of justice... that shadow which can pass from lifetime to lifetime."

He took a deep breath, his eyes finding George, Joe, and Theresa. "And so balance—some effort to restore balance, the harmony of nature—needs to be made. Forgiveness is crucial, but that doesn't preclude justice. God forgives, and still, those are the laws of karma. Balance. Justice is necessary, or people will go mad, quite mad."

James's voice softened, taking on an almost reverent quality. "There is an event that is hard to describe, so I'll just say it. Hiawatha came to raise the five nations up to such a level of pure energy, through a kind of osmosis, it rippled through the land through form and people, and so held the vibration for 500 years and counting. And in this time, the blessing was sealed into the North American continent as treasure in the bank, if you will, to hold the space for a country to be made that could glow enough God light that people around the world would feel the call to come here—to bury our sins in the earth, to absorb and love us back to normal, to 'ordinary times.'"

The room was utterly still, each person hanging on James's every word. He continued, his voice gaining strength. "I believe the Native American people held that light for this to happen. I believe it is time—so far past time—to make an offering to the people, to the line of people, and through them to their ancestors. To offer this Stupa, with the prayers on all the clay tiles, in gratitude to the Ojibwa people, and so all Native Americans, for them to have and hold in whatever way they would like."

There was a collective gasp from his friends at the table. George drew in a breath but barely moved; Joe and Theresa were likewise listening intently.

James paused, looked at Emma, then back to the elders, and in a private, more personal tone: "This will not be the first time in our shared history the Ojibwa have stepped forward in courage..." James nodded to Emma, then sat down and looked at Em. She stood, her fingers brushing against the smooth wood of the table as she rose.

The room was quiet, the soft hum of the air conditioning a whisper beneath the weight of silence. She looked around, meeting the eyes of her friends, lingering on Joe and Theresa Cloud before finally settling on her father's weathered face.

For a moment, she was that little girl again, showing him her first attempt at a coil pot, seeking his approval. George's eyes, dark and deep as the night sky, gave nothing away. Emma swallowed, her throat suddenly dry.

She glanced down, her gaze catching on the turquoise and silver bracelet encircling her wrist—a gift from her grandmother, a piece of home she carried with her always, right alongside the silver bracelet from James.

When she looked up again, her voice was clear and strong, carrying to every corner of the room.

"My great-great-great-grandfather walked with Chief Buffalo to Washington," she began, her words measured and deliberate. "They journeyed through a world that saw them as less than human, risking their lives to stand before President Fillmore and describe the truth of their nation—of the different tribes connected as one nation. And as one nation, they had purpose. The Creator has a plan for us to live in this way."

Emma stood still as she spoke, her hands quiet at her sides; she was aware James had moved his hand closer to hers on the table, for support. She continued, "They didn't go with weapons or threats. They went with courage, with hope, with the belief that if they could just be seen—truly seen—as people, truth could dispel the lie that they were as nothing, not deserving of our own land. They showed President Fillmore the map of our nation on a birchbark, which is sacred to our people. They showed him how the tribes, with different insignia in different areas of the land, were actually connected by blood as one nation—perhaps in the same way the different states are connected to the U.S.A."

She paused, her eyes finding James. He nodded, almost imperceptibly. She continued:

"Now, we stand at another crossroads," Emma continued, her voice gaining momentum. "We're being offered a gift, yes, but also a challenge. To take a risk, to step into the unknown, to believe that by opening our hearts and our lands this time, we can change the world."

Emma turned to face her father and the Clouds directly. "The journey to Washington was a leap of faith in the power of truth. This Stupa, this offering—it's another leap. But isn't that what we do? Isn't that who we are? People who dare to believe in a better world, even when the path seems impossible?"

The room was silent, but Emma could feel the energy shifting, like the air before a thunderstorm. She took a deep breath, her final words coming from a place deep within her.

"We took a chance once, and it saved our people. Maybe... maybe it's time to take another... to save all the people."

As Emma sat down, she felt, rather than saw, her father's slight nod. It wasn't approval, not yet, but it was acknowledgment. And for now, that was enough.

James's eyes met Emma's for a brief moment, then he stood and offered, without preamble, "I've saved some money, set aside for a rainy day. Well, the rain is falling. If Epoch does not want to pay for the cost of our installation and maintenance, I will. In the coming years it will, eventually, be self-sustained with solar and wind energy. The building itself will require minimal maintenance. If there is expansion later, Emma has a proposal for that to be self-sustaining as well. The Stupa will be made in such a way that will have minimal financial impact, and to last for hundreds of years. Emma has the stats on that."

Emma cleared her throat and said, "Yes, all the information is in the packets we have for you all."

James nodded, a small smile playing on his lips. "There you have it. There are other details that can be sorted, but the long list of issues virtually disappears, as you are your own nation, with your own rules. You can expand it to something like Emma's vision, or not. It may just simply sit and be... in whatever way you want. It would be up to you."

He looked to Emma; she nodded, and so he said softly, "We... humbly ask you to accept this offering, if you are able."

With those words, James sat down next to Emma, his hand finding hers under the table. The room fell into a profound silence, stunned with yet another unexpected turn in the road. All eyes turned to George, Joe, and Theresa, waiting to see how they would respond to this monumental offer.

The Ojibwa elders sat perfectly still, their faces impassive, but their eyes alive with a mix of emotions—surprise, consideration, and something deeper, harder to define. The fate of the project, and more, rested in their hands.

* * *

After what seemed an eternity, Joe and Theresa bowed their heads together, their whispered conversation too low for anyone else to hear. The soft murmur of their conversation filled the air with an almost musical quality.

Suddenly, Joe turned to George, speaking in their native language. The words were unintelligible to the others, but their impact was immediately visible. George's head snapped up, his eyes widening with a mixture of surprise and keen interest.

George's gaze locked onto James, his dark eyes seeming to peer into the very depths of James's soul. "Who are you?" he asked, his voice carrying a weight far beyond the simple question.

James and Emma exchanged a puzzled glance, the unexpected query catching them off guard. Before they could respond, George repeated, his voice carrying a hint of urgency, "The elders want to know: Who are you?"

James felt the weight of the moment settle on his shoulders. He turned to Joe Cloud, then Theresa, searching the elders' eyes for a clue, a hint of what they were truly asking. In that moment of connection, understanding leaked into his conscious mind. Ah. It was a test, a probe into the depths of his intentions.

He nodded slightly to Joe, then to Theresa and George, acknowledging the gravity of their question. Turning to Emma, he spoke in a low voice meant only for her ears. "They're asking me if I'm aware of who I was—that I'd be saying these things, taking this action. If I was a hero warrior... back then."

Emma's eyes widened with understanding.

James closed his eyes, searching within himself for the truth. Images flashed through his mind—not of heroic deeds or great wisdom, but of mistakes, of wrong turns, of a soul stumbling through time, trying to find its way home.

When he opened his eyes, his voice was steady, filled with a quiet humility. "No hero. No Chief Joseph. More likely on the other side—some bloke in the New World, mucking it up, doing the wrong thing at every turn and trying to set it straight. That feels more like me."

The words hung in the air, raw and honest. George listened intently, his eyes never leaving James's face. Then, almost imperceptibly, he nodded, turning to confer once more with Joe and Theresa.

Their hushed conversation seemed to stretch for an eternity, the rest of the room frozen in anticipation. Finally, George turned back to the group, his eyes closed as if in deep meditation. When he spoke, his voice carried the weight of profound consideration.

"We are willing to take this offering to all the elders," he said slowly, each word carefully chosen. "There are positive aspects and challenges we will need to discuss and take our own vote. But we are willing, as you suggest, to try."

A collective exhale seemed to sweep through the room, the tension breaking like a wave against the shore. James felt Emma's hand tighten around his—a silent communication of shared relief and hope.

Alfred's voice broke through the moment, steady and pragmatic. "I believe we should take a break, for an hour now, to think deeply and come back and have the vote on which way we should go."

As the group began to stir, preparing to disperse for this crucial hour of reflection, James remained seated, the weight of the moment still heavy upon him. He looked around the room, taking in the thoughtful expressions on his colleagues' faces, the quiet intensity of the Ojibwa elders, the mix of hope alongside trepidation that seemed to infuse the body politic in the conference room on this fine Sunday afternoon.

As people began to file out of the room, James caught George's eye one last time. In that brief moment of connection, he saw something that gave him hope—a glimmer of understanding, of shared purpose.

The hour ahead would be one of deep contemplation for all of them. But as James finally rose to his feet, Emma by his side, he was at peace. Whatever the outcome, they had done their level best.

* * *

Chapter 42

Chicago — Epoch Alliance Office *— Mar. 9, 2003 — 1:45 p.m. — Vote*

As the conference room emptied for the break, James and Emma headed for a quiet corner—their own special corner now—at the end of the lobby by the high windows. Their heads were bent close in hushed conversation when George's approach drew their attention. They rose to greet him, Emma's movement a half-beat behind James.

George stood before them, his weathered face a map of wisdom and considered thought. For a moment, he seemed to weigh his words, the silence stretching between them like a living thing. Then, with a slight nod, as if coming to a decision, he spoke.

"We've decided to leave the conference," George said, his voice low but carrying easily to their ears. "Because we have a vested interest, we think the vote should be among the group. We're going to trust your group to vote as you feel directed to do, without undue influence."

James and Emma exchanged a quick glance, surprise and comprehension passing between them. It was up to their group to make the leap. Before they could respond, George continued, his tone shifting to something more personal, almost paternal.

"There is a mountain for each of us to climb," he said, his eyes holding James's gaze, "and this last mile you all must do on your own." And then to Emma: "Your mother is here, waiting at the motel. I know she'd like to see you both before we drive back."

"Wonderful, good, yes, of course, I'll call after the vote," Emma assured him.

Then, as an afterthought, George looked at James. "You have my blessing to marry my daughter."

The words felt very, very good to hear. James reached for Emma's hand as she leaned in close to him, but his mind had been wiped clean from the long day and couldn't think of one thing more to say except, "Thank you, sir."

Brief, but he meant it.

Emma, her eyes bright with unshod tears, stepped forward and wrapped her arms around her father. George returned the embrace, his usual stoic demeanor softening for a moment as he held his daughter close.

As George turned to leave, James found his voice again. "We'd like to get married in the mosaic Stupa, sir," he called after George, a hint of mischief creeping into his tone. "As, you know, an added incentive in your decision-making."

George paused, turning back to face James. A smile—rare and brilliant—spread across his face. "You *were* a scoundrel, weren't you?" he asked, his eyes twinkling with a mix of amusement and comprehension.

And with that as his parting shot, he turned and left.

James hugged Emma, then let her go to look at her, his eyes searching her face. "Did that just happen?" he asked, his voice barely above a whisper.

Emma nodded, a smile blooming on her face. "It did," she confirmed, her hand finding his and squeezing gently.

As the minutes ticked by, signaling the approaching end of the break, James and Emma turned together and walked back to the conference room.

* * *

The group filed back into the conference room quietly, not looking at each other, nor speaking. In fact, there was no outward sign, clue, or hint on which way they would lean. Even Emma and James wore impassive expressions—perhaps it was out of mutual respect, so as not to affect each other's state of mind in any way. Time would tell.

The comfortable chairs had rubber flooring protection, so there was virtually no sound as they were pulled across the wood floor. Everyone made their adjustments until they were all individually and collectively settled. They chose their place at the round table like this: Alfred, Mabel, Emma, James, Gerardo, Rhonda. No one appeared to be displaying a case of nerves; perhaps "pensive" would better describe the group mood.

This meeting had not gone as any of them imagined—not even James. He of course, knew he had a figurative atomic device in his pocket, and a general expectation of the result, but there was no way to gauge the range and impact of the explosion of a new idea. None. Now, Emma had gotten up to light speed right quick and *may* have had a feeling of how the tree branch *might* sway in the breeze—but the rest were hanging on to the side of the deep end of the pool. *What in the world will happen if I let go? Can I swim?* This logical question was ever present—of course it was—and completely natural.

James and Emma exchanged a glance, their hands briefly touching under the table before they settled into their places. The gentle brush of fingers—a tiny touchstone oasis in the desert of *what in the world happens next?*

Alfred cleared his throat softly. "Well then," he murmured, his voice barely above a whisper, "shall we begin?" He straightened in his chair and looked at each member of the team in turn. "We find ourselves at a crossroads," he began, his voice steady and measured. "The decision we make today will shape not just the future of our project, but potentially the future of cultural reconciliation and healing in our community and beyond."

No one made a comment, move, or sound; all eyes were on Alfred to observe how he would steer the ship.

He paused, his eyes sweeping across the faces before him once again. "Due to the weight of the issue, I suggest that the vote be unanimous. We will have one vote, and one vote only."

Mabel nodded solemnly from her seat.

The conference room, once buzzing with energy and possibility, now sat in a heavy silence. Around the table, faces etched with contemplation and conflict stared at nothing in particular, each lost in their own thoughts. The weight of the decision before them hung in the air like a tangible presence.

Gerardo, his usual jovial demeanor subdued, was the first to break the silence. "I believe the field has been narrowed down to three choices," he said, his voice uncharacteristically solemn. "Alfred's suggestion of refurbishing the sewing factory, Emma's suggestion of the Stupa on a plot of land, with the additional Monolithic domes tabled for a future date... and James's suggestion to give the wall and Stupa to the Ojibwa."

Alfred nodded, his silver hair catching the light as he moved. "I agree, those are the ones that will keep the design and work already done in place."

The room lapsed back into silence, each person turning over the options in their mind. Rhonda's voice—usually sharp and decisive—was tinged with a note of vulnerability as she spoke.

"It's a sacrifice, isn't it? We know it's a good idea, but it hurts to let it go."

A collective nod rippled around the table, even James and Emma joining in the gesture. Emma's voice was soft as she added, "It's true, we may never see it again. I can't deny it."

Alfred's eyes found James, searching his face. "James, you still want to do this?"

"Yes." James's answer was simple. One vote down—the easy one.

Gerardo leaned back in his chair, shaking his head in amazement. "Never in one million years would I have seen this coming, not even from you..." He directed this last part to James, who remained silent, having already said his piece.

"I kept running it around in my mind, like I'm looking for a way out," Gerardo continued, his hands resting on the top of the table as he spoke. "But you covered every exit, James, *every single damn one*. And either I'm the man I believe I am... or I am not. I either want to help in this totally invisible but proven way, or I do not."

Alfred's voice cut through Gerardo's musing. "So, do you want to vote for the Stupa to go to the Ojibwa?"

"Hell yes," Gerardo replied, a hint of his usual fire returning to his voice.

Alfred turned his gaze to Emma. "Emma, what do you have to say?"

Emma's eyes were distant, lost in thought for a moment before she spoke. "'Screw Paris,'" she said, a small smile playing on her lips. "I was just sitting here thinking of some advice my mother gave me not too long ago. It was a scene from that old movie *Love Story*. The guy's wife is dying, and he feels bad because he thinks he cheated her from the path that she originally wanted, and she says, 'Screw Paris.'"

Her voice grew stronger as she continued, "I get it now. He didn't cheat her because she never really wanted Paris—she wanted her heart's desire—and for me... I want there to be peace on earth, and even if this is just a token, representing a blessing, even if it is all in our imagination, and there is no power in it, I still want it. I want to try—maybe trying will make it real. Maybe that's part of the formula. 'Screw Paris.' I'm voting to send the offering if they will accept it."

All eyes turned to Rhonda and Alfred, and Mabel—the last three holdouts. Rhonda spoke first, her words coming out in a rush. "I admit I'm kind of pissed, and people will be more than pissed at us, but that doesn't mean we'd be doing the wrong thing. It's more likely they'll be mad because we upset the cart and started something new. Who ever heard of giving something like that away in a capitalist society? It's going to piss people off... but... I kinda love that."

A mischievous glint appeared in her eye as she continued, "I've always wanted to be a rebel... maybe it is as James said, and I was a revolutionary soldier or something, because I'm saying yes, let's try. I'm trying to imagine working on another version of an installation and all the time wondering... what if? Every time I see some bad news on the TV, wondering, *What if we had only tried? What if?* James lays this huge bug in our ear, and we will never be the same, because now we think we can actually make a difference in a way that's real. Sure, I'm pissed that we might lose it, but I can be pissed and still agree. Yes."

All eyes turned to Alfred. The elder statesman of the group took a deep breath before speaking. "Have you noticed that we are only talking about the proposal to the Ojibwa? None of us has mentioned another installation. Ever since the idea has been presented, it has dominated my thoughts. Even looking for issues against it, I couldn't dismiss it out of hand."

He paused, his eyes taking on a faraway look. "I'm getting older now, and I've tried many other forms of facilitating expression... except this. I'd like to try that now. If the Ojibwa accept, I say yes."

That left Mabel as the final vote; they all turned to her and waited.

"Oh, I'm not a holdout, I just wanted the drama of being last," Mabel said, and they all laughed. But then she gathered her thoughts to continue, "I would like to say... that any project that relies on the simple homespun craft of the unsigned artifact like quilting... gets my vote. Yes... make the offering to the Ojibwa and see what happens, put it in motion, or as Rhonda said, we'll always wonder... 'what if?' Yes."

Alfred nodded and said simply, "Very well, the vote is unanimous. The offering has been made and, if accepted"—and here he looked at Mabel for confirmation—she nodded, "Epoch Alliance will absorb the cost of installation and paying staff... but there is an angle that may put a crimp in your style, Rhonda. I don't believe we should do any publicity about this activity unless the Ojibwa give expressed and specific permission. The offer was for them to do as they like—which also includes public awareness of where it will be and why. It can still serve its function without applause, right, James? Emma?"

James nodded but said nothing, and so Emma said, "Yes."

"So no one may ever know..." Rhonda observed.

Alfred continued, "That may be how it unfolds. For all the world, it seems the tiles are boxed and on the shelf, and there they'll stay until Epoch Alliance decides their fate."

As Alfred's words reverberated in the air, a sense of finality settled over the room. James remained silent, suspecting he was "talked out" for three and a half months going forward. The decision had been made, not just with their words, but with their hearts. They had chosen the path of sacrifice and hope.

* * *

Chapter 43

It had been seventeen days since the Great Epoch Alliance Meeting, as it would heretofore be known to all and sundry, and if James was feeling a little nervous, he worked it off in learning a new skill. The loft space hummed with a quiet energy, the air thick with the scent of clay and the subtle tang of glazes. Golden, late-afternoon light filtered through the tall windows, casting bright pathways across the refurbished wooden floor and illuminating the dust motes that danced in the air like tiny, glittering constellations.

All in a day's work.

James had a good rudimentary grasp of color grading when it came to glazes and kiln firing, and was certainly considered above par...but after studying Em's work, he absolutely could not help but wonder—how do you do that? His fingers, stained with a rainbow of hues, moved with a mixture of confidence and uncertainty as he attempted to recreate the magic he'd seen in Emma's creations, to feel into the alchemy and science of how it worked.

And she, always the willing teacher, was giving him—er—private lessons in the studio section of his work loft. The space between them crackled with a fun-filled, electric connection, their bodies moving in an unconscious dance as they worked side by side.

Now that the brakes were off, so to speak, and they could be with each other in a natural way, without all the pining, moaning, and frustration, a path had opened between them, seeming to heighten that connection and make every moment together—both sacred and mundane—more enjoyable with each passing day.

In brief, they were having a blast.

James already had a working kiln, of course, and so she was over all the time anyway—practically lived there—and if she took one too many phone calls on her cell with her mom on the line while James was yodeling something in "ye olde English" in the background, well...all the more incentive to find that place where they could get married.

All the more reason and incentive for the Stupa to be approved by the council—hint.

Her mom was not subtle about how nervous she was that her only daughter was spending so much time with James. Personally, she liked him, but no parent is ever going to appreciate their child in a free-range situation, even if she was a full-grown woman.

Emma's presence had gradually seeped into every corner of the loft. Her favorite mug sat next to his on the cluttered counter, a bright splash of color against the industrial backdrop. A soft, well-worn sweater draped over the back of a chair, its fibers catching the light and seeming to glow with an inner warmth.

And so the cell phone calls with her mom went something like this: Emma would say, "Pressuring him is no good, Mom. He wants to get married, but he wants to get married in the Stupa—his mind's set on it. I'm not gonna say another word to him."

And so her mother would back away from the marriage talk temporarily... and instead say something like: "You know, honey, making a decision on the Stupa takes time—these things take time. The elder council has politics too, like, 'Who's going to be in charge? Should it be a minimal tourist attraction? Can people make reservations to come and see?' and so control the flow of people coming here... or just keep it cut off from the public entirely. As soon as they have the details wrapped up on how it could work, they will come to a decision. But that could take time. Can you afford that kind of time?" Her mom would ask in her best, most-direct-but-still-loving-her-daughter-mom tone.

Emma: "I know, Mom, I'm just kidding, trying to lighten things and put your mind at ease. James isn't going anywhere and I'm not either—we're done with that... and so please don't worry about us not being careful, or anything like that—"

And as she spoke, Emma's eyes drifted to James, taking in the line of his shoulder, the well-toned muscles in his arms, the concentration etched on his face as he worked. Nice.

Her mom laughed. "Oh, I'm not worried about you two, I'm worried about God. I think He'll spot you both as a fertile field and great landing place to grow a new life, and there will be absolutely nothing you can do to stop it. Now, a grandchild would be wonderful—have five—that would be my personal heaven, but being stable before the pressure of responsibility you can't imagine yet is best. So listen to your mother."

They had both laughed, but after thinking about it, Emma had begun to wonder if her mom was right.

Because about three days later, she found herself watching James in that particularly avid way—his muscular arms, all of the angles of him, hard and so, so appealing to her—his body flowing in harmony as he was working off steam in his studio. The afternoon light had shifted, casting a golden glow over

James's form, accentuating every line and nuance of his body. The air seemed to thicken, charged with an unspoken tension that made it challenging for Emma to breathe... without panting a wee bit.

He looked up to catch her watching him, and instantly got the message. Instantly. His eyes went that deep, deep brown with a sizzle inside. Emma put her hand on her womb... it actually felt hot... and stiffening up... and yearning toward him... oh dear God, her mom was right.

It was like a switch had been thrown. The heat seemed to radiate outward from her core, flowing like slow lava through her body, heightening her senses and setting her nerves alight. Of course, she'd been attracted to him before—that wasn't new—of course, they'd been enjoying each other very well indeed, but that all felt like a prelude now, a dress rehearsal in comparison. She felt her body wanting him for one pointed purpose.

Emma took a deep breath, hands trembling, and grabbed her coat. "Gotta go for a walk." The soft leather of her coat felt cool against her flushed skin, a stark contrast to the heat building inside her. She could hear him calling after her to "stop," "wait," "Em, where are you going?"

She couldn't wait for the elevator, so she headed for the stairs. She'd only made it down the first staircase when she heard his voice echoing in the stairwell, a mix of confusion and concern for her that tugged at her heart.

Emma turned, and there he was standing at the top of the stairs, his hair disheveled—a little long and hanging over high cheekbones—and his beautiful eyes looking with love into hers. She put her back up against the wall of the warehouse hallway as if to brace herself, to hang onto the wall to keep herself from flying at him. The rough texture of the bricks grounded her, a stark contrast to the liquid heat pooling in her womb, her back, her hips already beginning to arch toward him, lubricating the works to open for him... oh God...

She could see he knew what she wanted and said softly, as if to tame her, "It'll be alright, we'll be careful—have been before." His voice, low and soothing, seemed to caress her skin, making her hyper-aware of every inch of her body.

Emma managed to say, "James, something's happening... this is different... my mom warned me about this."

James's eyebrow lifted. "About me?" His confusion was evident in the slight furrow of his brow, the way his head tilted to look at her from a different angle.

Emma countered, "About nature... women... love to make babies... it's wild, but true..."

Her words hung in the air between them, heavy with implication and desire.

James spoke softly. "Okay, okay, I won't touch you, just don't go tearing out there like this... look, I'm backing up, please, Em, please, luv, don't leave in a tear."

And he did indeed back up into the loft. James was retreating, but his kindness, his concern for her... state, his loving nature—putting his own needs on hold—made it all suddenly too much, and she launched herself at him.

In that moment, as Emma closed the gap between them, the world narrowed to a single point of contact. The rest was a blur. The hard edges of the world faded away, leaving only the soft sensation of skin on skin, the mingling of breath, and the overwhelming tide of passion that swept them both away.

* * *

Needless to say, after that particular mid-morning meltdown and mutual exchange—as he would remember it forever fondly until the end of his days, and into his next life too—James kept his cell phone handy in his pocket or nearby on the table, and always within reach, just in case George or Alfred or anybody called with news about the Stupa.

He didn't feel concerned it would be rejected; he would abide by their decision, obviously. No—right now, his focus was on a suitable place to be married, if the Ojibwa would allow it, because he wanted to give Emma what she needed...and he needed too.

And if not the Stupa, they must make other plans.

Thank God he'd had the presence of mind to close the door, but they hadn't made it far past the kitchen area for an hour. That room still bore evidence of their passionate encounter—a knocked-over chair, orange juice on the floor, the faint imprint of flour-dusted hands on the counter and floor. And once the initial wave had been... addressed... then the sweet, soft time lying in bed together, feeding each other love in the quiet hours until morning. The rumpled sheets told their own story, a tangle of fabric that mirrored the intertwining of their lives.

James had been right all those years ago: Emma was intense. He smiled, and even blushed a little. She was so sweet, and so intense. The morning light caught the fine lines around his eyes, etched there by years of laughter and contemplation. He was the luckiest, most blessed bloke on the planet and would never complain about anything ever again, because God had given him Em. The room seemed to glow with his contentment, the very air vibrating with his joy.

He was watching her sleep now, waiting for the moment she would awake and, now satiated, they would see each other as people again—good friends too—and not someone to be consumed. Not that he was complaining, but he loved his best friend too. His eyes traced the contours of her face, memorizing every freckle, every eyelash.

Here—she was waking up now. He held his breath, and time seemed to slow as Emma stirred.

***

Very slowly, Emma opened her eyes and found herself looking right into him, the soft morning light catching the flecks of gold in his irises. She closed her eyes and put her hands over her face, the blush creeping up her neck visible even through her fingers. "Oh my goodness... oh, James... sorry..." The words came out muffled, tinged with embarrassment and residual desire.

He was chuckling, the sound warm and rich in the quiet room, pushing her hair back so he could see all of her precious face. His calloused fingers were gentle against her skin. Kissing her cheek, he breathed in the familiar scent of her. Emma was speaking between her hands, mumbling something he couldn't make out, her words lost in the cocoon of her palms.

"Was' that, luv?" James asked, his accent thicker in the intimacy of the moment. Emma moved one hand enough to say, her eye peeking out between her fingers, "I'm so embarrassed... and then... did I hurt you?" Her voice was a mixture of mortification and genuine concern.

James was laughing again, the bed shaking slightly with his mirth, and assured her he was in excellent shape. His eyes were merry and bright; if he was wearing a red stocking cap, he could have been a Christmas greeting—you know, if he had more clothes on.

Emma nodded her head, her hands finally falling away to reveal her flushed face. "Yes, you certainly are in *excellent* shape, which is how all this started... so it's your fault, right?" But her voice was light, a teasing lilt to her words. Her eyes roamed over him appreciatively, taking in the strong lines of his body.

"I'm all right... but how are you? You're not sorry, are you?" James asked softly, but he needed to know. His hand found hers under the covers, their fingers intertwining instinctively. He seemed to be holding his breath, waiting for her answer.

"Oh no, God, no, I would do it all again... probably will if we stay here like this. Hope that's okay. Maybe I've been feeling safer or something, not sure why this time was more... ah, intense."

Her words hung in the air, heavy with implication and promise. James nodded but said nothing, his thumb gently rubbing the back of her hand.

"Okay, let's get married right away," James decided. The words tumbled out, filling the space between them with a pathway.

"I'm not pressuring you at all... forget about my mom—" Emma started, her free hand touching his cheek.

"—Your mom is right. We'll both relax and have more fun once we're sanctified, committed, and otherwise set up proper," James finished, his voice low and earnest. The sunlight streaming through the window cast a warm glow on his face, highlighting the sincerity in his eyes.

"I thought you wanted to get married in the Stupa, if they allow it," Emma asked, her brow furrowing slightly. She shifted, the sheets rustling softly with her movement.

James shrugged, the motion rippling through the bed. "I do, that feels right, but if the timing is off, we can find some other place too. What do you want?" James asked, his brows pulling together, concern evident on his face.

Emma thought for a long moment, her eyes unfocused as she considered. The room was quiet, save for their breathing and the distant sounds of the city waking up outside. "Let's wait one more week. I'd like to get married in the completed Stupa. I think it's going to be extraordinary, and as you say, somebody has to begin the tradition—why not us?"

James observed, his voice thoughtful, "And what do we do about... us... this isn't going to go away?" His gaze was intense, searching her face for answers.

Emma took his hand, her fingers tracing the familiar calluses and lines. "No, it's not, thank goodness. Well... we've certainly waited for each other long enough. I can watch the calendar—the days before ovulation are the window. I can stay at my place then." Her voice was practical, but there was a hint of regret in her tone.

"Not sure I like the sound of that," James admitted, his grip on her hand tightening slightly. "We can be careful."

"Well, I won't go on the pill—it'll mess with my system, and nothing is one hundred percent except staying away from each other. But if it comes down to re-enacting the past ten years being far apart, then double no to that. And so, if something happens—you know, unexpected-like—we can get married right away. And if not, we wait until the Stupa is complete."

Emma's words were firm, her decision clear in her eyes.

"Sounds reasonable," James said, leaning in to kiss the tip of her nose. The gesture was tender, full of affection.

"I'm kinda hungry," Emma admitted, her stomach giving a soft growl as if on cue.

"Me too..." James breathed, his voice dropping an octave. He kissed her like he meant to end the conversation, the passion from earlier rekindling in an instant. The world outside faded away, leaving only the two of them in their cocoon of sheets and sunlight.

* * *

Chicago — Leona's Restaurant — *Mar. 27, 2003 — 3:30 p.m.*

Val arrived at Leona's before Sam, so she asked for a table by the front window to enjoy the bright light and clear skies Chicago was having today. The checkered tablecloths were painted in stripes of amber and shadow, a testament to the gorgeous weather outside. Val fidgeted with her napkin, smoothing imaginary wrinkles as she waited. The bell above the door chimed, and there he was—Sam, looking slightly windblown but undeniably handsome.

Val felt a jolt of surprise at her own reaction. Somehow, in the months they'd been apart, she'd forgotten just how attractive Sam was. Or rather, she realized, she'd grown so accustomed to his wit, warmth, and intelligence that his physical appearance had faded into the background. Now, seeing him framed in the doorway, the late afternoon sun catching his hair just so, it hit her anew.

The effect was a bit jarring, like rediscovering a favorite song and wondering how you'd ever forgotten the melody. It also made her wonder about something he'd said at their last meeting at her apartment, something about the downside of his physical appearance and dealing with the effect on some people. Well, she didn't want to be one of "some people," and truth be told, she didn't think she was, but still it was something to watch in her own nature.

"Sorry I'm late," he said, sliding into the booth across from her. "Editing ran long, got kinda sucked in." His voice, so familiar yet now charged with a new awareness, sent a small shiver of energy down her spine.

Val blinked, trying to shake off the unexpected rush of attraction. "No worries," she managed, proud of how steady her voice sounded. "I ordered you a Coke. Still your poison of choice?"

Sam's eyebrows rose in surprise. "You remembered."

"Hard to forget a grown man who giggles over fizzy drinks," Val replied, the hint of a smile softening her words. She was grateful for the familiar banter, a lifeline in suddenly choppy waters.

Their easy back-and-forth felt like muscle memory, comfortable despite the months of silence between them. Sam took a long sip of his drink, studying Val over the rim of his glass. She found herself wondering if he was experiencing a similar rediscovery, and the thought made her cheeks warm.

"So," he said finally, setting the Coke down. "To what do I owe the pleasure? Last I checked, I was persona non grata in the land of Val."

Val winced, the reminder of their estrangement cooling some of her rekindled attraction. "About that... I may have overreacted."

"May have?" Sam's tone was light, but there was a flicker of something in his eyes—hope, perhaps, or wariness. Or maybe it was a genuine question.

Val took a deep breath and opted to ignore that for the moment and stay on track. "Look, I didn't call you here to rehash dusty stuff. Alfred's throwing a party in Wilmette. He wants us both there."

Sam's brow furrowed. "Us? As in, you and me specifically?"

Val nodded. "Apparently, we're on some kind of VIP list. Don't ask me why."

"Huh." Sam leaned back, absently tracing patterns in the condensation on his glass. "And you couldn't just text me this because...?"

Val bit her lip. "There's more. I gave James a heads-up... and so James told Alfred that you saw some... sensitive information on my computer—when you returned those thumb drives."

Understanding dawned on Sam's face. "The Stupa research."

She nodded, tension coiling in her shoulders. "If you hear any rumors—"

"—I know nothing," Sam finished for her. "On my honor."

Relief washed over Val's features. "Thank you."

They lapsed into silence, the clatter of dishes and murmur of other diners filling the space between them. Finally, Sam spoke.

"Listen, Val. I know things got... complicated. But I want you to know, if you'd rather keep things strictly professional, I understand. No hard feelings, no awkward attempts to rekindle a friendship you're not interested in."

Val's eyes snapped to his face, searching. "Is that what you want?"

Sam's expression softened. "What I want and what's best aren't always the same thing."

Val nodded, processing. After a moment, she reached into her bag and pulled out a small envelope. "Here's the party details. I should get going."

As she pulled her things together to leave, Sam's voice stopped her. "Val? One more thing."

She turned, eyebrows raised in question.

"When the documentary's finished, if it ever gets finished—you'll be listed in the credits. As an editor, plus a couple other mentions too. It's not much, but... your insight was invaluable."

A small smile tugged at the corners of Val's mouth. "Thanks, Sam. That's... that means a lot."

As Val stood to leave, Sam's voice stopped her. "You're gonna make me eat here by myself?"

Val hesitated, her hand still on her purse. "I don't want to impose..."

Sam's eyes sparkled, a hint of his old charm peeking through. "It's spaghetti night, Val. You know I can't walk away from that. Besides, lunch is on me," he added, his tone softening, "consider it a thank-you for all your work on the project."

For a moment, Val teetered on the edge of decision. Then, with a small sigh that was equal parts resignation and relief, she slid back into the booth. "Well, when you put it that way... I do like to eat."

Sam's face lit up with a genuine smile, and Val felt something inside her chest loosen, just a fraction.

As they perused the menus, a slightly more comfortable silence settled between them. It was Sam who finally broke it. "So, I moved apartments," he said casually, not looking up from his menu.

Val's eyebrows rose. "Oh? Noisy neighbors? Rent hike?"

Sam shrugged, his eyes still fixed on the list of pasta dishes. "Something like that."

Before Val could probe further, their waiter appeared, notepad at the ready. They placed their orders—spaghetti and meatballs for Sam, fettuccine Alfredo for Val—and settled back into an awkward quiet.

"So," Val said, fiddling with her napkin, "how's the documentary coming along?"

Sam's face lit up, and he launched into an enthusiastic description of his latest edits. Val found herself leaning in, drawn in by his passion. As she reached for her water glass, her elbow caught the edge of her plate, sending the glass teetering off the table's edge.

In a blur of motion, Sam's hand shot out, snatching the glass from midair before it could shatter on the floor. A few drops splashed onto the tablecloth, but the disaster had been largely averted.

Val blinked, her mouth slightly agape. "How did you…?"

Sam set the glass back on the table with a sheepish grin. "Uh, just good reflexes, I guess."

But Val wasn't buying it. She narrowed her eyes, studying him. "That was more than just good reflexes, Sam. That was… I don't know, some kind of ninja move."

Sam shrugged, a hint of color rising in his cheeks. "Really no big deal, I rescue falling glasses all the time. Sometimes, I even practice on the quiet."

Val leaned back, crossing her arms, trying to suppress a smile. He was funny—that was funny—but she wanted to get to the bottom of this, so she didn't let go. "Wait, I remember now, you told me you took martial arts training. I thought it was kids' classes, but did you continue?"

Sam's attempt at nonchalance crumbled under Val's scrutiny. He looked around the room as if searching for a diversion, but finally opted for, "Okay, you got me. I may have kept up with it a bit more than I let on."

"A bit more?" Val pressed, her curiosity piqued. "What level are you?"

"It's not really about levels—"

"Sam."

He sighed, his shoulders slumping under the grilling and his innate desire to please her. "Fine. I have a black belt in Aikido. But it's not something I usually bring up in casual conversation." When she simply looked at him, he explained, "It's a great physical, mental discipline, great way to stay in shape. I recommend it to you—I think you'd be a natural."

"Are you saying I'm flabby?" Val drilled with a straight face.

"No, far from it..." Just as he was beginning to look flustered, a smile cracked on Val's face. "Oh, great gangsters, I'd kinda forgot how quick you are. I've missed you, Val."

Val couldn't help but chuckle at Sam's flustered expression. "I've missed you too," she admitted, surprising herself with the warmth in her voice. She leaned forward, resting her elbows on the table. "So, a black belt, huh? That's pretty impressive. How long did it take you to get there?"

She found herself genuinely curious, not just about the Aikido, but about all the little details of Sam's life she'd missed out on. It was like rediscovering an old favorite book and finding new chapters you'd somehow overlooked before.

"And don't think I didn't notice that smooth deflection," she added, her eyes twinkling with amusement. "Recommending Aikido to me? Nice try, but you're not getting off that easy. I want to hear all about it. I know when you started and why, but why did you stick with it all the way to black belt? Wait, sorry, I don't want to make you rehash emotional stuff—"

"Wait, let's fix a possible miscue right now, I was trying to say I don't have emotional stuff, I think, because of Aikido. The training puts things in proportion, it's not about throwing chops or high kicks, it's a Japanese art form on how to protect yourself and the attacker from injury. It really keeps your head straight about priorities."

"You know," she began, her voice thoughtful, "have you ever considered making a documentary about kids learning Aikido or martial arts? It seems like something that could really inspire people, especially with your perspective on it."

He set down his fork, giving Val his full attention. "I've actually thought about it," he admitted. "The transformative power of martial arts, especially for kids, is incredible. But..." he trailed off, his brow furrowing.

"But?" Val prompted gently.

Sam sighed, running a hand through his hair. "There are some serious ethical considerations. Putting kids on camera, making them identifiable to the public—it opens up a whole can of worms. Remember our discussions about documentary ethics?"

Val nodded, recalling their late-night debates over coffee and editing software. "The responsibility of the filmmaker to their subjects," she murmured.

"Exactly," Sam said, leaning forward. "With adults, there's informed consent. But kids? Even with parental permission, it feels like a gray area. And in today's digital age, once something's out there, it's out there forever."

Val was touched by Sam's thoughtfulness. "You've really considered this from all angles, haven't you?"

Sam shrugged, a self-deprecating smile tugging at his lips. "Occupational hazard, I guess. But it's important—we have a responsibility to our subjects, especially the vulnerable ones."

"It's admirable," Val said softly. "The way you think about these things."

Their eyes met across the table, and for a moment, the bustling restaurant faded away. Val saw a man of principle, trying his best to navigate a complex world with integrity.

"Maybe," she ventured, breaking the silence, "there's a way to tell that story without compromising anyone's privacy. A more abstract approach, or focusing on the instructors instead of the kids?"

Sam's face lit up with interest. "That's not a bad idea, actually. It could be a way to explore the impact without putting anyone at risk." He chuckled softly. "See, this is why I've missed our brainstorming sessions. You always bring a fresh perspective."

Val felt a blush creep up her cheeks, oddly pleased by the compliment. "Well," she said, trying to keep her tone light, "I guess you'll just have to keep me around for future projects then."

Sam's smile widened, reaching his eyes. "I guess I will," he agreed softly.

For a moment, they just looked at each other, the bustling restaurant fading into the background. Then Val cleared her throat, suddenly aware of how intense the moment had become. "So, uh, any other secret ninja skills I should know about? Throwing stars? Smoke bombs?"

Sam laughed, the tension breaking. "Sorry to disappoint, but my talents are strictly limited to catching falling glasses and the occasional pratfall."

Val laughed out loud, and Sam actually beamed—he'd made her laugh, God, he loved the sound.

"Any other hidden talents I should know about?" she asked, trying to keep her tone light.

Sam's eyes met hers, a hint of mischief dancing in their depths. "I guess you'll just have to stick around and find out."

The air between them seemed to crackle a little with that. Val's eyes widened a bit, and then she looked down. Sam might be hiding...what other sides of him she had yet to discover. It was exciting and terrifying all at once.

As they resumed their meal, Val couldn't help but steal glances at Sam. He was still the same man she'd known—kind, funny, passionate about his work. But now she was reminded of all the things about him that had first caught her attention. The quiet confidence, the hint of mystery, the way he could make her feel both completely at ease and delightfully off-balance.

Sam twirled a forkful of spaghetti, a look of pure bliss on his face as he took the first bite. "God, I've missed this place. It used to be my neighborhood stop," he mumbled around his mouthful of food.

Val enjoyed him devouring his food for a few moments and then focused on her own plate. "So," she said, hoping to keep the conversation going, "you never did tell me why you moved."

Sam was quiet for a moment, pushing a meatball around his plate. Finally, he looked up, meeting Val's gaze. "I needed a fresh start," he said simply. "Some distance from... old habits."

Understanding dawned on Val's face. "Oh," she said softly.

They ate in silence for a while, the weight of unspoken words hanging between them. As they finished their meals, Sam spoke again.

"I thought you were writing me off," he admitted, his voice low. "When months went by without a word..."

Val's fork clattered against her plate. "Sam, I—"

He held up a hand, cutting her off. "It's okay. I get it. Things were complicated. Are complicated," he corrected himself with a wry smile.

Val took a deep breath. "I needed time," she said finally. "To sort things out in my head. But I never meant to..." She trailed off, unsure how to finish and finally opted for the truth. "I'm sorry if I upset your life. I'm never usually that emotional at all. James was so scared for Alfred, and I've never seen that before—the guy is fearless in most ways. Emotion can be catchy, but I don't really know why... I melted down. I'm trying to say I'm sorry."

Sam set down his fork, his eyes softening as he listened to Val's apology. He took a moment to gather his thoughts, his gaze drifting to the window where the Chicago streets bustled with early evening activity. When he looked back at Val, there was a mix of understanding and something deeper in his expression.

"Val," he began, his voice gentle but firm, "you don't need to apologize for having emotions. That's part of being human. And honestly? Seeing that side of you... it wasn't upsetting. It was real."

He leaned forward slightly, his elbows resting on the table. The warm glow of the restaurant's lighting brightened his eyes, making them seem to dance as he spoke.

"I get it, you know? James being scared for Alfred—that's big. It's the kind of thing that shakes you, makes you question what's really important." Sam paused, a rueful smile tugging at his lips. "If anything, I should thank you. That... intensity, it made me take a hard look at my own life. Hence the move, the fresh start."

He reached for his water glass, taking a sip before continuing. "As for writing me off, well, I won't pretend it didn't sting. But I understand needing time. Hell, I needed it too—to figure out what I really want, what matters."

Sam's gaze met Val's, steady and sincere. "I'm glad you called, Val. Even if it was just about Alfred's party. It gave us a chance to clear the air, to...catch up."

He hesitated for a moment, then added softly, "And for what it's worth, I like that you can be emotional sometimes. It shows you care. About your friends, your work... maybe even about me?"

The last part was said with a hint of his old charm, a playful sparkle in his eye that seemed to ask, *Is that okay? Are we okay?*

Sam sat back, giving Val space to process his words. He picked up his fork again, twirling another bite of spaghetti, but his attention remained on Val, waiting to see how she'd respond to his olive branch.

Val took a deep breath, her eyes meeting Sam's. "Thanks for that, we're okay," she said softly, almost like it came as a surprise to her, a small smile tugging at her lips. "Maybe we could... I don't know, grab coffee sometime? Catch up properly?"

Sam's face lit up with a gentle smile. "I'd like that, Val. I'd like that a lot. In fact, maybe it can be your turn to answer my list questions... next time."

Her eyes widened slightly at that, and at her surprised expression Sam observed, "Ah... the tables can turn."

As the waiter approached with their check, Val glanced at her watch. "Oh, I should probably get going."

"Okay, avoid for now, but I find you interesting too, you know." And then he looked at her and smiled, happy to have his friend back.

"All right... and well-played," Val admitted and chuckled.

Sam settled the bill—this was his treat, after all—and then they gathered their things, a comfortable silence settling between them as they stepped out of Leona's. The city was transitioning into twilight, the streetlights flickering to life around them.

"So, I'll see you at Alfred's party?" Sam asked, turning to face Val.

Val nodded. "Wouldn't miss it."

For a moment, they stood there, neither quite ready to say goodbye. Then Sam cleared his throat. "How's your car running these days? Think it'll make it to Wilmette?"

Val grimaced. "Half and half. It's been making this weird noise lately, but I'm hoping it'll hold out until payday."

Sam's brow furrowed with concern. "Well, if you need a ride, let me know. It doesn't sound like a meeting you want to miss or end up grabbing a taxi for at the last minute."

As he spoke, Sam reached out, his hand lightly tapping the back of Val's hand in a gesture that was both casual and deliberate. The moment his fingers made contact, a frisson of energy seemed to pass between them. Val felt her breath catch, the warmth of his touch spreading through her like molten lava—that is, slow... but igniting every atom on the way.

Sam's eyes widened slightly; he'd felt it too, and frankly couldn't move from the spot, as if hit by a mini stun gun, his hand lingering for a heartbeat longer than necessary. The physical manifestation of their connection had somehow grown stronger in their time apart.

Val managed a smile, hoping her voice didn't betray the sudden racing of her heart or feeling breathless. "Thanks, Sam. I'll keep that in mind."

As they parted ways, Val couldn't help but glance back over her shoulder. Sam was still standing there, hands in his pockets, watching her go. She offered a small wave, which he returned with a lopsided smile.

Walking toward her temperamental car, Val found herself both unsettled, oddly elated, and her body pleasantly singing. The evening had not gone as expected, but somehow, that didn't seem like a bad thing... at all.

Because some essential dynamic element between them had changed—he had changed, she had changed, they had changed.

Maybe it was as simple as removing Olivia from his energy field, or whatever... and her growing up a bit too. Maybe, just maybe, there was hope for them after all.

* * *

Chapter 44

Wilmette, IL — Worthington Residence — *Apr. 5, 2003 — 1:00 p.m. — Invitation*

Mabel had invited everyone over to their place—that is, the house in Wilmette—because it was getting just a little warmer out, the air carrying a hint of spring's promise. The large backyard and patio stretched out invitingly, dappled sunlight dancing across the freshly mowed grass and newly bloomed flowers. There was plenty of room for guests to amble, the space seeming to expand with the potential for laughter and conversation.

Everyone was happy to come, of course, a palpable excitement buzzing through the phone lines as invitations were extended and accepted. This was to be an informal fun-and-facts party meetup, but she and Alfred decided to do it up right, their enthusiasm infusing every detail of the preparation. They felt young again, a spring in their step as they moved about the house, arranging chairs and laying out platters.

Their sweet boy was in love—that was apparent—and Alfred and Mabel wanted to celebrate James and Emma, and perhaps the coming spring as well. James's usual dry demeanor had been replaced by a barely contained joy that radiated from him like perpetual warmth from the sun. They were so happy; it was a catchy thing. James and Emma's joy bubble moved 'good feeling' like osmosis to a fifty-foot perimeter. The very air seemed to shimmer with contentment, each breath filling lungs with not just oxygen, but pure, unadulterated happiness. If that in itself wasn't worth a party, perhaps some updates and changes that might affect them all were.

In any case, the food was ready with plenty of variety, aromas of savory dishes mingling with the sweet scent of freshly baked desserts. All was prepared—every surface gleaming, every cushion plumped—the house holding its breath in anticipation of the gathering to come. Mabel felt wonderful, a warm glow of satisfaction settling in her chest as she surveyed her handiwork.

She heard the doorbell, its cheerful chime echoing through the house, and then her husband called out a "hello," his voice carrying a note of welcome that seemed to embrace the arriving guest. Ah, Rhonda was the first to arrive—always punctual, always put together. Mabel went to greet her, her steps light on the polished hardwood floors.

It felt like Christmas—that same bubbling excitement, that same sense of magic in the air. The house seemed to come alive, shaking off the last vestiges of winter's chill and opening its arms to the warmth of friendship and new beginnings.

* * *

Gerardo arrived next, and not that they needed food, but he had been instructed by his father at an early age to never arrive empty-handed to a party or social invitation, and so he brought cookies—tasty, crisp cookies from an eastern European bakery on Lincoln Ave. They had arranged them on a plate and everything, so there would be no additional work for Mabel. The plate was a delicate porcelain, its edges adorned with intricate blue flowers that seemed a good harbinger for the coming spring.

Alfred greeted him with a bear hug before Gerardo could hug him—that was a first. The embrace was warm and genuine,

Alfred's cardigan soft against Gerardo's cheek. The scent of Alfred's familiar cologne—a mix of sandalwood and something indefinably comforting—enveloped Gerardo, bringing a sense of home and belonging.

Gerardo wasn't sure what to expect since their last group meeting—the fateful Epoch Alliance Sunday—he half expected one and all to be somewhat downcast, but no, there was a merry, light quality in the air, almost as if a heavy load had been laid down. A feeling of freedom. The room seemed to buzz with an energy that was almost tangible, a lightness that lifted spirits and smoothed away worry lines.

Gerardo entered the living room, his heart lifting at the vision of Rhonda wearing a white sweater and blue jeans. It was a lighter color than her usual fare, and it suited her and put him in mind of that morning he'd seen her in that oversized white shirt. Never quite burned that image out of his brain. The soft white of Rhonda's sweater seemed to glow in the afternoon light, accentuating the warmth in her eyes and the slight flush on her cheeks.

"Hello, Rhon... you are looking fine, fine, fine," Gerardo observed, and refrained from a wolf whistle. His voice was rich with admiration, his eyes twinkling with barely contained delight.

Rhonda pushed lightly at his shoulder, her touch lingering for a moment longer than necessary. Her lips curved into a smile that held a hint of "maybe," and then she forgot her quip and instead said, "Thanks, you too."

"Who's here?" Gerardo asked, his eyes roaming the room, taking in the comfortable furnishings and the personal touches that made Alfred's and Mabel's home so welcoming.

"Do you mean, is Emma here? Is James lurking?" Rhonda's voice held a note of amusement, her eyebrow arching slightly as she studied Gerardo's face.

Gerardo smiled. "Maybe." The smile reached his eyes in a way that made him look boyish and charming.

Rhonda's voice dropped, and she asked, "Are you still mad at him?" Her tone was gentle, concern evident in the soft furrow of her brow.

Gerardo tilted his head and cracked his neck but said, "I'm not mad at him, as such. James shoots straight and goes for what he wants. I was mad at the situation… and this may sound crazy… but I'm a little pissed that I actually feel better. This past week especially, I find myself waking up feeling ten years younger. That Sunday I made one of the toughest calls in my life. And now we're all war buddies or something, a little giddy that we survived, maybe?" As he spoke, Gerardo's posture relaxed, the tension in his shoulders melting away.

"Or," Rhonda leaned in to say, "it's already working, and we are being forgiven." Her words were barely above a whisper, her breath warm against Gerardo's ear.

Gerardo breathed in and asked, "Can I kiss you on the cheek for saying that?" His eyes searched Rhonda's face, a mix of hope and nervousness flitting across his features.

Rhonda's brows went up, but she nodded, a faint blush coloring her cheeks.

As Gerardo gave her a small cheek kiss, Alfred came back into the room with a stack of folders he placed on the end table near his easy chair. The folders were a crisp manila, their edges neat and precise, a testament to Alfred's meticulous nature.

"Well, that's nice to see," Alfred observed, his voice warm with approval, his eyes twinkling with a mixture of amusement and affection as he regarded Gerardo and Rhonda.

The door chime sounded, its melodic tones echoing through the cozy living room. Alfred's face lit up, his eyes twinkling with anticipation. "Ah!" he exclaimed, "That's probably them."

But it wasn't James and Emma. Gerardo heard voices, but they weren't the familiar tones he was expecting. Instead, to everyone's surprise, it was Sam Petosky, the videographer, and Val, James's ever-efficient assistant. They stood framed in the doorway to the living room, Sam with his camera bag slung over his shoulder, Val clutching a sleek leather portfolio.

Sam and Val entered the room with a careful air of casualness, like two people who happened to arrive at the same moment but were trying not to make a big deal of it. They maintained a polite distance, not quite together but not apart either. It looked like they had arrived in the same Twinkie box but weren't in the same Twinkie package.

Their eyes met briefly before they turned to greet their hosts. Val's posture was professional, her smile warm but reserved; this was close to "poker face" Val—on guard until she understood the lay of the land. Sam seemed to follow suit; his demeanor was friendly yet reserved. They moved into the room in the way two stray cats might on a new turf—curious, but testing the welcome as they tread.

Gerardo leaned in close to Rhonda, his breath warm against her ear as he whispered, "I gotta admit that's a surprise."

Mabel had been observing from the kitchen doorway; she now picked up the plate of cookies Gerardo had brought. Her eyes widened with delight as she recognized the treats. "Oh!" she exclaimed, her voice filled with genuine pleasure. "Are those

Spritzes? I love Spritz. Thank you, Gerardo—may I lay them out? They will be perfect with the hot beverages."

The cookies glistened in the soft light, their delicate shapes promising a perfect blend of sweetness and crunch. Mabel's fingers hovered over them, as if reluctant to disturb the artful arrangement.

Alfred, ever the gracious host, was already escorting Sam and Val deeper into the living room, his hand resting lightly on Sam's shoulder, guiding them towards Gerardo and Rhonda. The room was awash in warm, golden light from the antique floor lamps, casting a cozy glow on the gathered group. "And you all know each other," he said, his voice warm, providing welcome.

Rhonda's gaze fell on Sam, her eyes taking in his tall frame and the way he held himself with a mixture of confidence and humility. His camera bag hung at his side, a constant companion that seemed as much a part of him as his left arm. "I'm not sure we've actually met formally," she said, her tone polite but with an underlying note of curiosity.

Sam was just as handsome as she remembered; Rhonda had noticed him on the perimeter of the studio and on location at the Field Museum, but had never actually met the man. As Rhonda's curiosity became apparent, Sam subtly shifted his stance, angling his body slightly towards Val. The movement was almost imperceptible, but it effectively included Val in the conversation.

Val performed the introductions with the efficiency and clarity of a seasoned ringmaster. Sam shook hands with Rhonda, his grip firm but not overbearing, and nodded to Gerardo, adding, "Thanks for the tip for the kiln firing, I got some great footage." His voice carried the enthusiasm of an artist who'd captured something special.

"Por nada...just hope you can use it someday," Gerardo offered with a grimace.

"Were you very disappointed that your doc is on the shelf?" Rhonda asked, her eyes searching Sam's face for any sign of frustration or regret.

Sam drew in a breath. "Well, I come from a background in the theatre, so I'm used to fast turn-around of fortune. Shows open and close, but I've never met a project that caved after so much hard work...I just don't believe it. I think something is going to happen."

"Is that your radar talking?" This was from Val, her tone genuinely curious.

Sam shrugged, settling into a stance of quiet confidence. He would say no more.

Gerardo, sensing an upcoming gap in conversation, turned to Alfred, his brow furrowing slightly as he asked, "What's up, Alfred? Who else is coming?"

Alfred neatly evaded the first part of the question, his eyes twinkling with a hint of mischief. He focused on the second part, his voice warm as he replied, "Well, James and Emma, of course, and they are bringing a couple of people."

As if on cue, the door chimes rang out again, their cheerful sound filling the room. This time Mabel was at the door, and her exclamation of pure delight meant James and Emma had arrived. There was a murmur of bright voices calling out hello, the air suddenly filled with the warmth of reunions and the rustle of embraces.

Mabel escorted James, Emma, Ted, and Maribel into the living room, her face beaming with joy—she was so pleased to have new people to play with.

James looked relaxed; he seemed to fill the room effortlessly, yet calm in his own skin—a man who knew himself—his hand casually placed on Emma's lower back. The gesture was both protective and possessive, a silent declaration of their bond. As for Em, her cheeks were flushed with happiness, her eyes bright, her dark hair so vibrant it fairly danced in the light, each strand seeming to catch and reflect the room's warm glow.

They both looked around the room, nodding to their friends, calling out "hello." Their voices blended in perfect harmony, as if they'd been practicing this duet for years.

Gerardo looked to Rhonda, inclining his head toward the other mod squad members, and she nodded, her words somewhat wistful: "Oh yeah, absolutely." And then, as if the thought had just occurred to her, "So that's what love looks like."

Rhonda looked at Gerardo, and he nodded, a silent understanding passing between them. "I'm happy for them," he said, his voice soft but sincere.

She nodded, but their sotto voce moment was soon lost in the sea of sound and greetings and introductions.

Ted and Maribel were the misnomers, but introductions were made all round, the room filled with a din of happy voices and clever banter. The air hummed with energy, a palpable sense of excitement and anticipation. Ted's booming laugh rang out as he shared a joke with Gerardo, while Maribel engaged in an animated conversation with Val about the latest developments in the project, their words tumbling over each other in a rush of shared enthusiasm.

Sam quietly pulled himself to the outskirts of the group, made sure his digital camera was on silent shutter, and took some discreet candid photos. He had a feeling this would be an event to mark, and so he did his best to do it—plus, free food. Always a plus. When Val noticed what he was doing, she would drift over now and again to touch base and make sure he was included in the general happy-go-lucky melee.

After the room settled somewhat, Mabel's voice rose above the chatter. "Please, everyone, help yourselves to light refreshments," she said, gesturing towards a table laden with an array of delectable treats. The Spritz cookies Gerardo had brought were artfully arranged on the plate he'd brought, surrounded by an assortment of fresh fruits and savory bites. "There will be a proper lunch later," Mabel continued, her tone warm and inviting. "Once you've got your snacks, please come back and take a seat in the living room."

The group moved towards the refreshment table, the soft clink of china and silverware mingling with the continued hum of conversation. James and Emma stood close together, their hands brushing as they reached for the same cookie, eliciting soft laughter from both. Sam hung back slightly, his eyes moving around the room as if mentally framing each moment. Val poked him in the arm, and as he leaned down to catch what she was saying, she handed him a small tray of treats. "Not from my purse this time," she assured him, her face solemn.

It took Sam a couple of seconds to remember the cheese puffs rolled in red paper from the Epoch party, and then he laughed and took the small plate from her.

As the room buzzed with conversation and laughter, James and Emma made their way to the seating area. With an almost synchronized swim-team movement, they bee-lined for the two-seater sofa, their hands brushing against each other as they sat down. Emma leaned into James subtly, a soft smile playing on her lips as he draped his arm casually on the back of the sofa behind her.

Gerardo, still bantering with Ted, caught this interaction out of the corner of his eye. He turned slightly, catching Rhonda's gaze. His eyebrow raised, nodding almost imperceptibly towards James and Emma and their cuddle-fest on the couch.

Rhonda slowly shook her head. She was happy for them—she was—but it would take some getting used to. "Totally besotted," she mouthed, her eyes twinkling with amusement and something akin to awe.

As everyone began to settle into the comfortable seats of the living room, there was a sense of anticipation in the air. Whatever reason Alfred and Mabel had to gather them here, it was clearly significant.

* * *

The mid-afternoon sun glowed through the windows of Alfred's living room, casting a warm, golden glow over the assembled group. The air hummed with anticipation, the soft murmur of conversation fading as all eyes turned to Alfred. He sat in his favorite armchair, a well-worn leather piece that seemed to cradle him like an old friend. His fingers traced the arm of the chair absently; he was winding up for a pitch.

Alfred's eyes twinkled as he gazed around the room, taking in each face with a mixture of fondness and barely contained excitement. The lines around his eyes crinkled with genuine pleasure as he began to speak, his voice warm and rich, filling the space with its reassuring timbre.

"My dear friends," he began, leaning forward slightly, "I can't tell you how happy I am to see you all here, to meet new faces and reconnect with old ones in this house, at this particular moment in time." He paused, his gaze lingering on James and Emma, nestled together on the two-seater sofa, their closeness life-affirming in itself.

Alfred's hands came together, fingers interlacing as he continued, "We've been through quite a journey together, haven't we? The highs, the lows, the unexpected turns..." He chuckled softly, the sound warm and inviting. "But through it all, I've seen a remarkable feat accomplished. The end result seems almost less important to me than the fact that we tried with every ounce of our beings to always do the right thing as we imagined it to be at the time." And here he glanced around the room, looking steadily into every person's eyes. "And that has inspired Mabel and myself."

Was everyone holding their individual breath? Yes—the atmosphere was charged as if waiting for the other shoe to drop. But which one, and where? Mabel was standing near the doorway, nodding encouragingly, her eyes shining with pride and affection.

"Recent events have made me reflect deeply on our purpose—on the legacy we want to leave," Alfred continued, his voice taking on a more serious tone. "And I've come to a decision. A decision that I believe will shape the future of not just our project, but of community art initiatives for years to come."

He paused, his eyes sweeping the room once more. James leaned forward, both hands in his lap now, as if bracing himself. Gerardo and Rhonda exchanged intrigued glances, while Ted's eyebrows shot up in curiosity.

"I've decided," Alfred said, his voice gaining strength, "that it's time for Epoch Alliance to evolve—to become something greater than we ever imagined. We're going to convert Epoch Alliance into a non-profit organization."

A collective gasp rippled through the room, followed by a buzz of excited whispers. Alfred held up a hand, smiling as he continued.

"This isn't just a legal change. It's a statement of intent, a declaration that, going forward, our work—our vision—will now be centered around community, about nurturing creativity and connection. By becoming a non-profit, we're committing to this vision for the long haul."

As the implications of his words began to sink in, the room buzzed with a new energy. This wasn't just a gathering—it was the beginning of something monumental, a transformation that would reshape their collective purpose.

Alfred sat back in his chair, basking in the warmth of his announcement. "Of course, there's a lot of work ahead: legal hurdles, restructuring, new ways of thinking about our projects. But I believe, with all my heart, that this is the right path forward. Because as we've so clearly seen, if we don't begin with this intention, who will?"

The room erupted in a mix of applause, questions, and excited chatter. James and Emma exchanged a look of surprise and wonder. Emma leaned in to whisper, "Did you know?" But James was already shaking his head—he hadn't any idea they were going in this direction.

Gerardo's face split into a wide grin, and he popped a cookie in his mouth. Rhonda's eyes gleamed with the possibilities this change presented.

As the initial excitement began to settle, Alfred leaned forward once more, his expression both serious and hopeful. "So, my friends, what do you say? Are you ready to embark on this new adventure with me?"

The answer was written on every face in the room. This was more than a new beginning—it was a renewal of purpose, a chance to create something truly lasting. It appeared to be a solid "yes."

* * *

Alfred's living room was bright with the relentless white light of early afternoon, energizing the assembled group. The air buzzed with the intensity of their discussion, the aroma of fresh coffee mingling with the sweet scent of Gerardo's Spritz cookies. It was a wonderful time of day to talk turkey. Or new business. Same thing.

For the next hour, the room was filled with the soft rustle of papers as everyone pored over the folders Mabel had distributed. Alfred's steady voice guided them through the outlined details, his words painting a picture of Epoch Alliance's future.

"There will be a reserve fund to stabilize the financial system for new Epoch Alliance," Alfred explained, his fingers tracing the relevant lines on the document before him. "We'll have flow from several income streams, but yes, we will need to begin in a conservative way."

Emma leaned forward, her brow furrowed in concentration as she made neat annotations in the margins of her folder. Beside her, James alternated between studying the documents, observing the reactions in the room, and occasionally lingering on Emma's focused profile.

Alfred continued, his voice taking on a note of enthusiasm, "Certain investments along the lines of supporting alternative energy sources, especially for electric cars, are foremost in planning for the long haul." Gerardo's eyes lit up at this, his mind already racing with possibilities for sustainable art projects.

"But for the short term," Alfred added, tempering the excitement with practicality, "I foresee that we can reasonably arrange for perhaps two new projects a year. This will build our reputation, roots, and make new contacts in the direction we would like to proceed."

The room fell into a contemplative silence as everyone absorbed this information. The tick of the antique clock on the mantelpiece seemed to grow louder, marking the passage of this crucial hour.

James broke the silence, his voice carrying a mix of curiosity and concern. "I know you must have already covered this, but the board? Will they go along with this? You know how some of them are."

All eyes turned to Alfred, the air thick with anticipation. Alfred's face softened into a reassuring smile, the creases around his eyes deepening. "Yes... thanks for asking, James, yes—let's clear that from our minds right away," he said, his tone warm and confident. "The members of the board will not stand in our way. Mabel and I began Epoch, and they recognized that. They have all agreed, and after the transition, which will take some time, the ones who wish to go in a different direction will resign. I have taken them at their word."

A collective sigh of relief whispered through the room. Shoulders visibly relaxed, and the atmosphere lightened considerably. Rhonda and Gerardo exchanged glances, a mix of surprise and approval in their eyes.

Ted, sitting up straighter in his chair, nodded thoughtfully. His posture and expression reflected his professional demeanor, despite being new to the group. He seemed to be carefully considering the implications of this transition, his mind no doubt already racing with potential design concepts for the new non-profit. But still—Alfred barely knew them. He looked to Maribel, who easily read his mind: *but what has this to do with us?*

Sam, seated quietly near the back of the room, remained still and attentive. His camera bag sat unopened at his feet, a silent reminder of his usual role. Yet today, he was here as more than just a documentarian, though the reason for his presence remained a mystery to most in the room.

There were still unanswered questions and cards to be played.

Right on time, Alfred held up one hand to hold the group's attention. "Many of you have a very good understanding of why you have been invited here, and to others it may seem a surprise. We will address all of the variables in short order, and the myriad of other details as well, but first, I believe my precious Mabel, as 'artist-in-residence' of the house, is best suited to address this next important—and possibly critical—issue for some."

As Alfred spoke, a subtle shift occurred in the room. Mabel moved from her position in the doorway, her steps deliberate and graceful. The soft rustle of her clothing mingled with the gentle creak of chairs as those seated turned to face her. She stood in the cleared space, bathed in sunlight, cradling a folded quilt in her arms. The fabric, even in its compressed state, seemed to shimmer with hidden colors and textures.

Those who had been present at the Sunday meeting straightened in their seats, recognition dawning in their eyes. Sam, Maribel, and Ted—newcomers to this particular aspect—leaned forward with heightened curiosity.

Her voice, soft yet clear, filled the room. "Well... Alfred called me 'Artist in Residence' of the family, and that's where I'll begin, because I've never thought of myself that way, and I really don't know of anyone who makes quilts that does."

With practiced ease, Mabel unfurled the quilt. The room collectively held its breath as the fabric cascaded open, revealing the intricate design that had, until now, existed only as a photograph for most present. Sam, demonstrating unexpected agility and quick reflexes, was on his feet in an instant. He positioned himself behind the quilt, his tall frame providing the perfect backdrop to display the full majesty of Mabel's creation.

As the quilt unfurled in its entirety, a soft gasp rippled through the room. The vivid colors and intricate patterns, now brought to life in three dimensions, seemed to dance in the sunlight. For those who had seen only the photograph, the reality was a revelation—each stitch, each carefully chosen fabric, told a story that no two-dimensional image could capture.

Emma's voice, filled with genuine awe, broke the reverent silence. "Oh, Mabel... that's wonderful... really beautiful."

A chorus of agreement followed. The newcomers—Maribel and Ted—wore expressions of delighted surprise, their eyes drinking in every detail of the masterpiece before them.

Mabel acknowledged the praise with a gentle nod, her eyes sparkling with joy and some knowledge specific to the moment she was about to share. As the initial wave of exclamations subsided, she spoke again, her words carrying a weight that seemed to settle over the room.

"It is wonderful and beautiful too... but it's not art."

The statement hung in the air, challenging and provocative. Those who had been present at the Sunday meeting exchanged knowing glances, while the newcomers' expressions shifted to intrigued curiosity. The quilt, still displayed in all its glory, seemed to take on a new significance.

As Mabel's statement hung in the air, a ripple of objections began to rise from her friends in the room. Their faces registered a mix of confusion and disagreement—brows furrowing and mouths opening to protest. But before anyone could voice their thoughts, Mabel raised her hand, the gesture both gentle and firm. The room fell silent, all eyes fixed on her weathered hand, steady and sure against the vibrant backdrop of the quilt.

"And I will tell you why." Mabel's voice was soft but clear, carrying effortlessly in the hushed room. "I didn't sign it. You can look all you want, but you won't find my signature."

As she spoke, several in the room leaned forward, eyes scanning the quilt's intricate patterns as if searching for a hidden signature. James looked at Emma and smiled a slow, quiet smile; he was beginning to get an impression of where Alfred and Mabel were heading.

"I have no personal stake in this whatsoever," Mabel continued, her words measured and thoughtful. "Everyone who knows me understands I made it, and I receive contemporary accolades—and that is absolutely fine—because if I was doing this for a living, I would need those contacts to continue to thrive and make more for other people to enjoy. And so I'll be known in my small community... but no one at all will remember me for this beautiful quilt in twenty years, and that is how it should be—because it never belonged to me anyway, not really."

As Mabel's words sank in, a palpable shift occurred in the room. Emma's eyes widened with understanding, a small smile playing at the corners of her mouth. Gerardo leaned back in his chair, his expression thoughtful, while Rhonda's fingers rested lightly on her knees, waiting for the "reveal."

Mabel paused, allowing her words to resonate. The quilt, still held aloft by Sam, seemed to take on a new significance—its beauty now intertwined with the philosophy Mabel was unfolding.

"You might say, 'But the idea—the idea to take pictures, turn them into vector graphics, and laser print them on material—that is unique,'" Mabel continued, her voice taking on a slightly playful tone. "And true, it is unique, because we haven't seen many, but that doesn't mean Sue Sally over in Best Burger, Oregon, isn't doing a similar project—albeit along the infinite variation principle. Did she see mine? No. Did she 'steal' my idea? Absolutely not. So how are we both using the same methods?"

Her eyes, twinkling with a mix of mischief and wisdom, swept the room before landing on Rhonda. "Rhonda, would you like to take a guess?"

Rhonda straightened in her chair, her brow furrowing in concentration—the only sound the soft rustle of fabric as Sam adjusted his grip on the quilt. After a moment, Rhonda ventured cautiously, "Well... just thinking out loud here... I'm going to assume that you and Sue Sally had the same goal—to make a very personal quilt—and no material you found was specific enough, so you made what you needed from scratch."

Alfred's voice, warm with pride and a hint of amusement, broke the thoughtful silence. "Now, why did I know you would grasp that so easily?"

The gentle chuckles subsided, leaving a warm, expectant silence in their wake. All eyes returned to Mabel, her petite frame standing tall against the backdrop of her vibrant quilt.

"I think that's the reason too," Mabel continued, her voice carrying a quiet certainty that commanded attention. "I suspect the word 'art' got attached to art galleries and ego satisfaction, and away from artisans, craftsmen, or... craftswomen—and the soulful reason we create."

Here, Mabel's gaze shifted to Alfred, their eyes meeting in a moment of profound connection. "To make someone you love so happy he will stay with you for as long as he possibly can."

The room fell into a hushed reverence, the only sound the soft rustle of fabric as Sam adjusted his grip on the quilt again. James leaned forward imperceptibly, his eyes wide with recognition. These were ideas he had discussed countless times with Emma and Alfred—playful debates that had stretched long into the night. But now, hearing them from Mabel's lips, they took on a new weight, a tangible reality that sent a shiver of excitement through his system.

Mabel's voice—barely above a whisper but filled with heartfelt conviction—broke the silence. "Both Alfred and I have become convinced we are already feeling the positive ripple effect from our last meeting—you know the one I mean—so can you imagine what might happen if we start to live it? Let go of pride, in all its forms and disguises. And so we have decided that this is the way the non-profit Epoch Alliance will be."

"We plan that the installations we will provide, and that all related forms of expression that have our specific brand on it, will remain 'unsigned,'" Mabel continued, her words painting a picture of a future James had only dared to imagine. "There will be no plaque listing the designers, no information relayed to the public on purpose."

James's mind whirled with the implications. He could feel the energy in the room shift—a mixture of excitement and apprehension rippling through the gathered friends and colleagues.

"That is, the names of the designers and craftsmen involved may be available as verification for additional work in other places," Mabel clarified, her eyes sweeping the room to gauge reactions. "We can confirm contributions so you will be able to get work in other places—your friends, contemporaries, and word of mouth will help you keep working—but the intent is, in general as time goes by, and without the names attached in an obvious way, for the work to stand as coming from all humanity itself."

As Mabel's words hung in the air, James felt a surge of emotions—surprise, excitement, and a touch of awe. This was the culmination of years of theoretical discussions, now suddenly, thrillingly real. He exchanged a meaningful glance with Emma, seeing in her eyes the same mix of wonder and anticipation that he felt.

The room buzzed with an electric energy, each person processing this radical vision in their own way, the air thick with the promise of a new dawn for art and creation.

Taking a deep breath, Mabel continued, her voice soft but steady. "We are talking about the unsigned pot found in an archaeological dig. We know our plan isn't perfect, of course—there will be so many adjustments in real time as we progress—but that is our intention. We also intend to rely more and more on sacred geometric forms."

As she spoke, James's gaze flickered to Emma, finding her already looking at him, her expression a mirror of his own amazement. This wasn't just theoretical anymore—it was becoming thrillingly, breathtakingly real.

"After our last meeting, Alfred and I did research, and even with the construction of recent Stupas, we could find no names—not one—of any of the Tibetan craftsmen. That's what we want; that is our goal." Mabel's eyes shone with quiet passion, her hands gesturing gently as if shaping the very air around her. "To let it truly and really be all about our intent to be reminded of the sacred aspects of creation, and not idolize the object—and that begins with removing idolizing the artist."

Gerardo shifted in his seat, his brow furrowed in deep thought, while Rhonda's fingers tapped a thoughtful rhythm on her knee.

"It's a lot to think about," Mabel acknowledged, her gaze sweeping the room with warmth and understanding. "We know and want you all to keep your jobs, have steady lives... and we will pay you too, but be forewarned—the exposure you may get for your work will be more limited."

James felt a surge of emotions—surprise, excitement, and a touch of awe. These were ideas he had toyed with, concepts he had imagined as part of some distant future. Now, hearing them articulated as a concrete plan, he felt a shiver of anticipation run down his spine.

"Lots to think about, talk about," Mabel concluded, her voice softening further, "but I think it's time for food—lots and lots of food. We love you all and hope you still want to work with us in some way."

And that was that—and now it was lunchtime.

* * *

Chapter 45

Wilmette, IL — Worthington Residence — *Apr. 5, 2003 — 3:30 p.m. — Ring the Bell*

The late afternoon sun cast long shadows across the well-manicured lawn of Alfred and Mabel's Wilmette backyard. James sat on the cool stone of the memorial bench, its surface worn smooth by years of contemplative visitors. The statue of Saint Francis stood nearby, a silent sentinel amongst the towering pines that provided the prerequisite green backdrop for a suburban garden.

James had deliberately chosen this secluded spot—away from prying eyes and perked ears—for a conversation he knew was imminent. His eyes, reflecting the dappled sunlight filtering through the pine needles, scanned the garden, anticipating the arrival of either Rhonda or—

"You!" Gerardo's voice cut through the tranquil atmosphere, sharp and urgent. "I wanna talk with you!"

James turned, a small smile playing at the corners of his mouth, his posture relaxed despite the tension in Gerardo's voice. "Right on time, mate," he said kindly, his tone a stark contrast to Gerardo's agitation.

Gerardo stood before him, his usual composed demeanor replaced by a struggle to control his own emotions. It wasn't a state of mind he experienced often, and so, for a few moments, he literally wasn't sure how to best express himself.

"Am I? Am I your friend? 'Cause honestly you've been flipping my world upside down, then right-side up, then sideways, and God knows where—or what—might happen next. And right now I'm not at all sure if I want to thump you, run you off the road, or name my first child after you, boy or girl—"

"Jamie works for both—" James offered, his tone light but his eyes watchful, carefully gauging Gerardo's state of mind.

"Don't interrupt me. Where was I?" Gerardo asked, his brow furrowing as he tried to recapture his train of thought. The gentle rustling of leaves seemed to mock his momentary confusion. "Oh yeah—getting ready to thump you, or kiss you... Are you pulling us all off the charts and into your own personal 'bloody insanity'? You just couldn't bear to be crazy all by yourself, so you have to... indoctrinate us all too?"

James leaned back slightly, the cool stone of the bench grounding him as he absorbed Gerardo's outburst. "Was there a question in there?" he asked, his voice soft with affection. He truly loved this guy and understood well the disorientation of having one's entire worldview shifted seemingly overnight.

Gerardo's expression softened slightly, the furrows in his brow easing as he took a deep breath. The scent of pine and freshly mowed grass seemed to sedate him somewhat, and James—calm as the stone bench he sat on—helped too. Gerardo took a deep breath. "Yeah... one or three questions," he said, his voice noticeably quieter.

James nodded, his posture open and receptive. "Well, have a sit down. But before we dig deep, I need to tell you—I had no idea they were going to do this today," he began, his words measured and sincere. "We've talked about it, I have debated with them both for years, and you've heard me too... but I have never even come close to suggesting anything like that—not in that way."

Gerardo studied him intently, the statue of Saint Francis seeming to watch over their exchange with benevolent interest. "Okay, I believe you," he said softly, "but I'm not letting you off the hook yet."

"Fair enough," James replied, a hint of relief in his voice. His eyes then caught movement beyond Gerardo. "Wait—here comes trouble..."

Emma approached, carrying two plates laden with food, while Rhonda followed close behind, balancing two bottles of beer. The savory aroma of grilled burgers wafted towards them, making James's stomach growl involuntarily.

Emma handed over the plates, her voice warm but firm as she relayed Mabel's instructions: "Mabel has commanded you both to eat while you talk—she wants no food to go to waste. It sounded like an order."

"Ta, thanks, luv," James responded, gratitude evident in his tone.

Rhonda distributed the beers, the glass bottles cool and slick with condensation. "Don't worry, we're not staying," she assured them. "Emma and I have our own conversation to have."

With that, the women turned and left, their footsteps fading on the gravel path. James and Gerardo were left alone once more, the weight of their impending conversation hanging in the air between them. They each took a bite of their burgers, buying time to organize their thoughts before speaking again.

With half his burger gone and just on the verge of thinking Gerardo would give it all a pass—and James would see his sunny disposition again—Gerardo asked without preamble, "So, are you in?"

Only the truth would do. "Yes." James's answer was simple, his voice steady and sure.

"Full tilt?"

A gentle breeze rustled the leaves of the nearby pines, as if nature itself was holding its breath, waiting for James's response.

"As much as they want from me," James said honestly. His fingers absently traced the cool, smooth surface of the stone bench, grounding himself in the moment.

"Still, you might not have known, but they must have figured they could count on you for that—or this would have been unimaginable."

James said nothing. He was waiting for the real issue to come out—what really was hurting Gerardo. He had an idea what it might be, but didn't want to put words in his mouth, so he waited.

Gerardo began. "In a way, we come from similar backgrounds—both working class. I know your family was barely middle class, and Newcastle can be rough. Also aware New York can be rough on immigrants, and helpful too—obviously, as you built a name for yourself. A name that I know has helped your folks after working their fingers to the bone, but it's your name that does it."

James could see the play of emotions across his friend's face, each word a struggle to say. This was breaking Gerardo's heart to think—let alone say out loud—but there was nothing to do except wait for him to complete his thought.

"Maybe that pulled us together at first," Gerardo continued. "Common background. But Jimmy—Jimmy the James—listen to me. You were poor, but I was dirt poor. Not just me—my family, my neighbors—everyone for miles. And so..."

Here Gerardo paused to gather his thoughts, to feel into what he was trying to say. When he found the thread, he continued, "When I started to rise, to be noticed, to have my name known, it wasn't just me—not just me—but when people read my name, they read all 'Jimenez's' everywhere. And that feeling of... appreciation, maybe, and respect flows to all the Jimenez's too. Plus, when someone hears that name—not me, but another Jimenez—they might link it to me and think, 'Wasn't there a good artist with that name?'"

After a few moments, and James still didn't answer, Gerardo continued—his voice soft now. He was sitting on the stone bench across from him and leaned forward to say this next part, the late afternoon light casting long shadows across the grass, creating an isolation tank around the two men.

"Jimmy... I know... you know... I know..." Gerardo might have worked the expansion into infinity, save for the expression on James's face.

James smiled at the convolution. Gerardo caught the joke and smiled, a momentary lightness dropping ten pounds of weight.

In this lighter state, Gerardo said the hardest words: "I know what Alfred and Mabel are doing is right—I know it. I also know my people would starve without some shred of pride to keep them afloat—starve in the mind. I know Alfred's vision is right, but I do not know if the timing is right for me."

As Gerardo spoke, a gentle breeze rustled through the pine needles overhead, carrying with it the faint scent of blooming flowers from a nearby bed. James's eyes never left Gerardo's face, taking in every nuance of his friend's expression—the furrow of his brow, the tightness around his mouth, the mix of conviction and uncertainty in his gaze.

The golden light of late afternoon softened, a prelude to dusk settling over Alfred and Mabel's garden. James leaned back on the cool stone bench, his eyes fixed on Gerardo's furrowed brow. The statue of Saint Francis stood sentinel, its weathered features seeming to listen with infinite patience.

After a moment of contemplative silence, James spoke, his voice low and measured. "Ger, mate, think back a tick. What did Alfred and Mabel actually offer?"

Gerardo's eyebrows raised, a flicker of confusion crossing his face. "What do you mean?"

"Did they ask you to quit your job? Abandon your life?"

"Well, no, but—"

James held up a hand, cutting him off gently. "They know change comes in degrees, like paint layered on canvas. Artists need to eat, pay rent—they are well aware."

A rueful smile played at the corners of Gerardo's mouth. "True enough."

"So why burn a bridge they're still building?" James leaned forward, his gaze intense. "The door's not locked, Ger. It's hanging wide open. They know what they're proposing is a seismic shift, but they don't want to blow people up. I'm not just talking about artists who work with them, but the public at large too. I believe they're talking subtle—one step at a time. But yeah, they are serious too."

"But you're all in."

"I am, but I don't count. I've had plenty of practice thinking about it for years and years. I'm all ready. Plus, as you say, I've money in the bank—I'll be all right for a while—so my sacrifice doesn't play, does it? In addition, I'm close to being tarred and feathered in this town anyway, so what do I have to lose? Not as much as you, Ger, and I admit it. I'm suggesting you're here because they have big plans for you, and I'm asking you to hang on to the edge of the pool for a while and just see."

Gerardo's shoulders relaxed slightly, the tension easing from his frame. "You're saying I don't have to decide everything right now?"

"Exactly. I really should stop using metaphors—they are a long and winding road. See? I just did it again." James nodded, a grin spreading across his face. "Sit with it. Let ideas percolate. Who knows? Might even bring your own projects to their table someday."

The setting sun painted the garden in warm hues, mirroring the spark of hope rekindling in Gerardo's eyes. He reached for his forgotten beer, raising it in a small toast. "To open doors, then?"

James clinked his bottle against Gerardo's. "And the courage to walk through them, when the time's right."

As twilight descended, the two friends sat in companionable silence, the weight of decisions yet unmade settling comfortably between them.

* * *

The path curved along the far side of Mabel's garden, where the light slipped between the pear trees in slim, unsettled shafts. Emma and Rhonda walked without hurry, each carrying some of Gerardo's cookies and other treats in a folded napkin, the sugar grit flaking against their fingers. Somewhere behind them, voices still floated from the patio, but here it was quieter—just the faint whisper of a breeze through tulip leaves and the soft thrum from the heart of earth itself.

Mabel's beds were stirring to life. Crocuses clung low to the stone edging like tiny jeweled cups, while daffodils—those perennial harbingers of unbridled joy—had already pushed their yellow trumpets toward the sun. Tulips stood in their sheaths of green, tips brushed faintly with the color to come. The soil smelled newly turned—a living scent, almost warm.

Rhonda paused beside a cluster of hyacinths, leaning in to breathe them, then turned her head toward Emma.

"You've changed."

It wasn't offered as a rebuke—more along the lines of observing the time of day—oh look, it's three o'clock.

Emma paused their stroll to ponder the proposal. She cocked her head a bit to the right to get a different view of Rhon. "Have I?"

"Yes." Rhonda straightened, cookie in one hand. She broke off a piece, placed it in her mouth, savored the flavor—then: "You're not the same woman you were before James. Not exactly. Do you feel that's true? Are you still... Emma?"

They walked a few steps more. Emma's gaze had gone to the flagstones underfoot, to the complex weave of the pink and white quartz laced with threads of light brown here and there—even now, and always, she absorbed the color and logged it inside her secret self—then said, "No... I'm still myself, but the one buried deep. So no, not the self I was before." A quiet breath. "How could I be?"

She looked at Rhonda, her brows pulling together as if focusing on an internal translation into woman-speak that made sense, and so Emma clarified, "How do you cross a desert... climb a mountain... or even look at a flower—any one of these spring bloomers—and remain the same?"

Rhonda kept her eyes on her, weighing something. "I always thought women took a man's name because of property.

Control. Or just tradition. But now..." She let it trail, then: "I wonder if it's something else. Do you lose a part of yourself? Or... become part of someone else? Are you part of James now?"

No accusation in it—just the kind of question that can only come from another woman, standing still enough to listen to the answer.

Emma stopped. The breeze moved her hair. "I don't know," she said after a moment. "I can tell you I'm happy. And..." She glanced at Rhonda, voice dropping as if she'd only just decided to say it. "I'm seeing colors, Rhonda. Colors I can't describe. Colors I didn't even know existed. I haven't told anyone that—not even James." Her eyes searched the garden ahead. "How does that happen?"

Rhonda's gaze followed hers to a bed of tulips pushing up through the soil—fat buds still closed, petals yellow with a fringe of red like a painter's last stroke. Hybrids. A marriage of colors some mischievous, perky pollinating bee arranged.

They lingered there.

When they started walking again, Rhonda's voice had turned inward. "If I work for Epoch as a non-profit... if I became part of the... invisible ensemble in that way, if I lose my name in that way... who would I be? Just a drop in a wide sea?" She kept her eyes ahead. "I wonder about that. About what I want. What does it mean to create something and not have my name on it? To disappear into the... clockwork. I didn't even know I cared about it."

Emma was quiet for a few steps, enjoying the feel of the flagstones. "Maybe it isn't just about that—or women and men. Maybe it's about what you can live with as a person. Some keep their names. Others let them go. For some it's loss... for others, a kind of freedom. But it's still you in the mix—nothing can alter that." She paused, then repeated, "It's about what we can live with."

Rhonda gave a short breath of a laugh. "Feels like fishing. You throw the line out. See what bites. Keep it or throw it back."

Emma's mouth curved. "That's how we eat."

Rhonda smiled, eyes still on the tulips. "I guess so."

She didn't sound entirely convinced. Emma shrugged, then patted her arm—just for the fun of being friends.

Mabel's voice rose from the patio, warm and clear.

"Rhonda!"

Rhonda's head lifted instantly, like a bird turning toward a familiar call.

"Excuse me," she said to Emma, and angled across the lawn toward the open patio doors where Alfred and Mabel stood waiting, side by side.

Emma slowed, then stopped in the grass, letting Rhonda walk ahead. She watched the three of them framed by the door—the easy way Rhonda moved toward them, as if returning to her rightful place. There was a warmth in their faces that made Emma think, unbidden, She's like their daughter.

Not just any daughter—one who would never walk away when the years caught up with them, when sickness, loneliness, or grief set in. The faithful one who would keep the light on in the kitchen, who would visit every day if they needed her. There's always one in a family like that.

And yet women do it. Over and over, through the generations. Out of love, out of duty, out of something unnamed that feels like both. And often, there is that one—always that one—who stays to the last.

Emma thought as she stood on the center of the lawn: how often it is the women who stay, who let their own name and singular identity be absorbed into the life of a man, into the lives around them, into the rhythm of children and a family's needs. The list of personal, idiosyncratic happy moments—where one indulges oneself—are gone when children come, when you have a family to care for. The quiet trade of personal hours—an afternoon in the park, a day entirely to oneself—for the endless tending of others.

And how, as you get older, when the children scatter or your husband dies before you, and the house empties, the years can narrow to a Christmas card maybe, a polite phone call perhaps, but most times nothing at all. Until one day there's an old folks home, and the days get smaller too. So small. And still, women do it. They will do it.

Her gaze drifted toward the far corner of the lawn, where James sat with Gerardo. They were talking in low tones, heads tipped toward each other in an ease born of long trust. She looked at him for a moment, at the curve of his shoulders, the calm that sat on him like sunlight. He didn't look up. But she did.

She looked up to the tops of the trees scratching the sky, the naked branches reaching into the pale blue yonder. A lovely blue sky as background and placeholder... and in-between the blue, she drew in a breath... there was another color... she didn't have a word for the iridescent shimmer she saw tucked deep inside the soft blue.

A breeze moved across the garden, brushing her cheek. An angel kiss, to be sure—that's what her mom called them. She looked down at the grass beneath her shoes—new blades of tender shoots, sprouting, bouncing green. Fun.

She smiled.

Whatever, she thought. Screw Paris.

And then, as she started toward the house to join the others, the thought came to her—suddenly, without preamble—it was the present she needed to give James. He'd been gifting her with so many precious tokens this past month, it was his turn to receive a wee blessing, and it was this: the rock. The sculpture of the layered colors of lava rock she'd made a decade ago. She needed to give that to him.

Now the question was where, when, and how. Hmmm.

And then she wondered, vaguely bemused with herself: *Why in the world did I wait until now?*

* * *

Chapter 46

Wilmette, IL — Worthington Residence — *Apr. 5, 2003 — 5:15 p.m. — Reveal*

"Hey, you two, there's cake! You don't want to miss cake!" Mabel's voice carried across the garden, breaking the contemplative atmosphere. She stood at the back door, framed by the warm light spilling from the house, her face hopeful as she looked toward the two men sitting on the stone benches.

"Yes, ma'am, this is true," James called back, his tone so light that Mabel visibly relaxed, her shoulders softening.

"Okay, don't forget the plates," she reminded them, her voice carrying a motherly warmth.

"Yes, ma'am," James and Gerardo chorused in unison, their voices blending in perfect synchronicity. The garden seemed to brighten with their renewed spirits, the twilight air filled with a sense of camaraderie.

They looked at each other, a mischievous glint in their eyes. James said, his voice tinged with boyish excitement, "I suddenly feel like we're eight years old and should race for the back door."

Gerardo laughed, the sound rich and genuine, echoing through the garden. James loved it, the joy infectious. Mabel clearly did too, because she said in a playful, motherly tone, "Don't run with scissors."

Their laughter rang out once more, filling the garden with mirth. They exchanged a quick glance, a silent agreement passing between them, and then—yes—they ran for the back door. Their feet pounded on the grass, stirring up the scent of earth and greenery.

"I won..." Gerardo breathed, his chest heaving slightly as they reached the door.

"Well, I was carrying the plates," James observed, a hint of mock defensiveness in his tone.

"Which you could have used for ballast, if you'd thought about it," Gerardo retorted, his eyes twinkling with amusement.

"Boys, boys," Mabel admonished, but her eyes were soft with pleasure at seeing them in a lighter mood. The warm light from the kitchen haloed her figure, highlighting the affection in her gaze.

Mabel continued, her voice carrying a note of excitement, "Everybody is in the living room. There's chocolate layered raspberry cake and some kind of light yellow cake too. Anyway, there are choices, and there are champagne flutes too—grab a glass, time for a toast."

As they entered the house, the aroma of sweet confections enveloped them. The living room buzzed with anticipation, faces turned expectantly toward James and Gerardo as they completed the circle. James rejoined Emma where she sat on the two-seated sofa, their bodies gravitating toward each other naturally.

Once all were settled, a hush fell over the room. Attention shifted to Alfred, standing tall and dignified at the center. The soft clink of champagne flutes and the subtle rustle of clothing were the only sounds as they waited for the toast, the air thick with expectation and the promise of new beginnings.

Alfred stood at the center of the room, his champagne flute catching the soft light from the crystal chandelier above. The atmosphere was charged with anticipation, a palpable energy humming through the gathered friends and colleagues.

"This is a moment I feel I've been living toward..." Alfred began, his voice rich with emotion. "Here—Mabel, come stand beside me. Please, let us all stand..."

There was a gentle rustle of fabric as everyone rose, the clink of glasses and murmur of movement filling the air. Mabel glided to Alfred's side, her presence adding a warmth to the tableau.

Once she had joined him and all were in place, he continued, his words measured and heartfelt.

"We have, of course, the obvious enterprise before us. I will not underestimate the work and challenges ahead—and perhaps personal sacrifice too. I won't attempt to diminish that. I will choose to lay it alongside what we hope to do. We are vanguards, make no mistake, and we can take a moment and pat ourselves on the back for it—but only a moment—because I'd like to turn our attention to an additional reason to celebrate. Mabel, my dear, my friends, please let us raise our glasses to the upcoming nuptials of our dear friends James and Emma..."

Everyone in the room fell into a stunned silence—eyes widened, mouths hung slightly agape, and all gazes swiveled to where James and Emma stood. They seemed frozen in place, the shock evident in their rigid postures.

Then, as if drawn by an invisible force, Emma's hand reached for James's lower arm. Her touch seemed to awaken him from his stupor. James turned to Emma, his eyes searching her face, a mix of confusion and dawning realization flickering across his features.

Alfred's voice cut through the tension, finishing his phrase with a hint of mischief in his tone: "In the Great Lakota Ojibwa Stupa."

For a heartbeat, the room remained suspended in disbelief. Then, like a dam breaking, emotion flooded through. James and Emma were suddenly in each other's arms, embracing tightly as if they'd never let go. Their bodies melded together, years of unspoken longing finally finding expression.

Maribel's voice rose above the growing commotion, confusion evident in her tone. "I don't understand—what is happening?"

Alfred and Mabel were laughing, their eyes twinkling with joy as they watched their dear friends embrace. Alfred's voice carried a note of amusement as he explained to the bewildered group, "It seems James offered an incentive to his future father-in-law—as soon as the agreement was made and the Stupa was in place, he would marry his daughter. It looks like George is going to hold his feet to the fire."

Gerardo's voice cut through the excitement, a hint of playful sarcasm in his words. "Well... I hope I'll be that happy at my shotgun wedding."

The room erupted in laughter, the sound mingling with the palpable joy emanating from James and Emma.

Ted's voice rose above the din, a mix of amusement and impatience in his tone. "Somebody pry them apart so we can congratulate them proper."

There was a blend of voices in excited chatter, general hugging all around, champagne flutes clinking, and the air filled with the warm glow of celebration. As their friends moved to surround the newly engaged couple in a general group hug, Sam discreetly pulled out his digital camera, made sure the shutter sound was off, and took some stills to commemorate the moment.

* * *

Alfred had one thing more to say. He cleared his throat to pull the focus back to home base, and once anchored there, his voice set a more serious and focused tone.

"Now we will address why all of us are here today. It is because everyone in this room, through one means or another, knows about the proposal to build the Stupa. James and Emma have given us your names and also high praise for your personal ethics, and so while you may not have known the plan was accepted, we wanted to include you in this announcement because we would like you onboard in whatever capacity you feel you can contribute going forward. Mabel and I don't believe in 'accidents'—we suspect we are a group for a reason."

"Yes," was Mabel's simple addition.

"I have absolutely no doubt that we can fulfill our promise," Alfred continued, "and that the people we entrusted in turn are in this project for a reason. There are no mistakes. But I must emphasize—say nothing about the building, or even a hint of the plan to build this Stupa, to anyone: not to the clerk in a store, your mom, or your best pal you've known since kindergarten. Lock it up."

The room hung on his every word, the earlier levity giving way to a focused attention. Alfred's eyes swept across the gathered faces, making sure his message was understood.

"You may think me overcautious, but consider this as if the peace of the whole world depended on honoring this agreement with the nations. If someone asks—Rhonda, if you get a call—you say, 'That old fart Alfred put them in storage and won't budge until he's found the right spot.' If any of you get calls from the inquiries we've made, obviously, ditto. 'Ole Alfred has had a snit.'"

A ripple of laughter broke the tension, the sound warm and genuine. The room seemed to breathe a collective sigh of relief, the weight of secrecy momentarily lifted by the shared mirth.

"Okay, enough on that—we'll talk later about more precise language to use. On the bright side, we'll have other projects in the works. Mabel and I were impressed with the wide variety of ideas on display at that fateful meeting, and so believe me, we are daydreaming about it. We will approach you all individually to the extent you would like to play; this is not an 'all or nothing' commitment. We start with good seeds, and you, my friends, are the best I have known. I thank God every day for you."

As Alfred spoke, nods of agreement rippled through the group. Some eyes glistened with emotion, the depth of Alfred's words touching something profound within them. The room seemed to glow with a shared sense of purpose and camaraderie.

"James," Alfred called out, his voice carrying a note of expectation, "you, in many ways—some obvious, some more subterranean—put this in motion. Is there something you'd like to say?"

All eyes turned to James, including those from the portrait of Alfred's dear dad, Tom, over the mantelpiece. All the folks onboard train Stupa fell into an expectant hush.

They could all see James looking inside himself for some scrap of syllables yet unsaid, his brow furrowed in concentration. But for the life of him, he only had one thing on his mind at the moment... and so, in his best London accent, he started to sing in his fair baritone:

"'I'm getting married in the morning... ding dong, the bells are going to chime...'"

He sang in the semi-mournful way, as in the musical, but the sweet twinkle in his eye said it all. As he continued, one by one, everyone joined in, their voices blending in a joyous, if slightly off-key, chorus. Even those who didn't know the words hummed along, caught up in the infectious spirit of the moment.

"'Girls come and kiss me... show how you'll miss me, but get me to the church, get me to the church, for God's sake, get me to the church... on time.'"

Val was crying. She couldn't sing along because she couldn't seem to stop crying. She, more than most present, had witnessed James and Emma's slow waltz toward each other, and now she was so happy for James, for Emma, for the twists and turns leading to a happy ending.

So grateful.

"Need a Kleenex?" Sam asked, handing her a sweet-smelling tissue. "Don't worry, I pulled it from the box on the end table, not my shirt pocket."

Val looked up at Sam. He was smiling, so she smiled too. It was a small smile, but a perfectly acceptable human response.

"Appreciate that, ta," she said.

* * *

Chapter 47

Chicago — Warehouse Loft — Assembly — *Apr. 7, 2003 — 8:00 a.m. —*
My Love

The warehouse work loft stood silent, a testament to months of abandoned creativity. Dust motes danced in the shafts of sunlight that pierced through the high windows, illuminating the organized chaos below. Templates sprawled across the floor, some completed with a mosaic of colorful tiles, others waiting patiently for their turn to come alive, all the work was covered by thick sheets of plastic for protection. Stacks of tiles in vertical portable trays stood like sentinels, guarding the artistic vision that had been put on hold.

There might have been a subterranean drum roll thrilling the subtext of the moment James, Emma, Gerardo, Rhonda, Val, and Sam gathered in the locked space. Their presence seemed to awaken the dormant energy of the room, stirring memories of bustling activity and creative fervor.

And then, as if of one collective mind they split off in pairs to their respective work stations to begin again. Emma took off her coat and rolled up her sleeves and gestured for Rhonda to join her at the long glaze station where the bottles were still lined up and ready to be of service.

Emma's voice broke the reverent silence, her tone warm and instructive as she guided Rhonda through the intricacies of their color-coding system. "See the codes? They correspond to the bottles on the table. Double-check, make sure twice, and get some color and bring it over to the floor, and paint the tile, like this." Her hands moved with practiced ease, demonstrating the technique. "I'll be here, watching, working with you. It'll be okay."

Rhonda's eyes followed Emma's movements, a mix of determination and slight apprehension in her gaze. "Okay, we're short-staffed and interns are out of the question, so I'll step up... but you're training Val too right?" She paused, her eyes scanning the room before landing on Sam. "And maybe Sam too, right, Sam?" Rhonda called out

Sam's laughter echoed through the loft, a warm sound that seemed to breathe life back into the space. "Where Val goes, I'm sure to follow."

All eyes turned to him, a moment of surprised silence falling over the group. Sam's cheeks colored slightly as he realized what he'd said. "Did I say that out loud?"

Emma's voice held a note of amusement as she replied, "Uh... yeah... well, that's great, extra welcome."

Sam looked a little shy but smiled, his camera held at the ready. "I need some establishing shots and close-ups first, okay?"

Emma nodded, her focus already returning to the task at hand. "Take your time, it'll be almost an hour, maybe more before you're on deck."

* * *

The warehouse work loft was humming now with quiet activity. It was as if the room itself was coming out of hibernation, and each person onboard Project Resurrect Hope was just along for the ride, absorbed in their assigned tasks. Rhonda sat cross-legged on the floor, her brow furrowed in concentration as she carefully applied color to the tiles before her. The soft scrape of her brush against the clay surface punctuated the ambient noise of the loft.

Upstairs, James moved with practiced ease around the kiln, the heat radiating from it creating a pocket of warmth in the cooler air of the second floor. His hands—steady and sure—carefully arranged clay pieces inside the kiln, each placement deliberate and precise. They had three kilns going now; using the Monster kiln was out of the question. It would raise too many questions, too many curious eyes—so they would need to process the remaining two thousand tiles in rotating shifts in three kilns without perpetually blowing the circuit breakers.

It could be done.

At the front of the loft, Gerardo stood before the projector, his silhouette looming large against the wall as he meticulously traced templates. The soft whir of the projector and the scratch of his pencil created a rhythmic backdrop to the focused silence.

The sudden slam of the front door shattered the quiet, causing all eyes to snap toward the entrance, bodies tensing with alert wariness. The collective breath of relief was almost audible as they recognized Val—her familiar slight figure a welcome sight.

Val waved, then turned to lock the steel door behind her with a resolute click. She carried a box filled with packages to the conference table, her voice ringing out across the loft. "Got some mail that was gathered in the office. Em! There's a box for you—looks important."

Emma left the work floor, trotting over while wiping her hands on her jeans. The sound of her footsteps echoed in the vast space as she approached the table. She picked up the sturdy cardboard box, her eyes scanning the return address with curiosity.

With careful movements, Emma opened the box, peeling away layers of bubble wrap. As the contents were revealed, her eyes widened with surprise and delight. A fired white clay tile of a dove emerged, its wing tucked in, regarding her with an expression of good humor and love.

"James! Come—you have to see this," Emma called out, her voice carrying a mix of excitement and wonder.

James, hearing her call from his perch on the second floor, hustled down to join her. He looked over her shoulder, a low whistle escaping his lips as he took in the beautiful tile. "Amazing. Who's it from?"

Emma's voice was soft, filled with a mixture of reverence and nostalgia. "Helmut..."

"Herzog?" James asked. "He's the only Helmut I know."

Emma nodded, her fingers tracing the edge of the tile gently. "There's a note... I contacted him months ago to ask if he wanted to contribute a tile... it must have been down in the office."

Emma unfolded the note, her fingers trembling slightly with anticipation. The soft rustle of paper echoed in the hushed space, all eyes drawn to the small square of white in Emma's hands. The afternoon light slanting through the high windows caught the edges of the paper—nature's own little floodlight.

Emma read each word carefully, not wanting to miss a precious drop. Her lips moved silently, forming the shapes of the words as she read. The loft around her faded away, and for a moment, she was transported back to her days as a student, hanging on every word of wisdom from her mentor.

As she finished reading, a soft gasp escaped her lips, and she looked up, her eyes shining with unshed tears. James leaned in closer, his presence a comforting warmth at her side.

"What does it say, Em?" he asked softly, his voice barely above a whisper.

Emma cleared her throat and began to read aloud, her voice wavering only a little around the edges of the words.

"*My Dear Emma,*

Time has a way of moving both slowly and quickly, doesn't it? It seems like yesterday you were in my classroom, your eyes alight with the passion for color that set you apart. And now, here you are, embarking on a journey that will touch countless lives.

This dove is my contribution to your mosaic. Let it serve as a reminder of the peace and unity your art will bring to the world. Remember, Emma, true art speaks to the soul, transcending language and culture. What you're creating is more than a mosaic—it's a bridge between hearts.

I am proud of you, meine Schülerin. Your colors have always sung, and now they will sing for the world.

Mit Liebe und Stolz,

Helmut Herzog"

As Emma's voice faded, the loft remained silent, the words hanging in the air like a benediction. The dove tile seemed to glow with new significance—a tangible link between past and present, teacher and student, individual and community.

"Wait, there's a postscript," Emma said, and then read, "*Gib James einen sanften Schubs in die richtige Richtung, von mir.*"

"Well, I heard my name, but what does it mean?" James asked.

Emma laughed. "He suggests 'give James a nudge in the right direction for me,' which is a kinder, gentler way of saying—"

"—Kick me in the ass?" James smiled. "Good ole Helmut knew how to turn a phrase to get results." But he was smiling. "I like the guy—he has guts. Wait!"

Emma looked up at him, her eyes glowing. "What?"

"I know exactly where it should go," James said.

They looked each other in the eyes, and immediately it clicked.

"Where the land meets the water..." Emma was saying, but James was already moving quick-fast to the continent template, gently moving the arrangement of tiles they'd tried earlier that morning out of the way. None of those attempts seemed to *print* in a way that satisfied either of them.

The spot was clear. Emma approached the template on the floor, carrying the dove tile as the precious offering it was. Once at the edge of the design, she handed it to James, and with his longer reach, he placed it in the waiting spot—the pause point between the edge of the land and the open water. It seemed to fall into place with an audible click.

He stepped back to stand beside Emma and have a look at the dove doing sentry duty—on guard now as an offering and pausing place for peace.

"Wow," Gerardo observed.

Emma nodded as James recalled, "I remember something you said months ago, Em. You were drawing the line about using every single tile, even the broken ones. You had a plan to save them all because every person who showed up and contributed deserved to be on that wall. We'd never know which person made the key to make the whole thing work."

Emma nodded and sat on the floor to get a different view and adjust some of the tiles. James joined her.

* * *

The warehouse loft, previously filled with the quiet intensity of focused work, suddenly thrummed with a new energy as Val strolled in from the office. Her presence seemed to shift the very air, breaking the contemplative silence that had settled over James and Emma. Val's eyes sparkled with mischief as she took in the sight of them sitting on the floor, lost in their shared moment of reflection.

"Hey! Yous twos' watching the dust grow? Let's get some juice going," Val called out, her native Chicago accent thick with playful exasperation. She moved with purpose toward the CD player, a stack of discs balanced precariously in her hand. With practiced ease, she flipped through the collection, selected one, and slid it into the tray.

The moment her finger pressed *play*, the loft exploded with sound. The unmistakable, funky vibe of guitar and saxophone filled every corner of the space, electrifying the atmosphere. It was *Pick up the Pieces*—the notes seeming to dance in the air, bringing life to every tile and template scattered across the floor.

Val, caught up in the infectious rhythm, began to slip and slide across the floor, pulling a surprised but willing Sam into a semi-dance groove—their movements a joyous rendition of some kind of avant-garde twist 'n' shout. Why not?

"You what?" James called out, his voice a mix of surprise and delight. "How'd you know that was our song?"

Val's smile was enigmatic, her voice carrying over the music as she replied, "A little bird told me."

James turned to Emma, only to find her consumed by laughter. She had rolled onto her side, her body shaking with mirth, the sound of her joy harmonizing perfectly with the music filling the loft. James tilted his head, watching her struggle to regain composure while simultaneously grooving to the beat. His observation was casual, tinged with amusement and affection: "I'm not sure if I should kiss you or call 911..."

Suddenly, as if propelled by the music itself, Emma sat up. She had regained some control—enough to point emphatically at the CD player. The verse was coming around, the familiar lyrics building to their crescendo.

Emma's voice joined the others in the room, singing along with unbridled enthusiasm: "Pick up the pieces... uh-huh... pick up the pieces, oh yeah... pick—"

In a swift, fluid motion, James leaned in and kissed her, cutting off her song mid-lyric. Emma responded with equal fervor, returning the kiss with a passion that seemed to match the intensity of the music swirling around them.

The rest of the team, caught up in the moment, finished the phrase that Emma and James had abandoned, their voices rising in joyous unison: "—pick up the pieces!"

The loft pulsed with life and energy, the music binding them all together in a moment of pure, unadulterated joy. It was as if the spirit of their project—the essence of what they were creating—had found voice in this song, in this moment of connection and celebration.

The mosaic at their feet seemed to shimmer in the fading daylight, each tile a willing witness to the love, dedication, and sheer joy of participating in life.

"Pick up the pieces... that's right..."

Nothing is lost.

* * *

Epilogue

Red Lake, MN – Great Lakota Ojibwa Stupa – *May 15, 2007 – 10:05 a.m. – Forgive*

Helmut Herzog leaned heavily on his cane as he approached the Great Lakota Ojibwa Stupa. He paused on the gravel pathway for a moment to get a good look from afar—and to catch his breath. The parking lot wasn't situated that far away, but when you were a man of seventy-eight, and more than a little vain about using a walker or another form of motorized transit, well... it was good to pause now and again to espy the scenery.

He believed he did it in a way that was discreet—just simply taking a look at the wild, tall woods—but when he felt his sweet daughter secure her hold on his elbow, making sure she had a certain grip to balance their weight together, of course he wasn't fooling her. He smiled at his sweet Beth. His daughter hadn't complained or chided him once during this long trip... she knew how important this journey—this pilgrimage—was to him.

The Minnesota sun felt warm on his weathered face. It was a good day, and he was feeling fine—just a little tired. Beth checked her hold once again on his arm, while his teenage grandson, Karl, walked slightly ahead, his youthful energy a stark contrast to Herzog's measured steps.

"Slowly, Papa," Beth murmured, her voice a mixture of concern and excitement.

Herzog nodded, his eyes never leaving the magnificent structure before him. He'd promised himself he would not leave this earth until he saw this work, and now, finally, public access was being allowed in a limited way—and he was here.

Emma had never told him what had happened to the mosaic project put in storage. They corresponded more than they spoke on the phone, but when they did, he would ask, and she would simply say she didn't know when it would all come together—which was a kind of truth. The dome had been completed by the middle of the summer in 2003, and the mosaic wall installed in the following months, with finishing touches wrapping up just before it started getting really cold.

Helmut knew the time frame from the documentary *Seeds of Dreams: An American Stupa*, which was released in 2006—only just last year. The doc detailed every aspect: from interviews with people building their personal tiles, to all the elements of assembly, to the party at the beginning of 2003, to literally going into a box for storage.

Sam Petosky's doc then picked up with the Stupa construction and tile installation but did not reveal the Stupa's location. It had been a mystery to Helmut—and the world at large—until Emma had called him just three months ago to invite him and his family to the opening ceremony and first day the Stupa would be available to an invited list from the public.

Going forward, the two nations—Lakota and Ojibwa—would allow reservations to be made in order to control the flow of people... or pilgrims... to the site. It was a good, logical way to begin—and then they would see. They would note if people were being respectful and monitor the situation as they saw fit.

Herzog nodded to his own thoughts. It was a good plan, especially after witnessing for himself the... purity of the Stupa...

the aura of innocence. Yes, he understood their concern and agreed.

Helmut looked at the structure—a simple round dome with a form, a layered topknot rising in soft waves to the sky, just enough of a lift upward to make one smile… like a bit of whimsy or levity. Ah! Levitate. That's what James was going after. And though there was no designer byline noted in the brochure, there was a soft indication in the documentary, by virtue of the amount of footage of James and Emma. There was no aggrandizement of them, no exalted status, but still, it was clear to Helmut this concept and design had come from James.

The seamless blend of traditional Stupa architecture with contemporary building techniques was even more breathtaking in person than it had been in *Seeds of Dreams*. Herzog had watched that film countless times since its release in early 2006, but nothing could have prepared him for the reality. Nothing.

He could feel his daughter's concern had grown because he hadn't tried to move forward, but he patted her hand. "I'm all right. I needed a good look, that's all… it's good medicine to see this. See? It's almost fifty yards around—more than enough space for community gatherings. The cardinal directions expand the perimeter, but still minimal impact to the earth. Good job. It… feels like coming home. Odd."

They continued their progress. His grandson had given up waiting, but now that they were on the move again, Karl returned to walk alongside. As they approached the entrance, Herzog looked for Emma's influence—and, to be honest, he couldn't see it yet. But to be fair, while he knew the intent and design came from James, the design per se really seemed to come more from a universal principle of form.

It was as if the designers were moot. Very, very interesting. A kind of elegant simplicity, but immensely satisfying to gaze upon.

"You see here"—he patted Beth's hand and pointed—"these are the cardinal directions. You can see the Tibetan influence married with traditional Native American symbols, which are really very similar. It is thought the Mongols crossed the Bering Strait and were the ancestors of the Native Nations—fascinating. Anyway, the carvings are on the outer perimeter, the low wall running around the Stupa itself—a sacred circle to hold the works in place."

He looked around the clearing but didn't see Emma or James. Well... Helmut was a little late. Maybe he'd missed an opening ceremony of some kind. No matter—he was so glad to be here now... and was sure he'd see them at some point. He must. He must speak with them both.

* * *

Inside the Stupa, Herzog found himself breathless. His first impression was surprise at the amount of natural light illuminating the entire interior.

"How... how did James bring natural light into the dome?" he asked his daughter, Beth.

She shrugged, then pointed up. "Look! A skylight is hidden under the top point, beneath the crest or whatever it is... still, there's a lot of light... oh, look at the far wall."

Herzog almost laughed out loud. "I think I saw that in the documentary, but it didn't register as seeing it in person. Look, he's placed secured windows high on the dome, on the far side."

Herzog turned to his daughter to explain the principle. "As we approached, we saw a solid dome. We were psychologically prepared for a certain experience—perhaps incandescent interior lighting—so we were shocked by the natural light... delighted by the light. We think we're in the dark, but no... we are not. Clever, clever man."

More than clever, really, and Herzog felt another odd pang of regret. *Mein Gott, mein Gott...* James had been so bright... but he'd been mercurial too—hard to pin down back then. It had put Herzog in mind of what a happy, clueless child might do with matches—nay, a flamethrower—and his beloved student Emma had been in the path. But looking at this space now... *mein Gott...*

And Helmut hadn't even really looked at the mosaic wall itself yet.

The wall began at his immediate right. It was built out slightly from the curve of the exterior wall, so it ran flat and then made a soft curve—bringing the eye, guiding the eye around the design. Reading from left to right: beginning with land, to water, to sky, to planets, to stars, to cosmos. But there were abstract forms planted in the flow of the design as well, to highlight and nod to events in humanity—common, everyday activities building up into the bigger picture as it wound around. It was as if humanity had built a snapshot or time capsule of our lives as we hope to be, in flow with the natural world, and was offering it up to God... and all, all beginning with the clay tiles, beginning with small, but never losing one's sense of self because of the connection.

The interior was a symphony of color and form in each tile—the color itself a story of harmony and contrast, yet part of a greater whole. The shifting, blending, and oft-times contrasting color infused joy through it all, much as it would looking at a full-color grand vista in nature versus a black-and-white rendition. Each clay tile was idiosyncratic and significant; each tile was treated with respect in color complexity.

Helmut stepped up close and saw many of the tiles had gone through two glaze-kiln firings. Some had layers of glaze, perhaps, demonstrating the level of care given to each tile... all pointing to how much every single one of us is loved. No one is overlooked, or too small for infinite consideration. We human beings are small—so small—in the reality of infinite, yet never lost, unseen, or unknown. Never losing one's sense of self because of the connection.

Helmut breathed deep and pulled a handkerchief out of his pocket to dab at his eyes.

The color—Emma's hand in the color—was a perfect complement to the design, seamlessly integrating, supporting, and expanding the layers of love in each molecule, playing in harmony with, well... God.

He recognized the dove tile—there, just there—as a bridge between land and water, and he felt truly humbled they had seen his offering in that way. A peace-maker point. Yes, he could see he had contributed an integral part of the complex concept—an unconscious key from his heart to make it work.

His grandson, Karl, who had been quiet until now, suddenly spoke up. "Opa, did you teach them to do this?"

Helmut looked inside himself to see. He remembered Emma struggling with the clay as it "talked back" to her, as he clearly remembered James saying... and James, who from the outset appeared to have so many techniques come easily to him, wondered aloud, "I'm not sure, Franklin. Good teachers, good schools open the door, point out ways to develop skills... and then learn how to get out of a student's way, so I'm not quite sure."

Franklin wrinkled his brow and said, "That doesn't make sense."

Helmut laughed. "I suppose not... it's okay, you can go ahead with your mom. There's a place for me to sit; I'd like to stay here for a while."

Franklin nodded and hurried away, and just as one vacuum emptied, Helmut turned—and it was instantly filled. But this time, by him.

It was James, himself, standing only a few feet away. He was older, of course—soft laugh lines, a crease or two on the brow, perhaps strands of silver at his temple—but it was him. Helmut would have known him anywhere. How could a person seem so unchanged and yet deeper... so deeper and matured? His eyes were still bright, of course, but now had depth. James smiled at him and stepped closer to say hello.

But instead of a greeting, which would have been expected under the circumstances, Helmut asked the first thing that came to mind—as if, without preamble, they were picking up a conversation from five minutes ago and not fifteen years. Helmut asked: "Tell me, James, and no darting about... no fancy-dancing words... how did you come up with this? What was the first place, the inception point?"

Helmut watched James smile, and it seemed they were back at James' interview for acceptance into Cooper Union. The admission process was tailor-made to different students. For James, his portfolio had been such an unusual mix of classic study and avant-garde experiments, Helmut had asked him to go to the back of the room and, using only the media they provided, create a work—any work at all—using the theme: *apple*.

Helmut had chosen that word probably because he'd had an apple for breakfast and it was foremost on his mind, but it had no particular significance other than that. The test was, of course, to see if James's work was... well, original. If he could complete an excellent rendering with specific intent on command.

Helmut could see James remembering too, because he said, "Apple—what an insane test."

"You got it done," Herzog replied softly.

James shrugged. "I wouldn't mind another crack at it now... might come up with something a tad better than an infinite cosmic landscape of undulating whites—which I couldn't get unless I had enough charcoal black laid down where there wasn't white, because, you know... apples are always white inside. The cosmic constant."

Herzog nodded. "It got you across the ocean and into a great college."

James nodded. "Good to see you too, by the way."

Herzog nodded a greeting and then made his request again. "Please don't stall, this isn't a test now. James... I would really like to know. It is important to me."

James nodded—the wise one now, the teacher too. "Well, then, let's sit, and I'll tell you the secret I haven't told anyone. Hmm, that's right, I haven't even told Em."

They were seated now, so James began. "I saw a movie when I was a kid—just a little bloke, maybe eight or nine. It was an old black-and-white classic called *The Incredible Shrinking Man*. And in it, this guy is out on the water with his wife; she goes below to the galley, but he stays on deck, and this strange, odd fog comes over the water—covers him, puzzles him, and feels strange on his skin, so he wipes it away. I remember that moment so clearly. Anyway, pretty soon he notices his clothes getting larger, then his wife is his same height—every day he's smaller and smaller until he shrinks down to live in a dollhouse.

"And all the time they're praying for a cure, and somehow he falls into the basement—lost forever now... and at the close of the movie, his life feels like nothing, a speck, smaller and smaller. And he's at the basement window, and now he's so small he can fit between the iron grid, so he steps out into the night and looks at the stars... and the stars, Helmut... the stars are the same, no matter what size he is. The stars are the same, and so is he—the very same man living in God's world under God's stars—both the same, big or small, and not forgotten."

They both looked at the tiles—all the small tiles in the expanse of the wall.

They sat in quiet, and then Helmut blew his nose and wiped his eyes again. Then, very softly, he said, "Thank you, James... I need to say something to you—"

"—Helmut?"

It was Emma. She was speaking softly to show respect in this space, but he could tell she was so pleased to see him. Helmut rose to meet her. She hugged him hard, and when she pulled back he could see she was showing—she was pregnant, perhaps five months.

James rose too, his eyes sparkling as he kissed her softly on the cheek. "Missed you."

Peeking out from between the pair was a little boy. He'd been holding his mother's hand, but now grabbed his dad's hand.

Helmut leaned slightly and asked, "And who's this?"

Emma laughed lightly. "This is our son, Thomas."

"Hello, Thomas," Herzog said.

Herzog's gaze moved between James and Emma, taking in their easy companionship—the way they stood together as a unit—young Thomas a physical manifestation of their bond. He felt a lump form in his throat; he looked down as he composed himself.

Thomas nodded and then pulled at his dad's hand. James instantly understood. "He wants to go play at the clay station. I'll let you two catch up." And then, leaning in to kiss Emma again on the cheek, he said in a low voice, "Be seeing you soon, right? Staying away from construction still going on, right?"

Emma kissed him back and said simply, "Right."

"See you, luv," and then, to Helmut, "Don't go anywhere far. See you later, Helmut." And then he was gone.

Helmut turned his full attention to Emma, who said, "You two were deep in discussion."

"Always."

"Seemed you were always shaking each other's boxes back then," Emma observed.

Instead of responding directly to that, Helmut said, "Congratulations," nodding toward Emma's womb. "On everything. You look wonderful. This is... wunderbar."

Emma's smile widened, her free hand moving unconsciously to rest and comfort the infant inside. "Thank you, Helmut. We're so glad you could join us. I'm so pleased to see you in person. I love our letters, but I like your face even more."

Herzog just smiled. "Thank you, Emma, I feel the same." Then he looked back at the wall, gazing with wonder, then to her, and said, "Emma, I'm not sure what to say—words seem artificial."

So instead, Helmut told her how the wall and the colors made him feel—how he felt... well, better, lighter, "almost like a child wanting to pick up my crayons and pencils and start all over again."

He told her how well she looked and asked about motherhood, and did she feel it affected the kind of work she did these days? She'd been sending him photos of her growing family—her son, and of course James—and her work too. But Helmut hadn't been prepared to witness how comfortable she seemed in her own skin—how strength and tenderness flowed from her in equal measure, and power too. She was quite a woman.

Emma asked him how he was doing now. What she meant, but didn't say, was *now that Berte was gone*. And so Helmut told her the truth: "Well enough, well enough. I get by. My daughter and grandson are a help, but I miss her terribly."

They left it at that, and Emma asked, "So, you feel refreshed enough to take a full tour? And see who's around?"

Helmut was indeed ready to resume his tour. He felt good.

* * *

As they made their way around the Stupa, Herzog was introduced to more of the team he'd come to know through the documentary. Gerardo—whose passionate description of his community art programs reminded Herzog of his own youthful idealism. Rhonda—whose sharp mind and organizational skills had clearly been instrumental in bringing this project to fruition.

There were Alfred and Mabel. These were the people that truly moved Herzog. Here were the visionaries, the ones who had dared to dream of art without ego. As Alfred described the journey of the Epoch Alliance in the documentary, Herzog felt a renewed faith in the power of art to transform communities as a humble echo and touch point—versus glamour and idolatry.

Sam, the documentarian, was there and easy to spot; it was his keen eye Herzog recognized as kindred to his own.

After watching *Seeds of Dreams* so many times, he felt he knew Sam well enough to ask him some personal questions about the footage placed in the doc versus footage left out. And did he ever plan an additional project for that extra footage?

Sam was so pleased to get the question. "Funny you should ask—you're exactly right. I've footage that is so funny, so entertaining, especially between those two—" and here Sam pointed at Emma—"you, and your mad husband, could be a project in itself, but also fodder for what's called a 'goodie reel.'"

"Oh, I know what that is," Emma interjected, "all the bloopers and side takes."

"Right. And in a doc it would be more along the lines of personal moments—too personal for the public, but what the family and inner circle would enjoy."

"Oh dear God," Emma commented, already scared.

Helmut laughed. "Well, Emma sent me some rather interesting letters about their situation while constructing and installing the tile templates, so I might have an idea."

"Oh dear God," Emma reiterated, in exactly the same tone.

"James thinks it's funny," Sam offered innocently.

"Oh, of course he would. He'd look like the master of his domain compared to what I was going through." Both men laughed, and Emma shook her head and asked, "So James has seen all this forbidden footage?"

"Not all... enough," Sam said, a little sheepish now. "I thought I should warn you—James thought it would be a funny surprise for your anniversary—"

"Well... that is kind of sweet—" Emma mused.

"—At a public party," Sam finished, "and seeing I owe you a hundred favors by now, and I pay my debts... I'm breaking security in giving you a heads-up."

Emma's lips came together in a thin line, but she said nothing for about thirty seconds. Finally: "Well, can we see it first?"

"You and the Prof?" Sam asked, with a side glance to Herzog.

"Why? How bad is it?" Emma was alarmed. "I wrote to Helmut about what was going on in the main view—it can't be worse than what goes in a letter, can it?"

"Oh no." Sam's reply was a little too airy, a little too reassuring.

"Well, let's have at it," Emma insisted.

"All right, I have my laptop, but we need to find a quiet space where we can't be heard," Sam advised.

"There's sound?" asked Emma. "Never mind—you have your shotgun mic, of course there's sound. I know a place. There is a small gazebo just outside the side door; we can go there—maybe it won't sound as loud outside."

Emma led the way, her arm linked with Helmut's, with Sam tagging behind, saying:

"In my defense, it looked like you two were working—I thought I was taping you both working together."

Oh boy.

* * *

They sat in the gazebo with their backs to the Stupa, the laptop resting on the ledge before them. The shade from the gazebo's roof provided ample cover, allowing them to see the screen clearly despite the bright outdoor light.

"Okay just bear in mind I've made only minimal cuts so far—" Sam explained, "just letting you know this is a rough cut."

"Sam," Emma warned

"Sorry, pressing play now," and he did.

* * *

The scene began as the exterior shot of the Red Lake Reservation with full view of the Stupa construction for context in the late afternoon light.

EXT. RED LAKE RESERVATION – STUPA CONSTRUCTION SITE – LATE AFTERNOON

The Minnesota sun hangs low in the sky, painting the rolling hills in hues of gold and amber. A half-finished Stupa rises from the earth, its white dome gleaming in the fading light. The air is thick with the scent of fresh cement and newly tilled soil.

JAMES and EMMA work side by side, trowels in hand, carefully applying cement to the wall. The CAMERA PANS across the bustling construction site, capturing the rhythmic scrape of their tools against the general background noise.

Emma pauses, wiping sweat from her brow, leaving a smear of cement. James glances at her, fighting a smile.

JAMES
You've got a bit of...

He gestures vaguely at his own forehead. Emma rolls her eyes.

EMMA
I'm covered in cement, James. A little more won't hurt.

They return to work. James shifts, his arm brushing against Emma's. She stiffens almost imperceptibly.

EMMA (CONT'D)
(low but pointed)
James, if you don't stop crowding me, I swear I'll—

JAMES
(innocently)
What? I'm just doing my job, luv.

James reaches across her to smooth cement. His arm brushes hers again. The CAMERA ZOOMS IN on their hands, capturing the subtle tension.

EMMA
(narrowing her eyes)
Your job doesn't require you to be practically on top of me. That's the second time you've "accidentally" touched my hand in the last five minutes.

JAMES
(muttering)
Who's counting?

James takes a small step back. Emma glances over her shoulder. The CAMERA PANS to reveal MICHAEL watching them intently, then to EMMA'S MOTHER busying herself with plants in the distance—now looking up to watch them too.

EMMA
My whole family is counting, James. You know the rules. If I get pregnant, that's it for me working on this project. I won't be allowed on the construction site, or up the scaffolding. We've clocked four months so far—four! We had to stop even before construction began so I'd be able to be working now—

James sighs, focusing on his trowel work.

JAMES
Shhh... shhh... I know, luv, I know. I'm feeling it too... but the nations were firm about having your hands with mine on this installation. They need to have a tribe member working on this, and you can't be going up and down scaffolding while pregnant. They will not have one casualty on this project—and I agree.

Emma stops work, takes a deep breath. The CAMERA PULLS BACK to reveal JAMES still working alongside, smoothing cement.

EMMA
Am I turning into a shrew? I am, aren't I?

JAMES
Shhh... shhh... no, luv, no. You're a good, good girl doing your job. See? Our cement is just about right for the next template section to be laid—sorry, poor choice of words.

EMMA
Okay, that was funny.

JAMES
Humor is almost as good as... you know, the other unnamed activity.

EMMA
Almost. Okay, new topic—entertain me, please.

JAMES
Right. So, let's talk about something else, shall we? The weather, perhaps? Lovely day for cement work, don't you think?

Emma snorts, but a smile tugs at her lips. They work in companionable silence. The CAMERA PULLS BACK to show the entire construction site, then slowly ZOOMS IN on James and Emma again.

JAMES (CONT'D)
(thoughtfully)
You know, there is something that's been on me mind... Val has been stalwart throughout, from the very beginning—lunches, scheduling, running errands—

EMMA
Love that green mug she gave you that first day. It set a lot in motion—

JAMES
Right, so I'm thinking... we really ought to do something nice for our Val. She's been a non-stop miracle worker.

EMMA
She has, hasn't she? Love that green mug with the yellow flowers—it sparked the whole public invitation to the public idea—

JAMES
Again with the mug... and agreed, there are so many critical, invisible facets people contribute. Hard to give everybody a present, but we can begin with her—

EMMA
She's always on the spot, gets it done before we even ask.

JAMES
Exactly. But what do you get for someone who's already got an Apple computer? We need to get her a great gift—what does she really want?

Emma pauses, her trowel hovering over the cement. Her eyes drift across the site. The CAMERA FOLLOWS her gaze around the interior of the Stupa and back to EMMA, who is looking right at the camera. She nudges JAMES and inclines her head toward SAM, who is filming them off-camera.

JAMES follows her line of vision, sees Sam holding the video camera, but the connection doesn't register.

JAMES (CONT'D)
What? A new video camera? I doubt we could afford anything better than what Sam's already got.

James raises his hand to signal "hello" to SAM. EMMA pulls JAMES' attention away and speaks privately.

EMMA
(shaking her head)
Not a what, James. A who.

JAMES looks back at SAM still pointing the camera in their direction.

JAMES
(eyes widening; voice lowered)
Who? Sam? Pretty sure you can't give a person as a gift, luv. There are, you know, laws about that.

EMMA
(voice low)
Not as a gift. But we could... create opportunities. Get them together enough times until Sam realizes what we already know—that Val is the best ever and great for him.

JAMES
(frowning)
Huh. That serious, huh? Who is this bloke anyway? What's his pedigree? What do we really know about Sam?

EMMA
(sighing)
You asked what she really wants. You've been watching them for almost a year—stop being her big brother and think about it.

James runs a hand through his hair, his expression conflicted.

JAMES
I don't know, Em. Meddling in people's lives...

EMMA
Not meddling. Just... facilitating. Look, we could—

JAMES
Even if you're right, how would we even go about it?

Emma's eyes gleam with mischief.

EMMA
Oh, I have a few ideas...

JAMES
(muttering)
I'm sure you do. Go on then—entertain us, let's hear them.

The CAMERA PULLS BACK as Emma begins outlining her plans, showing the Stupa rising around them as the sun dips lower on the horizon.

FADE TO:

EXT. STUPA CONSTRUCTION SITE – MIDDAY

James and Emma sit on overturned buckets, eating sandwiches. Emma is still going strong with her matchmaking plans.

EMMA
...and then we organize a stargazing night. Val mentions her interest in astronomy, and Sam offers to teach her about astrophotography.

JAMES
(chewing thoughtfully)
Isn't that a bit on the nose, luv?

EMMA
(waving him off)
Trust me, they'll never suspect a thing.

FADE TO:

EXT. STUPA CONSTRUCTION SITE - LATE AFTERNOON

James and Emma stand outside the Stupa, discussing the placement of the four cardinal directions. Emma gestures with a compass. As they banter, they back up to the edge of the woods to get a long view of how the cardinal point construction is pulling together.

EMMA
Now, for Gerardo and Rhonda, I'm thinking of a salsa dancing class. Gerardo mentions he's always wanted to learn, and Rhonda "reluctantly" agrees to be his partner.

JAMES
(chuckling)
Em, don't you think you're getting a bit carried away? Next, you'll be pairing off the entire construction crew.

EMMA
(grinning mischievously)
Oh, I've got that mapped out too—I drew a blueprint for best possible pairings.

JAMES
(holding up his hands in mock surrender)
Alright, that's it. You're just diverting all your sexual tension onto other people now.

EMMA
(laughing)
Well, duh.

James joins in the laughter. As it subsides, they find themselves standing near the edge of the woods. The CAMERA PANS to show the inviting darkness of the forest, then back to James and Emma.

Their eyes meet. The CAMERA ZOOMS IN on Emma's face, capturing her dilating pupils and slightly parted lips. Her body leans towards James.

JAMES
(voice husky)
Oh God, Em. We're not going to make it.

Their gazes shift to the woods, then back to each other. Emma bites her lip and takes James's hand.

EMMA
(barely audible)
Too hot... I need to cool...

They take a step towards the treeline. The CAMERA FOLLOWS them as the sounds of the construction site fade.

Suddenly, a booming voice shatters the moment. The CAMERA WHIPS AROUND to reveal Gerardo striding towards them.

GERARDO
Hey, you two! Where are you going?

GERARDO (CONT'D)
Your brother's looking for you, Em. Something about needing your opinion on the mosaic placement.

James and Emma exchange a look.

JAMES
Right. We'll be right there.

James gently tries to pull Emma away from the woods. Her feet won't move.

JAMES (CONT'D)
(softly)
As soon as all the tiles get laid... so can we.

EMMA
(whispering)
You promise?

JAMES
Oh, aye.

They walk back towards the Stupa; Gerardo walks beside them as a well-intentioned chaperone. Emma leans close to James.

EMMA
(reminding)
You promised.

JAMES
(eyes twinkling)
Oh, abso-fucking-lutely. Excuse the pun-ish.

Emma laughs, the sound carrying across the construction site. The CAMERA PULLS BACK to show the entire scene—the half-finished Stupa, the bustling workers, and James and Emma walking side by side, their hands occasionally brushing.

FADE OUT.

* * *

Sam reached over and stopped the video file from playing, looked at Emma, and shrugged, waiting for her reaction. The pavilion fell silent, save for the distant sounds of visitors exploring the Stupa.

"Uh… happy anniversary?" James's voice came from behind Emma. She turned to look at him, her eyebrows raised.

"That's not how I remember it," she observed, a hint of amusement in her tone. "I remember you were all over me that day, James—touching me all the time, driving me nuts."

James, his eyes twinkling with mischief, found it best to agree. "That's right, luv. Sam didn't get those parts."

"Hmm…" Emma mused, glancing at Sam and Helmut, who were trying their best to suppress smiles. "I guess if he got those parts, it would have been more realistic. But—" she paused, a reluctant grin spreading across her face "—it is funny."

"In a good way," Sam assured her quickly, his hands raised in mock surrender.

Emma turned back to James, her expression softening. "Please tell me we will never have to go through that again."

"Not on my lookout," James assured her, his hand coming to rest gently on her shoulder.

Emma's hand drifted to her swollen womb, a contented sigh escaping her lips. "Well, thank you for my anniversary present. It was very thoughtful."

James leaned down, placing a soft kiss on her temple. "Love you so much, kitten," he whispered.

Helmut watched this exchange with a mixture of amusement and something deeper—a recognition of the bond between them, forged through challenges and triumphs. He cleared his throat softly.

"You know, Emma," he began, his eyes twinkling, "your letters during that time painted quite a vivid picture. I believe you described James as a 'persistent octopus with boundary issues.'"

James let out a bark of laughter. "Did she now?"

Emma blushed, but her eyes danced with humor. "Well, you were! I swear, every time I turned around, there you were, finding some excuse to be in my personal space."

"Can you blame me?" James asked, his voice low and warm. "You were irresistible, covered in cement and all."

Sam chuckled, closing his laptop. "I think that's my cue to make myself scarce. Thanks, guys... and thanks for making me a gift to Val—I owe you both forever. She should be here soon, gotta go."

He smiled a shy smile and strode away, pulling out his trusty Sony camera as he walked.

Herzog paused, reaching into his jacket pocket. "Emma, speaking of letters, I brought something I thought you might like to see."

He pulled out a well-worn envelope, its edges softened with age. Emma recognized her own handwriting immediately, her eyes widening in surprise. "Is that...?"

Helmut nodded, a gentle smile on his face. "The letter you sent me, describing your... predicament. I thought perhaps we could read it together, for old times' sake."

James moved to stand behind Emma, his hands resting lightly on her shoulders. "This I've got to hear," he murmured.

As Helmut unfolded the letter, the years seemed to fall away. The sounds of the Stupa faded into the background, and for a moment, they were transported back to that time of frustration, longing, and barely contained desire.

Helmut held Emma's letter in his hands, his eyes twinkling with amusement as he began to read aloud. "My dear Professor Herzog," he began, his accent adding a musical quality to the words.

Emma blushed slightly, but her smile was radiant. "I can't believe I'm hearing you read this out loud," she laughed.

Helmut waved her off with a chuckle. "Nonsense, my dear. This is a masterpiece of storytelling." He cleared his throat and continued:

"Two weeks after the final approval of the Stupa blueprint, with the last of the tiles glued to the grid template, prepped for installation, destiny took an unexpected turn. The Ojibwa elders had insisted on having a tribal person present during all critical phases of installation, especially the mosaic wall, and James and I respected their wishes. But that meant we began our... abstinence as soon as we received their—well, 'request' is too light a word and 'ultimatum' is too heavy—so let's call it a strongly worded suggestion."

James chuckled, shaking his head. "Strongly worded indeed. I thought I might spontaneously combust."

Helmut raised an eyebrow but continued reading: "And so our reserves were stretched well before the actual work had even begun—at least three months. My mom pointed out that James wasn't the problem—well, of course he was from my point of view—but he had an iron will in some matters that went beyond ordinary. Besides, she said I was the one to watch. I would be the one to crack."

"Your mother knows you well," James teased, earning a playful swat from Emma.

762 NOTHING LOST COPY KDP VERSION

"Not because I had less willpower," Helmut read on, "but because it would be my body demanding to make a baby. There would be no choice for me, no 'free will' in the equation."

Emma nodded solemnly. "Dealing with James was like fighting a persistent octopus with boundary issues—with eight arms, each one trying to drag me off by the hair in a different direction."

James and Emma erupted in laughter at the unexpected simile. Helmut wiped a tear from his eye before continuing:

"But as soon as the final tiles were installed, set, polished, and perfect, and as soon as the moon rose high over the Minnesota landscape, we found ourselves drawn to the woods once more. And that, as they say, is that."

James moved to stand behind Emma, his hand resting gently on her shoulder. "It was as if the very earth conspired to bring us together," he said softly, echoing the words in the letter.

Helmut nodded, reading on: "The scent of pine, the whisper of the wind through the trees, and the knowledge that we'd come so far in our work... it was overwhelming... and pure love magic."

"We didn't plan it," Emma added, her voice tender with the memory. "But when it happened, it felt right... our love is a force of nature, unstoppable and awe-inspiring."

Helmut continued reading: "The tribe would have had to lock us up on opposite sides of the planet to stop that night, and no one really wanted to torture us. We had fulfilled our obligation in the main part... it was as if God had waited until the final tile had been polished in place before—kablam!"

Helmut chuckled, continuing to read: "When I told my mother about the pregnancy, she just smiled and said, 'When God has a baby lined up, that's that.' There's wisdom in those words, a recognition of forces beyond human control."

"Of course," Helmut read on, "the pregnancy meant changes to our carefully laid plans. I was no longer allowed on the construction site—a precaution that James himself insisted upon with unwavering resolve."

James nodded solemnly. "No tripping, no temptation for ill fate. I wouldn't even help her slip in the back door, just to have a wee look."

Emma rolled her eyes good-naturedly. "He was worse than my dad, if you can believe it."

Helmut smiled. "Oh, I like this next part. Listen to this: 'But I found a way to stay involved. We placed a bench in a safe zone, just close enough for me to contribute via walkie-talkie. James and I agreed I should be the one to oversee the installation of the four cardinal points outside the Stupa. The Tibetan and tribal people were taking that task personally, so it made sense for me to be the designer's eyes on watch... from the bench in the safe zone.'"

"And what a sight you were," James teased, "barking orders over the walkie-talkie like a general commanding her troops."

Emma laughed, then grew serious as Helmut read the final part of the letter:

"We're so happy, Helmut. About the baby, about being back together, about how far we've come with the Stupa. I made it through the critical phase; the energy from our hands is in the installation of the tiles. That's what the tribes wanted, and now... Helmut, if the tribes ever offer this up to the public, you must come. You'll be on the first list of invites. Sam is making the documentary, which will help you understand the scope. He won't be able to release it until the tribes and Epoch approve, and it's great, really great, but not the same as being here, going on pilgrimage and walking the grounds."

As Helmut set the letter down, a comfortable silence fell over the gazebo, each of them lost in thought, reflecting on the journey that had brought them to this point.

Finally, Helmut spoke, his voice filled with emotion. "My dear children, what you have accomplished... it's more than just art—or rather, it's art as it should be—a testament to love, to commitment, to the unexpected joy of new life. I am so grateful you invited me and my family."

Helmut looked around at the tall green pines and resumed, "And thank you for spending this time with me. I know you need to go around and speak with everyone; I'll be alright sitting here. My daughter has been keeping an eye on me, see? She's over there."

Emma and James turned, spotted Beth, and waved. Helmut continued, "I'd like to sit here, quiet, for a while and watch the people. I'd like to observe their expressions and how they respond to the space."

And so James held out his arm to help his wife to her feet, and they strolled away to leave Helmut Herzog with the birds, the bees, the trees, and the Great Lakota Ojibwa Stupa beyond.

* * *

Herzog felt comfortable on the weathered wooden bench. It was well constructed, with the back tilted slightly to accommodate the natural curve of the spine, his hands resting atop his cane as he surveyed the bustling Stupa grounds. The late afternoon sun cast a warm glow over the scene, lighting the way for the comings and goings of visitors and familiar faces.

Herzog watched from his bench as Alfred, Mabel, and Gerardo strolled the Stupa grounds. Well, that got his attention. Their animated conversation, punctuated by frequent stops and gestures, told him all he needed to know. Emma's recent letter had prepared him for this moment.

Alfred and Mabel were planning their retirement, Herzog mused. They had chosen Gerardo as their successor, believing he embodied the spirit of Epoch Alliance. Herzog recalled Emma's words: *Gerardo has the vision and the passion. Alfred says he's "made for the position and more."*

The choice had surprised Herzog initially. Surely James would have been the natural successor? But Emma had explained James's unexpected support for the decision. *He's perfectly happy with it, Professor,* she had written. *It's as if he knows there's something else waiting for us.*

Herzog observed Gerardo's animated gestures as he spoke with Alfred, imagining his reaction to the news. He could almost hear the young man's voice: *But what about James? Won't he feel passed over?*

Emma's letter had addressed this too. James had expressed a desire to study Stupa-building in Tibet. A monastery school located there that was devoted to sacred technology—he wanted to understand how energy moves fluidly through some forms, but not as well through others, to delve deeper into sacred art. Yet he was reluctant to leave his family for an extended period. It was a conundrum that intrigued Herzog.

As the trio paused near a flowering cherry tree, Herzog reflected on Emma's cryptic words: *There's something else, Professor. Something I can't quite put my finger on. It's as if James is waiting for something. Some greater purpose we can't see yet. Alfred told me he felt this too, as if James and myself were "off limits" somehow.*

The conversation by the cherry tree seemed to be winding down. Herzog saw Gerardo nod solemnly, then break into a wide grin. Acceptance, then enthusiasm. The future of Epoch Alliance was taking shape before his eyes.

As Alfred, Mabel, and Gerardo resumed their walk, disappearing around a bend in the path, Herzog's mind turned to James and Emma. What could be this unseen future? What could be a higher ground than this? There were endless possibilities, but it seemed they were waiting for something specific—perhaps only to be recognized when it arrived.

* * *

Herzog's attention shifted as he spotted Rhonda hurrying past him and down the path through the pines to where Gerardo, Alfred, and Mabel stood in the woods. Her attire was noticeably softer than in years past. Gone were the sharp suits and severe hairstyles he'd seen in photos—and even in the documentary itself—replaced by flowing fabrics and a relaxed demeanor. The change was striking, a visual representation of her personal growth... and perhaps burgeoning femininity.

Gerardo called out to her, his face lighting up in a way that sparked Herzog's memory. What was it? Now he remembered—Emma had told him a tale, an account of their relationship's turning point: the fateful snowstorm of 2004, as it was now known to be. Rhonda, stranded on her way to Michigan, had been saved by Gerardo's quick thinking and newly acquired four-wheel drive.

It was like something out of a romance novel, Helmut, Emma had written. *He actually went to a car lot and bought a four-wheel-drive truck to get to her—Gerardo keeping her on the phone, figuring out where the car went off the road around the Warren Dunes area; talking her through the blizzard. There are tragedies every year of people stranded and freezing, and you never think it can happen to you until it does. It was like something out of a movie—he was so scared for her, it woke them both up big time.*

Herzog watched as Rhonda joined the group, her hand naturally finding Gerardo's. Their easy intimacy was a far cry from the professional distance they'd once maintained. Emma's letter had hinted at their upcoming nuptials, to be held at the Lakota Ojibwa Stupa in winter.

Can you believe it, Professor? Emma had exclaimed in her letter. *Rhonda and Gerardo, married in the very place that brought us all together. It's real-life magic, love in action, closing a circle... pick your favorite phrase...*

As the group chatted, Herzog could see the way Rhonda had softened—not just in appearance, but in spirit. She was still the driving force behind Epoch Alliance's operations, but there was a new warmth to her efficiency. Gerardo's influence, no doubt.

Their story, Herzog mused, was a testament to the unexpected ways life could unfold—from colleagues to lovers, from professional distance to shared dreams. It was a profound transformation.

* * *

Herzog's contemplation was interrupted by a familiar voice.

"Professor Herzog? Is that you?"

He looked up to see Maribel speaking—with Zane, or no, he was known by his real name now... Ted, wasn't he? The family group was approaching, with their son William in tow and two daughters moving like satellites behind, as if so full of high spirits they couldn't be pinned down. The years had been kind to his former students; they both looked better, healthier than he remembered, their faces etched with laughter lines rather than worry.

"My goodness," Herzog exclaimed, with genuine warmth in his voice. "Maribel and Ted, now is it? Emma told me you go by your real name now... what a delightful surprise."

As they settled beside him, Herzog's eyes were drawn to young William. The boy's vibrant energy belied his past struggles. Herzog, acutely aware of life's fragility since losing his wife, felt a surge of empathy.

"And this must be William," he said softly. "Emma's told me about your journey."

Maribel's eyes widened slightly. "She has?"

Herzog nodded, deciding to broach the subject gently. "She mentioned a health scare. I hope you don't mind my asking... how is he doing now?"

Ted and Maribel exchanged a glance—a world of shared experience in that look.

"It was touch and go for a while. The doctors simply didn't know what to do—a kind of drastic anemia that lowered his immune system," Ted admitted, his voice low. Helmut noted Ted never spoke the word of a specific illness.

"But the treatments at the Stupa clinic..." Ted looked at his son, smiled softly, then looked to his former instructor to add, "They were a game-changer."

Maribel chimed in, her voice gaining enthusiasm. "It's actually what inspired me to study homeopathy... and nutrition too—benefits of protein, beef, bone marrow to help build mitochondria cells. I never imagined my interest would go in that direction, but life has a funny way of steering us, doesn't it?"

Herzog nodded, thinking of his own unexpected turns. "Indeed it does. And you, Ted? Emma tells me you're quite the ad man now."

Ted chuckled, his cheeks coloring slightly. "Who would've thought, right? But I've found a way to sneak art into the corporate world, and have that world support Epoch Alliance too. It's... fulfilling, in ways I never expected. And always working with Epoch, of course—both of us. Plus Bel has a book series too."

Herzog smiled. "Well, expect to hear from the alumni committee from Cooper; they'll want updates to the catalog."

Ted and Maribel exchanged a glance. Ted quipped, "Imagine that—*we lot* making it into the books."

As they chatted, Herzog marveled at the resilience of his former students. They had faced challenges that could have broken them, yet here they were, stronger and more vibrant than ever.

They bid farewell for now. Was Helmut going to stay for the big feast? He assured them he was—with his daughter and grandson—so they promised to resume their conversation then.

Herzog watched them walk away, William skipping between them. Their story, he reflected, was a testament to the human spirit's capacity for growth and adaptation. It was a reminder that even in the face of near-tragedy, life was a powerful force you could put your faith in.

* * *

Helmut looked at the sky. It was late afternoon now; the weather would start cooling, but the sky was clear. It seemed the outdoor picnic-dinner was going ahead as planned. People were starting to wander in from various areas and walking paths, congregating near the Stupa.

Herzog's attention was drawn to a couple strolling hand-in-hand near the Stupa's entrance. He squinted, recognition dawning slowly.

"Ah, that must be Val," he mused. "She looks different than she did in the documentary—more beautiful somehow, her face more symmetrical." He chuckled softly to himself. "Love has a way of doing that."

As he watched them, Herzog wracked his brain for the details Emma had shared about Val and Sam's tumultuous story. There was something about a film festival, wasn't there? He frowned, the specifics eluding him for a moment. Then, like a bolt of lightning, it all came rushing back.

The Sundance Film Festival of 2005. Sam's documentary *Seeds of Dreams: An American Stupa* was set to debut—a crowning achievement in his budding career. Val had been by his side throughout the entire process, her steady presence and sharp mind contributing immeasurably to the project's success. They were riding high, their relationship blossoming alongside their professional collaboration.

Then Olivia had swept back into Sam's life like a hurricane—all Hollywood glamour and calculated neediness. Herzog recalled Emma's vivid description of the actress: a fading star desperate for exposure, seeing Sam's rising profile as a life raft for her career.

"Poor Sam," Herzog muttered, shaking his head. "He never stood a chance against that kind of manipulation."

Sam had felt he owed Olivia a debt. It seemed she'd loaned him money to get his first good video camera—he'd paid her back with interest, but still, in an attempt at kindness and to even the score, he'd agreed to let Olivia be his escort to the festival. Val, ever gracious and understanding of Sam's sense of honor, had smiled and said it was fine. But Herzog, even hearing the story secondhand and later, had recognized the deep hurt beneath her calm exterior.

"It's a wonder they survived that," Herzog mused, watching as Sam now leaned in to whisper something in Val's ear, making her laugh.

He remembered Emma's animated recounting of what happened next—how James and Emma had decided to attend the festival at the last minute, dragging a reluctant Val, kicking and screaming, along with them. James, in particular, had been determined to set things right.

Herzog chuckled, picturing the scene Emma had described: James orchestrating a "full court press" to ensure Val ended up in the seat next to Sam at the premiere—not Olivia. The older man could almost hear James's gruff voice delivering the ultimatum to Sam afterward: *You get one save from Val's big brother. Just one.*

As Herzog reminisced about the Sundance incident, a smile played on his lips. He recalled Emma's amused tone as she recounted what had come to be known in their circle as *The Mystery of the Musical Chairs Affair.*

While Emma was taking Val to get her hair coiffured and bedecked in a classic-cut gown, James had been at it. He'd never fully revealed the details of how he'd managed to rearrange the seating, but rumors and theories had circulated for years. Some said he'd charmed the event staff; others whispered about an elaborate ruse involving a fake clipboard and an air of authority. The true sequence of events remained a delightful enigma, with James offering only a mischievous wink whenever the topic arose.

What was certain, however, was the outcome. Somehow, when the lights dimmed and the premiere began, Val found herself seated next to a pleasantly surprised Sam for the duration of the film and all photo ops, while a flustered Olivia was relegated to a seat several rows back.

The incident had become a favorite story at gatherings, with each retelling growing slightly more outlandish. James, for his part, seemed to relish the air of mystery, neither confirming nor denying the wilder speculations.

The Mystery of the Musical Chairs Affair had entered family legend as a testament to James's cunning, his loyalty to his friends, and his penchant for benevolent mischief. It was a reminder that sometimes, a little well-intentioned trickery could pave the way for love to flourish.

And it had been a close call. Herzog recalled Emma's somber tone as she'd explained how near Sam had come to losing Val forever. But somehow, they'd weathered the storm. Val's hurt had been acknowledged, Sam's eyes had been opened—to a sense of desperation in Olivia's nature, to his own penchant for being more than a little obtuse, and to how to ferret out the proper channel to repay an honorary obligation.

So the strength of their connection had ultimately prevailed. And Sam's own credo had been established too: he would say he'd been so relieved to see Val's natural beauty in that seat next to his in the theatre, he'd taken her hand and did not let it go. *In fact,* he would say, *I'm still holding it now, even when I'm not with her.*

"The Stupa must have some kind of matchmaking ability," Herzog thought wryly, watching as Sam and Val paused to admire the structure's intricate details. Their body language spoke volumes—the way they leaned into each other, the comfortable silence between them, the gentle brush of Sam's hand on Val's hair.

And there was something else interesting about the two of them. Herzog had seen early footage of them both from the doc, when they had appeared to be physically mismatched, but somehow over the years it was as if they had met somewhere in the middle and looked more like a blend of each other than their previous separate selves.

Another Stupa miracle? Who could say?

Their story, like so many others he'd witnessed today, was a testament to the power of second chances and the enduring nature of true connection. From near-disaster to this display of quiet devotion, Sam and Val's journey embodied the transformative spirit of the Great Lakota Ojibwa Stupa itself.

Herzog's mind drifted to the documentary that had inadvertently caused such turmoil. *Seeds of Dreams: An American Stupa* had gone on to receive critical acclaim, launching Sam's career in earnest. And Val's as well—they were both young, with years ahead, and the Epoch Alliance backing them too, so goodness knows what would be in store. But more importantly, the documentary had captured the birth of something truly special—not just the Stupa project, but the intricate web of relationships that had made it possible.

As the couple disappeared from view, Herzog settled back on his bench, a contented smile playing on his lips. Everyone appreciated a good love story.

Where was the popcorn when you needed some?

* * *

Helmut felt the need to stretch his legs but found he only had the energy for a short stroll of about forty feet. As the day was growing late, he sought another spot to rest. A young woman with Down syndrome settled beside him. Though her face held a youthful quality, she also looked weary. Her almond-shaped eyes caught Herzog off guard with their unexpected depth of wisdom.

"It's peaceful here, isn't it?" she said, her voice slightly slurred but clear.

Herzog nodded, sensing a kindred spirit. "It is. There's something about this place."

She smiled, her gaze fixed on the Stupa. "I always feel better when I'm here."

Herzog studied her profile, noting the subtle signs of premature aging beneath her youthful appearance. "Yes, I think I understand," he said softly. "I find comfort in beautiful places as I grow older."

She turned to him, her eyes shining. "Are you scared? Of... you know?"

Herzog was taken aback by her directness, but her open expression invited his honest answer. "Sometimes," he admitted. "But being here, today... it gives me hope. I feel very good."

The girl nodded slowly. "That's why I want to stay. I always feel better for weeks. If I stay, I'll always feel good—then Ma, Da, and James and Em won't be sad."

Herzog's breath caught as realization dawned. This was Sarah, James's sister. The documentary had shown her designing a clay tile—yes, he remembered now.

"Tell me, does being here really help you feel better?" Helmut wanted to know.

Sarah nodded emphatically. "Oh aye! The pain goes away... for a while. James says we can move here and live with them. He and Em have a cabin—a real cabin in the woods, just like in the movies—for when they visit here. And Da says maybe, and I think that means 'yes.'"

Herzog felt a lump form in his throat, understanding the implications. The Stupa—this labor of love—might, might be helping to extend Sarah's life, giving her more precious time with her family.

"That sounds wonderful, Sarah," Herzog said, his voice thick—he was thinking about his Berte, of course. "I hope that happens. 'Maybe' often means 'yes' when it's from your mom and dad."

"I should find Ma and Da. Oh, there they are—bye!"

Herzog nodded, rising as well. "It was a pleasure meeting you, Sarah. Thank you."

As she walked away, Herzog swallowed and thought about courage. This sweet girl—this Sarah—had an invisible kind of courage, the subterranean, permanent aspect of her nature that guided her day to day, that rose to the surface in activity such as talking to a lonesome old man. And he was lonesome—not that he lacked for company; his daughter and friends kept in touch—it was because decades ago he had betrayed his sacred role as teacher. He was lonesome for the man he should be.

He must walk and find James now. It was something Sarah would do—with bells on.

* * *

The Minnesota sun had begun its descent, casting long shadows across the grounds of the Great Lakota Ojibwa Stupa. Helmut Herzog, his cane planted firmly on the ground, gazed at the magnificent structure before him. It seemed he couldn't get enough of looking at it.

As the crowd thinned, Herzog spotted James standing alone, his eyes distant as he too studied the Stupa... meditating perhaps. But it was time—way past time—for the conversation he'd hoped for and dreaded in equal measure, so he must dare to intrude.

With a nod to his daughter Beth, who was back by his side, he silently asked for privacy, and so Herzog made his way to James.

"Might an old man join you again for a moment?" Herzog asked, his German accent still thick despite years in the States.

James turned, a warm smile spreading across his face. "Seems we always pick up where we leave off. Of course. Let's find a place to sit—it's been a long day."

They settled on a nearby bench, the Stupa looming before them like a silent guardian. For a while, they sat in companionable silence. Finally, Herzog spoke, his voice low and filled with emotion. "James, there's something I must tell you. Something I've carried for far too long."

James turned to him, his expression open and curious.

Herzog took a deep breath. "The dove tile I sent... it was for Emma, yes, but in my heart, I sent it to you."

James's eyebrows raised slightly, but he remained silent, allowing Herzog to continue.

"Back in Cooper, I saw something in you—a brilliance, almost supernatural. But it was untamed, wild... as if you could burn down the world and never notice doing it. And I feared... I feared what you might become if left unchecked. It is no excuse, but it put me in mind of how it was back in Germany, back then in those dark times..." Herzog's hands trembled slightly as he spoke. "When the opportunity for Dresden came for Emma, I believed in her—it was a singular opportunity—but I also saw a chance to save her, I thought, and... to break you, just a little. To prevent you from becoming what I feared."

James's face remained remarkably impassive, and then his eyes slowly, slowly filled with understanding.

Herzog continued, his voice thick with regret. "I've wondered for years if I had the right—if I was correct in my role as a tutor. I... I need to apologize, James. Before I leave this earth. I am so sorry if I overstepped."

A heavy silence fell between them. James's gaze drifted back to the Stupa, his mind clearly processing Herzog's words.

Finally, James spoke, his voice soft but firm. "I wondered about that... but... as you see, it all worked out." He gestured to the Stupa, to the people milling about, to Emma in the distance with their son. "So what thread would you pull out now? Pull a thread, change the past, and risk losing all this? Wish any of that away and what—risk losing my wife and son and the baby that's coming too? Not bloody likely."

He turned back to Herzog, a small smile playing on his lips. "So I suppose I should say, thanks."

Herzog's eyes widened in surprise, relief washing over his features.

James added, almost as an afterthought, "Emma never needs to know. She appreciated Dresden so much, so she never needs to know. And you and me? Well, we're square."

The weight of years seemed to lift from Herzog's shoulders. Tears welled in his eyes, a few escaping to roll down his weathered cheeks.

James reached out, placing a comforting hand on Herzog's arm. They sat like that for a while—two men connected, well, in the way all people are.

As the sun dipped lower, casting a golden glow over the Stupa, Herzog felt a deep sense of peace settle over him. He had witnessed something truly remarkable today—not just in the physical structure before him, but in the man sitting beside him, and Emma, his golden student, a walking glory of a woman.

Helmut could see James thinking now, could almost hear the wheels working some problem out. And when he spoke, his voice was soft with a new idea, as if testing it out and liking the feel of it on his tongue. "Helmut, I'd like you to consider staying for a while. There are cabins in the area—your whole family can stay. Emma had a vision years ago about adding a healing center. We've been studying and adding sacred geometric forms such as the Icosahedron, the Dodecahedron, and such to the homeopathic clinic, plus magnetic resonance and red light therapy too—all clinical grade. Having some interesting results. Please consider staying—you are welcome."

Helmut was surprised and... touched. Could an old man like him still learn a thing or two? He smiled at James and nodded. He couldn't find the words.

James stood, offering his hand to help Herzog up. "Shall we rejoin the others, Professor? I believe there's a celebration to be had. Let's sit next to each other at the dinner table and talk like the old friends we are." And then, in the tradition of respect for elders, he took Helmut's arm to hold him steady, but made certain the older man led the way.

As they drew closer to Emma, she waved and walked to greet them. She kissed her husband on the cheek, then walked to the other side of her mentor, kissed him too on the cheek, then took his left arm, and the three of them walked in this way as a tidy ensemble to greet their friends and family at the long outdoor dining table.

* * *

Acknowledgments

This book was shaped by many quiet influences—artists, craftspeople, and teachers who generously shared their knowledge of clay, color, and the meditative work of hands. I'm especially grateful to those who taught me, without ceremony, how to shape tiles that last and breathe.

I also want to offer particular thanks to a Native American man who, guided by the Holy Spirit, chose to open a sacred sweat lodge to a small number of non-Native participants—including me. His decision was neither casual nor common, especially in the 1980's, and the experience changed how I understood prayer, heat, humility, and community. I remain deeply grateful.

Finally, to the unnamed conversations, small kindnesses, fragments of memory, and spirit threads that helped shape this work: thank you. Any errors or simplifications in representation are entirely my own.